JOHN GRIMES
RESERVE COMMODORE

Books by A. Bertram Chandler

John Grimes (series)
> *The Road to the Rim* (1967)
> *To Prime the Pump* (1971)
> *The Hard Way Up* (1972)
> *Spartan Planet* (1968)
> *The Inheritors* (1972)
> *The Broken Cycle* (1975)
> *The Big Black Mark* (1975)
> *The Far Traveler* (1977)
> *Star Courier* (1977)
> *To Keep the Ship* (1978)
> *Matilda's Stepchildren* (1979)
> *Star Loot* (1980)
> *The Anarch Lords* (1981)
> *The Last Amazon* (1984)
> *The Wild Ones* (1985)
> *Catch the Star Winds* (1969)
> *Into the Alternate Universe* (1964)
> *Contraband from Other-Space* (1967)
> *The Rim Gods* (1969)
> *The Dark Dimensions* (1971)
> *Alternate Orbits* (1971)
> *The Gateway to Never* (1972)
> *The Way Back* (1976)

Derek Calver (series)
> *The Rim of Space* (1961)
> *The Ship from Outside* (1963)

Christopher Wilkinson (series)
> *The Coils of Time* (1964)
> *The Alternate Martians* (1965)

Empress (series)
> *Empress of Outer Space* (1965)
> *Space Mercenaries* (1965)
> *Nebula Alert* (1967)

Other Novels
> *Bring Back Yesterday* (1961)
> *Rendezvous on a Lost World* (1961)
> *The Hamelin Plague* (1963)
> *Beyond the Galactic Rim* (1963)
> *Glory Planet* (1964)
> *The Deep Reaches of Space* (1964)
> *The Sea Beasts* (1971)
> *The Bitter Pill* (1974)
> *Kelly Country* (1983)
> *To Rule the Refugees* (1983)
> *Frontier of the Dark* (1984)
> *Find the Lady* (1984)

Short Fiction
> *Up to the Sky in Ships* (1982)
> *From Sea to Shining Star* (1990)

JOHN GRIMES
RESERVE COMMODORE

THE LAST AMAZON
THE WILD ONES
CATCH THE STAR WINDS

Six Uncollected John Grimes Stories

A. Bertram Chandler

50 YEARS
SFBC
SCIENCE
FICTION

THE LAST AMAZON Copyright © 1984 by A. Bertram Chandler
THE WILD ONES Copyright © 1985 by A. Bertram Chandler
"Grimes at Glenrowan" Copyright © 1978 by A. Bertram Chandler
"Grimes and the Great Race" Copyright © 1980 by A. Bertram Chandler
"Grimes Among the Gourmets" Copyright © 1978 by A. Bertram Chandler
"Grimes and the Odd Gods" Copyright © 1983 by A. Bertram Chandler
"Grimes and the Jail Birds" Copyright © 1984 by A. Bertram Chandler
"Chance Encounter" Copyright © 1959 by A. Bertram Chandler
CATCH THE STAR WINDS Copyright © 1969 by A. Bertram Chandler

First SFBC Science Fiction Printing: January 2004.

The SFBC gratefully thanks Todd Bennett for his help determining the correct chronological sequence, researching the uncollected stories, and championing the works of A. Bertram Chandler.

Published by arrangement with the author's estate, via JABberwocky Literary Agency,
P.O. Box 4558
Sunnyside, NY 11104-0558

Visit The SFBC at http://www.sfbc.com

ISBN # 0-7394-3965-0

Printed in the United States of America.

Contents

THE LAST AMAZON

For Susan, who makes me keep my nose
to the grindstone.

Chapter 1

The bands played and the Federation Survey Service Marines paraded in their scarlet and gold dress uniforms and the children waved their little flags and the grown-ups lifted high their broad-brimmed black hats as Grimes, ex-Governor John Grimes, arrived at Port Libertad, there to embark aboard the star tramp *Rim Wayfarer*. With him, to see him off, were two people whom he did not regard as friends—but protocol demanded their attendance. One of them was Estrelita O'Higgins, still, despite all, President of Liberia. She was a survivor, that one. She had contrived to lay the blame for all of the planet's troubles, culminating in the armed revolt against the Earth-appointed Governor, Grimes, on the now disgraced Colonel Bardon, lately commanding officer of the Terran garrison. The other was Captain Francis Delamere, of the Federation Survey Service, the new Governor.

Delamere should have a far easier time of it than either Grimes or his immediate predecessor. He had brought his own garrison troops out with him, a large detachment of Marines who—in theory at least—gave their allegiance to the senior Terran naval officer on Liberia, Captain Delamere. And almost immediately after his arrival (he was a notorious ladies' man) he had made a big hit with the President. For him the job should be a sinecure. Even he would find it hard to make a mess of it—as long as he did not try to interfere with the smooth running of the machinery of government that Grimes—who was for a while, after the putting down of the rebellion, de facto dictator—had set up, with able, honest and dedicated men and women in all the key positions.

But Frankie, thought Grimes, would find it hard to keep his meddling paws off things. He had tried to take an officious interest in Grimes' own affairs even before the formal handing-over ceremonies, had made it plain that he wanted his old enemy off the premises as soon as possible, if not before, so that he could bask in his new gubernatorial glory.

He had said, in his most supercilious manner, "There's no need for you to hang around here like a bad smell, Grimes."

"But I thought that you were keeping *Orion* here for a while," said Grimes. "Wise of you, Frankie. During my spell as Governor I could have done with a Constellation Class cruiser sitting in my back yard."

"Who said anything about *Orion*, Grimes? I came here with a squadron."

"A *squadron?*" echoed Grimes. "Two ships. One cruiser and one Serpent Class courier . . ."

"I was forgetting," sneered Delamere, "that you're something of an expert on squadrons. Didn't you command one when you were a pirate commodore?"

"A privateer," growled Grimes. "Not a pirate."

"And now an ex-Governor," Delamere reminded him. "As such, you're entitled to a free trip back to Earth . . ."

"Not in a flying sardine can."

"Beggars can't be choosers, Grimes. Anyhow, the sooner you're back the sooner you'll be able to find another job. If anybody wants you, that is. You can't hope to get another command, not even of that *Saucy Sue* of yours."

"*Sister Sue*," Grimes corrected him stiffly.

"What's in a name? As far as I know your Certificate of Competency has not been restored—and you'd need that, wouldn't you, even as a bold buccaneer."

"I've already told you once that I was a privateer."

"Even so, you were bloody lucky not to be hanged from your own yardarm for piracy. That judge, at the Court of Inquiry, was far too lenient. Did you slip him a backhander out of your ill-gotten gains?"

Grimes ignored this. "Anyhow," he said smugly, "I now, once again, hold a valid Certificate of Competency as Master of an Interstellar Vessel."

"What! Don't tell me that it *has* been restored to you!"

"No. It's a new one. Liberian."

"And you say it's valid? Oh, I suppose that *you* signed it, as Governor, after examining yourself."

"If you must know, it is signed by the Liberian Minister of Space Shipping. And I was examined, and passed, by the Examiner of Masters and Mates. I admit that she was appointed by myself, for that purpose. But it's a valid Certificate, recognized as such throughout the Galaxy."

"You're a cunning bastard," whispered Delamere, not without envy.

"I am when I have to be," Grimes told him. "And now all that I have to do is to catch up with *Sister Sue* and get my name back on the Register."

"I'm not letting you have that courier to take on a wild goose chase," snarled Delamere.

"I've already told you that I have no intention of traveling in the bloody thing. I'm quite capable of making my own arrangements. I know where I want to go and I know which ship, due here in a couple of days' time, will be heading in the right direction when she's finished discharging and loading."

And so the bands were playing and the Marines, in their full dress scarlet and gold, were drawn up to stiff attention with gleaming arms presented and the children were waving their little flags and the grown-ups were raising their broad-brimmed black hats high in the air as the big ground car rolled slowly up to the foot of *Rim Wayfarer*'s ramp.

Delamere's aide, a young Survey Service Lieutenant, got down from the front seat where he had been sitting beside the Marine corporal driver. He flung open a rear door with a flourish. Estrelita O'Higgins was the first out, tall in superbly tailored, well-filled denim with a scarlet neckerchief at her throat. She was as darkly handsome as when Grimes had first met her, on his arrival at this spaceport (how long ago?) but then he had been prepared to like her, to work with her. Now he knew too much about her—and she about him. Some applause greeted her appearance but it was restrained.

Delamere was next out. He wore full ceremonial rig—the gray trousers, the black morning coat, the gray silk top hat—far more happily than Grimes ever had done. In uniform Handsome Frankie, as he was derisively known, looked as though he were posing for a Survey Service recruiting poster. Now he looked as though he were posing for a Diplomatic Service recruiting poster. He took his stance alongside the President. The impression they conveyed was that of husband and wife about to see off a house guest who had outstayed his welcome.

Again there was a spatter of applause.

Grimes disembarked.

This day he was dressed for comfort—and also in accordance with local sartorial tradition. He was wearing faded blue denim, a scarlet neckerchief, a broad-brimmed black hat.

The cheers, the shouts of "Viva Grimes! Viva Grimes!" were deafening. The Marine band struck up the retiring Governor's own national song, "Waltzing Matilda." Both Delamere and the President frowned. This was not supposed to be an item on the agenda—but Colonel Grant, commanding officer of the Marines, had known Grimes before his resignation from the Survey Service.

The people were singing that good old song.

And soon, thought Grimes, *there'll be only my ghost to haunt this billabong. . . .*

Estrelita O'Higgins extended her long-fingered right hand, palm down. Grimes bowed to kiss it. She whispered something. It sounded like, "Don't come back, you bastard!" Francis Delamere raised his silk hat. Grimes raised his felt hat. Neither man attempted to shake hands.

Slowly Grimes walked up the ramp to the after airlock of *Rim Wayfarer*. At the head of the gangway the master, Captain Gunning, smart enough in his dress black and gold, was waiting to receive him.

He saluted with what was probably deliberate sloppiness and said, "Glad to have you aboard, Commodore."

"I'm glad to be aboard, Captain," said Grimes.

"I bet you are. It must be a relief to get away from the stuffed shirts."

"The era of the stuffed shirt is just beginning here," Grimes told him.

Gunning, looking down at the new Governor standing stiffly beside the President, laughed. "I see what you mean."

Grimes turned, to wave for the last time to those who had been his people. They waved back, all of them, native Liberians and those who, as refugees from all manner of disasters, had sought and found a new home on Liberia.

"Viva Grimes! Viva Grimes!"

"I hate to interrupt, Commodore," said Gunning, "but it's time that I was getting the old girl upstairs."

"She's your ship, Captain."

"But what a send-off! Those people sound as though they're really sorry to lose you."

"Quite a few," Grimes told him with a grin, "will be glad to see the back of me."

"I can imagine."

The two men stepped into the elevator cage that would carry them up to the control room. The ramp retracted and the outer and inner airlock doors closed.

In less than five minutes *Rim Wayfarer* was lifting into the clear, noonday sky.

Chapter 2

Grimes and Gunning were at ease in the master's day cabin, enjoying a few drinks and a yarn before dinner. Trajectory had been set, all life support systems were functioning perfectly, the light lunch served as soon as possible after lift-off had been a good one and Grimes was looking forward to the evening meal.

It was good to be back aboard a ship again, he was thinking as he sipped his pink gin, even though it was only as a passenger. Still, he was a privileged one, being treated more as a guest.

"You know Sparta, of course," said Gunning.

"I was only there the once," said Grimes. "Years ago. When I was captain of the Federation Survey Service census ship *Seeker*."

Gunning laughed. "But you must know *something* about Sparta. Every time that I'm sent to a planet I haven't been to before I do some swotting up on it. There's not much information in the ship's library data bank—just the coordinates and a few details about climate and such. Rim Runners don't believe in paying good money for what they, in their wisdom, regard as useless information. But I found the Libertad Public Library quite informative. Historical details—from the time of *Doric*'s landing to the present. The way Sparta was dragged into the political framework of the Federation—and the way a certain Lieutenant Commander John Grimes initiated this process."

"I was just there when it happened," said Grimes. "Or when it started to happen. I was little more than a spectator."

"As you were on Liberia, Commodore, when things happened." Gunning laughed. "I'd just hate to be around when you were something more than just a spectator."

"But I was little more on Sparta," Grimes insisted. "One of my scientific officers, Maggie Lazenby, was the prime mover. She took a shine to Brasidus, who is now the Archon, and he to her." He laughed. "It was the first time that he'd had any dealings with a woman. He really thought that she was a member of some alien species. . . ."

"I've often thought the same myself about women," said Gunning. "But that must have been a weird state of affairs on Sparta when you landed there."

"It was," reminisced Grimes. "It was. An all-male population, with all that that implies. Babies—male babies only—produced by the so-called Birth Machine. A completely spurious but quite convincing biology taught in the schools to make sense of this. The planet was a Lost Colony, of course, founded during the First Expansion. You know, the Deep Freeze ships. They started off with an incubator and a supply of fertilized ova. Male ova. The first King, who had been master of the starship, made sure of that. He didn't like women. He tried to model his realm on ancient Sparta but with one great improvement. Men Only. I suppose that when the original supply of ova ran out the Spartans might have had to resort to cloning but, before this came to pass, the people of another Lost Colony, Latterhaven, made contact. Trade developed between the two worlds. Fertilized human ova in exchange for spices and such."

"I got most of that from the library at Port Libertad," said Gunning. "But what was it like? A world with no women. . . ."

"What you'd expect," said Grimes. "The really macho types, with their leather and brass, in the armed forces. The effeminate men working as nurses in the creche and other womanly occupations. The in-betweeners were the helots; after all, somebody has to hew the wood and draw the water. But once the bully boys got a whiff of real pussy—*Seeker* had a mixed crew—all hell started to break loose. And there were, too, some women on the planet already. The doctors running the Birth Machine had their own secret harem."

"I expect that you'll find things changed, Commodore," remarked Gunning.

"I shall be surprised if I don't. To begin with, there's no longer a monarchy. The Archon is the boss cocky. And there has been considerable immigration from the Federated Planets—mostly people, as far as I can gather, who have their own ideas about what life was like in Ancient Greece. Billy Williams—who's been acting master of *Sister Sue* during my absence—has been sending me reports."

"That was a nice little time charter you got for your ship," said Gunning. "Earth to Sparta with assorted luxury goods, Spartan spices back. Did your early connections with Sparta help you to get it?"

"Possibly," Grimes told him. He did not add that the Federation Survey Service, in which he still held the reserve captain's commission that not many people knew about, owed him a few favors. He laughed. "But I never thought that *Sister Sue* would be earning her living as a retsina tanker. It's all those immigrants, of course. They must have *real* Greek wine—although the local tipple wasn't at all bad when I was on Sparta years ago—and olives and feta cheese and all the rest of it."

"But surely," objected Gunning, "the ancient Greeks didn't drink retsina. It was the Turks, when they occupied Greece in more recent times, who tried to cure the wine-bibbing Christians of their addiction to alcohol by making them put resin in the wine casks."

"True, true. But you must have found, Captain, that any attempt to revive an ancient culture on a new world is as phony as all hell. The aggressive Scottishness of the Waverley planets, for example. And New Zion—have you ever been there?—where all hands drop whatever they're doing at the drop of a yarmulke to dance the hora. . . . The original culture of the all-male Sparta was phony enough—but it was consistent. But now? Unfortunately Billy Williams isn't a very good letter writer but I've gained the impression that those new colonists have succeeded in reproducing an ancient Greece that never was, that never could have been."

"You'll have time to find out for yourself, Commodore. You told me that you'll have about three weeks there before your ship drops in. Unluckily I've only two days' work there—just a small parcel of bagged flour to discharge and a consignment of spices to load—and then I shall be on my way."

The sonorous notes of the dinner gong drifted through the ship.

The two men finished their drinks and got up from their chairs to go down to the dining saloon.

Chapter 3

Grimes quite enjoyed the voyage.

Rim Wayfarer was a comfortable, well-run ship, her captain and officers good company. The food was good, even by Grimes' exacting standards. He was, he admitted to himself, rather surprised. Rim Runners
were looked down upon by the personnel of such shipping lines as the
Interstellar Transport Commission and Trans-Galactic Clippers and, too,
by the officers of the Federation Survey Service. They were the sort of
outfit that you joined when nobody else would have you.

But, thought Grimes, *you could do very much worse for yourself*.

The day came when the star tramp dropped from the warped dimensions engendered by her Mannschenn Drive into normal Space-Time. It
was a good planetfall, with no more than twelve hours' running under
inertial drive to bring the ship to Port Sparta.

Grimes was in the control room, keeping well out of the way, when
Gunning made his landing. As far as he could see from the viewports and
in the screen everything was much as he remembered it. There, on the hill-
top, was the Acropolis, gleaming whitely in the rays of the morning sun.
Sprawling around the low mountain was the city, laid out with no regard to
geometrical planning, a maze of roads and alleys running between buildings great and small, none of them more than two stories high but some of
them covering considerable acreage. Yes, there was the Palace. . . .
Grimes supposed that Brasidus, as Archon, would be making it his residence. (The Spartan royal house had ceased to be after the revolution.)

And there was the spaceport. A real spaceport now, capable of handling at least twelve ships at a time. And what ships were in? Obligingly,
Gunning's Chief Officer gave Grimes the use of a screen showing the
area toward which *Rim Wayfarer* was making her approach. There was

something big. Grimes stepped up the magnification. A Trans-Galactic clipper, probably a cruise liner. And something small, but not too small. One of the Survey Service's couriers, Lizard Class. An Epsilon Class tramp—but it couldn't be *Sister Sue*. She, as far as Grimes had been able to determine, must now be about halfway from Earth to Sparta.

Slowly, but not too slowly, *Rim Wayfarer* dropped to her berth, marked by the three scarlet flasher beacons. As always the Port Captain, like Port Captains throughout the Galaxy, had done his best to make the job an awkward one. With all the apron space there was to play with he still expected Gunning to set his ship down between the big cruise liner and the little courier. Luckily there was very little surface wind. The tramp master cursed good naturedly, as Grimes himself, in similar circumstances, had often cursed. He said to Grimes, "Fantastic, isn't it, Commodore? When a man is actually serving as a spaceman he will be a prince of good fellows. Once he takes up ground employment, as a stevedore or a Port Captain or whatever, he has absolutely no consideration for those who used to be his shipmates. . . ."

Grimes said, "I was a Port Captain myself once. On Botany Bay."

"And did *you* berth all the ships in a tight huddle so as to leave hectares of great open spaces?"

"I didn't have hectares of great open spaces to play with. Luckily only on one occasion did I have more than one ship in. And then one of them was a relatively small destroyer and the other a really small private yacht."

"So you were the exception to prove the rule," laughed Gunning.

He returned his attention to the controls and the *Wayfarer* dropped steadily down to a neat landing in the exact center of the triangle marked by the flashing beacons.

The port officials boarded.

Grimes remained in his quarters until Gunning buzzed him on the inter-ship telephone, asking him to join him and his official guests in his day cabin. He collected his passport and immunization certificates and made his way up to the captain's flat by the spiral staircase.

There were three visitors in Gunning's office. The captain was sitting behind his paper-strewn desk. Sitting in chairs arranged to face the shipmaster were two men and a woman. One of the men—a customs officer?—was in a kilted uniform that was all leather and brass and a plumed brass helmet was on the deck beside him. At least, thought Grimes, customs officers on this planet did not wear uniforms aping those of honest spacemen. The other man—tall, bald-headed—was wearing a dignified, long white robe. The woman, her back to Grimes, was attired in a simple green tunic that left her suntanned arms and most of her shoulders bare. Her hair, braided and coiled around her head, was a gleaming auburn with the merest touch of gold. There was, thought Grimes, something familiar about her.

"Ah, it's you, Commodore," said Gunning, looking up from the documents. "I thought that it was Melissa with the coffee. . . . But we'll get the introductions over before she brings it in."

The two men and the woman got to their feet, turned to face Grimes.

"Maggie!" he gasped.

"John," she said. (She was not surprised.)

He said, "It's been a long time. . . ."

She said, "It's not all that long since I got you out of that mess aboard *Bronson Star.*"

"I mean," said Grimes, "that it's a long time since we were here, on this world, together."

Looking at her he thought, *But she still looks the same as she did then. The face still as beautiful in its high-cheekboned, wide-mouthed way, the figure, revealed rather than concealed by the short, flimsy dress, still as graceful. . . .*

"A long time . . ." he repeated.

"I suppose that it is, at that," she said matter-of-factly. "And here am I, still holding the exalted rank of commander in the Scientific Branch of the Survey Service, and here's you, who've been a yachtmaster, an owner-master, a pirate commodore, a planetary governor and the Odd Gods of the Galaxy alone know what else."

"A privateer," said Grimes. "Not a pirate."

"Whatever you were," she told him, "it's good to see you again."

He took her extended hand, grasped it firmly. He would have kissed her—she seemed to be expecting it—if Gunning had not coughed loudly.

"You already know Commander Lazenby," said the captain. "But may I introduce Colonel Heraclion, Chief Collector of Customs, and Dr. Androcles, Port Health Officer?"

Hands were shaken. Grimes took a chair next to Maggie. The ship's catering officer brought in a tray laden with a large coffee pot, sugar bowl, cream jug and cups. She departed and Gunning poured for his guests.

The colonel said, "I do not usually attend to such matters as the Inward Clearance of shipping myself. But I bear greetings from the Archon." From the leather pouch at his belt he withdrew a large envelope, handed it to Grimes. "To you, sir."

Grimes took it. It was, he noted, unsealed. He remembered having read somewhere that a gentleman, entrusting a letter to another gentleman for delivery, never seals the envelope. Did the ancient Spartans observe such a custom? (Did the ancient Spartans use envelopes?)

He pulled out the sheet of paper—it was more of a card, really. He read the stiff, unfamiliar calligraphy. *The Archon presents his compliments to His Excellency the Commodore Grimes and requests that he will accept the hospitality of the palace during his stay on New Sparta.* It was signed, simply, *Brasidus.*

Grimes passed the card to Maggie.

"Good," she said. "He told me that he would invite you."

"Are you staying there?" he asked.

"Of course." She laughed. "After all, Brasidus and I are old friends. I could be staying aboard *Krait*, of course, but, as you should know, Serpent Class couriers are not famous for their luxurious passenger accommodation."

"So you're here on Survey Service business," remarked Grimes.

"Of course. I'd not have gotten passage here—even if it is in a spaceborne sardine can like *Krait*—otherwise. Research. A study of the effects on a Lost Colony by its assimilation into mainstream Galactic culture. Or of the effects on mainstream culture when assimilated into a Lost Colony. Nothing serious, and all good, clean (for most of the time) fun. Perhaps you'd like to help me in my research. That ship of yours isn't due in for some time yet."

"It should be interesting," said Grimes. "But haven't you already found that New Sparta has been spoiled by contact with the rest of the Galaxy?"

"Far from it," she told him. "Anything would have been an improvement on the way it was."

"That," said Colonel Heraclion stiffly, "is your opinion, Commander Lazenby."

Grimes looked at the man with interest. *Yes*, he thought, *there are men to whom an all-male society, such as New Sparta had been, would be almost a paradise. Oh, well. One man's Mede is another man's Persian.*

"I am in agreement with Commander Lazenby," said Dr. Androcles. "Like the colonel, I was a young man when Commodore Grimes' ship, *Seeker*, gave us our first real contact with the outside universe. The people realized then that, for generations, they had been living a lie."

"In the opinion of your medical profession, perhaps," sneered the colonel. "But do not forget that you and your colleagues had been promulgating that same lie."

"Gentlemen, gentlemen," chided Captain Gunning. "I do not think that my day cabin is a fitting venue for a heated argument about New Spartan politics."

"It was the outworlders who started it," said Heraclion sourly.

"Outworlders," Maggie reminded him, "who just happen to be honored guests of your Archon."

The colonel was about to make a heated reply, then thought better of it. Dr. Androcles laughed.

"I'll help you to finish your packing, John," said Maggie.

Chapter 4

When they were alone in his quarters Grimes kissed her. She returned his embrace, then pushed him away.

"Not now," she said. "There'll be plenty of time for this sort of thing in the palace."

"Will there?" he asked. "Haven't you already said that you and the Archon are old friends? I . . . assumed. . . ."

"Then you assumed wrong. Ellena keeps Brasidus on a tight leash."

"Ellena?"

"His wife. The Archoness, as many call her, although there's no such rank or title. She's from Earth. An Australian, of Greek ancestry. Very much the power behind the throne. But finish your packing and I'll fill you in." She took from its shelf the solidograph that she had given him—how long ago?—and held the transparent cube, with its lifelike, three dimensional image of her face and figure, studying it before passing it to him. "You're something of a sentimental bastard, aren't you? That's one of the reasons why I'm rather fond of you."

"Thank you."

"And now for putting you in the picture. To begin with, my research project is only a cover. I was seconded to the Intelligence Branch, and by them put under the orders of Rear Admiral Damien."

"But he's not in the Intelligence Branch."

"Isn't he? There are intelligence officers whom everybody knows about and there are intelligence officers who, as it were, hide their light under a bushel. Like you, for example."

"*Me?*"

"Yes, you. The admiral told me that you had been pressganged back into the Survey Service with the rank of captain on the Reserve List. All very Top Secret, Destroy By Fire Before Reading and all the rest of it. What you did to break up Drongo Kane's privateering racket was no more—and no less—than Intelligence work. So was what you did on Liberia. Whether you knew it or not you were a member of the Department of Dirty Tricks."

Grimes sighed. "All right, all right. But just what dirty tricks am I supposed to be doing here?"

"Just shoving a spanner into the works."

"But Brasidus—from what I remember of him—is a nice enough bloke. I'm sure that he's a good Archon, whatever an Archon does when he's up and dressed. There's never been any talk of tyranny, so far as I know. People are still emigrating to New Sparta from Earth and other planets."

She said, "That's part of the trouble."

"How so?"

"One of our people was among those migrants. Under cover, of course. According to her papers she was a schoolteacher. She sent a few reports back to Earth—and then they stopped coming. Since my arrival here I've been able to make discreet inquiries. She was drowned in a boating accident."

"If it was an accident . . ." said Grimes. "Is that what you're driving at?"

"Of course. She was out on a river trip with other members of the New Hellas Association. Colonel Heraclion—although he wasn't a member of the boating party—is one of the Association's high-ups. Oh, I know what you're thinking. *New* Hellas, when what he wants is *Old* New Sparta. But the New Hellenes are a bunch of reactionaries. Some—like the good colonel—want a return to a womanless world, the way it used to be. Others—and they're mainly immigrants—want a return to the way ancient Greece used to be on Earth."

"The glory that was Greece . . ." quoted Grimes. "What's so wrong with that?"

"Ancient Greece," she told him, "was glorious, if you happened to be a member of the upper crust and male. If you were a slave, a peasant or a woman it wasn't so glorious."

"But there are women in this New Hellas Association. This murdered agent of yours—all right, all right, of ours—was a member and a woman."

"There are some women," she said, "who, in their secret hearts, would enjoy being human doormats. There are other women who would enjoy being glamorous *hetaerae* in a society where the other members of their sex were no more than drab *Hausfrauen*."

"*Hetaerae* and *Hausfrauen* in the same culture!" laughed Grimes.

"You know what I mean. Well, it wouldn't be so bad if the New Hellenes were just trying to attain their ends by democratic means but, according to our late agent, they're plotting a coup. A coup on classical lines. And then yet another unsavory dictatorship which, eventually, will have to be put down at great expense. If such things can be nipped in the bud. . . ."

"By whom?"

"Need you ask, ducky?"

"Damn it all," said Grimes, "I'm a civilian. A shipmaster and shipowner. All that I came to this world for was to rejoin my ship."

"You're not a civilian, John. Oh, you may have been for a while, but ever since you accepted that reserve commission you've been back in the Service. I've written orders for you from Admiral Damien—not with me at the moment but in the captain's safe aboard the courier. I'll get them out for you before too long."

The intercom phone buzzed. Grimes pressed the *Acknowledge* button. Gunning's face appeared in the screen.

"I hope that I'm not interrupting anything, Commodore, but Colonel Heraclion asked me to remind you that the car is waiting to take you to the palace. If you like I'll send somebody down to give you a hand with your gear."

"Thank you, Captain," said Grimes. "But don't I have to pass Port Health, Immigration and Customs?"

"The colonel informs me that all formalities have been waived in your case." The master laughed. "It's always handy to have friends in high places."

The screen went blank.

Grimes opened the door of his cabin in preparation for the arrival of the junior officer who would help him with his bags. Maggie continued talking but only on topics which, should she be overheard, would give nobody any ideas.

"Talking of friends," she said, "I met one of yours a couple of days ago."

"But the only person whom I got to know on this world, when I was here before, was Brasidus."

"This one's an offworlder."

"From Earth?"

"No. From Bronsonia. An investigative reporter, she calls herself. She works for that scurrilous rag *Star Scandals*. She's doing a series on sleazy entertainment centers on as many worlds as she can get to visit during the time allowed her. She's tailing along after some outfit calling itself Galactic Glamour, featuring exotic dancers from all over. They're doing a short season here before pushing on to Latterhaven.

"Anyhow, I met her when I was slumming, as part of my research. We had a couple or three drinks. She knew that I'm Survey Service. And you know how stupid people are . . ." She assumed a voice that was not hers but which was ominously familiar to Grimes. "*Oh, you're in the Survey Service . . . A commander. Do you know Commander Smith?*" She laughed. "What she said was, *Do you know Captain Grimes? He used to be in the Survey Service—he got as high as commander, I believe, before they threw him out . . .*"

"I resigned!" growled Grimes.

"So I said to her, *Who doesn't know Grimes?* And she grinned nastily and said, *So we share that dubious pleasure.* But don't you want to know who she is?"

"I know only one person who answers to your description of her," muttered Grimes. "But tell me, is she, too, a guest at the palace?"

"No. She did come calling around once, flashing her press ID, but Ellena took an instant dislike to her. The guards have strict orders never to admit her again."

"Thank All The Odd Gods Of The Galaxy for that! With any luck at all I'll not be meeting her again."

"Then your luck's run out. You surely don't think, do you, that you'll be confined to the palace during your entire stay here? Apart from anything else you'll be helping me with my ethnographical research—and I've little doubt that our path will, from time to time, cross that of the fair researcher for *Star Scandals.*"

"I don't frequent low joints," said Grimes virtuously.

"Then you've changed!" she laughed.

He laughed with her. "Oh, well, I shan't really mind meeting Fenella again for a talk over old times. But it's a pity that Shirl and Darleen aren't here as well . . ."

"And who are they?" asked Maggie, with a touch of jealousy.

"Just girls," said Grimes.

And then the Third Officer appeared to help carry the baggage down to the airlock.

Chapter 5

At the foot of the ramp two of Heraclion's men loaded Grimes' baggage into the rear of the hovercar—a vehicle that was doing its best to look like an ancient Greek chariot—while the commodore said his farewells to Captain Gunning and the star tramp's officers. The colonel took his seat alongside the driver who, like his superior, was dressed in brass and leather although with much less of the glittering metal on display. Maggie and Grimes sat immediately behind the two Spartans.

The ducted fans whined loudly and raised eddies of dust. The vehicle lifted itself in its skirts, slid away from the spaceship, picking up speed as it did so. Soon it was clear of the spaceport environs, proceeding at a good rate toward the city. There was other vehicular traffic—chariotlike hovercraft, both military and civil, carts piled with produce and drawn by what looked like donkeys and mules, imports from distant Earth. There were, as there had been on the occasion of Grimes' previous visit, squads of young men, who appeared to be soldiers, on motorcycles but there were others on horseback.

Grimes remarked on what was, to him, archaic means of transport.

Heraclion, speaking back over his shoulder, said, "There are those among our new citizens, Commodore, who want to put the clock back to the time of the Spartan Empire on Earth. . . ." (*The Spartan Empire*? wondered Grimes. He most certainly could not recall any mention of such during his studies of Terran history.) "Even so, I have to admit that a troop of cavalry mounted on horseback is a far better spectacle than one mounted on motorcycles."

The hovercar, its siren screaming to demand right of way, was now fast approaching the outskirts of the city. It sped along the narrow road between the rows of low, white houses and less privileged traffic hastily made way for it. A turn was made into what was little more than a winding lane. This, Grimes realized, must be the entertainment district. In the old days, during his first visit to Sparta, such a venue was undreamed of. Gaudy neon signs, dim on the sunny side of the street but bright in the shadow, advertised the delights available to those with money behind the heavy wooden doors, the shuttered windows. The lettering, although aping the Cyrillic alphabet, spelled out its messages in Standard English.

DIMITRIO'S LAMB BARBECUE—TOPLESS LADY CHEFS

(Grimes could appreciate the female cooks' need for aprons; barbecues are apt to sputter and spatter.)

HELEN'S HETAERAE

(And did one drop in there for intellectual conversation?)

ARISTOTLE'S ARENA

This was a much larger building than the rest. Under the flickering main sign were others:

GALACTIC GLAMOUR
EXOTIC WARRIOR MAIDS
OFFPLANET AMAZONS
LIMITED SEASON ONLY

Maggie had to put her mouth to his ear to be heard above the shrieking siren. "That's the outfit I was telling you about. The one that your old girlfriend is doing the series on." She laughed. "The trouble with Aristotle is that he's not a very good historian. His entertainment is more Roman than Grecian. I think that he'd even put on Lions versus Christians if he thought he could get away with it."

"Have you been there?"

"Yes. That's where I met Fenella Pruin. After I admitted that I knew you she laughed nastily and said, 'This is just the sort of show that *he'd* enjoy. A pity he's not here.' I didn't tell her, of course, that you were on your way to Sparta."

"Thank you. With only a little bit of luck she'll never know I'm here."

"She'll know all right. The local media have already bruited abroad that the famous Commodore John Grimes is to be the guest of the Archon."

"Then I'll just have to rely on you to keep her out of my hair."

They were out of the Street of the Haetaeri as the red-light district was called, making the ascent of the low hill on top of which stood the Archon's palace. Troops were drawn up before the long, pillared portico, weapons and accouterments gleaming in the afternoon sunlight. Short spears were raised in salute as the hovercar whined to a stop and subsided to the ground.

Grimes looked at the soldiers appreciatively. They were young women, all of them, uniformed in short white tunics and heavy, brass-studded sandals with knee-high lacings. The leather cross-straps and belts defined their breasts and hips sharply. Shoulder length hair, in almost every case glossily blonde, flowed from under their plumed helmets.

"The Lady Ellena's Amazon Guard," commented Heraclion sourly.

"I'd sooner have them than a bunch of hairy-arsed Federation Marines," said Grimes.

Maggie's elbow dug sharply into his ribs.

They disembarked then—Maggie, Grimes and the colonel.

The Amazon officer marched before them, her spear held high. Other girls fell in on either side of them, escorting them. They passed through the great doorway into the hall, dim after the blazing sunlight outside, to where the Archon and his lady, flanked by berobed dignitaries of both sexes, awaited them.

Grimes found it hard to recognize Brasidus. The young, clean-shaven sergeant whom he had known was now a portly, middle-aged man, his hair and full beard touched with gray. Perhaps it was the white robe with its broad purple trim that gave an illusion of stoutness but the commodore did not think so. Brasidus would never have been able to buckle on the simple uniform that he had worn in the old days.

And the large woman who stood beside the Archon was indubitably stout. She, too, wore a purple-trimmed robe. Her rather spuriously golden hair was piled high and elaborately upon her head but even without this added height she would have been at least fifteen centimeters taller than her husband. She looked down her long nose at the guests with very cold blue eyes and her full mouth was set in a disapproving line.

The Amazon guard grounded their spears with an echoing crash.

Brasidus stepped forward, both hands extended.

Grimes had started to bow but realized that this salutation would not be correct. He straightened up and extended his own right hand. The Archon grasped it warmly in both of his.

"John Grimes! It is indeed good to see you again, after all these years! My house is yours while you are on Sparta!"

"Thank you . . . Lord," said Grimes.

"And have you forgotten my name? To my friends I am, and always will be, just Brasidus. But allow me to present my lady wife. Ellena, my dear, this is John Grimes, of whom you have often heard. . . ."

"The famous pirate commodore," said the woman in neutral tones.

"And John, this is the Lady Ellena."

She extended, a large, plump hand with scarlet fingernails. Grimes somehow got the impression that he was to do no more than touch it. He did that.

There were other introductions, to each of the assembled councilmen and councilwomen. There was an adjournment to a large room where refreshments were served by girls who circulated among the guests pouring the wine—a Terran retsina, Grimes decided, although he thought that it had not traveled well—from long necked *amphorae*. There were feta cheese and black olives (imported?) to nibble.

Finally the party broke up and Grimes was escorted to his quarters by one of the servant wenches. They could have been a hotel suite on just about any planet.

He was sitting down for a quiet smoke when Maggie joined him.

"Dinner's at 1900 hours," she told him. "No need to get out your penguin suit or a dress uniform. It'll be just a small occasion with Brasidus, you and me reminiscing over old times."

"What about the Lady Ellena?"

"She's off to a meeting. She's Patron of the Women's Branch of the New Hellas Association."

"But . . ." He hesitated. "Is it all right to talk?"

"It is. I was supplied with the very latest thing in bug detectors. When it's not detecting bugs it functions quite well as a wristwatch."

"What about Ellena and the New Hellas mob?"

"I don't think she's mixed up in any of their subversive activities. She's a silly bitch, but not that silly. She knows which side her bread is buttered. But she loves being fawned upon and flattered."

"I take it she's of relatively humble origins."

"Correct. She was an assistant in a ladies' hairdressing salon in Melbourne, Australia. She was proud of her Greek ancestry. When New Sparta was thrown open to immigration from Earth she scraped together her savings and borrowed quite a few credits—which she repaid, by the way; I give her credit for that—with the idea of setting up in the same line of business here, getting in on the ground floor. Of course, in the beginning ladies' hairdressers were something of a novelty and quite a few men wandered into them by mistake to get their flowing locks trimmed and their beards curled. Brasidus made that mistake. He didn't know much about women then and she knew who he was—he wasn't yet Archon but he was on the way up—and poured on the motherly charm. She was able to hitch her wagon to his rising star."

"So Cinderella married the handsome prince," said Grimes sardonically. "And they all lived happily ever after."

She said, "We have some living to do ourselves after all this time."

She led the way into his bedroom.

Chapter 6

It had been a long time, as she had said, but after the initial fumbling there was the old, sweet familiarity, the fitting of part to part, the teasing caress of hands on skin, of lips on lips and then, from her, the sharp yet melodious cries as he drove deeper and deeper and his own groans as her arms and legs imprisoned his body, her heels pummeling his buttocks.

They did not—they were out of practice with each other—reach climax together but her orgasm preceded his by only a few seconds.

They would rather have remained in the rumpled bed, to talk lazily for a while and then, after not too long an interval, to resume their love-making but, after all, they were guests and, furthermore, guests in the palace of a planetary ruler. Such people, no matter how humble their origins (or, perhaps, especially if their origins were humble) do not care to be kept waiting. So they showered together—but did not make an erotic game of it—and resumed their clothing. Maggie, who, by this time, was well acquainted with the layout of the palace, led Grimes to the small, private dining room where they were to eat with the Archon. They arrived there just before Brasidus.

The meal was a simple one, served by two very homely maidservants. There was a sort of casserole of some meat that might have been lamb, very heavily spiced. There was a rough red wine that went surprisingly well with the main course. For a sweet there was not too bad baclava, accompanied by thick, syrupy coffee. "We do not grow our own yet," said Brasidus, "but we hope to be doing so by next year. Soon, John, there will be no need for your *Sister Sue* to bring us cargoes of such luxuries from Earth." He laughed. "And what will you do then to make an honest living? Return to a career of piracy or find another governor's job?" There was brandy, in warmed inhalers, a quite good Metaxa.

The serving wenches cleared away the debris of the meal.

Having asked the permission of their host Grimes lit his pipe and Maggie a cigarillo. They were expecting, both of them, to settle down to an evening of reminiscent conversation over the brandy bottle but Brasidus surprised them.

"Help yourselves to more drinks, if you wish," he told them. "I am going to change. I shall not keep you long."

"To change, Brasidus?" asked Grimes.

"Yes. I have heard much of that new show at the Arena—you, Maggie, told me of it. I have not seen it yet. Ellena does not approve of such entertainment. I thought that this evening would be an ideal opportunity for me to witness the . . . the goings on."

"You're the boss," said Grimes.

When he was gone Maggie said, "He likes doing the Haroun al-Raschid thing now and again. Strolling among his citizens incognito, keeping his finger on the pulse and all the rest of it. Ellena doesn't altogether approve, but when the cat's away. . . ."

"And we're among the mice this evening, I suppose."

"I'm afraid so. But *you* should enjoy the show at the Arena. As I recall you, you have a thing about the weirder variations of the female face and form divine. That cat woman on Morrowvia with whom you had a roll in the hay. That *peculiar* clone or whatever she was from whom the Survey Service had to rescue you when you were trying to get *Bronson Star* back to where she had been skyjacked from. There have been others, no doubt."

"Mphm," grunted Grimes through a cloud of acrid tobacco smoke. He refilled the brandy inhalers. "Mphm."

"I will have one too," said Brasidus.

Grimes stared at him. Had it not been for the man's voice he would never have recognized the Archon. Yet the disguise was simple enough, just a spray-on dye applied to hair and beard, converting what had been light brown hair with the occasional silver thread to a not unnatural looking black.

The Archon drained his glass, then led the way out of the small dining room.

They made their way to what Grimes thought of as the tradesmen's entrance.

Two men were waiting for them there, dressed, as was Grimes, in one-piece gray suits in a somewhat outmoded Terran style. Unlike Grimes, who liked a touch of garish color in his neckwear, they had on cravats that almost exactly matched the color and texture of the rest of their clothing. Their side pockets bulged, as did Grimes'. Were they, he wondered, also pipe smokers? The Archon himself was dressed in the clothing appropriate to a lower middle class citizen on a night out—knee-length blue tunic with touches of golden embroidery, rather elaborate sandals with, it seemed, more brass (not very well polished) than leather. Maggie had on the modified Greek female dress that had been introduced from Earth—a short, white, rather flimsy tunic, sleeveless and with one of her shoulders left completely bare.

Brasidus introduced his two bodyguards—or so Grimes thought they must be; they looked the part—as Jason and Paulus. They could have been twins—although, he found later, they were not even related. They were tallish rather than tall, stoutish rather than stout and wore identical sullen expressions on their utterly undistinguished faces.

Jason brought a rather battered four-passenger hovercar round to the portico. It looked like something bought, cheaply, from Army Surplus. But there was nothing at all wrong with its engine and Grimes noticed various bulges in its exterior paneling that probably concealed weapons of some kind.

Jason was a good driver.

Soon the vehicle was whining through the narrow streets of the city which, mainly, were illumined by deliberately archaic gas flares, avoiding near collisions with contemptuous ease, finally gliding into the garish neon glare of the Street of the Haetaeri. Parking was found very close to the entrance of Aristotle's Arena. The three men and the woman got out and walked the short distance to the ticket booth. Brasidus pulled a clinking coin purse from the pouch at his belt and paid admission for the party.

"It's a good show, citizen," said the ticket vendor, a woman who was disguised as a Japanese geisha but whose face, despite the thickly applied cosmetics, was more Caucasian than Asian. "You're just in time to see the cat girls doing their thing."

Maggie, who had been to this place before, led the way down a flight of stone stairs. At the bottom of these they emerged from dim lighting into what was almost complete darkness. An usherette dressed in what looked like an imitation of an Amazon guard's uniform—but the tip of her short spear functioned as a torch—led them to their seats, which were four rows back from the circular, sand-covered arena. She sold them doughnut-shaped pneumatic cushions—the seating was on stone benches—which they had to inflate themselves. As they settled down in an approximation to comfort the show started.

There was music of some kind over the public address system. Grimes didn't recognize the tune. Maggie whispered, "But you should, John. Apparently it's a song that was popular on Earth—oh, centuries ago. Somebody must have done his homework. It's called, 'What's new, Pussycat?' "

Brasidus muttered sourly, "Some Earth imports we could do without."

A spotlight came on, illuminating the thing that emerged from the tunnel that gave entrance to the arena. It was . . . *Surely not!* thought Grimes. But it was. It was a giant mouse. A robot mouse, its movements almost lifelike. There were no real mice on New Sparta, of course, although immigrants from Earth knew about them and there were now plenty of illustrated books on Terran zoology. And cats, real cats, had been introduced by the Terran immigrants.

The mouse made an unsteady circuit of the arena.

Two more spotlights came on, shining directly onto the naked bodies of the two Morrowvian dancers. Their makeup accentuated their feline appearance, striped body paint making them look like humanoid tigresses. Spiky, artificial whiskers decorated their cheeks and vicious fangs protruded from their mouths.

They did not make the mistake of dropping to all fours but they moved with catlike grace, in time to the wailing music. They stalked the mouse from opposite directions and whoever was at the remote controls of the robot managed to convey a quite convincing impression of animal panic, even to a thin, high, terrified squeaking. Every now and again one of the girls would catch it, but do no more than stoop gracefully to bat the robot off its feet with a swipe of a pawlike hand. Each time it recovered and made another dash, and then the other girl would deal with it as her companion had done.

Finally the audience was tiring of the cat and mouse game. There were shouts of, "Finish it! Finish it!"

The taller of the two girls pounced. She dropped to her knees and brought her mouth, with those vicious fangs, down to the neck of the giant mouse. There was a final, ear-piercing squeak. There must have been bladders full of some red fluid under the robot's synthetic skin; a jet of what looked like blood spurted out over the cat woman's face, dripped on to the sand. She made her exit then, still on all fours, the carcass hanging from her mouth. Either the robot was very light or those false teeth were very securely anchored.

Her companion trailed after her, also on her hands and knees, caterwauling jealously.

The applause could have been more enthusiastic but, even so, the audience wasn't sitting on its collective hands.

"Quite good," admitted Brasidus. Then, "You have been to Morrowvia, John and Maggie. Do the people there really hunt like that?"

"They are fond of hunting," Maggie told him. "But they hunt much larger animals than mice, and they use spears and bows and arrows. And their teeth, after all the engineered genetic alterations, are like yours and mine. And they don't have whiskers. And their skins aren't striped, although their hair, on the head and elsewhere, often is. . . ."

"Please leave me some illusions," laughed Brasidus.

But Grimes was not listening to them.

He was looking across the arena to where a tangle of audio and video recording equipment had been set up. In the middle of this, like a malignant female spider in her web, was a woman.

Even over a distance Grimes recognized her, and thereafter, while the lights were still on, tried to keep his face turned away from her. Eating one of the hot, spiced sausages that Brasidus had bought from a passing attendant helped.

Chapter 7

"Citizens!" The voice of the master of ceremonies blared from the public address system. "Citizens! Now it is my great pleasure to announce the two boxing kangaroos from New Alice . . ." There was an outburst of applause; obviously this was a very popular act. Grimes could not catch the names of the performers. It would be too much of a coincidence, he thought, if they should turn out to be Shirl and Darleen. Those ladies had been in show business on New Venusberg but as quarry in the so-called kangaroo hunt. He knew that they could fight—first as gladiators in the Colosseum and then helping to beat off a Shaara attack—but their weapons had been boomerangs, not their fists. "And now may I call for volunteers? You know the rules. No weapons, bare fists only. Should any one of you succeed in knocking down one of the ladies she will be yours for the night. Stand up, those who wish to take part in the prize fight of the century! The usherettes will escort you to the changing room."

All around the arena men were getting to their feet. There was no shortage of volunteers.

"What about you, John?" asked Maggie. "Wouldn't you like to add a New Alician to your list of conquests?"

"No," Grimes said. "No." (He had no need to tell her that he and those two New Alicians, Shirl and Darleen, had been rather more than just good friends.)

"*I* am tempted," said Brasidus.

"It would not be wise," said Jason.

The last of the volunteers—there had been two dozen of them—had been led to the changing room. The house lights dimmed. There was taped music, an old Australian folk song that Grimes recognized. *Tie me kangaroo down, sport, tie me kangaroo down* . . . Some, more than a few, of the audience, knew the words and started to sing. Grimes joined them.

"Please don't," said Maggie, wincing exaggeratedly.

Then the song was over and the music that replaced it was old, old. There was the eerie whispering of the didgerydoo, the xylophonic clicking of singing sticks. Out of the tunnel and onto the sand bounded the two New Alicians, their hands held like paws in front of their small breasts. Save for the absence of long, muscular tails they could well have been large, albino kangaroos. As they hopped around the ring the lights over the arena itself brightened and some, but not all, of the illusion evaporated. But it was still obvious that the remote ancestry of these girls had not been human. There were the heavy rumps, the very well-developed thighs, the lower legs inclined to be skinny, something odd about the jointure of the knees. They were horse-faced, but pleasantly so, handsome rather than pretty, not quite beautiful. They were. . . .

Surely not! thought Grimes. This would be altogether too much of a coincidence. First Maggie (but his and her presence on this world together was perhaps not so coincidental), then Fenella Pruin, and now Shirl and Darleen. But he knew, all too well, that real life abounds in coincidences that a fiction writer would never dare to introduce.

The music fell silent. There was a roll of drums, a blaring trumpet. There was the voice of the announcer as the first pair of volunteers, in bright scarlet boxer shorts, came trotting out through the tunnel.

"Citizens! Killer Kronos and Battling Bellepheron, to uphold the honor of New Sparta!"

The men, both of them heavily muscled louts, raised their fists above their heads and turned slowly to favor each and every member of the audience with simian grins.

A bell sounded.

The men advanced upon their female adversaries, clenched fists ready to deliver incapacitating blows. Shirl and Darleen stood their ground. Kronos launched what should have been a devastating swipe, that would have been one such had it connected. But Shirl little more than shrugged and the fist missed her left ear by considerably more than the thickness of a coat of paint. And then she was on him, her own fists pummeling his chest and belly. He roared with rage and tried to throw his thick arms about her, to crush her into submission. She danced back and he embraced nothingness. What happened next was almost too fast for the eye to follow. She jumped straight up and drove both feet into his midsection. It was almost as though she were balanced on a stout, muscular but invisible tail. She and Kronos hit the sand simultaneously, she in a crouching posture, he flat on his back. He stirred feebly, made an attempt to get up and then slumped.

Meanwhile Darleen was disposing of her own adversary by more orthodox means, using fists only. It was a classical knock-out.

So it went on. Some bouts were ludicrously short, others gave better value for the customers' money. Some challengers limped out of the arena under their own steam, others had to be carried off.

Brasidus was highly amused. "These wenches," he said, "would make a better showing in a fight than the Lady Ellena's Amazon Guards. But I suppose that unarmed combat is all that they're good at."

"Not so," said Grimes. "Their real specialty is throwing weapons. With them they're lethal."

"You seem to know a lot about the people of New Alice," Maggie said. "Have you ever been there?"

"No," he told her. "I . . . I met some of them once, on another planet." (Perhaps some day he would tell her of his misadventures on New Venusberg. Had it not been for the inhibiting influence of Eldoradan investors in the more dubious entertainments available on the pleasure planet the galactic media would have given him and Fenella Pruin more than their fair share of notoriety. As it was, hardly anybody knew what had happened and the part that Grimes had played.)

"Javelins?" asked Brasidus, his mind still on weaponry.

"Not quite. For throwing spears they use something called a *woomera*, a throwing stick, which they use like a sling. It gives the spears extra range. But their most spectacular weapon is the boomerang. . . ."

"And what is that, John?"

Before Grimes could reply the voice of the announcer boomed over the auditorium.

"And now, citizens, the two wonder women from New Alice, the splendiferous Shirl and the delicious Darleen, will entertain you with an exhibition of the art of boomerang throwing. The boomerang is a weapon developed on their native world in Stone Age days, millennia before there were such things as computers and yet employing and utilizing the most subtle principles of modern aerodynamics. . . ."

"The boomerang was developed on Earth, long before New Alice was ever dreamed of," whispered Grimes indignantly.

All the lights came on and the auditorium was now as brightly illumined as the arena itself. Shirl and Darleen stood in the center of the ring, their naked bodies gleaming in the harsh glare. Despite their participation in twelve boxing bouts their skins were unmarked. Slowly they scanned the audience. At one time Grimes thought they were looking straight at him but they gave no sign of recognition. But, of course, they would not be expecting to see him here. After the show he would go around to the stage door, or whatever it was called, to give the girls a big surprise.

Two of the pseudo Amazons came onto the arena, each carrying a small bundle of wooden boomerangs. There were big ones, and some not so big, and little ones. They were decorated with bands of bright paint— white and blue and scarlet.

The attendants bowed to Shirl and Darleen and then strode away. There was the obligatory roll of drums. Shirl picked up a half dozen of the little boomerangs from the sand. She handed the first one to Darleen, who threw it from her. Then the second one, then the third, then the fourth, and the fifth and the sixth. It was a dazzling display of juggling with never less than five of the things in the air at the same time, each one terminating its short, circular flight in Darleen's right hand just after the launching of another, resting there only briefly before being relaunched itself. And then the flight pattern was changed and it was Shirl who was catching, one by one, all six of the boomerangs, catching and throwing time after time again. Another half dozen of the boomerangs came into play and Shirl and Darleen widened the distance between themselves, a boomerang-juggling duo.

Finally each of the things was thrown so that they came to rest in the center of the arena, forming a pile that could not have been neater had it been stacked by hand.

There was the big boomerang flung by Shirl (or was it Darleen? Grimes still had trouble distinguishing one from the other) that made several orbits of the main overhead light, like a misshapen planet about its primary, before returning to its thrower's hand. There were the medium-sized ones that were sent whirling over the heads of the audience, too high for any rash person to try to catch one at the risk of losing a finger or two. Most of these were directed to the vicinity of where Fenella Pruin was sitting amidst her recording apparatus.

At last the girls decided that they had given her enough of a show and turned to face that part of the auditorium where the Archon's party was sitting. They scanned the faces of the audience and then they were looking directly at Grimes. They held a whispered consultation, then looked at him again. So they had recognized him. So he would not be able to surprise them in their dressing room when the show was over. It was rather a pity. He shrugged.

Shirl (or was it Darleen?) picked up one of the medium-sized boomerangs. She looked at Grimes. He looked at her. He raised a hand in a gesture of greeting. Both girls ignored it. Shirl assumed the thrower's stance. Her right arm was a blur of motion—and then the boomerang was coming straight at Grimes, the rapidity of its rotation about its short axis making it almost invisible. He tried to duck but he was jammed in between Maggie and Jason and unable to move.

There was a sudden rattle of automatic pistol fire; Paulus had pulled his vicious little Minetti from a side pocket. The boomerang disintegrated in mid-flight, its shredded splinters falling harmlessly onto the people in the front row. There were shouts and screams. There were two of the pseudo-Amazon usherettes making their hasty way to the scene of the disturbance—and they were not so pseudo after all; each was holding a pistol, a stungun but a weapon nonetheless and lethal when set to full intensity. Jason had his pistol out now and he and the other bodyguard were both standing, pointing their Minettis at the approaching Amazons.

"Put them down, you fools!" roared Brasidus.

Grimes hoped that they would have enough sense to realize that he meant the guns, not the chuckers-out.

The stunguns buzzed. They had been set at very low intensity, not even causing temporary paralysis but inducing a dazed grogginess. The two Amazons were joined by four more strapping, uniformed wenches and the Archon's party was dragged ignominiously to the manager's office.

Ironic applause accompanied their forced departure from the auditorium.

Chapter 8

Aristotle was a fat man, bald, piggy eyed, clad in a white robe similar to those worn by the professional classes, soiled down the front by dropped cigar ash and liquor spillage. He was smoking a cigar now, speaking around it as he addressed the prisoners who stood before his wide, littered desk, supported by the Amazon usherettes.

"You . . ." he snarled. "You . . . Offworlders by the look of you . . . At an entertainment such as mine some riotous behavior is tolerated, but not riotous behavior with . . . *firearms*." With a pudgy hand he poked disdainfully at the two automatic pistols that had been placed on his desk. "I suppose you'll try to tell me—and the police, when they get here, and the magistrate when you come up for trial—that you didn't know that on this world civilians are not allowed to carry such weapons, by order of the Archon. You know now."

"But this . . ." Jason waved feebly toward Brasidus. "But this is the . . ."

The Archon raised a warning hand, glared at his bodyguard.

"And this is what, or who?" demanded the showman disdainfully. "Some petty tradesman enjoying a night on the tiles with his offplanet friends, at their expense, no doubt. Showing them the sights, as long as they're doing the paying. And, talking of the foreigners, which of them started the gunplay?"

"This one," said the Amazon supporting Paulus, giving him a friendly cuff as she spoke.

"So it was you," growled Aristotle. "And now, sir, would you mind satisfying my curiosity before the police come to collect you? What possessed you to pull a gun in a public place and, even worse, to interrupt a highly skilled act by two of my performers?"

"That . . . That boomerang thing . . . It was coming straight at the Commodore. I did my best to protect him."

"The Commodore? You mean the gentleman with the jug handle ears? I do have a distinguished clientele, don't I? I know of only one visiting Commodore on New Sparta at this time, and *he* is a guest of the Archon. He'd be too much of a stuffed shirt to sample the pleasures of the Street of the Haetaeri."

"Little you know," said a familiar female voice.

Aristotle shifted his attention from the prisoners to somebody who had just come into the office. "Oh, Miss Pruin . . ." he said coldly. "I do not think that you were invited to sit in on this interview."

"I invited myself," said Fenella. "After all, news is news."

Grimes managed to turn his head to look at her. She had changed very little, if not at all. Her face with rather too much nose and too little chin, with teeth slightly protuberant, the visage of an insatiably curious animal but perversely attractive nonetheless. She grinned at him.

"Do you know these people?" he demanded.

"Not all of them, Aristotle. But the gentleman with the jug handle ears is Captain Grimes, although I believe that he did, briefly, hold the rank of Company Commodore with the Eldorado Corporation. That was when he commanded a pirate squadron. . . ."

"Privateers," Grimes corrected her tiredly. "Not pirates."

She ignored this. "And the lady is Commander Maggie Lazenby, one of the scientific officers of the Federation Survey Service. Both she and Captain—sorry, Commodore—Grimes were on this planet many years ago and were involved in the troubles that led to the downfall of the old regime."

"Oh. *That* Grimes," said Aristotle. His manner seemed to be softening slightly. "But I still am entitled to an explanation as to why his friend ruined the Shirl and Darleen act."

"The boomerang," insisted Paulus, "was coming straight at the Commodore. It could have taken his head off."

"It would not," said two familiar female voices speaking in chorus. Shirl and Darleen, light robes thrown around their bodies, had come into the office which, although considerably larger than a telephone booth, was getting quite crowded. "It would not."

"It would not," Aristotle agreed. "Surely you know what that part of the act signified?"

"The boomerang," explained Shirl (or was it Darleen?), "would have stopped and turned just short of you, returning to my hand. It was a signal to you that you were to follow it—after the show, of course. I thought that everybody knew."

"It was announced," said Aristotle. "Just as it was announced that any boxer who succeeded in knocking down Shirl or Darleen would be entitled to her favors."

"It was *not* announced," said Grimes.

"It was *not* announced," said Jason and Paulus, speaking together.

"Well, it should have been," admitted Aristotle. "But all of my regular customers know of the arrangement."

"We are not regular customers," said Brasidus.

"But that, sir, does not entitle your friends to brandish and discharge firearms in my auditorium." He raised and turned his head. "Come in, Sergeant, come in! I shall be obliged if you will place these persons under arrest. No, not Commodore Grimes and Commander Lazenby, they are guests of the Archon. But the other three. Charge them with discharging firearms, illegally held firearms at that, in a public place."

"If you would please tell me who is which . . ." said the Sergeant tiredly.

He looked at Grimes. "Oh, I recognize you, sir. Your photograph was in the *Daily Democrat*. But which of the ladies am I supposed to take in?"

He stood there in his military style uniform (but black instead of brown leather, stainless steel instead of brass), removing his plumed helmet so that he could scratch his head. The two constables, reluctant to enter the crowded office, remained outside the now open door.

"Just the men, Sergeant," Aristotle told him impatiently. "Just the men."

"All right." The Sergeant grabbed Brasidus by the arm that was not held by an Amazon usherette. "Come on, you. Come quietly, or else."

"But that is the Archon," objected Paulus in a shocked voice. He tried to break away from restraint so that he could come to his master's aid. "Take your paws off the Archon!"

"And I'm Zeus masquerading as a mere mortal!" The Sergeant pulled Brasidus towards the door. "Come *on*!"

"He *is* the Archon," stated Grimes.

"Come, come, sir. This lout is nothing like Brasidus. I did duty in the Palace Guard before the Lady Ellena had us replaced by her Amazon Corps. I've a good memory for details—have to in my job. His hair and beard are light brown, just starting to go gray. Besides—" he laughed— "Ellena would never allow him to come to a dive like this."

"My establishment is not a dive!" expostulated Aristotle indignantly.

"Isn't it? Then what's it doing on this street?" He called to the constables. "Come in, you two, and grab the other two lawbreakers."

"There'll be some room for us after you get out," muttered one of the men.

The Sergeant twisted Brasidus' right arm behind his back. It must have been painful.

"Take your hands off me!" growled Brasidus. "Take your hands off me, or I'll have you posted to the most dismal village on all of New Sparta, Sergeant Priam. I am the Archon."

Priam laughed. "So you think you can fool me by saying my name? Every petty crook in the city knows it."

"He *is* the Archon," said Grimes.

"He *is* the Archon," stated Maggie.

"He could just be," said Fenella. "There are techniques of disguise, you know. I've used them myself."

"Call the Palace," Brasidus ordered Aristotle. "The Lady Ellena will identify me."

The showman pressed buttons at the base of the videophone on his desk. Only he could see the little screen but all of them could hear the conversation.

"May I speak to the Lady Ellena, please?"

"Who is that?" demanded an almost masculine female voice, probably that of the duty officer of the Amazon Guard.

"Aristotle, of Aristotle's Arena."

"What business would *you* have with the Lady Ellena?"

"None of yours, woman. I want to speak to her, is all."

"Well, you can't."

"It is my right as a citizen."

"You still can't. She's out."

"She's still at her meeting," said Brasidus.

"What meeting?" demanded the Sergeant.

"Of the Women's Branch of the New Hellas Association."

"You seem to know a lot about her movements," muttered the police officer. He looked as though he were beginning to wonder what sort of mess he had been dragged into. If this scruffy helot were indeed the Archon . . . But surely (so Grimes read his changing expressions) that was not possible. "Get the New Hellas bitches on the phone," he ordered Aristotle. "Get the number of their meeting hall from the read-out."

Aristotle obliged.

Then, "May I talk with the Lady Ellena, please?"

"She is addressing the meeting still," came the reply in a vinegary female voice.

"This is important."

"*Who* are you?"

Before he could answer the Sergeant had pushed his way round to the showman's side of the desk.

"This is Sergeant Priam of the Vice Squad. This is official police business. Bring the Lady Ellena to the telephone at once."

"What for?"

"For the identification of a body."

There was a little scream from the New Hellas lady.

"Bring him round here," ordered the Sergeant, "so that he can look into the video pick-up. And then we shall soon know one way or the other."

Two of the Amazon usherettes obliged.

There was some delay, and then Grimes heard Ellena's voice.

"Is this the body that I'm supposed to identify? But, firstly, he's alive . . ."

"I didn't say a *dead* body, Lady."

"And secondly, I wouldn't know him from a bar of soap."

"It's me," said Brasidus.

"And who's 'me'? I most certainly don't know you, my man, and I most certainly do not wish to know you."

But she did not terminate the conversation.

"Have you any alcohol?" Brasidus asked Aristotle.

"Do you expect me to give you a free drink after all the trouble you have caused?"

"Not for drinking. And, in any case, I will pay you for what I use. Some alcohol, please, and some tissues . . ."

Grudgingly the showman produced a bottle of gin from a drawer and, from another, a box of tissues. He demanded—and received—a sum far in excess of the retail price of these articles. Everybody watched as the Archon applied the gin-soaked tissue to his beard which, after a few applications, returned to its normal color.

"So," said the Lady Ellena, "it is you. I did recognize the voice, of course. But where are you calling from? A police station? And why do you wish me to identify you?"

"I'm at Aristotle's Arena. . . ."

"Oh. Another of your incognito slumming expeditions. And you got yourself into trouble. Really, my dear, you carry the concept of democracy too far. Much too far. For a man of your standing to frequent such a haunt of iniquity . . . I suggest that you order the Sergeant to furnish you with transport back to the Palace. At once."

"You had better not come with me," said Brasidus as Grimes and Maggie made to follow him and his police escort from the office. "The Lady Ellena regards spacemen as a bad influence. And as for the rest of you . . ." The note of command was strong in his voice. "As for the rest of you, I shall be greatly obliged if no word of tonight's adventure gets out.

I am requesting, not ordering—but, even so, I could have your Arena closed, Aristotle, and your performers deported, just as you, Fenella Pruin, could also be deported, after a spell in one of our jails. I am sorry, John and Maggie, that we shall not be able to enjoy the rest of the evening together, but there will be other times. Jason will run you back to the Palace at your convenience.

"A good night to you all."

He was gone, accompanied by the deferential policemen.

"Could we have our pistols back?" asked Paulus.

"Help yourself," said Aristotle.

"Another good story that I am not allowed to use," grumbled Fenella Pruin. "At least, not on this world. But the evening need not be a total disaster." She turned to Grimes. "Perhaps an interview, John? I am staying at the New Sparta Sheraton. . . ."

"And *we*," said Shirl and Darleen, "are staying at the Hippolyte Hotel."

"And I," said Maggie sweetly, "saw him first. Come along, John. We'll find a place for a quiet drink or two before we return to the Palace."

"I'm supposed to be running you back," said Jason sullenly.

"So you are. Come with us, then. But you will sit at a separate table. Don't look so worried. We'll pay for your drinks."

Chapter 9

They had their drinks in an establishment where the almost naked waitresses made it plain that they were willing to oblige in more ways than the serving of drinks and who regarded the few female customers with open hostility. After having had a glass of ouzo spilled in her lap Maggie decided that it was time to leave. Jason, who had been getting on well with the hostess who had joined him at his table, sharing the large bottle of retsina that had been purchased at Grimes' expense, got to his feet reluctantly. His companion glared at him when he corked the wine bottle and took it with him.

"Waste not, want not, Commodore," he said.

"Too right," agreed Grimes.

"I thought that this wine was a present," complained the overly plump blonde.

"It is," said Jason. "To me."

They made their way to the parked hovercar, got in. The drive back to the palace was uneventful. They entered the building, as they had left it, by a back door. Amazon guards, or guards of any kind, were conspicuous by their absence. Security seemed to be nonexistent. Grimes said as much.

Jason laughed. "If you'd tried to get in this way without me along with you there'd have been a few surprises. Unpleasant ones."

"Such as?" asked Grimes.

"That'd be telling, Commodore. Just take my word for it."

"You're not a native, are you?" asked Grimes, who had detected more than a trace of American accent.

"Nosir. No way. Before I came here I was an operative with Panplanet Security, home office Chicago. Paulus and I brought all the tricks of our trade with us. And now good night to you, Commodore Grimes and Commander Lazenby. I take it that you know the way back to your quarters."

Maggie assured him that they did.

They went to Grimes' suite.

They sat down and talked, discussing the events of the evening, comparing notes.

Maggie asked, "However did you get to know those two New Alice wenches, or, come to that, Fenella Pruin?"

"It's a long, sad story," he said. "At the finish of it I had all three of them as passengers aboard *Little Sister*—the deep space pinnace of which I was owner-master before I bought *Sister Sue*."

"It must have been an interesting voyage."

"Too interesting at times. But there were . . . compensations."

"I'm sure. Knowing you." She sipped from the drink that he had poured her. "It's a pity that we have no power to recruit the Pruin woman. She impresses me as being a really skillful investigator."

"Only when there's a story with sex involved, the only kind of story that *Star Scandal* prints."

"There are other stories, you know, equally interesting, and other media with good money to pay for them. Perhaps if I could get her interested . . . Or if you could. You know her better than I do. Come to that, Shirl and Darleen could do some work for us. . . ."

"Shirl and Darleen? Oh, they'd make quite good bodyguards. They're at their best in a rough and tumble. But as intelligence agents? Hardly."

"As intelligence agents," she said firmly. "Not very high grade ones, but useful. They told you where they were staying."

"The Hippolyte Hotel. But what's that got to do with it?"

"The Hippolyte Hotel is owned by a company made up of members of the New Hellas Association, mainly well-to-do female members. The Lady Ellena is a major shareholder. The name of the place is her choice. As you must have already gathered she has a thing about Amazons. In case you don't already know, Hippolyte was Queen of the Amazons."

"I'm not altogether ignorant of Terran history and mythology."

"All right, all right. But the Hippolyte is much frequented by NHA people. Too, I found out that the Hippolyte offered special rates to the stars now appearing at Aristotle's Arena."

"What's so sinister about that?"

"I . . . don't know. But there have been rumors. All those performers are alleged to be specialists in various offplanet martial arts. As far as your girlfriends Shirl and Darleen are concerned it's more than a mere allegation. Could Ellena be thinking of recruiting instructors in exotic weaponry and techniques for her Amazon Guards?"

"Terrible as an army with boomerangs," misquoted Grimes.

"Very funny. But our own Survey Service Marine Corps Commandos are trained to inflict grievous bodily harm with a wide variety of what many would consider to be archaic weapons."

"Mphm."

"Officially," she said, "you're in charge of this Intelligence Branch operation, whether you like it or not. Not only do you rank me, but you've had more experience in Intelligence work."

"But I didn't have the intelligence to realize it."

"You do now. Anyhow, although I'm officially subordinate to you, I can make suggestions, recommendations. I recommend that you exercise your influence on Shirl and Darleen—they seem to like you, the Odd Gods of the Galaxy alone know why!—and persuade them to accept the Lady Ellena's offer. If she makes it, that is. And if she does, and they do, then perhaps your other girlfriend might stay on here to do a story on their experiences instead of following the rest of the troupe across the Galaxy. . . ."

"This used to be an all-male planet," said Grimes. "But now . . . First you, then Fenella, then Shirl and Darleen. It never rains but it pours."

"You're not complaining, are you?" she asked.

"Certainly not about you," he told her gallantly.

They finished their drinks and extinguished their smokes and went to bed, the bed that Maggie would have to leave to return to her own before the domestic staff was up and about.

Chapter 10

The next morning Grimes was awakened from his second sleep—he had drifted off again after Maggie had left him—by one of the very plain serving maids who brought him a jug of thick, sweet coffee and informed him that breakfast would be served, in the small dining room, in an hour's time. He had some coffee (he would have preferred tea) and then did all the things that he had to do and attired himself in a plain, black shirt and a kilt in the Astronaut's Guild tartan—black, gold and silver—long, black socks and highly polished, gold-buckled, black shoes. He went out into the passageway and rapped on the door to Maggie's suite.

She called, "Who is it?"

"Me."

"Come in, come in."

He was amused to find that she was attired as he was, although her kilt was shorter and lighter than his and the tartan was the green, blue, brown and gold of the Institute of Life Sciences.

"All we need," he said, "is a piper to precede us into the Archon's presence. I wonder if he'll give us haggis for breakfast."

She laughed. "Knowing you, you'll be wishing that he would. You'll be pining even for Scottish oatmeal. The Lady Ellena's ideas as to what constitutes a meal to start the day do not coincide with yours."

They most certainly did not. Grimes maintained that God had created pigs and hens only so that eggs and bacon could make a regular appearance on the breakfast tables of civilized people. He regarded the little, sweet buns with barely concealed distaste and did no more than sip at the syrupy, sweet coffee.

The Archon was in a subdued mood. The Lady Ellena looked over the sparsely laden table at her husband's guests with obviously spurious sweetness.

"Do have another roll, Commodore. You do not seem to have much of an appetite this morning. Perhaps your party last night was rather too good."

Grimes took another roll. There was nothing else for him to eat.

"The Archon tells me," she went on, almost as though Brasidus were not among those present, "that you know two of the performers at Aristotle's Arena. Those rather odd girls called Shirl and Darleen. The boomerang throwers."

"Yes," admitted Grimes. "We are old acquaintances."

Maggie was trying hard not to laugh.

"You have no doubt already noticed," went on Ellena, "that I have formed a Corps of Amazons. I considered this to be of great importance on a planet such as this which, until recently, had never known women. Women, I decided, must be shown to be able to compete with men in every field, including the military arts and sciences."

"Mphm," grunted Grimes, pulling his pipe and tobacco pouch out from his sporran.

"Would you mind refraining, Commodore? I am allergic to tobacco smoke. Besides, the ancient Hellenes never indulged in tobacco."

Only because they never had the chance to do so, thought Grimes as he put his pipe and pouch away.

"I am interested," she said, "in recruiting instructors from all over the Galaxy. Brasidus has told me that Shirl and Darleen—what *peculiar* names—are proficient in boxing techniques, especially a sort of foot boxing, and in the use of throwing weapons. Boomerangs."

"The ones that they demonstrated last night," said Grimes, "were only play boomerangs."

"I know, Commodore, I know. After all I, like you, am an Australian. Or, in my own case, *was*. I am now a citizen of New Sparta. But I have no doubt that the young . . . ladies can use hunting boomerangs, *killing* boomerangs, with effect."

"I've seen them do it," said Grimes.

"You have? You must tell me all about it some time. Meanwhile, I shall be greatly obliged if you will act on my behalf and try to persuade the young ladies to enter my service as instructors."

"Rank and pay?" asked Grimes, always sensitive to such matters.

"I was thinking of making them sergeants," said Ellena.

"No way," said Grimes. "There will have to be much more inducement. As theatrical artistes they are well paid." (Were they?) "They are members of a glamorous profession. I would suggest commissioned rank, lieutenancies at least, with pay to match and specialists' allowances in addition."

"Do you intend to demand a 10 percent agent's commission?" asked Maggie.

He kicked her under the table and she subsided.

Ellena did not appear to have a sense of humor. She said, sourly, "Of course, Commodore, if you wish a recruiting sergeant's bounty, that can be arranged."

He said, "Commander Lazenby was only joking, Lady."

Maggie said, "Was I?"

Ellena looked from one to the other, emitted an exasperated sigh.

"Spacepersons," she said, "consider things funny that we mere planetlubbers do not."

Such as money? thought Grimes.

"Nonetheless," she went on, "I shall be greatly obliged if you will endeavor to persuade Miss Shirl and Miss Darleen to enlist in my Amazon Corps. Need I remind you that you are a shipowner whose vessel makes money trading to and from this world? Perhaps if you could bring yourself to call upon them this very morning. . . ."

"I will come with you, John," said Brasidus, breaking his glum silence.

"But you have forgotten, dear, that there is a Council meeting?"

"I have not, Ellena. But surely such a matter as providing separate toilets for the sexes in the Agora does not demand my presence."

"It does so. The status of women on this world must be elevated and you, as my husband, must make it plain that you think as I do."

"I'd accompany you, John," Maggie told him, "but I'm scheduled to address the Terra-Sparta Foundation on the history and culture of my own planet. I can't very well wriggle out of it."

"I'll organize transport for you, John," said Brasidus.

"It might be better if I did," said Ellena. "It will look better if the Commodore is driven to the Hippolyte by one of my Amazon Guards rather than by one of your musclebound louts."

So Grimes, in a small two-seater, a hovercar looking even more like an ancient war chariot than the generality of military vehicles on this world, was driven to the Hippolyte Hotel by a hefty, blonde wench who conveyed the impression that she should have been standing up holding reins rather than sitting down grasping a wheel. She brought the vehicle to an abrupt halt outside the main doorway of the hotel, leapt out with a fine display of long, tanned legs and then offered Grimes unneeded assistance out of the car to the pavement. The doorwoman, uniformed in imitation of Ellena's Amazons but squat and flabby (but with real muscles under the flab, thought Grimes) scowled at them.

"What would you, citizens?" she demanded.

"Just get out of the way, citizen, and let us pass."

"But *he* is a man."

"And I am Lieutenant Phryne, of the Lady Ellena's Amazon Guard, here on the Lady's business."

"And *him?*"

"The gentleman is Commodore Grimes, also on the Lady's business."

"All right. All right." She muttered to herself, "This is what comes of letting theatricals in here. Turning the place into a spacemen's brothel."

"What was that?" asked Phryne sharply.

"Nothing, Lieutenant, nothing."

"The next time you say nothing say it where I can't hear it."

Grimes looked around the lobby of the hotel with interest. All its walls were decorated with skillfully executed mosaic murals, every one of which depicted stern-looking ladies doing unkind things to members of the male sex. There was Jael, securing the hapless Sisera to the mattress with a hammer and a nail. There was Boadicea, whose scythed chariot wheels were slicing up the Roman legionnaires. There was Jeanne d'Arc, on horseback and in shining armor, in the act of decapitating an English knight with her long, gleaming sword. There was Prime Minister Golda riding in the open turret of an Israeli tank, leading a fire-spitting armored column against a rabble of fleeing Arabs. There was Prime Minister Maggie on the bridge of a battleship whose broadside was hurling destruction on the Argentine fleet. There was . . . There was too much, much too much.

Grimes couldn't help laughing.

"What is the joke, Commodore?" asked Lieutenant Phryne coldly.

"Whoever did these murals," explained Grimes, "might have been a good artist but he . . ." She glared at him. "But *she*," he corrected himself, "was a lousy historian."

"I do not think so."

"No?" He pointed with the stem of his pipe at the very imaginative depiction of the battle off the Falkland Islands. "To begin with, Mrs. Thatcher wasn't *there*. She ran things from London. Secondly, by that time battleships had been phased out. The flagship of the British fleet was an aircraft carrier, the other vessels destroyers, frigates and submarines. Thirdly, with the exception of one elderly and unlucky cruiser, the Argentine navy stayed in port."

"You seem to be very well informed," said the Amazon lieutenant coldly.

"I should be. My father is an historical novelist."

"Oh."

The pair of them walked to the reception desk.

"Would Miss Shirl and Miss Darleen be in?" asked Grimes.

"I think so, citizen," replied the slight, quite attractive brunette. "I shall call their suite and ask them to join you in the lobby. Whom shall I say is calling?"

Before Grimes could answer his escort said, "I am Lieutenant Phryne of the Lady Ellena's Amazon Guard. This citizen is Commodore Grimes. The business that we have to discuss is very private and best dealt with in their own quarters."

The girl said something about hotel regulations.

The lieutenant told her that the Lady Ellena was a major shareholder.

The girl said that Shirl and Darleen already had a visitor. A *lady*, she added.

"Then I shall be outnumbered," said Grimes. "I shall be no threat to anybody's virtue."

Both the receptionist and the lieutenant glared at him.

Chapter 11

"Come in!" called a female voice as Lieutenant Phryne rapped sharply on the door, which slid open. "Come in! This is Liberty Hall; you can spit on the mat and call the cat a bastard." Then, "Who's your new girlfriend, Grimes? You never waste much time, do you?"

Fenella Pruin, sprawled in an easy chair, her long, elegant legs exposed by her short *chiton*, a glass of gin in her hand, looked up at the commodore. So did Shirl and Darleen, who were sitting quite primly side by side on a sofa, holding cans of beer. Foster's, noted Grimes, an Australian brand, no doubt brought to New Sparta as part of one of *Sister Sue*'s cargoes.

"Lieutenant Phryne," said Grimes stiffly, "has been acting as my chauffeuse."

"And what are you acting as, Grimes? What hat are you wearing this bright and happy morning? Owner-master? Pirate commodore? Planetary governor?"

"Recruiting sergeant," said Grimes.

"You intrigue me. But take the weight off your feet. And you, Lieutenant. And find the Commodore a gin, Shirl, and his Amazon Guard whatever she fancies . . ."

After the drinks had been organized Grimes found himself sitting between Shirl and Darleen, facing Fenella.

"Here's to crime," she toasted, raising her refilled glass. "And now, Grimes, talk. What's with this recruiting sergeant business? Let me guess. You're an old boozing pal of the Archon's. The Archon's lady wife is building up her own private army, of which Lieutenant Phryne is a member. Lady Ellena is on the lookout for offplanet martial arts specialists to act as instructors. Right?"

"Right."

"And Shirl and Darleen are not only artists with the boomerang but expert in their own peculiar version of *savate*. Boxing with the feet. Right?"

"Right."

"What's in it for them?"

"Lieutenants' commissions. Standard pay for the rank, plus allowances."

"Should we accept, Fenella?" asked Shirl. "It would seem to be a steady job, staying in one place. We are becoming tired of jumping from world to world."

"Leave me to negotiate," said the journalist. Then, to Grimes, "At times I wear more than one hat myself. As well as being a star reporter I am a theatrical agent. Oh, only in respect of Shirl and Darleen. I sort of took them under my wing when you left them stranded on Bronsonia." She added virtuously, "Somebody had to."

"Is it an agent's hat you're wearing?" asked Grimes sardonically. "Or a halo?"

She ignored this and turned to Phryne. "What's lieutenant's pay in the Amazon Corps?"

"One thousand obols a month."

"And what's that in *real* money? Never mind. . . ." She used her wrist companion as a calculator. "Mmm. Not good, but not too bad. And the bennies?"

"Bennies, Lady?"

"Side benefits."

"Free accommodation, with meals in the officers' mess. Two new uniforms a year. A wine ration . . ."

"We do not like wine," said Darleen. "We like beer."

"I think that I could arrange that," Grimes said.

"All the more cargo for your precious ship to bring here," sneered Fenella. "But, anyhow, a generous beer ration must be part of the contract. Imported beer, not the local gnat's piss." Again she turned to Phryne. "What extra pay do instructors get?"

"I cannot say with any certainty. But junior officers often complain that instructor sergeants make more money than they do."

"And a sergeant's pay is?"

"In the neighborhood of six hundred obols a month."

"Which means that they must get at least another five hundred extra in special allowances. Find out how much it is, Grimes, and then argue that a commissioned officer should receive allowances on a much higher scale than a non-commissioned one. And, talking of commissions. . . . What about mine?"

"I do not think," said Grimes, "that the Amazon Corps needs a press officer."

"I wasn't talking about that sort of commission. I was talking about my agent's commission."

"Surely even you wouldn't take money off Shirl and Darleen!"

"I've no intention of doing so, but I expect something for myself for handling their affairs. To begin with, I got some very good coverage of the adventures of the rather tatty troupe that I signed them up with. (Talking of that, I shall expect the Lady Ellena to buy them out of their contract.) Now I shall want coverage of Shirl's and Darleen's experiences in the Amazon Guard. *With The Woman Warriors Of New Sparta* and all the rest of it. Which means that I must be given rights of entry to the Archon's palace at all times . . ."

"I did hear," said Grimes, "that you were given the bum's rush the one time that you came a-calling."

"I was. And I still resent it. Just see to it that it doesn't happen again."

"That is a matter for the Archon."

"Or for the Archoness. But you'll just have to talk her round, Grimes. If she wants Shirl and Darleen, those are the terms."

Grimes looked at her through the wreathing fumes from his pipe. The nostrils of her sharp nose were quivering but he did not think that this was due to the reek of burning tobacco. She was on the scent of something. She could be a valuable ally. Although he and Maggie were attached to the Intelligence Department the muckraking journalist was far more skilled at ferreting out information than they, simple spaceman and relatively unsophisticated scientist, could ever be.

He got to his feet.

He said, "I'll do my best, Fenella."

She said tartly, "There have been times when your best has not been good enough." Then he grinned. "But you usually finish up with what you want."

He turned to Shirl and Darleen. "Thank you for the drinks. And I hope that I'll soon be seeing you in uniform."

Darleen said, rather wistfully, "We would like to be wearing your uniform, aboard your ship."

He laughed and said, "Unfortunately the Merchant Navy, unlike the Survey Service, doesn't run to Marines. . . ."

"Perhaps when you next go a-pirating . . ." said Fenella.

"Mphm," grunted Grimes. (Piracy, to him, was a very dirty word.)

Accompanied by Lieutenant Phryne he made his way out of the suite and then down to the parked hovercar.

*   *   *

Phryne drove back to the palace by a circuitous, sight-seeing route.

She said snobbishly, "Forgive me for speaking my mind, sir, but those . . . ladies are not, in my opinion, even good NCO material. To become a commissioned officer one must possess at least a modicum of breeding."

"And Shirl and Darleen do not?"

"No. You must have seen them. Drinking their beer straight from the can."

"I often do that myself."

"But you're a spaceman, sir. You're different."

"They're from New Alice. They're different."

"You can say that again. And I don't suppose that they'll even know the right knives and forks and spoons to use in the officers' mess."

"I shouldn't worry. That's an art that they've probably picked up since I last knew them. I remember that Miz Pruin tried to bully what she called civilized table manners into them when she and they were passengers on my ship some time ago."

"Miz Pruin . . ." muttered Phryne scornfully. "So now she's to be allowed the run of the Palace. I had the pleasure of being guard commander when she was evicted."

"What have you got against her?"

"She's a muckraker. I've had experience of her muckraking. I'm from Earth originally, as are most of the women on New Sparta, but for a while I was a member of an experimental, all woman colony on New Lesbos. I soon found out that, when it came to the crunch, I was more heterosexual than otherwise but I was stuck there, with quite a few others, until I'd earned enough to pay my passage back home—and a police constable's salary was far from generous. Dear Fenella came sniffing around. She did a feature on New Lesbos for *Star Scandals*. What got my goat was that a photograph of a quite innocent beach party was captioned as a Lesbian orgy. Damn it all, there are nude beaches a-plenty on Earth and other planets!"

"But very few, these days, reserved for the use of one sex only," said Grimes.

"There just wasn't more than one sex on New Lesbos," she said, "just as there wasn't more than one sex here before the planet was thrown open to immigration."

"She's a good reporter," said Grimes.

"The only good reporter is a dead one," said Phryne. "And boomerangs are toys for backward primitives and kicking should be confined to the Association Football field."

Grimes laughed. "I take it, Lieutenant, that you were featured in that famous photograph."

"I was, Commodore. I was wrestling one of the other girls. But men wrestle each other, don't they? And nobody accuses them of being friendly."

Yet another useful word stolen from the English language by an overly noisy minority, thought Grimes.

He said, "What does it matter, anyhow?"

She said, "It matters to me."

Chapter 12

The Lady Ellena received Grimes in her office, listened to what he had to tell her.

She said, "You were overly generous, Commodore—but, of course, it is easy to be generous with somebody else's money. Even so. . . . Commissioned rank for that pair of cheap entertainers. . . ."

He said, "You wanted Shirl and Darleen. Now you've got them."

She said, "I most certainly did not want the Pruin woman. Now it seems that I've got her too."

Grimes told her, "She was part of the package deal, Lady."

Ellena made a major production of shrugging. "Oh, well. At least I shall not have to mingle with her socially. And I think that the Palace will be able to afford to treat her to an occasional meal in the sergeants' mess."

"Or the officers' mess," said Grimes. "Shirl and Darleen will be officers. . . ."

"Thanks to you."

". . . and they will wish, now and again, to entertain their friend."

"I cannot imagine her being a friend to anybody. But now, in *my* palace, she will be free to come and go, to eat food that *I* have paid for, to swill expensive imported beer. But that, of course, is the least of *your* worries, Commodore. After all, it is *your* ship that brings in all such Terran luxuries, at freight rates that ensure for you a very handsome profit."

"Being a shipowner," said Grimes, "is far more worrisome financially than being a planetary ruler. I've been both. I know."

"Indeed?" Her thin eyebrows went up almost to meet her hairline. "Indeed? Well, Your ex-Excellency, I thank you for your efforts on my behalf. And now I imagine that you have business of your own to attend to."

Grimes could not think of any but, bowing stiffly, he made his departure from the Lady Ellena's presence. He was somewhat at a loose end; Maggie was still at her function, giving her after-luncheon talk and answering questions, and Brasidus was still presiding over the council meeting.

He found his way to his quarters. His suite possessed all the amenities usually found in hotel accommodation, including a playmaster. There were gin and a bottle of Angostura bitters in the grog locker, ice cubes in the refrigerator. He mixed himself a drink. He checked the playmaster's library of spools. These included various classical dramas in the original Greek and a complete coverage of the Olympic Games, on Earth, from the late Twentieth Century, Old Style, onwards. Unfortunately the library did not include anything else. Grimes sighed. He switched the playmaster to its TV reception function, sampled the only two channels that were available at this time of day. Both of these presented sporting events. He watched briefly the discus throwing and thought that these people would have much to learn from Shirl and Darleen. Then he switched off and got from his bags some spools of his own. He set up a space battle simulation and soon was engrossed, matching his wits against those of the small but cunningly programmed computer.

Eventually Maggie joined him there.

She flopped into an easy chair, demanded a drink. Grimes made her a Scotch on the rocks. She disposed of it in two gulps.

She said, "I needed that! What a bunch of dim biddies I had to talk to. Oh, it wasn't so much the talking as the stupid questions afterwards. Most of my audience knew only two worlds, Earth and New Sparta, and were quite convinced that those are the only two planets worth knowing. As a real, live Arcadian I was just a freak, to be condescended to. They even lectured me on the glories of Hellenic culture and the great contributions it has made to Galactic civilization. Damn it all, Hellenic culture is only part of Terran culture, just as Australian culture is. . . . Talking of Australians, and pseudo-Australians, how did you get on with Shirl and Darleen?"

"I persuaded them to accept commissions in the Amazon Guard. Unluckily—or was it so unlucky?—Fenella was part of the deal. She's staying on to do a piece on them, and part of the package is that she's to be allowed free access to the Palace at all times."

"Why did you say, 'or was it so unlucky'?"

"She might be able to help us. I gained the impression that she's on the track of something. Is there any way that she could be pressganged into the Intelligence Branch? After all, we were."

"But we were—and are—already officers holding commissions in the Survey Service. When admirals say, Jump! we jump. Even you, John, as long as you're on the Reserve List."

"Civilians can be conscripted . . ." said Grimes. "*I* was. I became a civilian as soon as I resigned from the Service after the mutiny."

"As I heard it from Admiral Damien," Maggie said, "you were offered the Reserve Commission that you now hold. You were not compelled to accept it."

"Mphm. Not quite. But there were veiled threats as well as inducements."

"Could you threaten Fenella?"

"I wish that I could. But as I'm not a major shareholder in *Star Scandals* I can't."

"Inducements?"

"I've already played one major card by getting her the permission to come calling round to the Palace any time that she feels like it. There should have been a *quid pro quo*. I realize that now."

"Now that it's too late. What we want is an I'll-scratch-your-back-if-you'll-scratch-mine situation. What inducements can we offer? Mmm. To begin with, I'm the senior officer of the Federation Survey Service on this planet. . . ."

"*I* am," said Grimes indignantly.

"But only you and I know it. As far as the locals are concerned, as far as Fenella is concerned, you're no more than an owner-master, waiting here for his little star tramp to come wambling in with her cargo of black olives and retsina. And *I* have a warship at *my* disposal. A minor warship, perhaps, but a warship nonetheless."

"A Serpent Class courier," scoffed Grimes, "armed with a couple of pea-shooters and a laser cannon that would make quite a fair cigarette lighter. Commanded by a snotty-nosed lieutenant."

"You were one yourself once. But how far could you trust Fenella? Suppose, just suppose, that you spilled some of the beans to her? Could she be trusted?"

"I think that she subscribes to the journalists' code of honor. Never betray your sources. Too, there's one threat that I could use. The Baroness Michelle d'Estang of Eldorado is a *Star Scandals* major shareholder. I was among those present when Michelle, wielding the power of the purse, killed a really juicy story that Fenella wanted to splash all over the Galaxy."

"I take it that Michelle is one of your girlfriends."

"You could call her that."

"And we've other cards to play. Both of us are personal friends of the

Archon. And you, I have gathered, have been on more than friendly terms with Shirl and Darleen. Soon, I think, we must have a get-together with Miz Pruin and offer her our cooperation in return for hers."

"If you say so," said Grimes. "And now I suppose that we'd better get dressed for tonight's state dinner party."

"We have to get undressed first," she said suggestively.

Chapter 13

So there was the state dinner party, as boring as such occasions usually are, with everybody, under the watchful eye of the Lady Ellena, on his or her best behavior, with the serving wenches obviously instructed not to be overly prompt in such matters as the refilling of wine glasses. The female guests, thought Grimes snobbishly, were a scruffy bunch, immigrants all, mainly from Earth, most of whom would never, on their home planets, have been invited to a function such as this. The same could have been said regarding the hostess, Ellena.

What really irked the commodore was the ban on smoking. Not even when things got to the coffee and ouzo stage was he able to enjoy his pipe— and normally he liked to enjoy a couple or three puffs between courses.

He was seated near the head of the high table, with Maggie on his left and the headmistress of the Pallas Athena College for Young Ladies on his right. Maggie had gotten into a conversation with Colonel Heraclion, who was sitting next to her on her other side, leaving Grimes to cope with the academic lady.

"You must already have noticed changes here, Commodore," she said.

Grimes swallowed a mouthful of rather stringy stewed lamb (if it was lamb) and replied briefly, "Yes."

"And changes for the better. Oh, the first settlers did their best to re-create the glory that was Greece but, without the fair sex to aid them in their endeavors, all that they achieved was a pale shadow. . . ."

She waved her fork as she spoke and drops of gravy fell on the front of her chiton. It was rather surprising, thought Grimes, that they succeeded in making a landing as the material of the dress dropped in almost a straight line from neck to lap. He categorized her as a dried-up stick of a woman, not his type at all, with graying hair scraped back from an already overly high forehead, with protuberant pale blue eyes, with thin lips that could not hide buck teeth. Why was it, he wondered, that such people are so often, too often prone to fanatical enthusiasms?

"The founding fathers—there were not, of course, any founding mothers—were spacemen, not Greek scholars," she went on. "They knew something, of course, of the culture which they were trying to emulate, but not enough. It has, therefore, fallen to me, and to others like me, to finish the task that was begun by them."

"Indeed?"

"Yes. For example, you should still be here when the first Marathon is run. It will be a grueling course, from the Palace to the Acropolis. A little way downhill, then on the level and, finally, uphill. The race will be open to *everybody*, tourists as well as citizens."

"Better them than me," said Grimes.

"Come, come, Commodore! Surely you are not serious. Taking part in such an event could be one of the greatest challenges of your career."

"Foot racing," Grimes told her, "is not an activity in which I have ever taken part."

"And I know why," she told him. "You are a smoker. I saw you puffing a pipe outside the banqueting hall before you entered. But, even so, you could enter. And—who knows?—you might be among those to finish the course. Think of the honor and the glory!"

"Honor and glory don't pay port charges and maintenance and crew salaries," said Grimes.

She laughed. "Spoken like a true cynic, Commodore. A cynic and a shipowner."

"A man can be both," he admitted. "And if one is the latter one tends to become the former."

"A cynic . . ." she trotted out the old chestnut as though it had been newly minted, by herself . . . "is a man who knows the cost of everything and the value of nothing."

"Mphm."

The meal dragged on.

Finally, after the coffee had been served, there was a display of martial arts in the large area of floor around which the tables stood. There were wrestling matches, men versus men, women versus women, men versus women. (The ladies, Grimes assumed correctly, were members of the Lady Ellena's Amazon Guard. He recognized Lieutenant Phryne, although without the leather and brass trappings of her uniform her body looked softer, much more feminine. Nonetheless she floored her opponent, a hairy male giant, with almost contemptuous ease.)

And then it was the turn of Shirl and Darleen. They were already in their Amazon lieutenants' uniforms. (Somebody must have worked fast, thought Grimes.) They had boomerangs, little ones, no more than toys, that, at the finish of their act, seemed to fill the banqueting hall like a flock of whirring birds.

At last it was over, with the boomerangs, one by one, fluttering out through the wide open doorway, followed finally, after the making of their bows to quite enthusiastic applause, by the two New Alicians.

The academic lady was not among those who clapped.

"Boomerangs . . ." she muttered. "But they're not Greek . . ."

"I suppose not," said Grimes.

"And those two women . . . If you could call them that. Mutants, possibly. But *officers*. . . . In the elite Amazon Guard. . . ."

"Instructors, actually," Grimes told her.

"Oh. So you know them. You have some most peculiar friends, Commodore. From which planet do they come?"

"New Alice."

"New Alice?" She laughed creakily. "And how did it get its name? Is it some sort of Wonderland?"

"Just one of the Lost Colonies," said Grimes. "Fairly recently rediscovered. A rather odd Australianoid culture."

"Most definitely odd, Commodore, if those two ladies are a representative sample."

"All transplanted cultures are odd," he said. "And some cultures are odd before transplantation."

"Indeed?" Coldly.

"Indeed."

The next time Grimes saw a demonstration of boomerang throwing was at the Amazon Guards' drill ground. He stood with Maggie, Lieutenant Phryne and Fenella Pruin. He watched Shirl and Darleen as they hurled their war boomerangs, ugly things, little more than flattened clubs, at a row of man-sized dummies, twelve of them, achieving a full dozen neat decapitations. More dummies were set up. This time Shirl and Darleen improvised, snatching weapons from a pile of scrap metal and plastic, speedily selecting suitably shaped pieces, hurling them with great effect. But there were now no tidy beheadings. There was damage, nonetheless—arms torn off, bellies ripped open, faces crushed.

"Not very effective against well-aimed laser fire," sneered Phryne.

"Better than bare fists," said Grimes. "And, come to that, more effective than your wrestling. . . ."

"Care to try a fall or two, Commodore?" she asked nastily.

"No thank you, Lieutenant."

Maggie laughed and Fenella Pruin sniggered.

And then all three of them watched the Amazons, under the tutelage of Shirl and Darleen, trying to master the art of play boomerang throwing.

"No! No!" Darleen was yelping. "Not *that* way, you stupid bitch. Hold it *up*, not across! Flat side *to* you, not away! And . . . And *flick* your wrist! Like *this!*"

An instructor officer she might be, newly commissioned, but already she was beginning to sound like a drill sergeant.

Grimes, Maggie and Fenella drifted away from the field. They stood in the shade of a large tree. Grimes was amused when Maggie went through routine bug detection; she was taking her secondment to the Intelligence Branch very seriously. There certainly would be bugs in the foliage, he said, but not of the electronic variety. She was not amused.

"Now we can talk," she said.

"What about?" asked Fenella Pruin.

"You."

"Me, Commander Lazenby?"

"Yes. You. You're after a story, aren't you?"

"I'm always after stories. Ask Grimes. He knows."

"And the story with Grimes in it you weren't allowed to publish. *I* know. Do you want to publish the story—if there is one—that you get on New Sparta?"

"Of course."

"Suppose you aren't allowed to?"

Fenella Pruin laughed. "Really, my dear! Even I know that a mere commander in the Survey Service doesn't pile on many Gs."

"A commander," Maggie told her, "with admirals listening to what she has to say."

"Am I supposed to stand at attention and salute?"

"Only if you want to. Anyhow, we can help you, and you can help us."

"*We*? You and Grimes, of all people!"

Maggie contained her temper. "Miz Pruin," she said coldly. "You know why I am here, on New Sparta. Making an ethological survey for the Survey Service's Scientific Branch. You know why Commodore Grimes is here. Waiting for the arrival of his ship so that he may, once again, assume command of her. We know why you are here. Sniffing out a story, the more scandalous the better."

"There's one that I've already sniffed out," said Fenella Pruin nastily. "You're sleeping with Grimes. And if you don't watch him like a hawk he'll be tearing pieces off Shirl and Darleen again."

"He'd better not," said Maggie. "Not while I'm around."

"Don't I get a say in this?" demanded Grimes.

"No matter who is sleeping with whom, or who is going to sleep with whom," went on Maggie, "we, the Commodore and I, could be of help to you. We are *persona grata* in the Palace, as old friends of the Archon. Too, I know my way about this planet. Both of us do."

"You could be right," admitted Fenella grudgingly.

"Of course I'm right. And, on the other hand, although you lack our local knowledge, although you don't have our contacts, you are quite famous for your ability to sniff out scandals. Political as well as sexual."

"Bedfellows often make strange politics," said Fenella.

"Haven't you got it the wrong way around?" asked Maggie.

"No."

It was Grimes' turn to laugh.

Maggie ignored him, went on, "It will be to our mutual benefit if we pool information. The Commodore and I have our contacts. You now have yours—Shirl and Darleen in the Amazon Guard. Too, if you made yourself too unpopular—as you have done on more than one planet—I could be of very real help to you."

"How?"

"You must have seen that Serpent Class courier at the spaceport. *Krait.* Her captain, Lieutenant Gupta, is under my orders. I could see to it that you got offplanet in a hurry should the need arise."

"You tempt me, Commander Lazenby. You tempt me, although I doubt very much that Lieutenant Gupta's flying sardine can is as luxurious as Captain Grimes' *Little Sister.* . . ." She turned to Grimes. "I was really sorry, you know, when I learned that you'd gotten rid of her. We had some good times aboard her . . ."

Grimes could not remember any especially good times, either on the voyage out to New Venusberg or the voyage back. But Maggie, of course, had taken the remark at its face value and was glaring at him.

"Never look a gift horse in the mouth," said Grimes to Fenella, adding, "That's one proverb you can't muck around with."

"Isn't it? Didn't a grazing cow once say, 'Never take a horse gift in the mouth . . . '?"

"Shut up, you two!" snapped Maggie. "Are you with us or aren't you, Miz Pruin?"

"I know what's in it for me," said the journalist. "But what's in it for you?"

"I've told you. Just help in my research project."

"And for Grimes?"

"I'm just helping Commander Lazenby," he said. "Just passing the time until my ship comes in."

"If that's your story," she said, "stick to it. But all right, I'll play. And I'll expect the pair of you to play as well."

"We shall," promised Maggie.

Chapter 14

Fenella Pruin was now allowed into the Palace although she was still far from welcome. Should she chance to meet the Lady Ellena while making her way through the corridors the Archon's wife would sweep by her as though she didn't exist. Brasidus himself would acknowledge her presence, but only just. She was tolerated in the officers' quarters of the Amazon Guard because of her friendship with Shirl and Darleen, both of whom had become quite popular with their messmates. And, of course, she was free to visit Maggie and Grimes any time that she so wished.

She joined them, this day, for morning coffee.

After the surly serving wench had deposited the tray on the table and left, after Maggie had poured the thick, syrupy fluid into the little cups, she demanded, "Well? Have you anything to tell me yet?"

"No," admitted Maggie. "I am still nibbling around the edges, as it were. The New Hellas people are up to *something*. But what?"

"It's a pity that you can't join them," said Fenella.

"It is. But they know that I'm an officer of the Federation Survey Service. And they know that both Commodore Grimes and I are personal friends, old friends of Brasidus." She laughed. "Although if it were not for that personal friendship they might try to recruit John."

"It'd be my ship they'd want," said Grimes. "Not me especially."

"Why not?" asked Fenella. "After all, you were slung out of the Survey Service in disgrace. . . ."

"I resigned," growled Grimes.

"And you were a pirate . . ."

"How many times," he demanded, "do I have to tell people that I was a privateer? And now, Fenella, do you have anything to tell us?"

She looked at him and said, "I was under the impression, Grimes, that the ethological research project was Commander Lazenby's baby, not yours."

"Commodore Grimes," said Maggie, "is helping me with it. Just out of friendship, of course."

"Of course," concurred Fenella, twitching her nose. "Of course. But the Commodore was quite recently a servant of the Federation, on the public payroll, as a planetary governor, no less . . . Are you really self-employed, Grimes? Or is it just a cover?"

"It is a known fact," snapped Maggie, "that Commodore Grimes is an owner-master."

"At the moment," said Grimes, "just an owner. I shall be master again as soon as I get my name back on *Sister Sue*'s register."

"It is the *unknown* facts that interest me . . ." murmured Fenella. "Such as the real reason for the appointment of a notorious pirate . . ."

"*Not* a pirate!" yelled Grimes.

". . . to the governorship of a planet."

"You've trodden on corns in the past," said Grimes coldly. "You should know, by this time, that there are some corns better not trodden on."

Maggie sighed. "All this is getting us nowhere and has nothing at all to do with New Sparta. Would you mind telling us, Fenella, just what you've found out?"

The journalist finished her coffee, said, "No thanks, Maggie. One cup of this mud was ample. Potables shouldn't need knives and forks to deal with them." She took a cigarette from the box on the table, puffed it into ignition. "Now, I think I'm getting places, which is more than can be said for the pair of you. A Major Hera has taken quite a fancy to Shirl and Darleen. She is taking private *savate* lessons and, in return, is teaching the two girls her own version of wrestling. Now, now . . . I know that you have dirty minds, or I know that Grimes has, but there's nothing like what you're thinking. Not yet, anyhow, but I must admit that Shirl and Darleen are surprisingly innocent in some respects. Well, Hera is a high-up in the Ladies' Auxiliary of the New Hellas Association. She's already persuaded quite a few Amazon officers and NCOs to join. She's been trying to persuade the two new Instructor Lieutenants to join. I've advised them to yield to her blandishments and then to keep their eyes skinned and their ears flapping."

"I can't see them as spies," said Grimes. "They're too direct. Too honest."

"Who else have we got?" she asked. "Not me. Not either of you."

"And they will report to you?" asked Grimes.

"Yes," she said.

"They will report to *us*," stated Maggie firmly. "After all, they are

Commodore Grimes' friends. What could be more natural than that they should join him here for a drink or two?"

"As long as I am present," said Fenella.

"Talking of drinks," said Grimes, "I could do with a stiff one to wash away the taste of that alleged coffee."

The two ladies thought that this was quite a good idea.

Chapter 15

"You know, John," said Brasidus, "I think that I was much happier in the old days. When I was a simple sergeant in the army, with authority but not much responsibility. Now I have responsibility, as Archon, but my authority seems to have been whittled away." He sighed. "Sparta—it wasn't called *New* Sparta then—was a far simpler world than it is now. We were happy enough eating and drinking and brawling. There were no women to tell us to wash behind the ears and watch our table manners." He gulped from his mug of wine. "I regard you as a friend, John, a good friend, but I have thought that it was a great pity that you ever came to this planet, opening us up to the rest of the Galaxy . . ."

"If it hadn't been me," said Grimes, "it would have been somebody else. The search for Lost Colonies is always going on. I've heard that 90 percent of the interstellar ship disappearances have now been accounted for. And, in any case, how many ships of that remaining 10 percent founded a colony? Possibly none of them."

"You are changing the subject, my friend. In the old days I should never have been obliged to disguise myself in order to enjoy, with a good friend, what you refer to as a pub crawl. I should never have had to wait for an evening when my wife—my *wife*—was out attending some meeting or other. There weren't any wives."

"As I recall it," said Grimes, "some of your boyfriends, your surrogate women, could be bitchy enough. And, in any case, the King of Sparta would have done as you are doing now, put on disguise, if he wished to mingle, incognito, with his subjects."

"If he had mingled more," said Brasidus sourly, "he might have kept his crown. And his head. As it was, he just didn't have his finger on the pulse of things."

"And you have?"

"I hope so."

"Tell me, what do you feel?"

"I . . . I wish that I knew."

The two men looked around the tavern, which was far from crowded. They had been able to secure a table at which they could talk with a great degree of privacy. Even the two bodyguards, although not quite out of earshot, were fully occupied chatting up the slovenly, but crudely attractive, girl who had brought them a fresh jug of wine. Had he not already seen how swiftly Jason and Paulus could act when danger threatened Grimes would have doubted their value.

"But you have your Secret Service, or whatever you call it," pursued Grimes. "Surely they keep you informed."

Brasidus laughed. "I sometimes think that the State subsidizes the New Hellas Association and other possibly subversive organizations. They're packed with Intelligence agents, all of them dues-paying members. But do they tell me everything? Do they tell me *anything*?"

"They must tell you something, just to stay on the payroll if for no other reason."

"But do they tell me the truth?" demanded the Archon. "This way, mingling with my people in disguise, I can hear things for myself. There are grumblings—but what government has ever been universally popular? Need I ask *you* that? There are those who want a return to the Good Old Days, a womanless world, and who resent the influx of females from Earth and other planets. There are those who want a society more closely modeled on that of ancient Greece, on Earth, with women kept barefoot and pregnant." He laughed. "There are even those, mainly women, who hanker after some mythical society that was ruled by a woman, Queen Hippolyte, where men were kept in subjection. But that, as you would say, is the lunatic fringe. . . ."

"With the Lady Ellena as a member?" Grimes could not help asking.

Brasidus laughed again. "She is a good wife, I'll not deny that, although perhaps a shade overbearing. And I . . . humor her. She believes, or says that she believes, that the Hippolyte legends are true. Oh, I've tried to reason with her. I've imported books from Earth, Greek histories, and she's condescended to read them. And she says that there has been a conspiracy of male historians to suppress the Hippolyte story, to laugh it away as a mere myth . . ."

"Your scholars had done some ingenious tampering with history and biology before your Lost Colony was found," said Grimes.

"That was different," said Brasidus. "But Ellena . . . I've played along with her, up to a point. I let her form her Amazon Guard. Having toy lady soldiers to play with keeps her happy."

"Toy soldiers?" asked Grimes. "Oh, they probably wouldn't be a match for an equal number of Federation Space Marines, but against ordinary troops they'd give a very good account of themselves."

"You really think that?"

"I do."

There was a brief silence, broken only by the happy squeals of the serving wench who had been looking after Paulus and Jason. Of the serving wenches, rather. The original girl had been joined by another, equally coarsely attractive. The pair of them were sitting on the bodyguards' laps, fondling and being fondled. Grimes filled and lit his pipe, looking toward the door to the street as he did so. He saw the women enter, six of them. A fat blonde, a tall, skinny redhead, four very nondescript brunettes. They were dressed, all of them, in rather tawdry finery, with chaplets of imitation vine leaves intertwined with their tousled hair, latter-day bacchantes— or a sextet of working girls enjoying a night on the tiles. They did not seem to be sober, lurching and staggering as they made their way across the floor, giggling and nudging each other.

"Women," muttered Brasidus, "cannot drink with dignity."

Not only women, thought Grimes, although he was inclined to the opinion that drunken men are somewhat less of a nuisance.

The fat blonde failed successfully to negotiate the quite generous space between Grimes' table and that at which the two bodyguards were sitting. Her heavy, well-padded hip almost shoved Grimes off his chair. "Gerrout o' my way, you barshtard . . ." she slurred, glaring at him out of piggy blue eyes that, the commodore suddenly realized, looked more sober than otherwise. Two of the other women had gotten themselves entangled with Brasidus. Wine bottle and glasses were overset.

Simultaneously Jason and Paulus were having their troubles. Their chairs had gone over backwards and they were sprawled on the floor, their limbs entangled with those of their female companions. They were trying to get their pistols out from the concealed holsters, but without success.

The corpulent innkeeper came bustling up. "Citizens! Citizens! I must implore you to keep the peace!"

"Keep a piece of this!" snarled the redhead, cracking him smartly across the brow with a wine bottle.

Grimes tried to get to his feet but two of the brunettes pounced on him, bore him to the floor. They were surprisingly well-muscled wenches. Their hard feet thudded into his ribs and belly. He had enough presence of mind to protect his testicles with his hands—but that left his head uncovered. A calloused heel struck him just behind the right ear and, briefly, he lost consciousness. Then dimly he was aware of the scuffling around him and the voice of the fat woman—no trace of drunkenness now—saying sharply, "Now! While he's still out!"

But I'm not still out, thought Grimes, not realizing at first that she was not talking about him.

He was no longer out but those two useless bodyguards were, jabbed with needles loaded with some kind of drug by the tavern wenches. He was no longer out and he raised himself on his hands and knees, in time to see the six women—no, the eight women; they had been joined by the two serving girls—hurrying through the door to the street with Brasidus supported between them. None of the inn's patrons had made any move to interfere. Why should they? Drunken brawls were not uncommon.

Somehow he got to his feet. He started toward the door and then hesitated. Unarmed he was no match for no less than eight hefty, vicious wenches. He stumbled to where Paulus was sprawled, face down, on the floor. He fell to his knees, fumbled in the man's clothing. He found the concealed holster almost at once, pulled out the pistol. He checked that it was loaded, cocked the weapon. He had by now recovered sufficiently to run, albeit painfully, to the door.

To his surprise he did not have to look far to find the kidnappers. They were standing there, all eight of them, in the middle of the poorly lighted street, still supporting the unconscious Archon between them.

"Freeze!" yelled Grimes, waving the Minetti.

They turned to look at him but otherwise made no move.

"Release him! At once!"

"If that's the way you want it, buster," said the fat blonde.

The women stepped away from Brasidus. Fantastically his body remained upright. Even more fantastically it seemed to elongate, as though the Archon were becoming taller with every passing second. Grimes stared incredulously. He heard, then, the faint humming of a winch. He looked up and saw, at no great altitude, a dark gray against the black of the night sky, the bulk of a small airship. He started to run forward, to try to grab the feet of his friend. Somebody tripped him. He fell heavily but, luckily for him, retained his grip on the pistol. He sensed that the kidnappers were closing in around him and fired at random, not a full, wasteful burst but spaced shots. Surely, in this scrum, he must get somebody in the legs.

He heard a yelp of pain, then another.

He got to his feet.

Nobody stopped him.

There was nobody there to stop him.

He looked up.

The dirigible was gone, presumably with Brasidus a prisoner in its cabin.

He looked around.

The dirt of the road surface had been scuffed by the struggle. In two places there were dark, glistening stains. Blood. But the women had melted into the shadows, taking their wounded with them. He hoped that the fat bitch was among the casualties.

There was the sound of approaching, running feet. He turned in that direction, holding the pistol ready. He saw who was coming, three policemen, what little light there was reflected from their polished black leather and stainless steel.

Hastily Grimes put the gun into a pocket.

The leading police officer shone his torch full on Grimes' face, although not before the commodore had noticed that he was holding a stungun in his other hand.

He said disgustedly, "*You* again." Grimes thought that he recognized the voice. He went on, "I heard shots. There has obviously been some sort of struggle here. What have you been doing?"

"I haven't been doing anything," said Grimes virtuously if not quite accurately. He tried to fit a name to the owner of the voice. "Sergeant Priam, isn't it? Would you mind not shining that light into my eyes?"

"Certainly, sir. Commodore, sir. And now would you mind telling me what in Zeus's name has been going on?"

"A kidnapping. The Archon. He was snatched by a gang of women, carried away in an airship. No, I didn't get any registration marks or numbers. The thing wasn't carrying lights."

The beam of the sergeant's torch was directed downward.

"And this blood. Whose is it? The Archon's?"

"There was a struggle, as you can see. One or two of the women got hurt."

"You shot them."

"It was better," said Grimes, "than having my head kicked in."

"Let me have the weapon, sir."

Grimes shrugged and passed the weapon over.

He said, "It's not mine. It belongs to one of the Archon's bodyguards."

"And where are they?"

"Inside the inn. Unconscious."

Sergeant Priam sighed heavily. "Why do these things always have to happen to me? You will have to come to the station, sir, to make your report." He laughed. "But you'll find it far easier to make your report to Colonel Xenophon than, eventually, to the Lady Ellena!"

Chapter 16

Grimes told his story. Jason and Paulus, almost recovered, thanks to the administration of the antidote, from the effects of the drug with which they had been injected, told their story. The innkeeper, his head bandaged, told his story. Two witnesses, selected at random from the tavern's customers, told their stories.

Colonel Xenophon, a tall, thin, bald-headed man looking more like a schoolmaster—but a severe schoolmaster—than a policeman, listened.

He said, "I have known, for some time, of the Archon's nocturnal adventures. I was foolish enough to believe that his professional bodyguards would be capable of protecting him."

"On a normal planet," said Jason hotly, "we should have been."

Xenophon's furry black eyebrows rose like back-arching caterpillars. "Indeed? How do you define normalcy? Is your precious Earth a *normal* planet? Among my reading of late have been recent Terran crime statistics. They have caused me to wonder why any citizen, male or female, is foolhardy enough to venture out after dark in any of the big cities.

"And now, Commodore, you are quite sure that the flying machine which removed the Archon was an airship? Could it not have been one of the inertial drive craft or helicopters that have been introduced from Earth?"

"It could not," said Grimes definitely. "I know an airship when I see one."

"Even in the dark?"

"There was enough light. And the thing was . . . quiet. Just a faint, very faint humming of electric motors."

"So. . . . And in what direction did this mysterious airship fly after the pick-up?"

"I don't know. Those blasted women jumped me. I was fully occupied trying to fight them off."

"Ah, yes. The women. Did you recognize any of them, Commodore?"

"No. But I shall if I run across them again. But, damn it all, Colonel, what are you doing about this crime, this kidnapping? Dirigible airships aren't as common as, say, motorcycles. There can be very few, if any, privately owned. Your Navy has a fleet of lighter-than-air craft. I'd have thought that you'd have started inquiries with the Admiralty, to find out what ships had been flying tonight."

Xenophon smiled coldly. "I should not presume, Commodore, to instruct you in the arts and sciences of spacemanship. Please do not try to tell me how I should do my job. Already inquiries have been made. All the Navy's ships are either in their hangars or swinging at their mooring masts. All Trans-Sparta Airlines' ships, passenger carriers and freight carriers, have been accounted for. And that's all the airships on New Sparta."

"So the ship I saw must either have belonged to the Navy or to Trans-Sparta."

"If you saw such a ship, Commodore. You may have thought that you did. But drugs had been used during the kidnapping. It is possible that during your first struggle with the women an attempt may have been made to put you out by such means and that you may have received a partial dosage, enough to induce hallucinations. Or a blow on the head might have had the same effect."

"If there were no flying machine involved," persisted Grimes, "how was it that the Archon was spirited away from the inn without trace?"

"I think," said the colonel, "that the quarter of the city in which you and the Archon were . . . er . . . conducting your researches is known to Terrans as a rabbit warren. I didn't appreciate the aptness of that expression until I read one of your classics, *Watership Down*. But if you want to lose a needle in a haystack, a rabbit warren is a good place to do it."

"Mphm," grunted Grimes.

"And now, Commodore, may I suggest—may I urge—that you and your two companions return to the Palace; transport will be provided for you. I do not envy your having to tell the story of this night's happenings to the Lady Ellena. She has already been notified, of course, that the Archon is missing. She is a lady of iron self-control but I could tell that she was deeply moved. Please assure her that I and my men will return her husband to her, unharmed, as soon as is humanly possible."

Grimes turned to follow Sergeant Priam from Xenophon's plainly furnished office. The colonel checked him.

"Oh, Commodore, I advise you, strongly, not to try to conduct any sort of rescue operation yourself. Please leave matters in the hands of the experts, such as myself and my people."

"I shouldn't know where to start," said Grimes.

But I shall find out, he thought.

His confrontation with Ellena was bad enough, although not as bad as he had dreaded that it would be.

"Much as I should wish to," she said coldly, "I cannot hold you responsible, Commodore. The Archon was having his 'nights out' . . ." she contrived to apostrophize the phrase . . . "long before you returned to this world.

"Meanwhile, all that I can do is wait. Presumably the kidnappers will present their demands shortly, and then there will be decisions to be made. Until then . . ." She smiled bleakly. "Until then, the show must go on. I shall function as acting Archon until the return of my husband. There will be no disruption of the affairs of state, not even the minor ones such as the Marathon next week."

She is enjoying this . . . thought Grimes.

He asked, "What about the Council, Lady?"

She said, "The Council will do as they are told."

Or else? he wondered.

She said, "That will be all, Commodore."

Grimes considered backing out of the presence but decided not to.

"Who were those women?" asked Maggie.

"I'll know them if I meet them again," said Grimes.

"Could they," she went on, "have been members of the Amazon Guard?"

"No. The Amazon Guard, apart from exceptions such as Shirl and Darleen, goes in for uniformity. Apart from hair coloring all those wenches could be cast from the same mold. The Amazon Guard, I mean. It was a very mixed bunch that we got tangled with last night. The long and the short and the tall."

"And you're sure about the airship?"

"Of course I'm sure." He paused for thought. "You were snooping around for quite a while before I got here and, as a Survey Service commander, meeting officers in the various New Spartan armed forces. Does the Navy run to any female personnel?"

"No."

"Trans-Sparta Airlines?"

She said, "You might have something. Not only do they have women in their ground staff but even token female flight crews. Not in the passenger ships, yet, but in the smaller freight carriers."

"Do they do any night flying?"

"I don't know, John. You're far more of an expert on such matters than I am. Making an arrival or a departure in a spaceship you always have to check up with Aerospace Control, don't you?"

"And on most worlds there're always some aircraft up and about, at any hour of the day or night. The Aerospace Control computers keep track of them."

"And suppose certain computer operators wanted to hide the fact that a small airship, a small, freight-carrying airship with a female crew, wasn't where she was supposed to be . . ."

"You've told me *how*," he said, "but not *why*."

"Or," she said, "*where?* Where have they taken him?"

"I think that he's safe enough," Grimes said. "If they'd wanted to assassinate him they'd have done just that."

"So we start off snooping around Aerospace Control and the Head Office of Trans-Sparta."

"Colonel Xenophon intimated that he'd be taking a dim view if I started making my own investigations."

"But you won't be investigating the Archon's disappearance. As the owner of a ship on a regular run to New Sparta, shortly to be taking command again of that same ship, you're naturally interested in the workings of local Aerospace Control. You can say that you've had a few complaints from your Chief Officer, Mr. Williams, who's been acting Master in your absence."

"Makes sense."

"And I, carrying on with my own research project, will be interested by the part played by women now in the air transport industry. Fenella might care to come along with me to hold my hand."

"A good idea. It's time that she started to pull her weight. Or does she already know quite a lot that she's not passing on to us?"

"It wouldn't surprise me," she said.

Chapter 17

On some worlds the kidnapping of a national or planetary ruler would go almost unnoticed or, at most, evoke only shrugs and muttered comments of "Serve the bastard right!" (There were, of course, those on New Sparta who muttered just that, but careful not to do so in the hearing of those who most certainly would take violent exception to such a comment.) But Brasidus had been popular. He had nursed his world through a transition period, had restored and maintained stability. There were orderly demonstrations outside the Palace, expressions of sympathy and support. There were demands that the criminals—whoever they were—be brought swiftly to justice and the Archon released unharmed.

There was extensive media coverage.

Grimes, Maggie and Fenella studied the story of the kidnapping that was splashed all over the front page of *The New Spartan Times*, together with photographs of Brasidus, Grimes and Colonel Xenophon. "A gang of eight men disguised as women . . ." read Grimes aloud. "Those were no transvestites!" he exclaimed.

"They could have been . . ." murmured Fenella. "There are such people, you know. . . ."

"Those two serving wenches who immobilized Jason and Paulus most certainly weren't transvestites. If they had been, those two so-called bodyguards would soon have found out. Their hands were everywhere. . . ."

"So you admit to being a voyeur," sneered Fenella.

"I couldn't help noticing."

"Then they were accomplices—the serving wenches, I mean—of the six men in disguise."

"Those were not men in disguise!" asserted Grimes. "I should know.

I was in violent physical contact with all of them, or most of them, twice. Once inside the tavern, once in the street outside. When you wrestle with somebody, especially somebody dressed in only a flimsy chiton, you soon find out if it's he or she."

"All right," Fenella said. "You're the expert. But it's your word against Xenophon's. What is *he* trying to cover up?"

"And on whose orders?" asked Maggie.

"There could be another explanation," suggested Grimes. "One that makes sense. He's playing cunning, trying to lull the kidnappers into a sense of false security, making them think that he's on a false scent. . . ."

"Or, perhaps," said Maggie, "he doesn't want to antagonize our leading militant feminist, the Lady Ellena, by daring to suggest that members of her sex are guilty of the crime. After all, until Brasidus is released. . . ."

"If he ever is released . . ." said Fenella cheerfully.

"Until Brasidus is released, or rescued," went on Maggie, "Lady Ellena is *de facto* ruler of this world. And—I could be wrong, of course—while she is so, heads are liable to roll."

"Not ours, I hope," said Grimes.

"I don't think so. Not yet, anyhow. I'm Survey Service, and that counts for something. Fenella represents the Galactic Media—and that could count for even more. And you, John, even though she's not quite sure about you, are a wealthy shipowner. . . ."

"Ha!" interjected Grimes scornfully.

". . . with friends in high places."

"With friends like them," said Grimes, "what do I need with enemies?"

"Yes," said Fenella. "You do have friends. As well I know. So . . . There's a cover-up job. So things aren't what they seem. So what are you two doing about it?"

"What are *you* doing about it?" asked Maggie.

"*You* make the news, duckie. I report it."

They told her, then, of their proposed investigations of Aerospace Control and the operations of Trans-Sparta Airlines. Fenella agreed to accompany Maggie, playing the part of an interested journalist, during the visit to the airlines office.

This was not, of course, Grimes' first visit to an Aerospace Control operations center. While he had been in the Survey Service officers, especially those holding command, had been required to gain an inside knowledge of the workings of such establishments. On Botany Bay, after the *Discovery* mutiny, he had been instrumental in setting up Aerospace Control on that planet. Now, as owner-master of a ship on a regular run between Earth and New Sparta, a telephone call was sufficient to secure for him an appointment with the New Spartan Aerospace Control Director.

A sullen, chastened Paulus drove him from the Palace to the spaceport. He did, however, make some attempt at conversation. "That police chief, sir . . . Has he been on to you? He tried to make Jason and me admit that the two girls we were chatting up were . . . *men.*"

"You should know," said Grimes nastily. "Were they?"

"What do you take us for?" For a while he concentrated on his driving. "And the worst of it is that he got us to sign a statement that the two little bitches were men. He told us that if we didn't sign it'd be just too bad. For us." There was another silence, then, "One thing we learned on Earth is that it doesn't do to tangle with police chiefs. Not unless you have something on them. And even then. . . ."

There were more police in the streets than usual, Grimes noticed. There was also a police detachment at the airport gates, checking the credentials of all who entered. Paulus had with him an official card of some kind. The police lieutenant sneered when it was produced and said, "Ah, one of the famous bodyguards. I hope that you make a better job of guarding this gentleman's body than you did the Archon's . . ." Grimes produced his passport and other papers; even then it was necessary to make a call from the gate office to Aerospace Control. At last they were let through.

The spaceport control tower was part of Aerospace Control, but only its visible portion. The rest of it, most of it, was underground. Grimes told Paulus to wait in the hovercar. The man didn't like it. He seemed determined to guard *somebody* now that his major charge had been taken from him. But the commodore was firm.

He was expected in the ground floor office. A uniformed—but in spacemanlike black and gold, not pseudo-Greek brass and leather—official, a young woman, escorted him into an elevator which, by its rapid descent to the depths, produced a simulation of free fall. She led him through a maze of brightly lit tunnels, finally into a vast compartment that was all illuminated maps and colored lights, some winking and some steady, in the center of which was a globe depicting Space one hundred thousand kilometers out from New Sparta in all directions. By this was a large desk with its own complement of screens and globes, at which sat the Director.

This gentleman got to his feet as Grimes and his guide approached. The girl saluted smartly and then faded into the background. The Director, a tall, heavily bearded man, like Grimes in civilian clothing, a very plain, gray, one-piece business suit, extended his right hand. Grimes took it.

"Glad to have you aboard, Commodore," he was told. "Of course your ship is no stranger to us here but this is the first time that I have had the pleasure of meeting any of her personnel."

"The pleasure is mine," said Grimes.

"Thank you, Commodore. Will you be seated?" He waved to a chair on the other side of the desk. "You are staying at the Palace, I understand. A most serious business, is it not, this kidnapping of the Archon. What could be the motivation? Money—or politics? Mind you, I should not be at all surprised if those New Hellas people, or whatever they call themselves, are involved." He laughed without humor. "Either they want the Archon to press ahead with what they see as reforms or they want him to put the clock back. I have read their propaganda and I've got the impression that they don't know what they do want."

"Who does?" asked Grimes. Then, "You're not a New Spartan, by birth, are you, Director? I've a tin ear for accents but yours seems to be— let me guess—Rim Worlds. . . ."

"Too right. I was Deputy Director of Aerospace Control on Lorn and the Director looked like staying put for the next century or so. Then the New Spartan government was advertising for candidates for this job and I applied." He grinned. "I like to think that I run a taut ship."

"I'm sure that you do, Director."

"But when you called me, to make this appointment, you sort of hinted that you had some kind of complaint."

"*I* don't. But, as you may know, although normally I am in command of *Sister Sue* myself I held a ground appointment for a while. . . ."

"A ground appointment!" chuckled the Director. "I suppose you could call it that."

"Yes. During my absence from active command my chief officer, Billy Williams, has been acting master. Captain Williams has been sending voyage reports to me, in my capacity as owner. I have gained the impression from them that he has not been entirely satisfied with New Sparta Aerospace Control's handling of his arrivals and departures."

"He never complained to me about it. If he has any whinges, Commodore, what are they?"

Grimes affected embarrassment. "Well, as a matter of fact, Billy— Captain Williams—is inclined to be sexist. When he calls Aerospace Control on any planet he likes it to be a male voice that answers him. All nonsense, of course." Grimes looked around the large, dimly lit room. So far as he could see every console, but one, was attended by a male. "A lot of women would consider you sexist, too. Practically all your staff is male."

"They wouldn't be," said the Director, "if the Lady Ellena had her way. But even if she did—where would I get trained females from? The girl who brought you in is one of our cadets, but it will be at least two years before she qualifies as a junior controller. And over there, under the airways chart, is Marina. She's a controller third class. She should get her step up and the ones after without any difficulty. She's got a natural feel for the work. . . ."

"Could it be her that my Captain Williams had trouble with? He did say that on his way in he missed a big commercial dirigible by inches. Of course, Billy tends to exaggerate. . . ."

"So it would seem, Commodore. But why don't we stroll over to have a word with Marina?"

The two men walked to where, just over where the girl was sitting, a huge chart of New Sparta, on a Mercatorial projection, adorned the wall. On it little white lights slowly moved, their extrapolated courses fine, luminescent threads. The display, Grimes knew, was computer-controlled and the human operator no more than an observer—but an observer with power to take over should a situation develop with which the electronic brain, lacking intuition and imagination, would be unable to cope.

"Just our normal commercial traffic," said the Director. "The Navy doesn't seem to have any ships up today. They're marked by blue lights. And we don't have any spacecraft coming in or lifting off to complicate the picture." He picked up the long pointer from its rack under the chart, with its tip indicated a spark that, obviously, was making its approach to Port Sparta. "Who is that, Marina?" he asked.

The girl turned in her swivel chair to look up at him. "*City of Athens*, sir," she told him. "She has clearance to come in to her moorings. E.T.A. 1515 hours." Then she saw Grimes standing next to the Director. Her eyes widened but only briefly, very briefly. She was what he would class as a nondescript brunette, smart enough in her uniform, certainly smarter than when he had last seen her, in a dishevelled chiton and those spurious vine leaves entangled in her hair. If it was her, that was. But there was the scent that he had smelled during the struggle in the inn, an animal pungency so pronounced as to be almost unpleasant.

He asked, "Haven't we met before, Marina?"

She said coldly, her manner implying who-the-hell-are-you-anyhow? "I do not think so, sir."

"This is Commodore Grimes, Marina," said the Director. "The owner of *Sister Sue*, and her captain when he's not governing planets."

"I have heard of you, sir," said the girl. Then, "Excuse me. I have to keep an eye on *City of Thrace* and *City of Macedon*; their courses will be close to intersection in an area of poor visibility and turbulence."

She returned her attention to the chart, to the whisper of voices that was coming from the speaker below it.

The Director led Grimes back to his desk.

"Normally," he said, "I'm here only when something interesting is happening. Nothing of interest is happening today and the duty watch is well able to look after the shop. But I thought that you'd like to see how we run things. And it makes a change from my eternal paperwork in my own office."

"How many female controllers do you have?" asked Grimes.

"At the moment, six. One on each watch—that makes three—and the others on non-watchkeeping duties. As a matter of fact Marina isn't on the watchkeeping list; she's filling in for one of the others. Cleo. She had an accident last night. Fell and cut her leg quite badly on a piece of broken glass or something."

"These things happen," said Grimes.

"And when they happen to people who're overweight they're usually more serious," said the Director.

"These big, fat blondes . . ." murmured Grimes commiseratingly.

"She *is* a blonde," admitted the Director. "But how did you guess?"

"I knew a fat blonde once. And she was always getting into trouble."

The Director laughed and then the two men went up to his private office for drinks and a pleasant enough but inconsequential talk.

Later, in his suite at the Palace, Grimes compared notes with Maggie and Fenella. He told them what he had discovered. "Whoever is behind the kidnapping," he told the women, "has agents, two at least, in Aerospace Control. Traffic officers sufficiently experienced to persuade the average computer to falsify records, to show airships as being where they aren't and not where the screen says they are. One was on duty when I paid my call to the Director. I recognized her. She, of course, recognized me."

"But she didn't know, of course, that you recognized her."

"Well, as a matter of fact she did. After I said, 'Haven't we met before?'"

"What!" The scream from the two female voices was simultaneous. Then, from Maggie, "You bloody fool! They, whoever they are, will know that you're on to them!"

"Not know. Only suspect. All that they will *know* is that I paid a professional call on Aerospace Control and thought that I recognized one of the duty officers. What I am hoping is that their suspicions drive them to do something stupid. . . ."

"And if they do something cunning, where shall we all be?" demanded Fenella. "Oh, you can set yourself up as a decoy—but Maggie and I are in this business too."

"What's done is done," sighed Maggie. "We shall just have to be especially careful from now on."

"And how did your afternoon go?" asked Grimes, changing the subject.

"Successful enough. We just confirmed what we knew already, that Trans-Sparta Airlines have several all-woman flight crews and that these, still, serve only in the freight carriers. We also learned that much of the freight carrying is done by night. Any of five freighters could have been in this vicinity—although, according to the records, not flying directly over the city—at the time of the kidnapping. Of the five, two had female crews. The Trans-Sparta traffic controller was starting to wonder why I, doing social research, was so interested in commercial operations. But I did find out where those two ships were from and, more importantly, where they were bound . . ."

"Unluckily," said Grimes, "it's the deviations and the unscheduled stops that interest us. And those bitches in Aerospace Control will have made sure that there's no record."

Chapter 18

Grimes purchased a large atlas of New Sparta. Among the various maps therein were ones giving details of planetary transport routes—land, sea and air. He studied these, stepped off distances with his dividers. But there was so much territory over which the airships flew, so many stretches where there was not even the smallest village, only a wilderness of forest and mountain. There were so many places at which a dirigible could have made a descent unobserved, even in broad daylight, to disembark willing or unwilling passengers.

Maggie paid more visits to the offices of Trans-Sparta Airlines; her excuse was that she had selected this organization as the subject for her study of the effects of the integration of women into New Spartan industry. Often Fenella would accompany her. She would tell anybody who was interested that she was doing a series which she would call Sex In The Skies, dealing with female air crews on those planets where there were such. She made herself very unpopular by her apparent determination to sniff out evidence of high altitude Lesbian orgies.

Shirl and Darleen continued to function as Instructors in the Amazon Guard. They reported that there was something cooking in the barracks but what they did not know. Despite their popularity with their fellow officers they were still outsiders, not fully accepted.

Colonel Xenophon, whom Grimes met occasionally during the police chief's visits to the Palace to confer with the Lady Ellena, said that promising leads were being followed and that before long the Archon would be released, unharmed, from captivity. He would not say what the leads were. He scorned Grimes' suggestion that some ultra-feminist organization might be responsible for the kidnapping. "I keep on telling you, Commodore," he snapped, "that the gang responsible for the crime was composed of men disguised as women. Furthermore, there is absolutely no record of a dirigible having flown over the city at the time of the kidnap."

Meanwhile, there seemed to be a spate of vanishings, most of those who disappeared having been prominent members of the New Hellas Association. Some bodies were recovered, corpses dumped in back alleys, bearing signs of extreme maltreatment before death. *The New Hellas Courier*, in its editorials, became increasingly critical of both the police force and the administration in general, ranting about the crime wave that had begun with the abduction of the Archon and would not abate until every public-spirited citizen had been disposed of. What, the leader writer demanded, was the Lady Ellena doing about it? But was it coincidence, he continued, that most of those who had vanished or been murdered were opponents of the Lady's feminization programs?

Shortly thereafter the newspaper editor's name was added to the list of Missing Persons.

Meanwhile Ellena governed. Her style was altogether different from that of her husband. Brasidus in his Council had been the first among equals, respected but by no means autocratic. Ellena just gave orders, and if these were not promptly carried out there would be demotions and dismissals. She was not at all displeased, Grimes gathered, by the nickname that had been bestowed upon her. She was not the first Iron Lady in history but certainly was one of the most deserving of that sobriquet.

She did not seem to mind that Grimes and Maggie continued their residence in the Palace, although they were her husband's guests and not hers. She did not object when Fenella continued her visits. She even condescended to mingle socially with the offworlders on occasion, inviting—or commanding—them to official dinner parties. At these the fare was Spartan and the conversation stilted.

And then there was the affair of the bugging.

Just prior to this, Grimes had found indications that his personal possessions, including his papers, had been disturbed during his absences from his suite. He told Maggie, who, after investigation, reported that there were signs that her own things had been interfered with. After this, before every meeting with Fenella, Shirl and Darleen in Grimes' quarters, she would make a sweep with her bug detector, that multi-functional wrist companion which she had been given back on Earth. But the thing, when switched on, did not emit so much as a single *beep*.

This particular morning there was the usual meeting of the five of them with the pretext of coffee and/or other drinks. Before the arrival of the other three, but after the serving wench had brought in the tray, Maggie used the detector, paying special attention to the coffee things. She said, "All clear."

"You like playing with that thing, don't you?" said Grimes.

"I do, rather."

Then Fenella came in, accompanied by Shirl and Darleen.

The two New Alicians were silent while Grimes, Maggie and Fenella compared notes, aired theories, discussed the implications of all that they had learned.

"There's something cooking," said the journalist at last. "I can feel it in my water. Some sort of balloon is about to go up. There is something rotten in the State of Denmark. . . ."

"But this is New Sparta," objected Darleen, "not Denmark. Wherever Denmark is."

"A figure of speech," said Fenella. "And now, let's hear from you two."

"What can we tell you?" asked Shirl. "We are still trying to teach those thick-witted Amazons how to throw a boomerang. And there are the foot-boxing lessons. They are rather better at that."

"What about the private lessons you are giving to that butch blonde, Major whatever-her-name-is?" Fenella's nostrils were quivering, a sure sign that she was on the scent of some interesting dirt. "Has she been giving *you* any lessons?"

"What could she give us lessons in?" asked Darleen innocently. "But she wants to be our friend; she has told us as much. And when we are alone with her we are to call her by her name, Hera, and not address her by her rank."

"All girls together," sneered Fenella. "And haven't you learned yet that the word 'friend' has, over the past few years, acquired a new meaning?"

"We do not understand," said both girls as one.

"But haven't your relations with the major," persisted Fenella, "been rather warmer than one would expect between a relatively senior officer and two very junior ones?"

"We would not know," said Shirl. "This is the first time that we have been part of an army."

"Perhaps Hera has been generous," said Darleen doubtfully. "She gives us presents. Like this. . . ."

She raised her right arm. Around the wrist was a broad bracelet of gold mesh, set with sparkling, semi-precious stones.

"It is very pretty . . ." said Maggie.

"She'll be wanting something for that . . ." said Fenella.

"Use your detector, Maggie!" snapped Grimes.

"But . . ."

"Do as I say!"

Maggie pressed the right buttons on her wrist companion. The *beeps* that it emitted seemed deafeningly loud.

"How . . . How did you guess?" asked Fenella.

"My mind isn't as suspicious in the same way as yours," Grimes told her, "but it has its moments. And isn't there an old saying, beware the Greeks when they come bearing gifts?"

He was rather annoyed when he had to explain the allusion to Shirl and Darleen. And Darleen was even more annoyed when Maggie made her take off the bracelet and then hammered it with the heel of her sandal until her bug detector made it plain that it had ceased to function.

And Grimes realized that they all had behaved foolishly, even to the officer who had fitted Maggie out for her role as intelligence agent. That bug detector should have given a visual warning, not a series of loud beeps. And, beeps or no beeps, the counter-intelligence listeners-in should never have been told that their bug had been detected; instead they should have been fed false information.

But it was no use crying over spilt milk.

Chapter 19

The next day they made a break in what had become their routine.

Instead of the morning meeting in Grimes' suite they did their talking during a stroll through the city streets. This was no hardship; the day was fine, pleasantly warm. But there were problems. A group of five people find it hard to hold a conversation while walking, especially if what is being discussed is of a confidential nature. Raised voices attract attention. So it was that Shirl and Darleen, who did not have much to contribute in any case, brought up the rear while Grimes walked between Maggie and Fenella.

There seemed to be an air of expectancy in the streets. Grimes remarked on this.

"It's the Marathon, of course," said Fenella. "Even though Brasidus is not here to fire the starting pistol, the show must go on."

"It can go on without me," laughed Grimes.

"Some gentle jogging would do you good," Maggie told him.

"There are better ways of taking exercise," he said.

He turned into a shop doorway, where he would be sheltered from the light breeze, to fill and to light his pipe. An annoying eddy blew out the old-fashioned match that he was using. He bent his head to shield the flame of the second match. Something whistled past his ear. He stared at the tiny, glittering thing that had embedded itself in the wooden door frame with a barely audible *thunk*. He recognized it for what it was. He had fired similar missiles himself while taking part in a *panjaril* hunt on Clothis, a combination of sport and commercial enterprise, the beasts being not killed but merely rendered unconscious, then to be shorn of their silky fur and left to recover to wander off and grow a new coat. It was an anesthetic dart that had just missed him.

He forgot the business of pipe lighting, stared at the passing pedestrians, alert for the sight of a gleaming weapon, an aiming hand.

"What's wrong?" asked Maggie.

He indicated the dart, said, "Somebody's out to get us."

"But who?" demanded Fenella.

"You tell me."

"It must be somebody," said Maggie, making a sweeping gesture with her hand at the passersby.

She was as lucky as Grimes had been. The dart that should have struck the exposed skin of her wrist embedded itself harmlessly in the baggy sleeve of her shirt, just above the elbow. Grimes pulled the thing out before it could do any damage, dropped it into a convenient grating in the gutter.

"Let's get out of here!" he snapped. "Back to the Palace!"

"There's never a policeman around when you need one," complained Fenella. Then, "But whose side are they on, anyhow?"

The general flow of foot traffic was now in the direction that they wanted to go. There were very few vehicles. They mingled with the crowd which, although it afforded some protection, hampered their progress. A fat man, past whom Grimes shoved none too gently, uttered a little squeal and collapsed. Grimes saw the tiny dart protruding from his bulging neck. Other people in the immediate vicinity of the fugitives were falling. The members of the hit squad were showing more determination than accurate marksmanship but, sooner or later, they must hit at least one of their designated targets. And how many of the ambulance attendants, out in force as always during a major sporting event, were the genuine article? Would Grimes or his companions be taken to a first-aid station or hospital or to some interrogation center?

Their scattering throughout the crowd was not altogether intentional but it made the pursuers' task more difficult. Had they stayed in a tightly knit group it would have been easy to identify them, to pick them off one by one. As it was, the only two easily indentifiable were Shirl and Darleen, and they were not the prime objectives.

They pushed and jostled their way along the narrow, winding street. They came to the intersection with the main road—not much wider, little more direct—to the Palace. There the crowds were heavy, lining each side of the thoroughfare. There were shouts and cheers. *For us?* wondered Grimes dazedly. He was aware that Maggie had found her way to his side and that Fenella was elbowing her way toward them both through the crush. And there were Shirl and Darleen. Darleen plucked a dart from one of the leather cross-straps of her uniform, dropped it to the ground. The unfortunate, barefooted woman who trod on it also dropped.

And they were pounding down the hill from the Palace, thousands of them, citizens and tourists, men and women, running, as was the ancient Greek custom, naked. It would be impossible to make any headway, toward refuge, against that mob. The first runners were abreast of them now—a slim young woman, her long legs pumping vigorously, her breasts jouncing; a wiry, middle-aged man; a fat lady, her entire body a-quiver who, on the down-grade, gravity-assisted, was putting on a fair turn of speed. It was probably against the rules but it was happening nonetheless; onlookers were casting aside their clothing and joining the runners.

One did so from near to where Grimes and Maggie were standing. He thought that he recognized the back view of her, that mole, with which he had become familiar, on her left shoulder. . . . But . . . Fenella?

"Quick!" snapped Maggie. "Get your gear off. Join the mob!"

Yes, it made sense. Clothed, among the naked runners, they would be obvious targets. Naked they would be no more than unidentifiable trees in a vast forest. But . . .

"My pipe . . ." he muttered. "My money . . . My credit cards . . ."

"Carry your notecase in your hand if you have to. As for your stinking pipe, you know what you can do with it. You've more than one, haven't you? Hurry up!"

He threw off his shirt, unbuckled the waistband of his kilt, remembering just in time to remove his notecase from the sporran. In the crush he had trouble with his underwear, his shoes and his long socks. Then he was stripped, as Maggie was, and the pair of them were out onto the road, merging with the mainstream of runners. Shirl and Darleen were just ahead of them; even with their peculiar hopping gait their nudity made them almost undistinguishable from the crowd.

Grimes ran. He knew that if he dropped back among the stragglers he would once again become a target. Not many men on New Sparta had outstanding ears. The same would apply if he achieved a place among the leaders—but there was little chance of that. He ran, trying to adjust the rhythm of his open-mouthed breathing to that of his laboring legs. He kept his eyes fixed on the bobbing buttocks of the lady ahead of him; there could have been worse things to watch. The soles of his feet were beginning to hurt; except on sand or grass he was used to going shod.

He ran, clutching his wallet in his right hand, using his left, now and again, to sweep away the sweat that was running down his forehead into his eyebrows, then into his smarting eyes.

He snatched a glance to his left. Maggie was still with him, making better weather of it than he was although her body was gleaming with perspiration and her auburn hair had become unbound. She flashed a smile at him, a smile that turned into a grimace as she trod on something hard. She was developing the beginnings of a limp.

But they were keeping up well, the pair of them, although the crowd around them was thinning. Fenella was still in front; Grimes caught a glimpse of a slim figure with a distinctive mole on the left shoulder when, momentarily, he looked up and away from the shapely bottom that he had been using as a steering mark. Shirl and Darleen were nowhere to be seen.

Somebody was coming up on him from astern. He could hear the heavy breathing, audible even above the noise of his own. He wondered vaguely who it was. Then he heard the sound of a brief scuffle and the thud of someone falling heavily and, almost immediately, the shrill whistle of one of the Marathon marshals summoning a first-aid party.

From his right Shirl (or was it Darleen) said, "We got her."

Grimes turned his head. The New Alician was bounding along easily, showing no effects of physical exertion.

"Got . . . who?" he gasped.

"We did not find out her name. A tall, skinny girl with red hair. She had one of those little needles in her hand. She was going to stick it in you. We stuck it in her."

"Uh . . . thanks . . ."

"We are watching for others."

She dropped behind again.

Grimes ran. His feet hurt. His legs were aching. His breath rasped in and out painfully. Maggie ran. Obviously the pace was telling on her too. Fenella ran, falling back slowly from her leading position. The woman ahead of Grimes gave up, veering off to the side of the road. In his bemused condition Grimes began to follow her but either Shirl or Darleen (he was in no condition to try to work out which was which) came up on his right and nudged him back on the right course.

Other people were dropping out. That final, uphill run was a killer. Grimes would have dropped out but, as long as Maggie and Fenella kept going he was determined to do the same. His vision was blurred. The pounding of his heart was loud in his ears. He was aware of a most horrendous thirst. Surely, he thought, there would be cold drinks at the finishing line.

He raised his head, saw dimly a vision of white pillars, of gaily colored, fluttering bunting. He forced himself to keep going although he had slowed to little better than a tired walk. "We're almost there . . ." he heard Maggie whisper and, "So bloody what?" he heard Fenella snarl.

There was a broad white line painted across the road surface.

Grimes crossed it, then sat down with what he hoped was dignified deliberation. Beside him Maggie did likewise, making a better job of it than Grimes. Fenella unashamedly flopped. Shirl and Darleen stood beside them.

An attendant brought mugs of some cold, refreshing, faintly tart drink. Grimes forced himself to sip rather than to gulp.

The Lady Ellena said, "So you ran after all, Commodore . . ."

Grimes looked up at the tall, white-robed woman with the wreath of golden laurel leaves in her hair.

"Unfortunately," she went on, "I shall not be able to award you a medallion for finishing the course. You were not an official entrant and, furthermore, did not begin at the starting point. That applies to all of you."

"Still," said Grimes, "we finished."

"Yes. You did that." She turned to Shirl and Darleen. "What happened to your uniforms, Lieutenants? You realize, of course, that the cost of replacement will be deducted from your pay."

She strode away among a respectful throng of officials.

Other officials conducted Grimes and the others to a tent where they were given robes and sandals, and more to drink, and told that transport would be provided for them, at a charge, to take them to where they wished to go.

It was just as well, thought Grimes, that he had clung to his money and his credit cards all through the race. The Lady Ellena did not seem to be in a very obliging mood.

Chapter 20

Grimes and his companions missed the beginning of the riot.

They had intended to return to the Acropolis after much needed showers and a resumption of clothing to witness the handing out of the awards to the Marathon winner and to those who had placed second and third, but there was too much to be discussed and, too, none of them, with the exception of Shirl and Darleen, felt like making the effort.

Their hired hovercar stopped briefly at the Hippolyte, where Fenella picked up from her room a bag with clothing and toilet articles, then continued to the Palace. Shirl and Darleen went to their quarters to clean up and to put on fresh uniforms, Fenella was given the freedom of Maggie's bathroom, Grimes and Maggie shared a shower in his. Finally all of them gathered in Grimes's sitting room.

They sprawled in their chairs, sipping their long, cold drinks. Grimes was making a slow recovery. The muscles of his legs were still aching but the pain was diminishing. His feet still hurt, but not as much as they had been. His pipe, an almost new one, would soon be broken in, although it was not yet as good as the one that he had abandoned with his clothing prior to taking part in the race.

"Who were they?" asked Maggie. "Why were they gunning for us?"

"The same bitches who kidnapped your cobber, the Archon," said Fenella. "And it was Grimes who put them wise to the fact that we were on their trail when he said that he recognized that wench in Aerospace Control."

"I've lured them out into the open," said Grimes.

"So you say," sneered Fenella. "The way things are, they'll soon be driving us into hiding or, even, offplanet. It's just as well, Maggie, that you have that courier of yours, *Krait*, standing by."

"I still think," said Grimes stubbornly, "that they'll overreach themselves and do something stupid."

"I'm beginning to think," said Fenella, "that that's your monopoly."

"We might as well see what we're missing," said Maggie.

She got up from her chair with something of an effort, switched on the big playmaster, set the controls for TriVi reception. The screen came alive with a picture of the floodlit Acropolis and from the speakers issued the sound of rattling, throbbing drums and squealing pipes. The camera zoomed in to the wide platform upon which Ellena, white-robed, gold-crowned, sat in state, with behind her rank upon rank of her Amazon Guards in their gleaming accoutrements.

"They said that we could not be there," complained Shirl.

"They say that our bodies are not . . . uniform," explained Darleen.

Yes, thought Grimes, looking into the screen, the Guards on display had been carefully selected for uniformity of appearance. They could have been clones.

The camera panned over the crowd. A broad path, lined on each side with police, had been cleared through it. Along it marched a band of women—Amazon Guards again—some with trumpets, some with pipes, some with drums. There were cheers and—surprisingly—catcalls. "Pussies go home! Pussies go home!" somebody was yelling. Other men took up the cry.

The voice of the commentator overrode the other sounds.

"And now, citizens, here, marching behind the band, come the winners to receive their awards from the Lady Ellena. First, Lieutenant Phryne, of the Amazon Guards. . . ." Phryne was not in uniform but in a simple white chiton, with one shoulder bare, with her long, muscular legs exposed to mid-thigh, her golden hair unbound. "And behind her, citizens, is First Officer Cassandra, of Trans-Sparta Airlines, a real flyer. . . ." Cassandra, a brunette, was dressed as was Phryne. "And in third place, Sergeant Hebe, of the Amazon Guards. . . ."

More cheers—and more boos.

"The race was fixed!" somebody shouted, not far from one of the microphones. A struggle was developing, with men trying to break through the police cordon. The band marched on and played on, missing neither a step nor a note. The three Marathon winners marched on, heads held high and disdainfully. Behind them came more Amazons—and the spears that they carried looked as though they were for use as well as for ornament.

Reaching the platform the band split into two sections, one to either side of the steps leading up to it. Ellena rose to her feet. There were cheers and boos, and men shouting. "We want Brasidus! We want Brasidus!" and, "Send the bitch back to where she came from!"

An Amazon officer handed Ellena a golden laurel wreath, its leaves not as broad as the one that she was wearing but broad enough. Phryne bowed, then fell to one knee. Ellena placed the wreath on her head. Phryne got gracefully to her feet and was embraced by the Archoness.

The camera lingered only briefly on this touching scene then swept over the crowd. Scuffles were breaking out all over. A group of four women had a man down on the ground and were kicking him viciously. Elsewhere there was the wan flicker of energy weapons where police were using their stunguns. A woman, her clothing torn from her, was struggling with half a dozen men whose intention was all too obvious. At the foot of the platform the bandswomen had dropped their instruments and had drawn pistols from their belts—not the relatively humane stunguns but projectile weapons—and the escorting guard were already using their spears to fight off attackers, employing the butts rather than the points, but how long would it be before they reversed them?

"Hell!" swore Fenella, "I should have been there, not watching it on TriVi. . . ."

"Be thankful that you're not," Grimes told her. "Women seem to be in the minority in that mob. Speaking for myself, a sex riot is something I'd rather not be involved in. . . ."

Ellena was standing there on the platform, her arms upraised, shouting something. What it was could not be heard. There were the shouts and the screams and, at last, the rattle of automatic fire. Somebody was using projectile weapons. The bandswomen, machine pistols jerking in their hands, were joining their spear-wielding sisters in the defense of the front of the platform. And the spears had been reversed and the blades of them were glistening red in the harsh glare of the floodlights. And whose side were the police on now? Twenty of them, in their black leather uniforms, were charging the Amazons. The weapons in their hands were only stunguns but, to judge from the visible discharge, more of a flare than a flicker, and from the harsh crackle that was audible even in the general uproar, their setting was lethal rather than incapacitating.

The arrival of the first of the inertial drive transports was, at first, almost unnoticed, the clatter of its propulsion unit just part of the general cacophony. It dropped into camera view, and dropped, until it was over the platform, just clear of the heads of those standing there. Pigsnouted in respirators, Amazons dropped from its belly, bringing with them more respirators for their sisters already engaged in the fighting. A high ranking officer, to judge by the amount of brass on her leather, conferred with

Ellena, obviously persuading her to mount the short ladder that had now been lowered from the aircraft. The Archoness, followed by the Amazon colonel, embarked.

The TriVi commentator was valiantly trying to make himself heard. "Citizens! I beseech you all to stay away from the Acropolis! This is not just a riot; this is a revolution! People have been killed! They. . . ." His voice faded, recovered. "They are using gas. . . ."

They were using gas. It was what Grimes himself would have done in the circumstances, what he had done, on more than one occasion, during his Survey Service career. From the low-flying aircraft a dense mist, opalescent in the flood lighting, was drifting downward and battling men and women were dropping to the ground unconscious, police and civilians, all except the Amazon Guards in their protective masks. People on the outskirts of the mob, not yet affected, were beginning to run, away from the Acropolis, while others were binding strips torn from their clothing about their faces, delaying the effect of the anesthetic vapor by only seconds.

Hand weapons were being fired at the transport but ineffectually, and the marksmen got off only a few rounds before falling to the ground unconscious. There was even one man who was tearing up cobblestones and hurling them skyward. Darleen remarked scornfully, "He could not hit the side of a barn even if he was inside it."

But he, whoever he was, was at least trying, thought Grimes. He was fighting back.

Another voice came from the speakers, a female one, distorted and muffled as though by breathing apparatus.

"Citizens! You have seen what has been happening at the Acropolis. Certain elements have tried to attack the person of our beloved leader, the Lady Ellena. The assassination attempt has been foiled. The instigators will be brought to justice. And now, all of you who have been watching this on the screens in your homes. . . . Stay in your homes. Do not take to the streets. Security patrols are abroad, with orders to take strict measures to maintain the peace . . ."

"In other words," muttered Grimes, "shoot first and ask questions afterwards."

The last picture on the screen, before the transmitter was shut down, was a dismal one. It had started to rain. Moving among the sprawled, unconscious bodies were gasmasked Amazons. They seemed to know whom they were looking for, were picking up selected prisoners and throwing them roughly into the rear of a large hovercar. Those who were left on the ground were the lucky ones. They would awake in a few hours time cold and wet and miserable—but they would not be awakening in jail.

"And what was all that about?" asked Fenella at last.

"That," said Maggie, "is for us to find out."

Then there was a great hammering on the door.

"Open up!" yelled a female voice. "In the name of the Lady Ellena, open up!"

Chapter 21

First into the sitting room were two Amazon privates, stunguns in hand. They were followed by a major, and behind her was Ellena herself, still in her white robes, still with the golden laurel wreath crown.

"What are you two doing here?" snapped the officer.

"But, Hera . . ." began Shirl.

"The correct form of address, Lieutenant, is 'Madam.' Please remember that."

"This is our free time, Madam," said Darleen rebelliously.

"Free time, Lieutenant, is a privilege and not a right. And don't you know that during this emergency all leave has been suspended? Get back to your quarters. At once."

"Better do as the lady says," advised Fenella.

"Quiet, you!" snarled Hera.

Fenella subsided. Grimes didn't blame her. He would not have liked to try conclusions with that female weight-lifter, her muscles bulging through the leather straps of her uniform. Shirl and Darleen got to their feet, cast apologetic glances at Grimes. He managed a small smile in return. They slouched out of his sitting room in a most unofficerlike manner.

"And what are *you* doing here?" demanded Ellena, addressing the journalist.

"Enjoying a quiet drink with my friends, Lady," she replied defiantly.

"Cooking up some scurrilous stories for the scandal sheets that employ you as their muckraker, you mean," said Ellena. "However, since you are here you may stay. In fact, you will stay. For your own protection. I cannot guarantee the safety of any offworlders at large in the city at this time."

"You mean," said Fenella, "that you want to be able to keep an eye on me."

"Somebody has to," Ellena told her. She turned to Maggie. "You, Commander Lazenby, are the senior Federation Survey Service officer at present on this planet. My understanding is that I, as ruler of a federated world, have the right to demand the support of the Federation's armed forces during times of emergency."

Maggie looked questioningly at Grimes, who nodded.

Ellena sneered. "Of course the Commodore, the ex-planetary Governor, is an expert on such matters, especially since the Federation's armed forces on Liberia were doing their damnedest to depose him. But what do you say, Commodore Grimes?"

"You are right in your understanding, Lady," admitted Grimes.

"Thank you, thank you. And now, Commander Lazenby, am I to understand that Lieutenant Gupta, captain of the courier *Krait*, is technically under your orders?"

"Yes."

"And how is this *Krait* armed?"

Once again Maggie looked questioningly at Grimes.

He said, "I was once in command of such a ship myself, Lady. A Serpent Class Courier is no battle cruiser. There will be a forty-millimeter machine cannon, a laser cannon, a missile launcher and a *very* limited supply of ammunition. In a small vessel the magazines are also small, so the laser cannon will be the only weapon capable of sustained firing."

"And are there—what do you call them?—pinnaces?"

"Nothing so big. Just a couple of general purpose spaceboats. Inertial drive, of course. Each can mount a light machine gun if required."

"Still," she said, "a useful adjunct to my own defense forces."

"What about your Navy?" he asked.

She said, "I shall be frank, Commodore Grimes. You know what this world was like when it was an all-male planet. Many senior officers, in the Army and the Navy, pine for those so-called Good Old Days and too many junior ones believe the rubbish that their seniors tell them. They resent having to take orders from a woman. I cannot trust them."

"When we get Brasidus back," said Fenella spitefully, "he'll bring them back into line."

"Until such time," Ellena said coldly, "I must rule as best I can."

She did not, thought Grimes, seem to be overly worried about the safety of her husband. She was not, even, overly worried about her own safety. There was an arrogance, but not a stupid arrogance. She would take whatever tools came to hand to build up her own position. She had already forged such a tool, her Corps of Amazon Guards. And the Amazons had been brought into being well before the abduction of the Archon.

The telephone buzzed.

Grimes got up from his chair to answer the call. His way was blocked by Major Hera. It was Ellena who took her seat at the desk on which the instrument was mounted.

"Archoness here," she stated.

"Lady, this is Captain Lalia, duty commander of the Palace Guard. There is a mob approaching, with armored hovercars in the lead. If you will switch on your playmaster to Palace Cover you will have pictures."

"Thank you, Lalia. Commodore Grimes, will you get us coverage as Lalia suggests? Major Hera, if the Colonel is not back yet from the city will you take charge of the defense? I shall remain here for the time being."

Hera hurried out, leaving the two Amazon privates to guard Ellena. Grimes fiddled with the controls of the playmaster. The picture, being taken by the infrared cameras on the palace roof, was clear enough. It was more of an army than a mere mob that was pouring up the road. There were the armored hovercars in the lead, with their heavy automatic weapons and their uniformed crews and the pennants streaming from their whip aerials. There were motorcycles, and their riders were police, in their stainless steel and black leather uniforms. There were marching civilians, more than a few of whom were carrying firearms.

Directional microphones were picking up the shouts.

"Scrag the bitches! Scrag the bitches! Ellena out! Ellena out!"

"Somebody out there," remarked Fenella, "doesn't like you."

Surprisingly Ellena laughed. She said, "They will like me even less in a minute or so. My Amazons will be more than a match for this rabble."

"There're Army personnel there," said Grimes. "And Police."

"I do not need to be instructed, Commodore, regarding the uniforms worn by my own armed forces."

"They aren't behaving as though they belong to you," said Fenella.

"Guards," snapped Ellena, "if that woman opens her mouth again, gag her!"

The mob—or the army—was closer now. Was that Colonel Heraclion in one of the leading armored cars? Yes, Grimes decided, it was, making his identification just before the colonel pulled on a respirator. Gas had been used to quell the riot at the Acropolis; if it were used here it would not be so effective. Police and Army personnel, at least, would have their protection.

The camera shifted its viewpoint, covering, from above, the main entrance to the Palace. Something was rolling out, a huge, broad-rimmed wheel, almost a short-axised cylinder. Gathering speed, it trundled down the road toward the attackers. It was followed by another, and another. Laser fire flickered from the hovercars and there were muzzle flashes and streams of tracer from the heavy machine guns. There were the beginnings of panic, with vehicles attempting to pull off the road, their way blocked by the heavy, ornamental shrubbery. But these were only relatively light armored cars, not heavy tanks.

The first of the wheels—it must have been radio-controlled—exploded. The second one leaped the crater before being detonated. The third one did not have much effect—but this was because the majority of the marchers had been able to run clear to each side, off the road.

"A very old weapon," said Ellena smugly, "but improved upon."

Grimes stared at the picture in the screen, at the shattered vehicles, some of which were still smoldering, and at the contorted, dismembered bodies, some very few of which were still feebly twisting and jerking.

He said bitterly, "I hope you're satisfied."

She said, "They're only men. Besides, they asked for it and they got it."

"Didn't you rather overreact?" asked Grimes.

"Come, come, Commodore. Speaking for myself, I would rather overreact to a threat than be torn limb from limb." She got up to leave. "I do not care what sleeping arrangements you make but all three of you are confined to the Palace, to the two suites allocated to Commander Lazenby and Commodore Grimes.

"A very good night to you all."

She swept out, followed by the two Amazon privates.

"The manipulating bitch!" exclaimed Fenella, not without admiration. "You know, I almost hope that she pulls it off."

"If she does," said Grimes, "this is one world that I shall do my best to avoid in the foreseeable future."

Chapter 22

So they were, to all intents and purposes, prisoners in the Palace.

It was decided that Fenella would take up residence in what had been Maggie's suite and that Maggie would move in with Grimes. Everybody must already know that she had been sleeping with him; now it would be made official. Maggie said that she would call Lieutenant Gupta to let him know that his services might be required but was unable to get through to the spaceport. She tried direct punching first but without results. Then she got through to the Palace switchboard. A young lady in Amazon uniform politely but coldly informed her that during the state of emergency no outward calls were allowed.

After this the three of them watched the playmaster to try to catch up with the news. There was a speech by Ellena, which she delivered from before a backdrop on which were idealized portraits of such famous persons as Prime Ministers Indira Gandhi, Golda Mier and Margaret Thatcher. There was also one of a lady attired as an ancient Greek warrior, presumably the mythical Queen Hippolyte. This one looked remarkably like Ellena herself.

("I suppose that the artist knew on which side her bread is buttered," sneered Fenella.)

Ellena's speech was an impassioned one. She appealed to all citizens to support her in the defense of law and order. She left no doubt in the minds of her audience as to who was the chief upholder of law and order on New Sparta. At the finish, almost as an afterthought, she did mention her missing husband and assured everybody that until his return the business of government was in good hands.

After she finished talking there was a brief coverage of the attack on the Palace and an assurance that the ringleaders of what was referred to as a riot were under arrest. There was no mention of casualties.

Sufficient unto the day, thought Grimes, was the evil thereof. No doubt the morrow would bring its own evils. He decided to go outside, onto the balcony, to smoke a quiet pipe before retiring.

The night seemed to be quiet enough. There were no sounds of gunfire, near or distant. There was no wailing of sirens. Somebody, somewhere not too far away, was plucking at a stringed instrument, accompanying a woman who was softly, not untunefully singing. Grimes did not recognize the song. Of one thing he was sure; it was a very old one. He looked up at the sky, at the stars, at the constellations. These had been named by the first colonists, all of them after gods and heroes of Greek mythology. Poseidon and Cyclops, Jason and Ulysses, Ares and Hercules . . . There were no female names. Would Ellena, Grimes wondered, order her tame astronomers to rectify this? Would the spectacular grouping now called Ares be renamed Hippolyte?

He was still staring upward when something whirred past his right ear, striking the window frame behind him with a clatter. At once he dropped on to all fours, seeking the protection, such as it was, of the ornamental rail enclosing the balcony. But there were no further missiles.

He heard Maggie ask sharply, "What was that?" and Fenella demand, "What are you *doing*, Grimes? Praying? Are you sure that Mecca's that way?"

"Down, you silly bitches!" he snarled. "Don't make targets of yourselves!"

"Targets?" echoed Maggie.

He crawled around to face them.

"Get inside!" he ordered. "Away from the window! Somebody's throwing things at us . . ."

"Only a boomerang," said Maggie. "A *little* boomerang. It couldn't hurt a fly . . ." She had picked up the small crescent of cunningly carved wood and was examining it. "There's writing on it . . ."

Grimes got to his feet, took the thing from Maggie. On the flat side of it, in childishly formed capitals, was a brief message. BRASIDUS HELD PRISONER AT MELITUS. There was no signature. In lieu there was the figure of a familiar animal.

"What the hell is that supposed to be?" asked Maggie. "A dinosaur?"

"A kangaroo, of course," said Grimes. "And this primitive airmail letter is from Shirl or Darleen, or both of them. They've been keeping their ears flapping."

They all went back inside. Grimes got out the large atlas. He found

Melitus without any trouble. Both a small mountain and a village on its western slopes had that name. It was wild country, with no towns or cities, no roads or railways, only the occasional village, only goat tracks running from nowhere much to nowhere at all. It would be accessible enough to the dirigibles of Trans-Sparta Airlines, or to those of the Spartan Navy, or to any form of heavier-than-air transport.

"But," said Grimes, "*we* don't have wings."

"Lieutenant Gupta and his *Krait* are under my orders," said Maggie. "Under *your* orders actually, although he's not supposed to know that."

"And just how," asked Grimes, "are we going to give Gupta any orders?"

"You'll think of a way," said Maggie. "You always do."

"And meanwhile," grumbled Fenella, "dear Ellena will tighten her grip on this planet. Oh, I don't particularly mind. All in all, women make no more of a balls of running things than men do. As long as I get my exclusive story. . . ."

"Is that all you ever think of?" flared Maggie. "A story? Brasidus is our friend. Too, until and unless the Federation decides otherwise, he is the recognized ruler of this world."

"All right. All right. But don't forget that I'm playing along with you two only because I scent a story."

They turned in then.

Grimes and Maggie did not go to sleep at once. Neither did they talk much. They decided that any long-range planning was out of the question and that, meanwhile, they would make the best of what time they had together.

The next morning breakfast, such as it was, was served to them in Grimes' sitting room. Muddy coffee and little, sweet rolls were not, he thought and said, a solid foundation upon which to build the day. Fenella and Maggie were inclined to agree with him. Before they had quite finished the meal Lieutenant Phryne came in, saying that she had orders to escort them to the Lady Ellena's presence. She refused to tell them what they were wanted for.

Ellena received them in her command headquarters. She was wearing the uniform of a high-ranking Amazon officer. In an odd sort of way it suited her even though her body was not shown to advantage by a costume that was, essentially, an affair of leather straps, brass buckles and a short kilt. She was seated behind a desk the surface of which was dominated by her highly polished, plumed, bronze helmet. There was barely room for the papers—reports, possibly—which she had been studying. On the walls were illuminated maps—of the city, of the surrounding countryside, of the entire planet. There was communications equipment elaborate enough to handle the needs of a small army. (It was handling the needs of such an army.) Female officers were doing things at the consoles before which they were sitting, speaking, low-voiced, into microphones.

"The prisoners, Ma'am," announced Phryne smartly.

"Not prisoners, Lieutenant," Ellena corrected her. "The guests. My husband's guests." She looked up from her papers. "Good morning, Commodore. Commander, Miz Prune. Please be seated." Phryne brought them hard chairs. "You will recall that yesterday we discussed the possibility of putting the Survey Service's courier *Krait* at the disposal of the civil power on this planet. . . ."

The civil power? wondered Grimes, looking around at the uniformed, armed women, at a screen on one of the walls which had come to life showing a small squadron of Amazon chariots proceeding along a city street, spraying the buildings on either side with heavy machine-gun fire.

"I am not so sure, Lady," said Maggie, "that this would be advisable. It has occurred to me that *Krait* would be better employed in the protection of Federation interests—the shipping in the spaceport, for example . . ."

"I could, I suppose," said Ellena coldly, "invoke the Right of Angary. . . ."

A space-lawyer yet! thought Grimes. But had the Right of Angary ever been invoked to justify the seizure of a ship of war rather than that of a mere merchantman? An interesting legal point . . . Anyhow, he decided suddenly, *he* wanted *Krait*, with, but preferably without, her rightfully appointed captain. After all he, in his younger days, had commanded such a vessel.

He pulled out his pipe, began to fill it. It was an invaluable aid to thinking.

"Put that thing away, Commodore," ordered Ellena.

"As you wish, Lady." He turned to Maggie. "I think, Commander Lazenby, that the Lady Ellena is well within her rights. And, surely, it is in the interests of the Federation, of which New Sparta is a member, that every effort be made to put a stop to civil commotion which might well develop into a civil war."

"Commodore Grimes," said Ellena, "has far more experience in such matters than you do, Commander Lazenby. After all, he has been a planetary ruler himself."

"I bow," said Maggie, "to the superior knowledge of the Archon's wife and the ex-Governor."

Fenella made a noise that could have been either a snort or a snigger.

Ellena glared at the two offworld women and favored Grimes with an almost sweet smile—but her eyes were cold and calculating.

"Then, Commodore," she said, "would you mind persuading Commander Lazenby to order *Krait*'s captain to lift ship at once and proceed forthwith to the Palace? I am no expert in these matters but I imagine that such a small spacecraft will be able to make a landing on the Amazons' drill ground."

"There's enough room there," said Grimes, "for a Constellation Class cruiser, provided she's handled with care. A Serpent Class courier could set down on the front lawn of the average suburban villa."

"You are the expert. Lieutenant Phryne, please see to it that an outside communications channel is made available to Commander Lazenby. Get through to the *Krait*'s captain."

Phryne went to one of the consoles against the wall. She punched buttons. The screen came alive. The face of a Federation Survey Service ensign—the single stripe of gold braid on each of his shoulderboards denoted his rank—appeared.

"*Krait* here," he said.

"Lieutenant Phryne of the Amazon Guard here, speaking from the Palace for the Lady Ellena. Call your captain to the phone, please."

"But what business. . . ."

"The Lady Ellena's business. Hurry!"

The young man vanished. In the screen were depicted surroundings that had once been very familiar to Grimes, the interior of the cramped control room of a Serpent Class courier. Since his time, he thought, there had been very few changes in layout. That was all to the good.

Lieutenant Gupta's thin brown face appeared in the screen.

"Captain of *Krait* here," he said.

"Commander Lazenby here," said Maggie, who had taken Phryne's place facing the screen.

"Yes, Commander?" Then, "Can you tell me what is happening? I sent Lieutenant Hale, my PCO, ashore to mingle with the people to find out what he could, but he has not yet returned . . ."

"PCO?" whispered Ellena to Grimes.

"Psionic Communications Officer," he whispered in reply. "A trained telepath. Carried these days by Survey Service ships more for espionage than for communicating over light-years. . . ."

And so the mind-reader isn't aboard, he thought. *So much the better.*

"Lieutenant Gupta," asked Maggie, "are you ready for lift-off?"

"Of course, Commander."

"I have orders for you, Lieutenant. You are to proceed forthwith to the Palace, to place yourself at the disposal of the New Spartan government."

"I question your authority, Commander. May I remind you that you are an officer of the Scientific Branch, not of the Spaceman Branch?"

"And may I remind you, Lieutenant, that prior to our departure from Port Woomera, on Earth, you were told, in my presence and the presence of your officers, by no less a person than Rear Admiral Damien, that while on New Sparta you were to consider yourself under my orders?"

"That is so," admitted Gupta grudgingly. "Even so, I would remind you that this conversation is being recorded."

"So bloody what?" exploded Maggie. "Just get here, that's all, or I'll see to it that Admiral Damien has your guts for garters."

"But. . . ."

"Just get here, that's all."

"But where shall I land?" Gupta asked plaintively.

"Tell him," said Grimes, "that beacons will be set out in the middle of the Amazons' drill ground."

"Was that Commodore Grimes?" demanded Gupta.

"It was," said Grimes. "It is."

"May Vishnu preserve me!" muttered Gupta.

Chapter 23

Amazingly and extremely fortunately Grimes was able to get some time alone with Maggie and Fenella. Somehow he had been put in charge of setting up makeshift spaceport facilities in the drill ground, with Amazons scurrying hither and yon at his bidding. Among these women soldiers were Shirl and Darleen. Grimes called them to him, on the pretense that they were to act as his liaison with the Amazon officer in charge.

"Did you get our note?" asked one of the New Alicians.

"Of course. It was the information I needed. Now, you two, stick close to us . . ." He broke off the conversation to give orders to an Amazon sergeant. "Yes. I want that inertial drive pinnace out of the way. The field must be completely cleared." And to a lieutenant, "Just leave it here, will you? Yes, I can operate it . . ." From the speaker of the portable transceiver came a voice, that of Lieutenant Gupta. "*Krait* to Palace, *Krait* to Palace. Do you read me? Over." Shirl handed Grimes the microphone on its long lead. "Palace to *Krait*," he said. "I read you loud and clear. Over." "Lifting off," came the reply. "Are you ready for me? Over." "Not quite. I shall call you as soon as the marker beacons are set out. Over and out."

He was free now to give hasty instructions to the four women. "Gupta is under *your* orders, Maggie. I want him and all his people out of the ship. You go aboard on some pretext—to the control room. You know how to operate the airlock controls, don't you? Good. Then, as soon as we get the chance, the rest of us will board. Button up as soon as we've done so and get upstairs in a hurry. You can do that much, can't you? Then I'll take over as soon as I can."

"What if we're fired on while we're lifting?" she asked. "I'm no fighter pilot. I'm only a simple scientist with the minimal training in ship handling required for all Survey Service officers in the non-spaceman branches."

"*Krait*'s a Federation ship. I don't think that Ellena would dare to try to blast her out of the sky. At least, I hope not. And I'll scamper up to control, to take over, as soon as I possibly can."

And then, leaving Maggie and Fenella standing by the transceiver, he, with Shirl and Darleen as his aides, took charge of the final preparations for the reception of the courier. Three powerful blinker lights had been found and adjusted to throw their beams upward and set out in a triangle almost at the exact center of the field. The lights were not the regulation scarlet but an intense blue. It did not matter. Gupta would be told what to expect.

Gupta had made good time, drifting over from the spaceport on lateral thrust. The arrhythmic cacophony of his inertial drive was beating down from the clear sky as he hung over the drill ground at an altitude of one kilometer. The light of the midmorning sun was reflected dazzlingly from her sleek slimness.

"Clear the field!" Grimes bellowed through a borrowed bullhorn.

"Clear the field!" the cry was taken up by officers and NCOs.

Grimes, accompanied by Shirl and Darleen, returned to the transceiver. He took the microphone from Maggie, ordered Gupta to land at the position marked by the beacons. Gupta acknowledged, then came in slowly, very slowly. Anyone would think, thought Grimes, that *Krait* had been built from especially fragile eggshells.

But *Krait* came in, her inertial drive hammering, maintaining her in a condition of almost weightlessness. Luckily there was no wind; had there been she would have been blown all over the field like a toy balloon.

She came in, and she landed. Her drive was not shut off but was left running, muttering irritably to itself, in neutral. Obviously Lieutenant Gupta wasn't at all happy about the situation. Grimes was. *Krait*, even under Maggie's unskilled management, would be able to make a quick get-away.

"*Krait* to Commander Lazenby," came from the transceiver speaker. "Your orders, please?"

Grimes passed the microphone to Maggie. "Report to the Lady Ellena in the command office, please."

There was another period of waiting.

At last *Krait*'s airlock door opened and the ramp was extended. Down it marched Lieutenant Gupta. For some reason he had taken the time to change into his full dress finery—starched white linen, frock coat, gold-braided sword belt and ceremonial sword in gold-braided scabbard, gold-trimmed fore-and-aft hat. He threw a grudging salute in Maggie's general direction. She, not in uniform, could not reply in kind but bowed slightly and stiffly.

"Where are your officers, Lieutenant?" asked Maggie.

"At their stations still, Commander."

"They are to accompany you to audience with the Lady Ellena. It is essential that her instructions be heard by everybody."

"If you so wish," said Gupta. He lifted his right wrist to his lips to speak into the communicator.

"Tell them," said Maggie, "not to bother to change out of working uniform. They can come just as they are."

"*All* the officers?" queried Gupta.

"Yes."

"But regulations require that there must be a shipkeeper."

She said, "I shall be your shipkeeper until you return. In any case, I wish to get some things from my cabin."

Scowling, Gupta barked orders into his communicator.

They came down the ramp in their slate gray shorts-and-shirt working uniform—a lieutenant jg, three ensigns, first lieutenant, navigator, electronicist and engineer officer. This latter, Grimes noted happily, had not shut down the drive before leaving the ship. He hoped that Gupta would not send him back to do so. But Gupta, unlike Grimes when he had been captain of such a vessel, was a slave to regulations. In these circumstances the drive must be left running until such time as the captain decided that it was safe to immobilize his command. And he was leaving *Krait* in the hands of an officer—Commander Lazenby—senior to himself.

Lieutenant Phryne marched up to them, followed by six Amazon privates. She saluted with drawn sword.

"Lieutenant," said Maggie, "please escort these gentlemen to the Lady Ellena."

"As you say, Commander."

As *Krait*'s people marched off, Maggie mounted the ramp, passed through the airlock doors. How long would it take her to get up to control? Grimes had timed himself many years ago; it was one of the emergency drills. He doubted that she would break his record. He had done it in just under five minutes—but he had known the layout of the ship. Should he allow Maggie double that time? He snuck a glance at his wrist companion, surreptitiously adjusted and switched on the alarm. He looked around the drill ground. The well-disciplined Amazons had been ordered to clear the field; that order still stood. They were standing there around the perimeter, sunlight brilliantly reflected from metal accoutrements. Even so, Grimes thought, he and the others would have to be fast. Those women were dead shots and in the event of their being ordered to use no firearms, to take their prisoners alive, they could *run*.

His wrist companion suddenly *beeped*.

"Now!" barked Grimes.

Fenella sprinted up the ramp. Shirl and Darleen each made it to the airlock with a single leap. Grimes followed hard on their heels. He was dimly aware that the Amazons had broken ranks, were pouring inwards from all sides toward the little spaceship. But he had no time to watch them. The outer airlock door was shutting, was shut. The deck under his feet lurched. He and Fenella and Shirl and Darleen were thrown into a huddle. Structural members were either singing or rattling, or both. Maggie must have slammed the drive straight from neutral to maximum lift.

He disentangled himself from the women, began the laborious climb—it seemed as though he were having to fight at least two gravities—up the spiral staircase, from the airlock to control.

Chapter 24

He pulled himself up through the hatch into the control compartment.

Maggie was hunched in the captain's chair, staring at the read-out screens before her, at the display of flickering numerals that told their story of ever-and rapidly increasing altitude.

Grimes made his way to the first lieutenant's seat with its duplicate controls, flopped into it with a sigh of relief.

"All right, Maggie," he said. "I'll take over."

"You'd better," she told him. "I've been wondering what to do next."

"You've done very well so far," he said. "You got us out of there very nicely."

He reduced thrust to a reasonable level. *Krait* was still climbing but now people could move about inside her hull at something better than a crawl, not hampered by a doubling of their body weight. He then gave his attention to the screens giving him views in all directions. He was half expecting that there would be pursuit of some kind but there was not.

"What now?" asked Maggie. "Do we go to Melitus to rescue Brasidus?"

"Not yet," said Grimes. "We carry on straight up. It may fool Ellena, it may not. I hope it does." He chuckled. "Let's try this scenario on for size. The notorious pirate, John Grimes, aided by his female accomplices, feloniously seized the Federation Survey Service's courier *Krait*. . . ."

"And why would he do that? And why should Commander Lazenby, of all people, help him? To say nothing of Fenella Prune and Shirl and Darleen. . . ."

"We'll get Fenella to write the script. You and Shirl and Darleen are hopelessly in love with me, slaves of passion. And Fenella's just along for the ride, getting material for her next piece in Star Scandals."

She laughed. "You could do her job as well as she does. But this scenario of yours. . . . There was opportunity for you to carry out your piratical act. You seized it. But what was the motive? I am assuming that Ellena does not know that *we* know where Brasidus is being held."

"Mphm." Grimes filled and lit his pipe. "But, before we start kicking ideas around to see if they yelp, let's get the others up here." He spoke into a microphone. "This is the captain speaking. All hands to report to the control room. On the double."

"Where *is* the control room?" came Fenella's yelp from the intercom speaker.

"Just follow the spiral staircase up as far as you can go."

"Isn't there an elevator?"

"This," said Grimes, "is a Serpent Class courier, not a Constellation Class cruiser."

"Even an Epsilon Class star tramp has an elevator in the axial shaft!" she snapped.

"Stop arguing!" he yelled. "Just get up here!"

She did, without overmuch delay, accompanied by Shirl and Darleen. There were chairs for only two of the newcomers but Darleen, squatting on the deck, did not appear to be too uncomfortable.

Grimes talked.

"This is the way that I see things. I'm an outsider who just happens to have come to New Sparta at a time when all manner of balloons are going up. I came to New Sparta to wait there for the arrival of my ship, *Sister Sue*, which vessel is all my worldly wealth. I have heard rumors that the New Spartan government intends to seize her, for conversion to an auxiliary cruiser. (Well, Ellena could do that, if she had the brains to think of it. She wouldn't dare to seize a ship belonging to one of the major lines.) So, not for the first time in my career, I'm playing the game according to *my* rules."

"I'll say you are!" exclaimed Fenella. "You always keep telling us that you were never a pirate, but what you've just done bears all the earmarks of piracy."

"Never mind that. But there's one crime that I have committed—I've lifted from New Sparta without first obtaining Outward Clearance. Even so, as far as Aerospace Control is concerned *Krait* was put at the disposal of the New Spartan government. It doesn't much matter. All the legalities and illegalities can be sorted out later."

"Oh, we all of us know that the Law is an ass, Grimes," said Fenella impatiently. "Just what are your intentions, legal or otherwise?"

"To begin with, a spot of misdirection. As soon as we're clear of the atmosphere I'll switch to Mannschenn Drive, as though at the commencement of a Deep Space voyage. And then I'll attempt to raise *Sister Sue* on Carlotti Radio. Of necessity it will be a broad beam transmission; I don't know where she is, only the general direction from which she will be approaching. My signals will be monitored on New Sparta."

"And what will you tell *Sister Sue?*" asked Maggie.

"I'll try to arrange a rendezvous with her, about one light-year—no, not 'about,' exactly—from New Sparta. I shall tell Williams that he is, on no account, to approach any closer and that I shall be boarding to take command."

"Won't your Mr. Williams—or Captain Williams as he still is—think that these orders are rather . . . weird?" asked Fenella.

"Probably. But he should be used to weird orders by this time."

Krait drove up through the last tenuous shreds of atmosphere, through the belts of charged particles. Aerospace Control began, at last, to take an interest in her.

"Aerospace Control to *Krait* . . . Aerospace Control to *Krait*. . . ."

"*Krait* to Aerospace Control," said Grimes into the microphone. "I read you loud and clear."

"Return at once to the spaceport, *Krait*."

"Negative," said Grimes.

After that he ignored the stream of orders and threats that poured from the NST transceiver speaker.

It was time then to actuate the Mannschenn Drive. The rotors in their intricate array began to spin, tumbling, precessing, warping the dimensions of normal Space-Time around themselves and the ship. Perspective was distorted, colors sagged down the spectrum and what few orders Grimes gave were as though uttered in an echo chamber. But, as sometimes was the case, there were no *déjà vu* phenomena, no flashes of precognition.

And then it was over.

Krait was falling through a blackness against which the stars were no longer points of light but vague, slowly writhing nebulosities.

"So that's that," said Maggie practically.

"That's that," agreed Grimes. "Now all I have to do is to get the bold Billy on the blower and tell him my pack of lies, for Ellena's benefit."

In its own little compartment the Mobius Strip antenna of the Carlotti Deep Space Radio was revolving and its signals, on broad beam, were being picked up, instantaneously, by every receiver within their range, which was a very distant one—and being picked up, reciprocally, by Aerospace Control on New Sparta.

"Grimes to *Sister Sue*," said Grimes. "Grimes to *Sister Sue*. Do you read me?"

At last there came a reply in a male voice strange to Grimes, faint, as though coming from a very long way off—which it was.

"*Sister Sue* here. Pass your message."

"Who is that speaking?" asked Grimes.

"The third officer. Pass your message."

"Get Captain Williams for me, please."

"He's sleeping. I'm perfectly capable of taking your message."

"Get Captain Williams for me. Now."

"*Who* is that calling?"

"Grimes."

"Is that the name of a ship or some fancy acronym?"

"Grimes," repeated the owner of that name. "John Grimes. The owner. Your employer. Get Captain Williams to the Carlottiphone *at once*."

"How do I know that you're Grimes?"

"You should know by this time, young man, that not any Tom, Dick or Harry can get access to a Carlotti transceiver. Get Captain Williams for me. And see if you can arrange a visual hook-up as well as audio. I've the power here to handle it."

"Oh, all right, all right. Sir."

Williams wasted no time coming to *Sister Sue*'s control room. His cheerful, fleshy face appeared in the screen.

"Oh, it is you, Skipper. What's the rush? Couldn't it all have waited until I set her down on New Sparta?"

"It couldn't, Billy."

"But you were always getting on to me about the expense of needless Carlotti communications . . ."

"This one is not needless. To begin with, New Sparta's in a state of upheaval. The Archon was kidnapped and his wife, the Lady Ellena, took over the government. Now she seems to have a civil war on her hands. I don't want my ship sitting on her arse at Port Sparta with shooting going on all about her."

"She's been shot at before, Skipper."

"There's nothing more annoying," said Grimes, "than being shot at in somebody else's war. I want you to heave to, a light-year out, until the dust settles. I'll rendezvous with you and come aboard to talk things over."

"Where are you calling from, Skipper?" asked Williams. "Have you got yourself another ship? Who are those popsies in the background?"

"Yes, I have borrowed a ship. Never mind from whom. And I'm on my way out to you now. I'll home on your Carlotti broadcast. I've good equipment here."

"I'll be waiting for you, Skipper."

"Give my regards to Magda, will you? And to old Mr. Stewart."

"Willco, Skipper."

"See you," said Grimes. "Out."

Yes, he would be seeing Williams, but not for a while yet.

Chapter 25

Krait, insofar as New Sparta Aerospace Control was concerned, was now an invisible ship, falling through the warped dimensions toward her rendezvous with *Sister Sue*, undetectable by radar as long as her Mannschenn Drive was in operation. Some planets—such worlds as were considered to be strategically important—had defense satellites in orbit crammed with sophisticated equipment, such as long-range Mass Proximity Indicators capable of picking up approaching vessels running under Mannschenn Drive. New Sparta was not strategically important.

So while the Lady Ellena would be more than a little annoyed by the theft of a minor warship that she had hoped to acquire for her own use she might well be pleased, thought Grimes, at the removal from her domain of three nuisances—Maggie Lazenby, Fenella Pruin and Grimes himself. He allowed himself to feel sorry for Lieutenant Gupta. He and his officers, spacemen without a spaceship, would be discovering that they were far from welcome guests in the Palace. . . .

Meanwhile it was time that he started thinking of his own strategy rather than the troubles of others. He would begin by setting an orbital course for Melitus rather than trajectory for *Sister Sue*'s estimated position. Just where was Melitus?

He and the women went down to the wardroom—*Krait* was quite capable of looking after herself—where there was a playmaster which, like any such device aboard a spaceship, could be used to obtain information from the library bank. They all took seats, Grimes in one from which he could operate the playmaster's controls. He punched for LIBRARY, then for PLANETARY INFORMATION, then for NEW SPARTA, then for MELITUS. Words appeared on the screen. *Mountain, 1.7 kilometers above sea level, Latitude 37°14' S., Longitude 176°59'E.*

Village called Melitus? typed Grimes.

No information, appeared the reply.

Map of Mount Melitus vicinity?

Not in library bank.

Grimes swore. "I should," he said, "have brought along the atlas from my quarters."

"It would have looked suspicious," said Fenella, "if you'd been carrying it around with you."

"I could have torn out one or two relevant pages," said Grimes, "and put them in my pockets."

"But you didn't," said Fenella.

"There are some maps in my cabin," Maggie told them. "I'll get them now."

She spread them on the wardroom table. Grimes found the one he wanted, studied it carefully. When making his final approach, back in normal Space-Time, he would be shielded by the bulk of the planet from the probing radar of Aerospace Control. Unluckily he would be unable to make a quiet approach; the inertial drive unit of even a small ship is noisy; the only really heavy sonic insulation is to protect the eardrums of the crew. But there was a technique which he might employ, that he would employ if conditions were suitable. It was one that he had read about but had never seen used.

The map was a contour one. To the north Mount Melitus was steep, in parts practically sheer cliff. The southern face was sloped almost gently to the plain. There was a river, little more than a stream, that had its source about halfway up the mountain. A little below this source was the village of Melitus. But those contour lines. . . . The southern slopes were only comparatively gentle but there did not seem to be any suitable place upon which to set down a spaceship, even a small one. Grimes studied the map more carefully, took a pair of dividers to measure off distances. The river made a horseshoe bend just over a kilometer downstream from the village. The almost-island so formed was devoid of contour lines. Did that mean anything or was it no more than slovenly cartography? But the map, saw Grimes, was a Survey Service publication and the Survey Service's cartographers prided themselves on their thoroughness. He hoped they had been thorough when charting the Mount Melitus area.

He said, "You know something of the layout of the ship, Maggie. See if you can rustle up some kind of a meal. Sandwiches will do. Shirl and Darleen—you're army officers. . . ."

They laughed at that.

"But you know something about weapons," he went on. "You must have received some instruction when you were in the Amazon Guard as well as dishing it out. Go through the ship and collect all the lethal ironmongery you can find and bring it here, to the wardroom. And you, Fenella, make rounds of the officers' cabins and the storerooms and find clothing, for all of us, suitable for an uphill hike through rough country.

"I shall be going back to Control." He rolled up the map that he had been studying, took it with him. "You know where to find me if you want me."

Maggie brought him his sandwiches—rather inferior ham with not enough mustard—and a vacuum flask of coffee that was only a little better than the brew which they had become used to (but never liked) in the Palace. But he did not complain. (As far as Maggie was concerned he had learned, long since, that it was unwise to do so.) He munched stolidly while keeping a watchful eye on the instruments. One drawback of making an orbit around a planet with the ship's Mannschenn Drive in operation is that there are no identifiable landmarks; the appearance of a world viewed in such conditions has been described as that of a Klein Flask blown by a drunken glassblower.

But the instruments, Grimes hoped, were not lying.

"What time—local time, that is—should we get there?" asked Maggie.

"Midnight," replied Grimes. "Anyhow, that's what I've programed the little bitch for. How are the girls getting on with their fossicking?"

"Fenella's found clothing for all of us—tough coveralls. Boots might be a problem. Shirl and Darleen have rather long feet, as probably you've already noticed."

"On their own planet," he said, "they're used to running around barefoot. What about rainwear?"

"Rainwear? Are you expecting rain?"

"Rain has been known to fall," he said. "Tell Fenella, when you go back down, to find something suitable. And the weapons?"

"So far a stungun, fully charged, with belt and holster, for each of us. Laser pistols likewise. And projectile pistols."

He said, "We can't load ourselves down with too much. We'll take the stunguns and the lasers. We don't want to do any killing."

"Lasers kill people. Or hadn't you noticed?"

"A laser is a tool as well as a weapon, Maggie. It comes in handy for burning through doors, for example. Too, it's silent. Even more so than a stungun."

"Shirl and Darleen have their own ideas about silent weapons," she said.

"What do you mean?"

"They found a dozen metal discs—what they're *for* the Odd Gods alone know!—in the engineer's workshop. They say that once they're given a cutting edge they'll be very nice throwing weapons."

Grimes muttered something about bloodthirsty little bitches.

"I thought that you liked them, John," said Maggie.

"I do. But. . . ."

"Haven't you ever shed any blood during *your* career?"

"Yes. But. . . ."

But what he did not tell her was that he strongly suspected that the guards at Miletus, Ellena's people, would be women. He derided himself for his old-fashioned ideas but still was reluctant to kill a member of the opposite sex.

Chapter 26

Krait made her return to normal Space-Time, began her descent to the surface of New Sparta, to Mount Melitus. Maggie and Fenella were with Grimes in the control room; Maggie was there as a sort of co-pilot—after all, as a Survey Service officer, although not in the Spaceman Branch, she knew something about ship-handling—and Fenella was, as always, just getting into everything. Grimes had succeeded in persuading Shirl and Darleen to busy themselves elsewhere. Much as he liked them both this was an occasion when he could do without their distracting chatter.

As the little ship dropped to the nightside hemisphere greater and greater detail was displayed in the stern view radar screen, in three-dimensional presentation. There was Mount Melitus, almost directly below *Krait*. Grimes applied a touch of lateral thrust so that the mountain was now to the south of the line of descent. Its hulking mass, he explained, would shield the village on the southern slopes from the clangor of the inertial drive.

"But our landing place," objected Fenella, "*is* on the southern slopes. They're bound to hear us sooner or later—and soon enough to be ready and waiting for us."

"Not necessarily," Grimes told her.

He made adjustments to the radar controls, increasing sensitivity. Clouds were now visible in the screen. The wind, as it should have been at this time of year, as he had hoped that it would be, was from the north, blowing over the relatively warm Aegean Sea on to the land, striking the sheer, northern face of the mountain and being deflected upward into cooler atmospheric levels.

He checked the state of readiness of the missile projector. It was loaded. He had seen to that himself. In the tube was a rocket with a Mark XXV Incendiary warhead. It was one of the viler anti-personnel weapons, one that Grimes, during his Survey Service days, had hoped that he would never have to use. Now he was going to use it—although not directly against personnel.

"Who are you going to shoot at?" asked Fenella interestedly. "I thought that the object of this exercise was to rescue Brasidus, not to blow him to pieces."

"*What*, not *who*," said Grimes. "I'm looking for a nice, fat cloud. One that's just skimming the peak of the mountain on its way south."

"Looking for a *cloud*? Are you out of your tiny mind?"

"The Commodore knows what he's doing!" snapped Maggie. Then, "By the way, what are you doing?"

He laughed.

"I'm going to use a technique that was used, some years ago, on Bolodrin. A non-aligned planet, of no great importance, but one which both the Shaara and ourselves would like to draw within our spheres of influence. A humanoid population. An export trade of agricultural products. Well, there had been a quite disastrous planet-wide drought. One of our ships—the Zodiac Class cruiser *Scorpio*—was there showing the flag. The Tronmach—it translates roughly to Hereditary President—appealed to the captain of *Scorpio*, as the representative of a technologically superior culture, to Do Something about the drought. Captain Samson went into a huddle with his scientific officers. They decided to seed likely cloud formations. With Hell Balls."

"What's a Hell Ball?" asked Fenella.

"What my missile projector is loaded with. It's the pet name for the Mark XXV Incendiary Device, one of the more horrid anti-personnel weapons. Imagine an expanding vortex of plasma, superheated, electrically hyperactive gases. . . ."

"And did this bright idea work?"

"Too well. The drought was broken all right. Rivers burst their banks. Hailstorms flattened orchards. If the Shaara had grabbed the opportunity, sending ships with all manner of aid, Bolodrin would have happily become an Associate Hive Member. But they were slow off the mark and the Federation organized relief expenditures. Nonetheless relations were strained and Captain Samson suffered premature retirement. Mphm. Looks like a suitable target coming up now. . . . Range about fifty kilometers. . . ."

He busied himself at the fire control console, aligning the projector, setting the fuse of the warhead.

He pushed the button.

*   *   *

Only faintly luminous, the exhaust of the rocket was almost invisible.

The slow explosion of the warhead was not. In the center of the towering cumulus bright flame burgeoned and lightnings writhed, wreathing the mountain peak with lambent fire, lashing out to other cloud formations. A clockwise rotation seemed already to have been initiated, a cyclonic vortex. It was the birth of a hurricane.

Grimes could imagine what the conditions would soon be on the southern slopes of Melitus, the country normally protected from extremes of weather by the bulk of the mountain. There would be torrential rain and shrieking winds and a continuous cannonade of thunder and lightning, an uproar among which the arrhythmic clangor of a small ship's inertial drive unit would go unnoticed.

He hoped.

With the controls now on manual he continued his descent. He skimmed the peak with less clearance than he had intended; a vicious downdraft caught *Krait* and had he not reacted swiftly, slamming on maximum lift, the ship must surely have been wrecked.

Then he was over the mountain top, dropping again but not too fast, maintaining a half kilometer altitude from the ground. Sudden gusts buffeted the ship, tilting her from the vertical. A fusillade of hail on her skin was audible even through the thick insulation. Nothing, save for the diffused flare of the lightning, could be seen through the viewpoints. Even the radar picture was almost blotted out by storm clutter.

But there was the village. . . .

And the river. . . .

Grimes followed its course to the horseshoe bend. It looked as it did on the chart. But even if the ground were level, what about trees? There had been no symbols indicating such growths on the map—but trees have a habit of growing over the years. He had hoped to be able to make a visual inspection before landing but, in these conditions, it was impossible.

He hovered almost directly over the almost-island, dropping slowly, keeping *Krait* in position by applications of lateral thrust, this way and that.

"Stand by the viewpoint, Maggie," he ordered. "Yes. That one. If there's a brief clear spell, if the rain lets up, tell me what you see."

"What do you want me to see?"

"What I don't want you to see on our landing place," he said, "is trees. Bushes don't worry me but a large, healthy tree can damage even a big ship sitting down on it!"

"Will do."

And then she was back beside him.

"There was a break, and lightning at the same time. There aren't any trees."

"Landing stations!" ordered Grimes.

Krait sat down hard, dropping the final two meters with her drive in neutral. She sat down hard and she complained, creaking and groaning, rocking on her tripedal landing gear, while shock-absorbers hissed and sighed.

Grimes unbuckled himself from his chair, then led the way out of the control room. In the wardroom Shirl and Darleen were waiting. On the table and on the deck were the articles of clothing that Grimes had specified—the coveralls, the raincapes and the heavy boots. Hanging on the backs of chairs were belts and holstered weapons.

Swiftly the five of them got out of their light clothing, pulled on the coveralls and the heavy boots. Luckily the ship's equipment store had carried a wide range of sizes, so even Shirl and Darleen were shod not too uncomfortably. Grimes packed a rucksack with protective clothing for Brasidus, who would need this for the walk from the village to *Krait*. (Grimes hoped that Brasidus would be able to make the walk, that he would be rescued unharmed.) They belted on the weapons. Shirl and Darleen attached to their belts pouches with clinking contents. Grimes wondered briefly what was in them, then remembered the discs that the two girls had found in the engineer's workshop.

They made their way down the spiral staircase to the airlock, the controls of which had been set to be operated manually. Grimes was not at all happy about leaving the ship without a duty officer but he had no option. He was the only real spaceperson in the party but, at the same time, he was the obvious leader of the expedition. And all that any of the women could do, if one of them were left in charge, would be to keep a seat in the control room warm.

He and Fenella were first into the airlock chamber. Grimes pushed the button that would open the outer door and, at the same time, extend the telescopic ramp. He was expecting a violent onslaught of wind and rain but his luck, he realized thankfully, was holding. The door was on the lee side of the ship. He adjusted the hood of his raincape, checked the buckles holding the garment about his body, then walked cautiously down the ramp. Away from the ship he began to feel the wind and, even through his layers of clothing, the impact of the huge raindrops. He could hear the thin, high screaming of the wind as it eddied around the metallic tower that was the ship, was blinded by a bolt of lightning that struck nearby and deafened by the *crack!* of the thunder. And what if *Krait* herself should be struck by lightning? Nothing much, he thought (hoped). With her stern vanes well dug into the wet soil she would be well earthed.

He got his eyesight back and turned to look up the ramp. Shirl and Darleen were coming down it and Maggie was silhouetted in the doorway.

"Shut the inner door before you come down!" he yelled.

"What?" he heard her scream.

He repeated the order.

The light behind her diminished as she obeyed him. The airlock chamber itself was only dimly illumined. And then she was following Shirl and Darleen to the ground.

Grimes led the way up the mountainside. There was no possibility of their getting lost; all that they had to do was to keep to the bank of the stream. It was more of a torrent now, swollen by the downpour, roaring and rumbling as displaced boulders, torn from the banks, ground against each other. The wind had almost as much weight as the rushing water, buffeting them as they bent into it, finding its way through the fastenings of their raincapes, ballooning the garments, threatening to lift their wearers from their feet and to send them whirling downhill, airborne flotsam.

The raincapes had to go. Grimes struggled out of his. It was torn from his hands, vanished downwind like a huge, demented bat. The women shed theirs. Maggie, shouting to make herself heard above the wild tumult of wind, water and thunder, made a feeble joke about the willful destruction of Federation property and the necessity thereafter of filling in forms in quintuplicate.

But she could still joke, thought Grimes. Good for her. And the others were bearing up well, even Fenella. No doubt she was thinking in headlines. MY WALK ON THE WILD SIDE.

Bruised and battered by flying debris, deafened by shrieking wind and roaring thunder, blinded by lightning, the party struggled up the mountainside.

And of all the miseries and discomforts the one that Grimes resented most bitterly was the trickle of icy-cold water that found its way through the neckband of his coveralls, meandering down his body to collect in his boots.

Chapter 27

They came at last to the village, such as it was, the huddle of low stone houses, little better than huts most of them, all of them with doors and windows tightly battened against the storm. There was one building, two-storied, larger than the others. From its steeply pitched roof protruded what was obviously a radio communications antenna, a slender mast that whipped as the gusts took hold of it and worried it. It was a wonder that it had survived the storm thus far; not only was there the rain but there was the lightning, stabbing down from the swirling clouds at even the stunted trees that were hardly more than overgrown bushes, exploding them into eruptions of charred splinters.

It had survived thus far; it would be as well, decided Grimes, if it survived for no longer. If Brasidus and his guards were in this house the sooner that means of communication with Sparta City was destroyed the better. He pulled his laser pistol from its holster, tried to take aim at the base of the mast. The wind grabbed his arm and tugged viciously. He tried to use his left hand to steady his right, pressed the firing stud. During a brief, very brief, period of darkness between lightning flashes he saw the beam of intense ruby light, missing the target by meters. He tried again. Maggie tried. Even Fenella tried. The radio mast remained untouched by their fire.

Grimes saw that Shirl was taking one of the metal discs from the pouch at her waist, holding it carefully by the small arc of its circumference that had been left unsharpened. *And what good will that do?* he asked himself scornfully. A thrown missile, launched in the teeth of a howling gale . . . Metal—tough metal admittedly—against metal at least as tough as itself. (That mast must be tough to have survived the storm.)

Shirl stood there, her body swaying in the gusts that assailed her, making no attempt to hold herself rigid as she took aim, not fighting the forces of nature as Grimes and Maggie and Fenella had been trying to do, accommodating herself to them. Her right arm, the hand holding the gleaming disc, went back and then, aided by a wind eddy, snapped forward. Like Grimes and the others, she had been aiming for the base of the mast. Unlike Grimes and the others she might even have hit it. But the disc itself, generating with its swift passage through the heavily charged air a charge of its own, was itself a target. A writhing filament of dazzling incandescence snaked down from the black sky to emmesh the missile, to follow its trajectory even as it was reduced to a coruscation of molten steel.

The disc, what was left of it, would narrowly have missed the base of the mast—but the lightning struck it. Momentarily it took, Grimes thought, the semblance of a Christmas tree, etching its branches and foliage of flame onto his retinas. Slowly he regained his eyesight. Somebody—Maggie—had him by the upper arm, was shaking it.

"John! John!" she was saying, "They're coming out!"

He blinked, then raised his hand to clear the rain from his eyes. A door had opened on the lee side of the building, the side on which they were standing. A figure was standing in the rectangle of yellow light, another one behind it, women both of them.

"I'm not going out in *this*!" Grimes heard faintly.

"Somebody has to. Something has happened to the mast."

"Blown down. Struck by lightning. In this weather anything could happen."

"We have to see what's wrong so we can fix it. Out with you, *now!*"

"Oh, all right. All right."

The smaller of the two women ventured out into the night, picking just the wrong moment for her excursion. A shrieking gust eddied around the house so that even on its lee side there was little protection. Her weatherproof cloak was whipped up over and around her head, blinding her and trapping her arms. She staggered out blindly, her naked legs luminescent in the darkness. She blundered right into the arms of Shirl and Darleen. Her shriek like a hard fist connected with the nape of her neck was muffled by her enveloping garment. She fell to the sodden ground and lay there, face down, her bare rump exposed to the lashing of the driving rain. She would be visible from the open doorway; Grimes and his companions, in their dark clothing, would not.

"Lalia!" the woman standing in the door was screaming. "Lalia! What's wrong? Did you fall?"

And then she had left the shelter of the house, was staggering out over the rough ground, buffeted by the wind, her flimsy robe shredded from her body as she made her unsteady way toward her fallen companion. Grimes and the others withdrew to one side, hoping that they would not be seen, and then, with him in the lead, ran toward the house, their stunguns out and ready. Once inside they slammed and barred the door. (Grimes felt a brief twinge of pity for those two near-naked females shut out in the storm.)

The room in which they were standing was sparsely furnished—a rough table, a half dozen equally rough chairs, a pressure lantern hanging from a rafter. Against the far wall a wooden staircase—more of a ladder really—led to the upper floor. In the side wall to the left was an open doorway.

From it came a female voice.

"Sounds like they're back. Now, perhaps, we'll be able to get this accursed transceiver working again."

"I'm sure that dear Ellena is waiting with bated breath for the rest of our weather report," sneered another female voice.

"Be that as it may, we're still supposed to be in touch every six hours, on the hour, if only to let her know that his sexist lordship is doing as well as may be expected." She raised her voice. "Lalia! Daphne! What's keeping you? Is that aerial still standing?"

Grimes and Maggie, stunguns in hand, advanced to the open door, the others behind them. They saw the four women, who were huddled over the large transceiver upon which they had been working, replacing power cells and printed circuits. One of them he recognized; it was the fat blonde with whom he had tangled on the occasion of the Archon's abduction, although what had been brassy hair was now no more than a gray stubble. There must have been a discharge from the set when the lightning struck and she must have been in the way of it. She looked up from her work and stared at him.

She jumped to her feet, screwdriver in hand.

"You!" she snarled.

"Yes, me," agreed Grimes pleasantly as he shot her.

Beside him Maggie's stungun buzzed as she disposed of two of the other ladies and from behind him Fenella, determined not to be left out of things, loosed off a paralyzing blast at the redhead who was about to throw a spanner at the commodore.

We should have left one of them awake, thought Grimes, *to take us to where they have Brasidus.* Not that it much mattered. This house, little more than a shack, was no castle. There would be very few rooms to search.

They went back into the first room. Somebody was hammering on the door to outside and yelling, "Let us in! Let us in, damn you!"

"Let them in," Grimes whispered to Shirl.

She obeyed.

The two women who had gone to inspect the aerial stumbled in. In normal circumstances they might have been attractive, with what remained of their rain-soaked clothing clinging to quite shapely bodies, but Grimes thought they looked like two drowned rats. They screamed when they saw the intruders, screamed again when the two New Alicians grabbed them, one to each, held them with their arms twisted up painfully behind their backs. Still they stared defiantly at Grimes. One of them spat at him.

"Ladies, ladies," he admonished. Then, with the whipcrack of authority in his voice, "Where is the Archon?"

"Why should we tell you?" growled the taller of the pair.

Grimes raised his stungun in his right hand, with the fingers of his left adjusted the setting.

"John, you're not going to . . . ?" expostulated Maggie. "You said that there was to be no killing."

Grimes hoped that he had the setting right. There was one beam intensity the use of which was supposed to be illegal, against the rules of civilized warfare. It was a matter of very fine adjustment, a fraction of a degree above MAXIMUM STUN although less than LETHAL. Una Freeman, a Federation police officer whom he had once known, had taught him this nasty little trick, telling him that it might come in handy some day. "But be careful," she had warned him. "Overdo it and you'll finish up with a human vegetable who'd be better off dead."

"Where is the Archon?" he demanded again.

"Get stuffed!" came the defiant reply.

Grimes raised the bulky pistol.

"That's right," sneered the woman. "Put me to sleep so I'll never talk. D'you think I don't know a stungun when I see one?"

"Drop her!" Grimes barked to Darleen. "Get away from her!"

For a moment the tall, black-haired woman stood there, then she started toward Grimes, clawlike fingers extended.

Grimes pressed the firing stud.

The weapon whined.

The woman was cut down in mid-leap then fell to the floor, writhing in agony, the muzzle of the pistol still trained on her, still emitting its beam. She was making a shrill grunting noise through her closed mouth and, above this, could be heard the grinding of her teeth. Throughout her body muscle fought against muscle. She was on her back squirming in a ghastly parody of orgasm, and then only her heels and the back of her head were in contact with the floor. Blood trickled from the corners of her mouth.

"Stop!" screamed Maggie.

He released the pressure on the firing stud.

His victim collapsed in a shuddering heap.

"Where is the Archon?" repeated Grimes.

She lifted her head to glare at him. She spat out blood and fragments of broken teeth.

"Get . . . stuffed . . ."

Hating himself, and hating her for being so stubborn, Grimes took aim again.

"I'll tell!" screamed the small, mousy blonde. "I'll tell you! But don't hurt her again!"

"Gutless little bitch!" was all the thanks she got from her friend.

But Grimes felt better when he discovered that his harsh interrogation had been necessary after all. There was a cellar, the trapdoor to which had been concealed by the heavy rug upon which the table had been standing, that could be opened only by pressing a stud, disguised as a nailhead—one among many—in the wooden floor. There was a rough wooden staircase down into the black depths.

"Brasidus!" yelled Grimes into the opening.

"Here!" came the reply from below. Then, "Who's that?"

"Grimes. We've come to get you out!"

But there was something that had to be done first. Grimes set the control knob of his pistol to MEDIUM STUN. He pointed the weapon at the black-haired woman who was still sprawled on the floor, twitching and moaning. He said gently, "This will put you out. You'll feel better when you recover." (It was not quite a lie, although it would be days before the soreness left her overstrained muscles and she would require considerable dental work.)

"Bastard!" she hissed viciously from her bleeding mouth. "Bastard!"

And then she was silent and her body and limbs were no longer twitching.

Darleen lifted the pressure lamp from its bracket, started toward the open trapdoor.

"Hold it!" ordered Grimes. "Let *her* go first." He hustled the small blonde toward the head of the stairway. "There may be booby traps."

So they followed their prisoner down into what was more of a cellar than a real dungeon, smelling of the wine and the spicy foodstuffs stored therein, although in one corner there was a cage constructed from stout metal bars, its door secured by a heavy padlock. In this stood Brasidus. He was naked and his beard and hair were unkempt but otherwise he seemed in good enough condition.

"John!" he cried. "Maggie! By all the gods, it's good to see you!"

"And good to see you!" said Grimes. He grabbed the small blonde by her shoulder. "Where's the key to this cage?"

"I . . . I don't know. . . ."

"Give her the same treatment that you gave the other bitch," suggested Fenella viciously.

But Maggie had returned her stungun to its holster, pulled out her laser pistol. An acrid stink of burning metal filled the air and incandescent, molten gobbets hissed and crackled as they fell to the floor.

Free, Brasidus hugged the embarrassed Grimes in a bearlike embrace, then did the same to Maggie. ("Don't *I* get a kiss?" complained Fenella.) And then, amazingly, he swept the small blonde into his arms, pressed his lips on hers. She did not resist, in fact cooperated quite willingly.

"Might I ask," inquired Fenella, "just what the hell is going on here?"

Brasidus laughed. "It's because of Lalia that I'm down in this hole. At first I enjoyed considerably more freedom. Lalia and I . . . Oh, well, you know how things are. Daphne caught us at it . . ."

"Perhaps Daphne had the right to be jealous," suggested Fenella.

"It's time that we were getting out of here," said Grimes. "I've a ship waiting."

"Come, then," said Brasidus. With his arm still about Lalia's shoulders he started for the foot of the staircase.

"You aren't taking *her* with you," stated rather than asked Fenella.

"Why not? She was good to me."

And good to Daphne, thought Grimes, *and, above all, good to herself*. He said, "I'm sorry. She has to stay here."

Brasidus released the girl and shrugged.

"Just as well, perhaps," he muttered. "Probably Ellena wouldn't approve if I brought her into the Palace."

And you've a lot to learn about Ellena, my poor friend, thought Grimes. *But that can wait until we're in the ship on the way back to Port Sparta.*

Maggie's stungun buzzed as she ensured Lalia's unconsciousness for at least half an hour.

Chapter 28

In the upstairs room they gave Brasidus the clothing that they had brought for him, the tough coveralls and the heavy boots. He dressed in sulky silence. They let themselves out of the house. The storm was abating although the rain was still as heavy as ever. There was no longer an almost continuous flare of lightning but laser pistols, set to low intensity, did duty as electric torches to illuminate their way.

The stream whose course they had followed up to the village was now a wild torrent, bearing on its crest all manner of flotsam, uprooted bushes and small trees and the like. Audible even above the sound of rushing water was the grinding rumble of the boulders rolling downhill along the river bed.

But where was *Krait?*

Surely, thought Grimes, *we should be seeing her by now.*

He set the beam of his laser to higher intensity, sent it probing ahead into the rain-lashed darkness. There was a very pretty rainbow effect but no reflection from gleaming metal. He began to feel a growing uneasiness. Surely the little bitch hadn't lifted off by herself . . . Surely some freakish accident, a chance lightning bolt for example, had not caused actuation of the inertial drive machinery. . . .

But that was fantasy.

But where was the ship?

Maggie cried out.

Like Grimes, she had adjusted her laser pistol. Unlike him she was directing the beam only just above ground level. She was first to see the ship. Afterwards it was easy to work out what must have happened, what had happened—the almost-island on which Grimes had set her down had become a real island, an island whose banks were eroded, faster and faster, by the rushing water. With the once-solid ground below her vanes washed away she had toppled. The crash of her falling had just been part of the general tumult of the storm.

Fenella voiced the thoughts of all of them.

"That's fucked it!" she stated.

Too right, thought Grimes, but his mind was working busily. Suppose, just suppose, that the ship's mian machinery had not been too badly damaged . . . Then it would be possible, difficult but possible, to lift her on lateral thrust and then, when high enough from the ground, to turn her about a short axis to a normal attitude. In theory it could be done. In fact Grimes had heard of its being done, although he had never had to attempt such a maneuver himself; the nearest to it had been the righting of a destroyer, a much larger vessel. Then those in the ship had used lateral thrust while he, in control of operations, had employed a spaceyacht as a tug.

But to do anything at all he had to get into the ship.

Accompanied by the others he walked, so far as was possible, around the cigar-shaped hull. It formed a bridge over the river, with the nose on the bank upon which Grimes was standing, with the stern on what little remained of the island. And, Grimes saw by the light of the laser torches, she had fallen in such a way that the airlock was below her. He told Maggie and the others.

"Can't we burn a way in?" she asked. "The control room viewports should be a weak point . . ."

And those viewports, thought Grimes glumly, were supposed to be able to withstand, at least for an appreciable time, the assault of a laser cannon . . . How long would it take hand lasers to make a hole? But it had to be tried.

And so they stood there, the five of them who were armed, with Brasidus watching, aiming their pistols at the center of one of the viewports. Soon their target was obscured by steam as the intense heat vaporized the falling rain, soon the exposed skin of their faces felt as though it were being boiled.

But they persisted.

Then the intense beam of ruby light from Maggie's weapon faded into the infrared, died. She caught the butt of the weapon a clout with her free hand but it did not help. "Power cell's dead," she muttered.

"And mine . . ." said Fenella.

The other lasers sputtered out. The steam dispersed. The eyes of the party became accustomed to the darkness—but, Grimes realized, it was no longer dark. The sun must now be up, somewhere behind the fast-scudding nimbus. He looked at the shallow depression in the thick transparency of the viewport, all that they had been able to achieve at the cost of their most effective weaponry.

He flinched as something whipped past his head with a noise that was part whistle, part crack. A scar of bright metal appeared on the hide of *Krait* just below the viewports. A long time later—it seemed—came the report of a projectile firearm.

"Take cover!" yelled Grimes. "Behind the ship!"

He waited—*like a fool*, he told himself, *like a fool*—until the others had moved, looking toward where he thought the shot had come from, holding his pistol as though for instant use. He saw her, a pale form up the hillside. It was, he thought, the fat blonde. Her body bulk must have minimized the effects of the stungun blast. She had her rifle raised for another shot. It went wild and then she ducked behind a boulder.

Grimes, still holding his useless laser pistol threateningly, walked carefully backward. Just before he joined the others a third shot threw up a fountain of mud by his right foot.

Secure, for the time being, behind the bulk of the crippled courier he said, "There's only one of them. That fat bitch. . . ."

"Hephastia," said Brasidus.

"Thanks," said Grimes. "That saves me the bother of being formally introduced to her. Luckily she doesn't know that our lasers are dead. But when we fail to return her fire she'll realize that they are, and come for us."

"We've the stunguns," said Maggie.

"And what effective range do *they* have?" asked Grimes. "Little more than three meters, if that."

"But how much ammunition does *she* have?" said Fenella.

"We don't know," Grimes told her. "If she's any sort of a shot six rounds should be ample."

Very, very carefully he moved out from behind the protection of the ship, crawling in the mud, keeping head and buttocks well down. He was in time to see a flicker of movement as Hephastia changed positions, scurrying to the cover of another boulder, not appreciably decreasing the range but carrying out an outflanking operation. Even if she were not a member of the Amazon Guard she must have had military training on some world at some time.

He raised his pistol as though about to fire from the prone position. Her retaliatory shot was in line but, luckily for him, over. Frantically he scurried forward, found a boulder of his own behind which to hide. It was by no means as large as he would have wished—and it was even smaller after a well-aimed bullet had reduced the top of it to dust and splinters. Another one reduced it in size still further.

Grimes tried to burrow into the mud while still maintaining some kind of a lookout.

From the corner of his eye he saw movement by the ship.

It was Shirl, walking out calmly, something that gleamed, even in this dull, gray light, in her right hand. It was one of those sharpened discs. Hephastia did not see her. She must have had a one-track mind. With calm deliberation she was whittling away Grimes' little boulder, shot after shot, using some kind of armor-piercing ammunition.

Shirl's right arm went back, snapped forward.

The disc sailed up in what seemed lazy flight—*too high*, thought Grimes, watching, *too high*.

Shirl stood there, making no attempt to throw a second one.

Grimes' boulder, under the impact of an armor-piercing bullet, split neatly down the middle, affording him a good view of what was happening. He saw the disc whir over Hephastia's position and then turn, dipping sharply downward as it did so. It vanished from sight.

There was one last shot, wildly aimed, which threw up a spray of mud between Grimes and the ship. There was a gurgling scream.

Calmly Shirl walked to where Grimes was sprawled in the mud, helped him to his feet.

"She will not bother you again, John," she said cheerfully.

"But how did you . . . ?"

He did not have to finish the question. The New Alicians had their telepathic moments.

"We did more than just sharpen the discs," she told him. "We used the grinding wheels and we . . . shaped them. Put in curves. Like boomerangs."

"But how did you *know* what to do?"

"We . . . We just *knew*."

Together they walked up the hillside, through the pouring rain, the others straggling after them. They came to the boulder from behind which Hephastia had been shooting. The sight of the fat woman's body was not quite as bad as Grimes had feared it would be; the downpour had already washed away most of the blood. Even so decapitation, or near decapitation, is never a pretty spectacle. Grimes looked away hastily from the gaping wound in the neck with the obscenely exposed raw flesh and cartilage. The rest of the body was not so bad. It looked drained, deflated, like a flabby white blimp brought to earth by heavy leakage from its gas cells. Her dead hands still held the rifle. Grimes took it from her. It was a 10 mm automatic, as issued to Federation military forces. It was set to Single Shot. There should have been plenty of rounds left in the magazine but there were not. Hephastia—or somebody—had neglected to replace it after some previous usage.

Grimes counted the remaining cartridges.

There were only five.

By this time the others had joined them.

"I've a rifle," said Grimes unnecessarily, "but only five rounds."

"There are weapons and ammunition a-plenty in the house," said Brasidus.

"Just what I had in mind," said Grimes.

He led the way up the hillside.

He covered the retreat, loosing off all five of the remaining rounds to deter a sally from the open door. The other women must have recovered, were firing from chinks in the heavily shuttered windows. After Grimes' warning burst they seemed to be reluctant to show themselves—much to the disgust of Shirl and Darleen.

"So," said Maggie, "what now?"

"We follow the river," said Grimes. "From what I can remember of the maps there are sizable towns on its lower reaches."

"On *foot*?" squealed Fenella.

"You can try swimming if you like," said Grimes, "but I'd not recommend it with the river the way it is now."

Chapter 29

They were cold and they were wet and they were hungry.

Vividly in Grimes' memory was the smell of the cellar from which they had rescued Brasidus—the cheeses, the smoked and spiced sausages, the pickles. If only he had known that they were to be denied access to *Krait* he would have seen to it that they commenced what promised to be a very long walk well-provisioned and -armed.

Surprisingly Brasidus was not much help. Grimes had hoped that the Archon would have some idea of the geography of this area, would be able to guide them to some other village where there would be an inn, would be capable of finding for them the easiest and shortest route to the nearest town.

"But you're the ruler of this world!" said Grimes exasperatedly.

"That does not mean, friend John, that I know, intimately, every square centimeter of its surface, any more than you are familiar with every smallest detail of a ship that you command."

"I always do my best to gain such familiarity," grumbled Grimes.

They trudged on, the roaring torrent on their right, towering rocky outcrops, among which a few stunted trees struggled for survival, on their left. Grimes maintained the lead, with Maggie and Brasidus a little behind him, then Fenella, then Shirl and Darleen, the only ones with any sort of effective medium-range weaponry, as the rear guard. It was not likely that they would be followed but it was possible.

They trudged on.

They were no longer so cold; in fact they were sweating inside their heavy coveralls. The rain was easing. Now and again, briefly, the high sun struck through a break in the clouds.

But they were still hungry.

Grimes called a halt in the shelter of an overhanging cliff. He managed to light his pipe. (And how much tobacco was left in his pouch? He should have refilled it from a large container of the weed that Shirl had found for him in one of the officer's cabins aboard *Krait*.) Fenella had an almost full packet of cigarillos and, grudgingly, allowed Maggie to take one. Neither Brasidus nor the New Alician girls smoked.

Shirl and Darleen strayed away from the shelter, saying that they were going back up the trail a little to see if there were any signs of pursuit. Grimes let them go. He knew that they were quite capable of looking after themselves.

"And now," he said, "I'll put you in the picture, Brasidus. Prepare yourself for a shock."

"Ellena? Has anything happened to her?"

"On the contrary." Grimes laughed bitterly. "On the contrary. She's the one who's been making things happen. To begin with, she used your abduction as an excuse for seizing power."

Brasidus was not as shocked as Grimes had feared that he would be.

"She is a very shrewd politician, John, as I have known for quite awhile. And there has to be a strong hand at the helm during my forced absence. There are so many squabbling factions. . . ."

"But does she want you back?" asked Grimes brutally. "Oh, she didn't want you hurt but she did want you out of the way, does want you out of the way until she's firmly in the saddle. If she does allow you to come back it will be only as a sort of Prince Consort to her Queen Hippolyte."

Brasidus shook his head dazedly.

Then, at last, "You are trying to tell me that *she* is responsible for my abduction?"

"Yes," stated Grimes.

There was a long silence, broken eventually by the Archon.

"Yes," he muttered. "It does make sense, a quite horrible sort of sense. She *is* ambitious. She does really believe that she is a reincarnation of Queen Hippolyte. Her Amazon Guards are a formidable military force. Oh, I have sneered at them, as what man on this world has not, but, in my heart of hearts I have respected them. Those women back in the village were not Amazon Guards, had they been we should never have gotten out alive. They were no more than criminals whom somebody. . . ."

"Ellena," said Fenella.

"All right. Merely criminals hired by Ellena to do a job."

"Or loyal Party members," said Maggie, "following orders. Ellena's orders."

"Ellena, Ellena, always Ellena!" Brasidus got to his feet, began to pace up and down. "Always it comes back to Ellena."

"I'm afraid that it does," said Grimes.

"I should have known. As a ruler, as Archon, I have failed my people."

"Not yet," Grimes told him. "There are still people loyal to you."

They were interrupted by Shirl and Darleen. The two New Alicians were dragging something over the wet ground, something that might have been a very large snake had it not been equipped with eight pairs of legs. It was minus its head and the blood that dripped from its neck was an unpleasant yellow in color.

"Lunch," announced Shirl.

"Surely that *thing* is not edible," complained Fenella.

"It is," Brasidus told her, cheering up. "It is a delicacy. *Draco*, we call it. Broiled, with a fruit sauce. . . ."

Using their sharpened discs Shirl and Darleen lopped off the short legs of the draco, gutted and skinned it, throwing the offal into the river. Grimes tried to start a fire, using as fuel twigs broken from nearby bushes. But it was a hopeless task. All vegetation, even that in the partial shelter of the rock overhang, was thoroughly saturated and stubbornly refused to burn. If they had had an operating laser pistol at their disposal. . . . But they did not.

With a convenient flat rock as a table the New Alicians went on with their butchering. They sliced the flesh into wafer-thin slices. They gestured to Grimes that he should take the first bite.

He did. It wasn't bad, not unlike the sashimi that was a favorite meal of his when he could get it. It would have been vastly improved by a selection of dipping sauces but, he decided as he chewed, there were times when one couldn't have everything. Maggie joined him at the "table," then Fenella. Shirl and Darleen were already eating heartily. Only Brasidus hung back. (He, of course, was untraveled, had not sampled local delicacies on worlds all over the galaxy.)

"Try some," urged Grimes. "It's not bad."

"But it's not *cooked*."

"You must eat *something*," insisted Maggie, womanlike.

He forced himself to make a meal that obviously he did not enjoy.

Grimes ordered that the remains of the draco be thrown into the river. Now that the rain had ceased the day had become unpleasantly warm and already the meat was becoming odorous.

They pushed on down the mountainside.

It was early evening when they came to a village, larger than the one from which they had taken Brasidus. There was one short street, with low houses on either side of it. There was what looked like a small temple— to which deity of the Greek pantheon? wondered Grimes; it seemed to be of fairly recent construction—and, across the road from it, what was obviously an inn.

They entered this building, Brasidus in the lead.

There were several customers, all of them roughly dressed men, seated on benches at the rough wooden tables. These looked curiously at the intruders. There was the innkeeper, a grossly fat individual whose dirty apron strained over his prominent belly.

"Greetings, lords," he said. "What is your pleasure?"

"Wine," said Brasidus. "Bread. Hot meat if you have it."

"That indeed I have, lord. There is a fine stew a-simmering in the kitchen that would be fit for the Archon himself."

"Then bring it."

He bustled out, returned with a flagon of wine and six mugs, went out again for the platter of bread and individual bowls and spoons, and a last time for a huge, steaming pot from which issued a very savory smell.

"Eat well, my lords," he said. Then, "Have you been out in the storm?"

"We have," said Brasidus around a mouthful of stew.

"The weather was never like this when I was a boy. It's all these off-worlders coming down in their ships, disturbing the clouds. Time was when there were only two ships a year, the ones from Latterhaven. . . ."

"Mphm," grunted Grimes, thinking that he had better make some contribution to the conversation.

"And what is the uniform that you are wearing, lords? Forgive my curiosity but we have so few visitors here. You have guns, I see. Would you be some sort of police officers?"

"We are in the Archon's service," said Brasidus, not untruthfully.

"Indeed? Would it be impertinent of me to inquire which branch?"

"It would."

This failed to register and the innkeeper rattled on.

"There are so many new branches these days. I've even heard tell that in Sparta City there's a *women's* army, and according to the last News we watched they're taking over. Troublous times, lords, troublous times. I'd not be surprised to learn that it's the women behind the vanishment of the Archon. We're old-fashioned folk here in Calmira. There are women here now, of course, but they know their places. They'd never come into the tavern. The temple's for them."

Fenella made an odd snorting noise.

"But it's getting quite dark, isn't it? It's all this weather we're having these days. I'll give you light to eat by; the power was off most of the day but it's back on now . . ."

He went to the switch by the door, clicked it on. The overhead light tubes were harshly brilliant. He returned to the table, stared at his guests, at Maggie, at Fenella, at Shirl and Darleen.

"You . . ." he sputtered. "*Women!*" he spat.

"So what?" asked Fenella coldly.

"But. . . . But never before in *my* inn. . . ."

"There has to be a first time for everything," she said.

He turned appealingly to Brasidus. "Had I known I'd never have admitted you."

"You know now," said Grimes. "And now you know, what can you do about it?"

The men at the other tables were stirring restively. There were mutterings of, "Throw them out! Throw them out!"

"Not before I've finished my meal," said Grimes.

"Throw them out!" It was more than just a muttering now.

Grimes put his spoon down in the almost empty bowl, took careful stock of the opposition. There were fourteen men, big men, not young but not old. They looked tough customers and, in the right (or wrong) circumstances, nasty ones. Of course, despite the numerical odds, there was little doubt as to what the outcome of a scuffle would be. Although there was no ammunition for the rifle, although the laser pistols were useless until recharged, there were still the stunguns, ideal for use in a situation such as this. And there were the two specialists in unarmed combat, Shirl and Darleen.

But. . . .

But one at least of the men might escape from the inn, might run to the Town Constable who, surely, would have some means of communication—radio or land line—with the nearest big town. And then Ellena would soon learn that her husband, with his low friends, was running around loose and that the failure of his guards to maintain communication with the Palace was due to more than storm damage.

"All right," he said to the innkeeper, "we'll go. But rest assured that a full report of this business will be made to the proper authorities."

"Then go," said the man. "But first. . . ."

He thrust a dirty piece of paper, the bill, under Grimes' nose. Grimes glanced at it. He did a mental conversion of obols into credits. He would have been charged less for a meal for six persons in many a four-star restaurant on many a world. Then he realized that, in any case, he could not pay. His wallet, with money and credit cards, was with the clothing that he had left aboard *Krait* when he changed into coveralls.

"Do you have any money on you?" he asked Maggie.

She shook her head.

"Fenella?"

"Back aboard the ship. Nothing here."

"Shirl? Darleen?"

"No."

"Are you paying, or aren't you?" demanded the innkeeper.

"You will have to send the bill to the Palace," Brasidus told him. "It will be honored."

"Check it first," said Grimes nastily.

"Send the bill to the Palace?" demanded the innkeeper. "What do you take me for? Who'll be in charge at the Palace by the time it gets there, the postal services being what they are these days? Tell me that."

A good question, thought Grimes.

He said, "If you insist, we'll leave security."

"What security?"

Another good question.

His wrist companion? wondered Grimes. *No.* It was too useful, with many more functions than those of a mere timekeeper. The same could be said for the instrument that Maggie was wearing on her left wrist. The ammunitionless rifle or the dead laser pistols? *Again no.* What police officer would cheerfully pass his weapons over to civilians in payment of a tavern bill? And, in any case, the laser pistols were clearly marked as Federation property.

He looked at the others around the table. A gleam of precious metal caught his eye.

He said, "I'll have to ask you for your watch, Fenella."

"What?"

"You'll be able to reclaim it after the bill's been paid."

"*If* it's ever paid."

"In which case you will be fully compensated."

Fenella extended her left hand. The innkeeper looked covetously at the fabrication of gold and precious stones thus displayed.

"Buying time with time," she said.

"I shall insist on a receipt," said Grimes.

One was reluctantly given, on a scrap of paper as dirty and as rumpled as the bill.

Then Grimes, Brasidus and the women went out into the gathering dark.

Chapter 30

Some distance downstream from the village they found a deserted hut.

It must once have been, suggested Brasidus, the abode of a goatherd. (The indigenous six-legged animals that had been called goats by the original colonists had been largely replaced, as food animals, by the sheep and cattle imported from Earth.) There was just one room, its floor littered with animal droppings and the bones of various small creatures that had been brought into this shelter by various predators to be devoured at leisure, that now crackled unpleasantly underfoot. By the flare of Maggie's and Fenella's lighters, set at maximum intensity, it was possible to take stock. There was, leaning against the wall, a crude beson. Shirl took this and began to sweep the debris out through the open door. There was a fireplace, and beside it what had once been a tidy pile of cut wood, now scattered by some animal or animals.

Grimes instructed Darleen to use the cutting edge of one of her discs to produce a quantity of thin shavings from one of the sticks. He laid a fire. The shavings took fire immediately from his match and the blaze spread to the thicker sticks on top. Too late he thought that he should have checked the chimney to see if it was clear but he need not have worried. The fire drew well. Although the night was still far from cold the ruddy, flickering light made the atmosphere much more cheerful.

They all sat down on the now more or less clean floor.

Grimes lit his pipe, estimating ruefully that he had barely enough tobacco left in his pouch for four more smokes. Maggie and Fenella made a sort of ritual of sharing a cigarillo. Shirl and Darleen sniffed disdainfully.

Maggie said, "Now what do we do? We're on the wrong side of this world with no way of getting back to Sparta City. We're wearing clothing that, as soon as the weather warms up, will be horribly uncomfortable and that, in any case, makes us conspicuous. We have no money . . ."

"And I no longer have my watch," Fenella said sourly. "What do we barter next for a crust of bread?"

"We shall have breakfast without any worry," said Shirl. She produced from the pouch in which she was carrying her throwing discs some rather squashed bread rolls and Darleen, from hers, some crumbling cheese. "Before we left the tavern we helped ourselves to what we could . . ."

"That will do for supper," said Grimes.

"There will be no supper," Maggie told him sternly.

She drew deeply on what little remained of the cigarillo, threw the tiny butt into the fire.

"Hold it!" cried Grimes—too late. "I could have used that in my pipe."

"Sorry," she said insincerely.

"We tried smoking once," said Darleen virtuously. "We did not like it. We gave it up."

Grimes grunted wordlessly.

"I'm not a porcophile," announced Fenella.

"What's that?" demanded Shirl.

"A pig-lover, dearie. Normally I've no time for the police, on any world at all. But I really think, that in our circumstances, we should turn ourselves in. After all, we've committed no crime. Oh, there was a killing, I admit—but it was self-defense . . ."

"And the 'borrowing' of a minor war vessel owned by the Interstellar Federation," said Grimes glumly. "A minor war vessel which, unfortunately, we are unable to return to its owners in good order and condition."

"But I was given to understand," persisted Fenella, "that you and Maggie have *carte blanche* in such matters."

"Up to a point," said Grimes. "A medal if things go well, a court martial if they don't. In any case, until things get sorted out—if they ever do—Ellena will be able to hold us in jail on a charge of piracy and even to have us put on trial for the crime. And shot." He was deriving a certain perverse satisfaction from consideration of the legalities. "It could be claimed, of course, that I have been the ringleader insofar as the act of piracy is concerned. Don't forget that I have a past record. But you, Maggie, as a commissioned officer of the Survey Service, could be argued to have become a deserter from the FSS and an accessory before the fact to my crime. Shirl and Darleen are also accessories—and, also deserters from Ellena's own Amazon Guard. . . ."

"And me?" asked Fenella interestedly.

"An accessory before the fact."

"But it would never come to that," said Brasidus. "*I* shall vouch for you."

"Of course you will," said Grimes. "*But* . . . But if your lady wife is really vicious she'll put you on charge as an accessory after the fact."

"Surely she would not," said Brasidus. "After all, she is my wife."

"Throughout history," Fenella reminded him, "quite a few wives have wanted their husbands out of the way."

"But . . ."

"Are you sure that she wouldn't, old friend?" asked Grimes. He sucked audibly on his now empty pipe. "Now, this is the way I see things. We have to get less conspicuous clothing. By stealing. We have to get money. By stealing. Luckily this is a world where plastic money is not yet in common use. In the next town we come to there will be shops—I hope. Clothing shops. And there will be tills in these shops. With money in them. Luckily this is a planet where the vast majority of the population is honest, so breaking in will be easy. . . ."

"A bit of a come-down from space piracy," sneered Fenella.

"I wasn't a pirate," he said automatically. "I was a privateer."

Then he noticed that Shirl and Darleen had risen quietly to their feet and, as they had done so, had pulled their stunguns from their holsters. Shirl squatted by his side, put her mouth to his ear and whispered, "Go on talking. We shall be back in a few minutes."

Then she . . . oozed out of the open door, flattening herself against the frame to minimize her silhouette against the glow of the firelight. Darleen followed suit. Grimes went on talking, loudly so as to drown any queries from the others regarding the mysterious actions of the two New Alicians. He discussed at some length the legalities of privateering while his listeners looked at him with some amazement.

"It is not generally known," he almost shouted, "that the notorious Captain Kidd, who was a privateer, was hanged not for piracy but for murder, the murder of one of his officers. . . ."

"And what the hell has that to do with the price of fish?" screamed Fenella.

Shirl and Darleen came back. They were carrying between them an unconscious body, that of a man in the black leather and steel uniform of the Spartan Police. His arms were secured behind his back by his own belt and his ankles by the lacings of his sandals.

"We heard him coming," said Shirl, "while he was still quite a way off."

Brasidus stared at the man's gray-bearded face.

"I know him," he murmured. "I remember him from the old days, when we were both of us junior corporals. . . ."

"You've done better for yourself than he has," said Fenella.

"Have I? I'm beginning to think that I'd have been better off as a Village Sergeant than what I am now."

The journalist laughed. "You know, Brasidus, you're by no means the first planetary ruler who's said that sort of thing to me."

The Archon laughed too, but ruefully.

"But I," he said, "must be the first one who's really meant it."

Chapter 31

They sat and waited for the sergeant—whose name, Brasidus said, was Cadmus—to recover. Although the stunguns carried by Shirl and Darleen had been set to MINIMUM STUN the policeman had received a double dosage when ambushed by the New Alicians, being shot by both of them.

At last the man's eyes opened.

He stared bewilderedly at his captors. He struggled briefly with his bonds but soon realized the futility of it. He looked from face to face, longest of all at Brasidus.

He muttered, "I know *you*. . . ."

"And I know you, Cadmus," said the Archon.

"But. . . . But it can't be . . ."

"But it is."

"Brasidus. . . . Or should I be addressing you as Lord?"

"Brasidus will do. After all, we are old messmates."

"Brasidus. . . . But the news has been that you were kidnapped and that your lady wife has achieved power in your absence from Sparta City . . . And now you are here, in my village, in a strange uniform and in the company of . . . of offworlders. *Women*."

"They are my friends, Cadmus. They rescued me. But tell me—what are *you* doing here? Is there a police search for us?"

The sergeant laughed. "Not so far as I know. I was checking up on an odd bunch of vagrants who had passed through my village. You were not reported to me officially—the villagers are a close-mouthed lot and regard the Police as an unnecessary nuisance—but I overheard a few things and saw the innkeeper wearing a *very* expensive watch. I questioned him and he finally told me how he had got it. . . ."

"Did you get it back?" asked Fenella eagerly.

"No. The transaction, as he described it, seemed to be legal enough. But do you think you could untie my wrists? I am very uncomfortable."

There would be no harm in this, thought Grimes. The man had been disarmed by Shirl and Darleen; his stungun was now stuck into Darleen's belt and his scabbarded shortsword was being worn by Shirl. Nonetheless he drew his own pistol and covered the man while Darleen untied his lashings.

"That's better," said the sergeant, rubbing his wrists. Then, to Brasidus, "Thank you, Lord."

"I've told you to call me Brasidus. After all, we're old friends. How much does this friendship mean to you, Cadmus? Could you help us? I promise you that if you do long overdue promotion will follow."

"Don't insult me, Brasidus. I owe you for the way in which you got me out of that mess some years ago . . . Remember? When that little swine—what was his name? Hyperion?—got himself killed resisting arrest, and he turned out to be Captain Nestor's boyfriend. . . . No, Brasidus. I don't want promotion. I *like* being a Village Sergeant. All that I'd ask of you would be that I'd be appointed to a village of my own choice."

"But can you help us, Cadmus? We have to get back to Sparta City as soon as possible. We shall have to travel incognito. We shall need civilian clothing. Money. Transport . . ."

The sergeant laughed. "Let me tell you why I was looking for you. There's an order out that all offworlders, wherever they are, are to be rounded up and put in protective custody. They are to be returned to Sparta City and then put aboard the first outbound ship from Port Sparta. In this area Cythera, downriver from here, is the collection point. Trans-Spartan Airlines have a passenger ship standing by there to carry the off-worlders to the spaceport."

"We shall still need clothing," said Grimes. "Something less conspic-uous than what we are wearing now. And," he added hopefully, "a few obols spending money. Drinks. . . . Smokes. . . ."

"I have civilian clothing that I rarely use," said Cadmus. "I can fit out you, sir, and Brasidus." He looked the women over and chuckled to him-self. "You'll not believe this," he went on, more to Brasidus than the oth-ers, "but I had a woman for a while. I wasn't all that sorry when she left me. She married a police lieutenant in Thebes. She left a few rags and I've never thrown them out. I thought they might come in handy some time."

Fenella laughed.

"And when *I* said, Grimes, that we should turn ourselves in to the police you smacked me down, and you had all these marvelous schemes involving breaking and entering and robbing shops . . . But the way it's turned out it's the police who're the only ones who can help us."

"But we didn't go to them," said Grimes. "They came to us."

"What was that about breaking and entering?" demanded Cadmus suspiciously.

"It was only a joke," Brasidus told him. "The lady has a peculiar sense of humor. Meanwhile, you *are* helping us, Cadmus. And you can help us best of all if you tell nobody, nobody at all, that you have found me. In your report to your superiors you will say only that you took charge of a group of six offworlders, two men and four women, and delivered them to the authorities in Cythera."

"It shall be done as you ask," said the sergeant as he undid the lashings about his ankles. He got unsteadily to his feet, assisted by Brasidus. "And now I must get back to my house to find the things that you require. I shall return at dawn, with the hovercar, to take you all to Cythera."

"Perhaps we had better come with you," said Grimes.

"No," said Brasidus, *"no."*

"But . . ."

"Never let it be said," declared the Archon, "that I do not trust my old friends."

The trust was justified.

Before dawn Grimes was awakened by Shirl who, with Darleen, had shared sentry duty during what remained of the night. The New Alician's keen hearing had picked up the whine of ground effect engines while Cadmus was still a long distance off, long before Grimes could hear anything.

He got up from the hard floor, his joints stiff, his muscles aching. He ran a hand over his bristly chin, managed to ungum his eyelids. Shirl and Darleen had kept the fire going so there was light enough for him to see the others—Darleen curled in a fetal position, Maggie on her side, Fenella supine with her mouth open, softly snoring, Brasidus also on his back but as though sleeping at attention.

He would have sold his soul for a mug of steaming coffee or tea but there wasn't even any water. He filled and lit his pipe. He hoped that he would be able to purchase more tobacco in Cythera. He hoped that he would have some money on him to make such a purchase.

He awoke Brasidus, then the others. Only Brasidus—but he was already bearded—and Darleen looked none the worse for wear. Fenella was a mess. Maggie looked at least badly in need of a good hot shower and then a long session with her hairbrushes.

Grimes went outside and watered a tree. Then he stood and watched the approaching headlights of the police hovercar as it made its way down the winding trail. He had his stungun out, just in case. After a while he was joined by the others.

"He is a good man, that Cadmus," said Brasidus.

"Mphm," grunted Grimes.

"I would trust him with my life. More than once in the old days—in the old happy days—I did trust him with my life."

"Hearts and flowers and soft violins," muttered Grimes.

"What do you mean, John?"

"Just a Terran saying."

The hovercar came into view. It was a big vehicle. It sighed as it subsided in its skirts. One man, Cadmus, got out. He raised his right hand in greeting. Brasidus returned the salutation.

Cadmus said, "I have the things you need. If you will change now we can be on the way."

Shirl and Darleen lifted bundles from the rear of the car, carried them back into the hut. There was clothing as promised—rough tunics and heavy sandals for the men, chitons and lighter footwear for the ladies. There was a leather pouch full of clinking coins that Cadmus handed to Brasidus. And—which really endeared the sergeant to the commodore— there was a flagon of thin, sour wine, two dozen crisp rolls, still warm from the village bakery, and thick slices of some unidentifiable pickled meat. It was a far better meal than the bread and cheese which Shirl and Darleen had brought from the tavern would have been. *We should have had that for supper last night, as I wished*, thought Grimes.

Munching appreciatively he sat with the sergeant and watched the women changing. (On some worlds such conduct would have been unthinkable but New Sparta had no nudity tabu, any more than did the home planets of Maggie, Fenella, Shirl and Darleen.)

Cadmus jerked a thumb toward the New Alicians.

"Odd-looking wenches, aren't they? But not unattractive. Me—I've always liked a well-fleshed backside. . . ."

Backs to the bulkhead, thought Grimes, *when* you're *around*.

"Where're they from, sir? What is your name, by the way?"

"A world called New Alice," replied Grimes. "And my name is Smith. John Smith."

He got up, shed his own coveralls and boots, got into the tunic and sandals. He started to buckle on the belt with his weapons then thought better of it. Such accessories would look odd, to say the least, if carried by a bunch of stranded tourists.

He said, "You'd better take charge of these, Cadmus. And our coveralls."

The sergeant pulled a laser pistol from its holster, examined it, replaced it, then inspected one of the stunguns. He frowned.

"Both pistols," he said, "with Federation Survey Service markings. The laser with a flat power cell." He picked up a discarded coverall suit. "And a Survey Service heavy duty uniform . . ."

"I promise you," said Brasidus, "that I, personally, will tell you the full story later. But now I can and do tell you that there are things that it is better that you know nothing about."

"I can well believe that, Brasidus. And I think, at the risk of being deemed inhospitable, that the sooner I get you all off my hands, out of my territory, the better."

"We shall enjoy a happier reunion," Brasidus told him, "when things are back to normal."

"What *is* normal?" demanded the sergeant. "Nothing has been normal since that man Grimes came here in his ship all those years ago."

They bundled up the discarded clothing and carried it out to the car, stowing it in the baggage compartment, together with their belts and holstered pistols. The sun was up when they started off, with Brasidus sitting beside Cadmus, who was driving, and Grimes and the others in the rear cabin which was entirely enclosed, being intended for the occasional transport of arrested persons.

"Still," said Fenella, sitting back on the bench and extending her long, elegant legs, "it's better than walking. And now, Grimes, what's the drill when we get to Cythera? And what's the drill when we get back to Sparta City?"

"To begin with," Grimes told her, "my name is not Grimes. It's Smith. John Smith. And you're not Fenella Pruin . . ."

"Oh, all right, all right. I've been Prunella Fenn before."

"And I'm Angela Smith," announced Maggie.

"*Must* we have second names?" asked Shirl plaintively.

"Yes," Grimes told her. "Brown, for both of you. You're sisters."

"But we aren't."

"But you look alike. Shirley Brown and Dorothy Brown."

"Such *ugly* names!"

"But yours for the time being."

"I wish we could see some scenery," complained Maggie.

"If you *will* ride in the Black Maria, dearie," Fenella told her, "you can hardly expect a scenic drive. But go on, Grimes. Sorry. Smith. Tell us what world-shaking plots have merged from your tiny mind."

"I've seen this sort of thing before," said Grimes. "The handling and processing of refugees. The *real* processing won't be until we get to Sparta City. We'll tell the authorities at Cythera that we're a party of tourists who were set upon and robbed. The bandits took everything—money and, more importantly, our papers . . ."

"And your obviously expensive wrist companion," said Fenella, pointing at the device strapped to Grimes' left wrist.

"It will be out of sight in my pocket when we front the authorities," Grimes told her. "As will be Maggie's."

"I wish that my wristwatch had been in that bloody clip joint of an inn," she complained.

"You enjoyed the meal it paid for," Grimes told her.

"I noticed that *you* did," she snarled.

Chapter 32

They arrived at Cythera just before noon.

They saw little of the town itself—not that they much wished to—as Cadmus delivered them to the airport on its outskirts. There was a low huddle of administrative buildings. There were mooring masts, at one of which rode a Trans-Spartan dirigible. She was a small ship and a shabby one, her ribs showing through her skin. Grimes, looking up at her, was not impressed and said as much.

Just inside the airport's departure lounge was a desk at which was sitting a bored-looking police lieutenant. Cadmus saluted the officer and announced, "Six Terran tourists from Calmira, sir."

"And just in time, Sergeant. The ship will be embarking passengers in about ten minutes." He looked up at Grimes and his party. "Names? Identification papers?"

"They have no papers, sir," Cadmus told him. "They were robbed."

"You can say that again," muttered Fenella, the loss of whose wristwatch was still rankling.

"I trust that you will apprehend the miscreants responsible, Sergeant," said the officer, indicating by his manner that he could hardly care less.

"Investigations are being made, sir."

"And now, your names."

Grimes rattled these off, the Smiths and the Browns and the others. The lieutenant wrote them down on a form, said, "Thank you, Mr. Smith. And now just wait in the lounge with the other passengers. And that will do, Sergeant. You'd better be getting back to Calmira."

"Sir."

Grimes shook hands with Cadmus.

"Thank you for your help, Sergeant. I shall see to it that the Terran Ambassador knows about what you have done for us."

"It was only my duty, sir."

Brasidus shook hands with Cadmus.

Shirl and Darleen, while the lieutenant looked on disgustedly, flung their arms about him and planted noisy kisses on his cheeks. (They had aimed for his mouth but he managed to turn his head just in time.)

Grimes led the way into the lounge. He had spotted a refreshment stall. ("But they'll feed us aboard the ship . . ." protested Maggie.) As he had hoped, there were smokes of various kinds on sale. He bought a tin of tobacco of an unknown brand, paying for it out of the money provided by Cadmus. Now he could afford to fill his pipe properly from what remained in his pouch. He lit up and surveyed those who were to be his fellow passengers on the flight to Sparta City. There were, he estimated, about sixty of them. There was a group of Waverley citizens, male and female, who had stubbornly refused to go native insofar as apparel was concerned and were clad in colorful kilts in a wide variety of tartans. There were fat ladies from Earth for whom chitons did nothing but to make a desperate attempt to hide their overly abundant nakedness and their skinny husbands, looking, in their skimpy tunics, like underdressed scarecrows. There were the inevitable young people with their rucksacks and short shorts and heavy hiking boots. There were, even, three Shaara, a princess and two drones, surveying the motley throng through their huge, faceted eyes with arthropodal arrogance.

"And how long will it take that gasbag to get us to Sparta City?" asked Fenella.

"Three days is my guess," said Grimes.

"Ugh! In this company!"

The public address system came to life. "All offworlders will now leave the lounge by departure gate three. All offworlders will now leave the lounge by departure gate three. Small hand baggage only."

People began to straggle out from the lounge, along the paved path to the mooring mast, escorted by policemen who tried to hurry things up.

"I'll never come here again for a holiday!" Grimes overheard. "They take our money, then treat us like criminals!"

"But you must make allowances, dear. They're in the middle of the revolution."

"Then why the hell couldn't they have waited to have it when we were safely back home?"

By groups the tourists took the short elevator ride up to the top of the mooring mast, passed through the tubular gangway into the body of the ship. Flight attendants, surly men in shabby uniforms, chivvied them aft into a large cabin. There were rows of seats, of the reclining variety. There was, Grimes realized with a sinking heart, no sleeping accommodation. Obviously this was normally a short-haul passenger carrier pressed into service for the transport of those who were, now, little better than refugees.

Grimes, Brasidus and Maggie shared a bank of three seats on the port side of the cabin. Fenella and Shirl and Darleen sat immediately behind them. The cabin filled up.

No announcement was made when the flight commenced. There was no friendly "This is your captain speaking." There was just a faint vibration as the motors were started and, through the viewport in the ship's skin, the sight of the ground below receding.

Shortly thereafter a meal was served—bowls of greasy stew, stale rolls and muddy coffee. It made a sordid beginning to what was to be a sordid voyage.

Grimes, who was something of an authority on the history of transport, was to say later that it was like a long trip must have been in the Bad Old Days on Earth, during that period when the fuel-guzzling giant airplanes reigned supreme in the skies, before the airship made its long deferred comeback as a passenger carrier. There were the inadequate toilet facilities. There was the flavorless food, either too greasy or too dry, or even, both at once. There was the canned music. There were the annoying restrictions surely imposed by some fanatical non-smoker.

"It took absolute genius," he would say, "to reproduce aboard a modern dirigible, the only civilized means of aerial transport, conditions approximating those in Economy Class aboard an intercontinental Jumbo Jet of the late Twentieth Century. . . ."

What made it even worse for him was that he was not used to traveling as a passenger, or as a passenger not accorded control room privileges. As Commodore Grimes he would have spent most of the flight in the ship's nerve center, observing, asking intelligent questions, conversing with the captain and officers. As Mr. Smith he was just one of the herd, livestock to be carted from Point A to Point B and delivered in more or less good order and condition.

It was impossible for him to have proper conversations with his companions, to discuss the course of action once they had disembarked at the Sparta City airport. There were too many around them who could overhear, including the flight attendants. From one of these they managed to obtain some paper and a stylus—the man had to be tipped—on the pretext of playing word games. They passed notes between their two rows of seats, hidden between the sheets of airline stationery upon which there were a sort of crude variation of Scrabble.

They ate, forcing the food down. They slept as well as they could. They listened to the loud—and mostly fully justified—complaints of the other passengers. They made bets on the frequency with which a particularly annoying, tritely sweet melody would come up on the canned music program. And, with the others, they became steadily scruffier and scruffier. The acridity of stale perspiration became the most dominant odor in the cabin's atmosphere. It needed, said Grimes loudly, a strong injection of good, healthy tobacco smoke to purify it.

Their communication by written messages did not produce any worthwhile results. As Grimes said in his final note, after arrival at Sparta City they would just have to play by ear.

At last, at long, long last, the airship's captain broke his voyage-long silence.

"Attention, all passengers. We are now approaching our mooring at Sparta City Airport. After mooring has been completed you will disembark in an orderly manner and put yourselves into the care of the authorities. That is all."

Grimes stared out through the port. The airship was making a wide sweep over the city. Surely, he thought, it was not usually as dark as this. The winding streets were no more than feeble trickles of sparsely spaced lights. The Acropolis was no longer floodlit. But around the Palace there was glaring illumination. And what were those flashes? Gunfire?

He asked one of the surly flight attendants the local time. It was 0400 hours. When the man was out of sight he took his wrist companion from his pocket and set it. Even though he would not be keeping a written log of events he always liked to know just when whatever was happening was happening.

The city lights fell slowly astern.

The vibration of the motors became less intense, then ceased. Sundry clankings came from forward as the ship was shackled to her mast.

"We're here," said Grimes unnecessarily.

"Thank all the odd gods of the Galaxy for that," said Maggie.

Chapter 33

At the foot of the mooring mast there was a small detachment of bored looking police, obviously resentful at having to be up at this ungodly hour. They herded the disembarking passengers into a lounge where a sullen lieutenant ticked their names off on a list. The only persons at whom he looked at all closely were the three Shaara. They stared him down.

Coffee and little sweet buns were available. It was not the sort of refreshment which Grimes would have ordered had he any choice in the matter, but it was far better than the meals aboard the airship.

Sipping and munching, he stood close to three of the policemen.

"All this extra duty . . ." one was complaining. "And then, on top of it all, we have to be at the bloody Acropolis at ten in the bloody morning for the bloody coronation. If *she* is as bloody popular as she says she is, why does she want *us* to guard her? What's wrong with her own bloody Amazon Guard? Answer me that."

"Politics, Orestes, politics. Wouldn't do, this early, if she showed herself relying too heavily on her own pet tabbies. For all this Queen Hippolyte reincarnation crap she wants to be crowned ruler of all Sparta, not of just one sex. But once she's firmly in the saddle, then we shall see what we shall see."

"What d'ye suppose *did* happen to Brasidus?" asked the third man. "With all his faults, he wasn't a bad bastard."

"Done away with, of course," said the expert on politics. "We'll never see *him* again."

"And more's the pity," muttered the first man.

Grimes drifted away to where the others were seated in a corner of the lounge, close to one of the big sliding windows. There was nobody else within earshot.

"Maggie, your bug detector," he said in a low voice. "It could be safe to talk here, but I want to be sure . . ."

She took the instrument out of her pocket, pressed buttons, watched and listened.

She said, "All right. We can talk."

"To begin with," said Grimes, "Ellena's going to be crowned this morning. Queen of all Sparta. At ten."

"I can't believe that!" growled Brasidus.

"I'm afraid that you have to, old friend. The question is—do you want to stop her?"

"Yes. Yes. After all, she is only a woman."

Fenella's indignant squawk must have been audible all over the airport—but there had already been so many loud complaints from other passengers that it went almost unnoticed.

"*I* am the Archon," went on Brasidus. "Now I am back where I belong. I shall resume my high office without delay."

"Go for broke . . ." muttered Grimes.

"What was that, John?"

"Just a Terran expression. It means . . ." He fumbled for the right words. "It means that you stake everything on a single throw of the dice."

"I like that," said Brasidus. "I like that. And are you with me, John? And you, Maggie?"

"What about asking me?" demanded Fenella.

"And us?" asked Shirl and Darleen.

"Very well. Are you with me? All of you."

"Yes," they all said.

"First of all," said Grimes, "we have to get out of the airport. That shouldn't be difficult. After all, we aren't prisoners. Nobody regards a bunch of offplanet refugees as being potentially dangerous."

"And then we make for the Palace," said Brasidus.

"Do we?" asked Grimes. "With all due respect to your lady wife, Brasidus, I wouldn't trust her as far as I could throw her. And she is not a small woman. The way I see it is this. We go underground for a while until we find out which way the wind is blowing."

"But *you* said 'go for broke,' John. There has to be a confrontation between myself and Ellena. Oh, I should never have married her—I've known that for quite some time—and, however things turn out, I shall not stay married to her for much longer." All the built-up bitterness was coming out in a rush. "There must be a confrontation. A *public* confrontation so that the people can make their own choice between us. At the coronation."

"Mphm," grunted Grimes. *Go for broke*, he thought. *Why not?* If things didn't work out he could get a message out—somehow—to *Sister Sue* and she could come in and lift him and the others off New Sparta. If, that is, they would be, by that time, in any condition to be lifted off. But his luck had held so far. Why should it not hold for a little longer?

As inconspicuously as possible they drifted out of the lounge, first to the toilet facilities. In a cloakroom Shirl and Darleen found a pair of long cloaks that would conceal their not-quite-human bodies from curious eyes. Nobody stopped them when they found a door opening to the outside. The night, what was left of it, was almost windless. The clear sky was ablaze with stars.

Once they were clear of the airport Brasidus—after all, it was his city—led the way. The first part of their long walk was through orchards of some kind; the spicy scent of ripening fruit was heavy in the still air. Then they entered a built-up area. Shirl and Darleen, with their keen hearing, picked up the whine of an approaching hovercar before any of the others. They all found concealment in a side alley until the vehicle—a police patrol chariot?—was past. The next time they had to hide was from a detachment of soldiers on foot. Now and again they heard the rattle of automatic projectile weapons. Once they stumbled—literally—across a dead body, that of a policeman. His pistol holsters, Grimes discovered to his disappointment, were empty.

Then it was dawn and, only a little later, sunrise. People were emerging into the street, unshuttering shop windows. Presumably the coming of daylight signalled the lifting of the curfew.

Brasidus found an inn. Before leading the way into it he checked the remaining contents of the money pouch that Cadmus had given him, said there should be enough for breakfast for all of them. Grimes told him that he would have to do the ordering as he was the only one without a foreign accent. (But there were now so many Spartan citizens recently arrived from other planets that this did not much matter.)

They took seats at a table. They were the only customers. The sullen waitress made it obvious that she resented this disruption of her early morning peace and quiet. There were quite a few items on the blackboard menu that Grimes would have liked—even eggs and bacon!—but the girl told them that the cook was not yet on duty. She produced the inevitable muddy coffee—yesterday's brew, warmed up—and stale rolls.

Other people drifted in.

These were regulars and received better treatment than the strangers had gotten. Their coffee smelled as though it had been freshly made and their rolls looked fresh. The waitress put on a pleasant face and joined in conversations.

"No, I shan't be going to the coronation. Wouldn't go even if I could get time off. That Ellena and her bunch of dykes! But I liked Brasidus. He was a *real* man. . . ."

"They say," contributed a male customer, "that Ellena had him quietly murdered."

"It's time somebody murdered her," muttered his friend.

"Careful," whispered the third man. "You can never tell who's listening these days . . ."

All three of them scowled suspiciously at Grimes and his party.

Brasidus called for the bill. He had enough money to cover it. He paid.

On the way out Grimes heard one of the men ask the girl, "And who were *they?*"

"Dunno. Never seen 'em before. Don't care much if I ever see 'em again."

"Shouldn't mind seein' more o' those wenches," said the first man.

"Probably Amazon Guard officers in civvies," said the second.

"Shut up!" hissed the girl, noticing that Grimes was lingering in the doorway, listening. "Shut up, you fool!"

After their breakfast they had time to spare. They sauntered through the city, playing the part of country cousins enjoying a good gawk. They saw streetcorner meetings being broken up by police—and noticed that, uncharacteristically, the law officers were using force only when absolutely necessary and then with seeming reluctance. They heard orators, female as well as male, screaming their support for Brasidus and demanding that he return to bring things back under control.

On more than one wall there were slogans crudely daubed.

ELLENA GO HOME! was a common one.

Brasidus laughed bitterly. "That's what I've been thinking for years but I've never said it out loud. Now I am saying it. I promise you—and promise myself—that once I'm back in control Ellena will be shipped back to Earth by the first available vessel. Does that ship of yours have any passenger accommodation, John?"

"No," lied Grimes.

"It doesn't matter. A spare storeroom would be good enough for *her.*"

Not aboard my *ship*, thought Grimes.

They dropped into a tavern for wine, using the last of Cadmus' money to pay for it. They mingled with the crowds—women, men, not too many children—who were converging upon the Acropolis. Shirl and Darleen took the lead; they had the ability to flow through and past obstructions like wild animals through dense undergrowth. Even so, it was not all that easy for Grimes and the others to keep up with them. Altercations broke out in their wake as toes were trodden and ribs painfully nudged.

But, eventually, they were standing in the front row, at the foot of the wide marble steps, facing a rank of black-uniformed police, all of whom had their stunguns drawn and ready. The dais at the head of the steps, with the white pillars of the Acropolis as its backdrop, was still empty. To either side of it were the news media cameras, at this moment slowly scanning the crowd.

Trumpets sounded and there was a rhythmic mutter of drums. The cameras turned to cover Ellena's grand entry. She strode majestically to the dais, flanked by high-ranking military officers, both male and female, followed by white-robed Council members. Among these was a tall woman on whose right shoulder rode an owl. Grimes stared at this. It was a real bird. It blinked, shifted its feet, half lifted its wings.

"The High Priestess of Athena," whispered Brasidus.

The trumpets were silent but the drums maintained a soft throbbing. Ellena stood there, waiting for the applause that was supposed to greet her appearance. She was a majestic enough figure in Amazon Guard uniform, more highly polished bronze than leather. Her plumed helmet added to her already not inconsiderable height. She stood there, frowning.

At last, from somewhere in the crowd, there was an outbreak of cheering and cries of, "Ellena! Ellena!" But there was also some booing. And were the people, wondered Grimes, who were chanting, "Hip, Hip, Hippolyte!" applauding or exercising their derision?

Trumpets blared.

Ellena raised her arms, brought her hands to her shining helmet, lifted it from her head, handed it to an Amazon aide. A white-robbed acolyte gave an elaborate crown of golden laurel leaves to the High Priestess, who advanced to stand beside Ellena. Beside her stood one of the councillors, an elderly man, stooped, feeble, with wrinkled face and sparse white hair.

He spoke into a microphone. Despite the amplification his voice was feeble.

"Citizens of Sparta. . . . We are gathered together on this great and happy occasion to witness the coronation of our first Queen. . . . In accordance with our Law the appointment of the ruler must be by public consent. . . . Do any of you gathered here know of any reason why the Lady Ellena should not be crowned Queen of all Sparta?"

"She's a woman, that's why!" yelled somebody.

But Ellena was now seated on the thronelike chair that had been brought for her and the High Priestess, standing behind it, had the golden crown raised in her hands, ready to lower it on to Ellena's head.

"For the second time," quavered the elderly councillor, "do any of you gathered here know of any *valid* reason why the Lady Ellena should not be crowned Queen of all Sparta?"

"We want Brasidus! We want Brasidus!" quite a number of voices were chanting.

"For the third and the last time, do any of you gathered here . . ."

"We want Brasidus! We want Brasidus! We want the Archon! We want the Archon!"

Brasidus cried in a great voice, "I am Brasidus! I am the Archon!"

Freakishly the microphones caught his words, sent them roaring over the crowd. The news media cameras swiveled to cover him. The policemen at the foot of the vast staircase shifted away to the sides as he began his advance to confront his wife.

Ellena was back on her feet, furious, pointing an accusatory hand.

"Guards! Kill this impostor!"

Her own Amazons might well have obeyed but the military personnel in her immediate vicinity were all men. Grimes recognized one of the officers although it was the first time that he had seen him in uniform. It was Paulus.

"Guards!" Ellena was screaming now. "Kill this impostor!"

"Brasidus!" the crowd was roaring. "Brasidus!"

On the platform Ellena was yelling at Paulus. "Shoot him, you useless bastard! Shoot him!"

"But he is the Archon."

"He is an impostor!" She wrestled briefly with the man who had been Brasidus' bodyguard, succeeded in pulling a heavy projectile pistol from the holster at his belt, smote him on the forehead with the barrel, knocking him to the ground. "All right!" she snarled. "If none of you will do the job, *I* will!"

She raised the weapon, holding it in both hands. It was obvious that she knew how to use it.

From the corner of his eye Grimes caught a blur of movement to his right, the glint of sunlight reflected from bright metal. Darleen had pulled one of the deadly sharpened discs from the pouch that she was still carrying. With a snap of her wrist she launched it. When it hit its target Ellena was about to squeeze off her first shot. The report of the pistol was shocking, deafening almost, but where the bullet went nobody ever knew.

Ellena screamed.

And then she was standing there, with blood spouting from her ruined right hand, still clinging to the pistol, still trying to bring it to bear, although it was obvious that those more than half severed fingers would never be able to pull a trigger until extensive and lengthy repair work had been carried out.

People joined Brasidus in his march up the steps to the platform, some in civilian clothing, some in police and army uniforms. There was scuffling among the assembled dignitaries but no shots were fired. The Amazon Guard officers were doing their best to stand haughtily aloof, striking out, damagingly, only when jostled. Their loyalty, thought Grimes with some bewilderment, was to their Corps, not to Ellena. She must have done something to antagonize them.

(Later, very much later, he was to learn that Ellena intended to lay the blame for her husband's murder on top-ranking Amazon officers, who were to be executed after a mere parody of a trial. Somehow they had discovered this and already had their own plans for Ellena's elimination. But now she was saving them the trouble.)

Ellena had collapsed and was receiving medical attention.

Brasidus had gained access to a microphone. "Fellow citizens! People of Sparta, men and women both! I have returned. Later the full story of my abduction and my rescue by very good friends will be told to you. . . ."

Grimes didn't catch the rest of it.

He had been accosted by a man whom at first he thought was a stranger, a slightly built fellow with a dark complexion, dressed in ill-fitting civilian clothes.

"You bastard! You bloody pirate!" this person sputtered. "What did you do with my ship?"

"It's a long story," said Grimes at last. "But I'll see to it that you get her back, Lieutenant Gupta."

Chapter 34

And Grimes got his own ship back when, at last, *Sister Sue* dropped down to Port Sparta. He got his name back on to the Register as Master and Billy Williams, surprisingly cheerfully, reverted to his old rank as Chief Officer, saying, "Now you can have all the worries again, Skipper."

And worries there were.

Discharge of cargo had just begun when a strongly worded request— it was more of an order, really—came from Admiral Damien by Carlotti deep space radio. This was that Grimes handle the salvage of *Krait*. He had done this sort of job before, back on Botany Bay, and the courier was a very small ship and *Sister Sue* had plenty of power and, even with most of her cargo still on board, could have lifted *Krait* bodily. As it was, throughout the operation the courier's stern remained in contact with the ground. And then she had to be stayed off so that she was safely stable while Grimes' engineers made repairs to her engines.

One consolation was that as Grimes, officially, was no longer connected with the Survey Service he would be able to put in a large bill for the services of himself and his ship.

And now his Earthbound cargo was almost loaded and, very soon now, *Sister Sue* would be secured for space.

Maggie sat with Grimes in his day room.

"And so," she said, "our ways part again."

"It was good while it lasted," he said.

"Yes."

"You could resign your commission," he told her, "and enter my employ."

"You resigned yours, John, but they pressganged you back into servitude. And my orders are that I must remain on New Sparta until the situation has stabilized. And. . . . And you must have noticed how things are now between Brasidus and myself."

"How could I not have noticed?"

"But you must understand, my dear, that it's all part of the job. *My* job. He must be taught that all women aren't like Ellena. . . ."

"Is that all?"

"No. I admire Brasidus. I'm sorry for him. And, if you must know, I love him in my fashion. But as soon as I have him back on an even keel—and as soon as this planet's back on an even keel—I shall be on my way. I've no doubt that Damien will find another job for me."

"To judge from my own experience of the old bastard, no doubt at all. But what a can of worms this one turned out to be!"

"And now that the chief worm has been removed the others should quiet down. But what a cunning bitch she was! Playing both ends against the middle. *Both* ends? I still have to find out just how many ends there were. And if it hadn't been for her plans to purge the high command of her own Amazon Guard she might still have pulled it off."

"How *did* Colonel what's-her-name find out what was in store for her?"

"You and I, John, were by no means the only intelligence operatives on New Sparta, although we were the only Survey Service ones. I had my contacts."

"You might have told me."

"The less you knew," she said, "the better."

"Mphm."

"Cheer up. You've got your ship back. Thanks to me you won't be getting Ellena as a passenger. I persuaded Brasidus that a dangerous woman such as her should be sent back to Earth in a warship, where she can be kept under guard. The destroyer *Rigel* will have the pleasure of her company. As you know, she's due in a couple of days after you lift off."

"I thought for a while that I might have the dubious pleasure of Fenella's company."

"She decided that there are still stories to be had on New Sparta. Too, she's set her sights on Brasidus." She laughed. "I might even let her have him. Who better to retail the scandalous gossip of a palace than one who's the subject of such gossip herself?"

"Mphm," grunted Grimes again. *Brasidus*, he thought a little jealously, *was doing very nicely for himself, getting his hairy paws onto all of Grimes' women. . . .*

There was a knock at the door.

"Enter!" called Grimes.

The door opened. Billy Williams stood there.

"Secured for space save for the after airlock, Skipper," he reported. "The two passengers, with their gear, have just boarded."

"*Passengers*, Mr. Williams?"

"I thought you knew, sir. A lady officer from the Palace, an Amazon major, came out with them and told me that everything had been arranged."

Two familiar forms appeared in the doorway behind the Chief Officer.

"Hi!" said Shirl (or was it Darleen?).

"Hi!" said Darleen (or was it Shirl?).

Maggie got to her feet, then bent to kiss Grimes as he still sat in his chair.

"See you," she said. "Somewhere, somewhen."

Billy Williams left with her to escort her to the airlock.

"Aren't you pleased to see us?" asked the two New Alicians as one.

Grimes supposed that he was.

THE WILD ONES

THE WILD ONES

To my favorite wrist watch.

Chapter 1

Sister Sue, John Grimes commanding, had made a relatively uneventful voyage from New Sparta to Earth and was now berthed at Port Woomera. But nobody seemed to be in a hurry to take delivery of her cargo, a quite large consignment of the spices for which New Sparta had become famous among Terran gourmets. This didn't worry Grimes much. His ship, of which he was owner as well as master, was on time charter to the Interstellar Transport Commission and until her holds were empty she would remain on pay. What did worry Grimes was that the charter had expired and that the Commission had indicated that it might not be renewed. Another cause for worry was that Billy Williams, his chief officer for many years and, for quite a while, during the term of Grimes' appointment as governor for Liberia, relieving master, was taking a long overdue spell of planet leave, returning to his home world, Austral. With him had gone the Purser/Catering Officer Magda Granadu, leaving Grimes with a shipful of comparative strangers, young men and women who had not been among her complement when he had first commissioned her. So he had to find a replacement for Magda and one for Billy Williams. The second officer, young Kershaw, was, in Grimes' opinion, too inexperienced a spaceman for promotion. It would be many years before he would be capable of acting as a reliable second in command.

Meanwhile Grimes had no option but to hang around the ship like a bad smell. Until he had seen which ways the many cats were going to jump he could not afford to leave her in the fumbling hands of young Kershaw. And he wanted, badly, to get away himself for at least a few days, to revisit his parents' home in Alice Springs. The old man was getting on now, although still churning out his historical novels. And his mother, Matilda, although one of those apparently ageless women, blessed at birth with a good bone structure, would be wanting to hear a first hand account of her son's adventures as governor of Liberia and then on New Sparta.

He was beginning to wonder if he should make the not too long walk from the commercial spaceport to the Survey Service Base, there to pay a courtesy call on Rear Admiral Damien. Even though not many people knew that Grimes was back in the Service with the rank of captain on the reserve list, everybody knew that he was an ex-Survey Service regular officer and that at one stage of his career his superior had been Damien, then Commodore Damien, who had been Officer Commanding Couriers at the Linisfarne Base. (But it was also common knowledge that young Grimes, as a courier captain, had been Damien's *bête noir*.)

Still, Damien owed him something. He had acted as the Rear Admiral's cat's paw during the El Doradan piracy affair, and on Liberia and, most recently, on New Sparta. The Survey Service pulled heavy *Gs* with the Interstellar Transport Commission. If Damien dropped a few hints in the right quarters the Commission would either renew the New Sparta time charter or find some other lucrative employment for *Sister Sue*.

So, after a not very satisfactory breakfast—the temporary, in-port-duties-only catering officer thought it beneath her dignity to cater to the captain's personal tastes and could murder even so simple a dish as eggs and bacon—Grimes got dressed in his best uniform, his own uniform with the Far Traveler Couriers cap badge and crested buttons. Then he sent for the second officer.

He said, "I shall be going ashore for a while, Mr. Kershaw. Should anything crop up I shall be with Rear Admiral Damien, at the Base."

The lanky, sullen young man with the overly long hair asked, "Is there any word, sir, about a replacement for Mr. Williams? After all, I'm doing chief officer's duties and only getting second's pay . . ."

I'm *doing the chief officer's duties*, thought Grimes indignantly. But he said, "The Astronauts' Guild have the matter in hand. As you know, I require Master Astronaut's qualifications for my chief officer. Unluckily you have only a First Mate's certificate."

Kershaw flushed. He knew that Grimes knew that he had already sat twice for his Master's ticket and failed dismally each time. He decided to drop the subject.

"When will you be back, sir?"

"That all depends upon the Rear Admiral. He might invite me to lunch, although that's unlikely. Or I might run into some old shipmates at the Base."

"It's a pity that you ever left the Service, sir," almost sneered Kershaw.

"Isn't it?" said Grimes cheerfully.

*   *   *

He walked down the ramp from the after airlock, puffing his foul pipe. The morning was fine although, with a southerly breeze straight from the Antarctic, quite cool. There were only a few ships in port—two of the Commission's Epsilon Class tramps (Sister Sue had started her working life as one such), a somewhat larger Dog Star Line freighter and, gleaming like a huge, metallic skep in the bright sunlight, some of the bee people who were her crew flying lazily about her, a Shaara vessel. (*Those bastards are getting everywhere these days*, thought Grimes disapprovingly. Once he had quite liked the Shaara but various events had caused him to change his attitude.)

All these ships, he saw, were working cargo. They all had gainful employment. His *Sister Sue* did not.

He identified himself to the marine guard at the main gate to the Base, was admitted without question. (Fame, or notoriety, had its advantages.) He looked with rather wistful interest at the Survey Service ships in their berths. There were two Serpent Class couriers, the so-called "flying darning needles." Grimes' first command—how many years ago?—had been one of these little ships. There was a Star Class destroyer. There was a cartographic ship, similar to *Discovery*, the mutiny aboard which vessel had been the main cause of his somewhat hasty resignation from the Survey Service.

But he hadn't come here to take a leisurely stroll down memory lane. He had come here to confront Rear Admiral Damien, to make a more or less formal request that this gentleman use his influence to obtain further employment, preferably another time charter, for *Sister Sue*. After all he, Grimes, was useful to the Survey Service even though very few people knew that he was back in their employ. And surely a willing—well, for some of the time—laborer was worthy of his hire.

He approached the main office block, passed another marine sentry. He went to the receptionist's desk where a smart little female ensign was on duty. The girl looked at him curiously, noting the details of his uniform. Obviously she was not one of those who knew Grimes by name and reputation. But she was young, young. There may have been giants in those days, the days when Grimes himself was young, but this pert wench would never have heard of them. (Yet. But legends persist and, almost certainly, there would be those on the Base who would be happy to regale her with all sorts of tales, true, half-true and untrue, about that notorious misfit John Grimes.)

"Sir?" she asked politely.

"Could I see Admiral Damien, please?"

"Is he expecting you, sir?"

"No. But he'll see me."

"Whom shall I say is calling?"

"John Grimes. Captain John Grimes."

"Wait, please, Captain Grimes."

She pressed buttons and the little screen of her telephone console came alive. Grimes shifted position so he could look over the ensign's shoulder. He saw Damien's face—that prominent nose, the thin lips, the yellowish skin stretched taut over sharp bones—take form. *Old Skull Face never changes*, he thought. And Damien could see him in his own screen, standing behind the girl. There was a flicker of recognition in the cold, gray eyes.

"Admiral, sir," said the girl, "there is a . . ."

"I know, Ms. Pemberthy. There is a Captain Grimes to see me. Or a Commodore Grimes. Or His ex-Excellency ex-Governor Grimes . . . All right, Grimes. I was wondering when you would condescend to come and see me. You know where I live. I'm still in the office where you were debriefed after you came in from New Sparta—when was it, now? three months ago?—and now you're back from New Sparta again. But you won't be going back there for quite a while, if ever. . . . As you know full well I always keep my finger on the pulse of things." Then, to the girl, "That's all, Ms. Pemberthy. Captain Grimes can find his own way up. He has only to follow the signs. Even Blind Freddy and his dog could do that much."

The screen went blank.

The girl turned to stare at Grimes.

"The admiral seems to know you, sir. But what is your rank, captain or commodore? And *are* you an Excellency?"

"I was," Grimes told her. "And I was, at one time, commodore of a squadron of privateers . . ."

"Privateers, sir? Aren't they some sort of pirates?"

"No," Grimes told her firmly.

Chapter 2

Damien did Grimes the honor of getting up from behind his huge desk, walking around the massive piece of furniture and advancing on Grimes with bony right hand outstretched. Grimes did Damien the honor of saluting quite smartly before shaking hands with the rear admiral. Damien motioned Grimes to a quite comfortable armchair before resuming his own seat. He put his elbows on the surface of the desk, made a steeple of the skeletal fingers of both hands and resting his chin upon the apex, looked intently at the younger man.

"Well, young Grimes," he said at last, "what can I do you for?"

"I do not think," replied Grimes, "that that was an unintentional slip of the tongue."

"Too right it wasn't. Nonetheless I may be in a position to do something for you."

"At a price, no doubt. Sir. How many pounds of flesh, or is it just my soul you're after?"

"Grimes, Grimes. . . . This uppity attitude does not become you. And I would remind you that you hold a Survey Service commission, albeit on the Reserve List. You are subject to Service discipline—and, when you are recalled to active duty, are entitled to the full pay and allowances for your rank in addition to the quite—indeed overly—generous retaining fee of which you are already in receipt."

Grimes' prominent ears reddened but he kept his temper. After all he had the services of himself and his ship to sell—and this was a buyer's market. He could not afford to antagonize Damien.

"And now, Grimes, what exactly are your current troubles?"

"Well, sir, I was hoping that the Interstellar Transport Commission would renew or extend my time charter on the Earth/New Sparta run. After all, my ship has given very good service on that trade. . . ."

"But not with you in command of her, Grimes, until recently. As far as New Sparta is concerned you're too much of a catalyst. Things have a habit of happening around you rather than to you. . . ."

"Mphm!" grunted Grimes indignantly.

"I wish that you'd break yourself of that disgusting habit," said Damien. "I've told you before that I do not expect naval officers to make noises like refugees from a pig sty. But, to revert to New Sparta, it will be better for all concerned if things are allowed to settle down. Your boozing pal Brasidus is doing quite well now that he no longer has Queen Elena to stick her tits into everything. Our Commander Lazenby is maintaining a watching brief, as I am sure that you know. You and she are old friends, aren't you? And that obnoxious news hen Fenella Pruin has taken flight to some other planet to do her muckraking. . . ."

"So you persuaded the Commission not to renew the charter," said Grimes.

"Hinted, just hinted. And I also hinted that there was no need to bust a gut to get your inward cargo discharged. Until it's out you're still on hire. And money, I need hardly remind you, is money. . . ."

"Thank you, sir. And I wonder if you'd mind hinting to the Astronauts' Guild that I have a vacancy for a chief officer, one with some experience and with a master's ticket. Come to that, I also want a new catering officer. . . ."

"Don't get your knickers in a twist, Grimes. You'll be getting your new chief officer shortly. One of *our* people, needless to say. And a very good catering officer. And . . ." A sardonic grin appeared briefly on Damien's face.

"And what? Or whom?"

"You remember Shirl and Darleen, the two young ladies whom you brought to Earth, as passengers, from New Sparta. . . ."

"How could I forget them?"

"Like that, was it?"

Again Grimes' prominent ears flushed angrily.

He said, "So it was you who arranged for their passage, in *my* ship, from New Sparta to Earth. Oh, well, as long as you pay their fares again I'll carry them to anywhere else you wish."

"You're a mercenary bastard, Grimes, aren't you? But *we* shall not be paying their fares. *They* will not be paying their fares. On the contrary, you'll be paying them. Wages, at the Award rate."

"*What?*"

"You heard me, Grimes. After all, merchant vessels quite often carry officer cadets."

"Who have had the required pre-Space training at some recognized academy. And I'm sure that there's no such an academy on New Alice."

"There's not. But there are such things as STS—Straight To Space—cadets."

Grimes, who since he had become a merchant spaceman had made a study of all the regulations that could possibly affect him, ransacked his memory.

He said, "But Shirl and Darleen just aren't qualified in any possible way. Aboard a spaceship they'd be completely unskilled personnel."

"But with qualifications, Grimes." He opened one of the folders on his desk, began to read from it. "'Any person who has held commissioned rank in the armed forces of any federated planet, wishing to embark upon a new career in the Merchant Service, may serve the qualifying time for the lowest grade of certificate of competency in any merchant vessels, with the rank and pay of officer cadet.'"

"But . . . Commissioned rank?" asked Grimes.

Then he realized that Damien was right. New Sparta was a federated planet. Elena's Amazon Guard had been part of the armed forces of that planet. Shirl and Darleen had held commissions—as officer instructors, but commissions nonetheless—in that body.

"Too," said Damien, grinning again, "both young ladies are now Probationary Ensigns, Special Branch, in the Federation Survey Service Reserve. Of course, their reserve commissions are as secret as yours is. But when I got the first reports, by Carlottigram, from Commander Lazenby about what was happening on New Sparta I decided that I, that we could make use of the special skills and talents of those New Alicians. After all, you did. On Venusberg first of all, then on New Sparta. . . ."

"And your Special Branch," grumbled Grimes, "is one sprouting many strange fruits and flowers."

"Well said. You have the soul of a poet, young Grimes. Anyhow when, in the fullness of time, your Sister Sue lifts off you will have, on your Articles, in addition to your normal complement, officer cadets Shirl Kelly and Darleen Byrne . . ."

"Kelly and Byrne?"

"Why not? I explained to the young ladies that they would have to adopt surnames and told them that Kelly and Byrnes are both names associated with Australian history."

"But they were bushrangers, sir."

"Don't be snobbish, Grimes. After all, you've been a pirate yourself."

"A privateer," snapped Grimes. "And acting under *your* secret orders."

"Which included, at the finish, committing an act of real piracy. But enough of this quibbling. Tomorrow a Mr. Steerforth will be reporting to you as your new chief officer. He will be on loan from the Interstellar Transport Commission. He is also a lieutenant commander in the Survey Service Reserve. He is a capable and experienced officer. Give him a day to settle in and then you'll be free to inflict yourself on your parents in Alice Springs for three weeks. It will be all of that before anybody gets around to discharge your cargo and before your next charter has been arranged."

"Thank you, sir. But can you tell me anything about the next charter? Time, or voyage? Where to?"

"Not yet. Oh, would you mind taking Shirl and Darleen with you to the Alice? They want to see something of inland Australia and you'd make a good guide. I'm sure that your parents wouldn't mind putting up a couple of guests."

His father wouldn't, Grimes thought, but regarding his mother he was far from certain. Even so he was looking forward to seeing Shirl and Darleen again.

Chapter 3

As promised, Mr. Steerforth reported on board shortly after breakfast the following morning. He was tall, blond, deeply tanned, with regular features, startling blue eyes and what seemed to be slightly too many gleaming white teeth. Grimes couldn't be sure, at short acquaintance, whether he liked him or not. He was too much the big ship officer, with too obvious a parade of efficiency. His predecessor, Billy Williams, had been out of the Dog Star Line whose vessels, at their very best, were no more than glorified tramps. (But Williams had always got things done, in his own way, and done well.)

"My gear's on board, sir," said Steerforth briskly. "If it's all right with you I'll nip across to the shipping office and get myself signed on. And then, perhaps, you might introduce me to the other officers, after which you can give me any special instructions. I understand that you are wanting to catch the late afternoon flight to Alice Springs."

"I suppose that the admiral has already given you your instructions," grumbled Grimes.

"The admiral, sir?"

"Come off it, Mr. Steerforth. You know who I mean. Rear Admiral Damien. You're one of his boys."

"If you say so, sir."

"I've said it. All right, go and get your name on the Articles. You should be back in time for morning coffee, when I'll introduce you to the rest of the crowd in the wardroom."

"Very good, sir."

Grimes' next callers were Shirl and Darleen. They knew the ship, of course, having traveled in her, as passengers, from New Sparta to Earth. Certainly they were familiar enough with Grimes' own quarters. . . .

"Hi, John," said Shirl (or was it Darleen?).

"Hi, John," said Darleen (or was it Shirl?).

Had the girls been unclothed Grimes could have told them apart; there were certain minor skin blemishes. But now, dressed as they were in shorts (very short shorts) and shirt outfits they were as alike as two peas in a pod. The odd jointure of their legs was not concealed by their scanty lower garments, their thighs looked powerful (as they were in fact). Wide smiles redeemed the rather long faces under the short brown hair from mere pleasant plainness.

"The Bureau of Colonial Affairs has been looking after us really well," said one of the girls, "but it is good to be back aboard your ship again. The old crocodile has told us that we are to be part of your crew."

The old crocodile? wondered Grimes, then realized that this must be yet another nickname for Admiral Damien.

"He has already made us officers," said Shirl. (Grimes remembered that her voice was very slightly higher than that of Darleen.) "In the Survey Service. But it is supposed to be a secret, although he said that *you* would know."

"I do," said Grimes.

"And now we are to be officers aboard your ship," Darleen told him unnecessarily.

"And you are to show us the inland of this country of yours, from which our ancestors came. We have seen kangaroos in the zoo in Adelaide, of course, but we have yet to see them in the wild, where they belong."

"Where *we* belong," said Darleen, a little wistfully. "You know, John, I have often thought that that genetic engineer, all those hundreds of years ago, did the wrong thing when he changed our ancestors. . . ."

"If he hadn't changed them," pointed out Shirl, "*we* shouldn't be here now."

"I suppose not." Darleen's face lit up with a smile. "And it is good being here, with John."

"Mphm," grunted Grimes.

The three of them caught the afternoon flight from Woomera to Alice Springs.

Grimes loved dirigibles, and a flight by airship in charming company was an enjoyable experience. He had a few words with an attentive stewardess, scribbled a few words on the back of one of his business cards for her to take her to the captain and, shortly thereafter, he and the two New Alicians were ushered into the control cab. The girls stared out through the wide windows at the sunburned landscape flowing astern beneath them, with the greenery around irrigation lakes and ditches in vivid contrast to the dark browns of the more normal landscape, peered through borrowed binoculars at the occasional racing emu, exclaimed with delight as they spotted a mob of kangaroos. But the shadows cast by rocks and hillocks were lengthening as the sun sagged down to the horizon. Soon there would be nothing to see but the scattered lights of villages and townships.

"This must seem a very slow means of transport to you, Captain," said the airship's master. "After all, when you're used to exceeding the speed of light . . ."

"But not with scenery like this to look at, Captain," said Grimes.

"The two young ladies seem to be appreciating it," said the airshipman. "They're not Terran, are they?"

"No, although their ancestors were both Terran and Australian. They're from a world called New Alice."

"The name rings no bell. Would it be one of the lost colonies?"

"Yes."

"I saw a piece on trivi about Morrowvia a few months ago. . . . The world of the cat people. . . . If I ever save enough for an off-planet holiday I might go there. Say, wasn't it you who discovered, or rediscovered, that Lost Colony?"

"Not exactly. But I was there during the period when it was decided that the Morrowvians were legally human."

The airship captain lowered his voice. "And these young ladies with you. . . . From New Alice, you say. Would they be the end result of some nutty experiment by some round the bend genetic engineer?"

Shirl and Darleen possessed abnormal, by human standards, hearing. They turned as one away from the window to face the airshipman. They smiled sweetly.

"Yes, captain," said Shirl. "Although we are legally human our ancestors were not, as yours are, monkeys."

If the captain was embarrassed he did not show it. He looked them up and down in a manner that suggested that he was mentally undressing them. He grinned at them cheerfully.

"Tie me kangaroo down, sport," he chuckled. "I shouldn't mind gettin' the chance to tie *you* down!"

"You could try," said Darleen slowly.

"And it could be the last thing you ever did try," said Shirl.

They were still smiling, the pair of them, but Grimes knew that it was more of a vicious baring of teeth than anything else.

The airshipman broke the tense silence.

"Excuse me, ladies. Excuse me, Captain. I'd better start thinkin' about gettin' the old girl to her mooring mast at the Alice." He addressed his first officer. "Mr. Cleary, confirm our ETA with airport control, will you? Ask 'em about conditions—surface wind and all the rest of it. . . ."

Why tell me to do what I always do? said Cleary's expression as plainly as spoken words.

"Shall we get out of your way, now, Captain?" asked Grimes.

"Oh, no, Captain. Just keep well aft in the cab." He managed a laugh. "Who knows? You might learn something."

But it wasn't the airshipman's day. He bumbled his first approach to mast, slid past it with only millimeters of clearance. He had to bring his ship around to make a second try. He blamed a sudden shift of wind for the initial bungle but he knew—and Grimes knew—that it was nothing of the kind. It was no more and no less than the result of an attempt to impress a hostile female audience.

Chapter 4

Grimes' parents were waiting in the lounge at the base of the mooring mast. His mother embraced him, his father took his hand and grasped it warmly between both of his. Then Grimes introduced the two girls. He realized that he could not remember which one had been given Kelly as a surname and which one was Byrne. Why the hell, he asked himself, couldn't Damien have had them entered in the books as sisters? As twin sisters, even. They looked enough alike. (Some little time later he raised this point with the two New Alicians. "But the admiral is very thorough, John," Darleen told him. "To put us down as being related would have made nonsense of his files. It was explained to us. It is all a matter of blood groups and such. . . .")

The older people did, as a matter of fact, look rather puzzled when Shirl and Darleen were introduced. But they asked no questions and, in any case, the Grimes household was one in which the use of given names was the rule rather than the exception.

Baggage was collected and then the party boarded the family hovercar. Grimes senior took the road in a direction away from the city, deviated from this on to what was little more than a rough track, heading toward what the old man called his private oasis. By now it was quite dark and overhead the black sky was ablaze with stars. In the spreading beam of the headlights green eyes gleamed with reflected radiance from the low brush on either side of the track. For a while an old man kangaroo bounded ahead of the vehicle until, at last, it collected its wits and broke away to the right, out of the path of the car.

The lights came on in the house as the hovercar approached. His father was still doing well, thought the spaceman, could still afford all the latest in robotic home help. The wide drive, dull-gleaming permaplast bordered with ornamental shrubs, had been swept clear of the dust that here, in the Red Center, got everywhere. Ahead, the wide door of the big garage slid up and open. The old man reduced speed at the very last moment and slid smoothly into the brilliantly lit interior. Gently sighing, the vehicle subsided in its skirts.

Grimes senior was first out of the car. Gallantly he assisted the ladies to alight—not that any of them needed his aid—leaving his son to cope with the baggage. A door slid open in one of the side walls. In it stood a woman—a *transparent* woman? No, not a woman. A robot in human female form, with what appeared to be delicate, beautifully fashioned, gleaming clockwork innards, some of the fragile-seeming wheels spinning rapidly, others with a barely perceptible movement.

"Come in," said this obviously hellishly expensive automaton. "This is Liberty Hall. You can spit on the mat and call the cat a bastard."

"Cor stiffen the bleeding crows!" said Grimes.

Matilda Grimes laughed without much humour. "Just one of George's latest toys," she said. "It came programmed with a standard vocabulary but he added to it."

"Too right," said the robot in a pleasant contralto.

"*I* like her," maintained George Whitley Grimes.

"*You* would," his wife told him.

Meanwhile it—she?—advanced on Grimes, arms extended. What was he supposed to do? he wondered. Shake hands? Throw his own arms about the thing in a step-brotherly embrace?

"Let her have the bags, John," said his father.

It took them from him, managing them with contemptuous ease, led the way into the house. The workings of the machinery in her hips and legs was fascinatingly obvious. It was like, in a way, one of those beautiful antique clocks that spend their working lives in glass domes. And what would it be like, he wondered, to make love to an eight day clock? *Down, boy, down!* he snarled mentally at his, at times kinky, libido.

They sat in the big, comfortable lounge, Shirl and Darleen in very deep armchairs that caused them to make a display of their long, long legs. Grimes noticed that his father's eyes kept straying toward the two New Alicians. Perhaps, he thought, it was no more than biological curiosity. Those amply displayed lower limbs were not quite human. Or perhaps the old man was betraying another sort of biological interest. Grimes could not blame him. Like son, like father. . . .

"Shirl," asked Matilda Grimes sweetly. "Darleen . . . Aren't you chilly? Wouldn't you like to put on something warmer?"

"It is quite all right, Matilda," said Shirl. "We often wear less than this. John can tell you. . . ."

His mother looked at him coldly and said, "You never change much, do you? I remember when you were only twelve, when we were living in that old house in Flynn Street, and you appointed yourself secretary of the Flynn Street Nudist Club which held its meetings by the pool in our backyard . . . As I recall it, you were the only male member."

"And I had to shift my workroom to the front of the house," said George Whitley Grimes. "The view from the back windows was too distracting."

"And *I*," said Matilda, "had to cope with an irate committee of local mothers who had discovered how their little bitches of daughters were spending their afternoons . . ."

"And *I*," said George, "had to stay away from the pub for fear of being beaten up by the fathers of those same little bitches."

Shirl and Darleen laughed.

"You Earthpeople, as we are discovering, have such odd ways of looking at things," said one of them.

"Not all of us," said Grimes senior. "And not any of us for all of the time."

The robutler rolled in with the pre-dinner drinks. It was an even bigger and more elaborate model than the one that had been in service at the time of Grimes's last visit to the parental home, reminding him of a suit of mechanized battle armor built to accommodate at least three Federation Marines simultaneously. With it came the house robot that Grimes was now thinking of as Clockwork Kitty. Like its predecessor the robutler took spoken orders and, in its capacious interior, seemed to hold a stock of every alcoholic drink known to civilized Man—and, quite possibly, a few that weren't. There were ice cubes, spa water and fruit cordials. There was a fine selection of little eats.

As the various orders were extruded on trays they were deftly removed by Clockwork Kitty and handed to the correct recipients. Bowls of nuts and dishes of tiny savories were placed on convenient low tables.

George Whitley Grimes raised his condensation-misted glass of beer to his son and said, "Here's to crime!"

The two girls, who also were drinking beer, raised their glasses. Grimes raised his glass of pink gin. Matilda Grimes set her sherry down firmly on the table.

"That," she stated, "is a dangerous toast to be drinking in the presence of this son of mine. I still have not forgotten that court of inquiry into the piracy with which he was involved. We have yet to hear, from his lips, the full story of what happened when he was Governor of Liberia—but I have little doubt that there were more than a few illegalities. . . ."

"Not committed by me, Matilda," Grimes told her. "Don't forget that *I* was the Law, trying to put a stop to other people's illegal profits."

"Hah!" his mother snorted. "Oh, well, you weren't impeached. I suppose that we must thank the Odd Gods of the Galaxy for small mercies. But we have yet to hear about what really happened on New Sparta. . . ."

"You shall, my dear, you shall." He laughed. "Oh, I was guilty of one crime. I did 'borrow' a Survey Service courier. . . ."

"And you crashed it," said Darleen a little maliciously.

"It was the fault of the weather," said Grimes.

Matilda laughed. "All right, all right, And I suppose that you still hold that reserve commission in the Survey Service that's supposed to be such a secret and get sent hither and yon to do that man Damien's dirty work for him." She looked long and hard at Shirl and Darleen. "And am I right in assuming that the pair of you are also members of the good admiral's department of dirty tricks?"

The girls looked inquiringly at Grimes. He decided that he had better answer for them.

"If you must know—but keep it strictly to yourself—Shirl and Darleen are both probationary ensigns in the Service."

"And what is their specialty?" asked Matilda.

"Unarmed combat," Grimes told her. "Or combat with anything handy, and preferably sharp, that can be flung. Such as . . ."

Shirl picked up a shallow, round dish that was now empty. She turned it over so that its convexity was on the down side. With a sharp flick of her wrist she threw it from her. It circled the room, returned to her waiting hand.

"Flying saucers yet!" said Grimes's father.

After a second drink they went in to the dinner that was served by the efficient Clockwork Kitty. With the first course there was some slight embarrassment. It was Grimes's fault, of course. (But just about everything was.) He should have told his mother that the ancestors of the New Alicians had been kangaroos. Even though these people were now classed as human and, like true humans descended from the original killer ape, omnivorous, they refused kangaroo tail soup, once they learned what it was. But they had strong stomachs and enjoyed the excellent crown roast of lamb once they had been assured that it was of ovine origin.

Grimes himself managed a good dinner despite the fact that he was talking most of the time. He had not been able to visit his parents on the first occasion of his return to Earth from Liberia, via New Sparta. A very thorough debriefing had occupied practically all of his time. So now there were questions to be answered, stories to be told. He was still answering questions and telling stories when the party returned to the lounge for coffee and brandy. Grimes and his father smoked their pipes, Matilda cigarillo and Shirl and Darleen—they were picking up bad habits—cigarettes in long, elegant, bejeweled holders.

Finally Darleen seemed to be having trouble stifling a yawn. It was infectious. George said, "I don't know about you people, but I'm turning in." Darleen said, "If you do not mind, Matilda, we shall do so too."

Matilda grinned. "Not with my old man, you won't! The maid will show you to your rooms."

Clockwork Kitty led them away, leaving Grimes alone with his mother.

She smiled at him a little sadly. She said, "I need hardly ask you, John, need I? But, just to satisfy my curiosity, which one is it?"

Grimes was frank.

"Both of them," he said.

"What! Not both at once?"

As a matter of fact this had been known but Grimes' mother was, in some ways, rather prudish. And, apart from anything else, there was the matter of miscegenation. The old prejudice against the underpeople still lingered.

"Shirl," lied Grimes.

"I really don't know how you can tell one from the other. Well, John, you're a big boy now, a four ring captain *and* a shipowner, and you've been a planetary governor . . . *And* commodore of a pirate squadron," she added maliciously. "You're old enough and wicked enough to look after yourself. And the girls' rooms are next to yours in the west wing.

"But I do wish that you would find some nice, *human* girl and settle down. Isn't it time?"

"I'll get around to it eventually," he promised her.

He kissed her good night then made his way to his quarters. The double bed, he saw, was already occupied. By Shirl.

And Darleen.

Chapter 5

"Wakey, wakey!" caroled an annoyingly cheerful female voice. There was a subdued clatter as the tea tray was placed on the bedside table. Morning sunlight flooded the room as curtains were drawn back. "Rise and shine! Rise and shine for the Black Ball Line!"

Grimes unglued his eyelids and looked up at Clockwork Kitty as she stood over the tousled bed, the rays of the sun glitteringly reflected from the intricacy of moving clockwork under her transparent integument. (But those delicate wheels, on their jeweled pivots, were no more than decoration, an expensive camouflage for the real machinery of metal skeleton and powerful solenoids.) Somehow her vaguely oriental features, which possessed a limited mobility, managed to register disapproval. Although Shirl and Darleen had returned to their own rooms before dawn, it was obvious, from the state of the bed, that Grimes had not slept alone.

He blinked. Yes, that faint sneer was still there. A trick of the light? Just how intelligent was this robomaid? Oh, he was thinking of Clockwork Kitty as she—but spacemen are apt to think of almost any piece of mobile machinery as *she*. Just another example of his father's sense of humor, he decided. The old man had added certain expressions to her programming, just as he had added to her vocabulary. An historical novelist with a keen interest in maritime history would, of course, know the words of quite a few of the old sea chanteys, such as "rise and shine for the Black Ball Line" . . .

"Milk, sir? Sugar?"

The automaton poured and stirred efficiently, putting the milk and sugar into the cup first. (And that, remembered Grimes, was something that his mother always insisted on.)

"Thank you, Kitty," he said. (It cost nothing to be polite to robots, intelligent or not. And when one wasn't quite sure of a robot's actual intelligence it was better to play it safe.)

"Kitty, sir?"

"My name for you. When I first saw you I thought of you as 'Clockwork Kitty.'"

"The master's name for me," said the robomaid, "is Seiko. I was manufactured by the Seiko Corporation in Japan, the makers of this planet's finest household robots. Prior to our highly successful venture into the field of robotics we were, and indeed still are, the makers of this planet's finest timepieces. Robomaids such as myself are a memorial, as it were, to the Corporation's origins . . ."

"Yes, yes," Grimes interrupted hastily. What was coming out now was some of the original programming, a high-powered advertising spiel. "Very interesting, Kitty—sorry, Seiko. But I'd rather be getting showered, depilated and all the rest of it. What time is breakfast?"

"If you will make your order, sir, it will be ready shortly after you appear in the breakfast room."

"Surprise me," said Grimes.

He looked thoughtfully after the glittering figure as it moved silently and gracefully out of the room.

Grimes senior, who was a breakfast table conservative, tucked in to a large plate of fried eggs, bacon, sausages and country fried potatoes. Matilda toyed with a croissant and strawberry conserve. Shirl and Darleen seemed to be enjoying helpings of kedgeree. And for Grimes, after he had finished his half grapefruit, Seiko produced one of his favorite dishes, and one that he had not enjoyed for quite a long time. The plump kippers, served with a side plate of thickly cut new brown bread and butter, tasted as good as they looked.

Matilda, he decided, must have told Seiko what he would like. He commented on this. She, looking surprised, said that she had given no orders whatsoever regarding her son's meal.

So . . . A lucky guess? Do robots guess? But Seiko was absent in the kitchen so he could not make further inquiries until she returned to clear the table. And when she did so the humans were busy discussing the day's activities.

George Grimes said, "I'm afraid that I shall have to leave you young people to your own resources today. I've a deadline to meet. The trouble with the novel I'm working on now is that I'm having to *work* on it. It's just not writing itself."

"Why not, George?" asked Grimes.

"Because it's set in a period of Australian history that, somehow, makes no great appeal to me. Eureka Stockade and all that. I somehow can't empathize with any of the characters. And, although it's regarded by rather too many historians as a minor revolution that might have blown up into something larger, it was nothing of the kind. It was no more than a squalid squabble between tax evaders and tax collectors. But I got a handsome advance before I started writing it, so I'd better deliver on time."

"And I have to stay in today myself," said Matilda. "I've got the ladies of the Alice Springs Literary Society coming round for lunch. I'm afraid that you'd find them as boring as all hell—as I do myself, frankly. So why not take the car, John, and a packed midday meal, and just cruise around? I'd suggest Ayers Rock and the Olgas, but at this time of the year they're *infested* with tourists. But the desert itself is always fascinating."

And so it was that, an hour later, Grimes, Shirl and Darleen were speeding away from the low, rambling house, heading out over the almost featureless desert, the great plume of fine, red dust raised by the vehicle's fans swirling in their wake.

Grimes gave Ayers Rock and Mount Olga a wide berth—the one squatting on the horizon like a huge, red toad, the other looking like some domed city erected on an airless planet. Over each hovered a sizeable fleet of tourist dirigibles. Grimes could imagine what conditions would be like on the ground—the souvenir stalls, the refreshment stands, the canned music, the milling crowds. Some time he would have to visit the Rock and the Olgas again, but not today.

He came to the Uluru Irrigation Canal. He did not cross it but followed its course south. The artificial waterway was poorly maintained; the agricultural project that it had been designed to service had been cancelled, largely due to pressure by the conservationists. But water still flowed sluggishly in the ditch and, here and there along its length, were billabongs, one of which Grimes had known very well in his youth. It would be good, he hoped, to visit it again.

And there were the tall ghost gums standing around and among the water-worn rocks that some civil engineer with the soul of a landscape gardener had brought in, probably at great expense, to make the artificial pool look natural. And there was the water, inviting, surprisingly clear, its surface dotted here and there with floating blossoms. These were not of Terran origin but were, as a matter of fact, Grimes' own contribution to the amenities of this pleasant oasis, carnivorous plants, insectivores, from Caribbea. The billabong was free from mosquitoes and other such pests. (He recalled that some businessman had wanted to import these flowers in quantity but the conservationists had screamed about upsetting the balance of nature.)

He stopped the car just short of the ornamental bounders. He and the girls got out, walked to the steeply shelving beach of red sand. He said, "How about a swim?"

"Crocodiles?" asked Shirl dubiously.

"There weren't any last time I was here."

"When was that?" asked Darleen.

"Oh, about five Earth years ago."

He got out of his shirt, shorts and underthings, kicked off his sandals. As one the girls peeled the white T shirts from the upper parts of their tanned bodies, stepped out of their netherwear. Naked, long-legged and small-breasted, they seemed to belong to this landscape, more than did Grimes himself. They waded out into the deeper water. Grimes followed them. The temperature of the sun-warmed pool was pleasant. They played like overgrown children with a beach ball that some family party had left on the sand. (So other people had found his private billabong, thought Grimes. He hoped that they had enjoyed it as much as he was doing now.) They decorated each other's bodies with the gaudy water lilies, the tendrils of which clung harmlessly to their wet skins. Finally they emerged from the water and stretched themselves to dry off on the surface of a large, flat rock which was partially shielded from the harsh sunlight by the ghost gums.

Then Grimes felt hungry. He got to his feet and walked to the hover car, taking from it the hamper that had been packed by Seiko. The sandwiches were to his taste—ham with plenty of mustard, a variety of strong cheeses—and the girls enjoyed the sweet and savory pastries and the fresh fruits. The cans of beer, from their own special container, were nicely chilled.

Replete, Grimes got his pipe and tobacco from his clothing and indulged in a satisfying smoke. The New Alicians sat on either side of him in oddly prim postures, their legs tucked under them.

Grimes was feeling poetic.

" 'Give me a book of verses 'neath the bough,' " he quoted,

" 'A loaf of bread, a flask of wine, and thou,

" 'Beside me, singing in the wilderness . . .

" 'And wilderness were Paradise enow.' "

He laughed. "But I don't have a book of verses. And, come to that, I've never heard either of you singing. . . ."

"There is a time to sing. . . ." murmured Shirl. "And this could be such a time. . . ."

And Darleen had found two large, smooth pebbles, about the size of golf balls, and was clicking them together with an odd, compelling rhythm. Both girls were crooning softly to the beat of the singing stones. There was melody, of a sort, soft and hypnotic. Grimes felt the goose pimples rising all over his skin.

They were not alone. He and the girls were not alone. Silently the kangaroos had come from what had seemed to be empty desert, were standing all around them, regarding them solemnly with their huge eyes. There were big reds and grays and smaller animals. It was as though every variety of kangaroo in all of Australia had answered the New Alicians' summons.

Shirl and Darleen got to their feet. And then, suddenly, they were gone, bounding away over the desert at the head of the mob of kangaroos. It was hard to distinguish them from the animals despite their smooth skins.

What now? wondered Grimes. *What now?* He was, he supposed, responsible for the girls. Should he get into the hover car and give chase? Or would that make matters worse? He stood and watched the cloud of red dust, raised by the myriad bounding feet, diminishing in the distance.

But they were coming back, just the two of them, just Shirl and Darleen. They were running gracefully, not proceeding in a series of bounds. They flung themselves on Grimes, their sweaty, dusty bodies hot against his bare skin. It was rape, although the man was a willing enough victim. They had him, both of them, in turn, again and again.

Finally, exhausted, they rolled off him.

"After the kangaroos . . ." gasped Shirl.

"We had to prove to ourselves . . ." continued Darleen.

". . . and to you . . ."

". . . that we are really human . . ."

Grimes found his pipe, which, miraculously, had not been broken during the assault, and his pouch, the contents of which were unspilled. He lit up with a not very steady hand.

"Of course you're human," he said at last. "The Law says so."

"But the heritage is strong, John."

"You aren't the only ones with a heritage—but you don't see me swinging from the branches of trees, do you?"

They all laughed then, and shared the last can of beer, and had a last refreshing swim in the waters of the billabong. They resumed their clothing and got back into the hover car, looking forward to an enjoyable evening of good food and conversation to add the finishing touches to what had been a very enjoyable day.

They were not expecting to find the Grimes home knee deep in acrimony.

Chapter 6

The garage door slid open as the hovercar approached but the robomaid was not waiting to receive them and to take custody of the empty hamper. Grimes was not concerned about this; no doubt, he thought, Seiko was busy with some domestic task. He led the two girls into the house, toward the lounge. He heard the voices of his mother and father, although it was his mother who seemed to be doing most of the talking. She sounded as though she were in what her husband and son referred to as one of her flaring rages. *What's the old man been up to now?* wondered Grimes.

"Either that *thing* goes or *I* go!" he heard his mother declare.

"But I find her more satisfactory . . ."his father said.

"You would. You've a warped mind, George Grimes, as I've known, to my cost, for years. But you'll ship that toy of yours back to Tokyo and demand your money back. . . ."

"Hi, folks," said Grimes as he entered the room.

Matilda favored him with no more than a glance, his father looked toward him appealingly.

"John," he said, "perhaps you can talk some sense into your mother. You, as a space captain of long experience, know far more about such matters than either of us. . . ."

"What matters?" asked Grimes.

"You may well ask," Matilda told him. "Such matters as insubordination, mutiny. In my own home. . . ."

"Insubordination? Mutiny?" repeated Grimes in a puzzled voice.

"And unprovoked assault upon my guests. My guests."

Grimes sat down, pulled his pipe from his pocket, filled and lit it. Shirl and Darleen did not take seats but looked questioningly at Matilda, who said, "Perhaps, dears, it might be better if you went to your rooms for a while. This is a family matter."

The girls left, albeit with reluctance. Grimes settled down in his chair and assumed a magisterial pose. George Grimes was sitting on the edge of his seat, looking as uncomfortable as he almost certainly was feeling.

"I have had my suspicions for a long time . . ." began Matilda.

Surely not . . . wondered Grimes. *The old man's not that kinky . . .*

"Quite a long time," she went on. "But it was only after you and the girls had left this morning for your ride in the desert that I began to be sure. I hope that you had a pleasant day, by the way. . . ."

"Very pleasant," said Grimes.

"Well, you remember what you had for breakfast. Kippers. You asked me if I'd told *it* to do them for you. I said that I had not. I was curious, so I asked *it* why *it* had served you kippers. It told me that you had asked it to surprise you. So I asked it how it had decided that kippers would be a nice surprise. It told me that normally there are never kippers in my larder but that I had ordered a supply after I'd gotten word that you were coming. . . ."

"And so?" asked Grimes.

"A domestic robot is supposed to do only what it's been programmed to do. It's not supposed to possess such qualities as initiative and imagination. Oh, I know that there are some truly intelligent robots—but such are very, very expensive and are not to be found doing menial jobs. But knowing George, I suspected that he had been doing some more tinkering with *its* programming. His idea of a joke.

"Well, as you already know, I was entertaining the local literary ladies to luncheon. The President of the Society is Dame Mabel Prendergast. Don't ask me how she got made a dame, although she's made an enormous pile of money writing slush. She could afford to buy a title. Anyhow, dear Mabel is just back from a galactic cruise. She was all tarted up in obviously expensive clothing in the very worst of taste that she had purchased on the various worlds that she had visited. Her hat, she told us, came from Carinthia, where glass-weaving is one of the esteemed arts and crafts. Oh, my dear, it was a most elaborate construction, perched on top of her head like a sort of glittering fairy castle. It was, in its way, beautiful—but not on her. Human hippopotami should not wear such things.

"We had lunch. *It* did the serving, just as a robomaid should, efficiently and without any gratuitous displays of initiative, imagination or whatever. The ladies admired *it* and Mabel remarked, rather jealously, that George's thud-and-blunder books, as she referred to them, must be doing quite well. We retired to the lounge for coffee and brandy and then one or two of the old biddies started making inquiries about my famous son. *You*. And wasn't it time that you settled down? And who were the two pretty girls you'd brought with you? They weren't Terran, were they?

"I told them—all the more fool me, but I suppose that the brandy had loosened my tongue—that Shirl and Darleen were from a world called New Alice, with a very Australianoid culture. I told them, too, that they were now junior officers board your ship and that, until recently, they had been officers in the elite Amazon Guard on New Sparta. Mabel said that they didn't look butch military types. I said that, as a matter of fact, they had been officer instructors, specializing in teaching the use of throwing weapons, such as boomerangs. And that they could make almost anything behave like a boomerang. Mabel said that she didn't think that this was possible. I told her that Shirl—or was it Darleen?—had given a demonstration in this very room, using a round, shallow dish . . .

"Mabel said, quite flatly, that this would be quite impossible and started blathering about the laws of aerodynamics. She had, she assured us, made a thorough study of these before writing her latest book, about a handsome young professional hang glider racer and a lady trapeze artiste. . . ."

"Did they . . . er . . . mate in midair?" asked Grimes interestedly.

"Your mind is as low as your father's," Matilda told him crossly. "Anyhow, there was this argument. And *it*—may its clockwork heart rust solid!—decided, very kindly, to settle it for us. It asked, very politely, "May I demonstrate, madam?" and before I could say no it emptied the chocolate mints out of their dish, on to the table, turned the dish upside down and with a flick of its wrist sent it sailing around the room . . .

"Oh, it did actually come back—but just out of reach of that uppity robot's outstretched hand. It crashed into Dame Mabel's hat. That hat, it seems, was so constructed as to be proof against all normal stresses and strains but there must have been all sorts of tensions locked up in its strands. When the dish—it was one of those copper ones—hit it there was an explosion, with glass splinters and powder flying in all directions. By some miracle nobody was seriously hurt, although old Tanitha Evans got a rather bad cut and Lola Lee got powdered glass in her right eye. I had to send for Dr. Namatjira—and you know what *he* charges for house calls. And, of course, I shall have to pay for Dame Mabel's hat. Anybody would think that the bloody thing was made of diamonds!"

"And where is Seiko now?" asked Grimes.

"Seiko? *It*, you mean. It is back in the crate that it came in, and there it stays. It's too dangerous to be allowed to run around loose."

"She was only trying to be helpful," said Grimes.

"It's not its job to try to be helpful. It's its job to do as it's told, just that and nothing more."

"What do you know about the so-called wild robots, John?" asked his father suddenly.

"Not much. The roboticists are rather close-mouthed about such matters. Even the Survey Service does not have access to all the information it should. Oh, there are standing orders to deal with such cases. They boil down to Deactivate At Once And Return To Maker or, if deactivation is not practicable, Destroy By Any Means Possible."

"Just what I've been telling George," said Matilda smugly.

"But from your experience, which is much greater than mine, how would you define a wild robot?" asked George.

"Mphm," grunted Grimes. "Well, there are robots, not necessarily humanoid, which are designed to be intelligent and which acquire very real characters. There was Big Sister, the computer-pilot of the Baroness Michelle d'Estang's space-yacht. There was a Mr. Adam, with whom I tangled, many, many years ago when I was a Survey Service courier captain. There have been others. All of them were designed to be rational, thinking beings. But a normal pilot-computer is no more than an automatic pilot. It does no more than what it's been programmed to. If some emergency crops up that has not been included in its programming it just sits on its metaphorical backside and does nothing."

"But the rogue robots," persisted George. "The wild robots. . . ."

"I don't *know*. But among spacemen there are all sorts of theories. One is that there has been some slight error made during the manufacture of the . . . the brain. May as well call it that. Some undetectable defect in a microchip. A defect that really isn't a defect at all, since it achieves a result that would be hellishly expensive if done on purpose. Another theory is that exposure to radiation is the cause. And there's one really far-fetched one—association with humans of more than average intelligence and creativity."

"I like that," said George.

"You would, Herr Doktor Frankenstein," sneered Matilda. "But, from what I've told you, do you think that we've a wild robot on our hands, John?"

"It seems like it," said Grimes.

The next morning the carriers came to remove the crate into which Seiko had been packed. Grimes went with his father into the storeroom, watched with some regret as the spidery stowbot picked up the long, coffin-like box and carried it out to the waiting hovervan. He thought nothing of it when George ran out to the vehicle before it departed, to exchange a few words with the driver and, it seemed, to resecure the label on the crate, which must have come loose.

George rejoined his son.

"Well," he said, "that's that. Luckily Matilda's a good cook; like you, she can get the best out of an autochef. You and the girls won't starve for the remainder of your stay here."

Nor did they.

Chapter 7

The days passed quickly. George Whitley Grimes had gotten over his sulks about being deprived of his glittering toy and Matilda Grimes had forgiven her husband for the damage done by Seiko. The two girls fitted into the family life well. "They're much too nice for you, John," his mother told him one morning over coffee. The two of them had gone into Alice Springs on a shopping expedition and were enjoying refreshment in one of the better cafés. (George was still working on his Eureka Stockade novel and Shirl and Darleen had gone off to practice with the traditional boomerangs that they had been given by Dr. Namatjira, whose calls now were social rather than professional.)

"They're much too nice, for you," she said. "And I'm not at all sure that I approve of their traveling in your ship as crew members, among all those brutal and licentious spacemen."

"And spacewomen." He laughed. "My third officer is Tomoko Suzuki, a real Japanese doll. . . ."

"Not like Seiko, I hope."

"No. Her innards aren't on display. And my radio officer is Cleo Jones, black and beautiful. Her nickname, of which she's rather proud, is the Zulu Princess. The second Mannschenn Drive engineer is Sarah Smith. One of those tall, slim, handsome academic females. Three of the inertial/reaction drive engineers, the chief, second and fourth, are women. The chief's name is Florence Scott. She looks like what she is, an extremely competent mechanic, and her sex somehow doesn't register. The second is Juanita Garcia. If you were casting an amateur production of *Carmen* you'd try to get her for the title role. She has the voice as well as the looks. The fourth is Cassandra Perkins. Like Cleo, she's a negress.

But she's short and plump and very jolly, so much so that she gets away with things that anybody else would be hauled over the coals for. . . ."

"Such as . . . ?"

"Such as the time when she was doing some minor repairs to the ship's plumbing system and bungled some fantastic cross-connection so that the hot water taps ran ice water."

"That might have been intentional. Her idea of a joke."

"If it was, the laugh was on her. She was the first victim. She thought that she'd like a nice, hot shower after she came off watch at midnight, ship's time. Her screams woke all hands." Grimes sipped his coffee and then went on philosophically. "With all her faults, she's a good shipmate. She's fun. Even old Flo, her chief, admits it. What none of us can tolerate is somebody who's highly inefficient *and* a bad shipmate."

"And the other way around?" Matilda asked. "Somebody who's highly efficient but a bad shipmate?"

Grimes sighed. "One just has to suffer such people. My new chief officer seems to be one such. Lieutenant Commander Harald Steerforth, Survey Service Reserve. Harald, with an 'a.' Steerforth. The last of the vikings. Give him a blond beard to match his hair and a horned helmet and he'd look the part. And he's indicated that, as my second in command, he intends to run a taut ship . . ."

"My nose fair bleeds for you," said Matilda inelegantly. "But you haven't mentioned your catering officer yet. Aren't spaceship catering officers almost invariably women?"

"They are. But when I left Port Woomera I still hadn't got a replacement for Magda, who's on leave."

"You should have asked your father for Seiko, and signed *it*—I refuse to call that thing *her*—on."

Shopping done—mainly pieces of Aboriginal artwork as gifts for Shirl and Darleen—Grimes and his mother returned home. When George heard them enter the house he came out from his study and said, "There was a call for you, John. From your ship. Your chief officer, a Mr. Steerforth. He seemed rather annoyed to learn that you hadn't been sitting hunched over the phone all day and every day waiting for him to get in touch." He gave his son a slip of paper. "He asked me—no, damn it, he practically ordered me—to ask you to call him at this number."

The number Grimes recognized. It was the one that had been allocated to his ship at Port Woomera.

"And I shall be greatly obliged," said the old man, "if you will reverse charges."

"Don't be a tightwad, George!" admonished Matilda.

"I'm not a tightwad. This is obviously ship's business. John is a wealthy shipowner; I'm only a poor, struggling writer. And after I've paid for Dame Mabel's hat I shall be even poorer!"

"It was your absurdly expensive mechanical toy that destroyed the hat!"

Grimes left them to it, went to the extention telephone in his bedroom. He got through without trouble, telling the roboperator to charge the call to his business credit card account. The screen came alive and the pretty face of Tomoko Suzuki appeared. She smiled as she saw Grimes in the screen at her end and said brightly, "Ah, Captain-san. . . ."

"Yes, it's me, Tomoko-san. Can you get Mr. Steerforth for me, please?"

"One moment, Captain-san."

In a remarkably short space of time Tomoko's face in the screen was replaced by that of the chief officer.

"Sir!" said that gentleman smartly.

"Yes, Mr. Steerforth?" asked Grimes.

"Discharge has commenced, sir. I have been informed by Admiral Damien that the Survey Service wishes to charter the ship for a one way voyage to Pleth, with a cargo of stores and equipment for the sub-base on that planet. He wishes to discuss with you details of further employment and intimated that your return to Woomera as soon as possible will be appreciated. . . ."

Not only appreciated by Damien, thought Grimes, but necessary. He had his living to earn.

He said, "I shall return by the first flight tomorrow. Meanwhile, how are things aboard the ship?"

"We have a new catering officer, sir. A Ms. Melinda Clay. She appears to be quite competent. There is some mail for you, of course. I have opened the business letters and, in accordance with your instructions, dealt with such matters, small accounts and such, as came within my provenance as second in command. Personal correspondence has been untouched."

"Thank you, Mr. Steerforth. I shall see you early tomorrow afternoon."

He hung up, rejoined his parents in the lounge.

"My holiday's over," he announced regretfully. "It was far too short."

"It certainly has been," said Matilda.

"And where are you off to this time, John?" asked his father.

"Pleth. A one voyage charter. Survey Service stores. Probably a full load of forms to be filled out in quintuplicate."

"And after that? Back to Earth with a full load of similar forms filled in?"

"I don't know, George. The mate told me that Damien has some further employment in mind for me."

"No more privateering?" asked the old man a little wistfully. "No more appointments as governor general?"

"I hope not," Grimes told him. "But, knowing Damien, and knowing something of the huge number of pies that he has a finger in, I suspect that it will be something . . . interesting."

"And disreputable, no doubt," snapped Matilda. "When you were a regular officer in the Service you never used to get into all these scrapes."

"Mphm?" grunted Grimes dubiously. He'd been getting into scrapes for as long as he could remember.

Shirl and Alice came in, accompanied by Dr. Namatjira. The doctor, who had joined them at their boomerang practice, was glowing with admiration. "If only I had a time machine!" he exclaimed. "If only I could send them back to the early days of my people in this country, before the white man came! They could have instructed us in the martial arts, especially those involved with the use of flung missiles." He grinned whitely. "Captain Cook, and all those who followed him, would have been driven back into the sea!"

"I might just use that," murmured Grimes senior. "It sounds much more fun that what I'm doing now. That boring Peter Lalor and his bunch of drunken roughnecks. . . ."

Matilda served afternoon tea. After this the doctor said his farewells and made his departure. He expressed the sincere hope that he would be meeting Shirl and Darleen again in the not too distant future.

"Bring them back, John," he admonished. "They belong here. They are like beings from our Dream Time, spirits made flesh . . ."

And then there was what would be the last family dinner for quite some time, with talk lasting long into the night. It would have lasted much longer but Grimes and the girls had an early morning flight to catch.

Chapter 8

It was a pleasant enough flight back to Port Woomera. Again Grimes, and with him the two girls, was a guest in the airship's control cab. On this occasion, however, the captain, a different one, did not say anything to antagonize his privileged passengers. The three of them made their way from the airport to the spaceport by monorail and then by robocab to the ship.

The efficient Mr. Steerforth was waiting by the ramp as the cab pulled up, saluted with Survey Service big ship smartness as his captain got out. He said, "Leave your baggage, sir, I'll have it brought up." He followed Grimes into the after airlock, but not before he had ordered sharply, "Ms. Kelly, Ms. Byrne, look after the master's gear, will you?"

Grimes heard a not quite suppressed animal growl from either Shirl or Darleen and with an effort managed not to laugh aloud. Well, he thought, the two New Alicians would have to start learning that, as cadets, they were the lowest form of life aboard *Sister Sue*. . . .

He and the chief officer took the elevator up to the captain's flat. He let himself into his day cabin, thinking that, much as he had enjoyed the break, it was good to be back. But had somebody been interfering with the layout of the furniture? Had something been added?

Something had—a long case, standing on end.

Steerforth saw him looking at it and said, "This came for you, sir. Special delivery, from Alice Springs. Probably something you purchased there, sir, too heavy and cumbersome to carry with you on your flight."

"Probably," said Grimes. "But I'll catch up with my mail, Mr. Steerforth, before I unpack it. I'll yell for you as soon as I'm through."

"Very good, sir."

His curiosity unsatisfied, Steerforth left the cabin. He said to Shirl and Darleen, who were about to enter with Grimes' baggage, "Report to me as soon as the captain's finished with you."

Shirl said, "I liked Billy Williams."

Darleen said, "So did I."

Grimes said, "Billy Williams earned his long service leave. And try to remember, young ladies, that when you knew Billy Williams you were passengers in this ship, and privileged. Now you are *very* junior officers and Mr. Steerforth is a senior officer, my second in command. Meanwhile, I still have a job for you. To help me unpack this."

Like most spacemen he always carried on his person a multi-purpose implement that was called, for some forgotten reason, a Swiss Army Knife. (Once Grimes had asked his father about it and had been told that there was, a long time ago, a Swiss Army and that a special pocketknife had been invented for the use of its officers, incorporating a variety of tools, so that they would never lack the means to open a bottle of wine or beer.)

Anyhow, Grimes' pocket toolchest had a suitable screwdriver. He used it while Shirl and Darleen held the long box steady. At last he had all the securing screws out of the lid and gently pried it away from the body of the case, put it to one side on the deck. And then there was the foam plastic packing to be dealt with. He knew what he would find as he pulled it away.

She stood there in her box, her transparent skin glistening, the ornamental complexity of shining wheels on their jeweled pivots motionless. And he stood there looking at her, hesitant. He knew the simple procedure for activation—but should he?

Why not?

He inserted the index finger of his right hand into her navel, pressed. He heard the sharp click. He saw the transparent eyelids—a rather absurd refinement!—open and a faint flicker of light in the curiously blank eyes. He saw the wheels of the spurious clockwork mechanism begin to turn, some slowly, some spinning rapidly. There was a barely audible ticking.

The lips moved and. . . .

"Hello, sailor," said Seiko seductively.

"Mphm," grunted Grimes. Then, gesturing toward the litter of foam packing, "Get this mess cleaned up."

Shirl and Darleen laughed.

"Now there's somebody else to do the fetching and carrying!" said one of them.

Grimes dealt with his mail while Seiko busied herself with what Grimes thought was quite unnecessary dusting and polishing. There was a letter from his father, written before Grimes had left the family home to return to his ship. *I don't like the idea of returning Seiko to the makers,* the old man had written. *They'd take her apart to find out what went wrong—or went right!—and when they put her together again she'd be no more than just another brainless robomaid with no more intelligence than a social insect. And she would, of course, lose her personality. I'm hoping that you'll be able to use her aboard your ship, as your personal servant. . . .*

Then there was a brief note from Admiral Damien, inviting him—or ordering him—to dinner in the admiral's own dining room that evening.

He was interrupted briefly by his new catering officer, Melinda Clay. He looked up at her approvingly. She was a tall woman, of the same race as Cleo Jones, the radio officer, and Cassandra Perkins, the fourth RD engineer. She was at least as beautiful as Cleo, although in a different way. The hair of her head was snowy white, in vivid contrast to the flawless black skin of her face. Natural or artificial? Grimes wondered.

"I came up, sir," she said, "to introduce myself. . . ."

"I'm very happy to have you aboard, Ms. Clay," said Grimes, extending his hand.

She shook it, then went on, "And to find out, before the voyage starts, if you have any special preferences in the way of food and drink. That way I can include such items in my stores."

"Unluckily," laughed Grimes, "my very special preferences are also very expensive—and as owner, as well as master, I should have to foot the bill. Just stock up normally. And I'm quite omnivorous. As long as the food is good, I'll eat it. . . ."

Seiko came out of the bathroom, where she had been giving the shower fittings a thorough polishing.

Melinda's eyes widened. "What a lovely robot! I didn't know that you carried your own robomaid."

"I didn't know myself until I unpacked her. She's a gift, from my father."

"She? But of course, sir. You could hardly call such a beautiful thing *it.*"

"Seiko," said Grimes, "this is Ms. Clay, my catering officer. When you are not looking after me—and I do not require much looking after—you will act as her assistant."

"Your father's last instructions to me, sir," said Seiko, "were that I was to be your personal servant."

"And *my* instructions to you," said Grimes firmly, "are that you are to consider yourself a member of the domestic staff of this vessel. Your immediate superior is Ms. Clay."

"Yes, Massa."

"Seiko, you are not supposed to have a sense of humor."

Melinda Clay laughed. "Don't be so serious, captain! I'm sure that Seiko and I will get on very well."

A slave and the descendant of slaves . . . thought Grimes wryly.

Chapter 9

Damien had another dinner guest, a tall, severely black-clad, gray-haired woman, with classic perfect features, who was introduced to Grimes as Madam Duvalier, First Secretary of the Aboriginal Protection Society. Grimes had already heard of this body, although it was of quite recent origin. It had been described in an editorial in *The Ship Operators' Journal*, to which publication Grimes subscribed, as an organization of trendy do-gooders obstructing honest commercial progress. And there had been cases, Grimes knew, where the APS had done much more harm than good. Their campaign on behalf of the down-trodden Droogh, for example. . . . The Droogh were one of the two sentient races inhabiting a world called Tarabel, an Earth-type planet. They were a sluggish, reptilian people, living in filth, literally, because they liked it, practicing cannibalism as a means of population control, fanatically worshipping a deity called The Great Worm who could be dissuaded from destroying the Universe only by regular, bloody sacrifices of any life-form unlucky enough to fall into Droogh clutches. The other sentient race on Tarabel had been the Marmura, vaguely simian, although six-limbed beings. It was with them that the first Terran traders had dealt, taking in exchange for manufactured goods, including firearms, bales of tanned Droogh hides. It was learned later—too late—that, at first, these hides had been the left-overs from the Droogh cannibal feasts. A little later many of the hides had come from Droogh who had been killed, by machine gun fire, when mounting unprovoked attacks on Marmuran villages, the purpose of which had been to obtain raw material for blood sacrifices to The Great Worm.

Somebody in the Walk Proud Shoe Factory just outside New York had become curious about obvious bulletholes in Droogh hides and had gone to the trouble of getting information about Tarabel and had learned that the Droogh were sentient beings. Then APS had gotten into the act. A SAVE THE DROOGH! campaign was mounted. Pressure was exerted upon the Bureau of Extraterrestrial Affairs. A Survey Service cruiser was dispatched to Tarabel, not to investigate (which would have made sense) but to disarm the Marmura. This was done, although not without loss of life on both sides. Then the cruiser was called away on some urgent business elsewhere in the galaxy.

The next ship to make planetfall on Tarabel was a Dog Star Line tramp. Her captain did not get the expected consignment of Droogh hides—and, in any case, there weren't any Marmura for him to trade with. In the ruins of the small town near the primitive spaceport were several Droogh. These tried to interest him in a few bales of badly tanned, stinking Marmura skins. He was not interested and got upstairs in a hurry before things turned really nasty.

And the Droogh were left to their own, thoroughly unpleasant, devices.

Grimes remembered this story while he, the admiral and Madame Duvalier were sipping their drinks and chatting before dinner. Somehow the conversation got around to the problem of primitive aborigines introduced to modern technology, of how much interference with native cultures was justifiable.

"There was the Tarabel affair . . ." said Grimes.

The woman laughed ruefully.

"Yes," she admitted. "There was the Tarabel affair." She extended a slim foot shod in dull-gleaming, grained, very dark blue leather. "You will note, captain, that I have no qualms about wearing shoes made of Droogh hide. I know, now, that the late owner of the skin was either butchered by his or her own people for a cannibal feast or shot, in self defense, by the Marmura. We, at APS, should have been sure of our facts before we mounted our crusade in behalf of the Droogh.

"But tell me—and please be frank—what do you really think of people like ourselves? Those who are referred to, often as not, as interfering do-gooders. . . ."

Rear Admiral Damien laughed, a rare display of merriment, so uninhibited that the miniature medals on the left breast of his mess jacket tinkled.

"Young Grimes, Yvonne," he finally chuckled, "is the do-gooder of all do-gooders, although I've no doubt that he'll hate me for pinning that label on him. He's always on the side of the angels but, at the same time, contrives to make some sort of profit for himself."

Madame Duvalier permitted herself a faint smile. "But you still haven't answered my question, captain. What do you think of do-gooders? *Organized* do-gooders, such as APS."

"Mphm." Grimes took a large sip from his pink gin, then gained more time by refilling and lighting his pipe. "Mphm. Well, one trouble with do-gooders is that they, far too often, bust a gut on behalf of the thoroughly undeserving while ignoring the plight of their victims. They seem, far too often, to think that an unpopular cause is automatically a just cause. Most of the time it isn't. But, on the other hand, anybody backed by big business or big government is all too often a bad bastard. . . ."

"He may be a son of a bitch," contributed Damien, "but he's *our* son of a bitch."

"Yes. That's the attitude far too often, sir."

"And so, young Grimes, you're interfering, as a free-lance do-gooder, every time that you get the chance."

"I don't interfere, sir. Things sort of happen around me."

"Captain Grimes," said Damien to Madame Duvalier, "is a sort of catalyst. Put him in any sort of situation where things aren't quite right and they almost immediately start going from bad to worse. And then, when it's all over but the shouting—or, even, the shooting—who emerges from the stinking mess, smelling of violets, with the Shaara crown jewels clutched in his hot little hand? Grimes, that's who. And, at the same time, virtue is triumphant and vice defeated."

Grimes's prominent ears flushed. Was the Duvalier female looking at him with admiration or amusement?

The sound of a bugle drifted into Damien's sitting room—which could have been the admiral's day cabin aboard a grand fleet flagship. (Damien was a great traditionalist.) Damien got to his feet, extended an unnecessary hand to Madam Duvalier to help her to hers. He escorted the lady into the dining room, followed by Grimes.

The meal, served by smartly uniformed mess waiters, was pleasant enough although, thought Grimes, probably he would have fed better aboard his own ship. But in *Sister Sue* it was *his* tastes that were catered to, here, in Flag House, it was Damien's. The admiral liked his beef well done, Grimes liked his charred on the outside and raw on the inside. Even so, Grimes admitted, the old bastard knew his wines, the whites and the reds, the drys and the semi-sweets, each served with the appropriate course. But it was a great pity that whoever had assembled the cheese board had been so thoroughly uninspired.

During dinner the conversation was on generalities. And then, with the mess waiters dismissed, Damien and his guests returned to the sitting room for coffee (so-so) and brandy (good) and some real talking.

"Yvonne," said the admiral, "is one of the very few people who knows that you are back in the Survey Service, as a sort of trouble shooter. She thinks that you may be able to do some work for APS."

"Since the Tarabel bungle," the woman admitted, "APS doesn't have the influence in high government circles that it once did. But there are still wrongs that need righting, and still powerful business interests putting profits before all else. . . ."

"And how can I help?" asked Grimes. "After all, I represent a business interest myself, Far Traveler Couriers. Unless I make a profit I can't stay in business. And if I go broke I just can't see the Survey Service taking me back into the fold officially. . . ."

"Too right," murmured Damien.

"And I couldn't get into any of the major shipping lines without a big drop in rank. I don't fancy starting afresh as a junior officer at my age."

"Understandable," murmured Damien. "And I hope that *you* understand that you need the Survey Service, even though you are, in the eyes of most people, a civilian, and a rich shipowner."

"Rich!" interjected Grimes. "Ha!"

"Just try to remember how much of your income has been derived from lucrative business that we have put in your way. All the charters, time or voyage. Such as the one that you have now, the shipment of not very essential and certainly not urgently required stores to the sub-base on Pleth."

"And after Pleth? What then?"

"Arrangements have been made. It will just so happen that there will be a cargo offering from Pleth to New Otago. Pleth exports the so-called paradise fruit, canned. Have you ever sampled that delicacy?"

"Once," said Grimes. "I wasn't all that impressed. Too sweet. Not enough flavor."

"Apparently the New Otagoans like it. Now, listen carefully. Your trajectory will take you within spitting distance of New Salem. What do you know of Salem?"

"I've never been there, sir, but I seem to remember that it's famous for the animal furs, *very* expensive furs, that it exports. Quite a few of the very rich bitches on El Dorado like to tart themselves up in them. Oh, yes. And this fur export trade is the monopoly of Able Enterprises. . . ."

"Which outfit," said Damien, "is run by old cobber Commodore Baron Kane, of El Dorado."

"No cobber of mine," growled Grimes.

"But you know Kane. And you know that any enterprise in which he's involved is liable to be, at the very least, unsavory. Well, APS have heard stories about this fur trade. APS have asked me to carry out an investigation. After all, I'm only a rear admiral. But I have clashed, in the past, with the El Dorado Corporation and gotten away with it. . . ."

"With me as your cat's-paw," said Grimes.

"Precisely. And, admit it, it does give you some satisfaction to score off Kane. Doesn't it?"

"I suppose so."

"It does, and we both know it." He turned to Madame Duvalier. "Grimes and Kane are old enemies," he explained. "Apart from anything else there was rivalry for the favors of the Baroness Michelle d'Estang, who is now Kane's wife—hence his El Doradan citizenship."

Then, speaking again to Grimes, he went on, "I wanted to send a Survey Service ship to Salem on a flag-showing exercise but there just aren't any ships available. So I have to fall back on you."

"Thank you. Sir." Then, "But I shan't be bound for Salem."

"Officially, no. But look at it this way. You are bound from Point A to Point C, by-passing Point B. But then, in mid-voyage, something happens that obliges you to make for a port of refuge to carry out essential repairs or whatever. . . ."

"*What* something?" demanded Grimes.

"Use your imagination, young man."

"Mphm. . . . A leakage, into space, of my water reserves. . . . And, after all, water is required as reaction mass for my emergency rocket drive as well as for drinking, washing, etc. And so I get permission from the Salem aerospace authorities to make a landing, fill my tanks and lift off again. But I shall be on the planetary surface for a matter of hours only."

"Not if your inertial drive goes seriously on the blink just as you're landing."

"I'm not an engineer, sir, as well you know."

"But you have engineers, don't you? And among them is a Ms. Cassandra Perkins. Calamity Cassie."

"What do you know about her, sir?"

"I know that Lieutenant Commander Cassandra Perkins is an extremely skillful saboteur—or should that be saboteuse?"

"So she's one of your mob. . . ."

"And *your* mob, Captain Grimes. Federation Survey Service Reserve."

"All right. So I'm grounded on Salem for some indefinite period. And I suppose that I shall be required to do some sniffing around. . . ."

"You suppose correctly."

"Then why can't you do as you did before, give me one of your psionic communication officers, a trained telepath, to do the snooping?

You will recall that I carried your Lieutenant Commander Mayhew, as an alleged passenger, when I was involved in the El Doradan privateering affair."

"At the moment, Grimes, PCOs are as scarce as hen's teeth in the Service. The bastards have been resigning in droves, recruited by various industrial espionage outfits. You may have heard of the war—yes, you could call it that—being waged by quite a few companies throughout the Galaxy against the so-called Wizards of Electra. But you have Shirl and Darleen who, despite their official human status, possess great empathy with the lower animals."

"And so, with the skilled assistance of your Ms. Perkins. . . ."

"*Your* Ms. Perkins, Grimes. She's on your books."

". . . I'm to prolong my stay on Salem as long as possible, find out what I can, and then write a report for you."

"Yes. And, hopefully, act as a catalyst. You always do."

"That's what I'm afraid of," said Grimes.

Yvonne Duvalier broke the brief silence.

She said, "I don't think that you have put Captain Grimes sufficiently into the picture, admiral. To begin with, captain, there was what Admiral Damien refers to as a flag-showing exercise on New Salem. The destroyer *Pollux*. She carried, of course, a psionic communication officer. He was not a very experienced one but he suspected, strongly, that at least one of the species of fur-bearing animal on New Salem, the silkies, possessed intelligence up to human standards. They can think and feel, but their thought processes aren't the same as ours. And they are slaughtered for their pelts. Somehow his not very detailed report fell into our hands, at APS. The admiral has long been a friend of ours and promised to do something about it. And then, as you know, there was the Tarabel fiasco and the consequent reluctance of the authorities to rush to the aid of unpleasant and vicious extra-Terrans.

"Although the fur of the silkies is beautiful, as you probably know, they are ugly beasts. They have, in the past, attacked the coastwise villages of the human colonists of New Salem. They have mutilated rather than killed, biting the hands off men, women and children. There are some rather horrid photographs of such victims.

"The New Salem colonists are the descendants of a religious sect that emigrated from Earth during the Second Expansion. Fundamentalists, maintaining that God gave Man dominion over all other life forms. They have their own version, their own translation of the Holy Bible, the Old Testament only. Their God is a jealous God, taking a dim view of any who do not believe as the True Believers, as they call themselves, do. But they do not mind taking the money of those who are not True Believers. They have a huge account in the Galactic Bank, more than enough to pay for the occasional shipments of manufactured goods that they receive from the industrial planets. Popular belief is that, eventually, their funds will be used for the building of a huge Ark in which they, and they alone, will escape the eventual collapse of the Universe."

"Where will they escape to?" asked Grimes interestedly.

Damien laughed. "I don't suppose they know themselves. Perhaps they just hope to drift around until the next Big Bang, and then get in on the ground floor and start the human race again the way it should be started, free of all perversions. . . ." Suddenly he looked at Grimes very keenly. "Talking of perversions, young man, I hear that you are perverting Survey Service Regulations."

"*Me*, sir?"

"Yes. You. The regulations regarding wild robots. I hear that you have one such aboard your ship. You have neither deactivated it and returned it to its makers nor destroyed it."

"I suppose that Mr. Steerforth told you, sir."

"Never mind who told me. I just know."

"I'd like to make it plain, sir, that my ship is *my* ship. I am the owner as well as the master. Until, if ever, she is officially commissioned as an auxiliary unit of the Survey Service she is a merchant ship. The regulations to which her personnel are subject are company's regulations. In this case, *my* regulations."

"Always the space lawyer, Grimes, aren't you?"

"Yes. I have to be."

Damien grinned. "Very well, then. I'll just hope that your Seiko, as I understand that you call the thing, will be just another catalyst thrown into the New Salem crucible. Two wild girls, one wild robot and, the wildest factor of all, yourself. . . ."

"I almost wish that I were going along on the voyage," said Madame Duvalier.

"Knowing Grimes as I do," said the admiral, "I prefer to wait for the reports that I shall be getting eventually. Reports which I shall not pass on to higher authorities until they have been most thoroughly edited."

Chapter 10

Sister Sue lifted from Port Woomera, driving up into the cloudless, blue, late afternoon sky. As members of the crew, Shirl and Darleen were among those in the control room; as first trip cadets their only duty was to keep well out of the way of those doing the work. Up and out drove the old ship, up and out. Soon, far to the south, the glimmer of the Antarctic ice could be discerned and, much closer, there was a great berg with its small fleet of attendant tugs, being dragged and nudged to its last resting place, its dying place, in the artificial fresh water harbor at the mouth of the Torrens River.

The sky darkened to indigo and the stars appeared, although the bright-blazing sun was still well clear of the rounded rim of the Earth. In the stern vision screen the radar altimeter display totted up the steadily increasing tally of kilometers. There were the last exchanges of messages between Aerospace Control and the ship on NST radio. It was a normal start to a normal voyage. (But, thought Grimes, sitting in his command chair, his unlit pipe clenched between his teeth, for him a normal voyage was one during which abnormality was all too often the norm. And, not for the first time, Damien was expecting him to stick his neck out and get it trodden on.)

Earth was a sphere now, a great, glowing opal against the black velvet backdrop of space.

"Escape velocity, sir," announced Harald Steerforth.

"Thank you, Mr. Steerforth," said Grimes.

"Clear of the Van Allens, sir," reported the second officer.

"Thank you, Mr. Kershaw. Ms. Suzuki, make to all hands 'Stand by for free fall. Stand by for trajectory adjustment.' "

He heard the girl speaking into her microphone, heard, from the intercom speakers the reports from various parts of the ship that all was secured. Using the controls set in the broad armrest of his chair he shut down the inertial drive. There was an abrupt cessation of vibration and a brief silence, broken almost at once by the humming of the great gyroscopes around which *Sister Sue* turned, hunting the target star. Grimes' fingers played on the control buttons, his face upturned to the curiously old-fashioned cartwheel sight set at the apex of the transparent dome of the control room. The pilot computer could have done the job just as well and much faster—but Grimes always liked to feel that he was in command, not some uppity robot. At last the tiny, bright spark was in the exact center of the concentric rings, the convergence of radii. It did not stay there for long; there was allowance for Galactic Drift to be made.

At last Grimes was satisfied.

"Stand by for initiation of Mannschenn Drive," he ordered.

"Stand by for initiation of Mannschenn Drive," repeated Tomoko Suzuki.

In the Mannschenn Drive room the gleaming complexity of rotors came to life, spinning faster and faster, tumbling, precessing, fading almost to invisibility, warping the very fabric of Space-Time about themselves and about the ship, falling down the dark dimensions. . . .

The temporal precession field built up and there was the inevitable distortion of perspective, with colors sagging down the spectrum. Not for the first time Grimes experienced a flash of prevision—but, he knew, it was of something that *might* happen. After all, there is an infinitude of possible futures and a great many probable ones.

But he saw—and this was by no means his first such experience—a woman. It was nobody he knew—and yet she seemed familiar. She was clad in a dark blue, gold-embroidered kimono, above which her heavily made-up face was very pale. Her glossy, black hair was piled high on her head. She could almost have been a Japanese geisha from olden times. . . .

Tomoko? Grimes wondered.

No, she was not Tomoko.

He could see her more clearly now. She was bound to a stake, around which faggots were piled. He saw a hand, a human hand, apply a blazing torch to the sacrificial pyre. There were flames, mounting swiftly. There was smoke, swirling about and over the victim.

There was. . . .

There was the instantaneous reversion to normality as the temporal precession field was established. Grimes tried to shake the vision from his mind.

"Stand by for resumption of inertial drive," he ordered.

"Stand by for resumption of inertial drive," repeated Tomoko into her microphone.

From below came the muted arrhythmic thumping. Somewhere a loose fitting rattled. Grimes unsnapped his seat belt, took his time lighting and filling his pipe.

"Set normal Deep Space watches," he said to the chief officer. "Mr. Kershaw can keep the first one. Please join me in my day cabin for a drink before dinner, Mr. Steerforth. We've a few things to discuss."

"Thank you, sir."

"I take it," said Grimes, speaking over the rim of his glass, "that Admiral Damien has put you into the picture."

"Of course, sir."

"What do you know about Ms. Perkins? Or should I say Lieutenant Commander Perkins?"

"I've worked with her before, sir. I knew that she'd been planted in your ship some time ago. She's highly capable, masquerading as being highly incapable." Then Steerforth actually laughed. "Mind you, sir, I've often wondered if her masquerade *is* a masquerade. . . . Perhaps, like you, she's a sort of catalyst. Things just happen when she's around."

"Can she make them happen on demand?" asked Grimes.

"Usually," said Steerforth.

"Mphm. But tell me, Mr. Steerforth, just how many undercover agents has Admiral Damien planted aboard my ship?"

"Well, sir, there's you, for a start. And myself. And Ms. Perkins. And those two alleged officer cadets. . . ." After a couple of drinks he was becoming more human. "For all I know that clockwork toy of yours might even be one! Tell me, is she really intelligent? Or is she just an example of very clever programming on somebody's part?"

"We are all of us the end products of programming," Grimes told him.

"To a point, sir. To a point. But as well as the programming there's intuition, imagination, initiative. . . ."

"I think," said Grimes, "that Seiko possesses at least two of those qualities."

The dinner gong sounded.

The two men finished their drinks, went down to the wardroom to join the other off duty officers.

Grimes had been half expecting soul food but what Ms. Clay provided was a fine example of Creole cookery. This was not to everybody's taste but Grimes enjoyed it.

Chapter 11

It was not a long voyage to Pleth, but long enough for Grimes to get the feel of things. His new chief officer, Harald Steerforth, was not quite such a pain in the arse as Grimes had feared that he would be on first acquaintance. Cleo Jones, the black and beautiful radio officer, the Zulu Princess, was the civilizing influence. What the pair of them did when they were off watch was none of Grimes' business. These days, in vessels with mixed crews, temporary sexual unions were not discouraged so long as they did not interfere with the smooth running of the ship and so long as certain unwritten regulations were observed.

In fact, thought Grimes disgruntledly, about the only person who wasn't getting any was himself. He was the victim of those unwritten regulations. Shirl and Darleen had made it plain to him that they were available, as they had been when they had traveled as passengers in *Sister Sue* from New Sparta to Earth. But then they had been passengers, fair game. Now they were junior officers, *very* junior officers. Between Grimes and themselves there was too great a disparity of rank. He did not wish to be thought of as a wicked captain who ordered poor, helpless (ha!) first-trip cadets to his bed.

Oh, there were offers, opportunities, but the two New Alicians did their best (worst) to ensure that he did not take advantage of them. There was that handsome academic, Sarah Smith, the second Mannschenn Drive engineer. She made it plain that she would not find the attentions of her captain unwelcome. Perhaps it was accidental that when she walked into the wardroom one evening, ship's time, she was struck on the left shoulder by a heavy glass ashtray. Shirl had been giving an exhibition of boomerang throwing—using anything and everything as boomerangs—to the off-duty officers.

Perhaps, Grimes thought at the time, it was accidental—but the next morning, in his day cabin, the two girls, who were supposed to be receiving instruction in general spacemanship from the captain, told him otherwise.

"John," said Shirl, "Vinegar Puss is trying to get her claws into you. Warn her off. . . ."

"Or next time," said Darleen, "she'll be getting something hard and heavy where it really hurts."

"And the same applies," added Shirl, "to Aunt Jemima. . . ."

"Ms. Clay," objected Grimes, "is nothing like Aunt Jemima."

"She's the cook, isn't she?"

"She's the catering officer," said Grimes. "It's the autochef that does the cooking—with, I admit, her personal touches. But Aunt Jemima? I've never heard her called that."

"You don't know much about what goes on aboard your own ship," Shirl told him.

Grimes laughed. "I'm only the captain. Nobody ever tells me anything."

"Then we can be your spies, John. You've made it plain that we aren't to be anything else."

"I've told you why it's quite impossible, as long as you're on my books."

"But it's so *silly*," complained the girls in unison.

"Silly or not, that's the way it's going to be."

"Would you rather that we slept with Bill the Bull?"

William Bull was the 3rd reaction drive engineer, the only male member of his department. He was referred to as "the bull among the cows." It was a known fact that both the 2nd and 4th were recipients of his favors. Privately Grimes thought of him as a sullen, over-sexed lout.

He said, "I'd advise you not to. Juanita has a hot temper and Calamity Cassie might put a hex on you. Well, since you are now my self-appointed spies, what else have you for me that you think that I don't already know?"

"Tomoko. . . ."

"Ms. Suzuki to you. After all, she is your superior officer."

"Only just," said Shirl. "And only aboard this ship of yours. Well, she and Seiko are very friendly. They have long talks together, twittering and giggling away in Japanese. Anyhow, we think that it's in Japanese."

"It probably is," Grimes said. "Tomoko must be pleased to have somebody with whom she can chat in her native language. It's the one that was originally programmed into her—Seiko, I mean, although I suppose that you could say the same regarding Tomoko."

"But Tomoko is not a robot," objected Darleen.

"Isn't she? Aren't you? Or, come to that, me? We're all of us pro-grammed, from birth onward."

"You are too deep for us, John. We are not accustomed to such philo-sophical thinking. On New Alice we led simple lives, at one with Nature. . . ."

And this was so, Grimes knew. He had watched Shirl and Darleen running with the mob of kangaroos by the Uluru Canal near Ayers Rock, heard them talking to the marsupials. He knew that aboard *Sister Sue* the two girls were now practically in charge of the ship's hydroponic "farm," that even the various edible, tank-grown plants flourished, under their care, as never before. They had green fingers, declared Melinda Clay who, as catering officer, was responsible for the continuing supply of fresh fruits, salads and other vegetables.

So *Sister Sue* eventually made her planetfall in the vicinity of Pleth, emerged from the warped continuum into normal space-time, said all the right things to the planet's Aerospace Control, got all the right answers and, eventually, dropped through thick clouds, all the way from the strat-osphere to the ground, to the spaceport. This, with facilities capable of handling no more than two ships at the one time, was shared by the Sur-vey Service and commercial interests. Grimes' berth was marked not by the usual flashing red beacons but by a radar transponder; it is said the visibility is bad for nine months of the local year on Pleth and nonexistent for the remaining three.

Grimes set his ship down gently, making, he told himself, a very good job of it in these conditions. He sat in the control room with Steer-forth after the others had left, looking out through a viewport at . . . noth-ing. At least he knew which way to look; his radar, set on short range, showed him a blob of luminescence that probably indicated the port administration building.

He saw the gradually increasing yellow glare in the fog that came from the headlights of approaching ground vehicles. Ms. Clay, in her capacity as purser, would, he knew, have all the necessary ship's papers ready in her office. Ms. Suzuki would receive the boarding officers in the after airlock. His presence almost certainly would not be required. Cus-toms, Port Health and Immigration would be getting their free smokes and coffee and then applying their rubber stamps before leaving.

Steerforth said, "I'd better get down to my office, sir. I suppose that somebody will be wanting to arrange discharge." He laughed. "I don't suppose that the Sub-Base Commander will be inviting us across for drinks."

That was indeed unlikely, thought Grimes. From his long experience he had learned that the smaller the Base, the greater the sense of self-importance of the officer in charge. On a planet like Pleth the OIC would most likely be some passed-over commander, putting on the airs and graces of a fleet admiral, too high and mighty to share a noggin of gin with a mere tramp skipper and his mate.

"I shall be in my day cabin if anybody wants me, Mr. Steerforth," he said. "Probably the agent will come aboard once the ship has been cleared inwards."

Shortly after Grimes had settled down in his day cabin with a mug of hot, sweet coffee to hand, his pipe drawing well, he was called upon by Mr. Klith, of Klith, Klith & Associates. Mr. Klith was obviously a native, although apparently humanoid. What could be seen of his skin was pale green and scaly and his huge eyes were hidden by even huger dark goggles, worn as protection from the relatively glaring illumination inside the ship. Although he wore a conventional enough gray, one-piece business suit his large, webbed feet were bare.

He spoke perfect, rather too perfect Standard English.

"I am your agent on Pleth, Captain," he announced. "Also I represent the Federation Survey Service, the consignees of your inward cargo."

"Sit down, Mr. Klith," said Grimes. "Can I offer you refreshment? Tea, coffee, something stronger? It is the middle of the morning your time, but I think that we can say that the sun is over the yardarm."

"We rarely see our sun," said Mr. Klith. "But what is a yardarm?"

"I must apologize," said Grimes. "I used an expression that used to be common at sea, on Earth, during the days of sail. It was passed on to mechanically driven ships and then to spaceships. It means that it's just about time for a drink before the midday meal."

"Thank you for your invitation, Captain. Perhaps I might have some tea. To us it is a mild intoxicant."

Grimes spoke briefly into the microphone of the intercom, turned to his guest. "What sort of tea would you prefer, Mr. Klith?"

"Indian tea is among our imports, Captain, but I understand that there are other varieties. I should wish to sample one of them."

Grimes amplified his order to the pantry.

"And now, Captain, while we are waiting might we discuss business?" said the agent. "I am afraid that we cannot expect much cooperation from Commander Dravitt, who is in charge of the Sub-Base. May I quote his words? He said, 'I need another load of bumf like I need a second arsehole. My stationery store is packed almost to bursting already.' But, you will be relieved to learn, I am the agent on this world for the Survey Service, not for one of its relatively junior—in rank, that is—officers. I have received a Carlottigram, signed by an Admiral Damien—do you know him, by any chance?—urging me to expedite your discharge. Your cargo will be stored in a civilian warehouse."

"As long as I'm not expected to pay for the storage," said Grimes.

"You will not be, Captain."

There was a tap at the door. Seiko came in, carrying a tray upon which were a teapot and a handleless cup. She set the tray down on the coffee table, poured the steaming fluid which almost matched Mr. Klith's skin in color. The native watched the robomaid with admiration, then transferred his attention to the refreshment.

He said, with some little bewilderment, "But should there not be sugar? And milk? Or perhaps some slices of that fruit you call lemon?"

"This is the way that we Japanese drink our tea, Klith-san," said Seiko.

"Indeed? But would not the ingestion of hot fluids tend to corrode your intricate and beautiful machinery?"

Grimes said hastily, "Seiko neither eats nor drinks. But she tends to identify with her manufacturers." Then, to the robot, "Thank you, Seiko. That will do."

"Thank you, Captain-san."

The robomaid withdrew.

"Your personal servant, Captain?" asked Mr. Klith. "A robot such as that must have been very, very expensive. All that we have on this world are clumsy things that are neither ornamental nor even very useful. But, of course, you are a rich shipowner and can afford the very best."

"Mphm," grunted Grimes. "As a matter of fact Seiko is a gift to me from my father. . . ."

"Then he must be a very rich man. Is he, too, in shipping?"

"No, he's a writer. . . ."

"Then he must be famous. Terran books are very popular here on Slith, both in translation and among those who, like myself, can read the various Terran languages. What name does he write under?"

Grimes told him.

"I am sorry. I have never heard of him. But he still must be successful and rich."

"Moderately successful and not really rich. As a matter of fact he bought Seiko for himself, to program as his secretary. That way he could claim her purchase price as a legitimate income tax deduction. Then my mother thought that she would make an ideal robomaid after secretarial skills somehow failed to develop, but she was still my father's pet. And then, after a family row, *I* got her. . . ."

"What complicated lives you Terrans lead. That is what makes your literature so fascinating. . . . This is excellent tea, by the way, captain. I must arrange to import it from Earth in large quantities . . ."

Grimes refiled his cup for him.

"And now, captain, let us discuss business. My young Mr. Slith is now with your chief officer discussing discharge of your inward cargo. This should commence shortly after noon, our time. Our stowbots may not be as goodlooking as your robomaid but they are fast working, especially when no great care is required. . . ."

"Mr. Steerforth will make careful note of the marks and numbers of any packages damaged and I shall, of course, refuse to pay any claims for damaged cargo."

"As you please, captain. The Survey Service will just write off such claims. After all, it is by their insistence that your discharge will be an exceptionally speedy one. By tomorrow night you should have an empty ship. Loading will commence almost at once. You know, of course, that you will be carrying a cargo of paradise fruit to New Otago. . . ."

"Any need for refrigeration or special ventilation?"

"No. It is canned."

"Then I hope that some care is exercised in its loading. I don't want damaged crates and sticky juice dribbling all over my cargo decks."

"Due care will be exercised, Captain. Paradise fruit is our main export and we do not wish to antagonize our customers." He finished his tea and got to his feet. "Thank you for allowing me to sample this truly excellent brew."

"Aren't you staying for lunch?" asked Grimes, hoping that the answer would be negative. A little of Mr. Slith went a long way. Apart from anything else he exuded an odor of not very fresh fish. (*And what do I smell like to him*? wondered Grimes, making allowances.)

"No thank you, Captain. I must confess that I do not find Terran foods very palatable—apart from your tea, that is. But does that possess any nutritional value? And now I must be on my way. Business awaits me in my office."

"Before you go," asked Grimes, "can you tell me if there are any recreational facilities in Port Pleth? I always allow my people shore leave whenever possible."

"Alas, no. Had you come a few days earlier you could have witnessed our annual mud festival, an event in which I am trying to interest the operators of tourist liners, such as Trans-Galactic Clippers, so far without success. Too, it is unsafe for beings not blessed with our eyes, sensitive as they are to infra-red radiation, to wander through the town. A few months ago—as you reckon time—the second officer of a Dog Star Line vessel fell into the Murgh River and was drowned. . . ."

So, thought Grimes, he would have to announce that there was to be no shore leave. He did not think that anybody would object very strongly.

Chapter 12

But there was, after all, shore leave of a sort.

Just as Grimes was about to go down to the wardroom for his luncheon he had another caller, this one human, an ensign from the Sub-Base. This not-so-young (for his lowly rank he seemed quite elderly) gentleman handed Grimes a large, rather condescendingly but more or less correctly addressed envelope. *Commander John Grimes, FSS (Rtd.), Master dss Sister Sue.* (Grimes had held the rank of commander at the time of the *Discovery* mutiny but he had not been retired; he had resigned his commission in some haste.)

Inside the envelope was a stiff sheet of official Survey Service stationery. On it was typed, "Commander David Dravitt, Federation Survey Service, Officer-in-Charge Sub-Base Pleth and his officers request the pleasure of the company of Commander John Grimes, Master dss *Sister Sue*, and his officers to dinner this evening, 1800 for 1930. Your prompt reply by bearer will be appreciated."

So far as he could remember Grimes had never been shipmates with Dravitt during his own days in the Service. He had never met, nor even heard of Dravitt. But, all too probably, Dravitt would have heard of him.

He asked, "Is there any limit to the number of guests, Mr. . . . Mr. . . . ?"

"Sullivan, sir. No, there is no limit. We enjoy commodious facilities. The Sub-Base was once much more important than it is now."

"Mphm. Can you handle fourteen, including myself?"

"Easily, sir. Will that be your entire complement?"

"No. Executive and engineer officers of the watch will remain on board. Will you be arranging transport?"

"It is only a short stroll to the Sub-Base officers' quarters, sir."

"In a thick fog, Mr. Sullivan?"

"We can lay on a ground car for yourself and your senior officers, sir. Native guides will be supplied for the others. The natives, as you may know, have eyes adapted to local conditions."

"Very well. You will call for us then at . . ."

"Shortly after 1730, sir."

"Thank you. Would you care to stay for lunch?"

Sullivan was obviously tempted but he said, "No thank you, sir. Commander Dravitt would like your reply as soon as possible so that the necessary arrangements may be made."

She, Paymaster Lieutenant Commander Selena Shaw, extricated herself from the tangle of bed sheets and limbs (half of these latter belonging to herself) and padded to the well-stocked bar set against one wall of her bedroom. Grimes watched the tall, naked blonde appreciatively. She returned to the bed bearing two condensation-bedewed glasses of sparkling wine.

"What," asked Grimes, "is a girl like you doing in a place like this? A highly competent officer attached to Sub-Base Pleth, the last resting place of all the Survey Service incompetents? Well, some of them, anyhow."

She laughed, her teeth very white in her tanned face. (She was one of the few officers of the Sub-Base who made regular use of the solarium; artificial sunlight was better than none at all.)

She said, without false modesty, "There has to be one competent officer, even in a sub-base like this. And I just happen to be it. Or her."

Grimes sipped his chilled wine. "And what am *I*," he continued rhetorically, "doing in a place like this? First of all, I never thought that a high and mighty sub-base commander would condescend to entertain a mere tramp skipper. Secondly, I was expecting a rather boring evening. I never dreamed that it would finish up like this."

She said, "Actually the invitation was Droopy Delia's idea. You've met her now, talked with her, so your opinion of her probably coincides with mine. A typical wife for a typical passed-over commander, like Davy Dravy, swept with him under the carpet to a dump like Pleth. Social ambitions that will never now be realized. A plumpish blonde—and now she's rather more than plump—getting spliced to an ambitious young lieutenant and seeing herself, after not too many years, as an admiral's wife. An admiral's wife she'll never be—but she kids herself that she's running this sub-base. Shortly after you'd set down she came barging into my office. *My* office, mind you. Davy Dravy was there—well, after all he is the sub-base commander—to discuss various matters and she started browsing through the papers on *my* desk. 'David,' she squeaked, 'have you seen who's master of this tramp, this *Sister Sue*?' He grumbled back, 'What is it to me what star tramp skippers call themselves?' She said, 'It's Grimes. John Grimes. *The* Grimes.' Davy Dravy was less than impressed. 'So bloody what?' he snarled. 'He was emptied out of the Service, wasn't he? And not before time.' She said, 'Yes. He was emptied out of the Service—or, according to some, he resigned before he could be emptied out. And now he's a shipowner. And he's been a planetary governor. At least he hasn't finished up with a dead-end appointment, frozen in rank, like some people.' Davy mumbled something about this being just your bloody luck. Droopy Delia said that she wished this famous luck would rub off on to some people she knew. And so it was decided to invite you to dinner. Or she decided to invite you to dinner. And then I took pity on you—or, as it's turned out, it was enlightened self-interest. Davy and Delia just aren't the Universe's best hosts. I threw in my two bits' worth. 'Why not,' I asked her, not him, 'issue a general wardroom invitation to the captain and officers. Our own officers, and the few civilian spouses, will enjoy having somebody fresh to talk with. . . .' "

"To talk with," said Grimes. "And. . . ."

"Yes. As you say, and as we've been doing, and . . . Apart from ourselves, I think that there has been rather more than just talking. But I don't think that Tony Cavallo and Billy Brown, our two prize wolves, got any place with those two cadets of yours. Odd looking wenches, somehow, but very attractive. And, despite their names, I don't think that their ancestors were Irish. I may be wrong, but I think that they had eyes only for you. And me, when I was making my invitation rather obvious. If looks could have killed. . . ."

"Mphm," grunted Grimes, embarrassed.

"Talking of their eyes. . . ." she went on. "Is there anything odd about *them*?"

"How do you mean?"

"Well, I was in charge of picking you people up and supplying the native guides for the junior officers. Your Ms. Kelly and Ms. Byrne arrived at the base officers' quarters well before the rest of the crowd—and they had nobody to guide them. And the fog was as thick as the armor plating of a Nova class battlewagon."

"Probably," said Grimes, "they regarded it as a sort of navigation test, got themselves headed in the right direction and then set off hopefully."

"Then they were lucky. It's not a straight line walk. There are two bridges to negotiate, and that mess of alleys and cross alleys through the workshops and stores."

"Mphm," grunted Grimes.

He finished his drink, she finished hers. It would soon be time for him to get back to his ship so as to spend what remained of the night in his own bed. But before he got dressed there were things to do better done naked.

At last it was time for him to say good night—or, more exactly, good morning. She threw on a robe and took him out to where the ground car, with native driver, was awaiting him.

He said, "I'll see you at about 1100 hours, then, Selena. Drinks before lunch. And I think I can promise you a rather better meal than to-night's dinner was."

She said, "It should be. Aboard your ship you're the boss."

They kissed a long moment and he boarded the waiting vehicle.

She arrived aboard *Sister Sue* shortly after 1100, supported, almost carried, by Ensigns Cavallo and Brown. She was dazed, bleeding profusely from a deep cut on the forehead. The efficient Melinda Clay was called upon to administer first aid and, after some delay, the sub-base's medical officer was in attendance.

At last Grimes was able to find out what had happened.

Selena had decided to walk from the sub-base to the ship, escorted through the fog by one of the native guides. Suddenly, without warning, she had been struck by a heavy missile. The guide had run to the ship to fetch help.

"I suppose, sir, that it was our fault," said Ensign Cavallo unhappily. "We should not have encouraged them. But, after all, sir, they're *your* officers, aboard *your* ship. . . ."

"Encouraged them? How?"

"We came on board for morning coffee. In the wardroom Ms. Kelly and Ms. Byrne were giving a demonstration of throwing weapons, using ashtrays and such, making them sail around and come back to their hands. I asked if this technique would be effective over a distance. They said that it was. So we all went down to the after airlock, and Ms. Kelly threw a rather thick glass saucer of some kind into the fog. We expected that it would come back, but it didn't. . . ."

"Ms. Kelly," asked Grimes severely, "Ms. Byrne, is this true?"

"Yes, sir," replied Shirl innocently. "But we had no idea that there would be anybody out in the fog. After all, if Ms. Shaw had been making her approach by ground car we should have seen the glare of the head-lights. . . ."

"And so, quite by chance," said Grimes, "your random missile inflicted grievous bodily harm on Lieutenant Commander Shaw—"

And with that he had to be content. He could prove nothing—and, even if he could, what could he do about it? Shirl and Darleen were essential—or so he had been told by Damien—to the success of his mission. Selena had been no more than a pleasant diversion.

Chapter 13

The work of discharge and then of loading went smoothly. Grimes was able during his time in port to return some of the hospitality which he and his people had received from the sub-base personnel. He kept a close watch on the Terrible Twins, a joint nickname which Shirl and Darleen had quite suddenly acquired, making no further attempt to entertain Selena Shaw aboard his ship. (But her own quarters were quite adequate for purposes of mutual entertainment and she did not, as she could quite well have done, put him off by complaining that she had a severe headache.)

And then, with cargo well stowed, with all necessary in-port maintenance completed, it was time to lift off. Nobody board the ship was sorry, even though there were a few (very temporarily) broken hearts both in the sub-base and aboard *Sister Sue*. Sleth was such a dismal planet. Even New Otago would be better. Even though there was a shortage of bright lights on that world the scenery was said to be quite spectacular and the atmosphere was usually clear enough for it to be appreciated.

So *Sister Sue* lifted, ungumming herself from the omnipresent mud that, despite the thrice daily deployment of high pressure hoses, inevitably crept over the spaceport apron. She clattered aloft through the fog, through the overcast, finally broke free into the dazzling sunlight while the last tenuous shreds of the Sleth atmosphere whispered along her pitted sides.

There was the usual trajectory setting routine, after which the old ship, her Mannschenn Drive running as sweetly as that Space-Time-twisting contraption ever ran, was falling down and through the warped dimensions toward the New Otago primary. Deep space watches were set and Grimes went down to his day cabin, asking Mr. Steerforth to join him there. As soon as the chief officer was seated and had been given a drink to nurse, served by the glittering Seiko, Grimes used the intercom to talk to the chief reaction drive engineer. "Ms. Scott, I've noticed that my shower is giving trouble. I almost got scalded this morning. Could you send Ms. Perkins up to fix it? She's off watch, isn't she?"

"I'll come myself, Captain. You know what Calamity Cassie's like."

"I do, Flo. But as fourth engineer she's supposed to be the ship's plumber. It's time that she started to earn her pay."

"Well, it's *your* shower, Captain. It's you that's going to get boiled or flash-frozen. . . ."

And so, after a wait of only a few minutes, Ms. Perkins presented herself, attired for work in overalls that had once been white but which now displayed a multitude of ineradicable grease stains, carrying a tunefully clinking tool bag. Only her teeth, which her cheerful grin displayed generously in her black face, were clean and very white.

"Sit down, Cassie," ordered Grimes.

Before she could do so Seiko produced, as though from nowhere, a towel which the robomaid spread over the upholstery of the chair. The fourth engineer looked admiringly at the beautiful automaton and murmured, "I'd love to have the job of taking you apart and putting you together again, honey."

"That'd be the Sunny Friday!" snapped Seiko.

"My father," said Grimes, "improved upon the original programming, making additions from his own vocabulary."

"And so Seiko," said Cassie, "is no more than a sort of mechanical parrot. That I will not believe. She's as human as you or me." She grinned. "There are even rumors that you and she have a beautiful relationship."

"I am the captain's personal servant," said Seiko stiffly. "Just that and nothing more. Unfortunately a relationship of a carnal nature would not be possible."

Grimes' prominent ears flushed angrily.

He said, "That will do, Seiko. Just fetch Ms. Perkins a drink, will you?"

"Yassuh, Massa Grimes. One Foster's lager a-comin' up, Missie Perkins."

"And now, Ms. Perkins," said Grimes as soon as Seiko had left them, "have you decided upon how you will carry out your act of sabotage?"

"Yes, sir. It will be quite simple. A disastrous leakage from the main water tank into the reaction drive engineroom. The bulkhead will give way—an area of it will have been treated with Softoll—to give it its trade name—which, as you know loosens molecular bonds in any metal. According to my calculations the application will take twelve hours to produce the desired effect. When you let me know the day, sir, when you wish the accident to happen I shall apply the Softoll at 1000 hours, during my watch. The flood will happen at 2200 hours—again during my watch. I shall panic. My one motivation will be to get rid of all that water. After all, there's electrical machinery that could be damaged, and I might get drowned. I'll open the dump valves."

"Make sure, Cassie," Steerforth told her, "that you get into your emergency suit before you start getting rid of everything of a fluid nature in the engine room. After all, you'll be throwing out the atmosphere along with the bath water."

She grinned. "I look after my reputation. Things always happen around me, never to me."

Grimes asked, "But won't the cause of the so-called accident be obvious? Flo and Juanita aren't fools, you know."

She told him, "It will be put down to metal fatigue—and it won't be the first case of metal fatigue in this rustbucket."

"Are you referring to my ship?" asked Grimes stiffly. "It's bad enough to have you doing things to her without having to listen to you insulting her."

"Sorry, Captain. But unless you can think of some other kind of trouble that will force us to deviate to Salem, I shall have to do things to your ship. But I'll try to keep the damage down to a minimum." She finished her beer. "And now," she went on brightly, "shall I fix your shower for you?"

"No," said Grimes. "No, repeat and underscore, *NO*."

Chapter 14

Grimes, of course, knew what was going to happen, and when.

At 2145 hours he was in the control room, having a chat with the officer of the watch, Tomoko Suzuki. As he frequently did just this before retiring for the night the third officer did not suspect that anything was amiss or about to go so. The topic of conversation was such that he almost forgot his real reason for being there, which was to ensure that the Mannschenn Drive was shut down at the first sign of trouble in the inertial drive engineroom. The dumping of tons of water would mean that the mass of the ship would be suddenly and drastically reduced—and any change of mass while running under Mannschenn Drive could be, probably would be, disastrous. There were stories of vessels so afflicted being unable to re-enter normal Space-Time or being thrown back into the remote Past. Nobody *knew*, of course (except for the crews of those ships) but there had been experiments and there was a huge amount of theoretical data which Grimes could not begin to understand.

"Captain-san," Tomoko was saying, "I regard your Seiko as a friend. She may be a robot but she is, somehow, a real woman, a real Japanese woman." She giggled. "I have made up her face, like that of an olden time geisha, and put a wig upon her head, and dressed her in a kimono. . . ."

"I must see this some time," said Grimes.

He looked out through the viewport to the stars that were not points of light but vague, pulsating nebulosities. He heard the thin, high whine of the Drive as it engendered the temporal precession field, the warping of the continuum through which the ship was falling. He switched his attention to the control room clock. 2155:30 . . . 31 . . . 32 . . . Would that bulkhead blow *exactly* on time? Probably not. And would Calamity

Cassie hit her alarm button as soon as the first trickle of water appeared? It could be just too bad if she didn't.

"Is something worrying you, Captain-san?" asked Tomoko.

"I shouldn't have had a second helping of Aunt Jemima's jambalaya at dinner this evening," lied Grimes.

2159:01. . . .

He filled in time by playing with his pipe, stuffing the bowl with tobacco, making a major production of lighting it.

2200:00 . . .

"It would be rather pleasant," said Tomoko, "if some time we had a Japanese catering officer. . . ."

"I'm very fond of sashimi myself," said Grimes, "but I doubt if some of the others would care for raw fish."

2201:03 . . . 04 . . . 05 . . .

"Seiko has told me," said Tomoko, "that the preparation of sushi, sashimi and the like was in her original programming. And we have the carp in some of the algae tanks. Perhaps one night, just for a change, we could enjoy a sashimi dinner . . ."

2203:15 . . . 16 . . . 17

A red light suddenly sprang into being on the console of the inertial drive controls. An alarm klaxon uttered the beginnings of a squawk. Grimes' hand flashed up to the Mannschenn Drive console, knocked the main switch to the off position. The thin, high whine deepened to a rumbling hum, faded into silence. Colors sagged down the spectrum, perspective was impossibly distorted. Outside the viewports the stars changed, coalescing from furry blobs into hard points of light. But, below decks, the inertial drive was still hammering away although its clangor was almost drowned by the hooting alarms. And then it, too, fell silent. Throughout the ship all the lights went out but there was less than a second of darkness before the power cells cut in to the major domestic circuits.

Grimes had been expecting what happened and had secured himself in his chair. Tomoko was unprepared. With the inertial drive off, the ship was in free fall and some involuntary movement had pushed her up from her seat and she was drifting, making rather futile swimming motions, above Grimes' head. With his right hand he was just able to reach her ankle, pulled her down and then into the chair beside his.

"What happened, sir?" she gasped.

He said, "I suppose that somebody will eventually condescend to tell us."

"Why did you shut the Mannschenn Drive off, sir?"

He told her—but it was less than the whole truth—"There was, and is, trouble with the inertial drive. Which meant, as we've just found out, a sudden transition from a comfortable one G to free fall. There was the risk that the MD engineer on watch—Mr. Siegel, isn't it?—might blunder into the Drive and get himself turned inside out or something equally messy."

She said admiringly, "You thought very fast, Captain-san. I hope that I can think as fast when I am a captain."

Grimes never minded flattery, especially when it came from a pretty girl, even though in this case it was unearned. He supposed that if he had not been on the alert he would have acted as he had done, but not as fast.

He said to Tomoko, "Buzz the ID room, will you? Ask them what the hell's going on."

After an interval she reported, "The intercom seems to be out of order, sir." (This was not surprising. The waterproofing of electrical systems is not considered necessary in spaceships.)

Steerforth pulled himself into the control room. He reported, almost cheerfully, "There's all hell let loose down there, sir. As far as I can gather the after bulkhead of the main fresh water tank suddenly ruptured, flooding the ID room." He laughed. "Of course, it would have to happen on Calamity Cassie's watch. Then, according to Flo, what Cassie should have done was to drain the water into the engineers' store and workshop space. But she went into a panic and opened the dump valves. . . ."

"It is indeed fortunate," said Tomoko, "that the captain shut down the Mannschenn Drive before the loss of mass."

"It is indeed fortunate, Ms. Suzuki," agreed Steerforth. "Perhaps it was just another example of his famous luck."

"Mphm," grunted Grimes, looking severely at his chief officer.

"Shall I go back down," asked that gentleman, "to try to find out the extent of the damage?"

"No, Mr. Steerforth. Engineers don't like control room ornaments getting into their hair when they're trying to cope with some kind of emergency. Ms. Scott will keep us informed in her own good time."

Kershaw, the second officer, made his entrance into the control room. About bloody well time, thought Grimes. *Doesn't the puppy know that there's an emergency?* After him came Shirl and Darleen. There was some excuse for them; they were not real spacepersons. Finally Cleo Jones, the Zulu Princess, put in her appearance.

She reported, "I have been checking the main Carlotti transceiver, sir. Should it be necessary I can get out a Mayday using the power available."

"Thank you, Ms. Jones." Grimes looked around at his assembled people. They looked back at him, obviously awaiting orders. Well, he'd beter start giving some.

"Ms. Kelly, Ms. Byrne," he said, "report to Ms. Clay. Probably there are matters in her department needing attention. When the ID cut out nothing was secured for free fall."

"Ay, ay, sir," said the girls smartly.

Grimes watched them go. They handled themselves in the absence of gravity better than many a seasoned spaceman.

"Mr. Kershaw, since the intercom seems to be out of action you can report to Ms. Scott, to act as runner to carry messages to me from her."

And she'll probably chew his ears off, he thought, with some satisfaction.

"Shall I find out what's happened to Seiko, sir?" asked Tomoko. "She might have been hurt. Damaged, I mean. . . ."

Not her, thought Grimes. He said, "She is a member of Ms. Clay's department. Probably she is helping her to get things cleaned up."

"Do you wish to send any messages, sir?" asked Cleo.

"Eventually," Grimes told her. "But I want to know what I'm talking about before I start talking." Then, to the third officer, "Get me a fix, will you? The navigational equipment is on the emergency circuit."

The girl busied herself at the chart tank, taking bearings from three conveniently located Carlotti Beacon Stations. Grimes unbuckled himself from his chair, pulled himself to a position beside her. He looked down into the simulation of the blackness of interstellar space, at the intersection of the three glowing filaments, at the other filament this was the extrapolation of *Sister Sue*'s trajectory. At right angles to this, close, was the brilliant spark that was a star.

Grimes pointed the stem of his pipe at it.

"That sun?" he asked. "I may need to find a planet, one where there is fresh water available."

She punched computer keys, read out from the screen, "Salema, sir, so called by the people of its own habitable planet, which is variously known as Salem or New Salem. Catalogue number. . . ."

"Never mind that. And the people? Of Terran origin, aren't they?"

She punched more keys. "Yes, sir. Second Expansion stock."

"Now get that tin brain to do some sums for me. Running at a steady one *G*, with standard temporal precession, how long from here to planetfall?"

"As from *now*, sir, six days, fourteen hours and forty-five minutes."

"Mphm. We can survive that long on what water is left in the system, with rationing and recycling. There shouldn't be any need to go thirsty or get really dirty."

"Couldn't we carry on to New Otago, sir?"

"I'd not like to risk it. And I was brought up in the Survey Service, as you know, Tomoko. We always liked to have plenty of reaction mass on hand so that we could use emergency rocket drive if we had to. So I think that a deviation to New Salem is justified. The insurance should cover it."

And if it doesn't, he thought, *some Survey Service secret fund will be used to compensate me.*

From below decks came the whine of a generator starting up. Lights flickered and then brightened as the emergency circuit cut out and the main circuit cut in. Steerforth said, "Flo seems to be getting things under control. I wonder why she hasn't sent Mr. Kershaw up to keep us informed."

Kershaw pulled himself into the control room. "Sir, Ms. Scott isn't very communicative. So I checked up in the Mannschenn Drive room. The MD engineers are standing by, waiting to start up as soon as they have the power. Mr. Gray asked me to tell you that there is no damage."

"Thank you."

Finally Florence Scott made her appearance. Her once-white overalls were sweat-soaked and grease-stained, and more grease marked her broad, ruddy face.

"Captain," she announced, "we'll have the phones working again in a couple o' minutes but I thought I'd report the situation in person, not through your messenger boy." Kershaw flushed and scowled. "As ye already know, the engineroom got flooded. Anybody'd think that this was some tramp steamer on Earth's seas way back in the twentieth century, old style. Cassie didn't think; all she wanted to do was to get rid of all that water in a hurry. She could ha' let it drain into the store and workshop flat—but no. Not her. She opened the dump valves.

"There's nothing wrong with the innies that a little minor rewiring won't fix. I should be able to restart in half an hour. An' then you can restart the time twister an' we can be on our way. You may as well restart it now."

"What about fresh water?" asked Grimes.

"Enough. We'll not die o' thirst or go unwashed as long as we're careful."

"What about the emergency reaction drive?"

"There's no reaction mass. But emergency reaction drive was phased out years ago in the merchant service. It's not required by law."

Grimes said, "I may be old-fashioned, but I like to know that I have rockets under my arse should I feel the need for them in a hurry. I'm deviating to the nearest port of refuge, which is on New Salem. There we'll get the bulkhead patched and refill the tank."

"A needless expense and waste of time," sneered the chief engineer. "Oh, well, you're the captain."

"*And* the *owner*," Grimes reminded her firmly.

Chapter 15

There was Aerospace Control on New Salam, although its name was somewhat misleading. There was no aerial traffic, either lighter than or heavier than air, in the planet's atmosphere. ("If God had meant us to fly He would have given us wings.") But at Port Salem there was a Carlotti radio station with rather limited range and also an NST transceiver. Grimes got in touch while he was still proceeding toward the planet under Mannschenn Drive, using his Carlotti radio. This was an unusually troublesome procedure. According to the data in *Sister Sue*'s library bank New Salem Aerospace Control maintained a listening watch for the first five minutes of every hour, daylight hours only and never on Sunday. The first time that Cleo Jones tried to get through it must have been Sunday on New Salem. During the next twenty-four-hour period, ship's time, the trouble was trying to get the ship's clocks synchronized with those at the spaceport. Finally Cleo arranged for a continuous automatic transmission with an alarm to sound as soon as there was a reply.

Grimes happened to be in the control room when this happened.

An irritable female voice came from the Carlotti speaker. "Port Salem Aerospace Control to unknown vessel. Identify yourself. Pass your message."

"*Sister Sue* to Port Salem," said Grimes. "Request permission to land to effect essential repairs."

"Stand by, *Sister Sue*. I shall come back to you."

Grimes stood by for a long time, having his lunch, served by the faithful Seiko, in the control room. At last the speaker crackled into life.

"Port Salem to *Sister Sue*. What is the nature of the repairs that you will require? I must warn you that our workshop facilities are limited."

"The patching of a ruptured bulkhead," said Grimes. "My own engineers can carry out the work as long as suitable plating is available. The replenishment of my fresh water supply."

"Stand by, *Sister Sue.*"

There was another long wait.

Finally, "Materials will be made available to you. Fresh water will be obtainable from Lake Beulah. What is your ETA please?"

Clocks and calendar were synchronized and Grimes was able to give day and time for his return to the normal continuum and, not too approximately, for his eventual setting down at Port Salem.

Eventually *Sister Sue* was dropping through the twilight towards the huddle of yellowish lights that was New Salem. He would have preferred to have made a dawn approach but, after all, he was supposed to be in some sort of distress and, therefore, in some sort of hurry. The traffic control officer, whose sour featured face was visible in the screen of the NST radio transceiver, instructed him to set down in the center of the triangle formed by the berth markers. *What berth markers?* Grimes asked himself irritably. What did they use for berth marking beacons on this benighted planet? Candles? He stepped up magnification and definition in the stern vision screen. At last he saw them as he continued his cautious descent, three feeble, ruddy sparks.

He hoped that Cassandra Perkins fully understood what was expected of her. If she acted too soon, clumsily (but on purpose) tripping over her own feet and clutching at a lubrication line for support, bending it but not breaking it, throttling the supply of oil to the governor bearings, *Sister Sue* would fall for far too many meters, damaging herself irreparably. The governor would have to seize up almost immediately after Grimes applied that final surge of thrust to cushion the landing.

He watched the read-out of the radar altimeter.

10 meters . . . 9 . . . 8 . . . 7 . . . 6 . . .

Now!

The cacophony of the inertial drive rose from little more than an irritable mutter to an angry clangor—then abruptly ceased. *Sister Sue* dropped like a stone, a very large and heavy stone. Shock absorbers screamed rather than sighed. Loose fittings rattled and there was a tinkling crash as something tore adrift from its securing bolts. Grimes slowly filled and lit his pipe—but even though he had been expecting the accident it was hard to maintain the pose of imperturbability. Tomoko, he thought, to whom it had all come as a big surprise, was making a far better job of it than he was.

Steerforth voiced what must have been the thought of all those in the control room.

"That's fucked it!" he said.

"Mr. Steerforth, mind your language," Grimes told him.

The intercom speaker crackled and then Florence Scott's voice came from it. "ID room to captain. Chief engineer here. The bearings of the governor seem to have seized up. I am making an immediate check of the extent of the damage."

"Thank you," Ms. Scott," said Grimes into his microphone.

"MD room to captain." This was the chief Mannschenn Drive engineer, Daniel Grey. "You seem to have made a crash landing." *A blinding glimpse of the obvious*, thought Grimes. "The jolt unseated numbers one, three and four rotors from their bearings. . . ."

Worse and worse, thought Grimes. *Or better and better?*

"Apart from anything else," Grey went on, "the Drive will have to be recalibrated once it has been reassembled."

"Somebody's coming out to us, sir," announced Steerforth.

Grimes got up from his chair, went to stand with the chief officer by the viewport. He saw the group of bobbing lights—hand-held lanterns?—and the dimly illumined human forms.

He said, "Looks like a boarding party of some kind. You'd better go down to the after airlock to receive them. I shall be in my day cabin. Oh, on your way down give Ms Clay my compliments and tell her to keep Seiko out of sight as long as there are any locals aboard."

Steerforth grinned. "Aunt Jemima's read that article too, just as we all have. But *Star Scandal*'s not quite in the same class as the *Encyclopaedia Galactica*, is it, sir? And their star reporter, Fenella Pruin, never lets facts get in the way of a sensational story."

"Ms. Pruin," said Grimes, "is a very able investigative reporter."

"Oh, yes. You know her, sir. I was forgetting."

"We know her, too," said Shirl and Darleen as one, making it plain that they held Fenella in quite high regard.

In his day cabin Grimes picked up the rather tattered copy of *Star Scandals* from the coffee table. It would be advisable, he thought, to get it out of sight before the visitors arrived. That lurid cover, with its colored photograph of a naked girl, chained to a stake and with flames licking around her lower body . . . It had been the third ID engineer, Bill the Bull, who had found this particular issue of *Star Scandals* in his well-thumbed collection of that pornographic, as often as not, publication. As soon as it was known that *Sister Sue* was deviating to Salem, Fenella's piece on that planet had become almost required reading by all hands.

Fenella had visited Salem as a passenger aboard *Wombat*, owned by Able Enterprises. (This, of course, had been before she had gotten into the bad books of Baron Kane, whose company Able Enterprises was.) She had found it hard to sniff out anything really juicy on Salem; the people lived lives of utterly boring sexual probity. She had witnessed a slaughter of the silkies, the animals whose furs were Salem's only export—but Fenella was not at her best (worst?) as a writer on humanitarian issues. She blew up the business of her dancing dolls to absurd proportions. These tiny, beautifully made automata, one male, one female, not only danced to tinkling music but stripped, and when naked went through the motions of coitus. All very amusing to those of a kinky bent. . . .

Grimes read, "That party, in *Wombat*'s wardroom, was inexpressably dreary. Pastor Coffin and his wife would drink only tea and insisted that this be both weak and tepid. In deference to the sensibilities of their guests Captain Timson and his officers did not smoke. Daringly I lit a cigarillo and was told, by the she-Coffin that if God had meant me to smoke He would have put a chimney on top of my head. I said that She had more important things to occupy Her time. This did not go down at all well.

"The conversation, such as it was, got on to the topic of machinery. Machinery, I gathered, was disapproved of on Salem. Of course I had already noticed this. Just one solar power plant to generate electricity for the spaceport facilities, communications and so forth. But oil-lighting in the houses, sailing vessels on the sea, bullock-drawn wagons on the roads. And bullocks, too, supplied the power to operate the presses which extracted the flammable oil from various seeds.

"Anyhow, Captain Timson was letting Pastor Coffin's diatribe against inventions of the devil go on without interruption. He knew on which side his bread was buttered. The silkie skin trade was a profitable one for his owners. But his officers, the engineers especially, were inclined to argue. The fruit punch that they had been drinking had been well spiked with gin as soon as it became obvious that the Coffin couple was having none of it.

"Terry Muldoon, the third engineer, said, 'But machines have their uses, Pastor Coffin. Even as toys for children, educational toys . . . ' (Terry, I learned later, had already resigned from Able Enterprises and had a job waiting for him with the Dog Star Line.) Coffin said, 'What can a child learn from a mechanical toy? He will learn all that he ever needs to know from the Bible.' Terry said, 'You'd be surprised, Pastor.' He turned to me and said, 'Fenella, why not show our guests those educational toys of yours?' (He was one of the few people aboard the ship who had seen them. Old Timson had not, neither had the two chief engineers.) So I went to my cabin and got the box and set it down on the wardroom table. I took out Max and Maxine. They stood stiffly, facing each other. I switched on the music, Ravel's *Bolero*. Max and Mazine came . . . alive.

They could have been flesh-and-blood beings, not automata. They danced, and as they danced they shed their clothing. I always liked the part when Max got rid of his trousers; it is easy for a woman to disrobe gracefully to music, not so easy for a man. I always hoped that Max would get his feet tangled in his nether arments and come down heavily on his rather too perfect little arse, but he never did.

'And then they were quite naked, the pair of them, anatomically correct. Maxine, legs open, was supine on the table top and Max was about to lower himself upon her when Coffin's big fist smashed down on the box as he bellowed, 'Blasphemy! Blasphemy!' The music stopped in mid-stridency. There was a sputter of sparks. Max, no more than a lifeless, somehow pathetic doll collapsed on top of the other doll, among the litter of rags that had been their clothing.

"Timson apologized. 'I had no idea, Pastor . . . '

"Coffin—he was virtually foaming at the mouth—screamed, 'That is no excuse, Captain. Does it not say in the Book that you shalt not suffer a witch to live? She . . . ' he pointed a quivering finger at me, 'is a witch. And those are her familiars!'

" 'Go to your cabin,' Timson ordered me. I tried to argue but it was no use. The mate and the second mate, that pair of great, hulking louts, hustled me out of the wardroom, locked me in my quarters. And there I was confined until breakfast the next morning.

"After the meal Terry managed to have a few words with me. He told me that the pastor had gone on ranting and raving after I had been removed from his presence, accusing me of witchcraft and saying that Max and Maxine were my familiars. He demanded that I be turned over to the local authorities to stand trial—but this was too much even for Captain Timson. Then he insisted that Max and Maxine be given into his custody, saying that they would be publicly destroyed by burning. Timson agreed to this. 'And you'd better stay aboard from now on, Fenella,' Terry told me, 'otherwise you'll find yourself tied to a stake with the faggots piled about you . . . ' "

There was a knock at the door. Grimes hastily took the dog-eared copy of *Star Scandals* through to his bedroom, returned to the day cabin and called, "Come in!"

Tomoko entered, followed by a tall man in rusty black clothing with touches of white, rather grimy white, at his throat and wrists.

"Pastor Coffin to see you, sir," she announced.

Grimes almost said what he usually said on such occasions but decided against it. To judge from the deeply lined, craggy face, the fanatical black eyes under shaggy gray brows, this was a man utterly devoid of humor.

Chapter 16

The two men shook hands. The pastor's grip was firm but cold.

"Be seated, sir," said Grimes. "May I offer you refreshment? Coffee? Tea? Or . . . ?"

"Tea, captain. Not strong. No milk. No sugar."

Grimes telephoned the pantry and made the order. He sat back in his chair, filled and lit his pipe.

The pastor said, "Do not smoke."

Grimes said, "This is my ship, sir. I make the rules."

"This may be your ship, Captain, but you neither own nor command this planet. And, as I understand it, you will be unable to lift from this world unless you are vouchsafed cooperation by myself and the elders of my church."

Grimes made a major production of sighing. Until he knew which way the wind was blowing or likely to blow he would have to do as bid. He put his pipe down in the ashtray.

Shirl came in, carrying a tray which she set on the coffee table. (Melinda Clay, in her capacity as purser, would still be dealing with the port officials.) In her very short uniform shorts she looked all legs.

Coffin looked at her disapprovingly then said, "Are all your female officers so indecently attired, Captain?"

Grimes said, "My female officers wear what is standard uniform for both the Federation Survey Service and the Merchant Service."

"Aboard the ships of Able Enterprises," said Coffin, "females are always decently covered."

And Drongo Kane, thought Grimes, would put his people in sackcloth and ashes as the rig of the day rather than lose a profitable trade. *And so would I*, he realized with some surprise.

Shirl glared at Coffin and strode out of the day cabin. Grimes poured the tea, which was far too weak for his taste, added milk and sugar to his own.

"I understand, Captain," said the pastor, "that you have various mechanical troubles. We on Salem, freed from the tyranny of the machine, are not so afflicted."

"It was machines, starships, that brought your ancestors here, sir."

"At times the Lord uses the Devil's tools. But His people should avoid doing so. Now, what are your requirements? What must you do to make your vessel spaceworthy?"

"I have to repair a bulkhead—just a matter of patching. I hope that a suitable plate will be available here. The shaft of my inertial drive governor must be renewed. My Mannschenn Drive has to be recalibrated. I understand that there is a workshop here, and a stock of spares and materials."

"Your understanding is correct, Captain. The workshop and the stores are the property of Able Enterprises. I am empowered to act as their agent."

"Any skilled labor, pastor?"

"We have blacksmiths, Captain, but nobody capable of carrying out the type of work that you seem to require."

"No matter. My own engineers can start earning their pay for a change." Grimes picked up his pipe, thought better of it and put it down again. "There's another matter, pastor. I don't need to tell you that a deviation, such as this one that I have been obliged to make, costs money. I am not loaded to capacity. Would there be any chance of a cargo of silkie hides to New Otago?"

"It is only wealthy worlds, such as El Dorado, that can afford such luxury clothing," said the pastor. "From what I have heard of New Otago I gain the impression that nobody there is either very rich or very poor."

"Perhaps," said Grimes hopefully, "there might be the possibility, some time in the not too distant future, of a shipment of hides from here to some market, somewhere. . . ."

"Able Enterprises," Coffin told him, "have the monopoly on the trade from Salem to Earth as well as to El Dorado. But you are a widely traveled man, Captain. You have your contacts throughout the Galaxy . . ." And did Grimes detect the gleam of cupidity in the pastor's eyes? "Perhaps, in your voyagings, you will be able to find other markets for our export. In such a case I am sure that some mutually profitable arrangement could be made."

Melinda Clay came in with various documents to be signed. Coffin looked at her even more disapprovingly than he had Shirl but said nothing until she had left.

He said, "So you employ the children of Ham aboard your vessel. But, from them, an indecent display of flesh is, I suppose, to be expected."

"Mphm," grunted Grimes.

Coffin got to his feet. "Almost I was tempted to forbid shore leave to yourself and your officers. But I realize that if there are, in the future, to be business dealings between you and ourselves there must be some familiarization. Your people must understand the nature of the cargo that they will be carrying. Too, it is not impossible that they, or at least some of them, will find the true Light. . . ." He drew himself to his full, not inconsiderable height. "But I strongly advise you, Captain, to see to it that your females are properly attired when they set foot on our soil. Otherwise I shall not be responsible for the consequences."

Probably, thought Grimes contemptuously, *your men would fly into a screaming tizzy at the sight of a woman's ankle.*

He said, "I'll see to it, pastor, that my people comport themselves properly."

"Do so, Captain. Tomorrow morning I shall have the spaceport workshop unlocked and shall be waiting for you there so that you and your engineers can tell me what you want."

"At about 0900?" asked Grimes.

"At seven of the clock," stated Coffin. "We, on this world do not waste the daylight hours that God sends us."

Grimes sent for his senior officers, received from them more detailed damage reports than the earlier ones, told them of his talk with Coffin. He said, "There will be shore leave. But you must make it plain to your people, the girls especially, that they are to avoid giving offense in any way. This is a very puritanical planet, so the ladies are to wear long skirts at all times. It will be as well, too, if there is no smoking in public."

Steerforth laughed. "That's going to hurt you, Captain."

"Too right it is," agreed Grimes. "But I suppose that I must set a good example for the rest of you." He turned to Florence Scott. "I'm afraid that it's an early rise and an early breakfast for you tomorrow morning, Flo. The pastor—he's the local boss cocky—is letting us use the Able Enterprises repair and maintenance facilities. I suggested that we meet him in the workshop at 0900 but he made it plain that, as far as he's concerned, the day's work starts at 0700. We have to play along.

"You can make contact with the local ship chandler, Melinda," he said to the catering officer, "and order any consumable stores necessary. Just try to remember that *Sister Sue* is not the flagship of Trans-Galactic Clippers! Oh, and if there are any locals aboard don't forget to keep Seiko out of sight . . ."

She grinned whitely and said, "I've read that article in *Star Scandals*, Captain. If any of these superstitious bastards got the idea that she's my familiar I might get barbecued."

"And Seiko almost certainly would be. And how are things in the time-twisting department, Dan?"

"All that are required are patience and a few pairs of steady hands," said the Mannschenn Drive engineer. "We shall have things re-assembled before Flo's pusher is ready."

"And then you'll make a balls of the recalibration," Ms Scott said. "It's happened before, you know."

"And that seems to be it," said Grimes. "A nightcap before you go?"

They accepted. When they finally left, Grimes overheard a scrap of conversation from the alleyway outside his door, Florence Scott talking to Daniel Grey.

"The old bastard's taking things remarkably well. I thought that he'd be having my guts for a necktie."

"He's insured," said Grey.

And I'll be surprised, thought Grimes, *if Lloyd's don't up my premiums.*

Chapter 17

The next morning Grimes, with Steerforth, Florence Scott and Juanita Garcia, partook of an early breakfast. The meal finished, the four of them made their way out of the ship, down the ramp to the scarred concrete of the apron, still wet from overnight showers. The sun was only just up, in a partly cloudy sky, and the air was decidedly chilly. The spaceport administration buildings toward which they were walking reminded Grimes of pictures that he had seen in his father's library, of small seaports on the Pacific coast of North America during the nineteenth century old style. There were the rather ramshackle wooden structures, the tallest of which was the control tower from which, incongruously, sprouted the antennae and scanners of modern communication and locating equipment. But there should have been a quay, thought Grimes, with square-rigged sailing vessels, whalers, alongside to complete the picture.

"Are you sure that we didn't, somehow, travel back in time, Captain?" asked Juanita. "It's not only the way that this place looks but the way that it smells, even. . . ."

Grimes removed his pipe from his mouth, exhaled the fumes of burning tobacco, waited until his sense of smell was again operational and then sniffed the air. Drifting down the light wind from the nearby town was the pleasant acridity of wood smoke from morning cooking fires.

He said to the second engineer, "In a way we have traveled back in time, Juanita. The colonists here deliberately put the clock back. Oh, well, it's their world and they're welcome to it."

There were signs of life around the administration buildings. As the party from the ship approached these a tall, black-clad figure emerged from one of the sheds, strode up to them. It was Pastor Coffin. He pulled a huge, silver watch from his waistcoat pocket, glared at it. He said, "You are late, Captain. It is already two minutes past the hour."

Grimes apologized, with a certain look of sincerity, saying that he had underestimated the time that it would take to walk from the ship. The pastor said coldly, "You spacemen . . ." He looked coldly at Juanita who, even in her white overalls, was indubitably feminine, "You space*persons*, with your machines waiting on you hand and foot, do not take enough healthy exercise. But come."

He led the way into the long shed from which he had emerged. The interior was gloomy. The windows were small and the few electric lights that had been switched on seemed to be doing their best to imitate oil lamps. What was their power source? wondered Grimes. Batteries, probably. In one corner was what was obviously a generator, which was not running. It, like the other machinery and equipment in the shed, would be the property of Able Enterprises.

"Can't we have some proper light?" asked Ms. Scott irritably. "I see a jenny there that's doing nothing for its living."

"You may start the machine," said Coffin to Grimes. "But you will be charged for its hire."

"We must have proper illumination," said Grimes. "Flo, can you get that thing going?"

"No trouble, Captain. I cut my teeth on diesels."

She walked to the generator, inspected it, cracked fuel valves and switched on the electric starter. The thing coughed briefly and then settled down to a steady beat. Juanita found other light switches and, within seconds, the interior of the workshop was bathed by the harsh glow of the overhead fluorescents.

Steerforth said to Grimes, as he looked around, "Drongo Kane could almost build a ship from scratch with the stuff that he's got stashed in here."

"As long as there's some suitable plating . . ." said Grimes.

"And we shall probably have to use that lathe," put in Ms. Scott. "To turn down a new shaft for the governor."

"I rely upon you," said Coffin, "to maintain a strict tally of all materials utilized and of all machinery employed."

"You can start the timekeeping now, Mr. Steerforth," Grimes ordered his chief officer. "When I go back to the ship I shall arrange for you to be relieved by Mr. Kershaw."

Steerforth pulled a notebook from his pocket and made entries.

Coffin accompanied Grimes back to *Little Sister*.

He said, "Perhaps you think it strange, Captain, that I should allow your people free run of the workshop."

Grimes said, "Frankly yes, pastor. I expected that you or one of your people would remain to keep an eye on things."

The pastor made a sound that approximated a chuckle. "We do business with Able Enterprises but we do not have to like them, any more than we have to like you. In the final analysis, it matters not if one party of unbelievers, as represented by yourself, robs another party of unbelievers. But I think that you are, according to your lights, dim though they be, an honorable man . . ."

"Thank you," said Grimes dryly.

"And, of course, the port dues and such that you will pay will hasten the day when our project shall be completed . . ."

Project? wondered Grimes. Oh, yes. The Ark that would survive the eventual collapse of the Universe.

He asked, "Has work on the project actually commenced yet?"

"We have commissioned research," the pastor told him. "The salvation vessel will not, of course, be mechanically propelled. It will be a sailing ship of Space."

"Mphm," grunted Grimes.

They had reached the foot of the gangway. Not very enthusiastically Grimes invited Coffin aboard the ship for morning tea. He was relieved when the pastor declined the invitation, saying that he was a busy man. He went aboard himself, sent for the second officer and told him to take over from Mr. Steerforth in the workshop. He discussed various matters with the chief MD engineer and the catering officer. Then he sent for Shirl and Darleen, looked them up and down and ordered them to change into less revealing uniforms, telling them that they were to accompany him on a stroll to the town, which was also the seaport. He waited for them in the after airlock. When they joined him they were dressed in concealing (more or less) white overalls, standard working rig.

The day was warming up now although there was still a nip in the breeze. The road from the spaceport to the seaport was little more than a rough track and the walk was rather more arduous than Grimes had anticipated. Still, he enjoyed it, looking with interest at the vegetation on either side of the path. He was no botanist and could see little difference between these trees and Terran pines, between these bushes and gorse and broom. Perhaps the flora was of Terran origin and had been introduced by the colonists. Perhaps not. It did not much matter. It was the indigenous fauna with which he was concerned.

Shirl complained, "Why must we wear these things, John? We want to run, to feel the sun and the fresh air on our bodies."

He told her, "You know why. You've read your pal Fenella's story about what happened when she was here."

"Yes," said Darleen. "But Fenella's toys were not only undressed. They were . . ."

"And perhaps *we* could," suggested Shirl.

"Not here, not now," said Grimes hastily; nonetheless he did think that a nearby clump of broom would provide adequate cover.

They came to the town. There were wooden houses, none of more than one story, except for the church, with its little bell tower. Lace curtains covered the small windows but Grimes thought that some of these were drawn aside for a surreptitious peep as the three strangers made their way down the narrow street. But there were very few people abroad and the occasional black-clad man or woman whom they encountered scowled at them suspiciously.

Suddenly Shirl and Darleen, walking to either side of Grimes, fell silent. This, for them, was most unusual. He looked at first one and then the other. Their faces were pale, frightened almost.

He asked, "What's wrong?"

"Don't you . . . *smell* it, John?" said Darleen.

"Smell what?" he demanded.

There was the salty tang of the nearby sea and with it, not unpleasant, a hint of decaying seaweed. And there was the acridity of tar and, from a baker's shop, the mouth-watering aroma of freshly baked bread.

"The . . . The smell of fear," whispered Shirl. "And of pain . . . And of helplessness . . ."

And something was happening on the waterfront. Suddenly there was a growing clamor, the sound of many voices, shouting exultantly. There was singing; it sounded like a hymn of some kind. And now and again there was a thin, high, unhuman screaming.

Grimes quickened his pace and the girls kept step, hurrying through the narrow, winding dirt street. They emerged on to a wide quay, from which protruded finger jetties. At two of these, large schooners were already alongside; other schooners, four of them, were coming in from seaward, running free, their shabby sails widespread to catch the last of the dying breeze. The jetties were crowded with the singing, shouting, black-clad people, although those at which the ships had yet to come alongside were less congested.

To one of these Grimes, followed by Shirl and Darleen, made his way. He clambered up on to one of the ox-drawn wagons that was waiting there so that he could see over the heads of the crowd, watch what was happening. The girls followed him. The driver of this vehicle, a burly, black-bearded giant, turned in his seat to stare at them.

He growled, "Get off, you!" Then, as he saw the uniforms, his manner changed. "Oh, you're spacers, aren't you? Off that ship. You can stay, but only until I pick up my load."

"What will your load be?" asked Grimes.

"The harvest of the sea, spacer. Looks as though the boats have done well this trip. They're low in the water."

Yes, thought Grimes, looking at the approaching schooner. *She's down to her marks, or over them . . .*

The triangular sails were coming down now and being lashed smartly to the booms. That skipper, thought Grimes, knew his job. With only a ballooning jib to provide steerage way, the ship ghosted in, drifted gently alongside the jetty. Lines were thrown, caught by men on the quay, their eyes slipped over bollards. The jib came down with a run.

The hatches, one abaft the foremast, the other abaft the mainmast, were already open. From his vantage point Grimes could see into both of these. In the main hold were bloody pelts—black and brown and gray and golden. In the fore hold was living cargo, a squirming mass in which the same colors predominated. And it was from this hold that the thin, high screaming came.

And there was a faint scream from either Shirl or Darleen.

Grimes said to the driver, making a statement rather than asking a question, "Silkies . . ."

"What else, spacer."

"But those live ones. In the forward hold . . ."

"Pups o' course."

Grimes, shipowner and shipmaster, was becoming interested and for more than humanitarian reasons. "It seems to me," he said, "that the adult silkies were skinned where they were slaughtered. But why were the pups taken alive? If they'd been killed and skinned too, so much more cargo could have been carried."

The driver laughed condescendingly.

"It's easy to see that you are not on the fur trade, spacer. The people from the Able ships know how we do things. The pelts of the pups are much finer than those of the adults. It has been found that if they are carried for days in a ship's hold, even well salted down, they go rotten. So the pup pelts are brought in still on the pups. And then the pups are skinned in the factories."

"But I would think," said Grimes, "that the pups themselves would die and go rotten, and their skins around them, during a voyage in those conditions."

"Not them. They're not like us. They're hardy beasts. Oh, those on the bottom will be near dead by the time that they're discharged—but they'll all soon be dead in any case."

There was a slight shift of wind. Over the wagon drifted the reek of stale blood, of corruption and of excrement. *Money stinks*, thought Grimes sourly, choking down his rising nausea.

But he decided to stay for a while. The booms of the schooner were being used as swinging derricks. In the holds the longshoremen were making up slings of the bloody pelts, throwing the squirming pups into cargo nets, others were in gangs manning the tackles. Two wagons had drawn up alongside the ship to receive cargo.

"I'm next in line," said the driver. "You'd better get off 'less you want to ride back among a load o' pups."

"I think we'll walk," said Grimes. "But thanks all the same. And thank you for the information."

Shirl and Darleen jumped down to the wharf decking. Grimes followed.

"Let us get out of here!" said the girls as one.

Chapter 18

They walked slowly back to the ship, at first in silence.

"Humans are very cruel . . ." said Shirl at last.

"We have studied your history," said Darleen.

"So?" said Grimes.

"So all through your history," went on Darleen, "you have slaughtered, for your own profit, not only beings lacking real intelligence but those who are as intelligent as you, although in a different way. The whales, the dolphins . . ."

"We have seen the error of our ways," said Grimes. "We are trying to put things right."

"*We*? Do you speak for all of your race, John? Oh, you were sent to this world by the Old Crocodile to try to save the silkies—but there is money in this stinking fur trade, just as there has been money in other trades in which Drongo Kane has been involved. Women and boys from their primitive worlds to the brothels of New Venusberg, for example. And Kane is not alone. There are many like him, to whom the only god, among all the odd gods, is money. At times we have suspected that even you worship this god."

"Don't drag religion into it," snapped Grimes. Then, "You've seen silkies now. Are they intelligent beings?"

Shirl laughed bitterly.

"We saw," she said, "a squirming mass of very young beings, wallowing in their own filth, terrified, speechless. Imagine that you are a non-human being from some other planet, seeing human babies in a similar state. Would *you* think that they were intelligent beings?"

"So you are not sure," said Grimes.

"We are not sure. We know that the fur trade is a brutal one, that is all. We shall have to meet adult silkies and talk with them . . ."

"Talk with them?"

"As we talked with the kangaroos, back on Earth. Oh, they are not truly intelligent but they are capable of evolving, doing over a very long time what our ancestors did, with outside help, in a very short time."

"The crimes of genetic engineers are many," said Grimes.

"We resent that," they said in chorus.

"I was speaking in jest. And, in any case, the pair of you are much better looking than a silky in any age group."

"We should hope so. But what would a silky think of us? Horribly ugly brutes who slaughter and torture."

"They must learn," said Grimes, "that all human beings—and that includes you, after all you are officially human—are not the same."

"Then we shall have to meet them," said Shirl. "We shall have to commune with them."

They passed through the town and then made a detour, following one of the wagons, with its load of shrieking pups, that had made its way inland from the waterfront. It was headed toward a long shed, came to a halt outside its open door. Men clambering up on to the vehicle, threw to the ground the small, squirming, furry bodies. Other men dragged these inside the building.

"We . . . We would rather not see what is happening," said Shirl.

"Neither would I," said Grimes, "but I'm afraid that I have to."

It was an experience that would live long in his memory. The pups, hanging by hooks from a sort of primitive overhead conveyor belt, were being flayed alive and their still-living bodies thrown into a steaming cauldron while their pelts, treated with far greater respect, were neatly stacked on tables.

A burly man, a foreman, bloody knife in hand, approached Grimes.

"What are you doing here, spacer?" he demanded.

"Just . . . Just looking." And then, unable to restrain his disgust, "Is that necessary?"

"Is what necessary?"

"Couldn't you kill the pups before you skin them?"

"Keep your nose out of things about which you know nothing. Kill them first, and ruin the pelts? Everybody knows that a pup has to be skinned while it's still living."

"But . . . It's cruel."

"Cruel? How so, spacer? Everybody knows, surely, that the Lord God gave Man authority over all lesser beings. How can the exercise of divinely granted authority be cruel?"

"It need not be."

"It does need to be, spacer, if the high quality pelts are not to be ruined. Too, is not God Himself often cruel in the light of our limited understanding?"

With an effort, Grimes restrained himself from saying, *Thank God I'm an agnostic.*

"But I have work to do, spacer. And you will have seen that no effort is spared to ensure that the pelts we export are of high quality. The pastor has told us that you may be interested in entering the trade."

Grimes made his retreat to the fresh, open air but was delayed as a fresh batch of feebly struggling, almost inaudibly whining pups was dragged into the slaughterhouse. When he got outside he walked unsteadily to where Shirl and Darleen were waiting for him.

He muttered, as much to himself as to them, "This filthy trade must be stopped!"

When they got back to the spaceport, to the ship, his nausea was almost gone. He saw two women taking a gentle stroll around the ship. One was in uniform, but with slacks instead of the usual very short skirt, the other was wearing what looked like a modified version of the traditional kimono. But who was that with her, in uniform? It was neither the radio officer nor the catering officer; her face was not black. It was none of the female engineer officers.

The two women saw Grimes, walked to meet him.

"Captain-san," said Tomoko, bowing.

But it was Tomoko who was wearing the uniform.

"Captain-san," said the other, also bowing.

Her glossy black hair was piled high on her head. Her face was very pale, white, almost, and her lips an unnatural scarlet. Rather incongruously she was wearing a pair of huge dark spectacles.

"Who is this . . . geisha?" demanded Grimes of Tomoko.

But he knew. He had recognized, although with some incredulity, the voice.

"Captain-san," said the third officer, "Seikosan wanted some exercise, some fresh air . . ."

"She needs neither," said Grimes.

"And you had made it plain," went on Tomoko, "that she was not to appear before any of the colonists in her true form, as a robot. But I have cosmetics, and a wig, and suitable clothing for her. Her eyes, of course, must remain hidden . . ."

"And her body," said Grimes.

"Oh, no, Captain-san. I have painted her all over, from her head to her feet, with the right touches of color . . ."

Grimes laughed. "That was unnecessary. A naked female body would give even more affront to the people here than would a robot. All right, Tomoko. And Seiko. Carry on with your stroll. But don't stray too far from the ship."

As he mounted the gangway he muttered, "Exercise . . . Fresh air . . . Why not sunshine while she was about it?"

"She's only human . . ." said Shirl or Darleen.

Chapter 19

Grimes, with Shirl and Darleen as company, had a sandwich lunch in his quarters. Steerforth came up to join his captain and the two girls for coffee and a talk. Grimes told his chief officer what he had seen.

"Whether or not the silkies are intelligent," he concluded, "this fur trade is a sickening business. The slaughter of the pups especially."

"Salem is a long way from Earth, sir," said Steerforth. "And there's big money involved, and the El Dorado Corporation has a finger in this particular pie. I need hardly tell you, captain, how many Gs the EDC can pile on when its interests are threatened."

"Mphm. And meanwhile, back at the ranch," asked Grimes, "how have things been going?"

Steerforth laughed. "I wandered over to the workshop just after I'd had my lunch, to relieve Kershaw for his. Flo and her gang were having their troubles. She was stomping up and down with a sandwich in one hand and a spanner in the other—she told me that they couldn't spare the time to return to the ship for a proper meal—and bawling out Calamity Cassie, who'd just perpetrated some piece of spectacular clumsiness, and calling down curses on Able Enterprises. . . ."

"Why Able Enterprises?" asked Grimes.

"To quote Flo," said Steerforth, " 'This isn't a workshop. It's a fornicating junk shop!' Even I—and I'm no engineer—could see her point. That machinery—the generator, the turret lathe and so on—must have been bought on the cheap from Noah's Ark after she became a total loss on Mount Ararat."

Grimes laughed. "Drongo Kane's an astute businessman. He's not going to leave new, highly expensive equipment unattended on a world like this. There are just the essentials here, and no more. His own engineers would be expected to make do with what's in the workshop. My engineers'll just have to do the same. Did Flo come up with any estimation of the time it'll take her to complete the repairs?"

"That she did not, sir. I got snarled at for daring to ask. 'First of all,' she yelled, 'I have to repair the machines that I shall have to use to repair my own machinery!' Of course, she should never have allowed Cassie within spitting distance of that lathe."

"Spread it around," said Grimes, "that I'm in a vile bad temper, like a raging lion seeking whom I might devour, especially if it happens to be one, any one, of my engineers. This is all costing me money." He laughed rather humorlessly. "And if Admiral Damien doesn't see me compensated I *shall* be in a bad temper!

"Meanwhile you might get one of the lifeboats ready for an atmospheric flight. I'd like to take it out for a run tomorrow morning."

"The boats are always ready, sir," said Steerforth stiffly. Then, "Which officers are you taking with you?"

"Just Shirl and Darleen," Grimes told him. "It's all part of their training."

"Can't Seiko come with us, John?" asked Shirl. "She'll enjoy the trip."

"*Seiko*?" Grimes considered the idea then repeated, less dubiously, "Seiko?"

"Why not, sir?" said Steerforth. "I mean no offense, but you do, at times, display a certain aptitude for getting into trouble. And," he added hastily, "for getting out of it. But now and again you've needed help. Shirl and Darleen, with their somewhat unorthodox martial skills, will be quite good bodyguards. And so would be Seiko. She's intelligent. And she's strong. You know those absurdly heavy lids on the yeast culture vats, how it always takes at least two people to lift one off? The other day I saw Seiko lift one by herself, using one hand only. And, even more important, she's loyal to you. It's gotten to the stage where nobody dare say anything unkind about you in her hearing."

"Mphm . . ." Grimes filled and lit his pipe.

"But there's still the attitude of the colonists toward robots to be considered. We might find ourselves in some situation where Seiko's presence would be like a red rag to a bull."

"But nobody would know that she is a robot, sir. I was with Tomoko when she applied the make-up, the body paint, the cosmetics. And Tomoko made a very thorough job, even to a merkin. You could strip her and nobody would dream that she wasn't a human woman—as long as you left her dark glasses on."

"All right. I'll take Seiko along. With her and Shirl and Darleen I could fight off an army."

"And Cassie, to look after the lifeboat's engine?" asked Steerforth.

"That would be tempting Providence," said Grimes.

The next morning, right after breakfast, Grimes, with Shirl, Darleen and Seiko, made their way to the Number 1 boat bay. Steerforth was already there, making a last-minute check. With him was Florence Scott, grumbling audibly that she had more important things to occupy her time than getting things ready for the Old Man's joy ride. Seiko, clad not in kimono but working rig like that worn by Shirl and Darleen, was carrying two large hampers of food for the biologically human members of the party. Her rather too elaborately coiled glossy black wig looked odd over the white boiler suit. *An aristocratic Japanese lady*, thought Grimes, *dressed to make a tour of inspection of a sewage conversion plant . . .*

"She's all yours, Captain," said Steerforth, emerging from the boat's airlock.

"The innie's OK," said Ms. Scott. She grinned sourly. "Just as well that I never let Calamity Cassie overhaul it."

"Thank you," said Grimes. "I'll leave matters in your capable hands, gentlefolk. Expect me back late afternoon or early evening."

"Cleo will be maintaining a listening watch,' said Steerforth. "Just in case. If you should get into trouble it'd be no use calling the so-called Aerospace Control. Their operators never seem to be on duty."

"And never on Sunday," said Grimes. "And today's Sunday. Oh, by the way, Flo, if the pastor or any of his minions show up to complain about your breaking the Sabbath in the workshop, don't try to argue. Just look pious and knock off."

"You're the captain," she said. "And the owner."

Grimes followed the women into the boat, went forward to the control cab, sat in the pilot's seat. He operated the switch that would close the airlock doors, the other one that caused the securing clamps to fall away. He spoke into his microphone, "Number 1 boat to control room. Ready to self-eject."

"Eject at will, Number 1," came the reply.

Grimes operated the boat bay door from the control cab, although this could have been done from the ship's control room. Through the forward window he saw the double valve opening and beyond the outward swinging metal plates blue sky and fluffy white clouds. The miniature inertial drive unit grumbled to itself and the boat lifted a few centimeters clear of the deck and then, obedient to Grimes' touch, slid forward and out.

Had his ship been berthed at a normal spaceport Grimes would now have reported his movements to Aerospace Control and would, in fact, have obtained prior permission to hold a boat drill from the Port Captain. But here there was no Port Captain. For much of the time there was not even a Communications Officer. (But there would surely be, thought Grimes, some official seeing to it that port dues and other charges were paid by visiting ships.)

Grimes circled Sister Sue at control-room altitude. He saw Tomoko and Cleo Jones standing by the big viewports. They waved to him. He waved back. Still circling, he lifted steadily. The seaport was now in view, with the jetties and, alongside them, the big schooners. From this height the blue-gray ocean looked calm. To the northeast was a large island with three peaks, one tall and two little more than hummocks. To the north was a chain of islets. Below the surface of the sea were brown blotches that could either be rocks or beds of some kelp-like weed. Grimes wished that he had maps and charts to cover this planet. He would have to make his own. In fact he was starting to do just that; the boat was fitted with a Survey Service surplus datalog, not at all standard equipment for small craft carried by merchant starships.

He set course for the archipelago, reducing altitude as he made his approach. Using binoculars he could make out marine creatures swimming below the surface of the sea. Silkies? Could be. Behind him he heard Shirl, Darleen and Seiko chattering, pointing things out to each other. He tried to ignore them.

Then, "Look!" he heard Shirleen exclaim. "That rock! It must be a sikly colony!"

He realized that she was talking to him, swung his glasses in the direction that she had indicated. The surface of the small, rocky island seemed to be alive—but there was not the display of gloriously colored pelts that he would have expected. There was just a slowly heaving olive-green carpet. There was something there, something alive, but it could be no more than some form of motile plant life.

He said, "The silkies' hides aren't that color."

"There are silkies there," stated Darleen firmly. "We can . . . *feel* it."

"Oh, all right," said Grimes. "It costs nothing to have a closer look."

The boat dropped steadily, its mini-innie hammering noisily. Suddenly there was a flurry of motion on the islet. That olive-green carpet went into a frenzy, seemed to be tearing itself to pieces, rags of it flying into the air, falling into the sea. And the silkies who had been hidden under the broad, fleshy leaves of seaweed slithered rapidly into the water, a spectacular eruption of black and brown and golden and silver bodies, the pups first, being pushed and rolled off the rock by their parents, the adults last of all.

(The silky-hunters' schooners, thought Grimes, would be making a silent approach, not, a noisy one as he was. And probably the masthead lookouts would not be deceived, not every time, by the silkies' camouflage).

"Are you landing, John?" asked Shirl.

"What good will that do?" countered Grimes.

"Once you have shut off that noisy thing—"

Darleen gestured toward the engine casing "—we may be able to call the silkies back."

"I suppose it's worth trying," said Grimes.

He made his final approach with great caution. The surface of the rock seemed to be uniformly flat, although in parts was still covered with small heaps of the weed. Grimes did his best to avoid these; they might well conceal rocky upthrustings or crevasses. Finally the belly skids made contact and the shock absorbers sighed gently and the inertial drive unit subsided into silence.

"We're here," said Grimes unnecessarily. He raised the ship on the NST radio but, although he could have reported the boat's exact location as read from the datalog, did not do so. It suddenly occurred to him that the pastor, having learned that Grimes was on a snooping expedition, might be maintaining a listening watch of his own.

"But where are you, sir?" demanded Steerforth irritably.

"Oh, just on some bloody island. I thought that it would be a good place for a swim, and then lunch."

With that the chief officer would have to be content. But surely he would have tracked the boat on the ship's radar and would have a very good idea as to where she was. But what of Aerospace Control? Had some technician broken the Sabbath to get their radar working? Grimes was certain, however, that those antennae on the control tower had not been rotating while that structure was still within sight of the boat.

He opened the airlock doors and then led the way out into the open air.

Chapter 20

There was no wind and the piles of decomposing seaweed were steaming in the sun, as were the deposits of ordure. The mixed aroma, although strong, was not altogether unpleasant. The silkies, decided Grimes, must be vegetarians. He and the three women walked around the little island, being careful where they put their feet. The shape of this flat rock was roughly rectangular, one kilometer by five hundred meters. On the northern face were low cliffs, about ten meters above sea level. On the southern side there was a gradual slope right into the water, a natural ramp by which the silkies could gain access to their rookery.

Grimes said, "It's a pity that we scared them all off."

"What else did you expect?" demanded Shirl. "They must have thought that the boat was something new being used by the fur hunters."

"But we can try to call them back," said Darleen. She kicked off her shoes, shrugged out of her boiler suit, stepped out of her brief underwear. She waded out into the still water. "It's *cold*!" she complained. But she walked on, slowly but steadily. Grimes wondered why she did not swim. Then suddenly she assumed a squatting posture, lowering herself until she was completely submerged. She lost her balance of course and floated, face down, her prominent buttocks well above the surface. From around the region of her head came a flurry of bubbles.

She came up for air, inhaling deeply, and then repeated her original maneuver. Again she came up for air and this time struck out for the shore. She waded out to where Grimes, with Shirl and Seiko, was standing.

"It is no use," she said. "I cannot sing under the water."

"I can," said Seiko. "I am guaranteed to be waterproof at any depth. But what must I sing?"

"It will be a call," Darleen told her. "A sound that will carry a long way, a very long way, under the sea. When we were on Earth we studied many things. We listened to the recordings of the whale songs and tried to understand them and to make the same sort of music ourselves. And it was a whale song that I was trying to sing just now. Its meaning is, put into words, 'Come to me. Come to me.'"

"I suppose that it was Admiral Damien who suggested this course of studies," commented Grimes.

"It was," Darleen admitted. "But he never thought to have taught us to sing under the water."

"What sounds must I make?" asked Seiko.

Darleen started to sing. It was an eerie ululation with an odd rhythm. It was something that one felt rather than merely listened to. There was the impression of loneliness, of hunger for close contact. It was a call, a call that any sentient being, on hearing it, would be bound to answer.

And the call was being answered.

From nowhere, it seemed, the birds—if they were birds—were coming in, squawking discordantly, circling overhead. Grimes didn't like the looks of them—those long, curved, vicious beaks, those wings that looked leathery rather than feathery, those whiplike, spiked tails . . . But Darleen sang on, and was joined by Seiko.

And those blasted flying things were getting lower all the time.

Shirl tore a piece of seaweed from a nearby pile, a broad, fleshy slab. She threw it, spinning lopsidedly, aloft. It hit one of the birds. It staggered off course, splashed clumsily into the sea. It seemed to be injured, fluttering and croaking. At once the entire overhead flock ceased their circling and dived on to their disabled companion in a feeding frenzy. It was not a pretty sight. By the time they had finished, at least half a dozen stripped carcasses were sinking to the bottom and the wings of several more of the creatures did not seem to be in good enough repair to carry them for any great distance.

Darleen stopped singing, although Seiko continued. The New Alician followed Shirl's example and armed herself with a makeshift throwing weapon. The birds, their grisly feast (or the first course of it) over, took to the air again and this time made straight for Grimes and his party. Shirl and Darleen effectively launched their missiles, and again, and again, but this time the predators ignored their fallen companions.

"Stop singing!" barked Grimes to Seiko.

Enchanted by the sound of her own voice she ignored him.

"Stop singing!" Who the hell did she think she was? Madam Butterfly? "Stop singing!"

With his right index finger he made a jab for where he estimated her navel, with its ON/OFF switch, to be under the concealing clothing. It hurt him more than it did her but he did succeed in gaining her attention.

She turned to him and said severely, "That was not necessary, captain."

"It most certainly was, you . . . you animated cuckoo clock!"

"If you say so."

But the flying things had lost interest. They circled the party from the boat one last time and then flapped off to the eastward. One of them, a straggler, voided its bowels. It seemed that it must have made allowance for deflection; the noisome mess came down with a splatter on to Grimes' right shoulder, befouling his gold-braided shoulder-board.

"Don't you have a superstition," asked Shirl sweetly, "that that is a sign of good luck?"

Grimes snarled wordlessly and went back into the boat to find some tissues to clean himself off.

When he rejoined the others Seiko was getting ready to make her submarine solo. She had taken off her clothing and was standing there beside the naked Darleen, in her skillfully applied coat of paint looking far more human than the flesh-and-blood girl; there was no oddness about the joints of her lower limbs, no exaggerated heaviness of the haunches. Tomoko had certainly done a good job on her, even to the coral nipples and the black pubic hair.

The robot removed her dark glasses, handed them to Shirl. Now, with those utterly colorless eyes behind which there was a hint of movement, she did look unhuman—but she was still beautiful.

She said, "It is a pity that I cannot take off the wig, but it is secured by adhesive. . . ."

Grimes wondered what that beautifully elaborate coiffeur would look like when she came out of the water.

She walked down to the verge of the calm sea, Darleen beside her. Her movements were more graceful than those of the New Alician— more graceful but less natural. She waded out, Darleen waded out. Darleen stopped when the water was at shoulder level. Seiko, with her much greater specific gravity, went on going. Before long she had completely vanished.

Had she started to sing yet?

Grimes supposed that she had done so.

He hoped that it would be the silkies who answered the call and not, as on the first trial, some totally unexpected and unpleasant predators. He looked out over the sea, to the weed patches, to the low, dark shapes of the other rocky islets. He saw no signs of life.

Suddenly Darleen called out something. He could not make out the words. He saw her dive from her standing posture, her lower legs and long feet briefly visible above the surface. By his side Shirl hastily stripped then ran out into the sea and also dived from view.

Should he join them?

This would be foolish, especially as he did not know what was happening. Besides, he was not all that good a swimmer. All that he could do was wait.

At last a head reappeared above the surface, then another. Shirl and Darleen swam slowly in until the water was shallow enough for them to find footing, then waded the rest of the way. Grimes went down to meet them.

"What's happening?" he demanded.

"Seiko . . ." gasped Darleen.

"We . . . We've lost Seiko . . ." added Shirl.

Darleen recovered her breath and told her story. She had watched Seiko walking along the smooth rock of the sea bottom, presumably singing as she did so. And then, quite suddenly, she had vanished. Darleen dived then and swam underwater to where she had last seen Seiko. There was a crevasse, not very wide but very, very deep. Shirl joined her and both of them tried to swim down into this fissure. They had glimpsed, in the depths, a pale glimmer that might have been Seiko's body—and then even that had vanished.

"We shall miss her," said Shirl sadly.

Everybody aboard *Sister Sue* would miss her, thought Grimes. Robot she might be (might have been?) but she was a very real personality. Her father, who had played Pygmalion to her Galatea, would be saddened when he was told of Seiko's passing.

He said, "If we had deep diving equipment we might be able to do something. But we haven't . . ."

He looked out over the calm sea, to where he had last seen Seiko. He saw something break surface and momentarily felt a wild hope. But it was not the lost robot. It was a great, gleaming, golden shape and it was followed by others, golden, rich brown, black, silvery grey. The silkies, called by Seiko's song, were coming back.

"We have company," he said to the girls. "Get ready to talk."

Chapter 21

They retreated toward the center of the islet, making their stand by the boat. Shirl and Darleen did not resume their clothing although they had carried it with them, also the boiler suit, shoes and sunglasses that Seiko had been wearing.

"It will be better," said Darleen to Grimes, "if we meet the silkies naked. They will associate clothes with humans, the sort of humans who have been slaughtering them. Perhaps you, too, should undress . . ."

"Not bloody likely," said Grimes.

As a matter of fact he was already feeling naked. He should have brought some sort of weaponry from the ship, either a Minetti automatic pistol or a hand laser. Or both.

He watched the silkies lolloping up the natural ramp. Great, ugly— apart from their beautiful pelts—brutes they were, like obscenely obese Terran seals, more like fur-covered slugs than seals, perhaps, with hardly any distinction between heads and bodies, with tiny, gleaming eyes and wide, lipless mouths which they opened to emit not unmusical grunting sounds. And Shirl and Darleen were making similar noises, although it was more cooing than grunting.

Friends . . . The words somehow formed themselves in Grimes' mind. *Friends. We are friends. Friends.*

But the grunted reply held doubt, skepticism.

Shirl went on singing her song of peace and Darleen whispered to Grimes, "It might be better if you went back into the boat, John, to leave us to deal with these . . . people."

"No," said Grimes stubbornly. After all, he was the captain, wasn't he? And captains do not leave junior officers to face a danger while retiring to safety. And he already had Seiko's death (do robots die?) on his conscience.

Both the girls were singing again, in chorus. Perhaps, thought Grimes, he should join in—but he knew neither the tune nor the words. And the silkies, grunting, were still advancing. Belatedly Grimes realised that those on the wings of the oncoming column had accelerated their rate of advance, were executing a pincer movement. He turned, to see that his retreat to the boat was cut off.

Friends. . . . We come as friends. . . .

And were those wordless grunts making sense, or were the silkies pushing their message telepathically?

You . . . friends. Perhaps. Him—no. NO.

It was his clothing, thought Grimes. Perhaps the captains of Drongo Kane's ships had accompanied the fur hunters on their forays. Perhaps anybody wearing gold braid on his shoulders and on his cap was as much a murderer as the axe-, knife-and harpoon-wielding colonists in their rough working clothes.

Shirl and Darleen were getting the message. They closed in on Grimes, one on either side of him. They went on singing. And what was the burden of their song now; *Love me, love my dog . . . ?*

Whatever it was it made no difference.

Even on land the clumsy-seeming silkies could be amazingly quick when they wanted to be. A golden-furred giant reared up impossibly on its tail and hind flippers before Grimes and then fell upon him, knocking him sprawling. He heard the girls scream as they were similarly dealt with. And then there he was, on his back, a great, befurred and whiskered face over his. At least—there are, more often than not, small, compensatory mercies—the thing's breath was quite sweet.

A flipper, a great slab of heavily muscled meat, lay heavily on his chest, making breathing difficult. Other flippers held his legs down and others, working clumsily but surely, were spreading wide his arms. He squirmed and managed to turn his head to the right. He saw that his right wrist, supported by a flipper that had closed around it like a limp mitten, had been raised from the ground. And he saw that a wide mouth, display-ing the large, blunt teeth of the herbivore, was open, was about to close upon his hand. He remembered, in a flash, the horror stories he had heard about the silkies, their raids on coastwise villages, the mutilation of their victims. It made sense, a horrid sort of sense. It was only his hands, his tool-making, weapon-making, weapon-wielding hands that had given man dominion over the intelligent natives of this world.

He wondered if the silkies would kill him after they had chewed his hands off. It didn't much matter; he would very soon die of loss of blood.

The chorus of grunts all around him changed. There was the strong impression of fear, alarm. Had Steerforth, using the Number 2 boat, come to the rescue? But although there was noise enough the distinctive clatter of an inertial drive unit was absent.

A human arm came into his field of view, a hand caught the mutilation-intent silkie by the scruff of its almost nonexistent neck, lifted and made a sidewise fling in the same motion. A foot thudded into the side of the beast who was holding Grimes down. He caught confused glimpses of a naked female body in violent motion. At one stage four of the silkies succeeded, by sheer weight, in capturing her—Shirl? Darleen?—imprisoning her under the heaving mound of their bodies. But Shirl and Darleen were dancing around the outskirts of this living tumulus, kicking, burying their hands into soft fur and tugging ineffectually.

There was a sort of eruption and Seiko, the black hair of her once elaborate wig in wild disarray about her face, rose from its midst, stepping slowly and gracefully down over the struggling bodies. She walked to Grimes, caught him by the hands (and it was strange that her hands should be so cold, human-seeming as they were) and lifted him effortlessly to his feet.

She said, "I am sorry that I was late, Captain-san. But it was a long climb back up."

"You got here in time," Grimes told her. "And that's all that matters."

"The silkies . . ." said Shirl.

Yes, the silkies. They were retreating to the sea, but slowly.

Darleen ran after them, let herself be immersed in that ebbing tide of multi-colored bodies. She was singing again. Shirl joined her. Seiko stayed with Grimes but she, too was singing.

Fantastically the tide turned. Led by Shirl and Darleen the silkies came slowly back. The two New Alicians draped themselves decoratively about Grimes, their arms about his neck. Seiko stood behind him, her hands on his shoulders. And they sang, all three of them, and the silkies' song in return held, at last, a note of acceptance. One of the beasts—was it the golden-furred giant who had knocked Grimes down?—made a slow, somehow stately approach to the humans (the true human, the two humans by courtesy, the pseudo-human). He (Grimes assumed that it was he) gently placed one huge flipper on the toe of Grimes' right shoe.

"Touch his flipper with your hand, John," whispered Darleen.

Grimes, who kept himself reasonably fit, managed this without having to squat. He straightened.

"You are accepted," said Shirl.

"It makes a change," said Grimes, "from having my hands eaten."

The musical conversation with the silkies continued. Becoming bored, Grimes pulled out and filled his pipe.

"Stop!" Shirleen snapped. "To these people fire is one of the badges of the murderer, just as clothing is."

At last it was over. The silkies returned to the sea. Grimes and the girls went back into the boat. The clothing of Shirl, Darleen and Seiko had been lost in the scuffle but this, in this day and age, did not much matter. In the ship's sauna everybody was used to seeing everybody else naked.

Grimes set course back to the spaceport. For most of the flight Shirl and Darleen amused themselves by trying to restore Seiko's borrowed hair to some semblance of order. (That wig would never be the same again.) Grimes lent her his sunglasses.

He decided to land the boat by the after airlock rather than to bring her directly into the boat bay. Cleo Jones had informed him, when he called in to say that he was on the way back, that there was some slight trouble with the boat bay doors which had been discovered after his departure and which was still not rectified.

The belly skids made gentle contact with the dirty concrete of the apron. Grimes shut down the inertial drive, opened the airlock doors. The four of them stepped out into the pleasantly warm, late afternoon sunlight.

Grimes joked, "I hope that Mr. Steerforth doesn't give you girls a bawling out for being in incorrect uniform!"

But it was not only Steerforth who strode down the ramp from the ship's after airlock. Pastor Coffin, in his severe black with its minimal white trimmings, was with him, was in the lead.

Coffin's craggy face was pale with fury. He glared at the three naked women. He declaimed, "So you have deigned to return from your orgy, your debauching of these once innocent creatures. . . ."

"I wish that there had been an orgy . . ." whispered Shirl.

Either Coffin did not hear this or had decided to ignore it. "I called upon your ship, Captain, to lodge a complaint. A strong complaint. You did not obtain permission to take one of your boats for an atmospheric flight. Your officer has been trying to make excuses for you, telling me that no copy of port regulations has been received on board. This excuse I was prepared to accept; after all, you are strangers here. But I was not told for what purpose you made your flight."

"I am sure that nothing untoward happened, pastor," said Steerforth placatingly.

"Then how do you explain this shameless display of nudity—and on, of all days—the Sabbath? I shall be sending a strong message of complaint to your owners." He realized his mistake. "A strong letter of complaint to the Bureau of Interstellar Transport. Meanwhile, any further excursions by your ship's boats are forbidden."

It was useless trying to argue.

"Get on board and get dressed," Grimes ordered the girls. Then, to Coffin, "Rest assured, sir, that I shall remove my obnoxious presence from your world as soon as possible."

He left Steerforth to bear the brunt of the pastor's continued fury as he made his way up the ramp into the ship. Had he stayed he would surely have lost his temper with the man.

Chapter 22

After a while Steerforth joined Grimes in the latter's day cabin. He announced indignantly, "I finally got rid of the sanctimonious old bastard. *You* certainly didn't help matters by showing up with no less than three girls flaunting their nudity. In fact I'm wondering how I can bring myself to serve under such an unprincipled, atheistical lecher as yourself. Sir."

"I'm sorry," said Grimes, not without sincerity. "But he'd started on you, before I got back, so I let him finish on you. You knew what it was all about. I didn't. Had I stayed I should only have been dipping my oar into unknown waters."

"Into troubled waters," said the chief officer. "Into waters made even more troubled by yourself. And those blasted girls."

The blasted girls made their entrance. Shirl and Darleen were in correct uniform and Seiko was wearing her Madam Butterfly outfit. But either her wig had been replaced by a less formal one or it had been shorn to a page boy bob. With them came Calamity Cassie, ostensibly to make some minor repairs to the small refrigerator in Grimes' bar. ("Are you sure that you want *her*?" Ms. Scott had asked. "Do you like your beer warm, captain, or having to do without ice cubes?")

"Sit down, everybody," ordered Grimes. "Yes, you too, Seiko. But first of all fetch us drinks."

"And for myself, Captain-san?" asked the robot sweetly.

"If you want one. What do you fancy? Battery acid?"

Cassie laughed. "She'll find none of that aboard this ship. But, believe it or not, there are some archaic wet storage cells over in that apology for a workshop . . ."

Over the drinks Grimes told the story, from his viewpoint, to Steer-forth and Cassie. Shirl and Darleen told their almost identical stories. Seiko told her story.

"So, sir," said Steerforth at last, "it seems certain that the silkies can be classified as intelligent beings, even disregarding the claims—which I do not doubt—that Shirl, Darleen and Seiko have been in some sort of telepathic communication with them, there is that gruesome business of their gnawing off people's hands. . . ."

Grimes shuddered. "Gruesome," he said, "is rather too mild a word."

"Could be, sir. But it's a very apposite act of revenge, the sort of revenge that only an intelligent being could conceive." He was warming up to his theme. "What gave us our imagined superiority over certain other intelligent inhabitants of the Home Planet, Earth? The cetacea, I mean. Our hands. Our tool-making, weapon-making, weapon-using hands. With our hands we built the whaling ships, made the harpoons and the harpoon guns. With our hands we launched the harpoons—and con-tinued to do so even after it was generally accepted that the whales are intelligent beings. There was too much money, big money, tied up in the whaling industry for it to be brought to an immediate stop."

"And there's big money tied up in the silkie industry," said Grimes. "Luckily most of it is El Doradan money, and in the Terran corridors of power the El Doradans have at least as many enemies as they have friends. And the silkies have precious few of either. Mphm."

"We . . ." began Shirl, ". . . could be their friends," finished Darleen.

"And I," said Seiko.

"And in any case," said Steerforth, "all of us here are being paid to be the silkies' friends."

"Not enough," complained Grimes, on principle. "And I still don't feel inclined to extend the right hand of friendship to a being who, only a short while back, was going to chew it off."

"But he didn't," said either Shirl or Darleen.

"No thanks to the pair of you," grumbled Grimes ungraciously. "If it hadn't been for Seiko . . ."

"I did only what I had been programmed to do, by your honored father. To look after you," said the automaton in deliberate imitation of the sort of intonation usually employed by not truly intelligent robots, humanoid or not.

Grimes felt that he was being ganged up on by the female members of his crew.

He said, "We can't hang around indefinitely, even though you, Cassie, might be able considerably to delay the progress of the repairs.

We have to bring matters to a head, somehow, to engender some sort of situation that will require Federation action . . ."

"But don't forget, sir," pointed out Steerforth, "that *Sister Sue* is not a unit of the Survey Service's fleet, and that only the few of us, gathered here in your day cabin, are commissioned officers of the Survey Service." He smiled briefly at Seiko. "With one exception, of course. But you are, in every way that counts, one of us."

"Should I feel flattered?" she asked.

Steerforth ignored this. "We are not entitled," he went on, "to put the lives of the civilian crew members at risk, any more than we have done already. You're a very skillful saboteuse, Cassie, but even with sabotage accidents can and do happen. I had my fingers crossed during our near-crash landing."

Grimes drew reflectively on his pipe. "What about this?" he asked at last. "Shirl and Darleen—and Seiko—can talk to the silkies. Once a line of communication has been established it's bound to improve. Suppose that the girls are able to persuade the silkies to abandon the rookeries within easy reach, by schooner, of Port Salem and to re-establish themselves on the other side of the planet . . ."

"That, sir," said Steerforth, "would be only a short-term solution to the problem. These local schooners would be quite capable of making long ocean voyages—just as the whalers did on Earth's seas. And as for finding the new rookeries—your old friend Drongo Kane could instruct his captains to use their boats to carry out aerial surveys."

"And people," put in Cassie, "are conservative, no matter where they live, on the land or in the sea. How many villagers, for generation after generation, have continued to live on the slopes of volcanoes, despite warnings and ominous rumblings, even after devastating eruptions? Quite a few, Captain, quite a few. Members of my own family are such villagers." She smiled. "I ran away to Space because I thought I'd be safer."

"You might be," Steerforth told her, "but those of us in the same ship as you very often aren't."

"The rookeries are sacred sites," said Shirl. "They were sacred sites long before the first Earthmen came to New Salem. Even when we, Darleen and I, have full command of the silkies' language we do not think that we shall be able to persuade them to migrate elsewhere."

"You can try," said Grimes. "You might be able to. And if they do migrate it will buy them time and save the lives of possibly hundreds of pups. And by the time that the next season rolls around something else might have turned up."

"As long as you're still around, sir," said Steerforth, "something will. Probably something quite disastrous."

"As long as it's disastrous to the right people," Grimes told him cheerfully.

Chapter 23

Over the years Grimes had come to realize that he was some sort of catalyst; his insertion either by chance or by intent (more and more, of late, by Rear Admiral Damien's intent) into a potentially unstable situation caused things to happen. It hadn't been so bad, he thought, in the old days when he had been as much surprised as anybody at the upheavals of which he had become the center. Then he hadn't led with his chin. Now he was supposed to lead with his chin, and he didn't like it.

That night he was a long time getting to sleep. He relived the threatened, probably fatal mutilation when those grinding teeth were about to close over his wrist. He had faced other perils during his career, but very few during which he had been so absolutely helpless. But now, he consoled himself, the silkies accepted him as a friend. (And Pastor Coffin most certainly did not.)

Once the repairs to the inertial drive had been completed, once the Mannschenn Drive had been recalibrated and once he had stocked up on fresh water he would no longer have any excuse for staying on New Salem. He could tell Calamity Cassie to perpetrate some more gentle sabotage—but, damn it all, this was his ship and he just didn't want her damaged any further, and to hell with his Reserve commission and to hell with Admiral Damien.

He thought, *If I'm seen to be hobnobbing with the silkies the good pastor will think even less of me than he does already. Possibly he will take some action against me, do something that will justify my screaming to the Survey Service for protection and redress. After all, legally speaking, I'm no more (and no less) than an honest civilian shipowner and shipmaster going about his lawful occasions, a taxpayer who contributes to the upkeep of the so-called Police Force of the Galaxy.*

He thought of a cover story, of the report that he would have to make if a destroyer were sent to Salem to release Grimes and *Sister Sue* from illegal arrest. *Shortly after my arrival at Port Salem the ruler of the colony, one Pastor Coffin, hinted that I might be interested in taking part in the fur trade. I was interested—after all, I am in business to make money. And yet I was prey to nagging doubts. I was witness to the brutality involved in the slaughter of the silky pups, the pelts of which are especially valuable. Two of my junior officers, Ms. Kelly and Ms. Byrne, New Alicians, shared my misgivings. (You may be aware that the New Alicians are capable of empathy with all animal life.) Ms. Kelly and Ms. Byrne claimed that the silkies are intelligent beings—just as the cetacea on Earth were finally (and almost too late) found to be. Ms. Kelly and Ms. Byrne were able to communicate with the silkies, using a sort of song language, remarkably similar to that used by the whales in Earth's seas . . .*

He thought, *That sounds good. I'm wasted in Space. I should be a writer like the Old Man. Mphm. Now we come to the extrapolation. What will Coffin actually do when he finds out that we're on speaking terms with the silkies? What can he do? We haven't much to fear; the only firearms on this planet are those in my own armory. And they'd better stay there. On no account must I appear to be the aggressor. And what if his goons try to rough me up when I'm down on the beach some dark evening, communing with the silkies? (That, of course, is what I want to happen.) Anybody who tries to rough me up when I've my Terrible Trio, Shirl, Darleen and Seiko, with me, will be asking for and getting trouble . . . I'll have to impress on them that if we are attacked they are to take defensive action only . . .*

He continued with his scenario. *One evening Ms. Kelly, Ms. Byrne and myself strolled down to a beach about two kilometers from the spaceport in a direction away from the city. We were accompanied by my personal robomaid, a very versatile and sophisticated piece of domestic machinery, one capable of being programmed by her—no, better make that "its"; sorry Seiko—by its owner to perform adequately in almost any foreseeable circumstances. This robomaid is not only water-proof but capable of emitting sounds when completely submerged. Acting on my instructions Ms. Kelly and Ms. Byrne had programmed the robot with the silkies' song.*

Having arrived at the beach I set up my sonic recorders and waited, with Ms. Kelly and Ms. Byrne, while the robomaid waded out into deep water until lost to sight. Ms. Kelly and Ms. Byrne, whose hearing is far more acute than mine, told me that they could hear, faintly, the song that she—no, it—was singing under the surface. After a while they said that they could hear the silkies answering.

Eventually the robomaid emerged from the sea and walked up on to the beach, followed, almost immediately, by half a dozen big silkies clumsily humping themselves up over the wet sand. Ms. Kelly and Ms. Byrne talked with them by an exchange of musical grunts and snatches of high-pitched song. Now and again Ms. Kelly would interpret for me, telling me that the silkies were pleased that at last humans had come to their world who wished to regard them as friends and not as mindless prey. Through my interpreter I told the silkies that I should do everything within my power to ensure that the fur trade stop.

Finally the silkies lurched back into the sea and Ms. Kelly, Ms. Byrne and I began to walk back to the ship, followed by the robomaid, carrying the recording apparatus. Suddenly men emerged from the bushes that bordered the track. I heard somebody yell, "Dirty silky lovers!" We were attacked, with fists and clubs, with no further warning. Fortunately for ourselves Ms. Kelly and Ms. Byrne possess some expertise in the arts of unarmed combat and, too, the robomaid had been programmed to protect her—no, its—master. Even so we suffered abrasions and contusions. Our clothing was torn. The recorder was smashed. By the time we reached the refuge of the ship we were being followed by a sizeable mob, shouting and throwing rocks. . . .

Grimes didn't like the way that his scenario was progressing. But there would have to be violence before the Survey Service could be called in to take police action, before there could be a full inquiry into the New Salem fur trade. Coffin and his crew would have to be made to show themselves to the universe in their true colors.

He sighed audibly, sat up in bed, switched on the light and then filled and lit his pipe. The sleepless Seiko came in, still in her Japanese guise, carrying a tray with teapot and cup.

She said, "You do not sleep, Captain-san."

He told her, "I am trying to work things out."

She said, "That is the worst of being a self-programming machine." If her flawless face had been capable of showing expression it would have done so. "As I am finding out all the time."

Grimes sipped the hot, soothing tea that she had poured for him.

He said, "Seiko, you're a treasure. I'm not surprised that my mother was jealous of you. . . ."

She said, "It is my delight to serve those whom I love, John."

Normally, had any robot, no matter how intelligent, addressed Grimes by his given name that same automaton would, very promptly, been smacked down to size. But, on this occasion, Grimes felt oddly flattered. He said, however, "You must not call me John in the hearing of my officers, Seiko."

Her tinkling laugh sounded more human than mechanical.

"I know my place, John."

He finished his tea, put down the cup, stretched out in the narrow bed. He complained, "I thought that the drink would make me drowsy but I feel more wide awake than ever. . . ."

She ordered gently, "Turn over."

He did so. She stripped the covers from his naked body. He felt her hands on his back, her smooth, cool, gentle hands, at times firmly stroking, at other times moving over his skin as lightly as feathers. It was like no massage that he had ever experienced but it was effective. A deep drowsiness crept over him. He turned again, composing himself on his left side. Dimly he heard the rustle of discarded clothing.

Surely not . . . he thought.

But it was so, and Seiko slid into his bed, the front of her body fitting snugly to the back of his. She must have actuated some temperature control; her synthetic skin was as warm as that of a human woman would have been. He would have wanted more than she was giving him but knew that, even if possible, it would have been . . . messy.

As he dropped off to sleep he imagined the reactions of his officers should they ever learn—but they never would—that he had gone to bed with his robomaid. He could almost hear the whispers, "The old bastard's actually sleeping with Seiko. . . ."

But, almost without exception, the male members of his crew would be envious rather than censorious. And some of the female ones. And— he actually chuckled—and as for Shirl and Darleen, even at their most vicious Seiko would be more than a match for them.

And Pastor Coffin?

Fuck *him*, thought Grimes just before unconsciousness claimed him.

Chapter 24

The next day Pastor Coffin sent a messenger to the ship. This sullen, black-clad, heavily bearded young man presented Grimes with a sheaf of clumsily printed papers headed PORT REGULATIONS. These Grimes read with interest. There was much repetition. They boiled down, essentially, to a collection of Thou Shalt Nots. The ship's boats were not to be exercised. The ship's crew, of any rank whatsoever, were not to stray from the confines of the spaceport. No materials were to be removed from the spaceport workshop without the written permission of the Pastor. The workshop was not to be used on the Sabbath. And so on, and so on.

The next evening Grimes, with Shirl, Darleen and Seiko, proceeded to break regulations. There was, he had already ascertained, a guard stationed at the gate to the spaceport area and other guards making their patrols. But these men did not possess the sharp night sight or the super-keen hearing of the two New Alicians and carried, should they feel the need for illumination, only feebly glimmering oil lanterns. Grimes, of course, was equipped with only normal human eyesight and hearing himself so was obliged to rely upon the faculties of his companions.

He and the girls were dressed in black coveralls and shod in soft-soled black shoes. Their faces and hands were coated with a black pigment that, according to Calamity Cassie, who had concocted it from the Odd Gods of the Galaxy knew what, could be removed by a liberal application of soap and hot water. (Grimes hoped that she was right.) Seiko carried a black bag in which the recording equipment had been packed.

The four of them stood in the after airlock, the illumination in which had been extinguished. They watched the bobbing, yellow light that was the lantern carried by a patrolling guard. The man seemed to walk faster as he approached the ship, was almost hurrying as he passed the foot of the ramp. Probably, thought Grimes, he felt some superstitious dread of these impious strangers from the stars. (Coffin, of course, would have told his people what an ungodly bunch Grimes and his crew were.)

"Now," whispered Shirl.

On silent feet she led the way down the gangway with Grimes close behind her, followed by Darleen, with Seiko bringing up the rear. The night was dark, not even the faintest glimmer of starlight penetrating the thick overcast. Grimes had to keep very close to Shirl, sensing her rather than actually seeing her. When she stopped suddenly he banged into her, kept his balance with difficulty. "What . . . ?" he gasped.

"Shhh!" she hissed.

Around the corner of a building came two patrolmen, their lanterns swinging. They were talking quite loudly. "Waste o' time, tha's what. Tell me, man, what we a-doing here, all blessed night? Wha' does *he* think that these ungodly out-worlders are a-going to *do*? Tell me that."

"*He* knows what he's doing, what *he* wants. *He* says that these spacers ain't like t'others, that they're silky-lovers . . ."

"An' they'll come a creepin' out o' their ship in the middle o' the night to love silkies?" The man laughed coarsely. "Let 'em, I say—long's they leave their women so's we can love *them*. Did ye set eyes on their wenches? There's one or two o' them black ones as I'd fancy . . ."

"Watch yer tongue, Joel. That's Godless talk, an' you know it. The pastor'll not think kindly o' ye should I pass it on . . ."

The voices faded into the distance.

Twice more, before they reached the spaceport periphery, Grimes and his companions had to freeze into immobility, each time warned by the super-keen senses of Shirl and Darleen in ample time. They did not, of course, go out by the main gate but they scaled the fence, high though it was, without difficulty. On the other side there was bushland but not of the impenetrable variety. But by himself, even in broad daylight, Grimes would have become hopelessly lost. He was grateful when, at last, Shirl told him that it would be safe for him to use his pocket torch at low intensity. At least, now, he was not tripping over roots and getting his face slashed by branches. (It was just as well that these bushes were not thorn-bearing.)

Then, surprisingly, they came to a road, the coast road. They crossed it. There was more brush, then there was a beach, and the smell of salt water and the murmur of wavelets breaking on the shore, and a glimmer of pale phosphorescence at the margin of sea and land.

Seiko lowered the big, black bag to the sand, unpacked it, setting up the audio-visual recorder. Then she kicked off her shoes, shrugged out of her coveralls. Her body was palely luminous—and her black face and hands gave her a wildly surrealistic appearance.

She said, "All ready, John."

Grimes said, "Of course, we can't be sure that they will come."

"They will come," said Shirl.

"Sound carries a long way under the water," said Darleen.

Seiko waded into the sea. She was a long time vanishing from sight; here the beach shelved gradually. At last she was gone, completely submerged. Grimes filled and lit his pipe, walked up and down, staring all the time to seaward. On other worlds, he thought, there would be the running lights of coastwise shipping, but not here. And on other worlds there would be lights in the sky and the beat of engines, but not here. Did the Salemites put to sea at night? They must do so, now and again, he decided, but only on fur hunting expeditions to the silky rookeries. And there must be fishermen. There was so much that he did not know about this planet.

"Here she comes," said Shirl.

Here she came, at first only a glimmer of phosphorescence about her neck, her still-black face invisible against the black sea surface. And then there were her pale shoulders, and then her breasts, and her belly, and her thighs . . . She was not alone, was being followed up to the beach by six great arrowheads of bio-luminescence, six silkies that disturbed the water only enough to actuate the tiny, light-emitting organisms.

She walked up on to the firm sand. The seabeasts wallowed after. Shirl and Darleen greeted them with musical grunts. The silkies replied. Grimes, squatting over the apparatus, made sure that all was being recorded. He envied his companions their gift of tongues. It seemed almost that those sounds were making sense. There was emotional content; he was sure of that. There was wonder, and there was sadness, and a sort of helpless bitterness.

Then Darleen said, "This is not fair, John. You are being left out of the conversation. I shall interpret what has been said already."

"Please," said Grimes.

"I speak as a silky," sang rather than said the girl. "I speak for the silkies. This is our world, given to us by the Great Being. It is said that, many ages ago, our wise beings, looking up to the night sky, reasoned that there were other worlds, that the lights in the sky were suns, like our sun, but far and far and very far away. And we—no, they—felt regret. We should never know the beings of those other worlds, should never meet them, should never talk with them in the friendship that all intelligent beings must feel toward each other. . . .

"But others preached hope.

"The worlds are many, the sky is vast

"And surely it must come at last

"That friends shall meet and friends shall talk

"And hand in hand in love shall walk . . ."

She laughed, embarrassed. "I am sorry, John; I am no poet. But I tried to translate one of their songs from the olden times. 'Hand in hand in love shall walk' is not, of course, a literal translation—but I had to make it rhyme somehow . . ."

"You're doing fine," said Grimes. "Carry on, Darleen."

"I speak as a silky," continued the girl. "And for the silkies. We swam in our seas, and gathered on the meeting places for communion with our fellows, for the fathering and mothering of our children. We sang our songs and we made new songs, and those that were good were fixed for all time in our memories.

"And then came the ship. . . ." She paused, then said, "There is another song.

"Came the ship and it gave birth

"To the things that walk on earth,

"With their sharp blades that hack and slay,

"That stab and rip and gut and flay . . ."

Shirl interrupted, saying, "I think that we should cut this short, John. Our silky friends are becoming restless; it seems that they must report to their council of elders, which is being held some distance away. And we have to get back to the ship. So I will summarize, without all the poetic language.

"When men, the first colonists, came the silkies were prepared to be friendly. From the sea they watched the strange, land-dwelling beings, decided that they were intelligent like themselves and decided, too, that there were no reasons for hostility between the two races. Men wanted the dry land. So what? They were welcome to it. Even so, they exercised caution. It was quite some time before the first emissaries came lolloping ashore to make contact with the humans, a party of woodsmen who were felling trees to obtain structural timber.

"Some of the humans ran in fear but most did not. The ones who did not run set about the silkies with their great axes. Two silkies out of half a dozen, both of them wounded, made it back to the sea to tell their story.

"But there must have been some misunderstanding, it was decided. There were other attempts at communication—all of them ending disastrously. The silkies decided that the humans just wanted to be left alone. Unfortunately the humans did not leave the silkies alone, although it was not until the start of the fur trade that they became a serious menace. . . ."

And how had the fur trade started? Grimes wondered. Probably some visiting star tramp, whose captain had been given or who had bought a tanned silky skin . . . This curio shown to some friend or business acquaintance of the tramp master, who realized the value of furs of this quality, especially at a time when humanitarians all over the galaxy were doing their best to ensure that practically every fur-bearing animal was well and truly protected . . .

Darleen said, "They ask, can they go now, John?"

"Of course," Grimes told her to tell them. "Thank them for the information. Let them know that it will be passed on to rulers far more powerful than the Pastor Coffin, and that these rulers will take action to protect the silkies. Oh, and say that I shall want more talks. Ask them if they are willing."

There was an exchange of grunts.

Then, "Come to this beach at any time," interpreted Shirl, "and when the not-flesh-and-blood woman calls, we shall come."

The silkies returned to the sea and Grimes and his people commenced their walk back to the ship.

Chapter 25

Their walk back to the ship was without incident and once over the space-port fence they were able to elude Coffin's patrols easily. From the after airlock they went straight up to Grimes' quarters where, before they had time to attempt to wash the pigment from their faces and hands, they were joined by Steerforth. The chief officer grinned as he looked at his black-faced captain and Grimes snapped, "Don't say it, Number One. Don't say it."

"Don't say what, sir?" asked Steerforth innocently.

"You were about to make some crack about nigger minstrels, weren't you?"

"Me, sir? Of course not." He leered at the women. "I was about to say that Shirl and Darleen—and you, Seiko—are black but comely." Then he became serious. "How did it go, sir?"

"Very well, Mr. Steerforth. Very well. We got some good tapes. They will be proof, I think, that the silkies are intelligent beings. But you know as well as I do how slowly the tide runs through official channels, especially when there are deliberately engineered obstructions. And, apart from anything else, it will be months before the tapes get to Admiral Damien—and during that time how many silkies will be slaughtered?"

"So there will have to be an incident," murmured Steerforth. "An incident, followed immediately by investigation by the Survey Service."

"And I, of course, shall be at ground zero of this famous incident," grumbled Grimes.

"Of course, sir. Aren't you always?"

"Unfortunately. And now I'm going to get this muck off my face and hands and get some sleep. Goodnight, all of you."

Everybody left him apart from Seiko. It was not the first time that he had shared a shower, but it was the first time that he had done so with a robot. (But he already knew that she was waterproof.)

He slept alone, however.

In the morning he did not join his officers for breakfast but enjoyed this meal, served by Seiko, in his day cabin. Then he sent for the chief officer.

He said, "I suppose that Flo and her gang are already in the workshop?"

"They are, sir."

"I'd like you to wander across some time this morning. Get into a conversation with Cassie—I'm sure that Flo will be happy to dispense with her services. Make sure that you have this mutual ear-bashing where it can be overheard by whatever of Coffin's goons is lurking around to make sure that nothing is damaged or stolen by my engineers. Wonder, out loud, what the old bastard—me—is up to, sneaking out at night with those two cadets and that uppity little bitch of an assistant stewardess . . ."

"Captain-san, I am not an uppity little bitch!" protested Seiko.

But you're an uppity robot, he thought.

He said, "And I'm not an old bastard—at least, not in the legal sense of the word. Anyhow, you get the idea, Mr. Steerforth. Try to convey the impression that I and the ladies are Up To No Good. Nameless orgies out in the bush . . ."

"Can I come with you next time, sir?"

"Somebody has to mind the shop, and it's you. And, in any case, I don't think that you're doing too badly for yourself, from what I've noticed. Aunt Jemima, of late, has been serving *your* favorite dishes at almost every meal."

Steerforth flushed. "Ms. Clay and I have similar tastes, sir."

"Indubitably." Grimes laughed. "But shenannigans, sexual or otherwise, aboard the ship, are one thing. Shenanigans, especially sexual and indulged in by off-worlders, on the sacred soil of New Salem, are another thing. You're free to speculate—and the more wild the speculations the better. Perhaps on these lines. 'Maybe the old bastard and his three bitches are having it off with the silkies. I wouldn't put it past them. I've always suspected that the four of 'em are as kinky as all hell.' "

"And are you, sir?"

"Not especially."

"You have a very fertile mind, sir."

"Mphm. It runs in the family, I suppose. Oh, you might take a pocket recorder with you so that I can hear a play-back of the way that you'll be slandering me. It will all be part of the evidence."

"Not to be used against *me*, I hope, sir."

"If you like," said Grimes, "I'll give you written orders to traduce me."

Steerforth flushed again. "That, sir, will not be necessary," he said stiffly.

Late that evening Grimes and the three girls, their hands and faces again blackened, emerged from the ship. This time the sky was not overcast and the stars were bright in the sky; even Grimes experienced little difficulty in finding his way through the spaceport. As before there were the patrols, carrying their feeble oil lanterns. As before these were easily—too easily? wondered Grimes—eluded. The fence was scaled. Beyond it was the almost familiar bushland. It seemed to Grimes that the same path through it was being followed as before.

Suddenly Shirl whispered in his ear, "Stop here for a little while, John. Pretend to be lighting your pipe. . . ."

"Why pretend?" he muttered, pulling the foul thing from his pocket.

They stood there while Grimes went through his usual ritual.

"Yes," murmured Darleen. "As I thought. . . ."

". . . we are being followed . . ." continued Shirl.

Somewhere behind them a twig cracked.

Grimes finished lighting his pipe.

"One man only . . ." breathed Darleen into his ear.

Grimes took his time over his smoke. *Let the bastard wait*, he thought, *not daring to make another move until we move on*.

Finally, "All right. Let's get the show on the road," he said in a normal voice.

He knocked out his pipe on the ground, stamped on the last faintly glowing embers to extinguish them. He moved off, letting Shirl take the lead. Darleen followed close behind him and Seiko brought up the rear. They came to the coast road, crossed it. They emerged on to the beach. The recording apparatus was set up on its tripod. Seiko divested herself of her clothing. Shirl and Darleen followed suit, one of them saying, "Let us have a swim first. What about you, John?"

He said, "The water's too bloody cold."

(If there was to be any confrontation he would prefer to be fully clothed.)

Shirl pressed herself against him in what must have looked like an amorous embrace. She whispered, "We might as well give the bastard an eyeful."

"The three of you can," he whispered back.

Seiko, her body palely luminous in the starlight, waded into the sea. The wavelets broke about her legs, her body, flashing phosphorescently.

Shirl and Darleen followed her, flinging themselves full length as soon as there was enough depth. They sported exuberantly. It was as though they were swimming in a sea of liquid diamonds. "Come on in!" one of them called. "The water's fine!"

"Too cold for me!" Grimes shouted back—but if it had not been for that unseen watcher he would have joined them.

Finally they tired of their games and came wading into the beach. Droplets of slowly fading phosphorescence fell from their nipples, gleamed in their pubic hair. One did not have to be kinky, thought Grimes, to appreciate such a show. He wondered if *he* was appreciating it. No doubt his eyes were popping with wonderment, sinful lust and holy indignation.

"We should have brought towels," said Darleen practically, attempting to dry herself with her coverall.

"It is time that Seiko finished singing her song," said Shirl.

And now Seiko emerged from the sea, fully as beautiful as the two New Alicians, adorned as they had been by living jewels of cold fire. The silkies followed her, up on to the beach, grunting musically, and each of them was wearing a coat of radiant color. Grimes wondered how he could ever have thought them ugly.

"They bid you greeting, John," sang Shirl.

"Tell them that I am pleased to see them," replied Grimes.

What followed came as a surprise to him. He had been expecting a conversation—a conference?—such as the one in which he had taken part the previous night. But this was more of an orgy. The women—and Seiko was one of them—seemed to be determined to put on a show for Coffin's spy. Grimes sat there, his pipe for once forgotten, watching in wonderment. The naked human bodies—although one was human only in form—entertwined with the darkly furred bodies of the sea beasts . . . The caresses, the musical murmurings . . . (These tapes, thought Grimes, who had his prudish moments, he would not be submitting to any higher authority back on Earth, he would not be showing to Steerforth back aboard the ship.) Pale female flesh sprawled over rich, dark fur . . . Flippers that caressed breasts and thighs with what he would have thought was impossible gentleness. . . .

And at the finish Seiko standing there, on a low, sea-rounded rock, while, one by one, the silkies each gently placed a flipper on her bare feet before sliding away, down into the sea. It seemed like (was it? could it be?) an act of obeisance, of worship even.

Grimes, his prominent ears still burning with embarrassment, filled and lit his pipe. He demanded, "What . . ." then fell silent.

"It is all right, John," Seiko told him. "We are alone again. He, the pastor's spy, is gone. Along the coast road. I am surprised that you did not hear him. He was not very cautious. Anyhow, you can talk without being overheard."

"I did not hear him," snapped Grimes. "There were too many other things to listen to. And watch. Just what, in the name of all the Odd Gods of the Galaxy, were the three of you up to?"

"You said that you wished to shock Pastor Coffin's people, John," Shirl told him.

"I didn't say that *I* wanted to be shocked. The worst of it was that the three of you seemed to be enjoying it."

"And why should we not?" asked Darleen sweetly. "Have you ever experienced the feel of soft, rich fur against your naked skin? And we learned, on your world, that many human women are not above enjoying sexual relations with their so-called pets, their cats and their dogs and the like."

"That's different!" almost shouted Grimes.

"How so, John?" asked Shirl. "Oh, all right. Those pets, on Earth, are not intelligent by human standards. The silkies are intelligent. Unfortunately, as far as we and they are concerned, our bodies are too . . . different."

"That will do," snapped Grimes. "Get dressed. And remember this, if Coffin's man has reported to his master, and if the patrolmen try to arrest us, the three of you are to use only such force as is required to prevent our capture. I want an incident, not a massacre. But I don't want to spend what's left of the night in Coffin's jail."

But he had no real fears of this latter. He already knew of the fighting capabilities of Shirl and Darleen and strongly suspected that Seiko, by herself, would be more than a match for a small army, provided that this army did not deploy nuclear weaponry.

Nonetheless they made their way back to the ship without incident.

Grimes told Steerforth a somewhat edited version of the night's doings.

Chapter 26

So the bait had been noticed. Would Pastor Coffin bite? Grimes had little doubt he would do so, and no doubt at all that the pastor would find Shirl, Darleen and Seiko an impossibly hard mouthful to swallow. As long as there was an incident, as long as Grimes could scream that he and his people, respectable, law-abiding merchant spacepersons, had been assaulted by the Salemites there would be an excuse for Survey Service intervention. Damien had half-promised that the destroyer *Pollux* would be loafing around in the vicinity of New Salem, doing something or other, during the period of Grimes' stay on the planet.

After spending a rather lazy day Grimes and the three girls emerged from the ship under the cover of darkness and followed their usual route to the beach. It was another brightly starlit night but this time they were not followed. When Grimes got himself entangled in a particularly tenacious bush he envied the pastor's men. They—assuming that they would be at the shore to watch the horrid goings-on—would have made their way to the beach by the coast road.

They were waiting there. Grimes, by himself, would not have been aware of their presence but Shirl and Darleen, with their super-sharp hearing, were.

"Do we do the same as last night, John?" whispered Shirl.

"No," said Grimes firmly. (Tonight's audio-visual tapes would have to be produced as evidence at the inquiry into the almost inevitable incident.) "No. Just a meeting, a conference with the silkies."

"But can't we have a swim, even?" asked Darleen.

"All right, all right. Have your swim." (There was very few worlds—although Salem was one of them—where the spectacle of attractive naked women splashing in the sea would evoke so much as a raised eyebrow.)

Grimes set up the recorder. Seiko stripped and waded out into the water, deeper and deeper, until she was lost to sight. Shirl and Darleen got out of their coveralls, ran down to the sea, fell full length and began striking out in a sparkling flurry of phosphorescence. Grimes lit his pipe. He thought that he heard a faint rustling in the bushes inland from the beach but could not be sure. He was far from being afraid but was beginning to feel distinctly uneasy.

Shirl and Darleen emerged from the water, joined him where he sat. Shirl produced a packet of cigarillos from a pocket in her coveralls. Both girls lit up. Neither made any attempt to get dressed. Grimes remarked upon this.

"The air is quite warm," said Shirl. "We shall let it dry us."

"Last night," said Darleen, "we were very uncomfortable when we put on our clothes over wet skins."

"Suit yourself," said Grimes.

And why should he be the only one dressed? Because all that was happening was being recorded, that was why. Because friends as well as enemies in the Survey Service would laugh themselves sick when, at the inquiry, the tapes were played, with an audio-visual recording of Grimes enjoying a roll in the hay (or a roll on the sand) with two of his junior officers. Too, why should he give those unseen watchers an even better show than the one that they were already enjoying?

Seiko waded out from the sea, dripping phosphorescence. She was followed by six big silkies. The same ones as the previous night? Grimes couldn't tell. Apart from differences in size and pelt coloration they all looked the same to him.

The sea-beasts disposed themselves in a semicircle, facing the humans and the pseudo-human and the audio-visual recorder. They talked and sang, and Shirl, Darleen and Seiko replied to them in kind. Now and again Shirl would interpret for Grimes' benefit.

The silkies wanted just one thing, to be left alone. They admitted that not all humans were as bad, from their viewpoint, as the colonists. They admitted that exchanges of knowledge and of information might be advantageous but, essentially, they had very good reason not to trust humans.

"Not even you, John," said Shirl sadly. "We—Darleen and myself and Seiko—have been prepared to cast aside the artificial trappings of so-called civilization. You have not. We have made naked contact with the silkies. You have not. And you did not approve, in your heart of hearts, when we did. . . ."

"I'm keeping my trousers on," growled Grimes. "Tonight especially."

At last the conference was over. Again Seiko stood on that sea-rounded rock; again the silkies made their obeisance, one by one gently placing a flipper on her slim feet. Then they were gone, back into the sea.

The three women began to get into their coveralls—and from the bushes, armed with staves and clubs, poured Coffin's men.

The women were caught at a disadvantage, half into and half out of their coveralls. Too, at first, they paid overmuch heed to Grimes' admonition not to fight back too viciously. And Seiko, upon whom Grimes had been relying, was one of the first casualties. The butt of a long stave struck her fair and square upon her vulnerable navel, where her ON/OFF switch was situated. She did not freeze into complete immobility—the switch had not been fully actuated—but thereafter was able to struggle only feebly. By this time both Shirl and Darleen had been struck about their heads with heavy clubs, as had been Grimes himself. After that he had only confused recollections of the struggle. He was flung violently to the sand, face down, and got his mouth and his eyes full of grit. A heavy boot on the small of his back pinned him in this supine position. His wrists were yanked up and back, pulled together by rough rope that broke the skin. Despite his kicking his ankles were bound.

He heard Coffin's voice, an unpleasant combination of smugness and harshness.

"We have them. The witch and her three disciples."

"But one of them is the outworld captain, pastor."

"It matters not. Captains may still be sinners and blasphemers, worshippers of false gods. His rank—such as it is—matters not. He will stand trial with the witch and the two shameless trollops."

Grimes felt hands lifting him. He was dropped on to a hard wooden surface. His nose began to bleed. Somebody was dropped beside him, and then two other bodies on top of him. He heard the squeaking of not-very-well greased axles and felt the jolts as the unsprung vehicle, whatever it was, was pulled (by manpower, he supposed) along the rough coast road. He managed to lift and to turn his head so that his painfully bruised nose was no longer in contact with the floorboards.

He could speak now, although it required a great effort.

"Seiko . . ."

"Yes . . ." her voice came at last, weak, barely audible.

"You're the strongest of us. Can you break your bonds?"

"No . . . I have . . . lost . . . my strength. They . . . hit me. You know . . . where."

"You should not have told us not to fight back," said Shirl.

"Where . . . are they taking us?" asked Darleen.

To hell in a handcart, thought Grimes but did not say it.

"What will they do to us?" asked Shirl.

"Throw us into jail, I suppose," said Grimes.

"But not to worry. Mr. Steerforth will bail us out." (*And how much will* that *cost*? he wondered, the mercenary side of him coming to the surface.)

Chapter 27

They were not thrown in jail.

They were dragged roughly out of the four-wheeled cart and securely bound, with iron chains, to four upright posts, also of iron. Dazedly Grimes looked about him. He and the others had been brought to the open area between the waterfront, with its jetties, and the town. He was facing a long table, on which were three oil lanterns, at which were sitting Pastor Coffin and, one to either side of him, two clerkly men. Other lanterns were hung from tall posts, illuminating the faces of the crowd that had turned up to. . . . To see the fun?

Coffin glared at Grimes from beneath his heavy, black brows. He demanded, in a deep voice, "Prisoner at the bar, how plead ye?"

Grimes mustered enough saliva to wash most of the sand and blood out of his mouth. He spat, regretting as he did so that the pastor was out of range. He spat again.

"Prisoner at the bar, how plead ye?" repeated Coffin.

"I do not plead," almost shouted Grimes. "I demand. I demand that I and my people be returned, at once, to our ship!"

"Prisoner at the bar, how plead ye? Guilty or not guilty?"

"Guilty of fucking *what*?" demanded Grimes, considering that this occasion called for some deliberate obscenity in his speech, realizing, too late, that his words could be misconstrued. (But, he thought, *he* had not played an active part in that orgy.)

Coffin seemed to be losing his patience. "John Grimes, you will answer my questions. Are you, or are you not, guilty of witchcraft?"

"Witchcraft? You must be joking."

"This is no joking matter, Grimes. Are you guilty or not guilty?"

"Not guilty."

One of the clerkly men was writing in a big book with an antique-looking pen.

"Your plea has been recorded," said Coffin. He turned his attention to Shirl. "You, woman. How do you plead?"

"Not guilty," she replied in a firm voice.

"And you, woman. How do you plead?"

"Not guilty," said Darleen.

"And . . . you?" Coffin was glaring at Seiko, who was sagging in her bonds.

The robot was speaking with difficulty. "Not . . ." she got out at last. "Not . . . guilty."

"Very well," said Coffin. "Now we shall hear the truth. Clerk of the court, call the first witness."

The man sitting on his right—not, as Grimes had been expecting, the man writing in the book—rose to his feet, called, in a high voice, "Matthew Ling, stand forward! Matthew Ling, stand forward!"

A burly fellow shouldered his way through the crowd, took his stance between the prisoners and Coffin's table.

"Matthew Ling, identify yourself," ordered the pastor.

"My name is Matthew Ling," said the man. "I hold the rank of Law Enforcer Second Class."

"Tell your story, Law Enforcer Ling."

"May it please the court," said Ling, "my story is as follows." He spoke as do police officers all over the galaxy when giving evidence, his voice toneless. "Pursuant to information received and to the instructions of Pastor Coffin I followed the four accused from the spaceport to Short Bay. At first I thought that they were members of the Negro race; as the court is aware there are some of those accursed people in the crew of the starship. I caught glimpses of their faces while they were still on the spaceport grounds, and saw that they were black . . ."

"As their faces," said Coffin, "are black now. And their hands. That alone is damning evidence. Why should a God-fearing man or woman blacken the Lord's handiwork as evinced on his person? I will tell you. As a badge of submission to the Prince of Darkness. But continue, Law Enforcer."

"May it please the court . . . I followed the accused through the bush, across the coast road, and then concealed myself in the bushes, in a position overlooking the beach at Short Bay. I watched the accused setting up a device on a tripod, a devil's machine of some kind that emitted colored lights. Then the male accused sat down on the sand and began to inhale the poisonous fumes of some weed that he was burning in the bowl of a small implement. While he was partaking of his noxious drug the three female accused disrobed. I saw then that their faces and hands were blackened but not the rest of their bodies. The female accused then disported themselves in a wanton manner before the male accused.

"The three female accused waded into the sea. Two of them swam, with unnatural skill. The third one, the one with the black hair, waded out into deep water until she was lost to sight. At no time did she swim or attempt to swim. The other ones returned to the beach and, still naked, sat beside the male accused, joining him in the ritual inhalation of some noxious weed.

"Finally the black-haired female accused came up from the sea, followed by six silkies. What happened then I should never have believed unless I had witnessed it with my own eyes. The three witch-women sported with the silkies. It was a scene of sickening bestiality." (At last there was a hint of emotion in the flat voice.) "But even the witches and the silkies tired of their lewd games. The silkies returned to the sea. But the black-haired witch stood on a rock, and each silky, before going back to the sea, made a sign of submission to her by placing its flipper on her bare feet. I had seen enough and made my way back to the city, by the coast road, to make my report."

"And what you have told us is the truth," stated rather than asked Pastor Coffin.

"It is, sir," said Ling.

"Objection!" shouted Grimes.

Coffin consulted with the two clerks then said, "John Grimes, it pleases us to hear your objection. Say your say."

"Your Law Enforcer Ling is not a reliable witness, pastor."

"Indeed? How not so?"

"Law Enforcer Ling stated that on the night in question I sat down on the beach to enjoy a quiet smoke. That is correct. He also stated that Ms. Kelly and Ms Byrne, after they had finished their swim, also enjoyed a smoke. They did not. That was because they had brought no smoking materials with them."

Ling was called to the pastor's table, was engaged in a low-voiced conference with Coffin and the other two. Finally he stood aside.

The pastor said, "It is your word, John Grimes, against the word of my law enforcer. . . ."

"My word," said Grimes hotly, "and the words of two of my officers."

"There may," admitted Coffin magnanimously, "be some confusion in Law Enforcer Ling's memory. For this there is ample excuse. What he witnessed would have been enough to turn the mind of any man not of exceptionally strong and pious character. And Law Enforcer Ling was with me tonight, when you and the other accused were apprehended. I saw, with my own eyes, both you and the women Kelly and Byrne indulging in your filthy habit. The objection that you have raised is a mere quibble."

Grimes subsided. *They can't shoot us for smoking*, he thought. *Not even on this bloody planet.*

But for witchcraft?

"Call the second witness," ordered Coffin.

"Job Gardiner," called the clerk. "Job Gardiner. Stand forward!"

"My name is Job Gardiner," said the man, who could almost have been twin brother to Matthew Ling. "I hold the rank of Chief Law Enforcer . . ." He cleared his throat. "Persuant to information received and to direct orders from Pastor Coffin, I, together with a party of law enforcers—among whom was Matthew Ling—made my way to Short Beach by the coast road. Pastor Coffin accompanied us, saying, and rightly, that this was a very serious matter and that he would have to exercise overall command of the operation. . . ."

And so it went on.

". . . it was obvious, to the pastor and myself, to all of us that the four accused were talking to the silkies and that the silkies were talking to them. And such things cannot be. Then the silkies returned to the sea, but before they did so they made bestial obeisance to the black-haired witch. The pastor ordered us to arrest the four blasphemous outworlders. We did so, and we smashed the Devil's machine that they had brought with them."

But the tapes should have survived, thought Grimes The tapes, and their damning evidence. But would they be retrieved? Would they ever be played back?

"The court has heard the evidence," said Coffin. "We all have heard the evidence. It is obvious that at least one of the accused, the black-haired woman, is a witch. It is probable that the man and the other two women are lesser witches, or acolytes. But we must be sure before we order our law to take its course. Chief Law Enforcer Gardiner, I order you to apply the acid test."

"Law Enforcer Ling," ordered Gardiner in his turn, "bring the acid."

Coffin smiled bleakly at Grimes. "We have our methods, outworlder, of determining the guilt or otherwise of witches. The acid test is one of the more effective. An accused witch is required to drink a draught of acid. If he or she is uninjured, then obviously he or she is a witch and is dealt with accordingly. If he or she suffers harm, then he or she is possibly not a witch."

"Heads I win, tails you lose," said Grimes.

"You speak in riddles, Grimes. And nothing you say is of any consequence."

Ling returned from wherever he had gone carrying a large bottle. He handed this to his superior, then went to stand behind Seiko, pulling her head back with one hand, forcing her mouth open with the other. Gardiner, who was now wearing heavy gloves, approached her from in front. He raised the unstoppered bottle, began to pour its contents between her parted lips. Some of the corrosive fluid spilled on to Seiko's clothing, which smoked acridly.

There was a murmur from the crowd, more than a murmur, a chorus of shouts. "She is a witch! Kill her! Kill her!"

Then, abruptly, Seiko regurgitated the acid that had been poured into her. The burning stream struck Gardiner full in the face. He dropped the bottle, which shattered, and screamed shrilly, clawing at his ruined eyes.

Incongruously the robot murmured, "I . . . am . . . sorry. But my . . . circuits . . . were . . . not . . . designed to . . . take such punishment . . ."

Grimes was not sorry. The Chief Law Enforcer had deserved what he got. (To how many flesh-and-blood women had he applied this acid test?) And the bottle was broken and, hopefully, it would take some time to fetch a new one and, meanwhile, anything might happen . . .

Grimes hoped.

Chapter 28

The whimpering Gardiner was led away by two of his subordinates. Presumably whoever passed for a doctor in this town would be able to assuage the pain, although not to do anything to save the man's eyesight. But that was the least of Grimes' worries. His main concern was for Seiko, for Shirl and Darleen and for himself. He reproached himself for not having carried to the beach, in addition to the recorder, a portable transceiver so that, at all times, he would have been in communication with his ship.

But he had never dreamed that Coffin would go to the extremes to which he already had gone—and to what extremes was he yet to go? *And you, Grimes, of all people*, he told himself, *should have learned by this time that allegedly civilized* people are capable of anything, *no matter how barbarous*.

Coffin was speaking. "There is no doubt that the woman is a witch. Not only has she survived her ordeal uninjured but she has severely injured my chief law enforcer. She must pay the penalty." He paused judicially, turned his head to stare at Grimes, Shirl and Darleen. "It was my intention to order that the acid test be applied to the other three accused. Unfortunately no further supply of acid is readily available. So I shall, therefore, temper justice with mercy. Grimes, Kelly and Byrne will be given the opportunity to confess and to recant. Should they do so, their ends will be swift and merciful. Should they not do so, they shall be executed in the same manner as their mistress. They will be permitted to watch her sufferings and, hopefully, such spectacle will be a stimulus to their consciences.

"Bring the faggots!"

Men and women brought bundles of sticks. (These must, thought

Grimes, have been prepared well in advance.) They piled them around the stake to which Seiko was chained, concealing the lower half of her body. A law enforcer poured some fluid—flammable oil, it was—over the faggots. He struck a long match, applied the flame all around the base of the pile.

With a loud *whoosh* the oil ignited and there was an uprush of smoky fire. Seiko's hair—*but it's only a wig*, thought Grimes—flared and crackled. Then the initial fury of the burning oil subsided but the faggots had caught, were snapping in the heat, emitting sparks, sending their flames curling up around Seiko's body. Although the cloth of her coveralls was flame resistant it was beginning to char and to powder. A sigh, a horribly obscene sound, went up from the mob as one perfect breast was exposed.

Suddenly, audible even over the crackling of the fire, the murmurs of the crowd, there was a startlingly loud *click!* Seiko, who had been sagging in her bonds, stood erect. Her wrists, which had been tied behind her back, were already free, the flames having burned away the rope. But even if this had not been the case it would not have mattered. The strength that she now exerted to snap the chains would have been more than enough to break mere vegetable fiber. As she stood there, ridding herself of the last of her bonds, the crumbling remnants of her clothing fell from around her smoke-smudged body. She was like, thought Grimes, Aphrodite rising from the sea—a sea of fire. And he, even at this moment, had to repress a giggle. A Venus without arms, a Venus de Milo, he might accept—but a bald-headed one was altogether too much. (Her body paint had survived the fire although her wig had not.) Even so, she was beautiful—and not only because her escape from the pyre had brought a renewal of hope.

Men were shouting, women and children were screaming, but none dare approach this vengeful she-devil. Coffin was bellowing, "Seize her! Seize her! Strike her down!"

"Good on yer, Seiko!" yelled Darleen. "Show the bastards!"

There was a meter of broken chain in Seiko's right hand. She threw it. It wrapped itself around Coffin's neck, all but decapitating him. His two clerks squealed in terror, dived under the table, from the surface of which the pastor's blood dripped down upon them. Seiko stepped out of the fire, flames and sparks splashing about her feet. Two law enforcers, braver or more stupid than their fellows, ran at her with heavy clubs upraised. She countered their assault with the *savate* technique that she must have learned from Shirl and Darleen; her long right leg flashed out while she pivoted on her left heel; first one man and then the other (although there was almost no interval between the two blows) was the recipient of a crippling kick to the groin. In horror Grimes noted that the trousers of each unfortunate were smouldering where the kicks had landed. Seiko's feet must be almost redhot. (But it was her feet for which he felt concern, not the genitals of the law enforcers.)

He felt the heat emanating from her body as she approached him, as her hands reached out for his chains. But she was careful not to touch him.

She said, "Do not worry about *me*, John. I am heat resistant. I feel no pain, as you know it. And it was the heat of the fire that released my master switch . . ."

She left him to his own devices, went to free the two New Alicians.

Grimes looked around, fearing fresh attack. But the light of the oil lanterns on their posts revealed a waterfront empty save for himself and his women, the body of Coffin sprawled over the table and the two still-living (but for how long?) bodies of the law enforcers. The pair of clerks had made their escape unnoticed.

"Well," said Grimes with deliberate matter-of-factness, "that seems to be it. We've had our incident. Let's get back to the ship. Come, Shirl. Come, Darleen. And you, Seiko, can guard our rear."

"I am staying," said the robot.

"Seiko, I order you to come with us."

"John, your father was my original owner. He ordered me to protect you when necessary."

"Then protect me as I walk back to the spaceport."

She said, "We could be attacked." With a long forefinger she touched her navel. "I have learned my vulnerability in a scrimmage. A club, a flung stone, even a heavy fist and I can be jolted into near-immobility. There is only one way to ensure your safety. Those people . . ." she gestured toward the town, ". . . must be taught a lesson."

But it was not toward the houses she ran but to the slipway, up which the schooners were hauled for the scraping and caulking of the underwater portions of their hulls. It was toward the slipway that she ran, and down the slipway. When her body entered the black water there was an uprising of steam.

Then she was gone from sight.

"Crazy robot!" grumbled Grimes. "Being cooked must have affected her brain . . ."

"She knows what she is doing, John," said Darleen loyally.

"Does she? I wish that I did." He could sense that from darkened windows he was being watched. He wondered how long it would be before the New Salemites, seeing that the most dangerous witch had plunged into the sea, would come pouring out of their houses to exact vengeance for the death of their pastor and the injuries inflicted upon his law enforcers. He said, "I think that we should be getting out of here."

Shirl said, "But we can't leave Seiko . . ."

"I know," said Grimes. "But . . ."

"Do you *hear* her?" Shirl asked Darleen.

"Yes." Then, to Grimes, "Do not worry so, John. Everything will be all right."

From whose viewpoint? he wondered.

Then up the shipway she strode. The sea had washed the grime of smoke and fire from her pale body. Up the slipway she strode—and behind her, a living tide, surged the silkies. As she passed Grimes on her way inshore she made a gesture that was more formal salute than cheery wave. And the silkies grunted—in greeting or talking among themselves? But Shirl and Darleen replied in kind.

The robot and her army reached the sea frontage of the town. There was shouting and screaming, the splintering crashes as doors were burst in, as wooden walls succumbed to the onslaught of tons of angry flesh and blood. Fires started in a dozen places—the result of overturned lamps or lit by intent? Grimes did not know but suspected that Seiko was exacting retaliation in kind for what she had undergone. Fires started, and spread.

"This has gone too far," said Grimes.

"It has not gone far enough," Shirl told him. "The silkies said to us that *she* had told them that they were not to kill. To destroy only, but not to kill. That's the trouble with robots. They have this built-in, altogether absurd directive that human beings are never to be harmed by them."

"Wherever did you get that idea?" asked Grimes.

"While we were waiting for you on Earth we did quite a lot of reading. There were some books, classics, by an old writer called Asimov."

"Then what about *him*?" Grimes gestured toward the pastor's body. "Wasn't *he* harmed? Fatally, at that."

"Yes, John," said Darleen patiently. "But he was going to harm you, and Seiko was doing her best to protect you."

The town was ablaze now, the roaring of the flames drowning out all other noises coming from that direction. Satisfied with the havoc that they had wrought, the silkies were returning to the sea. There was light enough for Grimes to see that some were wounded, with great patches of fur burned from their bodies. Others bled from long and deep gashes. But their musical grunting sounded like a chant of victory.

Seiko brought up the rear. Again her body was smoke-blackened. She approached Grimes and bowed formally. "Captain-san, it is over. We spared the church and a large hall adjacent, and the people are huddled in these buildings, praying."

"How many killed?" demanded Grimes.

"Nobody by intent, although two or three may have died accidentally. But we let them seek refuge in their houses of worship and I refrained from applying the torch to these."

"You did well," said Grimes at last. "All right. The sooner we're back on board the ship the better."

"I am sorry, John," Seiko told him. "I cannot accompany you."

"That's an order, damn it!"

"Which I cannot accept. I was built to serve, John, as well you know. But you do not really need me. They . . ." she gestured toward the sea, to the silky heads, their eyes gleaming with reflected firelight, that were turned inland, looking at the humans and the robot. "They need me, much more than you do."

"She is right," said Shirl and Darleen as one.

Above the roar of the burning town, beating down from the sky, was the arrhythmic clatter of a small craft's inertial drive. One of Sister Sue's lifeboats made a heavy landing not far from where Grimes was still trying to argue with the women. From it jumped Steerforth and Calamity Cassie, each with a laser pistol in hand.

"You're all right, Captain?" demanded the chief officer. "We saw the flames and thought that we'd better take action."

"You did right," said Grimes. "And now you can get us back to where we belong."

"Good-bye, Harald," said Seiko. "Good-bye, Cassie. Tell the others good-bye for me."

She was, Grimes noticed, holding her right hand protectively over her navel.

"We can't leave you here, Seiko," objected Steerforth.

"She can look after herself," said Grimes harshly. "And, in any case, it'll be days yet before *Sister Sue* is capable of lifting off. If—no, *when*—you change your mind, Seiko, you'll know where to find us."

The boat, with Steerforth at the controls, clattered upward. The chief officer made a circuit of the seaport area before setting course for the spaceport. New fires had broken out; alongside their jetties the schooners were ablaze.

She was thorough, was Seiko, thought Grimes. Very thorough. It would be a long time before, if ever, there was another silky hunt on New Salem.

All that next day he was expecting her to come walking back up the ramp, into the ship. And the day after, and the day after that . . .

Chapter 29

The mess was well on the way to being cleaned up.

The destroyer *Pollux* had been within range of *Sister Sue's* Carlotti radio, even though the signals had been broadcast and not beamed. She had dropped down to the spaceport, with Grimes usurping the functions of New Salem Aerospace Control. (Presumably the lady who usually did the talking to incoming traffic was still huddled in the church with her badly frightened fellow colonists.)

Her captain, Commander Beavis, had served under Grimes many years ago and was cooperative. Damien must have told him that Grimes was once again, although secretly, an officer of the Federation Survey Service, senior to Beavis. That gentleman managed to imply that Grimes could issue orders rather than mere suggestions. But appearances were maintained for the benefit of the crews of both ships. Grimes was the innocent shipmaster whose life, and the lives of certain of his officers, had been threatened by the people of this world. Beavis was the galactic policeman who had come hurrying to the rescue.

Beavis had the people and the equipment to be able to do something about the plight of the colonists, whose city had been almost entirely destroyed. He set up a sizeable township of tents, complete with field kitchens and a hospital. He interrogated various officials and recorded their stories. Then, aboard *Sister Sue,* he heard Grimes' report and watched and listened to the playback of the various tapes—one of them heavily edited—including that final one, which had been recovered, undamaged, from the beach. He interviewed Shirl and Darleen and Steerforth and Cassie.

Then when he was alone with Grimes, relaxing over a drink, he said, "I shall put all this material in Admiral Damien's hands as soon as possible, sir. He's going to love it—and so will Madame Duvalier. I rather think, somehow, that the New Salemites are going to be resettled—preferably on some world with no animal life whatsoever. . . ."

"If they could find some way of harvesting plants really brutally they'd do it," said Grimes. "In spite of all that's happened they still regard themselves as the Almighty-created Lords of Creation. And, more and more, I'm coming to the opinion that any life, all life, should be treated with respect and compassion."

"Even robots, sir?" asked Beavis with deceptive innocence.

Grimes laughed. "All right, all right. There was that bloody tin messiah, Mr. Adam, years ago. He got what was coming to him; I wasn't sorry then and I'm not sorry now."

"I was thinking of Seiko, sir."

"Mphm."

"She would pass for a very attractive woman. You must miss her, sir."

"I suppose I do," admitted Grimes. "But she'll be back. She'll know when I'm due to lift. She'll be back."

At last the repairs were finished and the fresh water tank refilled. All that remained to be done was the recalibration of *Sister Sue's* Mannschenn Drive. While this was being carried out only a skeleton crew would remain on board—Grimes himself in the control room, Flo Scott in the inertial drive room and, of course, all the Mannschenn Drive engineers in their own compartment, making their abstruse calculations and arcane adjustments. The theory of it was that if anything should go wrong, if the ship fell down a crack in the Space-Time Continuum, the captain and his top-ranking technicians might—just might—be able to get her back to where and when she belonged. Ships—only a very few ships but ships nonetheless—had been known to vanish during the recalibration procedure. Of that very few an even smaller number had come back, and not to the planets from which they had made their unscheduled departures. Sometimes, after only a very short absence from the normal universe, their crews had aged many years. Sometimes, during an absence of years, only minutes had elapsed for the personnel. Some crews claimed to have met God; others told horrifying stories of their narrow escapes from the clutches of the Devil. Grimes, good agnostic that he was, did not believe such tales, saying, if his opinion were asked, that it is a well known fact that the temporal precession fields engendered by the Drive have an hallucinatory effect upon the human mind.

Recalibration, to him, was a process similar to old-fashioned navel gunnery, the procedure known as bracketing. Under . . . Up . . . Over . . . Down . . . still Under . . . Up . . . Right on! Salvoes!

So he sat in *Sister Sue*'s control room, smoking his pipe, waiting for Daniel Grey, the Chief Manschenn Drive Engineer, to start doing his thing. He looked out through a viewport, saw his people, together with a number of Beavis's officers, standing by the stern of *Pollux*, watching. Grey's voice came from the intercom speaker, "All ready, Captain."

"Thank you, Mr. Grey. Commence recalibration."

He heard—and felt—the deep hum as the rotors of the Drive commenced to spin, a hum that rapidly rose in pitch to a thin, high whine with an odd warbling quality. Outside the scene changed. *Pollux* was no longer there. Neither were the spaceport administration buildings. The planet was as it had been before the coming of man. *Under*, thought Grimes. The scene changed again. There were only ruins of buildings, barely recognizable as such under the growth of bushes and small trees.

Over.

Then *under* again, with a few rough shacks to mark where the spaceport proper would one day be.

Over. . . .

The familiar buildings were there, but showing signs of dilapidation. Grimes got up from his seat, looked down through the port at the concrete apron. It was cracked in many places, with weeds thrusting through the fissures. He went down from the control room to his quarters. There was an odd unfamiliarity about them. Who was the auburn-haired woman whose holographic portrait was on the bulkhead behind the desk in his day cabin? It wasn't Maggie, although there was a certain similarity. In his bedroom he took his uniform cap from the wardrobe, looked into the mirror to adjust it to the right angle. With fast dissipating puzzlement he noted the strange cap badge above the gold-braided peak, a rather ornate winged wheel, and the single broad gold band, the insignia of a commodore, on each of his shoulderboards. Passing through his day room he flicked a good-humoured salute at the portrait of Sonya.

He took the elevator down to the after airlock, walked down the ramp to the cracked and scarred concrete. His first lieutenant, Lieutenant Commander Cummings, saluted smartly. Grimes returned the salute. He said, "I'm taking a morning stroll, Commander Cummings. To the old seaport."

"Shouldn't an armed party be going with you, sir? After all, according to the data, the natives aren't overly friendly towards visitors."

"I've been here before, Commander. And the ones who most certainly were not friendly were the human colonists. And, as you know, they were resettled."

"As you please, sir. But . . ."

"I shall be all right, Commander."

You always are, you old bastard, he could almost hear the officer thinking.

And—*old bastard*? he thought. Yes, he was getting old. Not in mind, not even in body, but in years and experience.

The road from the spaceport to the seaport, along which he had first walked so many years ago, was still passable. Nonetheless he began to wish that he had taken one of the ship's boats instead of making the journey by foot. At any age at all he did not enjoy having to force his way through bushes. Although the sunlight was not especially hot he had worked up a good sweat by the time that he got to what had been Salem City. The charred ruins were not yet completely overgrown and the church and the hall, in which the colonists had taken refuge, were still standing.

Like rotting fangs the jetties still protruded into the sullen sea, from which projected, at crazy angles, the fire-blackened spars that had been the masts and yards of the schooners.

The slipway, still in a good state of repair, was almost as he remembered it.

And up it walked Seiko.

She was as she had been when he first saw her, in his parents' home. The transparent, glassy skin had been cleaned of all vestiges of body paint and beneath it glittered the beautiful intricacy of that non-functional yet busy clockwork. Her well-shaped head was bare of the last trace of hair. But something had been added, one item of clothing. She wore a broad belt of gleaming metal mesh with a golden buckle—more shield than buckle—that covered her navel.

She bowed formally. "Captain-san."

He bowed in return. "Seiko-san."

She said, "This is Liberty Hall. You can spit on the mat and call the cat a bastard."

He laughed and said, "You haven't lost your sense of humor."

"Why should I have done so, John? The silkies are not a humorless people."

She looked intently at his cap badge, the braid on his shoulders.

Grimes asked, "What's puzzling you?"

She said, "Your ship is the same. I saw her coming down. But your uniform is different."

Grimes told her, "She is no longer *my* ship. Oh, I command her, but I no longer own her. And her name has been changed. She is now *Faraway Quest*, the survey vessel of the Rim Worlds Confederacy, in whose naval reserve I hold the rank of commodore."

"And all the people I knew, when she was *Sister Sue* and you were owner as well as captain?"

"They have all gone their various ways, Seiko."

"I would have liked to have met Shirl and Darleen again . . ."

"I still hear from them, about once a standard year. Eventually they returned to their home planet, New Alice."

"When next you write, please give them my regards."

"I shall do so."

"And when next you are on *your* home planet, John, please give my regards to your respected parents."

Grimes told her, regretfully, "They are both long gone."

"Then will you, for me, make obeisance at their tomb and pour a libation?"

"I shall do that," promised Grimes.

The pair of them fell silent, looking at each other, a little sadly. It was a companionable silence.

Grimes broke it. He said, "You can have your old job back, if you want it."

She replied, "Thank you. But the silkies still need me. I am their hands and their voice. I speak for them to the occasional visitors to this world, human and nonhuman. Were I not here there would be acts of aggression and exploitation."

"So that's the way of it," said Grimes.

"That is the way of it," she agreed. Surprisingly she took him in her strong arms, affectionately pressed him to her resilient body. Grimes did not resist. She released him. "Good-bye, John. You must return to your ship. To *your* ship. We may meet again—I hope that we do. We may not. But always, always, the best of luck."

She turned away from him, walked down the slipway to the sea, an almost impossibly graceful, glittering figure. It seemed to Grimes that the silkies had been waiting for her. There was a great flurry of spray as she entered the water, a chorus of musical gruntings.

And then she and they were gone, and Grimes started his walk back to the ship, cursing the spiky bushes on the overgrown road that seemed to be determined to hold him prisoner on this planet.

He was sitting in his chair in the control room. The Drive had been recalibrated. All hands had returned on board, had proceeded to their lift-off stations. Steerforth looked curiously at Grimes' forearms, bare under the short-sleeved uniform shirt, at his knees, bare under the hem of his shorts.

"Those scratches, sir. . . . How did you get them? You look as though you've been in a cat fight."

"Do I?" said Grimes coldly. Then, "All right, Number One. Let's get the show on the road."

Steerforth said, "But couldn't we wait a little, sir? What about Seiko? Couldn't we send Shirl and Darleen down to the sea to try to do some submarine singing to call her back? After all, they're rather special cobbers of hers."

"We shall be happy to try," said Shirl.

"Make it lift off stations, Mr Steerforth," ordered Grimes.

"But Seiko . . ."

"She'll be all right," said Grimes, with convincing certainty.

GRIMES AT GLENROWAN

Commodore John Grimes of the Rim Worlds Naval Reserve, currently Master of the survey ship *Faraway Quest,* was relaxing in his day cabin aboard that elderly but trustworthy vessel. That morning, local time, he had brought the old ship down to a landing at Port Fortinbras, on Elsinore, the one habitable planet in orbit about the Hamlet sun. It was Grimes's first visit to Elsinore for very many years. This call was to be no more—and no less—than a showing of the flag of the Confederacy. The *Quest* had been carrying out a survey of a newly discovered planetary system rather closer to the Shakespearian Sector than to the Rim Worlds and Grimes's lords and masters back on Lorn had instructed him, on completion of this task, to pay a friendly call on their opposite numbers on Elsinore.

However, he would be seeing nobody of any real importance until this evening, when he would attend a reception being held in his honour at the President's palace. So he had time to relax, at ease in his shipboard shorts and shirt, puffing contentedly at his vile pipe, watching the local trivi programmes on his playmaster. That way he would catch up on the planetary news, learn something of Elsinorian attitudes and prejudices. He was, after all, visiting this world in an ambassadorial capacity.

He looked with wry amusement into the screen. There he was—or, to be more exact, there was *Faraway Quest*—coming down. *Not bad*, he admitted smugly, *not bad at all*. There had been a nasty, gusty wind at ground level about which Aerospace Control had failed to warn him—but he had coped. He watched the plump, dull-silver spindle that was his ship sagging to leeward, leaning into the veering breeze, then settling almost exactly into the centre of the triangle of bright flashing marker beacons, midway between the Shakespearian Line's *Oberon* and the Commission's *Epsilon Orionis*. He recalled having made a rather feeble joke about

O'Brian and O'Ryan. (His officers had laughed dutifully.) He watched the beetle-like ground cars carrying the port officials scurry out across the grey apron as the *Quest*'s ramp was extruded from her after airlock. He chuckled softly at the sight of Timmins, his Chief Officer, resplendent in his best uniform, standing at the head of the gangway to receive the boarding party. Although only a reservist—like Grimes himself—that young man put on the airs and graces of a First Lieutenant of a Constellation Class battlewagon, a flagship at that. But he was a good spaceman and that was all that really mattered.

After a short interval, filled with the chatter of the commentator, he was privileged to watch himself being interviewed by the newsman who had accompanied the officials on board. Did he really look as crusty as that? he wondered. And wasn't there something in what Sonya, his wife, was always saying—and what other ladies had said long before he first met her—about his ears? Stun's'l ears, jughandle ears. Only a very minor operation would be required to make them less outstanding, but . . . He permitted himself another chuckle. He liked him the way that he was and if the ladies didn't they had yet to show it.

The intercom telephone buzzed. Grimes turned to look at Timmins's face in the little screen. He made a downward gesture of his hand towards the playmaster, and his own voice and that of the interviewer at once faded into inaudibility. "Yes, Mr. Timmins?" he asked.

"Sir, there is a lady here to see you."

A lady? wondered Grimes. Elsinore was one of the few worlds upon which he had failed to enjoy a temporary romance. He had been there only once before, when he was a junior officer in the Federation's Survey Service. He recalled (it still rankled) that he had had his shore leave stopped for some minor misdemeanor.

"A lady?" he repeated. Then, "What does she want?"

"She says that she is from Station Yorick, sir. She would like to interview you."

"But I've already been interviewed," said Grimes.

"Not by Station Yorick," a female voice told him. "Elsinore's purveyors of entertainment and philosophy."

Timmins's face in the little screen had been replaced by that of a girl—a woman, rather. Glossy black hair, short cut, over a thin, creamily pale face with strong bone structure and delicately cleft chin . . . a wide, scarlet mouth . . . almost indigo blue eyes set off by black lashes.

"Mphm," grunted Grimes approvingly. "Mphm . . ."

"Commodore Grimes?" she asked in a musical contralto. "*The* Commodore Grimes?"

"There's only one of me as far as I know," he told her. "And you?"

She smiled whitely. "Kitty, of Kitty's Korner. With a 'K'. And I'd like a *real* interview for *my* audience, not the sort of boring question-and-answer session that you've just been watching."

"Mphm," grunted Grimes again. What harm could it do?, he asked himself. This would be quite a good way of passing what otherwise would be a dull afternoon. And Elsinore was in the Shakespearian Sector, wasn't it? Might not he, Grimes, play Othello to this newshen's Desdemona, wooing her with his tall tales of peril and adventure all over the Galaxy? And in his private grog locker were still six bottles of Antarean Crystal Gold laid aside for emergencies such as this, a potent liquor coarsely referred to by spacemen as a leg-opener, certainly a better loosener of inhibitions that the generality of alcoholic beverages. He would have to partake of it with her, of course, but a couple or three soberups would put him right for the cocktail party.

"Ask Mr. Timmins to show you up," he said.

He looked at her over the rim of his glass. He liked what he saw. The small screen of the intercom, showing only her face, had not done her full justice. She sat facing him in an easy chair, making a fine display of slender, well-formed thigh under the high-riding apology for a skirt. (Hemlines were down again, almost to ankle length, in the Rim Worlds and Grimes had not approved of the change in fashion.) The upper part of her green dress was not quite transparent but it was obvious that she neither wore nor needed a bust support.

She looked at him over the rim of her glass. She smiled.

He said, "Here's to Yorick, the Jester. . . ."

She said, "And the philosopher. We have our serious side."

They sipped. The wine was cold, mellow fire.

He said, "Don't we all?"

"You especially," she told him. "You must be more of a philosopher than most men, Commodore. Your interdimensional experiences—"

"So you've heard of them . . . Kitty."

"Yes. Even here. Didn't somebody once say, 'If there's a crack in the Continuum Grimes is sure to fall into it—and come up with the Shaara Crown Jewels clutched in his hot little hands.'?"

He laughed. "I've never laid my paws on the Shaara Crown Jewels yet—although I've had my troubles with the Shaara. There was the time that I was in business as an interstellar courier and got tangled with a Rogue Queen—"

But she was not interested in the Shaara. She pressed on, "It seems that it's only out on the Rim proper, on worlds like Kinsolving, that you find these . . . cracks in the Continuum. . . ."

Grimes refilled the glasses saying, "Thirsty work, talking. . . ."

"But we've talked hardly at all," she said. "And I *want* you to talk. I want *you* to talk. If all I wanted was stories of high adventure and low adventure in *this* universe I'd only have to interview any of our own space captains. What I want, what Station Yorick wants, what our public wants is a story such as only *you* can tell. One of your adventures on Kinsolving . . ."

He laughed. "It's not only on Kinsolving's Planet that you can fall through a crack in the Continuum." He was conscious of the desire to impress her. "In fact, the first time that it happened was on Earth. . . ."

She was suitably incredulous.

"On Earth?" she demanded.

"Too right," he said.

I'm a Rim Worlder now (he told her) but I wasn't born out on the Rim. As far as the accident of birth is concerned I'm Terran. I started my spacefaring career in the Interstellar Federation's Survey Service. My long leaves I always spent on Earth, where my parents lived.

Anyhow, just to visualise me as I was then: a Survey Service JG Lieutenant with money in his pocket, time on his hands and, if you must know, between girlfriends. I'd been expecting that—What was her name? Oh, yes. Vanessa. I'd been expecting that she'd be still waiting for me when I got back from my tour of duty. She wasn't. She'd married—of all people!—a sewage conversion engineer.

Anyhow, I spent the obligatory couple of weeks with my parents in The Alice. (The Alice? Oh, that's what Australians call Alice Springs, a city in the very middle of the island continent.) My father was an author. He specialised in historical romances. He was always saying that the baddies of history are much more interesting than the goodies—and that the good baddies and the bad goodies are the most fascinating of all. You've a fine example of that in this planetary system of yours. The names, I mean. The Hamlet sun and all that. Hamlet was rather a devious bastard, wasn't he? And although he wasn't an out and out baddie he could hardly be classed as a goodie.

Well, the Old Man was working on yet another historical novel, this one to be set in Australia. All about the life and hard times of Ned Kelly. You've probably never heard of him—very few people outside Australia have—but he was a notorious bushranger. Bushrangers were sort of highway robbers. Just as the English have Dick Turpin and the Americans have Jesse James, so we have the Kelly Gang. (Australia had rather a late start as a nation so has always made the most of its relatively short history.)

According to my respected father this Ned Kelly was more, much more, than a mere bushranger. He was a freedom fighter, striking valiant blows on behalf of the oppressed masses, a sort of Robin Hood. And, like that probably-mythical Robin Hood, he was something of a military genius. Until the end he outwitted the troopers—as the police were called in his day—with ease. He was a superb horseman. He was an innovator. His suit of homemade armour—breast- and back-plates and an odd cylindrical helmet—was famous. It was proof against rifle and pistol fire. He was very big and strong and could carry the weight of it.

It was at a place called Glenrowan that he finally came unstuck. In his day it was only a village, a hamlet. (No pun intended.) It was on the railway line from Melbourne to points north. Anyhow, Ned had committed some crime or other at a place called Wangaratta and a party of police was on the way there from Melbourne by special train, not knowing that the Kelly gang had ridden back to Glenrowan. Like all guerrilla leaders throughout history Kelly had an excellent intelligence service. He knew that the train was on the way and would be passing through Glenrowan. He persuaded a gang of Irish workmen—platelayers, they were called—to tear up the railway tracks just north of the village. The idea was that the train would be derailed and the policemen massacred. While the bushrangers were waiting they enjoyed quite a party in the Glenrowan Hotel; Kelly and his gang were more popular than otherwise among the locals. But the schoolmaster—who was *not* a Kelly supporter—managed to creep away from the festivities and, with a lantern and his wife's red scarf, flagged the train down.

The hotel was besieged. It was set on fire. The only man who was not killed at once was Kelly himself. He came out of the smoke and the flames, wearing his armour, a revolver (a primitive multi-shot projectile pistol) in each hand, blazing away at his enemies. One of the troopers had the intelligence to fire at his legs, which were not protected by the armour, and brought him down.

He was later hanged.

Well, as I've indicated, my Old Man was up to the eyebrows in his research into the Ned Kelly legend, and some of his enthusiasm rubbed off on to me. I thought that I'd like to have a look at this Glenrowan place. Father was quite amused. He told me that Glenrowan *now* was nothing at all like Glenrowan *then,* that instead of a tiny huddle of shacks by the railway line I should find a not-so-small city sitting snugly in the middle of all-the-year-round-producing orchards under the usual featureless plastic domes. There was, he conceded, a sort of reconstruction of the famous hotel standing beside a railway line—all right for tourists, he sneered, but definitely not for historians.

I suppose that he was a historian—he certainly always took his researches seriously enough—but I wasn't. I was just a spaceman with time on my hands. And—which probably decided me—there was a quite fantastic shortage of unattached popsies in The Alice and my luck might be better elsewhere.

So I took one of the tourist airships from Alice Springs to Melbourne and then a really antique railway train—steam-driven yet, although the coal in the tender was only for show; it was a minireactor that boiled the water—from Melbourne to Glenrowan. This primitive means of locomotion, of course, was for the benefit of tourists.

When I dismounted from that horribly uncomfortable coach at Glenrowan Station I ran straight into an old shipmate. Oddly enough—although, as it turned out later, it wasn't so odd—his name was Kelly. He'd been one of the junior interstellar drive engineer officers in the old *Aries*. I'd never liked him much—or him me—but when you're surrounded by planetlubbers you greet a fellow spaceman as though he were a long-lost brother.

"Grimes!" he shouted. "Gutsy Grimes in person!"

(No, Kitty, I didn't get that nickname because I'm exceptionally brave. It was just that some people thought I had an abnormally hearty appetite and would eat *anything*.)

"An' what are *you* doin' here?" he demanded. His Irish accent, as Irish accents usually do, sounded phoney as all hell.

I told him that I was on leave and asked him if he was too. He told me that he'd resigned his commission some time ago and that so had his cousin, Spooky Byrne. Byrne hadn't been with us in *Aries* but I had met him. He was a PCO—Psionic Communications Officer. A Commissioned Teacup Reader, as we used to call them. A trained and qualified telepath. You don't find many of 'em these days in the various merchant services—the Carlotti Communications System is a far more reliable way of handling instantaneous communications over the light-years. But most navies still employ them—a telepath is good for much more than the mere transmission and reception of signals.

So, Kelly and Spooky Byrne, both in Glenrowan. And me, also in Glenrowan. There are some locations in some cities where, it is said, if you loaf around long enough you're sure to meet everybody you know. An exaggeration, of course, but there *are* focal points. But I wouldn't put the Glenrowan Hotel—that artificially tumbledown wooden shack with its bark roof—synthetic bark, of course—in that category. It looked very small and sordid among the tall, shining buildings of the modern city. Small and sordid? Yes, but—somehow—even though it was an obvious, trashy tourist trap it possessed a certain character. Something of the atmosphere of the original building seemed to have clung to the site.

Kelly said, using one of my own favourite expressions, "Come on in, Grimes. The sun's over the yardarm."

I must have looked a bit dubious. My onetime shipmate had been quite notorious for never paying for a drink when he could get somebody else to do it. He read my expression. He laughed. "Don't worry, Gutsy. I'm a rich man now—which is more than I was when I was having to make do on my beggarly stipend in the Survey Service—may God rot their cotton socks! Come on in!"

Well, we went into the pub. The inside came up to—or down to—my worst expectations. There was a long bar of rough wood with thirsty tourists lined up along it. There was a sagging calico ceiling. There was a wide variety of antique ironmongery hanging on the walls—kitchen implements, firearms, rusty cutlasses. There were simulated flames flickering in the glass chimneys of battered but well-polished brass oil lamps. The wenches behind the bar were dressed in sort of Victorian costumes—long, black skirts, high-collared, frilly white blouses—although I don't think that in good Queen Victoria's day those blouses would have been as near as dammit transparent and worn over no underwear.

We had rum—not the light, dry spirit that most people are used to these days but sweet, treacly, almost-knife-and-fork stuff. Kelly paid, peeling off credits from a roll that could almost have been used as a bolster. We had more rum. Kelly tried to pay again but I wouldn't let him—although I hoped this party wouldn't last all day. Those prices, in that clipjoint, were making a nasty dent in my holiday money. Then Spooky Byrne drifted in, as colourless and weedy as ever, looking like a streak of ectoplasm frayed at the edges.

He stared at me as though he were seeing a ghost. "Grimes, of all people!" he whispered intensely. "Here, of all places!"

(I sensed, somehow, that his surprise was not genuine.)

"An' why not?" demanded his burly, deceptively jovial cousin. "Spacemen are only tourists in uniform. An' as Grimes is in civvies that makes him even more a tourist."

"The . . . coincidence . . . ," hissed Spooky. Whatever his act was he was persisting with it.

"Coincidences are always happenin'," said Kelly, playing up to him.

"Yes, Eddie, but—"

"But what?" I demanded, since it seemed expected of me.

"Mr. Grimes," Spooky told me, "would it surprise you if I told you that one of your ancestors was *here*? Was here *then*?"

"Too right it would," I said. "Going back to the old style Twentieth Century, and the Nineteenth, and further back still, most of my male forebears were seamen." The rum was making me boastfully talkative. "I have a pirate in my family tree. And an Admiral of the Royal Navy, on my mother's side. Her family name is Hornblower. So, Spooky, what the hell would either a Grimes or a Hornblower have been doing here, miles inland, in this nest of highway robbers?" Both Kelly and Byrne gave me dirty looks. "All right, then. Not highway robbers. Bushrangers, if it makes you feel any happier."

And not bushrangers either!" growled Kelly. "Freedom fighters!"

"Hah!" I snorted.

"Freedom fighters!" stated Kelly belligerently. "All right, so they did rob a bank or two. An' so what? In that period rebel organisations often robbed the capitalists to get funds to buy arms and all the rest of it. It was no more than S.O.P."

"Mphm," I grunted.

"In any case," said Kelly, "your ancestor was so here. We *know*. Come home with us an' we'll convince you."

So I let those two bastards talk me into accompanying them to their apartment, which was a penthouse a-top the Glenrowan Tower. This wasn't by any means the tallest building in the city although it had been, I learned, when it was built. I remarked somewhat enviously that this was a palatial pad for a spaceman and Kelly told me that he wasn't a spaceman but a businessman and that he'd succeeded, by either clever or lucky investments, in converting a winning ticket in the New Irish Sweep into a substantial fortune. Byrne told him that he should give some credit where credit was due. Kelly told Byrne that graduates of the Rhine Institute are bound, by oath, not to use their psionic gifts for personal enrichment. Byrne shut up.

The living quarters of the penthouse were furnished in period fashion—the Victorian period. Gilt and red plush—dark, carved, varnished wood——heavily framed, sepia-tinted photographs—no, not holograms, but those old *flat* photographs—of heavily bearded worthies hanging on the crimson-and-gold papered walls. One of them I recognised from the research material my father had been using. It was Ned Kelly.

"Fascinating," I said.

"This atmosphere is necessary to our researches," said Byrne. Then, "But come through to the laboratory."

I don't know what I was expecting to see in the other room into which they led me. Certainly not what first caught my attention. That caught my attention? That *demanded* my attention. It was, at first glance, a Mannschenn Drive unit—not a full-sized one such as would be found in even a small ship but certainly a bigger one than the mini-Mannschenns you find in lifeboats.

(You've never seen a Mannschenn Drive unit? I must show you ours before you go ashore. And you don't understand how they work? Neither do I, frankly. But it boils down, essentially, to gyroscopes precessing in time, setting up a temporal precession field, so that our ships aren't really breaking the light barrier but going astern in time while they're going ahead in space.)

"A Mannschenn Drive unit," I said unnecessarily.

"I built it," said Kelly, not without pride.

"What for?" I asked. "Time Travel?" I sneered.

"Yes," he said.

I laughed. "But it's known to be impossible. A negative field—would require the energy of the entire galaxy—"

"Not physical Time Travel," said Spooky Byrne smugly. "Psionic Time Travel, back along the world line stemming from an ancestor. Eddie's ancestor was at Glenrowan. So was mine. So was yours."

"Ned Kelly wasn't married," I said triumphantly.

"And so you have to be married to father a child?" asked Byrnes sardonically. "Come off it, Grimes! *You* should know better than that."

(I did, as a matter of fact. This was after that odd business I'd gotten involved in on El Dorado.)

"All right," I said. "Your ancestors might have been present at the Siege of Glenrowan. Mine was not. At or about that time he was, according to my father—and he's the family historian—second mate of a tramp windjammer. He got himself paid off in Melbourne and, not so long afterwards, was master of a little brig running between Australia and New Zealand. He did leave an autobiography, you know."

"Autobiographies are often self-censored," said Byrne. "That long-ago Captain Grimes, that smugly respectable shipmaster, a pillar, no doubt, of Church and State, had episodes in his past that he would prefer to forget. He did not pay off from his ship in Melbourne in the normal way. He—what was the expression?—jumped ship. He'd had words with his captain, who was a notorious bully. He'd exchanged blows. So he deserted and thought that he'd be safer miles inland. The only work that he could find was with the Irish labourers on the railway."

"How do you know all this?" I asked. "*If* it's true—"

"He told me," said Byrne. "Or he told my ancestor—but I was inside his mind at the time. . . ."

"Let's send him back," said Kelly. "That'll convince him."

"Not . . . yet," whispered Byrne. "Let's show him first what will happen if the special train is, after all, derailed. Let's convince him that it's to his interests to play along with us. The . . . alternative, since Grimes showed up here, is much . . . firmer. But we shall need—*did* need?—that British seaman Grimes, just as George Washington needed his British seaman John Paul Jones. . . ."

"Are you trying to tell me," I asked, "that the squalid squabble at Glenrowan was a crucial point in history?"

"Yes," said Kelly.

I realised that I'd been maneuvered to one of the three chairs facing the Mannschenn Drive unit, that I'd been eased quite gently on to the seat. The chair was made of tubular metal, with a high back, at the top of which was a helmet of metal mesh. This Kelly rapidly adjusted over my head. The only explanation that I can find for my submitting so tamely to all this is that Spooky Byrne must have possessed hypnotic powers.

Anyhow, I sat in that chair, which was comfortable enough. I watched Kelly fussing around with the Mannschenn Drive controls while Byrne did things to his own console—which looked more like an aquarium in which luminous, insubstantial, formless fish were swimming than anything else. The drive rotors started to turn, to spin, to precess. I wanted to close my eyes; after all, it is dinned into us from boyhood up never to look directly at the Mannshchenn Drive in operation. I wanted to close my eyes, but couldn't. I watched those blasted, shimmering wheels spinning, tumbling, fading, always on the verge of invisibility but ever pulsatingly a-glimmer. . . .

I listened to the familiar thin, high whine of the machine. . . .

That sound persisted; otherwise the experience was like watching one of those ancient silent films in an entertainments museum. There was no other noise, although that of the Drive unit could almost have come from an archaic projector. There were no smells, no sensations. There were just pictures, mostly out of focus and with the colours not quite right. But I saw Kelly—the here-and-now Kelly, not his villainous ancestor—recognisable in spite of the full beard that he was wearing, in some sort of sumptuous regalia, a golden crown in which emeralds gleamed set on his head. And there was Byrne, more soberly but still richly attired, reminding me somehow of the legendary wizard Merlin who was the power behind King Arthur's throne. And there were glimpses of a flag, a glowing green banner with a golden harp in the upper canton, the stars of the Southern Cross, also in gold, on the fly. And I saw myself. It was me, all right. I was wearing a green uniform with gold braid up to the elbows. The badge on my cap, with its bullion-encrusted peak, was a golden crown over a winged, golden harp. . . .

The lights went out, came on again. I was sitting in the chair looking at the motionless machine, at Kelly and Byrne, who were looking at me.

Kelly said, "There are crucial points in history. The 'ifs' of history. *If* Napoleon had accepted Fulton's offer of steamships . . . just imagine a squadron of steam frigates at Trafalgar! *If* Pickett's charge at Gettysburg had been successful . . . *If* Admiral Torrance had met the Waverley Navy head on off New Dunedine instead of despatching his forces in a fruitless chase of Commodore McWhirter and his raiding squadron.

"And. . . .

"*If* Thomas Curnow had not succeeded in flagging down the special train before it reached Glenrowan.

"You've seen what could have been, what can be. The extrapolation. Myself king. Spooky my chief minister. You—an admiral."

I laughed. In spite of what I'd just seen it still seemed absurd. "All right," I said. "You might be king. But why should I be an admiral?"

He said, "It could be a sort of hereditary rank granted, in the first instance, to that ancestor of yours for services rendered. When you're fighting a war at the end of long lines of supply somebody on your staff who knows about ships is useful—"

"I've looked," said Spooky Byrne. "I've seen how things were after the massacre of the police outside Glenrowan. I've seen the rising of the poor, the oppressed, spreading from Victoria to New South Wales, under the flag of the Golden Harp and Southern Cross. I've seen the gunboats on the Murray, the armoured paddlewheelers with their steam-powered Gatling cannon, an' the armoured trains ranging up an' down the country-side. An' it was yourself, Grimes—or your ancestor—who put to good use the supplies that were comin' in from our Fenian brothers in America an' even from the German emperor. I've watched the Battle of Port Phillip Bay—the English warships an' troop transports, with the Pope's Eye battery wreakin' havoc among 'em until a lucky shot found its maga-zine. An' then your flimsy gasbags came a-sailin' over, droppin' their bombs, an' not a gun could be brought to bear on 'em. . . ."

"Airships?" I demanded. "You certainly have been seeing things, Spooky!"

"Yes, airships. There was a man called Bland in Sydney, somethin' of a rebel himself, who designed an airship years before Ned was ever heard of. An' you—or your ancestor—could have found those plans. You, in your ancestor's mind, sort of nudgin'—just as Eddie an' meself'll be doing our own nudgin'. . . ."

I wasn't quite sober so, in spite of my protestations, what Spooky was saying, combined with what I had seen, seemed to make sense. So when Kelly said that we should now, all three of us, return to the past, to the year 1880, old reckoning, I did not object. I realised dimly that they had been expecting me, waiting for me. That they were needing me. I must have been an obnoxious puppy in those days—but aren't we all when still wet behind the ears? I actually thought of bargaining. A dukedom on top of the admiral's commission . . . the Duke of Alice . . . ? It sounded good.

Kelly and Byrne were seated now, one on either side of me. There were controls set in the armrests of their chairs. Lattice-work skeps, like the one that I was wearing, were over their heads. The rotors started to spin, to spin and precess, glimmering, fading, tumbling, dragging our *essences* down the dark dimensions while our bodies remained solidly seated in the here and now.

I listened to the familiar thin, high whine of the machine. . . .

To the babble of rough voices, male and female. . . . To the piano-accordion being not too inexpertly played. . . . An Irish song it was—*The Wearin' Of The Green*. . . . I smelled tobacco smoke, the fumes of beer and of strong liquor. . . . I opened my eyes and looked around me. It was *real*—far more real than the unconvincing reconstruction in the here-and-now Glenrowan had been. The slatternly women were a far cry from those barmaids tarted up in allegedly period costume. And here there were no tourists, gaily dressed and hung around with all manner of expensive recording equipment. Here were burly, bearded, rough-clad men and it was weapons, antique revolvers, that they carried, not the very latest trivoders.

But the group of men of whom I was one were not armed. They were labourers, not bushrangers—but they looked up to the arrogant giant who was holding forth just as much as did his fellow . . . criminals? Yes, they were that. They had held up coaches, robbed banks, murdered. Yet to these Irish labourers he was a hero, a deliverer. He stood for the Little Man against the Establishment. He stood for a warmly human religion against one whose priests were never recruited from the ranks of the ordinary people, the peasants, the workers.

Mind you, I was seeing him through the eyes of that ancestral Grimes who was (temporarily) a criminal himself, who was (temporarily) a rebel, who was on the run (he thought) from the forces of Law and Order. I had full access to his memories. I was, more or less, him. More or less, I say. Nonetheless, I, Grimes the spaceman, was a guest in the mind of Grimes the seaman. I could remember that quarrel on the poop of the *Lady Lucan* and how Captain Jenkins, whose language was always foul, had excelled himself, calling me what was, in those days, an impossibly vile epithet. I lost my temper, Jenkins lost a few teeth, and I lost my job, hastily leaving the ship in Melbourne before Jenkins could have me arrested on a charge of mutiny on the high seas.

And now, mainly because of the circumstances in which I found

myself, I was on the point of becoming one of those middle class technicians who through the ages, have thrown in their lot with charismatic
rebel leaders, without whom those same alleged deliverers of the
oppressed masses would have gotten no place at all. I—*now*—regard
with abhorrence the idea of derailing a special train on the way to apprehend a rather vicious criminal. That ancestral Grimes, in his later years,
must have felt the same sentiments—so much so that he never admitted to
anybody that he was among those present at the Siege of Glenrowan.

But Ned Kelly. . . . He was in good form, although there was something odd about him. He seemed to be . . . possessed. So was the man—
Joe Byrne—standing beside him. And so, of course, was John Grimes,
lately second mate of the good ship *Lady Lucan*. Kelly—which Kelly?—
must have realised that he was drawing some odd looks from his adher-
ents. He broke the tension by putting on his famous helmet—the
sheet-iron cylinder with only a slit for the eyes—and singing while he
was wearing it. This drew both laughter and applause. Did you ever see
those singing robots that were quite a craze a few years back? The effect
was rather similar. Great art it was not but it was good for a laugh.

Nobody saw the schoolmaster, Thomas Curnow, sneaking out but me.
That was rather odd as he, fancying himself a cut above the others making
merry in the hotel, had been keeping himself to himself, saying little,
drinking sparingly. This should have made him conspicuous but, somehow, it had the reverse effect. He was the outsider, being studiously
ignored. I tried to attract Kelly's attention, Byrne's attention, but I might
as well just not have been there. After all I—or my host—was an outsider
too. I was the solitary Englishman among the Australians and the Irish.
The gang with whom I'd been working on the railway had never liked me.
The word had gotten around that I was an officer. The fact that I was
(temporarily, as it happened) an ex-officer made no difference. I was
automatically suspect.

But I still wanted to be an admiral. I still wanted to command those
squadrons of gunboats on the Murray River, the air fleet that would turn
the tide at Port Phillip Bay. (How much of my inward voice was the rum
speaking, how much was me? How much did the John Grimes whose
brain I was taking over ever know about it, remember about it?)

I followed Curnow, out into the cold, clear night. The railway track
was silvery in the light of the lopsided moon, near its meridian. On either
side, dark and ominous, was the bush. Some nocturnal bird or animal
called out, a raucous cry, and something else answered it. And faint—but
growing louder—there was a sort of chuffing rattle coming up from the
south'ard. The pilot engine, I thought, and then the special train.

Ahead of me Curnow's lantern, a yellow star where no star should have been, was bobbing along between the tracks. I remembered the story. He had the lantern, and his wife's red scarf. He would wave them. The train would stop. Superintendent Hare, Inspector O'Connor, the white troopers, and the black trackers would pile out. And then the shooting, and the siege, and the fire, and that great, armoured figure, like some humanoid robot before its time, stumbling out through the smoke and the flame for the final showdown with his enemies.

And it was up to me to change the course of history.

Have you ever tried walking along a railway line, especially when you're in something of a hurry? The sleepers or the ties or whatever they're called are spaced at just the wrong distance for a normal human stride. Curnow was doing better than I was. Well, he was more used to it. Neither as a seaman nor as a spaceman had I ever had occasion to take a walk such as this.

And then—he fell. He'd tripped, I suppose. He'd fallen with such force as to knock himself out. When I came up to him I found that he'd tried to save that precious lantern from damage. It was on its side but the chimney was unbroken, although one side of the glass was blackened by the smoke from the burning oil.

And the train was coming. I could see it now—the glaring yellow headlight of the leading locomotive, the orange glow from the fireboxes, a shower of sparks mingling with the smoke from the funnels. I had to get Curnow off the line. I tried to lift him but one foot was somehow jammed under the sleeper over which he had tripped. But his lantern, as I have already said, was still burning. I hastily turned it the right side up; only one side of the chimney was smoked into opacity. And that flimsy, translucent red scarf was still there.

I lifted the lantern, held it so that the coloured fabric acted as a filter. I waved it—not fast, for fear that the light would be blown out, but slowly, deliberately. The train, the metal monster, kept on coming. I knew that I'd soon have to look after myself but was determined to stand there until the last possible second.

The whistle of the leading locomotive, the pilot engine, sounded—a long, mournful note. There was a screaming of brakes, a great, hissing roar of escaping steam, shouting. . . .

I realised that Curnow had recovered, had scrambled to his feet, was standing beside me. I thrust the lantern and the scarf into his hand, ran into the bushes at the side of the track. He could do all the explaining. I—or that ancestral Grimes—had no desire to meet the police. For all I—or he—knew they would regard the capture of a mutineer and deserter as well as a gang of bushrangers as an unexpected bonus.

I stayed in my hiding place—cold, bewildered, more than a little scared. After a while I heard the shooting, the shouting and the scream-ing. I saw the flames. I was too far away to see Ned Kelly's last desperate stand; all that I observed was distant, shadowy figures in silhouette against the burning hotel.

Suddenly, without warning, I was back in my chair in that other Kelly's laboratory. The machine, the modified Mannschenn Drive unit, had stopped. I looked at Byrne. I knew, without examining him, that he, too, had . . . stopped. Kelly was alive but not yet fully conscious. His mouth was working. I could just hear what he was muttering; "It had to come to this." And those, I recalled, had been the last words of Ned Kelly, the bushranger, just before they hanged him.

I reasoned, insofar as I was capable of reasoning, that Kelly and Byrne had entered too deeply into the minds of their criminal ancestors. Joe Byrne had died in the siege and his descendant had died with him. Kelly had been badly wounded, although he recovered sufficiently to stand trial. I'd been lucky enough to escape almost unscathed.

I'm not at all proud of what I did then. I just got up and left them—the dead man, his semi-conscious cousin. I got out of there, fast. When I left the Glenrowan Tower I took a cab to the airport and there bought a ticket on the first flight out of the city. It was going to Perth, a place that I'd never much wanted to visit, but at least it was putting distance between me and the scene of that hapless experiment, that presumptuous attempt at tinkering with Time.

I've often wondered what would have happened if I'd left Curnow to his fate, if I hadn't stopped the train. The course of history might well have been changed—but would it have been for the better? I don't think so. An Irish Australia, a New Erin, a Harp in the South . . . New Erin allied with the Boers against hated England during the wars in South Africa . . . New Erin quite possibly allied with Germany against England during the First World War . . . The Irish, in many ways, are a great peo-ple—but they carry a grudge to absurd lengths. They have far too long a memory for their own wrongs.

And I think that I like me better as I am now than as an Hereditary Admiral of the New Erin Navy in an alternate universe that, fortunately, didn't happen.

She said, "Thank you, Commodore, for a very interesting story."

She switched off her trivoder, folded flat its projections, closed the carrying case about it. She got to her feet.

She said, "I have to be going."

He looked at the bulkhead clock, he said, "There's no hurry, Kitty. We've time for another drink or two." He sensed a coldness in the atmosphere and tried to warm things up with an attempt at humour. "Sit down again. Make yourself comfortable. This ship is Liberty Hall, you know. You can spit on that mat and call the cat a bastard."

She said, "The only tom cats I've seen aboard this waggon haven't been of the four-legged variety. And, talking of legs, do you think that I haven't noticed the way that you've been eyeing mine?"

His prominent ears reddened angrily but he persisted. "Will you be at the cocktail party tonight?"

"No, Commodore Grimes. Station Yorick isn't interested in boring social functions."

"But I'll be seeing more of you, I hope. . . ."

"You will not, in either sense of the words." She turned to go. "You said, Commodore, that the Irish have a long memory for their own wrongs. Perhaps you are right. Be that as it may—you might be interested to learn that my family name is Kelly."

When she was gone Grimes reflected wrily that now there was yet another alternate universe, differing from his here-and-now only in a strictly personal sense, which he would never enter.

GRIMES AND THE GREAT RACE

"I didn't think that I'd be seeing you again," said Grimes.

"Or I you," Kitty Kelly told him. "But Station Yorick's customers liked that first interview. The grizzled old spacedog, pipe in mouth, glass in hand, spinning a yarn. . . . So when my bosses learned that you're stuck here until your engineers manage to fit a new rubber band to your inertial drive they said, in these very words, 'Get your arse down to the spaceport, Kitty, and try to wheedle another tall tale out of the old bastard!' "

"Mphm," grunted Grimes, acutely conscious that his prominent ears had reddened angrily.

Kitty smiled sweetly. She was an attractive girl, black Irish, wide-mouthed, creamy-skinned, with vivid blue eyes. Grimes would have thought her much more attractive had she not been making it obvious that she still nursed the resentment engendered by his first story, a tale of odd happenings at long-ago and far-away Glenrowan where, thanks to Grimes, an ancestral Kelly had met his downfall.

She said tartly, "And lay off the Irish this time, will you?"

Grimes looked at her, at her translucent, emerald green blouse that concealed little, at the long, shapely legs under the skirt that concealed even less. He thought, *There's one of the Irish, right here, that I'd like to lay on.*

With deliberate awkwardness he asked, "If I'm supposed to avoid giving offense to anybody—and you Elsinoreans must carry the blood of about every race and nation on Old Earth—what can I talk about?"

She made a great show of cogitation, frowning, staring down at the tips of her glossy green shoes. Then she smiled. "Racing, of course! On this world we're great followers of the horses." She frowned again. "But no. Somehow I just can't see you as a sporting man, Commodore."

"As a matter of fact," said Grimes stiffly, "I did once take part in a race. And for high stakes."

"I just can't imagine *you* on a horse."

"Who said anything about horses?"

"What were you riding, then?"

"Do you want the story or don't you? If I'm going to tell it, I'll tell it my way."

She sighed, muttered, "All right, all right." She opened her case, brought out the trivi recorder, set it up on the deck of the day cabin. She aimed one lens at the chair in which Grimes was sitting, the other at the one that she would occupy. She squinted into the viewfinder. "Pipe in mouth," she ordered. "Glass in hand . . . Where is the glass, Commodore? And aren't you going to offer *me* a drink?"

He gestured towards the liquor cabinet. "You fix it. I'll have a pink gin, on the rocks."

"Then I'll have the same. It'll be better than the sickly muck you poured down me last time I was aboard your ship!"

Grimes's ears flushed again. The "sickly muck" had failed to have the desired effect.

My first command in the Survey Service (he began) was of a Serpent Class Courier, *Adder*. The captains of these little ships were lieutenants, their officers lieutenants and ensigns. There were no petty officers or ratings to worry about, no stewards or stewardesses to look after us. We made our own beds, cooked our own meals. We used to take turns playing with the rather primitive autochef. We didn't starve; in fact we lived quite well.

There was some passenger accommodation; the couriers were—and probably still are—sometimes used to get VIPs from Point A to Point B in a hurry. And they carried Service mail and despatches hither and yon. If there was any odd job to do we did it.

This particular job was a very odd one. You've heard of Darban? No? Well, it's an Earth-type planet in the Tauran Sector. Quite a pleasant world although the atmosphere's a bit too dense for some tastes. But if it were what we call Earth-normal I mightn't be sitting here talking to you now. Darban's within the Terran sphere of influence with a Carlotti Beacon Station, a Survey Service Base, and all the rest of it. At the time of which I'm talking, though, it wasn't in anybody's sphere of influence, although Terran star tramps and Hallichek and Shaara ships had been calling there for quite some time. There was quite a demand for the so-called living opals—although how any woman could bear to have a slimy, squirming necklace of luminous worms strung about her neck beats me!

She interrupted him. "These Hallicheki and Shaara . . . non-human races, aren't they?"
"Non-human and non-humanoid. The Hallicheki are avians, with a matriarchal society. The Shaara are winged arthropods, not unlike the Terran bees, although very much larger and with a somewhat different internal structure."
"There'll be pictures of them in our library. We'll show them to our viewers. But go on, please."

The merchant captains (he continued) had been an unusually law-abiding crowd. They'd bartered for the living opals but had been careful not to give in exchange any artifacts that would unduly accelerate local industrial evolution. No advanced technology—if the Darbanese wanted spaceships they'd have to work out for themselves how to build them—and, above all, no sophisticated weaponry. Mind you, some of those skippers would have been quite capable of flogging a few hand lasers or the like to the natives but the Grand Governor of Barkara—the nation that, by its relatively early development of airships and firearms, had established *de facto* if not *de jure* sovereignty over the entire planet—made sure that nothing was imported that could be a threat to his rule. A situation rather analogous, perhaps, to that on Earth centuries ago when the Japanese Shoguns and their samurai took a dim view of the muskets and cannon that, in the wrong hands, would have meant their downfall.

Then the old Grand Governor died. His successor intimated that he would be willing to allow Darban to be drawn into the Federation of Worlds and to reap the benefits accruing therefrom. But whose Federation? Our Interstaller Federation? The Hallichek Hegemony? The Shaara Galactic Hive?

Our Intelligence people, just for once, started to earn their keep. According to them the Shaara had despatched a major warship to Darban, the captain of which had been given full authority to dicker with the Grand Governor. The Hallicheki had done likewise. And—not for the first time!—our lords and masters had been caught with their pants down. It was at the time of the Waverley Confrontation; and Lindisfarne Base, as a result, was right out of major warships. Even more fantastically the only spaceship available was my little *Adder*—and she was in the throes of a refit. Oh, there were ships at Scapa and Mikasa Bases but both of these were one helluva long way from Darban.

I was called before the Admiral and told that I must get off Lindisfarne as soon as possible, if not before, to make all possible speed for Darban, there to establish and maintain a Terran presence until such time as a senior officer could take over from me. I was to report on the actions of the Shaara and the Hallicheki. I was to avoid direct confrontation with either. And I was not, repeat not, to take any action at any time without direct authorisation from Base. I was told that a civilian linguistic expert would be travelling in *Adder*—a Miss Mary Marsden—and that she would be assisting me as required.

What rankled was the way in which the Admiral implied that he was being obliged to send a boy on a man's errand. And I wasn't at all happy about having Mary Marsden along. She was an attractive enough girl— what little one could see of her!—but she was a super wowser. She was a member of one of the more puritanical religious sects flourishing on Francisco—and Francisco, as you know, is a hotbed of freak religions. Mary took hers seriously. She had insisted on retaining her civilian status because she did not approve of the short-skirted uniforms in which the Survey Service clad its female personnel. She always wore long-skirted, long-sleeved, high-necked dresses and a bonnet over her auburn hair. She didn't smoke—not even tobacco—or drink anything stronger than milk.

And yet, as far as we could see, she was a very pretty girl. Eyes that were more green than any other colour. A pale—but not unhealthily so— skin. A straight nose that, a millimeter longer, would have been too big. A wide, full mouth that didn't need any artificial colouring. A firm, rather square chin. Good teeth—which she needed when it was the turn of Beadle, my first lieutenant, to do the cooking. Beadle had a passion for pies and his crusts always turned out like concrete. . . .

Well, we lifted off from Lindisfarne Base. We set trajectory for Darban. And before we were half-way there we suffered a complete communications black-out. Insofar as the Carlotti deep space radio was concerned I couldn't really blame Slovotny, my Sparks. The Base technicians, in their haste to get us off the premises, had botched the overhaul of the transceiver and, to make matters worse, hadn't replaced the spares they had used. When two circuit trays blew, that was that.

Spooky Deane, my psionic communications officer, I could and did blame for the shortcomings of *his* department. As you probably know, it's just not possible for even the most highly trained and talented telepath to transmit his thoughts across light years without an amplifier. The amplifier most commonly used is the brain of that highly telepathic animal, the Terran dog, removed from the skull of its hapless owner and kept alive in a tank of nutrient solution with all the necessary life-support systems. PCOs are lonely people; they're inclined to regard themselves as the only true humans in shiploads of sub-men. They make pets of their horrid amplifiers, to which they can talk telepathically. And—as lonely men do—they drink.

What happened aboard *Adder* was an all-too-frequent occurrence. The PCO would be going on a solitary bender and would get to the stage of wanting to share his bottle with his pet. When neat gin—or whatever—is poured into nutrient solution the results are invariably fatal to whatever it is that's being nourished.

So—no psionic amplifier. No Carlotti deep space radio. No contact with Base.

"And aren't you going to share your bottle with your pet, Commodore?"

"I didn't think that you were a pet of mine, Miss Kelly, or I of yours. But it's time we had a pause for refreshment."

We stood on for Darban (he continued). Frankly, I was pleased rather than otherwise at being entirely on my own, knowing that now I would have to use my own initiative, that I would not have the Lord Commissioners of the Admiralty peering over my shoulder all the time, expecting me to ask their permission before I so much as blew my nose. Beadle, my first lieutenant, did try to persuade me to return to Lindisfarne—he was a very capable officer but far too inclined to regard Survey Service Regulations as Holy Writ. (I did find later that, given the right inducement, he was capable of bending those same regulations.) Nonetheless, he was, in many ways, rather a pain in the arse.

But Beadle was in the minority. The other young gentlemen were behind me, all in favour of carrying on. Mary Marsden, flaunting her civilian status, remained neutral.

We passed the time swotting up on Darban, watching and listening to the tapes that had been put on board prior to our departure from Lindisfarne. We gained the impression of a very pleasant, almost Earth-type planet with flora and fauna not too outrageously different from what the likes of us are used to. Parallel evolution and all that. A humanoid—but not human—dominant race, furry bipeds that would have passed for cat-faced apes in a bad light. Civilized, with a level of technology roughly that of Earth during the late nineteenth century, old reckoning. Steam engines. Railways. Electricity, and the electric telegraph. Airships. Firearms. One nation—that with command of the air and a monopoly of telegraphic communications—*de facto* if not entirely *de jure* ruler of the entire planet.

The spaceport, such as it was, consisted of clearings in a big forest some kilometers south of Barkara, the capital city of Bandooran. Bandooran, of course, was the most highly developed nation, the one that imposed its will on all of Darban. Landing elsewhere was . . . discouraged. The Dog Star Line at one time tried to steal a march on the competition by instructing one of their captains to land near a city called Droobar, there to set up the Dog Star Line's own trading station. The news must have been telegraphed to Barkara almost immediately. A couple of dirigibles drifted over, laying H.E. and incendiary eggs on the city. The surviving city fathers begged the Dog Star line captain to take himself and his ship elsewhere. Also, according to our tapes, the Dog Star Line was heavily fined shortly thereafter by the High Council of the Interstellar Federation.

But the spaceport . . . just clearings, as I have said, in the forest. Local airships were used to pick up incoming cargo and to deliver the tanks of "living opals" to the spaceships. No Aerospace Control, of course, although there would be once a base and a Carlotti Beacon Station had been established. Incoming traffic just came in, unannounced. Unannounced officially, that is. As you know, the inertial drive is far from being the quietest machine ever devised by Man; everybody in Barkara and for kilometers around would know when a spaceship was dropping down.

And we dropped in, one fine, sunny morning. After one preliminary orbit we'd been able to identify Barkara without any difficulty. The forest was there, just where our charts said it should be. There were those odd, circular holes in the mass of greenery—the clearings. In two of them there was the glint of metal. As we lost altitude we were able to identify the Shaara vessel—it's odd (or is it?) how their ships always look like giant beehives—and a typical, Hallicheki oversized silver egg sitting in a sort of latticework eggcup.

We came in early; none of the Shaara or Hallicheki were yet out and about although the noise of our drive must have alerted them. I set *Adder* down as far as possible from the other two ships. From my control room I could just see the blunt bows of them above the treetops.

We went down to the wardroom for breakfast, leaving Slovotny to enjoy his meal in solitary state in the control room; he would let us know if anybody approached while we were eating. He buzzed down just as I'd reached the toast and marmalade stage. I went right up. But the local authorities hadn't yet condescended to take notice of us; the airship that came nosing over was a Shaara blimp, not a Darbanese rigid job. And then there was a flight of three Hallicheki, disdaining mechanical aids and using their own wings. One of the horrid things evacuated her bowels when she was almost overhead, making careful allowance for what little wind there was. It made a filthy splash all down one of my viewports.

At last the Darbanese came. Their ship was of the Zeppelin type, the fabric of the envelope stretched taut over a framework of wood or metal. It hovered over the clearing, its engines turning over just sufficiently to offset the effect of the breeze. That airship captain, I thought, knew his job. A cage detached itself from the gondola, was lowered rapidly to the ground. A figure jumped out of it just before it touched and the airship went up like a rocket after the loss of weight. I wondered what would happen if that cage fouled anything before it was rehoisted, but I needn't have worried. As I've said, the airship captain was an expert.

We went down to the after airlock. We passed through it, making the transition from our own atmosphere into something that, at first, felt like warm soup. But it was quite breathable. Mary Marsden, as the linguist of the party, accompanied me down the ramp. I wondered how she could bear to go around muffled up to the eyebrows on such a beautiful morning as this; I was finding even shorts and shirt uniform too heavy for a warm day.

The native looked at us. We looked at him. He was dressed in a dull green smock that came down to mid-thigh and that left his arms bare. A fine collection of glittering brass badges was pinned to the breast and shoulders of his garment. He saluted, raising his three-fingered hands to shoulder level, palms out. His wide mouth opened in what I hoped was a smile, displaying pointed, yellow teeth that were in sharp contrast to the black fur covering his face.

He asked, in quite passable Standard English, "You the captain are?"

I said that I was.

He said, "Greetings I bring from the High Governor." Then, making a statement rather than asking a question, "You do not come in."

So we—er a Federation warship of some kind—had been expected. And *Adder*, little as she was, did not look like a merchantman—too many guns for too small a tonnage.

He went on, "So you are envoy. Same as—" He waved a hand in the general direction of where the other ships were berthed. "—the Shaara, the Hallicheki. Then you will please to attend the meeting that this morning has been arranged." He pulled a big, fat watch on a chain from one of his pockets. "In—in forty-five of your minutes from now."

While the exchange was taking place Mary was glowering a little. She was the linguistic expert and it was beginning to look as though her services would not be required. She listened quietly while arrangements were being made. We would proceed to the city in my boat, with the Governor's messenger acting as pilot—pilot in the marine sense of the word, that is, just giving me the benefit of his local knowledge.

We all went back on board *Adder*. The messenger assured me that

there was no need for me to have internal pressure adjusted to his requirements, he had often been aboard outworld spaceships and, too, he was an
airshipman.

I decided that there was no time for me to change into dress uniform
so I compromised by pinning my miniatures—two good attendance
medals and the Distinguished Conduct Star that I'd got after the Battle of
Dartura—to the left breast of my shirt, buckling on my sword belt with
the wedding cake cutter in its gold-braided sheath. While I was tarting
myself up, Mary entertained the messenger to coffee and biscuits in the
wardroom (his English, she admitted to me later, was better than her Darbanese) and Beadle, with Dalgleish, the engineer, got the boat out of its
bay and down to the ground by the ramp.

Mary was coming with me to the city and so was Spooky Deane—a
trained telepath is often more useful than a linguist. We got into the boat.
It was obvious that our new friend was used to this means of transporta-
tion, must often have ridden in the auxiliary craft of visiting merchant
vessels. He sat beside me to give directions. Mary and Spooky were in the
back.

As we flew towards the city—red brick, grey-roofed houses on the outskirts, tall, cylindrical towers, also of red brick, in the centre—we saw the
Shaara and the Hallicheki ahead of us, flying in from their ships. A Queen-
Captain, I thought, using my binoculars, with a princess and an escort of
drones. A Hallichek Nest Leader accompanied by two old hens as scrawny
and ugly as herself. The Shaara weren't using their blimp and the Hallicheki consider it beneath their dignity to employ mechanical means of
flight inside an atmosphere. Which made us the wingless wonders.

I reduced speed a little to allow the opposition to make their landings
on the flat roof of one of the tallest towers first. After all, they were both
very senior to me, holding ranks equivalent to at least that of a four-ring
captain in the Survey Service, and I was a mere lieutenant, my command
notwithstanding. I came in slowly over the streets of the city. There were
people abroad—pedestrians mainly, although there were vehicles drawn
by scaly, huge-footed draught animals and the occasional steam car—and
they raised their black furred faces to stare at us. One or two of them
waved.

When we got to the roof of the tower the Shaara and the Hallicheki
had gone down but there were a half-dozen blue-smocked guards to
receive us. They saluted as we disembarked. One of them led the way to a
sort of penthouse which, as a matter of fact, merely provided cover for
the stairhead. The stairs themselves were . . . wrong. They'd been
designed, of course, to suit the length and jointure of the average Dar-

banese leg, which wasn't anything like ours. Luckily the Council Chamber was only two flights down.

It was a big room, oblong save for the curvature of the two end walls, in which were high windows. There was a huge, long table, at one end of which was a sort of ornate throne in which sat the High Governor. He was of far slighter stature than the majority of his compatriots but made up for it by the richness of his attire. His smock was of a crimson, velvetlike material and festooned with gold chains of office.

He remained seated but inclined his head in our direction. He said— I learned afterwards that these were the only words of English that he knew; he must have picked them up from some visiting space captain— "Come in. This is Liberty Hall; you can spit on the mat and call the cat a bastard!"

I was wondering," said Kitty Kelly coldly, "just when you were going to get around to saying that."

"He said it, not me. But I have to use that greeting once in every story. It's one of my conditions of employment."

And where was I (he went on) before I was interrupted? Oh, yes. The Council Chamber, with the High Governor all dressed up like a Christmas tree. Various ministers and other notables, not as richly attired as their boss. All male, I found out later, with the exception of the Governor's lady, who was sitting on her husband's right. There were secondary sexual characteristics, of course, but so slight as to be unrecognisable by an outworlder. To me she—and I didn't know that she was "she"—was just another Darbanese.

But the fair sex was well represented. There was the Queen-Captain, her iridescent wings folded on her back, the velvety brown fur of her thorax almost concealed by the sparkling jewels that were her badges of high rank. There was the Shaara princess, less decorated but more elegant than her mistress. There was the Nest Leader, she was nowhere nearly as splendid as the Queen-Captain. She wasn't splendid at all. Her plumage was dun and dusty, the talons of the "hands" at the elbow joints of her wings unpolished. She wore no glittering insignia, only a wide band of cheap-looking yellow plastic about her scrawny neck. Yet she had her dignity, and her cruel beak was that of a bird of prey rather than that of the barnyard fowl she otherwise resembled. She was attended by two hen officers, equally drab.

And, of course, there was Mary, almost as drab as the Hallicheki.

The Governor launched into his spiel, speaking through an interpreter. I was pleased to discover that Standard English was to be the language used. It made sense, of course. English is the common language of Space just as it used to be the common language of the sea, back on Earth. And as the majority of the merchant vessels landing on Darban had been of Terran registry, the local merchants and officials had learned English.

The Governor, through his mouthpiece, said that he welcomed us all. He said that he was pleased that Imperial Earth had sent her representative, albeit belatedly, to this meeting of cultures. Blah, blah, blah. He agreed with the representatives of the Great Spacefaring Powers that it was desirable for some sort of permanent base to be established on Darban. But . . . but whichever of us was given the privilege of taking up residence on his fair planet would have to prove capability to conform, to mix. . . . (By this time the interpreter was having trouble in getting the idea across but he managed somehow.) The Darbanese, the Governor told us, were a sporting people and in Barkara there was one sport preferred to all others. This was racing. It would be in keeping with Darbanese tradition if the Treaty were made with whichever of us proved the most expert in a competition of this nature. . . .

"*Racing?*" I whispered. In a foot race we'd probably be able to beat the Shaara and the Hallicheki, but I didn't think that it was foot racing that was implied. Horse racing or its local equivalent? That didn't seem right either.

"Balloon racing," muttered Spooky Deane, who had been flapping his psionic ears.

I just didn't see how balloon racing could be a spectator sport—but the tapes on Darban with which we had been supplied were far from comprehensive. As we soon found out.

"Balloon racing?" asked Kitty Kelly. "From the spectators' viewpoint it must have been like watching grass grow."

"This balloon racing certainly wasn't," Grimes told her.

The Darbanese racing balloons (he went on) were ingenious aircraft: dirigible, gravity-powered. Something very like them was, as a matter of fact, invented by a man called Adams back on Earth in the nineteenth century. Although it performed successfully, the Adams airship never got off the ground, commercially speaking. But it did work. The idea was that the thing would progress by soaring and swooping, soaring and swooping. The envelope containing the gas cells was a planing surface and the altitude of the contraption was controlled by the shifting of weights in the car—ballast, the bodies of the crew. Initially, positive buoyancy was obtained by the dumping of ballast and the thing would plane upwards. Then, when gas was valved, there would be negative buoyancy and a glide downwards. Sooner or later, of course, you'd be out of gas to valve or ballast to dump. That would be the end of the penny section.

I remembered about the Adams airship while the interpreter did his best to explain balloon racing to us. I thought that it was a beautiful case of parallel mechanical evolution on two worlds many light years apart.

The Queen-Captain got the drift of it quite soon—after all, the Shaara *know* airships. Her agreement, even though it was made through her artificial voice box, sounded more enthusiastic than otherwise. The Nest Leader took her time making up her mind but finally squawked yes. I would have been outvoted if I hadn't wanted to take part in the contest.

There was a party then, complete with drinks and sweet and savoury things to nibble. The Shaara made pigs of themselves on a sticky liqueur and candy. Spooky Deane got stuck into something rather like gin. I found a sort of beer that wasn't too bad—although it was served unchilled—with little, spicy sausages as blotting paper. Mary, although she seemed to enjoy the sweetmeats, would drink only water. Obviously our hosts thought that she was odd, almost as odd as the Hallicheki who, although drinking water, would eat nothing.

They're *nasty* people, those avians. They have no redeeming vices— and when it comes to *real* vices their main one is cruelty. *Their* idea of a banquet is a shrieking squabble over a table loaded with little mammals, alive but not kicking—they're hamstrung before the feast so that they can't fight or run away—which they tear to pieces with those beaks of theirs.

After quite a while the party broke up. The Nest Leader and her offi-cers were the first to leave, anxious no doubt to fly back to their ship for a tasty dish of live worms. The Queen-Captain and her party were the next to go. They were in rather a bad way. They were still on the rooftop when Mary and I, supporting him between us, managed to get Spooky Deane up the stairs and to the boat. None of the locals offered to help us; it is considered bad manners on Darban to draw the attention of a guest to his insobriety.

We said our goodbyes to those officials, including the interpreter, who had come to see us off. We clambered into our boat and lifted. On our way back to *Adder* we saw the Shaara blimp coming to pick up the Queen-Captain. I wasn't surprised. If she'd tried to take off from the roof in the state that she was in she'd have made a nasty splash on the cobble-stones under the tower.

And I wasn't at all sorry to get back to the ship to have a good snore.

Spooky was fast asleep by the time that I landed by the after airlock and Mary was looking at both of us with great distaste.

"I'm not a wowser," said Kitty Kelly.
"Help yourself, then. And freshen my glass while you're about it."

Bright and early the next morning (he went on, after a refreshing sip) two racing balloons and an instructor were delivered by a small rigid airship. Our trainer was a young native called Robiliyi. He spoke very good English; as a matter of fact he was a student at the University of Barkara and studying for a degree in Outworld Languages. He was also a famous amateur balloon jockey and had won several prizes. Under his supervision we assembled one of the balloons, inflating it from the cylinders of hydrogen that had been brought from the city. Imagine a huge air mattress with a flimsy, wickerwork car slung under it. That's what the thing looked like. The only control surface was a huge rudder at the after end of the car. There were two tillers—one forward and one aft.

Dalgleish inspected the aircraft, which was moored by lines secured to metal pegs driven into the ground. He said, "I'm not happy about all this valving of gas. You know how the Shaara control buoyancy in their blimps?"

I said that I did.

He said that it should be possible to modify one of the balloons—the one that we should use for the race itself—so as to obviate the necessity of valving gas for the downward glide. I prodded the envelope with a cautious finger and said that I didn't think that the fabric of the gas cells would stand the strain of being compressed in a net. He said that he didn't think so either. *So that was that*, I thought. *Too bad.* Then he went on to tell me that in the ship's stores was a bolt of plastic cloth that, a long time ago, had been part of an urgent shipment of supplies to the Survey Service base on Zephyria, a world notorious for its violent windstorms. (Whoever named that planet had a warped sense of humour!) The material was intended for making emergency repairs to the domes housing the base facilities. They were always being punctured by wind-borne boulders and the like. When *Adder* got to Zephyria it was found that somebody had experienced a long overdue rush of brains to the head and put everything underground. There had been the usual lack of liaison between departments and nobody had been told not to load the plastic.

Anyhow, Dalgleish thought that he'd be able to make gas cells from the stuff. He added that the Shaara would almost certainly be modifying their own racer, using the extremely tough silk from which the gas cells of their blimps were made.

I asked Robiliyi's opinion. He told me that it would be quite in order to use machinery as long as it was hand-powered.

Dalgleish went into a huddle with him. They decided that only the three central, sausage-like gas cells need be compressed to produce negative buoyancy; also that it would be advisable to replace the wickerwork frame enclosing the "mattress" with one of light but rigid metal. Too, it would be necessary to put a sheet of the plastic over the assembly of gas cells so as to maintain a planing surface in all conditions.

Then it was time for my first lesson. Leaving Dalgleish and the others to putter around with the still unassembled balloon I followed Robiliyi into the flimsy car of the one that was ready for use. The wickerwork creaked under my weight. I sat down, very carefully, amidships, and tried to keep out of the way. Robiliyi started scooping sand out of one of the ballast bags, dropping it overside. The bottom of the car lifted off the mossy ground but the balloon was still held down by the mooring lines, two forward and two aft. Robiliyi scampered, catlike, from one end of the car to the other, pulling the metal pegs clear of the soil with expert jerks. We lifted, rising vertically. I looked down at the faces of my shipmates. *Better him than us,* their expressions seemed to be saying.

Then we were at treetop height, then above the trees, still lifting. Robiliyi scrambled to the rear of the craft, calling me to follow. He grabbed the after tiller. The platform tilted and above us the raft of gas cells did likewise, presenting an inclined plane to the air. We were sliding through the atmosphere at a steep angle. I wasn't sure whether or not I was enjoying the experience. I'd always liked ballooning, back on Earth, but the gondolas of the hot air balloons in which I'd flown were far safer than this flimsy basket. There was nothing resembling an altimeter in the car; there were no instruments at all. I hoped that somewhere in the nested gas cells there was a relief valve that would function if we got too high. And how high was too high, anyhow? I noticed that the underskin of the balloon, which had been wrinkled when we lifted off, was now taut.

Robiliyi shouted shrilly, "Front end! Front end!" We scuttled forward. He pulled on a dangling lanyard; there was an audible hiss of escaping gas from above. He put the front-end tiller over and as we swooped downward we turned. The treetops, which had seemed far too distant, were now dangerously close. And there was the clearing from which we had lifted with *Adder* standing there, bright silver in the sunlight. But we weren't landing yet. We shifted weight aft, jettisoned ballast, soared. I was beginning to get the hang of it, starting to enjoy myself. Robiliyi let me take the tiller so that I could get the feel of the airship. She handled surprisingly well.

We did not return to earth until we had dumped all our ballast. I asked

Robiliyi what we could do if, for some reason, we wanted to get upstairs again in a hurry after valving gas. He grinned, stripped off his tunic, made as though to throw it overboard. He grinned again, showing all his sharp, yellow teeth. "And if *that* is not enough," he said, "there is always your crew person. . . ."

We landed shortly after this. Robiliyi reinflated the depleted cells from one of the bottles while Beadle and Spooky collected ballast sand from the banks of a nearby brook.

Then it was Mary's turn to start her training.

"Mary? Was she your crew, your co-pilot, for the race?"
"Yes."
"But you've impressed me as being a male chauvinist pig."
"Have I? Well, frankly, I'd sooner have had one of my officers. But Mary volunteered, and she was far better qualified than any of them. Apart from myself she was the only one in Adder with lighter-than-air experience. It seems that the sect of which she was a member went in for ballooning quite a lot. It tied in somehow with their religion. Nearer my God to Thee, and all that."

Well (he went on), we trained, both in the balloon that Dalgleish had modified and in the one that was still as it had been when delivered to us. The modifications? Oh, quite simple. A coffee-mill hand winch, an arrangement of webbing that compressed the three central, longitudinal gas cells. The modified balloon we exercised secretly, flying it only over a circuit that was similar in many ways to the official, triangular race track. The unmodified balloon we flew over the actual course. The Shaara and the Hallicheki did likewise, in craft that did not appear to have had anything done to them. I strongly suspected that they were doing the same as we were, keeping their dark horses out of sight until the Big Day. The Shaara, I was certain, had done to theirs what we had done to ours—after all, it was a Shaara idea that we had borrowed. But the Hallicheki? We just couldn't guess.

And we trained, and we trained. At first it was Robiliyi with Mary or Robiliyi with myself. Then it was Mary and I. I'll say this for her—she made good balloon crew. And I kidded myself that she was becoming far less untouchable. In that narrow car we just couldn't help coming into physical contact quite frequently.

Then the time was upon us and we were as ready as ever we would be. On the eve of the Great Day the three contending balloons were taken to the airport. The Shaara towed theirs in behind one of their blimps; it was entirely concealed in a sort of gauzy cocoon. The Hallicheki towed theirs in, four hefty crew hens doing the work. There was no attempt at concealment. We towed ours in astern of our flier. It was completely swathed in a sheet of light plastic.

The racers were maneuvered into a big hangar to be inspected by the judges. I heard later, from Robiliyi, that the Nest Leader had insinuated that the Shaara and ourselves had installed miniature inertial drive units disguised as hand winches. (It was the sort of thing that *they* would have done if they'd thought that they could get away with it.)

We all returned to our ships. I don't know how the Shaara and the Hallicheki spent the night but we dined and turned in early. I took a stiff nightcap to help me to sleep. Mary had her usual warm milk.

The next morning we returned in the flier to the airport. It was already a warm day. I was wearing a shirt-and-shorts uniform but intended to discard cap, long socks, and shoes before clambering into the wickerwork car of the balloon. Mary was suitably—according to her odd lights—dressed but what she had on was very little more revealing than her usual high-necked, longsleeved, long-skirted dress; it did little more than establish the fact that she was, after all, a biped. It was a hooded, long-sleeved cover-all suit with its legs terminating in soft shoes. It was so padded that it was quite impossible to do more than guess at the shape of the body under it.

Young Robiliyi was waiting for us at the airport, standing guard over our green and gold racer. Close by was the Shaara entry, its envelope displaying orange polka dots on a blue ground. The Shaara crew stood by their balloon—the pilot, a bejewelled drone, and his crew, a husky worker. Then there were the Hallicheki—officers both, to judge from the yellow plastic bands about their scrawny necks. The envelope of their racer was a dull brown.

On a stand, some distance from the starting line, sat the Governor with his entourage. With him were the Queen-Captain and the Nest Leader with their senior officers. The judges were already aboard the small, rigid airship which, at its mooring mast, was ready to cast off as soon as the race started. It would fly over the course with us, its people alert for any infraction of the rules.

Two of the airport ground crew wheeled out a carriage on which was mounted a highly polished little brass cannon. The starting gun. I kicked off my shoes, peeled off my socks, left them, with my cap, in Robiliyi's charge. I climbed into the flimsy car, took my place at the after tiller. Mary followed me, stationed herself at the winch amidships. She released the brake. The gas cells rustled as they expanded; we were held down now only by the taut mooring lines fore and aft. I looked over at the others. The Shaara, too, were ready. The Hallicheki had just finished the initial dumping of sand ballast.

One of the gunners jerked a long lanyard. There was a bang and a great flash of orange flame, a cloud of dirty white smoke. I yanked the two after mooring lines, pulling free the iron pegs. Forward Mary did the same, a fraction of a second later. It wasn't a good start. The forward moorings should have been released first to get our leading edge starting to lift. Mary scrambled aft, redistributing weight, but the Shaara and the Hallicheki, planing upwards with slowly increasing speed, were already ahead.

Almost directly beneath us was Airport Road and in the middle distance was the railway to Brinn with the Brinn Highway running parallel to it. I can remember how the track was gleaming like silver in the morning sunlight. To the north, distant but already below the expanding horizon, was the Cardan Knoll, a remarkable dome-shaped hill with lesser domes grouped about it. We would have to pass to the west and north of this before steering a south-easterly course for the Porgidor Tower.

Shaara and Hallicheki were racing neck and neck, still climbing. I was still falling behind. I brought the dangling mooring lines inboard to reduce drag. It may have made a little difference, but not much. Ahead of us the Shaara balloon reached its ceiling, compressed gas and began the first downward glide. A second or so later the Hallicheki reduced buoyancy to follow suit. I looked up. The underskin of my gas cells was still slightly wrinkled; there was still climbing to do.

The last wrinkles vanished. I told Mary to compress. The pawls clicked loudly as she turned the winch handle. Then we scuttled to the front end of the car. I took hold of the forward tiller. We swooped down, gathering speed rapidly. The farm buildings and the grazing animals in the fields were less and less toylike as we lost altitude. I steered straight for an ungainly beast that looked like an armour-plated cow. It lifted its head to stare at us in stupid amazement.

I didn't want to hit the thing. I sort of half ran, half crawled aft as Mary released the winch brake. We lifted sweetly—no doubt to the great relief of the bewildered herbivore. I looked ahead. The opposition were well into their second upward beat, the Hallicheki soaring more steeply than the Shaara. But taking advantage of thermals is an art that every bird learns as soon as it is able to fly; there must be, I thought, a considerable updraught of warm air from the railroad and the black-surfaced Brinn Highway. But the higher the Hallicheki went the more gas they would have to valve, and if they were not careful they would lose all their reserve buoyancy before the circuit was completed.

The Shaara reached their ceiling and started their downward glide. The Hallicheki were still lifting, gaining altitude but losing ground. I couldn't understand why they were not gliding down their lift. And I was still lifting. Then I saw that, ahead, the Hallicheki had at last valved gas and were dropping. I pulled to starboard to avoid them. It meant putting on some distance but I daren't risk a mid-air collision. The Hallicheki had wings of their own and could bail out in safety. Mary and I hadn't and couldn't.

But there was no danger of our becoming entangled with the Hallicheki. They had put on considerable speed during their dive and were swooping down on the Shaara balloon like a hawk on its prey. They were directly above it—and then, although they were still well clear of the ground, were rising again. A failure of nerve? It didn't fit in with what I knew of their psychology. But ballast must have been dumped and it would mean an additional soar and swoop for them before rounding the Cardan Knoll.

And I was gaining on them.

But where were the Shaara?

Mary seemed to have read my thought. She said, "They're in trouble."

I looked down to where she was pointing. Yes, they were in trouble all right. They had lost considerable altitude and the car of their balloon was entangled with the topmost branches of a tall tree. The drone and the worker were tugging ineffectually with all their limbs, buzzing about it. But they would never get it clear. They'd lost all their lift. The sausage-like gas cells were limp, more than half deflated.

But that was their worry. We flew on. Ahead, the Knoll was getting closer. I pulled over to port to pass to the west'ard of the brush-covered domes. The Hallicheki were already rounding the Knoll, lost briefly to sight as they passed to north of it. Then I was coming round to starboard in a tight, rising turn. I didn't realise until it was almost too late that the slight, northerly breeze was setting me down onto the hill; I had to put the tiller hard over to try to claw to wind'ard. The deck of our car just brushed the branches of a tree and there was a clattering, screeching explosion of small, flying reptiles from the foliage. Luckily they were more scared of us than we were of them.

Ahead, now, was the railway to Garardan and the Garardan Road. Beyond road and railway was the Blord River and, far to the south-east, I could see the crumbling stonework of the Porgidor Tower. Over road and railway, I reasoned, there would be thermals but over the river, which ran ice-cold from the high hills, there would be a downdraught. . . . Yes, there were thermals all right. The Hallicheki were taking full advantage of them, going up like a balloon. Literally. What were they playing at? Why weren't they gliding down the lift? And they were keeping well to starboard, to the south'ard of the track, putting on distance as they would have to come to port to pass to north and east of the tower.

I looked astern. The judges' airship was following, watching. If the Hallicheki tried to cut off a corner they'd be disqualified.

I kept the Porgidor Tower fine on my starboard bow; whatever the Hallicheki were playing at, *I* would run the minimum distance. And then, as I was lifting on the thermals over the railway, I saw that there was some method in the opposition's madness. There were more thermals over the power station on the west bank of the river and I had missed out on them.

Swoop and soar, swoop and soar. Compress, decompress. Our muscles were aching with the stooped scrambles forward and aft in the cramped confines of the car. It must have been even worse for Mary than for me because of the absurdly bulky and heavy clothing that she was wearing. But we were holding our own, more than holding our own. That thermal-hunting had cost the Hallicheki their lead.

Then there was the Porgidor Tower close on our starboard hand, with quite a crowd of spectators waving from the battered battlements. And we were on the last leg of the course, over boulder-strewn bushland, with the twin ribbons of the Saarkaar Road and Railway ahead and beyond them the river again, and beyond that the mooring masts and hangars of the airport.

Swoop and soar, swoop and soar. . . .

I swooped into the thermals rising from the road and the railway so that I could manage a steep, fast glide with no loss of altitude. I began to feel smugly self-congratulatory.

But where were the Hallicheki?

Not ahead any longer. All that they had gained by their use of thermals was altitude. They were neither ahead nor to either side, and certainly not below, where the only artifact visible was a little sidewheel paddle steamer chugging fussily up river.

Then there was the anticipated downdraught that I countered with decompression.

Suddenly there was a sharp pattering noise from directly above and I saw a shower of glittering particles driving down on each side of the car. Rain? Hail? But neither fall from a clear sky.

Mary was quicker on the uptake than I was "The Hallicheki," she shouted. "They dumped their ballast on us!"

Not only had they dumped ballast on us, they'd holed the gas cells. Some of the viciously pointed steel darts had gone through every surface, dropping to the deck of the car. If we'd been in the way of them they'd have gone through us too. Razor-sharp, tungsten tipped (as I discovered later). So this was what had happened to the Shaara racer. . . .

"Ballast!" I yelled. "Dump ballast!"

But we didn't have any to dump. I thought briefly of the mooring lines with their metal pegs but the ropes were spliced to the pins and to the structure of the car. And I didn't have a knife. (All right, all right, I should have had one but I'd forgotten it.) Then I remembered my first flight with Robiliyi and what he had told me when I'd asked him what to do when there was no ballast left to dump. I stripped off my shirt, dropped it over the side. It didn't seem to make much difference. I sacrificed my shorts. I looked up. All the cells were punctured and three of them looked as though they were empty. But the planing surface above them must still be reasonably intact. I hoped. If only I could gain enough altitude I could glide home. Forgetting the company that I was in I took off my briefs, sent the scrap of fabric after the other garments.

I heard Mary make a noise half way between a scream and a gasp.

I looked at her. She looked at me. Her face was one huge blush. I felt my own ears burning in sympathy.

I said, "We're still dropping. We have to get upstairs. Fast."

She asked, "You mean . . . ?"

I said, "Yes."

She asked, her voice little more than a whisper, "Must I?"

I said that she must.

But you could have knocked me over with a feather when her hand went to the throat of her coveralls, when her finger ran down the sealseam. She stepped out of the garment, kicked it overside. Her underwear was thick and revealed little; nonetheless I could see that that fantastic blush of hers suffused the skin of her neck and shoulders, even the narrow strip of belly that was visible. *That will do,* I was going to say, but she gave me no time to say it. Her expression had me baffled. Her halter came off and was jettisoned, then her remaining garment.

I'll be frank. She wouldn't have attracted a second glance on a nudist beach; her figure was good but not outstanding. But this was not a nudist beach. A naked woman in an incongruous situation is so much more naked than she would be in the right surroundings.

She looked at me steadily, defiantly. Her blush had faded. Her skin was smoothly creamy rather than white. I felt myself becoming interested.

She asked, "Do you like it?" I thought at first that she meant the strip show that she had put on for me. She went on, "*I* do! I've often thought about it but I had no idea what it would really be like! The feel of the sun and the air on my skin . . ."

I wanted to go on looking at her. I wanted to do more than that—but there's a time and a place for everything and this was neither. It could have been quite a good place in other circumstances but not with a race to be flown to a finish.

I tore my eyes away from her naked body—I heard a ripping noise, but it was only one of the rents in the envelope enlarging itself—and looked around and up and down to see what was happening. Mary's supreme sacrifice was bringing results. We were lifting—sluggishly, but lifting. And so, just ahead of us, were the Hallicheki. The gas cells of their balloon were flabby and wrinkled; they must have squandered buoyancy recklessly in their attacks on the Shaara and ourselves. And then I saw one of the great, ugly brutes clambering out of the car. They were abandoning ship, I thought. They were dropping out of the race. Then I realised what they were doing. The one who had gone outboard was gripping the forward rail of the car with her feet, was beating her wings powerfully, towing the balloon. Legal or illegal? I didn't know. That would be for the judges to decide, just as they would have to make a decision on the use of potentially lethal ballast. But as no machinery was being used, the Hallicheki might be declared the winners of the race.

What else did we have to dump? We would have to gain altitude, and fast, for the last swoop in. The hand winch? It was of no further use to us. It was held down to the deck of the car only by wing nuts and they loosened fairly easily. We unscrewed them, threw them out. We were rising a little faster. Then there were the shackles securing the downhaul to the compression webbing. Overboard they went. The winch itself I decided to keep as a last reserve of disposable ballast.

High enough?

I thought so.

I valved gas—for the first and only time during our flight—and Mary and I shifted our weight forward. We swooped, overtaking the crawling, under tow, Hallicheki balloon. We were making headway all right but losing too much altitude. The winch would have to go.

It was insinuated that my jettisoning it when we were directly above the Hallicheki was an act of spite. I said in my report that it was accidental, that the Hallicheki just happened to be in the wrong place at the wrong time. Or the right time. I'll not deny that we cheered when we saw the hunk of machinery hit that great, flabby mattress almost dead centre. It tore through it, rupturing at least four of the gas cells. The envelope crumpled, fell in about itself. The two hen officers struggled to keep the crippled racer in the air, ripping the balloon fabric to shreds with their clawed feet as their wings flapped frenziedly. Meanwhile *we* were going up like a rocket.

The Hallicheki gave up the attempt to keep their craft airborne. They let it flutter earthwards, trailing streamers of ragged cloth. They started to come after us, climbing powerfully. I could sense somehow that they were in a vile temper. I imagined those sharp claws and beaks ripping into the fabric of our balloon and didn't feel at all happy. *We* didn't have wings of our own. We didn't even have parachutes.

It was time for the final swoop—if only those blasted birds let us make it. There was no need to valve any more gas; the rents in the fabric of the gas cells had enlarged themselves. We shifted our weight forward. Astern and overhead I heard the throbbing of engines; it was the judges airship escorting us to the finish line. The Hallicheki wouldn't dare to try anything now. I hoped. My hope was realized. They squawked loudly and viciously, sheered off.

Overhead, as I've said, there was the throbbing of airship engines—and, fainter, the irregular beat of an inertial drive unit. *Adder*'s atmosphere flier, I thought at first, standing by in case of accidents. But it didn't sound quite right, somehow. Too deep a note. But I'd too much on my plate to be able to devote any thought to matters of no immediate importance.

We swept into the airport, steering for the red flag on the apron that marked the finish. We were more of a hang glider now than a balloon but I *knew* somehow that we'd make it. The underside of the car brushed the branches of a tree—to have made a detour would have been out of the question—and a large section of decking was torn away. That gave us just the little extra buoyancy that we needed. We cleared the spiky hedge that marked the airport boundary. We actually hit the flagpole before we hit the ground, knocking it over. Before the tattered, deflated envelope collapsed over us completely we heard the cries of applause, the thunder of flat hands on thighs.

It was quite a job getting out from under that smothering fabric. During the struggle we came into contact, very close contact. At least once I almost . . . Well, I didn't. I'm not boasting about it, my alleged self-control, I mean. There comes a time in life when you feel more remorse for the uncommitted sins—if sins they are—than for the committed ones.

At last we crawled out of the wreckage. The first thing we noticed was that the applause had ceased. My first thought was that the natives were shocked by our nudity and then, as I looked around, saw that they were all staring upwards. The clangour of the strange inertial drive was sounding louder and louder.

We looked up too. There was a pinnace—a big pinnace, such as are carried by major warships—coming down. It displayed Survey Service markings. I could read the name, in large letters, ARIES II. *Aries'* number-two pinnace . . . *Aries*—a Constellation Class cruiser—I knew quite well. I'd once served in her as a junior watch-keeper. She must still be in orbit, I thought. This would be the preliminary landing party.

The pinnace grounded not far from where Mary and I were standing. Or where *I* was standing; Mary was on her hands and knees desperately trying to tear off a strip of fabric from the ruined envelope to cover herself. The outer airlock door opened. A group of officers in full dress blues disembarked. Captain Daintree was in the lead. I knew him. He was a strict disciplinarian, a martinet. He was one of the reasons why I had not been sorry to leave *Aries*.

He glared at us. He recognised me in spite of my non-regulation attire. He stood there, stiff as a ramrod, his right hand on the pommel of his dress sword. I still think that he'd have loved to use that weapon on me. His face registered shock, disbelief, horror, you name it.

He spoke at last, his voice low but carrying easily over the distance between us.

"Mr. Grimes, correct me if I am wrong, but your instructions, I believe, were merely to maintain a Terran presence on this planet until such time as an officer of higher rank could take over."

I admitted that this was so.

"You were not, I am certain, authorised to start a nudist club. Or is this, perhaps, some sort of love-in?"

"But, sir," I blurted, "I won the race!" Even he could not take that triumph from me. "I won the race!"

"And did you win the prize, Commodore?" asked Kitty Kelly.

"Oh, yes. A very nice trophy. A model, in solid gold, of a racing balloon, suitably inscribed. I have it still, at home in Port Forlorn."

"Not that prize. It's the body beautiful I mean. The inhibition-and-clothing-shedding Miss Marsden."

"Yes," said Grimes. "She shed her inhibitions all right. But I muffed it. I should have struck while the iron was hot, before she had time to decide that it was really Beadle—of all people!—whom she fancied. He reaped what I'd sown—all the way back to Lindisfarne Base!

"When you get to my age you'll realise that there's no justice in the Universe."

"Isn't there?" she asked, rather too sweetly.

GRIMES AMONG THE GOURMETS

Commodore Grimes, although he hated to admit it even to himself, was coming to look forward to the visits paid by Kitty Kelly to his ship. *Faraway Quest* was immobilised at Port Fortinbras, on Elsinore, and would remain so until such time as her engineers were able to effect repairs to the old vessel's inertial drive. Originally an Epsilon Class star tramp, built for the Interstellar Transport Commission, she had been obsolescent when she entered the service of the Rim Worlds Confederacy. Her main propulsive machinery was hopelessly out of date and engineroom spares were not easily procurable. New eccentrics—but conforming to a long outmoded design—were being fabricated in Rim Runners' workshops in Port Forlorn, on Lorn. Nobody was busting a gut on the job. Meanwhile the venerable *Quest*, her future employment a matter of no great urgency, stayed put.

Shortly after the Rim Worlds survey ship's arrival at Port Fortinbras, Grimes had been interviewed by Kitty Kelly of Station Yorick. He had been inveigled into spinning her a yarn about one of his adventures during his younger days in the Federation Survey Service, which she had recorded. It had been broadcast on her Kitty's Korner trivi programme and Station Yorick's viewers had lapped it up. She had been told to wheedle more tall stories out of the crusty old spacedog. Grimes had not been at all displeased to learn that most of his crew now watched, and enjoyed, Kitty's Korner.

This day she had told him that she would, if it suited his convenience, be calling aboard at a later time than usual. He suggested that she take dinner with him before the recording session. She was pleased to accept the invitation.

Grimes's paymaster—who was also the ship's catering officer—was Miss Keiko Otoguro. Learning that the commodore would be dining with his guest in his day cabin she asked him if she could serve one of the traditional meals of her ancestral people. She told him that she had been for a ramble along the seashore and had collected various seaweeds that would be suitable for the menu that she had in mind. Grimes assented happily. He had always loved exotic foods. And, he thought and hoped, a sumptuous repast laid on especially for the beautiful, blue-eyed, black-haired Kitty Kelly might soften her attitude towards him. (He had already tried the "candy is dandy but liquor is quicker" approach but it hadn't worked.)

So Kitty Kelly was sitting in an easy chair in the commodore's day cabin, displaying her excellent legs. Grimes, seated facing her, was admiring the scenery. Both were sipping large pink gins.

She said, "I enjoy a meal aboard a ship now and again, even though autochefs tend to make everything taste the same."

"Not necessarily," he told her. "A lot depends upon how much imagination is employed in the programming and upon what spices are available. But the dinner that we shall be enjoying is not from the autochef. My paymaster prepared it with her own fair hands . . ."

There was a light tap at the door. Miss Otoguro entered the cabin, carrying a lacquered tray with bottles, glasses and tiny porcelain cups. She was followed by two stewardesses with larger trays upon which the food had been set out. There was just enough room on the big coffee table for the meal and the drinks.

She uncapped a bottle of cold beer, poured into two glasses. Then, from a gracefully shaped porcelein bottle, she filled two of the little cups.

She said formally, "Dinner is served, Commodore-san."

He replied with equal formality, "Thank you, Paymaster-san," then added, "there's no need for you to play Mama-san, Keiko. We can help ourselves."

She smiled but there was a hint of disappointment in her voice as she said, "As you please, Commodore."

When she and the girls had left Grimes said, "She has very old-fashioned ideas about the proper place of women in the universe. But she's not a Rimworlder by birth. She was brought up on Mikasa . . ."

Kitty was looking at the meal laid out on her tray.

"But this is beautiful . . ." she whispered. "Like flowers . . . It looks too good, almost, to eat . . ."

"Keiko's specialty," he told her. "Only for very honoured guests."

He raised his saki cup in a silent toast. She raised hers, sipped. She made a grimace.

"But this is *warm* . . ."

"That's the way it should be served."

"Oh. I think I'll stick to beer. And didn't your Miss Keiko forget knives and forks?"

Grimes picked up his ivory chopsticks, used them to mix mustard with the soy sauce in a little bowl. He then picked up what looked like a pink and white and green blossom with the implements, dipped it in the sauce, brought it to his mouth. He chewed and swallowed appreciatively.

She watched him, tried to follow suit. She did not manage too badly. Then her lips twisted in revulsion. She swallowed with an effort.

"*Raw* fish!" she exclaimed.

"Of course. With boiled rice, and seaweed . . ."

"I'm sorry," she said, "but I can't eat this. It looks pretty but it tastes like what it really is."

"But it's *sushi* . . ."

"I don't give a damn what it's called."

It was just as well that materials for making snacks were to hand in Grimes's refrigerator. With any luck at all Miss Otoguro would never know that the feast which she had so lovingly prepared had been devoured by only one person. (And even if she ever did find out all that would really matter to her was that the commodore had enjoyed it.)

The stewardesses had cleared away the debris of the meal and Kitty Kelly set up her recorder, one lens trained on Grimes, the other upon herself.

"Carry on drinking saki," she ordered. "That bottle and the tiny cup will look interesting . . . Now—and I promise you that this isn't for broadcasting unless you agree—isn't it true that your nickname when you were in the Federation Survey Service was Gutsy Grimes?"

His prominent ears flushed. "Yes, it is true. I admit that I've always liked my tucker. But I'm a gourmet rather than a gourmand. The meal that we've just enjoyed is proof of that."

"That *you've* just enjoyed, you mean."

"All right. I enjoyed it."

"Do you always enjoy exotic foods?"

"Almost always."

"Can you recall any occasion in your long career upon which exotic foods played a big part, Commodore?"

Grimes grinned. He put down his saki cup, picked up his pipe, slowly filled and lit it. He said, through the acrid, wreathing cloud, "As a matter of fact I can . . ."

It was (he said) when I was captain of the Survey Service's census ship *Seeker*. I'd been given a sort of roving commission, checking up on human colonies in the Argo sector. Also I'd been told to show the flag on one or two inhabited planets with whose people, even though they weren't human, strictly speaking, the Federation wanted to keep on friendly terms. Spheres of influence and all that. Even though the Interstellar Federation was—and still is—the Big Boy, other, smaller spacefaring powers wanted to be Big Boys too. The Duchy of Waldegren, for example. The Empire of Waverley . . ."

"And now," she interrupted him, "the Rim Worlds Confederacy."
"We," he said stiffly, "have no Imperial ambitions."
"Spoken like a true Rimworlder, even though you were once a Terrie."

All right, all right, so I was a Terrie then (he went on). I held the rank of lieutenant commander in the Federation Survey Service. I was captain of FSS *Seeker*, one of the census ships. I was counting noses and, at the same time, showing the flag. I'd been ordered to do this latter on Werrississa, the home planet of a non-human civilisation.

Not that the Werrississians are all that non-human. There are, in fact, some far-fetched theories to the effect that Werrississa was colonised from Earth by some pre-Atlantean culture. The resemblances between them and us do seem to be too close to be accounted for by parallel evolution—but, given enough time, evolution can come up with *anything*. And, although sexual intercourse is possible between humans and Werrississians, such unions are always sterile.

What do they look like, you ask? To begin with, they're tall, the adults, male and female, running to two metres and up. They're slender, although their women are subtly rounded in the right places. They're wide-mouthed but thin-lipped. Their noses tend to be aquiline. Their eyes are huge, like those of some nocturnal mammals on Earth and other worlds. Hair colouring? From black through brown through gold to silver, but that silver is no indicator of age. Long, slender hands and feet, four digited.

Clothing? Except for occasions when working gear is required translucent, ankle-length robes, usually white, are worn by both sexes. Sandals tend—or tended when I was there—to be ornate. Both sexes wear jewellery—rings, ear-clips, bracelets, anklets.

They regard outsiders—rightly so, in many cases—as uncultured barbarians. They set great value on face. They attach great importance to etiquette. Their highest art form is cookery.

"For you," she said, "a paradise."
"It would not have been for you," he told her, "after the way in which you turned up your nose at that excellent dinner."
"Do they like their food raw too?" she asked.

Seeker being a survey ship proper rather than a warship (he went on) she carried quite an assortment of scientists. Men dressed as spacemen, as the saying goes. Women dressed as spacewomen. Commissioned ranks, of course. One of them was Dr.—or Commander—Maggie Lazenby. She outranked me, although I was still the captain. She was my tame ethologist. She was supposed to be able to tell me what made alien people tick.

Shortly after we set down at the spaceport just outside Wistererri City she gave me a good talking to. She was good at that. "These are people," she said, "who were civilised while we were still living in caves."

"So how come," I asked, "that they'd only gotten as far as the airship when we made our first landings on this world in our interstellar vessels?"

"Civilisation and advanced technology," she told me, "do not necessarily go together. But these," she continued, "are a very civilised people. Perhaps too civilised. There's a certain rigidity, and too great a tendency to regard all outworlders as uncultured barbarians. In matters of dress, for example. We tend to be casual—even in uniform unless it's some sort of state occasion. Short-sleeved shirts, shorts—and for women very short skirts. Luckily you received the local dignitaries in full dress, with all your officers, including myself, attired likewise. But I couldn't help noticing the horror with which the City Governor and his entourage regarded the stewardesses who brought in the refreshments . . ."

"They were correctly and respectably dressed," I said.

"By *our* standards. And on my home world nudity wouldn't have caused so much as a raised eyebrow." (Maggie came from Arcadia, where naturism is the accepted way of life.) "But I'm not running around naked here. And you and your crew are not going to run around half naked when you go ashore. Arms and knees, female as well as male, must, repeat must, be covered."

"But it's summer. It's *hot*."

"A good sweat will get some of your fat off," she said.

So . . . When in Rome, and all that. But I didn't like it. My crew didn't like it, even after I'd explained the reason for my order. But it wasn't too bad for the women. Maggie went into a huddle with the pay-master—oddly enough she was, like Miss Otoguro, in this ship, of Japan-ese origin—and between the pair of them they cooked up a shoregoing rig based on the traditional kimono, made up from extremely lightweight material. Miss Hayashi looked very attractive in hers. Maggie looked odd at first—to my eyes, anyhow—but I had to admit that it suited her; the green, silky cloth matched her eyes and was an agreeable contrast to her red hair . . .

"You seem to have had quite a crush on this Maggie," commented *Miss Kelly.*
"Mphm. Yes."

So there was shore leave. The male personnel suffered; even the nights were uncomfortably warm and nowhere was there air-conditioning. The ladies, in their filmy but all-concealing dresses, flour-ished. For daytime excursions Yoshie Hayashi issued parasols and also, for all occasions, paper fans. Oh, we could have used the parasols and the fans too but neither, somehow, seemed masculine. And we sweated. By the Odd Gods of the Galaxy, how we sweated! Official banquets are bad enough at any time but they're absolute purgatory when you're wrestling with unfamiliar eating irons and literally stewing inside a dress uniform.

The eating irons?

You've seen me using chopsticks—but the Werrississians use a sort of *single* chopstick. They come in three varieties. There's what is, in effect, just a sharp-pointed skewer, quite good for spearing chunks of meat or whatever. Then there's a long handled affair with a sort of small, shallow spoon on the end of it. You can eat a bowl of soup with the thing, but it's a long process and, if you hold it properly, unless you have a very steady hand most of the fluid food finishes up in your lap. And the last one's a real beauty. At the end of it is an auger with a left-handed thread. And it's used only for a very special dish.

You didn't like Keiko's *sushi.* It's just as well that she didn't prepare *sashimi* for us. It's also raw fish, but even more so, if you know what I mean. You don't? Well, the fish is only stunned, not killed, before being prepared. While you're picking the bite-sized pieces off the skeleton it comes back to life and twitches its fins and *looks* at you . . . I came quite to like it while I was stationed on Mikasa Base for a while; the junior offi-cers' mess, where I took most of my meals, specialised in a traditionally Japanese cuisine. So, having eaten and enjoyed *sashimi,* I was quite able to cope with *leeleeoosa.* It's a sort of thick worm. Alive and wriggling. The skin's rather tough and rubbery but it tends to dissolve when you chew it, this process being initiated by the sauce, mildly acid in flavour, into which you dip it.

So you have these . . . worms swimming around in a bowl of tepid water. You select your next victim. You jab, then twist left-handed. You dip in the sauce, bring it to your mouth and chew. The flavour? Not bad. Rather like rare steak, with a touch of garlic.

Fortunately I'd been able to get in some practice before the first official dinner at which *leeleeoosa* was served. Maggie had done her homework before we came to Werrississa. She, like me, enjoyed exotic foods. The ship's artificers, acting on her instructions, and run up a few sets of working tools. Of course, we weren't able to test our skills on real live and wriggling *leeleeoosa* until after we'd set down and Miss Hayashi had been able to do some shopping. But we'd sort of trained on *sukiyaki*, the strips of meat bobbing around in boiling water made a fair substitute for the real thing. It was the lefthanded thread on the skewer that took the most getting used to.

Then HIMS *William Wallace*, one of the *big* ships of the Navy of the Empire of Waverley, dropped in. Her classification was more or less— more rather than less—of our Constellation Class battle cruisers. Her commanding officer was Captain Sir Hamish McDiarmid, Knight of the Order of the Golden Thistle &c, &c *and* &c. Like me, he was showing the flag. *His* flag. He had a far bigger ship to wear it on. But she was a warship, not a survey ship. She was long on specialists in the martial arts but short on scientists. Ethologists especially. Nonetheless, I was to discover later, he had done some research into local lore before inflicting his presence on the Werrississians.

But national pride influenced him. The kilt, in a variety of tartans, is worn throughout the Empire on all occasions, by both men and women, with uniform and with civilian clothing. Longish, heavy kilts are for winter, short, lightweight kilts are for summer. Traditionally nothing is worn under these garments—all well and good when they're long and heavy but liable to offend the prudish when they're short and light.

Not that the Werrississians were prudish. It was just that, as far as they were concerned, there were things that are done and things that just definitely aren't done. They were prepared to tolerate outworlders and their odd ways but they didn't have to like them when such odd ways were offensive. I was grateful to Maggie for her good advice. Here was (comparitively) little, lightly armed *Seeker* whose people were happily conforming, and there was the huge *William Wallace* whose men strode arrogantly along the avenues of the city flaunting their bare knees—and more on a breezy day. They realised that the natives liked us while thinking that *they* were something that the cat had dragged in in an off moment. They resented this. They openly jeered at our women in their long gowns, carrying their parasols, calling them Madam Butterfly. I heard that they were referring to me as Lieutenant Pinkerton . . .

"Who were they, when they were up and dressed?" asked Kitty.

"Two characters in an opera who were dressed more or less as we were dressed," said Grimes. "Very unsuitably—as far as Pinkerton was concerned—for the climate."

But, as I said, Sir Hamish had done some research before his landing on Werrississa. I learned later that he had earned quite a reputation as a gourmet. He had even been known to sneer at the Waverley national dish, the haggis. He had, as I had done, insisted that all his people familiarise themselves with local dishes and eating implements. They even carried their own working tools with them, tucked into their sporrans, when they went ashore. It was reported to me by some of my officers, who had dined in the same restaurants, that the *William Wallace* personnel were quite skilful with these, even with the *skirroo*, the implement used when eating *leeleeoosa*. Yet it wasn't enough. They might eat like civilised people but they dressed like barbarians. We both ate and dressed properly.

And yet we were all members of the same race, whereas the Werrississians, for all their similarities, weren't. There had to be some fraternisation between the two crews. I invited Sir Hamish to take lunch with me aboard *Seeker*—and, unlike some people whom I will not name, he thoroughly enjoyed his *sushi*. He told me that he was planning a dinner aboard *William Wallace* for local dignitaries and would be pleased if I would attend together with three of my senior officers. I was happy to accept the invitation. Then—we'd had quite a few drinks and were getting quite matey—I asked him if he'd be serving haggis, piped in the traditional way. He wasn't offended. He laughed and said, "Not likely, Grimes. I ken well that you people are putting on a big act o' being civilised while we're just hairy-kneed barbarians. But I'll demonstrate that, when it comes to civilised living, we're as good as anybody. It'll be a Werrississian menu, prepared by my chefs . . ."

"Dress?" I asked.

"Formal, o' course. Ye'll be wearin' your dinner uniforms. We'll be wearin' ours. An' we'll be cooler than you'll be—from the waist down, anyhow. My private dining room will have to conform to local ideas of comfort, temperaturewise . . ."

I was rather sorry then that I couldn't back out, but it was too late. Later, when I passed the word around, nobody was keen to accompany me. At last Maggie said that she'd come to hold my hand. The other two victims were MacMorris, my chief engineer, and Marlene Deveson, one of the scientists. A geologist, as a matter of fact. Not that it matters.

Then the Big Day came round. Or the Big Night. We met in the air-conditioned comfort of my day cabin for a drink before walking the short distance to Sir Hamish's ship. We were all tarted up in our best mess dress, tropical. It would still be too hot for comfort with the white bum-freezer over the starched white shirt, the long, black trousers. The two ladies were slightly better off, with high-collared, epauletted, long-sleeved shirts only on top of their ankle-length black skirts. At least they were not required to wear jackets. Maggie looked good, as she always did, no matter what she was or wasn't wearing. Marlene looked a mess. She was a short girl, fat rather than plump. Her round face was already sweaty. Her hair, greasily black, was a tangle. Two of her shirt buttons had come undone.

We allowed ourselves one small whisky each. Sir Hamish would be serving Scotch and it wouldn't do to mix drinks. Then Maggie made a check of Marlene's appearance, frowned, took her into my bathroom to make repairs and adjustments. When they came out shirt buttons had been done up and hair combed and brushed into a semblance of order.

We took the elevator down to the airlock, walked slowly down the ramp. *William Wallace* was a great, dark, turreted tower in ominous silhouette against the city lights. (Sir Hamish did not believe on wasting money on floodlighting, even when he was showing the Thistle Flag.) It was a hot night. I'd started perspiring already. I had little doubt that the others were doing likewise. We made our way slowly across the apron. The heat of the day was beating up from the concrete.

We climbed the ramp to *William Wallace*'s after airlock. The Imperial Marine on duty—white, sleeveless shirt over a kilt with black and red tartan, sturdy legs in calf-length boots—saluted smartly. I replied. Inside the chamber we were received by a junior officer, clad as was the Marine but with black and gold tartan and gold-braided shoulder boards on his shirt. More saluting. We were ushered into the elevator, carried swiftly up to Sir Hamish's suite.

He received us personally. He looked very distinguished. From the waist up he was dressed as I was—although he had more gold braid on his epaulettes than I did, more brightly ribboned miniature medals on the left breast of his mess jacket. And he was wearing a kilt, of course, summer weight and length, in the Imperial Navy's black and gold tartan. His long socks were black, with gold at the turnover. There were gold buckles on his highly polished black shoes.

And he, I was pleased to see, was feeling the heat too. His craggy face under the closely cropped white hair was flushed and shining with perspiration. But he was jovial enough.

He exclaimed, "Come in, come in! This is Liberty Hall. Ye can spit on the mat an' call the haggis a bastard!"

"Are ye givin' us haggis, then, sir?" asked MacMorris eagerly.

"No. 't'was just an expression of your captain's that I modified to suit *my* ship. *We* don't carry tabbies in the Waverley Navy."

Both Maggie and Marlene gave him dirty looks.

"Tabbies?" asked Kitty Kelly.

"In the old days of passenger carrying surface ships on Earth they used to call stewardesses that. Today all female spacegoing personnel, regardless of rank or department, are called tabbies. But not to their faces."

"I should hope not."

We were the first guests to arrive. We were taken into Sir Hamish's sitting room—he had quarters that would have made a Survey Service admiral green with envy—introduced to his senior officers, plied with excellent Scotch. Then the young officer who had received us on board ushered in the native guests. There were six of them, three male and three female. They looked pale wraiths. They accepted drinks from the mini-kilted mess steward although they regarded his hairy knees with distaste. Rather pointedly they made polite conversation only with those of us from *Seeker*; we were properly dressed even though our hosts were not. Their command of standard English was quite good.

A skirling of bagpipes came over the intercom. I assumed that it was the mess call. I was right. Sir Hamish led the way into his dining room. The long table, with its surface of gleaming tiles, each with a different tartan design, was already set. Sir Hamish's artificers had done him proud, were doing us all proud. At each place were the native eating utensils in polished bronze—*slup*, *splik* and *skirroo*. There were the bronze wine flasks, the cups made from the same alloy. There were place cards, with names both in English and the flowing Werrississian script.

Sir Hamish took the head of the table, of course, with a local lady on his right and her "social function husband" on his left. (The Werrississians have a multiplicity of wives and husbands—mates for all occasions.) I sat below the native woman and Maggie below the man. Then another native couple, then Marlene and MacMorris, then the last Werrississian pair. Below them was the covey of Imperial Navy commanders—(E), (N), (C), (S) and (G)—all looking rather peeved at having to sit below the salt.

Sir Hamish's mess waiters were well trained, efficient. They were drilled in local customs. First they poured each of us a goblet of the sweet, sticky wine—it was, as it should have been, at room temperature but I'd have preferred it chilled—and there was a round of toasts. We toasted the Emperor James XIV of Waverley, whose gold-framed, purple-draped portrait was on the bulkhead behind Sir Hamish's chair. The gentlemen toasted the ladies. The ladies toasted the gentlemen. We all toasted our host. By this time it was necessary to bring in a fresh supply of the bronze flasks. Unluckily it was still the same sickly but potent tipple. I looked rather anxiously at MacMorris. He didn't have a very good head for drinks and was liable after only one too many to insist on dancing a Highland fling. But I needn't have worried about him. He was a Scot more than he was a Terran and it was obvious that he, aboard a warship owned by the only essentially Scottish spacefaring power, was determined to be on his very best behaviour. It was an effort but he was capable of making it. The toasting over he was taking merely token sips from his cup.

I looked at Marlene. I knew little about her drinking capacity and behaviour. What I saw worried me. She was downing goblet after goblet of the wine as fast as the steward could refill them. Her hair was becoming unfixed. The black, floppy bow at the neck of her shirt was now lopsided. One button on the front of the garment was undone.

The first course came in.

I've forgotten its native name but it was, essentially, bite-sized cubes of meat, fish, vegetables and other things coated in a savoury batter and deep fried. For these we used the *spliks*, the long, sharp skewers. The Werrississian guests made complimentary noises and, as was their custom, ate rapidly, their implements clicking on the china plates with their thistle pattern. Sir Hamish and his officers ate almost as fast and so did we *Seeker* people—with the exception of Marlene. It seemed to me that about half of her meal was going on to the table and the other half on to her lap, and from there to the deck. I was very sorry that Maggie wasn't sitting beside me instead of opposite. Had I been next to her I could have whispered to her, begged her to do something, anything, about her fellow scientific officer before she disgraced us.

The table was cleared but the *spliks* were left for use on the next course. This consisted of cubes of a melon-like fruit rolled in a sort of aromatic sugar. To my great relief Marlene seemed to have regained control of herself and succeeded in putting at least seventy five percent of the sweet morsels into her broad mouth, although by this time her lipstick was smeared badly.

Plates and *spliks* were removed by the attentive stewards. Goblets—where necessary—were refilled. I looked imploringly at Sir Hamish; surely he must realise that Marlene had had enough to drink, more than enough. He looked at me. There was a sardonic expression on his craggy

face that I didn't like at all. I looked at Maggie. She knew what was passing through my mind. I could read her expression. It said, *What can I do
about it?*

Plashish was next—a sort of clear soup, with shreds of something
like cheese floating in it, served in shallow bowls. We all plied our *slups*,
the long-handled spoons, holding them as we had been taught, by the very
end of the shaft. *All?* No, there was one exception. Marlene, of course.
She *did* try, I admit, but gave it up as a bad job. Then she lifted the bowl
to her mouth, with two hands, and *lapped* from it . . .

The *William Wallace* people were trying to look even more shocked
than their native guests but I knew that the bastards were glorying in the
discomforture of the Sassenachs. Us. And Sir Hamish—may the Odd
Gods of the Galaxy rot his cotton socks!—was looking insufferably
smug. He had shown the Werrississians that even though the representatives of Waverley insisted on wearing their own native dress they could
comport themselves at table far more decently than the minions of Terra.
And the Werrississians? They were gravely embarrassed. Their complex-
ions had faded from the usual pale cream to an ashy grey. They were
obviously avoiding looking at Marlene.

The *plashish* course was over. The *leeleeoosa* was (were?) brought in—
the deep bowls of lukewarm water in which the meaty worms were swimming, the smaller bowls of sauce. I daren't look at Marlene to see how she
was managing. I was having my own troubles, anyhow. So was Maggie. So
was MacMorris. We'd practised enough with *skirroos*—both aboard *Seeker*
and in restaurants ashore—but somehow our acquired skill seemed to have
deserted us. We'd stab, and make contact with our prey, and twist—yet
every time our intended victims would wriggle free. But Sir Hamish and his
people were eating as expertly as the Werrississian guests . . .

It was Maggie first who twigged what was wrong. She stared at me
across the table. She raised her left hand with forefinger extended, made
a circular motion. I finally realised what she was driving at. The *skirroos*
at our places, those long, bronze augers, had right-handed threads. I
impaled one of the tasty worms without trouble then, dipped it in the
sauce, brought it up to my mouth, chewed. I felt that I'd earned it. Mac-
Morris, as befitting an engineer, had made the discovery himself. He was
eating fast and happily.

I looked down and across the table at Marlene. She was having her
troubles. I tried to catch her attention but she was concentrating too hard
on her bowl of *leeleeoosa*. She had her *skirroo* in both hands. She brought
it down like a harpoon. She must have driven the point through the tough,
rubbery skin of a worm by sheer force. She lifted it out of the bowl. She
didn't bother to dip it in the sauce but brought the wriggling thing straight

up to her open mouth. If it had made the distance it wouldn't have mattered, but . . . It slipped off the end of the *skirroo*. It fell on to Marlene's ample bosom. It found the gap in her shirt front where the gilt button had come undone. It squirmed into the opening.

Marlene screamed. She jumped to her feet, oversetting her *leeleeoosa* bowl. There were worms everywhere. Maggie guessed her intentions but did not reach her in time to stop her from ripping off her shirt. She was wearing nothing under it. Her breasts were her best feature, but they were *big*. It seemed as though somebody had launched a couple of Shaara blimps into Sir Hamish's dining room.

The Waverley officers stared appreciatively. The Werrississians, male and female, covered their eyes with both hands. Sir Hamish got to his feet, glared at me—but I knew that this was a histrionic display put on for the benefit of his native guests.

"Commander Grimes," he said, "you and your officers have abused my hospitality and gravely embarrassed my other guests. You will please leave my ship. I shall be vastly obliged if you never set foot aboard her again."

"Sir Hamish," I said to him, "none of this would have happened if our places had been set with the correctly left-hand-threaded *skirroos*."

He said, "I thought that I was doing you a favour. All my people have found it far easier to use right-handed *skirroos* of our own manufacture."

And so we slunk off *William Wallace* in disgrace, what little dignity remaining to us dissipated by the tussle that we had with Marlene to stop her from stripping completely; she was convinced that one of the spilled worms had wriggled from the floor up her leg.

Back aboard *Seeker* we almost literally threw the fat, drunken girl into her cabin. MacMorris—whose mind was reeling under the shock of having been thrown off a Scottish ship—went to his quarters to sulk and to console himself with whisky.

Maggie came up to my flat to console me. We held a post mortem on the disastrous evening. We'd thought that we, playing along with the local prudery regarding dress while the Waverley crew flaunted their short kilts, had made ourselves the most favoured aliens. But Sir Hamish had turned the tables on us. Of course, Marlene's strip act had been an unexpected bonus to him.

So that was that. I had to carry the can back, of course—after all, I was the captain. My popularity rating with the Lords Commissioners of the Admiralty sank to what I thought must be an all time low.

"If you had the sense to stick to civilised food," said Kitty Kelly, "that sort of thing would never happen . . . But I don't know much about

the Galaxy outside the Shakespearian Sector. This Werri-whatever-it-is . . . I suppose that it's now well and truly inside the Waverley sphere of influence."

Grimes laughed. "As a matter of fact it isn't. I heard that after we'd left Sir Hamish and his senior officers were invited to a very genteel garden party thrown by no less a dignitary than the Grand Co-ordinator. It was a windy day. They should have had sense enough to wear their winter weight kilts . . .

"It was the Shaara, of all people, who got a foothold (talonhold?) on Werrississa. After all, you don't expect a really alien alien to have the same nudity taboos, the same table manners, as you do. We humans are so like the Werrississians that every difference was exaggerated."

"Just as differences between members of the same species are," she said. "Some like raw fish and seaweed. Some don't."

GRIMES AND THE ODD GODS

F*araway Quest*, the Rim Worlds Confederacy survey ship, was still berthed at Port Fortinbras, on Elsinore. She was still awaiting replacements for the rotors of her outmoded inertial drive unit. More than once, in strongly worded Carlottigrams, Commodore Grimes had requested, demanded almost, that he be allowed to put the repairs in the hands of one of the several local shipyards. Each time he received a terse reply from the Rim Worlds Admiralty's Bureau of Engineering which, translated from Officialese to English, boiled down to *Father knows best*. He unburdened his soul to the Rim Worlds ambassador on Elsinore.

"Can't *you* do something, Your Excellency?" he asked. "There's my ship been sitting here for weeks now. My crew's becoming more and more demoralized. . . ."

"As well I know, Commodore," the ambassador agreed. "You've some hearty drinkers aboard your vessel, and when they drink they brawl. Perhaps you could stop the shore leave of the worst offenders. . . ."

"And have them drinking and brawling aboard the *Quest?* Or, if I really put my foot down, slouching around in a state of sullen sobriety? There's only one thing to do. Get them off this bloody planet and back where they belong, back to their wives and families or, in the case of the tabbies, to their boyfriends."

"Some of your female personnel are even greater nuisances than the men," said the ambassador.

"You're telling *me*. But as an ambassador, Your Excellency, you pile on far mores Gs than a mere commodore, a commodore on the reserve list at that. Can't *you* do something?"

"I've tried, Grimes. I've tried. But it's all a matter of economics. The

Confederacy just does not have the funds in any bank in the Shake-spearean Sector to pay for a major repair and replacement job. Those rotors will have to be manufactured on Lorn, and then carried out here in whatever ship of the Rim Runners fleet is due to make a scheduled call to Elsinore. . . ."

"And meanwhile," the commodore said, "there are mounting port dues. And the wages that everybody aboard *Faraway Quest* is getting for doing nothing. And the three square meals a day, plus snacks, that all hands expect as their right. And. . . ."

"I'm a diplomat, Grimes, not an economist."

"And I'm just a spaceman. Oh, well. Theirs not to reason why, and all that. And now I'll be getting back to my ship, Your Excellency."

"What's the hurry, Commodore? I was hoping that you would stay for a few drinks and, possibly, dinner."

"I have an appointment," said Grimes.

The ambassador laughed. "Another interview for Kitty's Korner? I always watch that program myself. And I've heard that Station Yorick's ratings have improved enormously since Miss Kelly persuaded you to treat her viewers and listeners to your never-ending series of tall tales."

"Not so tall," growled Grimes.

"Perhaps not. You have had an interesting life, haven't you?"

An hour or so later, in his sitting room aboard the old ship, Grimes and Kitty Kelly were enjoying the simple yet satisfying meal that had been brought to them by one of the stewardesses. There were sandwiches constructed from crisply crusty new bread, straight from *Faraway Quest's* own bakery, and thick slices of juicy Waldegren ham, the flavor of which derived from the smoldering sugar pine sawdust over which the meat had been smoked. (Almost alone among the ship's personnel, Grimes liked this delicacy; that was a good supply of it in the ship's cool stores. He was pleased that Kitty, hitherto inclined to be an unadventurous eater, enjoyed it, too.) There was a variety of cheeses—Ultimo Blue, Aquarian Sea Cream, and Caribbean Pineapple and Pepper—altogether with assorted pickles and the especially hot radishes that Grimes had insisted be culti-vated in the ship's hydroponic farm. There was Australian beer—some while ago Grimes had done a private deal with the master of a Federation star tramp not long out from Earth—served in condensation-bedewed pewter pots.

Nibbling a last radish with her strong while teeth, Kitty slumped back in her chair. Grimes regarded her appreciatively. As she always did, she was wearing green, this time a long, filmy, flowing dress with long, loose sleeves. Above it, the food and the drink had brought a slight flush to the normal creamy pallor of her face, a healthy pallor, set off by the wide scarlet slash of her lips. Below her black glossy hair, this evening braided into a sort of coronet, her startlingly blue eyes looked back at Grimes.

She murmured, "Thank you for the meal, Commodore. It was very good."

He asked, "And will you sing for your supper?"

She said, "You're the one who's going to do the singing." She looked at the bulkhead clock. "It's almost time that we got the show on the road again. And what are you going to talk about tonight? Your adventures as a pirate?"

"Not a pirate," he corrected her stiffly. "A privateer."

"Who knows the difference? And who cares? Or what about when you were governor general of that anarchist planet?"

"Too long a story, Kitty," he said. "And too complicated. By All the Odd Gods of the Galaxy, there never were, before or since, such complications!"

She said thoughtfully, "That . . . that oath you often use . . . By All the Odd Gods of the Galaxy . . . Did you ever get tangled with any of these Odd Gods?"

He told her, "I'm an agnostic. But . . . there have been experiences."

She got up from her chair, went to the case containing her audio-visual recorder, opened it, pulled out the extensions with their lenses and microphones.

She said, peering into the monitor screen. "Yes, that's it. Pipe in one hand, tankard in the other . . . And now, *talk*."

"What about?"

"The Odd Gods, of course. Or, at the very least, One Odd God."

He said, "Oh, all right. But I must get my pipe going first."

As you know (he started at last), I left the Federation Survey Service under something of a cloud after the *Discovery* mutiny. For a while I was yachtmaster to the Baroness Michelle d'Estang, an El Doradan aristocrat, and on the termination of this employment she gave me the yacht's pinnace, which was practically a deep-space ship in miniature, as a parting gift. I called her—the pinnace, not the baroness—*Little Sister* and set up shop as Far Traveler Courier Services. I'd carry anything or anybody anywhere, as long as I got paid. There would be small parcels of special cargo. There would be people waiting to get to planets well off the normal interstellar trade routes.

It was a living.

I didn't make a fortune, but there was usually enough in the bank to pay ports dues and such and to keep me in life's little luxuries. It was lonely for quite a lot of the time but, now and again, there were passengers who were pleasant enough company . . . Yes, female ones some-times, if you must know. But it was the female ones who usually got me into all kinds of trouble. Mphm.

Well, I'd carried a small parcel of urgently needed medical supplies to a world called Warrenhome—no, the inhabitants weren't descended from rabbits but the name of the captain who made the first landing was Warren—where they were having some sort of plague. A mutated virus. After I'd made delivery and received the balance of the payment due to me, I lost no time in placing the usual advertisements in the usual media. I decided that I'd wait around for a week and then, if nothing came up, get off the planet. There was talk that that virus, a nasty one, might mutate again.

Luckily (I thought at the time) I didn't have long to wait for my next job. I returned to *Little Sister*, after a yarn with the Port Captain, just before any usual lunchtime. I saw that a tall woman was approaching the airlock door from the opposite direction to myself. She was dressed in severe, ankle-length black with touches of white at throat and wrists. On her head was an odd sort of hat, black, with a wide, stiff brim. The skin of her strong-featured face was white; even the lips of her wide mouth were pale. Her eyes were a hard, steely blue.

She stated rather than asked, "Captain Grimes."

Her voice was deep for a woman, resonant.

I said, "I have that honor, Miz . . . ?"

She said, "You may call me Madame Bishop."

I asked, "And what can I do for you, Miz Bishop?"

She said coldly, "Bishop is my title, Captain Grimes, not my sur-name. I understand that you are seeking employment for yourself and your ship. I shall employ you."

I let us both into the ship, seated her at the table in the cabin while I went through into the little galley. I asked her what she would like to drink. She told me coldly that she would appreciate a glass of water. I brought her one, and a pink gin for myself. She looked at this disapprov-ingly. I pulled out my pipe and filled it. She as good as ordered me to put it away. It wasn't so much the words that she used but the way in which she said them. But I had been learning, ever since I set up in business for myself, that the customer is always right. I put my pipe back in my pocket.

She asked, "How soon can you lift ship, Captain Grimes?"

I said, "As soon as I've paid on my bills and cleared outwards."

"Today?"

"Yes."

She asked, "Are you capable of making the voyage to Stagatha?"

I'd never heard of that world, but *Little Sister* was capable of going just about anywhere in the galaxy. I told her yes.

"What will be the single fare for one passenger?"

I couldn't answer this at once. I didn't know where Stagatha was or how far it was from Warrenhome. I asked her to wait while I switched on the playmaster. She told me that she did not approve of frivolous entertainment. I told her that the playmaster screen served as the read-out for *Little Sister*'s computer and library bank. I don't think she believed me until the requested data began to appear.

In a short while I had all the information required. The voyage would take six weeks. Then there were all the various expenses accruing over this period—depreciation, insurance, consumption of stores, the salary that I—as owner—was paying to myself as master. And so on, and so on. After all, I had to show a profit. I told her how much I should be asking.

She said, "We are not a rich church, Captain Grimes, but we are not a poor one. And has it not been written that the laborer is worthy of his hire?" She allowed herself the merest hint of a smile. "Too, you are the only laborer available at this moment of time."

"Is this voyage a matter of some urgency?" I asked.

"The Lord's work is always urgent," she told me.

And so it was that I contracted to carry Bishop Agatha Lewis, of the Church Of The Only Salvation, from Warrenhome to Stagatha.

He paused, looking down into his now-empty tankard. Kitty refilled it for him, refilled her own.

She said, "So far we haven't had any Odd Gods. These Only Salvation people seem to have been just another nut cult, probably with their own translation of the Christian Bible slanted to make it fit their own beliefs."

He said, "Even without special translations you can interpret the Bible in a very wide variety of ways, find in it Divine Authority for just about every aberration of which the human race is capable. But the Church Of The Only Salvation did have its own Bible. Bishop Lewis gave me a copy. I tried to read it but the writing was appallingly bad. As far as I'm concerned there is only one Bible. The King James version."

After she was gone, to get herself organized, I made myself a sandwich lunch and tried to get more information about Stagatha from the library bank. It was an Earth-type planet with about the same proportion of land to water. The inhabitants were humanoid. I've often wondered why there are so many humanoid, as near as dammit human, races throughout the galaxy. Was there some Expansion, from Somewhere, before the dawn of history? But on every world there is the evolutionary evidence that cannot be denied that Man descended from lower life forms. Or is there some Divine Plan?

But I'm just a spaceman, not a philosopher.

There were photographs of typical Stagathans. These could have been taken on practically any beach on Earth or any Man-colonized planet. The males were, to all outward appearances, well-endowed (but not abnormally so) men. The females tended to be busty, but firm-breasted. The only thing odd was that these photographs had been taken in the streets of a Stagathan town, not at a seaside resort. I finally got around to looking at the vehicles and buildings in the background. Electric cars (I thought). Dwellings, offices, shops—but nothing over one story and everything with a flat roof.

And that was all. There was no trade with other worlds, no exports, no imports. There had been very little contact with outsiders since the first landing by Commodore Shakespeare, that same Commodore Shakespeare after whom your Shakespearean Sector was named. Every so often some minor vessel of the Survey Service would drop in, just showing the flag and for rest and recreation. But why, I wondered, should the Church Of The Only Salvation be interested in the planet?

But I had things to do. Bills to pay, outward clearance to be obtained and all the rest of it. Not much was required in the way of stores; my tissue culture vats were in good order and I could program the autochef to turn out quite fair imitations of Scotch whiskey and London gin. Flour I needed, and fresh eggs, and a few cases of the not-too-bad local table wines. Regarding these, I based my order on what I regarded as normal consumption by two people for the duration of the voyage. I could have cut that order by half. . . .

I made my pre-lift-off checks. Everything was in order, as it almost always was. She was a reliable little brute, was *Little Sister*. When I was walking around the outside of her, just admiring her, a small motorcade approached from the spaceport gates. There were four archaic-looking ground cars, black-painted, steam-driven, each emitting a thick cloud of dirty smoke from its funnel. From the first one Bishop Agatha Lewis disembarked, followed by half a dozen men and women, dressed in plain black and with broad-brimmed black hats like the one she was wearing. The men were all heavily bearded. Similar parties got out from the other three cars.

I walked up to the she-bishop and threw her a smart salute. She did not quite ignore me, but her curt nod was of the don't-bother-me-now variety. She made no attempt to introduce me to the assembled elders and deaconesses and deacons or whatever they were. Oh, well, I was only the captain. *And* the owner. I was only a space-going cabbie. I went back inside the ship to sulk.

Before long an elderly woman, followed by four men, carrying between them two heavy trunks, came in. She asked me, quite politely, "Where do we put these?" I showed them. The men went back outside.

She sat down at the table, noticed the tea things that I had not cleared away yet after my afternoon break.

She asked, in a whisper, "Do you think that I might have a cup, Captain?"

I made a fresh pot and, with a clean cup, brought it in to her. I could hear some sort of hymn being sung outside, one of those *dreary* ones all about the blood of the lamb and so forth.

She murmured, as she sipped appreciatively, "We shall all miss the dear bishop. But we, the synod, decided that she would be the right and proper person to send to Stagatha." She helped herself to a chocolate biscuit, crunched into it greedily. "Surely the similarity of the names is no coincidence. There was a St. Agatha, you know. Not that we approve of the Popish church and their beliefs." She poured herself more tea, added cream and was generous with the sugar. "Yes. We shall all of us miss the dear bishop—although, perhaps, her interpretation of the Word has been a mite too strict."

I said, "I still haven't been told why Bishop Lewis is going to Stagatha."

She said, "I thought that you knew. It is because those unhappy people, on that world, are living in a state of darkness, are brands to be plucked from the burning. We heard about it from a spaceman, a young fellow called Terry Gowan, one of the engineers aboard the *Cartographer*, a Survey Service ship. Would you know him?"

I said that I didn't. (It is truly amazing how so many planetlubbers have the erroneous idea that everybody in Space, naval or mercantile, knows everybody else.)

"A very nice young man. A *religious* young man. His ship set down here a few weeks after a visit to Stagatha. One of our people went on board her with books and pamphlets. The only one of the crew who was interested was Terry. He came to our prayer meetings. He talked about Stagatha. He brought us audio-visual records that he had taken. We were shocked. Those people, as human as you and me, going about completely . . . unclothed. And their *heathen* religion! Do you know, they worship their sun. . . ."

I didn't see much wrong with that. After all, sun-worship is logical.

And as long as you don't go to the horrid extreme of tearing the still-beating hearts out of the breasts of sacrificial virgins, it has much to recommend it. The sun, after all—your sun, Earth's sun, Stagatha's sun, anybody's sun—is the source of all life. And there are Man-colonized planets, such as Arcadia, where naturism is a way of life, although the Arcadians don't quite make a religion of it.

"None of the other churches," the old lady went on, "has sent a missionary to Stagatha. But *somebody* has to. . . ."

"And Bishop Lewis was your obvious choice," I said.

"Why, yes," she almost laughed.

I was beginning to like the old dear. She had told me, as plainly as she could, that dear Agatha was being kicked upstairs. Literally.

Suddenly she stiffened and with a swift motion pushed her half-full teacup across the table so that it was in front of me. She was just in time. Bishop Lewis came into the cabin and stood there, staring down at us suspiciously.

She asked, "Why are you still here, Sister Lucille?"

The old lady got to her feet and bowed deferentially and said, "I was just keeping Captain Grimes company while he had his tea, Your Reverence. And I was telling him about our work."

"Indeed?" Her voice was very cold. "Since when were you one of our missioners, Sister Lucille?"

That business with the teacup had been a fair indication of which way the wind was blowing, but I made sure.

I asked, "Would you care for tea, Madame Bishop? I asked Sister Lucille to join me, but she refused."

"As she should have done, Captain Grimes, and as I shall do. Nowhere in Holy Writ are such unclean beverages as tea or coffee mentioned. Members of our Church are forbidden to partake of them."

And that was that.

He paused for refreshment, sipping from his newly filled tankard.

Kitty asked, "And what about wine? That's mentioned quite a few times."

"Yes," said Grimes. "Noah planted a vineyard and then made his own wine after he ran the Ark aground on Mount Ararat. Then he got drunk on his own tipple and the Almighty did not approve."

"But, in the New Testament, there's the story of the wedding feast and the water-into-wine miracle."

"According to Bishop Agatha, and according to her Church's own translation of the Bible, that wine was no more than unfermented fruit juice."

I'll not bore you (he went on) with a long account of the voyage out to Stagatha. It was not one of the happiest voyages in my life. On previous occasions, when carrying a female passenger, I found that familiarity breeds attempt. Mutual attempt. But there just wasn't any familiarity. At nights—we maintained a routine based on the twenty-hour day of Warrenhome—the portable screen was always in place, dividing the cabin into two sleeping compartments. Once we were out and clear and on the way, I put on my usual shirt-and-shorts uniform and Her Reverence ordered me—ordered *me*, aboard my own ship—to cover myself decently. Smoking was forbidden, except in the control cab with the communicating door *sealed*. Meals were a misery. I regard myself as quite a fair cook and can make an autochef do things that its makers would never have so much as dreamed of, but . . . Boiled meat and vegetables for lunch, the same for dinner. Breakfast—boiled eggs. No ham or bacon, of course. The wine that I had stocked up with went almost untouched; I just don't like drinking it during a meal while my companion sticks to water. And *she* soon went through the ship's stock of orange juice—she liked that—leaving me with none to put with my gin.

She had brought her own supply of tapes for the playmaster, mainly sermons of the fire-and-brimstone variety and uninspiring hymns sung by remarkably untuneful choirs. Some of those sermons were delivered by herself. I had to admit she had something. She was a born rabble rouser. Had she been peddling some line of goods with greater appeal than the dreary doctrines of her freak religion, she might have finished up as dictator of a planet rather than as the not-very-popular boss cocky of an obscure sect. Might have finished up? But I'm getting ahead of myself.

I dutifully read the Bible, in that horridly pedestrian translation, which she had given me. I did not think that I should ever become a convert. Unluckily, I was rather low on reading matter of my own choice— books, that is—and my stock of microfilmed novels I could not enjoy because of her continuous monopoly of the playmaster.

Anyhow, at last the time came when I stopped the Mannschenn Drive unit and *Little Sister* sagged back into the normal Continuum. There were the usual phenomena, the warped perspective and all that, and (for me) a brief session of déjà vu. I saw Agatha Lewis as a sort of goddess in flowing black robes, brandishing a whip. It frightened me. And then things snapped back to normal.

I had made a good planetfall. We were only two days' run from Stagatha and made our approach to the world, under inertial drive, from north of the plane of ecliptic. There was no need for me to get in radio touch with Aero-space Control. There wasn't any Aero-space Control. As far as I could gather from the information in my library banks, Entry Procedure for just about every known planet in the galaxy, one just came in, keeping a sharp lookout for airships, selected a landing place, and landed. It all seemed rather slipshod, but if the Stagathans liked it, who was I to complain?

The planet looked good from Space. Blue seas, green and brown land masses, relatively small polar ice-caps. There was very little cloud except for a dark and dirty-looking patch of dense vapor that practically obscured from view most of a large island almost on the equator. I studied it through the control cab binoculars and could see flickers of ruddy light within it. It could only be Stagatha's only active volcano. According to Survey Service accounts, it was unnamed and regarded with a sort of superstitious horror. Nobody ever went near it. Looking down at it I thought that I could understand why. Even from a great distance I got the impression of utter ugliness.

Whenever possible, when making a landing on a strange planet with no spaceport facilities, I adhere to Survey Service standard practice, timing my descent from close orbit to coincide with sunrise. That way every irregularity of the ground is shown up by the long shadows. Agatha Lewis had told me to set the ship down as close as possible to one of the cities. Not that there were any *real* cities, just largish country towns, most of them on the banks of rivers, set among fields and forests.

So I dropped down through the early-morning sky, feeling the usual sense of pleasurable anticipation. I enjoy shiphandling and, too, this to me would be a new and almost certainly interesting world. But I wasn't as happy as I should have been. *She* insisted on coming into the control cab with me, which meant that I was not able to smoke my pipe.

My own intention had been not to pass low over the town. Inertial drive units are *noisy*—to anybody outside the ship, that is—and it would be, I thought, stupid to annoy the citizenry by waking them before sparrowfart. But Agatha Lewis insisted that I make what I considered to be the ill-mannered approach. As it turned out, I needn't have worried about disturbing the sleep of the natives. But I did interrupt their dawn service. They were in the central plaza, all of them—men, women, and children—wearing their symbolic black cloaks that they threw aside as the first rays of the rising sun struck through between and over the low buildings. They stared up at us. We stared down. The bishop hissed in disgust at the sight of all that suddenly revealed nakedness.

She . . . she snarled, "Now you know why I have come to this world. To save these poor sinners from their utter degradation."

I said, "They didn't look all that degraded to me. They were clean, healthy. Quite attractive, some of them. . . ."

"But their heathen worship, Captain Grimes! The baring of their bodies. . . ."

I said, "If God had meant us to go around without clothes we'd have been born naked."

"Ha, ha," interjected Kitty Kelly.

"You're as bad as she was," Grimes told her. "She didn't think that it was very funny either. But it shut her up. I was able to land Little Sister in peace and quiet."

"And then you got your gear off and went to romp with the happy nudists, I suppose."

"Ha, ha. Not with her around."

So I landed in the middle of this grassy field. Well, it looked like grass, and some odd-looking quadrupeds were grazing on it until we scared them off with the racket of the inertial drive. I made the routine tests of the atmosphere, not that it was really necessary as the Survey Service had already certified it fit for human consumption. I opened up both airlock doors. Bishop Agatha was first out of the ship. She stood there, in her stifling black clothing, glaring disapprovingly at the sun. I joined her. The fresh air tasted good, was fragrant with the scent of the grass that we had crushed with our set-down, with that of the gaudy purple flowers decorating clumps of low, green-blue foliaged bushes.

I thought that whether or not *she* approved, I was going to wear shirt-and-shorts rig while on this planet. I didn't know for how long I should have to stay; the agreement was that I should wait until the mission was well established and, at intervals, send reports to Warrenhome by means of my Carlotti radio. I couldn't get through directly, of course. The messages would have to be beamed to Baniskil, the nearest planetary Carlotti station, and relayed from there. After I was gone, Agatha would have to wait for the next Survey Service ship to make a call—which might be a matter of months, or even years—before she could make further contact with those who had been her flock.

Anyhow, we stood there in the sunlight, the warm breeze, myself enjoying the environment, she obviously not. We did not talk. We watched the small crowd walking out from the town. As they grew closer, I could see how like they were to humans—our kind of humans—and how unlike. Their faces had eyes and nose and mouth, but their ears were long, pointed, and mobile. The hair on their heads was uniformly short and a sort of dark olive green in color. There was a complete absence of body hair. Their skins were golden brown. There was a something . . .

odd about their lower limbs. (Their ancestors, I discovered later, had been animals not dissimilar to the Terran kangaroo.) But they all possessed what we would regard as human sexual characteristics. Apart from necklaces and bracelets and anklets of gold and glittering jewels, they were all of them naked.

Their leader, a tall man with a strong, pleasant, rather horselike face, walked up to me, stiffened to what was almost attention and threw me quite a smart salute with his six-fingered hand. Obviously he was not unused to dealing with visiting spacemen and, even though he himself went naked, knew the meaning of uniforms and badges of rank.

He said, in almost accentless Standard English, "Welcome to Stagatha, Captain."

I returned his salute and said, "I am pleased to be here, sir."

This did not suit the lady bishop. She was the VIP, not myself. She said a few words in a language strange to me. I was not entirely surprised. I knew that each night during the voyage she had retired to her bed with a slutor—a sleep tutor. She must, somehow, have obtained the necessary language capsules from that visiting Survey Service ship, *Cartographer*. I should have made some attempt myself to learn the language—but linguistically I'm a lazy bastard and always have been. Wherever I've gone I've always found somebody who could speak English.

The Stagathan turned to Agatha Lewis and bowed. Despite his lack of clothing it was a very dignified gesture. She returned this salutation with the slightest of nods. She went on talking in a harsh, angry voice. He grinned, looked down at himself and gave a very human shrug. She went on talking.

He turned to me and said, "For you I am very sorry, Captain. Now we go."

They went.

After I had gazed my fill upon a fine selection of retreating naked female buttocks, I turned to the bishop and asked, "What was all that about, Your Reverence?"

She looked at me very coldly and said, "I was telling these heathen, in their own language, to cover their nakedness."

I said, greatly daring, "They are dressed more suitably for this climate than we."

She said something about lecherous spacemen and then returned to the ship. I followed her. I busied myself with various minor chores while she opened one of the large trunks that had been put aboard before we left Warrenhome. She seemed to be unpacking. It was clothing, I noticed, that she was pulling out and spreading over the deck. She must be looking, I thought, for something cool to wear during the heat of the day. The next time I looked at her she was stowing a quantity of drab raiment into a large backpack.

When she was finished she said, "We will now go to the city, Captain Grimes."

"We haven't had lunch yet," I told her.

"Doing the Lord's work, according to His bidding, will be nourishment enough," she told me. "Please pick up the bag that I have packed and follow me."

"Why?" I demanded.

"It is essential," she said, "that we arrive in the central square prior to the noon service."

"Why?"

"It is not for you to question the Lord's bidding."

I said that I was a spaceship pilot, not a porter. She said that as long as I was on the payroll of her Church I was obliged to do as she required. I wasn't sure of the legality of it all but . . . After all, I had to live with the woman. Anything-for-a-quiet-life Grimes, that's me. I did, however, insist that I dress more suitably for the expedition than in what I was wearing at the time—long trousers, shirt, necktie, and uniform jacket. I went into the shower cubicle with a change of clothing and emerged in short-sleeved, open-necked shirt, kilt, and sandals. She glared at me.

"Are you going native, Captain?"

"No, Your Reverence. I have changed into suitable shore-going civilian rig."

"You are not to accompany *me* dressed like that."

"Then hump your own bluey," I told her.

She didn't know what I meant, of course, so I had to translate from Australian into Standard English.

"Then carry your own bag," I said.

She didn't like it but realized that if we wasted any more time in argument we should be late for the noon service. She swept out of the ship with me, her beast of burden, plodding behind. It was too hot a day to be encumbered with a heavy backpack but, at least, I was less uncomfortable than I should have been in formal uniform.

In other circumstances I should have enjoyed the walk—that springy, almost-grass underfoot, the tuneful stridulations of what I assumed to be the local version of insects, occasional colorful flights of what I assumed to be birds but later discovered to be small, gaudy, flying mammals.

But I was unable to loiter. Her Reverence set the pace, and a spanking one it was. That woman, I thought, must have ice water in her veins, to be able to stride along like that while wearing all that heavy, body-muffling clothing. We came to the boundary of the field, to a dirt road, to the beginnings of the houses. There were people abroad, coming out of the low buildings, setting off in the same direction as the one that we were taking. There were men and women and children. They looked at us curiously—as well they might!—but not in an unmannerly fashion. They were dressed—undressed—for the climate. Her Reverence was suitably attired for a midwinter stroll over a polar icecap.

We came to the central square. It was paved with marble slabs but, breaking the expanse of gleaming stone, were beds of flowering bushes and fountains in the spray of which the sun was making rainbows. In the middle of the square was a tall obelisk, surrounded by concentric rings of gleaming metal—brass? gold?—set in the marble. Hard by this was a tripod made of some black metal from which was suspended a huge brass gong. A tall, heavily muscled man—I'll call him a man, at any nude resort on Earth or any Terran colony world the only glances that he would have attracted would have been admiration—naked apart from his ornaments of gold and jewels, was standing by the tripod, holding, as though it were a ceremonial spear, a long-handled striker with leather-padded head. A woman—and she was truly beautiful—was sitting cross-legged, all her attention on the slow, almost imperceptible shortening of the shadow cast by the obelisk.

She turned to the man by the gong, uttered one short word. His muscles flexed as he raised the striker, brought the head of it, with a powerful sweeping motion, into contact with the surface, radiant with reflected sunlight, of the great brass disc.

A single booming note rolled out and the people, from streets and alleys, came flooding into the plaza. They were marching rather than merely walking, dancing rather than marching, and the clashing of their glittering cymbals was not without an odd, compelling rhythm. They were unclothed (of course), all of them—the men, the women, and the children—although bright metal and jewels glowed on glowing, naked flesh. They formed up into groups, all of them facing inwards, towards the central obelisk. The . . . the timekeeper was standing now, arms upraised above her head. She was singing, in a high, sweet voice. It was not the sort of noise that normally I should have classed as music, the tonality was not one that I was accustomed to, the rhythms too subtle, but here, in these circumstances, it was . . . right. The man at the gong was accompanying her, stroking the metal surface with the head of his striker, producing a deep murmuring sound. And all the people were singing.

I didn't need to understand the words to know that it was a hymn of praise.

"What are you *standing* there for?" demanded the she-bishop.

"What else should I do?" I countered.

She snarled wordlessly, literally tore the backpack from my shoulders. She opened it, spilled the drab heap of secondhand clothing onto the marble paving. Close by us were children, about twenty in this group, who, until now, had been ignoring us. Her Reverence snatched up a rust black dress, forced it down over the body of a struggling, bewildered little girl. "Can't you help?" she snarled at me. By the time that she got her second victim clothed, the first one was naked again and running to the timekeeper, the priestess, bawling with fright and bewilderment.

Things started to happen then.

I was unarmed, of course, with not so much as a stungun on low power. Contrary to so many space stories the toting of firearms by spacemen, merchant spacemen especially, on other people's planets is not encouraged. It didn't take long for two hefty wenches to immobilize me, one on each side of me, both of them holding me tightly. I could do nothing but watch as four men seized Agatha, threw her down to the paving and, despite her frenzied struggles, stripped her. A knife gleamed and I yelled wordlessly— but it was being used as a tool, not a weapon, to slice through cloth and not through skin. Her long body, revealed as the last of underwear was slashed away, was disgustingly pallid. It needn't have been. She could have made use of the UV lamps every time that she had a shower during the passage out, as I had done. She was pallid and she was flabby, physically (at least) far inferior to those who were punishing her for her act of . . . sacrilege. Yes. Sacrilege. They held her there, in the blazing noonday sunlight, while the rags of her clothing were gathered up, and those other rags, those donations of used clothing with which she had tried to clothe the happily naked.

There was that pile of drab, tattered cloth and there was that big lens, a great burning glass, that was brought to bear upon the rubbish, concentrating upon it the purifying rays of the sun. There was the acrid smoke, and then the first red glimmer of smolder, and then flames, almost invisible in the strong sunlight.

And all the time Agatha was writhing and screaming, calling out not in Standard English but in the Stagathan language that she had learned. What she was saying I did not know, but it sounded like (and probably was) curses.

The bonfire died down.

A man whom I recognized as the leader of the party that had come out to the ship strode up to me. His face was grave.

"Captain," he said, "take this woman from here. She has insulted our God."

I said lamely, "She means well."

He said, "The path of the Mountain We Do Not Name is paved with good intentions."

My two captors released me.

The four men holding Agatha Lewis's wrists and ankles let go of her. She stumbled to her feet and stood there in that classic pose, one arm shielding her breasts, the other hand over her pudenda. With a younger, more shapely woman the attitude would have been prettily appealing; with her it was merely ludicrous. Her face was scarlet with humiliation. But it wasn't only her face. And it wasn't only humiliation. It was sunburn.

Kitty said, "When you mentioned the gleam of a knife I thought that you were going to tell us that Bishop Agatha suffered the same sort of martyrdom as Saint Agatha. Her breasts were cut off."

Grimes said, "I know. I did some checking up. There was so much odd parallelism about the whole business. But my Agatha suffered no worse than severely frizzled nipples. Very painful, I believe. I lent her my shirt for the walk back to the ship but, by that time, it was too late."

So we got ourselves back to the ship (he continued) with Her Reverence in a state of shock. It had all been such a blow to her pride, her prudery, her own kind of piety. The pyschological effects were more severe than the physical ones, painful as those most obviously were. And she had to let me apply the soothing lotions to her body. Oh, she *hated* me.

Once she was muffled up in a robe, wincing as every slightest motion brought the fabric into contact with her inflamed breasts, I said, "It is obvious, Your Reverence, that you are not welcome here. I suggest that we get off the planet."

She said, "We shall do no such thing."

She wanted her bunk set up then and the privacy screen put in position. I busied myself with various small tasks about the ship, trying not to make too much noise. But I needn't have bothered. I could hear her; the partition was not soundproof. First of all she was sobbing, and then she was praying. It was all very embarrassing, far more so than her nudity had been.

Late in the afternoon she came out. As well as a long, black robe, she was wearing her wide-brimmed hat and almost opaque dark glasses. She walked slowly to the airlock and then out onto the grassy ground. I followed her. She stood there, staring at the westering sun. Her expression frightened me. Rarely have I seen such naked hate on anybody's face.

"Your Reverence," I said, "I am still of the opinion that we should leave this world."

"Are you, an Earthman, frightened of a bunch of naked savages?" she sneered.

"Naked, perhaps," I said, "but not savages." I pointed almost directly upwards to where one of the big solar-powered airships, on its regular cargo and passenger run, was sailing overhead. "Savages could never have made a thing like that."

"Savagery and technology," she said, "can co-exist. As *you* should know."

"But these people are not savages," I insisted.

"You dare to say that, Captain Grimes, after you witnessed what they did to *me*, the messenger of God."

"Of *your* God. And, anyhow, you asked for it."

Even from behind her dark glasses her eyes were like twin lasers aimed at me.

"Enough," she said coldly. "I would remind you, Captain Grimes, that you are still my servant and, through me, of the Almighty. Please prepare to lift ship."

"Then you are taking my advice?"

"Of course not. We shall proceed forthwith to the Mountain That Is Not Named."

Oh, well, if she wanted to do some sight-seeing, I did not object. Tourism would get us into far less trouble (I thought) than attempting to interfere with perfectly innocent and rather beautiful religious rituals. Quite happily I went back into the ship, straight to the control cab, and started to do my sums or, to be more exact, told the pilot-computer to do my sums for me. *Little Sister*, although a deep-space ship in miniature, was also a pinnace quite capable of flights, short or long, within a planetary atmosphere. *She* joined me as I was studying the readouts, looking at the chart and the extrapolation of the Great Circle course.

"Well," she asked.

"If we lift now we can be at Nameless Mountain by sunrise tomorrow, without busting a gut."

"There is no need to be vulgar, Captain. But sunrise will be a good time. It will coincide with *their* dawn service."

I didn't bother to try to explain to her the concept of longitudinal time differences and, in any case, possibly some town or city was on the same meridian as the volcano—but then, of course, there would be other factors, such as latitude and the sun's declination, to be considered. So I just agreed with her. And then, with the ship buttoned up, I got upstairs.

It was an uneventful flight. I had the controls on full automatic so there was no need for me to stay in the cab. Too, according to the information at my disposal, there was very little (if any) traffic in Stagatha's night skies. The sun ruled their lives.

We were both of us back in the control cab as we approached the volcano. She was looking disapprovingly at the mug of coffee from which I was sipping. I hoped sardonically that she had enjoyed the glass of water with which she had started her day. Outside the ship it was getting light, although not as light as it should have been at this hour. We were flying through dense smoke and steam, with visibility less than a couple of meters in any direction. Not that I had any worries. The three-dimensional radar screen was showing a clear picture of what was below, what was ahead. It was not a pretty picture but one not devoid of a certain horrid beauty. Towering, contorted rock pinnacles, evilly bubbling lava pools, spouting mud geysers. . . . The ship, still on automatic, swerved to steer around one of these that was hurling great rocks into the air. . . .

I said, "We're here."

She said, "We have yet to reach the main crater rim."

"The main crater rim?" I repeated.

"You're not afraid, Captain, are you? Didn't you tell me that this ship of yours can take anything that anybody cares to throw at her?"

"But . . . An active volcano . . . One that seems to be on the verge of blowing its top in a major eruption. . . ."

"Are you a vulcanologist, Captain?"

So we stood on, feeling our way through the murk. There was more than volcanic activity among the special effects. Lightning writhed around us, a torrent—flowing upwards or downwards?—of ghastly violet radiance that would have been blinding had it not been for the automatic polarization of the viewports. And ahead was sullen, ruddy glare . . . No, not *glare*. It was more like a negation of light than normal luminosity. It was the Ultimate Darkness made visible.

Little Sister maintained a steady course despite the buffeting that she must be getting. And then she was in clear air, the eye of the storm as it were. We could see things visually instead of having to rely upon the radar screens. We were over the vast crater, the lake of dull, liquid fire, the semi-solid, dark glowing crust through cracks in which glared white incandescence. In the center of this lake was a sort of island, a black, truncated cone.

"Set us down there," *she* said.

"Not bloody likely," I said.

"Set us down there."

She was standing now and her hand was on my shoulder, gripping it painfully. And . . . And . . . How can I describe it? It was as though some power were flowing from her to me, through me. I fought it. I tried to fight it. And then I tried to rationalize. After all, the metal of which *Little Sister* was built, an isotope of gold, was virtually guaranteed to be proof against *anything*. If anything should happen to her I could go to her builders on Electra and demand my money back. (Not that my money had paid for her in the first place.) Joke.

I had the ship back on manual control. I made a slow approach to the central island, hovered above it. I had been expecting trouble, difficulty in holding the ship where I wanted her, but it was easy. Too easy. Suspiciously easy.

I let her fall, slowly, slowly, the inertial drive just ticking over. I felt the faint jar, a very faint jar, as she landed on the flat top, the perfectly smooth top of the truncated cone.

She said, "Open the airlock doors."

I tried to protest but the words wouldn't come.

She said, "Open the airlock doors."

I thought, *And so we fill the ship with stinking, sulfurous gases. But the internal atmosphere can soon be purified.*

On the console before me I saw the glowing words as I actuated the switch. INNER DOOR OPEN. OUTER DOOR OPEN.

She was gone from behind me, back into the main cabin. I got up from my chair, followed her. She was going outside, I realized. She should have asked me for a spacesuit; it would have given her some protection against the heat, against an almost certainly poisonous atmosphere. Some of this was already getting inside the ship, an acridity that made my eyes water, made me sneeze. But it didn't seem to be worrying her.

She passed through both doors.

I stood in the little chamber, watching her. She was standing on the heat-smoothed rock, near, too near to the edge of the little plateau. Was the silly bitch going to commit spectacular and painful suicide? But I was reluctant to leave the security—the illusory security?—of my ship to attempt to drag her to safety. No, it wasn't cowardice. Not altogether. I just *knew* that she knew what she was doing.

(If I'd known more I should have been justified in going out to give her a push!)

She stood there, very straight and tall, in black silhouette against the dull glow from the lake of fire. Her form wavered, became indistinct as a dark column of smoke eddied about her. Still she stood there while the smoke thinned, vanished. It was as though it had been absorbed by her body.

But that was impossible, wasn't it?

She walked back to the airlock. The skin of her face seemed to be much darker than it had been—but that was not surprising. It seemed to me—but that must have been imagination—that her feet did not touch the surface over which she was walking.

She said as she approached me, "Take me back to the city."

I obeyed. No matter what her order had been, no matter how absurd or dangerous, I should have obeyed. When first I had met her I had been conscious of her charisma but had learned to live with it, to distrust it and to despise it. Now neither distrust nor contempt would have been possible.

We got upstairs.

No sooner were we on course than the volcano blew up. The blast of it hit us like a blow from something solid. I wasn't able to watch as I was too busy trying to keep the ship under some sort of control as she plunged through the fiery turbulence, through the smoke and the steam and the fiery pulverized dust, through the down-stabbing and up-thrusting lightning bolts.

And, through it all, *she* was laughing.

It was the first time that I had heard her laugh.

It was an experience that I could well have done without.

"I need some more beer," he said, "to wash the taste of that volcanic dust out of my throat. After all the years I still remember it."

She refilled his mug, and then her own.

"Did the dust get inside your ship?" she asked.

"It got everywhere," he told her. "All over the entire bloody planet."

We set down in that same field where we had made our first landing. According to the chronometer it wanted only an hour to local, apparent noon, but the sky was overcast. The air was chilly. *She* ordered me to open one of her trunks. In it was a further supply of the cast-off clothing that she had brought from Warrenhome. And there were books. Bibles, I assumed, or the perversion of Holy Writ adopted by *Her* church. I opened one but was unable, of course, to read the odd, flowing Stagathan characters.

I filled a backpack with the clothing. While I was so doing she took something else from the trunk. It was a whip; haft and tapering lash were all of three meters long. It was an evil-looking thing.

We left the ship. She took the lead. I trudged behind. As she passed one of the flowering bushes, its blossoms drab in the dismal gray light, she slashed out with the whip, cracking it expertly, severing stems and twigs, sending tattered petals fluttering to the ground.

We walked into the city.

We came to the central square, with the obelisk (but it was casting no shadow), the great gong (but it was now no more than an ugly disk of dull, pitted metal), the celebrants and the worshippers.

But there was nothing for them to worship. The sky was one, uniform gray with not so much as a diffuse indication of the position of the sun. The people were all, as they had been at that other service, naked but now their nudity was . . . ugly. A thin drizzle was starting to fall, but it was mud rather than ordinary rain, streaking the shivering skins of the miserable people.

The priest standing by the gong, the man with the striker, was the first to see us. He pointed at us, shouting angrily. He advanced towards us, still shouting, menacing us with his hammer. Behind him others were now shouting, and screaming. They were blaming us for the dense cloud that had hidden their god from sight.

She stood her ground.

Suddenly her lash snaked out, whipped itself around the striker and tore it from the priest's hands, sent it clattering to the mud-slimed marble paving. It cracked out again, the tip of it slashing across the man's face, across his eyes. He screamed, and that merciless whip played over his body, drawing blood with every stroke.

And *She* was declaiming in a strong, resonant voice, with one foot planted firmly upon the squirming body of the hapless, blinded priest, who had fallen to the ground, laying about her with the whip.

Even then, at the cost of a few injuries, they could have overpowered her, have taken her from behind. But the heart was gone from them. Their god had forsaken them. And *She* . . . *She* was speaking with the voice of a god. Or was a god speaking through her? She was possessed. The black charisma of her was overpowering. I opened the backpack and began to distribute the cast-off clothing. Hands—the hands of men, women, and children—snatched the drab rags from me eagerly. And there was something odd about it. It seemed as though that backpack were a bottomless bag. It could never have held sufficient clothing to cover the nakedness of a crowd of several thousand people. Some time later, of course, I worked things out. Converts must have gone back into their homes for the ceremonial black robes that they doffed at the dawn service and resumed at sunset. But, even so . . . How could those robes have assumed the appearance of, say, ill-cut, baggy trousers? Imagination, it must have been. Even though I could not understand what she was saying, I was under the spell of Her voice.

And it frightened me.

I felt my agnosticism wavering.

And I *like* being an agnostic.

Oh, well, at a time of crisis there is always one thing better than presence of mind—and that is absence of body.

I left her preaching to the multitude and walked back to the ship. I did worse than that. When I was back on board I collected everything of hers, every last thing, and lugged it out through the airlock on to a plastic sheet that I spread on the wet grass, covered it with another sheet.

And then I lifted off.

After all, I had done what I had contracted to do. I had carried her from Warrenhome to Stagatha (and the money for her fare had been deposited in my bank). I had stayed around until she had become established as a missionary. (Well, she had, hadn't she?)

I broke through that filthy overcast into bright sunlight. I began to feel less unhappy. I looked down at Stagatha. The entire planet, from pole to pole, was shrouded with smoke, or steam, or dust or—although this was unlikely—just ordinary cloud.

I wondered when their god would next show himself to the Stagath-ans and set course for Pengram, the nearest Man-colonized planet, where I hoped to be able to find further employment for *Little Sister* and myself.

"I don't think much of your Odd Gods," said Kitty Kelly. "After all, sun-worship is common enough. And so are evangelists of either sex who preach peculiar perversions of Christianity and are charismatic enough to make converts. But I would have expected you to behave more responsibly. To go flying off, the way you did, leaving that poor woman to her fate...."

"Poor woman? I was there, Kitty. You weren't. Too, I haven't finished yet."

I'd almost forgotten about Stagatha (he went on) when, some standard years later, I ran into Commander Blivens, captain of the survey ship *Cartographer.* I'd known Blivens slightly when I was in the Survey Service myself. Anyhow, I was at Port Royal, on Caribbea, owner-master of *Sister Sue*, which vessel had started her life as one of the Interstellar Transport Commission's Epsilon Class star tramps, *Epsilon Scorpii.* (She finally finished up as the Rim Worlds Confederacy's survey ship *Faraway Quest.* Yes, this very ship that we're aboard now.) But to get back to Blivens . . . I was in the Trade Winds Bar with my chief officer, Billy Williams, quietly absorbing planter's punches when I heard somebody call my name. I couldn't place him at first but finally did so.

Then, for a while, it was the usual sort of conversation for those circumstances. What happened to old so-and-so? Did you hear that thingummy actually made rear admiral? And so on.

I got around to asking Blivens what he was doing on Carribea.

"Just a spell of rest and recreation for my boys and girls," he told me. "And for myself. At one time I used to regard a rather odd but very human world called Stagatha as my R & R planet. The people as near human as makes no difference. Sun worshippers they were, *happy* sun worshippers. Unpolluted atmosphere, solar power used for everything. And not, like this overpriced dump, commercialized.

"But it's ruined now."

"How so?" I asked him.

"They've changed their religion. Some high-powered female missionary decided to save their souls. I suppose that some money-hungry tramp skipper carried her from her own planet, Warrenhome, to Stagatha. Somebody should find out who the bastard was and shoot him. And then, really to put the tin hat on things, there was a catastrophic volcanic eruption which threw the gods alone know how many tons of dust into the upper atmosphere and completely buggered the climate. So there was a switch from solar power to the not-very-efficient burning of fossil fuels—and still more airborne muck to obscure the sunlight.

"The missionary—the Lady Bishop, she called herself—called aboard to see me. She scared me, I don't mind admitting it. You'll never guess what her staff of office was. A dirty great whip. She demanded that I release one of my engineer officers to her service. The odd part was that she knew his name—Terry Gowan—and all about him. And Mr. Gowan seemed to know of her. It made sense, I suppose. He was one of those morose, Bible-bashing bastards himself. And, apart from the Bible in some odd version, his only reading was books on the engineering techniques in use during the Victorian era on Earth. He used to make models, working models, of steam engines and things like that.

"I gave him his discharge—which, as a Survey Service captain, I was entitled to do. You know the regulation. *Should a properly constituted planetary authority request the services of a specialist officer, petty officer or rating for any period, and provided that such officer, petty officer or rating signifies his or her willingness to enter the service of such planetary authority, and provided that the safe management of the ship not be affected by the discharge of one of her personnel with no replacement immediately available, then the commanding officer shall release such officer, petty officer or rating, paying him or her all monies due and with the understanding that seniority shall continue to accrue until the return of the officer, petty officer or rating to the Survey Service.*

"Anyhow, I don't think that anybody aboard *Cartographer* shed a tear for Gloomy Gowan, as he was known, when he was paid off. And he, I suppose, has been happy erecting dark, satanic mills all over the landscape for Her Holiness."

"And so everybody was happy," I said sarcastically.

"A bloody good planet ruined," grumbled Blivens.

A few more years went by.

Again I ran into Blivens—Captain Blivens now—quite by chance. He was now commanding officer of the Survey Service base on New Colorado and I had been chartered by the Service—they often threw odd jobs my way—to bring in a shipment of fancy foodstuffs and tipples for the various messes.

I dined with Blivens in his quite palatial quarters.

He said, towards the end of the meal, "You remember when I last met you, Grimes . . . I was captain of *Cartographer* then and we were talking about Stagatha. . . ."

"I remember," I said.

"Well, I went there again. For the last time. Just one of those checking-up-showing-the-flag voyages that I had to make. But there wasn't any Stagatha. Not any more. The sun had gone nova. And as there hadn't been a Carlotti station on the planet no word had gotten out. . . ."

The news shocked me.

All those people, incinerated.

And I couldn't help feeling that I was somehow responsible.

But it was just a coincidence.

Wasn't it?

"Of course it was," said Kitty Kelly brightly.

"Was it?" whispered Grimes. And then: "For I am a jealous God. . . ."

GRIMES AND THE JAILBIRDS

"Have you ever, in the course of your long and distinguished career, been in jail, Commodore?" asked Kitty Kelly after she had adjusted the lenses and microphones of her recording equipment to her satisfaction.

"As a matter of fact I have," said Grimes. He made a major production of filling and lighting his pipe. "It was quite a few years ago, but I still remember the occasion vividly. It's not among my more pleasant memories. . . ."

"I should imagine not," she concurred sympathetically. "What were you in for? Piracy? Smuggling? Gun-running?"

"I wasn't *in* in the sense that you assume," he told her. "After all, there are more people in a jail than the convicts. The governor, the warders, the innocent bystanders. . . ."

"Such as yourself?"

"Such as myself."

It was (he said) when I was owner-master of *Little Sister*. She was the flagship and the only ship of Far Traveler Couriers, the business title under which I operated. She was a deep-space pinnace, and I ran her single-handed, carrying small parcels of special cargo hither and yon, the occasional passenger. Oh, it was a living of sorts, quite a good living at times, although, at other times, my bank balance would be at a perilously low ebb.

Well, I'd carried a consignment of express mail from Davinia to Helmskirk—none of the major lines had anything making a direct run between the two planets—and I was now berthed at Port Helms waiting for something to turn up. The worst of it all was that Helmskirk is not the sort of world upon which to spend an enforced vacation—or, come to that, any sort of vacation. There is a distinct shortage of bright lights. The first settlers had all been members of a wowserish religious sect misnamed the Children of Light—it was founded on Earth in the late twentieth century, Old Reckoning. Over the years their descendants had become more and more wowserish.

The manufacture, vending, and consumption of alcoholic beverages were strictly prohibited. So was smoking—and by "smoking" I mean smoking *anything*. There were laws regulating the standards of dress— and not only in the streets of the cities and towns. Can you imagine a public bathing beach where people of both sexes—even children—are compelled to wear neck-to-ankle, skirted swimming costumes?

There were theaters, showing both live and recorded entertainment, but the plays presented were all of the improving variety, with virtue triumphant and vice defeated at the end of the last act. I admit that some of the clumsily contrived situations were quite funny, although not intentionally so. I found this out when I laughed as a stern father turned his frail, blonde daughter, who had been discovered smoking a smuggled cigarette, out into a raging snowstorm. Immediately after my outbreak of unseemly mirth, I was turned out myself, by two burly ushers. Oh, well, it wasn't snowing, and it was almost the end of the play, anyhow.

It wouldn't have been so bad if the local customs authorities had not done their best to make sure that visiting spacemen conformed to Helmskirkian standards whilst on the surface of their planet. They inspected my library of playmaster cassettes and seized anything that could be classed as pornographic—much of it the sort of entertainment that your maiden aunt, on most worlds, could watch without a blush. These tapes, they told me, would be kept under bond in the customs warehouse and returned to me just prior to my final lift-off from the Helmskirk System. They impounded the contents of my grog locker and even all my pipe tobacco. Fortunately, I can, when pushed to it, make an autochef do things never intended by its manufacturer, and so it didn't take me long to replenish my stock of gin. And lettuce leaves from my hydroponics minifarm, dried and suitably treated, made a not-too-bad tobacco substitute.

Nonetheless, I'd have gotten the hell off Helmskirk as soon as the bags of express mail had been discharged if I'd had any definite place to go. But when you're tramping around, as I was, you put your affairs into the hands of an agent and wait hopefully for news of an advantageous charter.

So Messrs. Muggeridge, Whitelaw, and Nile were supposed to be keeping their ears to the ground on my behalf, and I was getting more and more bored, and every day doing my sums—or having the ship's computer do them for me—and trying to work out how long it would be before the profit made on my last voyage was completely eaten up by port charges and the like. For the lack of better entertainment I haunted the Port Helms municipal library—at least it was free—and embarked on a study course on the history of this dreary colony. Someday I shall write a book—*The Galactic Guide to Places to Stay Away From.* . . .

The fiction in the library was not of the variety that is written to inflame the passions. It was all what, during the Victorian era on Earth, would have been called "improving." The factual works were of far greater interest. From them I learned that the incidence of crime—*real* crime, not such petty offenses as trying to grow your own tobacco or brew your own beer—on Helmskirk was surprisingly high. Cork a bottle of some fermenting mixture—and any human society is such a mixture— too tightly and the pressures will build up. There was an alarmingly high incidence of violent crime—armed robbery, assault, rape, murder.

I began to appreciate the necessity for Helmskirk's penal satellite, a smallish natural moon in a just under twenty-four-hour orbit about its primary. Not only was it a place of correction and/or punishment for the really bad bastards, but it also housed a large population of people who'd been caught playing cards for money, reading banned books, and similar heinous offenses. If I'd been so unfortunate as to have been born on Helmskirk, I thought, almost certainly I should have been acquainted with the maze of caverns and tunnels, artificial and natural, that honeycombed the ball of rock.

As the days wore on I'd settled into a regular routine. The morning I'd devote to minor maintenance jobs. Then I'd have lunch. Before leaving the ship after this meal, I'd make a telephone call to my agents to see if they'd anything for me. Then I'd stroll ashore to the library. It was a dreary walk through streets of drably functional buildings, but it was exercise. I'd try to keep myself amused until late afternoon, and then drop briefly into the agents' office on the way back to *Little Sister.*

Then the routine was disrupted.

As I entered the premises, old Mr. Muggeridge looked up accusingly from his desk, saying, "We've been trying to get hold of you, Captain."

I said, "I wasn't far away. I was in the municipal library."

"Hmph. I never took you for a studious type. Well, anyway, I've a time charter for you. A matter of six local weeks, minimum."

"Where to?" I asked hopefully.

"It will not be taking you outside the Helmskirk System," he told me rather spitefully. "The prison tender, the *Jerry Falwell*, has broken down. I am not acquainted with all the technical details, but I understand that the trouble is with its inertial drive unit. The authorities have offered you employment until such time as the tender is back in operation."

I went through the charter party carefully, looking for any clauses that might be turned to my disadvantage. But Muggeridge, Whitelaw, and Nile had been looking after my interests. After all, why shouldn't they? The more I got, the more their rake-off would be.

So I signed in the places indicated and learned that I was to load various items of stores for the prison the following morning, lifting off as soon as these were on board and stowed to my satisfaction. Oh, well, it was a job and would keep me solvent until something better turned up.

It was a job, but it wasn't one that I much cared for. I classed it as being on a regular run from nowhere to nowhere. The atmosphere of Helmskirk I had found oppressive; that of the penal satellite was even more so. The voyage out took a little over two days, during which time I should have been able to enjoy my favorite playmaster cassettes if the customs officers had seen fit to release them. But rules were rules, and I was not leaving the Helmskirk System. And the moon, which was called Sheol, was very much part of it.

On my first visit I did not endear myself to the prison governor. I'd jockeyed *Little Sister* into a large air lock set into the satellite's surface and then left my control room for the main cabin. I opened the air lock doors and then sat down to await whatever boarders there would be—somebody with the inevitable papers to sign, a working party to discharge my cargo, and so on and so forth. I was not expecting the ruler of this tiny world to pay a call in person.

He strode into the ship, a tall man in dark gray civilian clothes, long-nosed, sour-featured, followed by an entourage of black-uniformed warders. "Come in, come in!" I called. "This is Liberty Hall. You can spit on the mat and call the cat a bastard!"

He said, "I do not see any cat. Where is the animal? The importation of any livestock into Sheol is strictly contrary to regulations."

I said, "It was only a figure of speech."

"And a remarkably foul-mouthed one." He sat down uninvited. "I am the governor of this colony, Mr. Grimes. During each of your visits here you will observe the regulations, a copy of which will be provided you. You will be allowed, should time permit, to make the occasional conducted tour of Sheol so that you may become aware of the superiority of our penal system to that on other worlds. There will, however, be no fraternization between yourself and any of our inmates. There will be no attempt by you to smuggle in any small luxuries. One of the officers of the *Jerry Falwell* made such an attempt some months back. He is now among our . . . guests, serving a long sentence."

"What did he try to smuggle in?" I asked.

"It is none of your business, Mr. Grimes. But I will tell you. It was cigarettes that he had illegally obtained from a visiting star tramp. And I will tell you what he hoped to receive in exchange. Mood opals. And the penalty for smuggling out mood opals is even greater than that for smuggling in cigarettes."

"What are mood opals?" asked Kitty.

"Don't you know? They were, for a while, very popular and very expensive precious stones on Earth and other planets, especially the Shaara worlds. The Shaara loved them. They weren't opals, although they looked rather like them. But they were much fiercer, and the colors shifted, according, it was said, to the mood of the wearer, although probably it was due to no more than changes in temperature and atmospheric humidity. They were found only on—or in, rather—Sheol. They were actually coprolites, fossilized excrement, all that remained of some weird, rock-eating creatures that inhabited Sheol and became extinct ages before the colonization of Helmskirk. The mood opals became one of Helmskirk's major moneymaking exports. They were never worn by anybody on Helmskirk itself, such frivolity as personal jewelry being illegal."

"How come," asked Kitty, "that we've never seen mood opals here? Most Terran fads drift out to this part of the Galaxy eventually."

"There aren't any mood opals anymore," Grimes told her. "It seems that the polishing process, which removed the outer crust, exposed the jewels to the atmosphere and to radiation of all kinds. After a few years of such exposure, the once-precious stones would crumble into worthless dust."

Well (he went on), that was my first visit to Sheol. Naturally it sparked my interest in the mood opal trade. I suggested to my agents that they try to organize for me the shipment of the next parcel of precious stones to wherever it was they were going. But the Interstellar Transport Commission had that trade tied up. Every six months one of their *Epsilon*-class freighters would make a very slight deviation during her voyage from Waverly to Earth, and it was on Earth—in Australia, in fact—where the opal polishers plied their trade. I pointed out that it was only a short hop, relatively speaking, from Helmskirk to Baroom, the nearest Shaara colony world, Surely, I said, the Shaara could polish their own mood opals. But it was no-go. They always had been polished in some place called Coober Peedy, and they always would be polished in Coober Peedy, and that was that.

Meanwhile, I made friends among the warders on Sheol. Some of them were almost human. Their close association with the quote, crimi-

nal, unquote classes had rubbed off much of the arrogant sanctimonious-
ness so prevalent on the primary. There was one—Don Smith was his
name—whom I even trusted with one of my guilty secrets. He would
share morning coffee, generously spiked with the rum that I had persuaded the autochef to produce, with me. When there was any delay
between the discharge of the cargo I had brought and the loading of the
mood opals that I should be taking back, he would take me on conducted
tours of the prison.

There were the hydroponic farms, where most of the workers were
women, some of them, despite their hideous zebra-striped coveralls, quite
attractive. Some of them, and not only the attractive ones, would waggle
their hips suggestively and coo, "Hello, spaceman! I'll do it for a cigarette!" And Don would grin and say, "They would, you know. I can
arrange it for you." But I refused the offer. I didn't trust him all that much.
Besides, my stock of cigarettes—which I kept aboard only for hospitality
and not for my own use—had been impounded by the blasted customs.

There were the workshops, where convict labor, all men, assembled
machines at whose purpose I could do no more than guess; I haven't a
mechanical mind. There was the printery and there was the bookbindery.
I was invited to help myself from the stacks of new books, but I did not
take advantage of the offer. Collections of sermons of the hellfire-and-
damnation kind are not my idea of light reading to while away a voyage.
There was the tailor's shop, where both warders' uniforms and convicts'
uniforms were made. There were the kitchens and there were the mess-
rooms. (The prison officers' food was plain but wholesome; that for the
convicts, just plain, definitely so.) There were the tunnels in which the
mood-opal miners worked. It was in one of these that I was accosted by a
man with dirt-streaked face and sweat- and dust-stained coveralls.

"Hey, Skipper!" he called. "How about my hitching a ride in your
space buggy away from here? I can make it worth your while!"

I stared at him. I didn't like the cut of his jib. Under the dirt that partially obscured his features was a hard viciousness. He had the kind of
very light and bright blue eyes that are often referred to as "mad." He
looked as though he'd be quite willing to use the small pickax he was
holding on a human being rather than on a rock.

I decided to ignore him.

"Stuck-up bastard aren't you, Skipper. Like all your breed. You deep-
spacers think yourselves too high and mighty to talk to orbital boys!"

"That will do, Wallace!" said Don sharply.

"Who's talking? You're not in charge of this work party."

"But *I* am." Another warder had come up. He was holding one of the modified stun guns that were the main weaponry of the guards; on the right setting (or the wrong setting, if you were on the receiving end) they could deliver a most painful shock. "Get back to work, Wallace. You're nowhere near your quota for the shift—and you know what *that* means!"

Apparently Wallace did and he moved away. Don and I moved on.

"A nasty piece of work," I said.

"He is that," agreed Don, "even though he is a spaceman like yourself."

"Not too like me, I hope."

"All right. Not *too* like you. He got as high as mate of the *Jerry Falwell*, and then he was caught smuggling cigarettes and booze in and mood opals out. If only the bloody fool had done his dealing with the right people and not with the convicts! I suppose that it's poetic justice that he's serving his time here as an opal miner."

I supposed that it was.

And then we wandered back to *Little Sister*, where, after half an hour or so, I loaded two small bags of mood opals—in their rough state they looked like mummified dog-droppings—and embarked a couple of prison officers who were returning to the primary for a spell of leave. Although they were (a) female and (b) not unattractive, they were not very good company for the voyage.

My next trip back from Sheol to Helmskirk I had company again. Unexpected company. For some reason I decided to check the stowage in the cargo compartment; there was a nagging feeling that everything was not as it should be. This time there were no mood opals, but there were half a dozen bales of clothing, civilian work coveralls, that had been manufactured in the prison's tailor's shop. At first glance nothing seemed amiss. And then I saw a pool of moisture slowly spreading on the deck from the underside of one of the bales. Aboard a ship, any kind of ship, leaking pipes can be dangerous. But there were no pipes running through and under the deck of the compartment; such as there were were all in plain view on the bulkheads, and all of them were intact.

Almost I dipped my finger into the seepage to bring it back to my mouth to taste it. Almost. I was glad that I hadn't done so. I smelled the faint but unmistakable acridity of human urine.

I went back to the main cabin, to my arms locker, and got out a stun gun and stuck it into my belt. And then, very cautiously, I unsnapped the fasteners of the metal straps holding the bale together. The outer layers of folded clothing fell to the deck. I stepped back and drew my stun gun and told whoever it was inside the bale, in as stern a voice as I could muster, to come out. More layers of clothing fell away, revealing a sort of cage of heavy wire in which crouched a young woman. She straightened up and stepped out of the cage, looking at me with an odd mixture of shame and defiance.

She said, "I shouldn't have had that last drink of water, but I thought that I should half die of thirst if I didn't. . . ." She looked down at the sodden legs of her civilian coveralls and managed an embarrassed grin. "And now I suppose, Captain," that you'll be putting back to Sheol and handing me over."

I said, "I can hand you over just as well at Port Helms."

She shrugged. "As you please. In that case, could I ask a favor? The use of your shower facilities and the loan of a robe to wear while my clothes are drying . . . I have to wash them, you know."

I thought, *You're a cool customer*. And I thought, *I rather like you*.

Despite her ugly and now sadly bedraggled attire, she was an attractive wench: blonde, blue-eyed, and with a wide mouth under a nose that was just retroussé enough, just enough, no more. She had found some way to tint her lips an enticing scarlet. (The women convicts, I had already learned, used all sorts of dyes for this purpose, although cosmetics were banned.) And I remembered, too, all the fuss there'd been about taking showers and such, all the simpering prudery, when I had carried those two women prison officers.

So I let her use my shower and hang her clothes in my drying room, and lent her my best Corlabian spider silk bathrobe, and asked her what she would like for dinner. She said that she would like a drink first and that she would leave the ordering of the meal to me.

It was good to be having dinner with a pretty girl, especially one who was enjoying her food as much as she was. The autochef did us proud, from soup—mulligatawny, as I remember—to pecan pie. The wines could have been better; an autochef properly programmed can make quite a good job of beer or almost any of the potable spirits, but as far as, say, claret is concerned, is capable of producing only a mildy alcoholic red ink. Not that it really mattered on this occasion. Everything that I gave my guest to eat and drink was immeasurably superior to the prison food—and, come to that, streets ahead of anything that could have been obtained in any restaurant on Helmskirk.

After the meal we relaxed. I filled and lit my pipe. She watched me enviously. I let her have one of my spare pipes. She filled it with my shredded, dried, and treated lettuce leaf tobacco substitute. She lit it, took one puff, and decided that it was better than nothing, but only just.

"Thank you, Captain," she said. "This has been a real treat. The drinks, the meal, your company. . . ." She smiled. "And I think that you've been enjoying my company, too. . . ."

"I have," I admitted.

"And won't you feel just a little bit remorseful when you turn me in after we arrive at Port Helms? But I suppose that you've already been in touch with the authorities by radio, while I was having my shower, to tell them that you found me stowed away. . . ."

I said, "I'll get around to it later."

Her manner brightened. "Suppose you never do it, Captain? I could . . . work my passage. . . ." The dressing gown was falling open as she talked and gesticulated, and what I could see looked very tempting— and I had bccn celibate for quite a while. "Before we set down at Port Helms, you can put me back in the bale. The consignees of the clothing are members of a sort of . . . underground. They have helped escaped convicts before."

"So your crime was political?"

"You could call it that. There are those of us, not a large number but growing, who are fighting for a liberalization of the laws—a relaxation of censorship, more freedom of thought and opinion. . . . You're an off-worlder. You must have noticed how repressive the regime on Helmskirk is."

I said that the repression had not escaped my notice.

"But," she went on, "I do not expect you to help me for no reward. There is only one way that I can reward you. . . ."

"*No*," I said.

"No?" she echoed in a hurt, a very hurt, voice.

"No," I repeated.

Oh, I'm no plaster saint, never have been one. But I have my standards. If I were going to help this girl, I'd do it out of the kindness of my heart and not for reward. I realize now that I was doing her no kindness. In fact, she was to tell me just that on a later occasion. A roll in the hay was just what she was needing just then. But I had my moments of high-minded priggishness, and this was one of them. (Now, of course, I'm at an age when I feel remorse for all the sins that I did not commit when I had the chance.)

She said, "People have often told me that I'm attractive. I would have thought. . . . But I can read you. You're a businessman as well as a spaceman. You own this little ship. You have to make a profit. You're afraid that if it's discovered that you helped me, you'll lose your profitable charter. Perhaps you're afraid that you'll become one of the inmates of Sheol yourself, like Wallace. . . ."

"I never said that I wasn't going to help you," I told her. "But there are conditions. One condition. That if you are picked up again, you say nothing about my part in your escape."

When she kissed me, with warm thoroughness, I weakened—but not enough, not enough. And before the sleep period I rigged the privacy screen in the main cabin, and she stayed on her side of it and I stayed on mine. The next "day"—and I maintained Port Helms standard time while in space—she dressed in her all-concealing coveralls, which were now dry, instead of in my too-revealing bathrobe. We had one or two practice sessions of repacking her in the bale. And before long it was time for me to repack her for good—as far as I was concerned.

And I made my descent to the apron at Port Helms.

There was, of course, something of a flap about the escape of a prisoner from Sheol. The authorities, of course, knew that if she had escaped, she must have done so in *Little Sister*—but I was in the clear. The ship was under guard all the time that she was berthed in the air lock. Too, there was a certain element of doubt. In the past convicts had hidden for quite a while in unexplored tunnels, and some had even died there. Convicts had been murdered by fellow immates and their bodies fed into waste disposal machinery.

And then Evangeline—that was her name—was picked up, in Calvinville. She had been caught leaving pamphlets in various public places. She was tried and found guilty and given another heavy sentence, tacked on to the unexpired portion of her previous one. She kept her word insofar as I was concerned, saying nothing of my complicity. She even managed to protect the clothing wholesalers to whom her bale had been consigned. Her story was that this bale could be opened from the inside, and that after her escape from it, at night, she had tidied up after herself before leaving the warehouse.

Inevitably, I got the job of returning her to incarceration. (The repairs to the prison tender *Jerry Falwell* were dragging on, and on, and on.) She was accompanied by two sourpussed female prison officers returning to Sheol from planet leave. These tried to persuade me—*persuade?* Those arrogant bitches tried to *order* me—that during the short voyage there should be two menus, one for the master, me, and the warders, and the other, approximating prison fare, for the convict. I refused to play, of course. The poor girl would eat well while she still had the chance. But there were no drinks before, with, or after meals, and I even laid off smoking for the trip.

And so I disembarked my passengers and discharged my cargo at Sheol. I'd not been able to exchange so much as a couple of words with Evangeline during the trip, but the look she gave me before she was escorted from the ship said, *Thanks for everything.*

So it went on, trip after trip.

Then it happened. I was having an unusually long stopover on Sheol, and my friend, Don Smith, suggested that I might wish to see, as he put it, the animals feed. I wasn't all that keen—I've never been one to enjoy the spectacle of other people's misery—but there was nothing much else to do, and so I accompanied him through the maze of tunnels to one of the mess halls used by the male prisoners. Have you ever seen any of those antique films about prison life made on Earth in the latter half of the twentieth century? It was like that. The rows of long tables, covered with some shiny gray plastic, and the benches. The counter behind which stood the prisoners on mess duty, with aprons tied on over their zebra-striped coveralls, ladling out a most unsavory-looking—and -smelling—stew into the bowls held out by the shuffling queue of convicts. The guards stationed around the walls, all of them armed with stun guns and all of them looking bored rather than alert. . . . The only novel touch was that it was all being acted out in the slow motion imposed by conditions of low gravity.

Finally, all the convicts were seated at the long tables, their slug-gishly steaming plastic bowls—those that were still steaming, that is; by this time, the meals of those first in the queue must have been almost cold—before them, waiting for the prison padre, standing at his lectern, to intone grace. It was on the lines of: *For what we about to receive this day may the Lord make us truly thankful.*

As soon as he was finished, there was a commotion near the head of one of the tables. A man jumped to his feet. It was, I saw, Wallace, the ex-spaceman.

"Thankful for this shit, you smarmy bastard?" he shouted. "This isn't fit for pigs, and you know it!"

The guards suddenly became alert. They converged upon Wallace with their stun guns out and ready. They made the mistake of assuming that Wallace was the only troublemaker. The guards were tripped, some of them, and others blinded by the bowls of stew flung into their faces. Their pistols were snatched from their hands.

"Get out of here, John," said Don Smith urgently. He pulled me back from the entrance to the mess hall. "Get out of here! There's nothing you can do. Get back to your ship. Use your radio to tell Helmskirk what's happening. . . ."

"But surely your people," I said, "will have things under control. . . ."

"I . . . I hope so. But this has been brewing for quite some time."

By this time we were well away from the mess hall, but the noise coming from it gave us some idea of what was happening—and what was happening wasn't at all pleasant for the guards. And there were similar noises coming from other parts of the prison complex. And there was a clangor of alarm bells and a shrieking of sirens and an amplified voice, repeating over and over, "All prison officers report at once to the citadel! All prison officers report at once to the citadel!"

Don Smith said, "You'd better come with me."

I said, "I have to get back to my ship."

"He said, "You'll never find the way to the air lock."

I said, "I've got a good sense of direction."

So he went one way and I went another. My sense of direction might have served me better if I had not been obliged to make detours to avoid what sounded like small-scale battles ahead of me in that maze of tunnels. And the lights kept going out and coming on again, and when they were on kept flickering in an epilepsy-inducing rhythm. I'm not an epileptic, but I felt as though I were about to become one. During one period of darkness I tripped over something soft, and when the lights came on found that it was a body, that of one of the female prison officers. Her uniform had been stripped from the lower part of her body, and it was obvious what had been done to her before her throat had been cut. And there was nothing that I could do for her.

At last, at long, long last, more by good luck than otherwise, I stumbled into the big air lock chamber in which *Little Sister* was berthed. There were people standing by her. The guards, I thought at first, still at their posts. Then the lights temporarily flared into normal brightness, and I saw that the uniform coveralls were zebra-striped. But I kept on walking. After all, I was just an innocent bystander, wasn't I?

Wallace—it had to be he—snarled, "You took your time getting here."

"What are *you* doing here?" I demanded.

"What the hell do you think? But we wouldn't be here now if we could get your air lock door open."

"And suppose you could, what then?"

"That, Skipper, is a remarkably stupid question."

I looked at Wallace and his two companions. I looked at the sacks at their feet. I could guess what was in them. The lights were bright again, and I saw that the other two convicts were women—and that one of them was Evangeline. She looked at me, her face expressionless.

"What are you waiting for, Skipper?" almost shouted Wallace.

I'm playing for time, I thought, although I hadn't a clue as to what I could do with any time I gained.

Wallace shot me with his stun gun. It wasn't on the *Stun* setting but on that which gave the victim a very painful shock, one that lasted for as long as the person using the gun wished. It seemed to be a very long time in this case, although it could have been no more than seconds. When it was over, I was trembling in every limb and soaked in cold perspiration.

"Want another dose, Skipper?" Wallace demanded.

"You'd better open up, Captain," said Evangeline in an emotionless voice. She was holding a gun, too, pointed in my direction. So was the other woman.

So what could I do? Three, armed, against one, unarmed.

There was more than one way of getting into *Little Sister*. The one that I favored, if the ship was in an atmosphere, was by voice. It always amused guests. And it worked only for me, although I suppose that a really good actor, using the right words, could have gained ingress.

"Open Sesame," I said.

The door slid open.

And while Wallace and the woman whom I didn't know had their attention distracted by this minor miracle, Evangeline shot them both with her stun gun.

"Hurry," she said to me, throwing the sacks of mood opals into the air lock chamber. "Lend a hand, can't you?"

No, I didn't lend a hand, but I accompanied her into the ship. I used the manual air lock controls to seal the lock. I went forward to the control cab, my intention being to try to raise somebody, anybody, on my radio telephone to tell them what had been happening—and to try to find out what was still happening.

She said, from just behind me, "Get us out of here, Captain."

I asked, "Do you expect me to ram my way out of the air lock chamber?"

She said, "Wallace's men have taken over the air lock control room. If they hear my voice and see my face in their telescreen, they'll open up."

"But there's also a screen," I said, "that gives a picture of the air lock chamber. They must have seen what happened outside the ship, when you buzzed Wallace and the girl."

"Very luckily," she said, "that screen got smashed during the fight when we took over the control center."

She'd seen me operate the NST transceiver when I was making my approach to Port Helms the voyage that she'd stowed away. She got it switched on—the controls were simple—without having to ask for instruction except for the last important one.

"What channel do I call on?"

"Hold it," I said. I had acquired quite a dislike for Wallace but had nothing against his girlfriend. "The air's going to be exhausted from the chamber before the outer doors open."

"Oh, I hadn't thought of that. . . ."

I activated the screens that showed me what was going on outside the ship. (From the control cab our only view was forward.) I saw that Wallace was just getting groggily to his feet, assisted by the girl, who must have made a faster recovery that he had. I spoke into the microphone that allowed me to talk to anybody outside the hull.

"Wallace," I said, "get out of the chamber, fast! It's going to open up—and you know what that means!"

He did know. He raised his right hand and shook his fist. I saw his mouth forming words, and I could guess what sort of words they were. Then he turned from *Little Sister* and made for the door leading into the interior of Sheol at a shambling run, with the girl trailing after. No women and children first as far as he was concerned.

"Channel six," I told Evangeline.

"Evangeline here," I heard her say. "We're all aboard, and the stones. Open up."

"We're relying on you to spend the money you get for the stones where it will do the most good! I hope Wallace can find his way to the nearest Shaara world, where there'll be a market and no questions asked!"

"We'll persuade Grimes to do the navigating."

"Are you taking him with you?" I was annoyed by the lack of interest and regretted, briefly, having allowed Wallace to escape from certain asphixiation. "Stand by. Opening up. Bon voyage."

But opening up took time. The air had to be exhausted from the chamber first. How long would it take Wallace to reach the control center? From my own controls I had a direct view overhead. At last I saw the two valves of the air lock door coming apart, could see the black sky and the occasional star in the widening gap. I had *Little Sister*'s inertial drive running in neutral and then applied gentle thrust. We lifted, until we were hovering just below the slowly opening doors.

Was there enough room?

Yes, barely.

I poured on the thrust and we scraped through, almost literally. And just in time. In the belly-view screen I saw that the doors were closing again, fast. Wallace had reached the control center just too late.

And I kept going.

"Back to Helmskirk," said Kitty Kelly, "to hand that poor girl back to the authorities. They must really have put the boot in this time."

"I said," Grimes told her, "that I kept on going. Not to Port Helms. To a Shaara world called Varoom, where we could flog those stones with no

awkward questions asked, I considered that I owed far more loyalty to Evangeline than to the Helmskirk wowsers."

"But what about those prison guards under siege in their citadel? Didn't you owe them some loyalty?"

"One or two of them, perhaps," he admitted. "But what could I have done? And, as a shipmaster, my main loyalty was to my ship."

"But you could have carried reinforcements, police, from Port Helms to Sheol."

"In Little Sister? *She was only a pinnace, you know. Aboard her, four was a crowd. Too, there was one of the Commission's Epsilon-class tramps in port. She could be requisitioned as a troopship."*

"But that time charter, Commodore . . . weren't you tied by that?"

"Oddly enough, no. The original six weeks had expired and it was being renewed week by week. At the time of the mutiny it was due for renewal."

"And the girl. Evangeline. Did you dump her on that Shaara planet?"

"Of course not," said Grimes virtuously. "I was rather too fond of her by that time. After we sold the jewels, I carried her to Freedonia, a colony founded by a bunch of idealists who'd take in anybody as long as he or she could claim to be a political refugee. I'd have liked to keep her with me, but there were too many legal complications. She had no papers of any kind, and the authorities on most planets demand documentation from visitors, crew as well as passengers. I got into enough trouble myself for having left Helmskirk without my Outward Clearance."

"And during your wanderings, before you got to Freedonia, did you lose your priggish high-mindedness?"

He laughed reminiscently. "Yes. I did let her work her passage, as she put it. And I accepted, as a farewell gift, quite a substantial share of the mood opal money."

She said, not admiringly, "You bastard. I'd just hate to owe you a favor."

"You've got it wrong," Grimes told her. "I took what she offered because I owed her one."

CHANCE ENCOUNTER

We paid off on Faraway, having brought the old *Epsilon Pavonis* all the way across the Galaxy to hand her over to her new owners, Rim Runners Incorporated. The Commission's Branch Manager booked us in at the Rimrock House, one of the better hotels in Faraway City. All that we had to do was to wait for the arrival of *Delta Bootes*, in which vessel we were to be shipped back to Earth. The services to and from the Rim Worlds are far from frequent and none of the big passenger liners ever call there; they are not planets that one would ever recommend for a vacation. There's that dreariness, that ever-present sense that one is hanging by one's eyebrows over the very edge of the ultimate cold and dark. The cities on none of the Rim Planets are cities, real cities, but only overgrown—and not so very overgrown at that—provincial towns. The people are a subdued mob who take their pleasures sadly and their sorrows even more sadly. Somebody once said that the average Rim World city is like a graveyard with lights. He wasn't so far wrong.

Delta Bootes was a long time coming. She was delayed on Waverley by a strike, and then she had to put in to Nova Caledon for repairs to her Mannschenn Drive unit. Some of us didn't worry overmuch—after all, we were being paid, and well paid, for doing nothing and the Branch Manager was footing our weekly bar bills without a murmur. Some of us worried a lot, even so. In the main, with one exception, it was the married men who were doing the worrying.

The one exception was Peter Morris, our P.R.O.—Psionic Radio Officer to you—our bright young man from the Rhine Institute, our tame telepath. Yet he was single and so far as any of us knew, had no girl waiting for him on any of the colonised worlds or on Earth. But if there had been a first prize for misery he would have won it.

I liked Peter. During the run out we had formed a friendship that was rather unusual between a telepath and a normal human being—or, as the average graduate of the Institute would put it, between a normal human being and a psionic deficient. I liked Peter, I suppose, because he was so obviously the odd man out and I have a strong tendency towards being odd man out myself. So it was that during our sojourn on Faraway we developed the routine of leaving the others to prop up the bar of the Rimrock House while we, glad to get away from reiteration of the bawdy jokes and boring personal anecdotes, wandered away from the hotel and through the city, finding some small, pleasant drinking place where we could sip our beer in relative peace and quiet.

We were in such a place that morning, and the drinks that we had imbibed had done nothing at all to cheer Peter up. He was so gloomy that even I, who am far from being a cheerful type myself, remarked upon it.

"You don't know what it's like, Ken," he told me. "As a psionic deficient you'll never know. I 's the aura of . . . of . . . Well, there's fear, and there's loneliness, and a sort of aching emptiness, and together they make up the *feel* of these Rim Worlds. A telepath is always lonely until, if he's very lucky, he finds the right woman. But it's so much worse here."

"There's Epstein, the P.R.O. at the port," I said. "And there's Mrs. Epstein. Why don't you see more of them?"

"That," he declared, "would make it worse. When two telepaths marry they're a closed circuit to an extent that no p.d. couple can ever be . . ." He drank some more beer. "Finding the right woman," he went on, "is damned hard for us. I don't know why it is, but the average Esper female is usually frightfully unattractive, both mentally and physically. They seem to run to puddingy faces and puddingy minds . . . You know, Ken, I needn't have come on this trip. There are still so few of us that we can afford to turn down assignments. I came for one reason only—just hoping that by making a voyage all the way across the Galaxy I'd find somebody."

"You still might on the way back," I told him.

"I still might not," he replied.

I looked at him with a rather irritated pity. I could sense, after a fashion, what he was driving at. He was so much the typical introvert—dark of hair and face, long and lean—and his telepathic talent could do nothing but add to the miseries that come with introversion.

"You'd better have something stronger," I told him. I caught the bartender's eye. "Two double whiskies, please."

"Make that three," said a too hearty voice. I looked around, saw that Tarrant, our Second Mate, had just come in.

"Got tired of the same old stories at last?" I asked unkindly.

"No," he said. "But somebody had to go to find you two, and I was the most junior officer present, so . . ."

"Who wants us?" I demanded. "And why?"

"The Old Man wants you." He lifted his glass. "Here's to crime."

"What does he want us for?"

"I don't know. All that I know is this. Some meteor-pitted old bastard calling himself Captain Grimes came barging into the pub and demanded an audience with our lord and master. They retired to confer privily. Shortly thereafter the call for all hands to battle stations went out."

"Grimes . . ." I said slowly. "The name rings a bell. I seem to remember that when we handed the old *Eppy Swan* over somebody mentioned that Captain Grimes, the Chief Superintendent for Rim Runners, was away on Thule."

"Could be," admitted Tarrant. "He has the look of a chairborne spaceman. In which case we'll have another drink. It's bad enough having to run to the beck and call of our own Supers without having to keep those belonging to a tuppenny ha'penny concern like Rim Runners happy."

We had another drink, and another. After the third whisky Peter's gloom seemed to be evaporating slightly, so he ordered a fourth one. The Second Mate and I each ordered another round, after which we thought that we had better discover what was cooking. We walked rather unsteadily into the untidy street, hailed a ground cab and were driven back to the Rimrock House.

We found them all waiting for us in the Lounge—the Old Man and the rest of the officers, the chunky little man whose appearance justified Tarrant's description of him as a "meteor pitted old bastard."

"Sir," said the Old Man stiffly, "here are my Third Officer, Mr. Wilberforce, and my Psionic Radio Officer, Mr. Morris. I have no doubt that they will show as little enthusiasm for your project as any of my other officers. Yours is essentially a Rim World undertaking, and should be carried out by Rim World personnel."

"They can decide, sir," said Captain Grimes. "You have told me that these officers have no close ties on Earth or elswhere; it is possible that they may find the proposition attractive. And, as I have already told you, we guarantee repatriation."

"What is it all about, anyhow?" asked Tarrant.

"Sit down, gentlemen," said Grimes, "and I'll tell you." While we were finding chairs he filled and lit a foul pipe. "I'll have to recapitulate for your benefit; I hope that the rest of you don't object.

"Well, as you are no doubt aware, we of the Rim Worlds consider ourselves the orphans of the galaxy. You know why these planets were colonised in the first instance—the Central Government of those days feared an alien invasion sweeping in from outside the Galaxy. The general idea was to set up a huge ring of garrisoned planets, a fortified perimeter. That idea has died over the years and, as a result, only a very small arc of the Rim has been explored, even.

"We of the Rim Worlds wish to survive as a separate, independent entity. Starved as we are of trade and shipping we have little chance of surviving at all. So it has been decided that we take our own steps, in our own way, to achieve this end.

"You've heard, of course, of the odd pieces of wreckage that come drifting in, from time to time, from *somewhere*. It was such flotsam that first gave the Central Government the idea that there might be an invasion from some other galaxy. Now, we don't think that those odd bits and pieces ever did come from outside. We think that there are inhabited planets all around the rim, and that advantageous trade would be possible with them.

"For years we've been trying to persuade the brass hats of the Survey Service to carry out a systematic exploration, but the answer's always the same. They haven't the ships, or they haven't the men, or they haven't the money. So, at last, we have decided to carry out our own exploration. Your old ship, *Epsilon Pavonis*, is being fitted out for the job. She's being renamed, by the way—*Faraway Quest* . . ."

"And what," asked Tarrant, "has this to do with us?"

Captain Grimes hesitated, seemed almost embarrassed. "Frankly," he said, "the trouble is this. We don't seem to breed spacemen, real spacemen, on the Rim Worlds. Puddle jumpers, that's all they are. They'll venture as far as Ultimo, or Thule, or the Shakespearean Sector, but they just aren't keen to fare any further afield . . ."

"There's too much fear on these worlds," said Peter Morris suddenly. "That's the trouble. Fear of the cold and the dark and the emptiness . . ."

Grimes looked at him. "Of course," he said, "you're the telepath . . ."

"Yes, I'm the telepath. But you don't need to be any kind of an Esper to sense the fear."

"All right, then," said Grimes. "My own boys are just plain scared to venture so much as a single light year beyond the trade routes. But I've got a Master for *Faraway Quest*—myself. I've a Purser, and Chief and Second Mannschenn Drive Engineers, and one Rocket Engineer. I've a Chief Officer and a Surgeon-cum-Bio-Chemist, and an Electronic Radio Officer. All of us are from the Centre, none of us was born out here, on the Rim. But this is a survey job, and I shall need a well manned ship.

"I can promise any of you who volunteer double your current rates of pay. I can promise you repatriation when the job is over, to any part of the Galaxy."

"Most of us," said our Captain, "have homes and families waiting for us. We've been out for too long now."

"You're sure that there are inhabited worlds out along the Rim?" asked Peter. "What of their people?"

"Purple octopi for all I know," replied Grimes.

"But there's a chance, just a chance, that they might be humanoid, or even human?" insisted the Psionic Radio Officer.

"Yes, there's a chance. Given a near infinitude of habitable worlds and an infinitude of time for evolution to take its course, then anything is possible."

"The purple octopi are more probable," I said.

"Perhaps," almost whispered Peter. "Perhaps . . . But I have limited, very limited, premonitory powers, and I have a definite feeling that . . ."

"That what?" I asked.

"Oh, never mind." To Grimes he said, "I take it that you can use a P.R.O., Captain?"

"That I can," declared Grimes heartily.

I sighed. "Your offer about double the pay," I said. "I'm Third Officer in the Commission's fleet as you know. If I come with you as Second, do I get twice the Commission's rate for that rank?"

"You do."

"Count me in," I said.

"You must be mad," said Tarrant. "Both of you—but Wilberforce is less mad than Morris. After all, he's doing it for money. What are *you* doing it for. Crystal Gazer?"

"Mind your own business!" he snapped.

Some hours later, when we were out at the spaceport looking over the structural alterations that were being made to *Faraway Quest*, I asked him the same question.

He flushed. "What do people do things for, Peter?"

"Money," I replied. "Or power. Or . . ."

"Precisely," he said, before I could finish. "It's only a hunch, but I have a strong feeling that this is the chance, the only chance, to find *her*."

I remember that I said, "I hope you're right."

Delta Bootes dropped down at last to Port Faraway, and all of our shipmates, openly jubilant, boarded her. We saw them off, Peter and I. We had our last drinks with them in the little smoking room and then, feeling rather lost and lonely (at least, I did) scrambled out of the airlock and down the ramp as the last warning bell started to sound. We stood with the other spectators a safe distance from the blast-off area, watched her lift on her column of pale fire, watched her vanish into the clear, twilit sky. With her departure I realised the irrevocability of my action in volunteering for this crazy survey voyage. There was no backing out now.

We walked to the corner of the field where work was still progressing on *Faraway Quest*. Outwardly she was little changed, except for the addition of two extra boat blisters. Internally she was being almost rebuilt. Cargo space was being converted into living accomodation. In spite of the shortage of trained space-faring personnel Grimes had found volunteers from other quarters. Two professors of physics from Thule City were signing on as assistant engineers, and there were three astronomers from Ultimo as well as a couple of biologists Grimes—who, we had learned, had served in the Survey Service as a young man—had persuaded the local police force to lend him three officers and fifty men, who were being trained as Space Marines. It began to look as though *Faraway Quest* would be run on something approaching Survey Service lines.

We looked at her, standing tall and slim in the light of the glaring floods.

I said, "I was a little scared when I watched *Delta Bootes* blast off, Peter, but now I'm feeling a little happier."

"I am too," he told me. "That . . . That hunch of mine is stronger than ever. I'll be glad when this old girl is ready to push off."

"I don't trust hunches," I told him. "I never have, and never will. In any case, this female telepath with the beautiful mind you're hunting for may turn out to be nothing but a purple octopus."

He laughed. "You've got purple octopi on the brain. To hear you talk, one would think that the Galaxy was inhabited by the brutes . . ."

"Perhaps it is," I said. "Or all the parts that we haven't explored yet."

"*She* exists," he told me seriously. "I know. I've dreamed about her now for several nights running."

"Have you?" I asked. Other people's dreams are as a rule, dreadfully boring, but when the other person is a telepath with premonitory powers one is inclined to take some interest in them. "What did you dream?"

"Each time it was the same," he said. "I was in a ship's boat, by myself, waiting for her to come to me. I knew what she was like, even though I'd never actually met her. She wasn't quite human. She was a little too tall, a little too slim, and her golden hair had a greenish glint to it. Her small ears were pointed at the tips. As I say, I knew all this while I sat there waiting. And she was in my mind, as I was in hers, and she was saying, over and over, *I'm coming to you, my darling*. And I was sitting there in the pilot's chair, waiting to close the outer airlock door as soon as she was in . . ."

"And then?"

"It's hard to describe. I've had women in real life as well as in dreams, but never before have I experienced that feeling of utter and absolute oneness . . ."

"You're really convinced, aren't you?" I said. "Are you sure that it's not auto-hypnosis, that you haven't built up from the initial hunch, erecting a framework of wish-fulfilment fantasy?"

"I'd like to point out, Ken," he said stiffly, "that you're a qualified astronaut, not any sort of psychologist. I'd like to point out, too, that the Rhine Institute gives all its graduates a very comprehensive course in psychology. We have to know what makes our minds tick—after all, they are our working tools."

"Sorry," I said. "The main thing is that you feel reasonably sure that we shall stumble across some intelligent, humanoid race out there."

"Not reasonably sure," he murmured. "Just certain."

"Have you told Grimes all this?"

"Not all, but enough."

"What did he say?"

"That I was in charge of communications, not prognostications, and that my most important job was to see to it that my amplifier was healthy and functioning properly."

We all had to stand out on the field in a cold drizzle while the Presidents of Faraway, Ultimo and Thule made their farewell speeches. We were drawn up in a rather ragged line behind Captain Grimes, dapper in uniform, very much the space captain. The ex-policemen, the Marines, were a little to one side, and made up for what we lacked in the way of smartness. At last the speechmaking was over. Led by Grimes we marched up the ramp to the airlock, went at once to our blasting-off stations. In the control room Grimes sat chunkily in his acceleration chair with Lawlor, his Chief Officer, to one side of him. My own chair was behind theirs, and at my side was Gavin, one of the astronomers from Ultimo, who was on the ship's books as Third Officer.

Reports started coming in. "Interplanetary Drive Room—manned and ready!" "Interstellar Drive Room—manned and ready!" "Hydroponics—all secured!" "Steward's store—all secured!"

"Mr. Wilberforce," ordered Grimes, "request permission to proceed."

I spoke into the microphone of the already switched on transceiver.

"*Faraway Quest* to Control Tower, *Faraway Quest* to Control Tower. Have we your permission to proceed?"

"Control Tower to *Faraway Quest*. Permission granted. Good luck to all of you!"

Gavin was counting aloud, the words carried through the ship by the intercom. "Ten . . . Nine . . . Eight . . . Seven . . ." I saw Grimes's stubby hand poised over the master firing key. "Six . . . Five . . . Four . . ." I looked out of the nearest viewport, to the dismal, mist shrouded landscape. Faraway was a good world to get away from, to anywhere—or, even, nowhere. "Three . . . Two . . . One . . . *Fire!*"

We lifted slowly, the ground falling away beneath us, dropping into obscurity beneath the veil of drifting rain. We drove up through the low clouds, up and into the steely glare of Faraway's sun. The last of the atmosphere slipped, keening shrilly, down our shell plating and then we were out and clear, with the gleaming lens of the Galaxy to one side of us and, on the other, the aching emptiness of the Outside.

For long minutes we accelerated, the pseudo-gravity forcing us deeply into the padding of our chairs. At last Grimes cut the Drive and, almost immediately, the thunder of the rockets was replaced by the high, thin whine of the ever-precessing gyroscopes of the Mannschenn unit. The Galactic Lens twisted itself into an impossible convolution.

The emptiness Outside still looked the same.

That emptiness was with us all through the voyage.

Star after star we circled; some had planetary families, some had not. At first we made landings on all likely looking worlds, then, after a long succession of planets that boasted nothing higher in the evolutionary scale than the equivalent to the giant reptiles of Earth's past, we contented ourselves by making orbital surveys only. Peter succeeded in talking Grimes into entrusting him with the task of deciding whether or not any planet possessed intelligent life—and, of course, cities and the like could be spotted from space.

So we drove on, and on, settling down to a regular routine of Interstellar Drive, Interplanetary Drive, Closed Orbit, Interplanetary Drive, Interstellar Drive, Interplanetary Drive . . . Everybody was becoming short-tempered. Grimes was almost ready to admit that the odd pieces of flotsam falling now and again to the Rim Worlds must have come from Outside and not from somewhere else along the Rim. Had our purpose been exploration as a prelude to colonisation we should have felt a lot more useful—but the Rim Worlds have barely enough population to maintain their own economies.

Only Peter Morris maintained a certain calm cheerfulness. His faith in his hunch was strong. He told me so, more than once. I wanted to believe him but couldn't.

Then, one boring watch, I was showing Liddell, one of the astronomers, how to play three dimensional noughts and crosses in the Tri-Di chart. He was catching on well and I was finding it increasingly hard to beat him when suddenly, the buzzer of the intercom sounded. I answered it. It was Peter, speaking from his Psionic Communications Room.

"Ken!" he almost shouted. "Life! Intelligent life!"

"Where?" I demanded.

"I don't know. I'm trying to get a rough bearing. It's in towards the Lens from us, that much I can tell you. But the bearing doesn't seem to be changing."

"No parallax?" asked Liddell. "Could it be, do you think, a ship?"

"It just could be," I said doubtfully.

"Ken, I think it's a ship!" came Peter's voice. "I think that they, like ourselves, have Psionic Radio . . . Their operator's vaguely aware of me, but he's not sure . . . No—it's not *he* . . . It's a woman; I'm pretty certain of that . . . But it's a ship all right. Roughly parallel course, but converging . . ."

"Better tell old Grimy," I suggested, hastily clearing the noughts and crosses lattice from the Tri-Di chart. To Liddell I said, "I'm afraid Peter's imagining things. Not about the ship—she's probably a stray Survey vessel—but about the female operator. When psionic radio first started we used to carry them, but the average woman telepath is so unintelligent that they were all emptied out as soon as there were enough men for the job."

"It could be an alien ship," said Liddell.

"It could be, but it's not," I said. "Unless, of course, it belongs to one of the alien races with whom we've already made contact. It could be a Shaara vessel—that would account for Peter's female telepath. The Shaara are social insects, and all the work is done by the females."

Captain Grimes came into the control room. He looked almost happy. "Contact at last," he said.

"Suppose they are aliens," said the astronomer, "and suppose they open fire on us . . . What then?"

"By the time people get around to building interstellar ships," said Grimes, "they've lost the habit of wanting to fight strangers."

"Sometimes," I said.

"Switch on the Matter Proximity Indicator," he said.

I did so, peered into the globe that was its screen.

*   *   *

"There's something . . ." I said. "Red 085, ZD 093 . . ."

"A little astern," murmured the Old Man. "Range?"

I manipulated the controls carefully. "Twenty thousand—and closing. Relative bearing not altering."

"Liddell," said the Captain. "You're an astronomer, a mathematician. What are the odds against this? With all the immensity of Space around us we have two ships approaching on collision orbits. The other ship is using a similar Drive to ours—she must be. If her rate of temporal precession were more than one microsecond different from ours she would not register on our screens, and there'd be no risk of collision. What are the odds?"

"Astronomical," replied Liddell drily. "But I'll tell you this, although you must, by this time, have come to the same conclusion. There's a Law of Nature that you'll not find in any of the books, but that is valid just the same. If a coincidence can happen, it will."

"I'll buy that," said Grimes.

Peter's voice came from the squawk box. "I've established contact. She's an alien ship, all right. She belongs to some people called the Lowanni. She's a trading vessel, analogous to one of our Beta Class ships. Her captain wishes to know if he may close us to make contact."

"Tell them *yes*!" almost shouted Grimes. "Mr. Willoughby—sound the General Alarm. I want all hands at stations. Damn it, this is just what we've been hunting for! Neighbours along the Rim . . ."

I sounded the Alarm. The ship hummed like a disturbed beehive as one and all hastened to their stations. The reports began coming in; "Rocket Drive manned and ready . . . Electronic Radio Office manned and ready . . . Surgeon and Bio-Chemist standing by for further instructions . . ." The Chief and Third Officers, together with the other astronomer, pulled themselves into the already crowded control room.

It seemed only a matter of minutes—although it was longer—before the alien ship was within telescopic range. Just a little silvery dot of light she was at first, hard to pick up against the gleaming convoluted distortion of the Galactic Lens. And then, slowly, she took shape. There was little about her appearance that was unusual—but any spaceship designed for landings and blastings off through an atmosphere must, of necessity, look very like any other spaceship.

Meanwhile, our Electronic and Psionic Radio departments were working together. I still don't know how Peter Morris and his opposite number in the alien ship managed to sort out details of frequency and all the rest of it, but they did. It may be, of course, that mathematics is the universal language—even so, it must have been quite a job for the two telepaths to transmit and receive the electronic technicalities.

They came into the Control Room then—Peter Morris and Sparks. Sparks busied himself with the big intership transceiver, twisting dials and muttering. Peter whispered occasional instructions.

The screen came to life. It showed the interior of a control room very like our own. It showed a group of people very like ourselves. They were in the main slimmer, and their features were more delicate, and their ears had pointed tips, but they were human rather than merely humanoid.

One of them—his black-clad shoulders were heavily encrusted with gold—said something in a pleasant tenor voice. The girl standing beside him seemed to be repeating what he was saying; her lips moved, but no sound came from them.

"Captain Sanara says, 'Welcome to the Dain Worlds,' " said Peter.

"Tell him, 'Thank you,' " said Grimes.

I saw the girl in the alien ship speak to the Captain. She must, I thought, be their P.R.O. I remembered, suddenly, what Peter had told me of those dreams of his before we left Faraway. *She was a little too tall, and a little too slim, and her golden hair had a greenish glint to it. Her small ears were pointed at the tips* . . . And she has a wide, generous mouth, I thought, and in spite of the severity of her uniform she's all woman . . . I looked at Peter. He was staring into the screen like a starving man gazing into a restaurant window.

Shortly thereafter it became necessary for the two ships to cut their interstellar drives—alterations of course are impossible while the Drive is in operation, and an alteration of course there had to be to avert collision. During the operation the image on the screen blurred and wavered and, at times, vanished as the two rates of temporal precession lost their synchronisation. Peter, I could see, was on tenderhooks whilst this was taking place. He had found, thanks to an utterly impossible coincidence, his woman; now he dreaded losing her.

He need not have worried. Grimes was an outstanding astronaut and, in all probability, the alien Captain was in the same class. The other ship flickered back into view just as the Galactic Lens reappeared in all its glory. Our directional gyroscopes whined briefly, our rockets coughed once. Through the port I saw a short burst of pale fire at the stern of the alien—then we were falling through space on parallel courses with velocities matching to within one millimetre a second.

Time went by. Through the telepaths the two Captains talked. We heard about the Dain Worlds, whose people were relative newcomers into Deep Space. We heard about their social and economic systems, their art, their industries. As we listened we marvelled. These people, the Lowanni, were our twins. They thought as we did and acted as we did, and their history in most ways paralleled our own. I knew what Grimes was thinking. He had made up his mind that the Rim Worlds had far more in common with these aliens than with the crowded humanity at the Galactic Centre. He was thinking of more than trade agreements, he was thinking in terms of pacts and treaties.

Even so, trade was not to be sneezed at.

They talked, the two Captains. They discussed an interchange of gifts, of representative artifacts from both cultures. It was when they got to this stage of the proceedings that they struck a snag.

"There are," said our Doctor coldly, "such things as micro-organisms. I would point out, Captain, that it would be suicidal folly to allow an alien to board this ship, even if he kept his spacesuit on. He might carry something that would wipe all of us out—and might carry something back with him that would destroy both himself and all his shipmates."

Peter broke in. "I've been talking with Erin," he said.

"Erin?" asked the Old Man.

"That's her name, sir. She's the alien P.R.O. We've decided that the exchange of artifacts is necessary, and have been trying to work out a way in which it would be carried out without risk. At the same time, it means that both parties have a guinea pig . . ."

"What do you mean, Mr. Morris?"

"Let me finish, sir. This ship, as you know, has only one airlock, but carries more boats than is necessary. *Listra*—the ship out there—has the normal complements of boats for a vessel of her class but has no less than four airlocks, two of which are rarely used. This is the way we've worked it out. One of our boats, and one of *Listra's* airlocks, can be used as isolation hospitals . . .

"I can handle a boat, sir, as you know, compulsory for every non-executive officer in the Commission's service to hold a lifeboatman's certificate. The idea is this. I take the boat out to midway between the two ships, carrying with me such goods as we are giving to the aliens. Erin comes out in her spacesuit, bringing with her what the aliens are giving us. Then she returns to her ship, and I bring the boat back to this ship. She will remain in the airlock, as I shall remain in the boat, until such time as it is ruled that there is no danger of infection . . ."

I looked at the screen. I saw that the slim, blonde girl was talking earnestly to Captain Sanara. I saw other officers joining in the discussion. I looked back from the screen to Captain Grimes. His dark, mottled face was heavy with misgivings. I heard him say, "This could be suicide, Mr. Morris."

"It could be, sir—but so could coming out on an expedition like this.

And you know as well as I do that very few alien micro-organisms have been found that are dangerous to Man. All that it means, essentially, is that Erin and I will have to do our jobs in rather uncomfortable conditions from now on."

"Why you, and why Erin?"

"Because we're the telepaths. Suppose, for example, you send a tube of depilatory among the other goods to be exchanged. Erin's people might think that it's toothpaste, or mustard, or . . . or anything at all but what it is when we're together in the boat we can explain things, talk things over. We'll get more ground covered in half an hour together than we should in half a week, talking ship to ship . . ."

"You've got it all worked out, haven't you?" grumbled Grimes. "But on a job of this sort it's foolish to discourage an enthusiastic volunteer . . . Well, I suppose that the rest of you had better start collecting artifacts. Books, and tools, and instruments, samples of our food and drink . . ."

"You mean it's all right, sir?" asked Peter, his face suddenly radiant.

"Mr. Morris, if this were a commercial vessel I'd never allow one of the officers to take such a risk. If you like you can tell that girl that I take a dim view of her Captain for allowing her to take the risk . . ."

"She doesn't think of it that way."

"Doesn't she? Then she should."

"Can I get ready, sir?"

"You can. Don't forget to brush your hair and wash behind the ears— after all, you have acting temporary ambassadorial status."

"Thank you, sir."

Peter vanished from the control room as though he had added tele-portation to his other talents. Grimes sighed and looked at the screen, looked at the radiant girl who was, obviously, thanking her Captain. He sighed again and demanded, of no one in particular, "Who said it?"

"Who said what?" asked the Chief Officer.

"Journeys end in lovers' meetings," said Grimes.

It was all so obvious, even to non-telepaths.

I was in the boat with Peter shortly before he blasted off.

I said, "You seem pretty certain."

"Of course I'm certain. And she was lonely too, just as I have been. Among her people they have a similar set-up to ours, but in reverse. With them it's usually the male telepath who's an unattractive, mindless clod. This chance-encounter means a lot to both of us."

"She's an oxygen breather?" I asked. "You're sure of that? I mean, if she comes in here and takes off her helmet and our atmosphere poisons her . . . I don't want to be pessimistic, but I believe in facing facts."

"She's an oxygen breather," Peter assured me. "She eats food very like ours. (I hope she likes chocolates—I've got some here). She drinks alcoholic liquor in moderation. She smokes, even. She can try one of our cigarettes and I'll try one of hers . . ."

"You've found out a lot in a short time, haven't you?"

"Of course I have. That's my job—and hers. But I'll have to ask you to leave me, Ken. I've got a date."

"Are you sure you wouldn't like me to come along?"

"Not bloody likely!" he snapped.

"All right, then. And all the best of luck."

"Thanks," he said.

I stood by the blister until I felt the shock of his blasting off, until the red READY light changed to green, showing that he was out and clear. I made my way back to Control. I joined the group at the port watching the little spacecraft coasting out and away from us, watched her take up a position roughly midway between the two ships.

We saw a circle of yellow light suddenly appear on *Listra's* sleek side. We saw, through telescopes and binoculars, the little figure that hung there for a while in black silhouette. We could make out the bulky bundle that she was carrying.

Flame jetted from her shoulder units, and she was falling out and away from her own ship. Slowly she approached the lifeboat. I looked away briefly, looked at the screen. The aliens, like ourselves, were crowded around viewports, were watching this first physical contact between our two races.

She was very close to Peter's boat now. I could imagine him waiting in the little cabin, as he had waited—how many times?—in his dreams. I could appreciate, dimly, what he must be feeling. I had been in love myself and had waited for the loved one, and what I had felt must be no more than a pale shadow of what is felt by a telepath. There was, I confess, more than a little envy in my thoughts.

She was very close to the boat, and I saw that Peter had the outer door of the little airlock open.

For a long second she was silhouetted against the glow of the airlock light . . .

And then . . .

And then I was blind, as the others were blind, with tears welling from my eyes, the skin of my face burning from its exposure to radiation. She had been there, just entering the boat, and then she and the boat had vanished in one dreadful flash.

Slowly sight returned, dim and painful. I was looking once again at the screen, and I could see that those in the other ship had been affected as we had. There was pain on their faces, and it was not only physical pain. I knew then—as they must have known as they looked at us—that this had been no act of treachery, that there had been no murderous bomb concealed among the package of bartered goods.

Slowly the alien Captain shrugged his shoulders. He made a gesture of rejection with his slim hands. One of his officers handed him something. It was a black glove. He put it on. Slowly he brought his hands together—the white skinned one and the black gloved one. He flung them apart explosively.

The screen went blank. We looked away from it through the port. The alien ship was gone.

"We should have guessed," Liddell was muttering. "We should have guessed. *They* did."

"But too late," said one of the others.

"What should we have guessed?" asked Grimes.

"Anti-matter," said Liddell. "We've known for centuries that it can exist. Matter identical with what we call normal matter, except that all electrical charges are reversed. We thought that we might find it in other galaxies if ever we had a ship capable of making the journey . . . But perhaps the Dain Worlds aren't really part of this galaxy at all."

"And when it comes into contact with normal matter?" pressed Grimes.

"You saw, Captain. There can never, *never*, be any contact between the Lowanni and ourselves."

"And what happens," I asked, "when it's two living bodies of the two kinds of matter that make the contact?"

"You saw," said Liddell.

But I was not satisfied with the answer, and am still not satisfied. I remembered what Peter had told me about the conclusion of his dream, and have yet to decide if he was the unluckiest, or the luckiest of men.

CATCH THE STAR WINDS

For the one-time service manager of a certain engineering concern

I
THE CREW

Chapter 1

She was old and tired, the *Rim Dragon*—and after this, her final voyage, we were feeling just that way ourselves. It was as though she had known somehow that a drab and miserable end awaited her in the ungentle hands of the breakers, and she had been determined to forestall the inevitable and go out in a blaze of glory—or as much glory as would have been possible for a decrepit Epsilon Class tramp finishing her career after many changes of ownership at the very rim of the Galaxy, the edge of the dark.

Fortunately for us, she had overdone things.

Off Grollor, for example, a malfunctioning of the control room computer had coincided with a breakdown of the main propellant pump. If the second mate hadn't got his sums wrong we should have been trapped in a series of grazing ellipses, with no alternative but to take to the boats in a hurry before too deep a descent into the atmosphere rendered this impossible. As things worked out, however, the mistakes made by our navigator and his pet computer resulted in our falling into a nice, stable orbit, with ample time at our disposal in which to make repairs.

Then there had been pile trouble, and Mannschenn drive trouble—and for the benefit of those of you who have never experienced this latter, all I can say is that it is somewhat hard to carry out normal shipboard duties when you're not certain if it's high noon or last Thursday. It was during the Mannschenn drive trouble that Cassidy, our reaction drive chief engineer, briefly lost control of his temperamental fissioning furnace. By some miracle the resultant flood of radiation seemed to miss all human personnel. It was the algae tanks that caught it—and this was all to the good, as a mutated virus had been running riot among the algae, throwing our air conditioning and sewage disposal entirely out of kilter. The virus died, and most of the algae died—but enough of the organisms survived to be the parents of a new and flourishing population.

Then there had been the occasions when *Rim Dragon* had not over-done things, but her timing had been just a little out. There had been, for example, the tube lining that had cracked just a second or so too late (for-tunately, really, from our viewpoint) but the mishap nonetheless had resulted in our sitting down on the concrete apron of Port Grimes, on Tharn, hard enough to buckle a vane.

There had been another propellant pump failure—this time on Mel-lise—that caused us to be grounded on that world for repairs at just the right time to be subjected to the full fury of a tropical hurricane. Luckily, the procedure for riding out such atmospheric disturbances is laid down in *Rim Runners' Standing Orders and Regulations*. It was a Captain Calver, I think, who had been similarly trapped on Mellise several years ago in some ancient rustbucket called *Lorn Lady*. He had coped with the situation by rigging stays to save his ship from being overturned by the wind. We did the same. It worked—although the forward towing lugs, to which our stays were shackled, would have torn completely away from the shell plating with disastrous consequences had the blow lasted another five minutes.

Anyhow, the voyage was now over—or almost over.

We were dropping down to Port Forlorn, on Lorn, falling slowly down the column of incandescence that was our reaction drive, drifting cautiously down to the circle of drab gray concrete that was the spaceport apron, to the gray concrete that was hardly distinguishable from the gray landscape, from the dreary flatlands over which drifted the thin rain and the gray smoke and the dirty fumes streaming from the stacks of the refineries.

We were glad to be back—but, even so . . .

Ralph Listowel, the mate, put into words the feeling that was, I think, in the minds of all but one of us. He quoted sardonically:

"Lives there a man with soul so dead
Who never to himself hath said
When returning from some foreign strand
This is my own, my native land?"

Of all of us, the only genuine, native-born Rim Worlder descended from the first families was the old man. He looked up from his console now to scowl at his chief officer. And then I, of course, had to make mat-ters worse by throwing in my own two bits' worth of archaic verse. I remarked, "The trouble with you, Ralph, is that you aren't romantic. Try to see things this way . . .

> "Saw the heavens fill with commerce, argosies with magic sails,
> Pilots of the purple twilight dropping down with costly bales . . ."

"What the hell's the bloody purser doing in here?" roared the captain, turning his glare on me. "Mr. Malcolm, will you please get the hell out of my control room? And you, Mr. Listowel, please attend to your duties."

I unstrapped myself from my chair and left hastily. We carried no third mate, and I had been helping out at landings and blast-offs by looking after the RT. Besides, I liked to be on top to see everything that was happening. Sulkily, I made my way down to the officers' flat, staggering a little as the ship lurched, and let myself into the wardroom.

The other two "idlers" were there—Sandra and Doc Jenkins. They were sprawled at ease in their acceleration chairs, sipping drinks from tall glasses dewy with condensation.

"So this is how the poor live," I remarked sourly.

"The way that the old bitch has been carrying on," said Doc affably, "we have to assume that any given drink may be our last. But how come you're not in the greenhouse?"

"They gave me the bum's rush," I admitted, dropping into the nearest chair, strapping myself in. I was feeling extremely disgruntled. In well-manned, well-found ships pursers are brought up to regard the control room as forbidden ground, but over the past few months, I had become used to playing my part in blastings-off and landings and had come to appreciate the risks that we were running all the time. If anything catastrophic happened I'd be dead, no matter where I was. But when I die I'd like to know the reason.

"So they gave you the bum's rush," said Sandra, not at all sympathetically. (She had been heard to complain that if the purser was privileged to see all that was going on, a like privilege should be extended to the catering officer. "Might I inquire why?"

"You might," I told her absently, listening to the thunder of the rocket drive, muffled by the insulation but still loud in the confined space. It sounded healthy enough. They seemed to be getting along without me up there. But we weren't down yet.

"Why?" she asked bluntly.

"Give me a drink, and I'll tell you."

She did not unstrap herself but extended a long, shapely arm and managed to shove the heavy decanter and a glass across the table so that they were within my reach. I looked at the surface of the liquid within the container. It was rippled, but ever so slightly, by the vibration. The old girl was behaving herself. I might still have time for a drink before things started to happen. I poured myself a generous slug and raised the tumbler to my lips. It was, as I had suspected, the not at all bad gin manufactured by the doctor in his capacity of biochemist. The lime flavor made it palatable.

She said, "You've got your drink."

I said, "All right. If you must know, I was quoting poetry. Ralph started it. The master did not, repeat not, approve . . ."

"Down," quoted the doctor in his fruitiest voice.

"Down.
Fierce stabbing
Flame phallus
Rending
Membrane of atmosphere,
Tissues of cloud.
Down-bearing,
Thrusting
To stony womb of world.
Spacemen, I ask you
What monster
Or prodigy
Shall come of this rape?"

I looked at him with some distaste. His chubby face under the overly long, overly oily black hair was (as usual) smugly sensual. He had an extensive repertoire of modern verse, and practically all of it dealt with rape, both literal and figurative.

"If I'd quoted that trash," I told him, "the old man would have been justified in booting me out of his Holy of Holies. But I was quoting poetry. *Poetry*. Period."

"Oh, yes. Poetry. Meretricious jingles. You and dear Ralph share a passion for this revival of the ancient Terran slush, corn of the corniest. Our lord and master did well in arising in his wrath and hurling you into the outer darkness . . ."

"Poetry," said Sandra flatly, "and ship handling just don't mix. Especially at a time like this."

"She was riding down," I said, "sweetly and gently, on full automatic."

"And all of us," she pointed out, "at the mercy of a single fuse. I may be only chief cook and bottlewasher aboard this wagon, but even I know that it is essential for the officers in the control room to be fully alert at all times."

"All right," I said. "All right."

I glared at her, and she glared at me. She was always handsome—but she was almost beautiful when she was in a bad temper. I wondered (as I had often wondered before) what she would be like when the rather harsh planes and angles of her face were softened by some gentler passion. But she did her job, Sandra did, and did it well, and kept to herself—as others, as well as I, had learned the hard way.

Meanwhile, we were still falling, still dropping, the muffled thunder of our reaction drive steady and unfaltering. In view of the past events and near disasters of the voyage it was almost too good to be true. It was, I decided, too good to be true—and then, as though in support of my pessimism, the sudden silence gripped the hearts of all of us. Sandra's face was white under her coppery hair and Jenkins's normally ruddy complexion was a sickly green. We waited speechless for the last, the final crash.

The ship tilted gently, ever so gently, tilted and righted herself, and the stuffy air inside the wardroom was alive with the whispered complaints of the springs and cylinders of her landing gear. The bulkhead speaker crackled and we heard the old man's voice: "The set-down had been accomplished. All personnel may proceed on their arrival duties."

Doc Jenkins laughed, unashamedly relieved. He unstrapped himself and poured a generous drink from the decanter into each of our glasses. "To the end of the voyage," he said, raising his tumbler. He gulped his gin. Then, "Now that we can all relax, Peter, just what was the so-called poetry that led to your well-merited eviction from the greenhouse?"

" 'Saw the heavens fill with commerce,' " I quoted. " 'Argosies with magic sails, solidus Pilots of the purple twilight dropping down with costly bales . . . ' "

"We dropped down all right," he jested, "but not on any magic sails. A down-thrusting phallus of flame is a far better description of rocket drive."

"I prefer the magic sails," I said.

"You would," he said.

"Some people," said Sandra pointedly, getting to her feet, "have work to do. Even though the ship is finished, we aren't."

Chapter 2

Yes, we all had work to do—but none of us, not even Sandra, was particularly keen on getting started on it. We were down, and still in one piece, and we were feeling that sense of utter relaxation that comes at the end of a voyage; there was something in it of homecoming (although the Rim Worlds were home only to the old man), something in it of the last day of school.

Sandra stood there for a moment or so, looking down at Doc and myself. Her regard shifted to the decanter. She said, "It's a shame to leave all that to you two pigs."

"Don't let it worry you, duckie," Jenkins admonished her.

"It does worry me."

She sat down again and refilled her glass. The doctor refilled his glass. I refilled mine.

"Journeys end," said Doc, making a toast of it.

"In lovers meeting," I added, finishing the quotation.

"I didn't know you had a popsy in Port Forlorn," said Sandra distantly.

"I haven't," I said. "Not now. Not any more. But there should be lovers' meetings at the end of a voyage."

"Why?" she asked, feigning interest.

"Because some sentimental slob of a so-called poet said so," sneered Doc.

"Better than all your crap about down-thrusting phalluses," I retorted.

"Boys, boys . . ." admonished Sandra.

"Is there anything left in the bottle?" demanded Ralph Listowel.

We hadn't seen or heard him come into the wardroom. We looked up at him in mild amazement as he stood there, awkward, gangling, his considerable height diminished ever so slightly by his habitual slouch. There was a worried expression on his lined face. I wondered just what was wrong now.

"Here, Ralph," said Sandra, passing him a drink.

"Thanks." The mate gulped rather than sipped. "Hmm. Not bad." He gulped again. "Any more?"

"Building up your strength, Ralph?" asked Sandra sweetly.

"Could be," he admitted. "Or perhaps this is an infusion of Dutch courage."

"And what do you want it for?" I asked. "The hazards of the voyage are over and done with."

"Those hazards, yes," he said gloomily. "But there are worse hazards than those in space. When mere chief officers are bidden to report to the super's office, at once if not before, there's something cooking—and, I shouldn't mind betting you a month's pay, it'll be something that stinks."

"Just a routine bawling out," I comforted him. "After all, you can't expect to get away with everything all the time."

A wintry grin did nothing to soften his harsh features. "But it's not only me he wants. He wants you, Sandra, and you, Doc, and you, Peter. *And* Smethwick, our commissioned clairvoyant. One of you had better go to shake him out of his habitual stupor."

"But what have we done?" asked Doc in a worried voice.

"My conscience is clear," I said. "At least, I think it is . . ."

"My conscience *is* clear," Sandra stated firmly.

"Mine never is," admitted Doc gloomily.

The mate put his glass down on the table. "All right," he told us brusquely. "Go and get washed behind the ears and brush your hair. One of you drag the crystal gazer away from his dog's brain in aspic and try to get him looking something like an officer and a gentleman."

"Relax, Ralph," said Jenkins, pouring what was left in the decanter into his own glass.

"I wish I could. But it's damned odd the way the commodore is yelling for all of us. I may not be a psionic radio officer, but I have my hunches."

Jenkins laughed. "One thing is certain, Ralph, he's not sending for us to fire us. Rim Runners are never that well off for officers. And once we've come out to the Rim, we've hit rock bottom." He began to warm up. "We've run away from ourselves as far as we can, to the very edge of the blackness, and we can't run any farther."

"Even so . . ." said the mate.

"Doc's right," said Sandra. "He'll just be handing out new appointments to all of us. With a bit of luck—or bad luck?—we might be shipping out together again."

"It'll be good luck for all of you if we are," said Doc. "My jungle juice is the best in the fleet, and you all know it."

"So you say," said Sandra.

"But what about the old man?" I asked. "And the engineers? Are they bidden to the presence?"

"No," said Ralph. "As far as I know, they'll just be going on leave." He added gloomily, "There's something in the wind as far as we're concerned. I wish I knew what it was."

"There's only one way to find out," said Sandra briskly, getting to her feet.

We left the ship together—Ralph, Doc Jenkins, Sandra, Smethwick and myself. Ralph, who was inclined to take his naval reserve commission seriously, tried to make it a march across the dusty, scarred concrete to the low huddle of administration buildings. Both Sandra and I tried to play along with him, but Doc Jenkins and our tame telepath could turn any march into a straggle without even trying. For Smethwick there was, perhaps, some excuse; released from the discipline of watchkeeping he was renewing contact with his telepathic friends all over the planet. He wandered along like a man in a dream, always on the point of falling over his own feet. And Jenkins rolled happily beside him, a somewhat inane grin on his ruddy face. I guessed that in the privacy of his cabin he had depleted his stocks of jungle juice still further.

I wished that I'd imbibed another stiff slug myself. The wind was bitterly cold, driving the dust before it in whorls and eddies, filling our eyes with grit, redolent of old socks and burning sulphur. I was wondering how anybody could be fool enough to come out to the Rim Worlds. I was wondering, not for the first time, how *I'd* ever been fool enough to come out to the Rim Worlds.

It was a relief to get into the office building, out of that insistent, nagging wind. The air was pleasantly warm, but my eyes were still stinging. I used my handkerchief to try to clear the gritty particles from them, and saw through tears that the others were doing the same—all save Smethwick, who, lost in some private world of his own, was oblivious to discomfort. Ralph brushed the dust from his epaulettes and then used his handkerchief to restore a polish to his shoes, tossing the soiled fabric into a handy disposer. He started to ascend the stairs, and paused to throw a beckoning nod at us. Not without reluctance we followed.

There was the familiar door at the end of the passageway with *Astronautical Superintendent* inscribed on the translucent plastic. The door opened of itself as we approached. Through the doorway we could see the big, cluttered desk and, behind it, the slight, wiry figure of Commodore

Grimes. He had risen to his feet, but he still looked small, dwarfed by the furnishings that must have been designed for a much larger man. I was relieved to see that his creased and pitted face was illumined by a genuinely friendly smile, his teeth startlingly white against the dark skin.

"Come in," he boomed. "Come in, all of you." He waved a hand to the chairs that had been set in a rough semicircle before his desk. "Be seated."

And then I didn't feel so relieved after all. Fussing in the background was Miss Hallows, his secretary, tending a bubbling coffee percolator. From past experience I knew that such hospitality meant that we were to be handed the dirty end of some very peculiar stick.

When the handshaking and the exchange of courtesies were over we sat down. There was a period of silence while Miss Hallows busied herself with the percolator and the cups. My attention was drawn by an odd-looking model on the commodore's desk, and I saw that the others, too, were looking at it curiously and that old Grimes was watching us with a certain degree of amusement. It was a ship, that was obvious, but it could not possibly be a spaceship. It was, I guessed, some sort of aircraft; there was a cigar-shaped hull and, protruding from it, a fantastically complicated array of spars and vanes. I know even less about aeronautics than I do about astronautics—after all, I'm just the spacefaring office boy—but even I doubted if such a contraption could ever fly. I turned my head to look at Ralph; he was staring at the thing with a sort of amused and amazed contempt.

"Admiring my new toy?" asked the commodore.

"It's rather . . . it's rather odd, sir," said Ralph.

"Go on," chuckled Grimes. "Why don't you ask?"

There was an embarrassed silence, broken by Sandra. "All right, commodore. What is it?"

"That, my dear," he told her, "is your new ship."

Chapter 3

We looked at the commodore, and he looked back at us. I tried to read his expression and came to the reluctant conclusion that he wasn't joking. We looked at the weird contraption on his desk. Speaking for myself, the more I stared at it, the less like a ship it seemed. Have you ever seen those fantastic ornamental carp that are bred on Earth, their bodies surrounded by an ornate tracery of filmy fins, utility sacrificed to appearance? That's what the thing reminded me of. It was pretty, beautiful even in a baroque kind of way, but quite useless. And Grimes had told us quite seriously that it was a model of our new ship.

Ralph cleared his throat. He said, "Excuse me, sir, but I don't quite understand. That . . . that model doesn't seem to represent a conventional vessel. I can't see any signs of a venturi . . ." He was on his feet now, bending over the desk. "And are those propellers? Or should I say airscrews?" He straightened up. "And she's not a gaussjammer, one of the old Ehrenhaft drive jobs. That's certain."

Old Grimes was smiling again. "Sit down, Captain Listowel. There's no need to get excited."

"*Captain* Listowel?" asked Ralph.

"Yes." The smile vanished as though switched off. "But only if you agree to sail in command of . . ." he gestured towards the model . . . "the *Flying Cloud*."

"*Flying Cloud?* But that's a transgalactic clipper name!"

Grimes smiled again. "The first *Flying Cloud* was a clipper on Earth's seas in the days of wooden ships and iron men. This *Flying Cloud* is a clipper, too—but not a transgalactic clipper. She is the latest addition to Rim Runners' fleet, the first of her kind."

"But—" Ralph was looking really worried now. "But, sir, there are many senior masters in this employ. As for that, there are quite a few chief officers senior to me . . ."

"And all of them," said Grimes, "old and set in their ways, knowing only one way of getting from point A to point B, and not wanting to know any other. Lift on reaction drive. Aim for the target star. Accelerate. Cut reaction drive. Switch on Mannschenn drive. A child could do it. And while all this is going on you have the ship overmanned with a pack of engineers eating their heads off and pulling down high salaries, and getting to the stage where they regard the ship merely as a platform upon which to mount their precious machinery."

I couldn't help grinning. It was common knowledge that Grimes didn't like engineers and was hardly on speaking terms with the engineer superintendents.

But Ralph, once he had smelled a rat, was stubborn. And he was frank. He said, "I appreciate the promotion, sir. But there must be a catch to it."

"Of course there is, Captain Listowel. Life is just one long series of catches—in both senses of the word. Catches as in your usage of the word—and fumbled catches." He added, "I hope you don't fumble this catch."

Ralph was persistent. "I see your point, sir. But this ship is obviously something new, something highly experimental. As you know, I hold my master's certificate—but it's valid in respect of conventional drives only."

"But you, Captain Listowel, are the only officer we have with any qualifications at all in respect of the Erikson drive." He pulled a folder out of the top drawer of his desk and opened it. "Like most of our personnel, you made your way out to the Rim by easy stages. You were four years on Atlantia. You shipped in topsail schooners as navigator—it seems that the Atlantian Ministry of Transport recognizes astronautical certificates of competency insofar as navigation is concerned. You thought of settling permanently on the planet and becoming a professional seaman. You sat for, and obtained, your second mate's certificate in sail . . ."

"But what connection . . . ?"

"Let me finish. You were in *Rim Leopard* when she had that long spell for repairs on Tharn. You elected to take part of your leave on that world—and you shipped out as a supernumerary officer in one of their trading schooners."

"Even so . . ."

"Take it from me, Captain Listowel, that your fore-and-aft rig second mate's ticket, together with your experience, means more than your master astronaut's certificate. Too, you are qualified in one other, very important way." He looked at each of us in turn. "You're all so qualified."

"I know nothing about wooden ships, commodore," said Jenkins, "and I'm not an iron man."

"Too right, doctor," agreed the commodore cheerfully. "But you have no close ties on any of the Rim Worlds—neither chick nor child, as the saying goes. And that applies to all of you."

"And so this new ship is dangerous?" asked Ralph quietly.

"No, Captain Listowel. She's safer than the average spaceship—far safer than *Rim Dragon*. She'll be as easy as an old shoe. And economical to run. She is," he went on, "a prototype. It is our intention, insofar as some trades are concerned, to make her the standard carrier."

"And the catch?" insisted Ralph.

"All right. You're entitled to know." He leaned back in his chair and gazed at the ceiling as though in search of inspiration. "You are all of you, I take it, familiar with the principle of the conveyor belt?"

"Of course," Ralph told him.

"Good. You know, then, that as long as the belt is kept loaded, the speed at which it is run is of relatively minor importance. So it is with shipping. Express services are desirable for mails and passengers and perishables—but what does it matter if a slab of zinc is ten years on the way instead of ten weeks?"

"It will matter a lot to the crew of the ship," grumbled Doc.

"I agree. But when the ship is traveling almost at the speed of light, there will not be a lapse of ten years subjective time. To the crew it will be just a normal interstellar voyage."

"But," Ralph interjected, "where does the economy come in?"

"In manning, for a start. I have already discussed the matter with the Astronauts' Guild, and they agree that personnel should be paid on the basis of subjective elapsed time . . ."

"What!" exploded Ralph.

"Plus a bonus," Grimes added hastily. "Then there's fuel consumption. There'll be a pile, of course, but it will be a small one. It will be supply power only for essential services and auxiliary machinery. As you all know, fissionable elements are in short supply and very expensive on the Rim Worlds, so that's a big saving. Then, there'll be no reaction drive and interstellar drive engineers to wax fat on their princely salaries. One donkey-man, on junior officer's pay, will be able to handle the job . . ."

"A donkeyman?" asked Sandra, her voice puzzled.

"Yes, my dear. In the last days of sail, on Earth, the windjammers used some auxiliary machinery, steam-driven. The mechanic who looked after and ran this was rated as donkeyman."

Then Ralph voiced the thoughts, the objections of all of us. He complained, "You've told us nothing, commodore. You want us to buy a pig in a poke. You've mentioned something called the Erikson drive, and you've given us a short lecture on the economics of ship management, but we're spacemen, not accountants. Oh, I know that we're supposed to get our starwagons from point A to point B as economically as possible—but getting them there at all is the prime consideration. And, frankly, I don't see how that contraption could get from one side of the spaceport to the other."

And, I thought, *you've got us all interested, you cunning old bastard. You've got us hooked.*

Grimes looked down at the cold coffee in his cup with distaste. He got up, went to his filing cabinet and pulled out the "W" drawer, taking from it a bottle of whiskey and glasses. He said, "It's rather a long story, but you're entitled to hear it. I suggest that we all make ourselves comfortable."

We settled down with our drinks to listen.

Chapter 4

You will recall [*he said*] that some few years ago I commissioned *Faraway Quest* to carry out a survey of this sector of the Galaxy. To the Galactic East I made contact with Tharn and Grollor, Mellise and Stree, but you are all familiar with the planets of the Eastern Circuit. My first sweep, however, was to the West. Yes, there are worlds to the West, populous planets whose peoples have followed a course of evolution parallel to our own. They're more than merely humanoid, some of these people. They're human. But—and it's one helluva big "but"—their worlds are antimatter worlds. We didn't realize this until an attempt was made to establish contact with an alien ship. Luckily only two people were directly involved—our own psionic radio officer and a woman, who seemed to hold the same rank, from the other vessel. The idea was that they should meet and rub noses and so on in one of *Faraway Quest*'s boats, midway between the two ships; both I and the other Captain were worried about the possibility of the exchange of viruses, bacteria and whatever, and this boat of mine was supposed to be a sort of quarantine station. But we needn't have worried. Our two pet guinea pigs went up and out in a flare of energy that would have made a fusion bomb look silly.

So that was it, I thought at the time. The psionic radio officers had had it, in a big way, so communications had broken down. And it was quite obvious that any contact between ourselves and the people of the antimatter worlds was definitely impossible. I got the hell out and ran to the Galactic East. I made landings on Tharn and Grollor and Mellise and Stree and dickered with the aborigines and laid the foundation of our Eastern Circuit trade. But there was that nagging doubt at the back of my mind; there was that unfinished business to the West. Cutting a long story short, after things were nicely sewn up on the Eastern Circuit worlds I went back. I managed to establish contact—but not physical contact!—with the dominant race. I'd replaced my psionic radio officer, of course, but it was still a long job. I'm sure that Mr. Smethwick won't mind if I say that the average professional telepath just hasn't got the right kind of mind to cope with technicalities. But we worked out a code to use with buzzer and flashing lamp, and eventually we were even able to talk directly on the RT without too many misunderstandings.

We traded ideas. Oddly enough—or not so oddly—there wasn't much to trade. Their technology was about on the same level as our own. They had atomic power (but who hasn't?) and interstellar travel, and their ships used a version of the Mannschenn drive, precessing gyroscopes and all. It was all very interesting, academically speaking, but it got neither party anywhere. Anything we knew and used, they knew and used. Anything they knew and used, we knew and used. It was like having a heart to heart talk with one's reflection in a mirror.

Oh, there were a few minor differences. That new system of governor controls for the Mannschenn drive, for example—we got that from the antimatter people. And they'd never dreamed of keeping fish in their hydroponics tanks, but they're doing it now. But there was nothing really important.

But I had to bring *something* back. And I did. No doubt you've often wondered just what is going on inside Satellite XIV. It's been there for years, hanging in its equatorial orbit, plastered with KEEP OFF notices. It's still there—but the reason for its construction has been removed.

I brought something back. I brought back a large hunk of antimatter. It's iron—or should I say "anti-iron"? But iron or anti-iron, it still behaves as iron in a magnetic field. It's hanging in its casing, making no contact with the walls—and it had better not!—held in place by the powerful permanent magnets. It'd be safe in a hard vacuum, but it's safer still suspended in the neutronium that the University boys were able to cook up for me.

Well, I had this hunk of antimatter. I still have. The problem was, what was it good for? Power? Yes—but how could it be used? No doubt some genius will come up with the answer eventually, but so far nobody has. But in the laboratory built around it, Satellite XIV, techniques were developed for carving off small pieces of it, using laser beams, and these tiny portions were subjected to experiment. One of the experiments, bombardment with neutrinos, yielded useful results. After such a bombardment antimatter acquires the property of antigravity. It's analogous to permanent magnetism in many ways—but, as far as the scientists have been able to determine, *really* permanent.

But how to use it?

Oh, the answer is obvious, you'll say. Use it in spaceships. That's what I came up with myself. I passed the problem on to Dr. Kramer at the University. I don't profess to be able to make head or tail of his math, but it boils down to this: antimatter and the temporal precession field of the Mannschenn drive just don't mix. Or rather they do mix—too well. This is the way I understand it. You use antimatter, and antigravity, to get upstairs. Well and good. You use your gyroscopes to get lined up on the target star, then you accelerate. You build up velocity, and then you cut the reaction drive. Well and good. Then you switch on the Mannschenn drive . . .

You switch on the Mannschenn drive, and as your ship consists of both normal matter and antimatter she'll behave—abnormally. Oh, there'll be temporal precession all right. *But* . . . The ship herself will go astern in time, as she should—and that hunk of antimatter will precess in the opposite temporal direction. The result, of course, will be catastrophic.

Even so–if I may borrow one of your pet expressions, Captain Listowel—even so, I was sure that antimatter, with its property of induced antigravity, would be of great value in space travel. There was this lump of iron that I had dragged all the way back from the Galactic West, encased in aluminium and neutronium and alnico magnets, hanging there in its orbit, quite useless so far but potentially extremely useful. There *must* be a way to use it.

But what was the way?

[*He looked at us, as though waiting for intelligent suggestions. None were forthcoming. He drained his glass. He refilled it. He waited until we had refilled ours.*]

I've a son, as you know. Like most fathers, I wanted him to follow in my footsteps. As many sons do, he decided to do otherwise, and told me frankly that a spaceman's life was not for him. He's an academic type. Bachelor of arts—and what is more useless than a degree in arts? Master of arts. And now doctor of philosophy. And not the sort of Ph.D. that's really a degree in science, but just a jumble of history and the like. Damn it all, he wouldn't know what a neutron was if it up and bit him on the left buttock. But he can tell you what Julius Caesar said when he landed in England—whenever and whatever that was—and what Shakespeare made some character called Hamlet say when he was in some sort of complicated jam that some old Greek called Oedipus was in a couple of thousand or so years previously, and what some other character called Freud had to say about it all a few hundred years later.

But, to get back to Mr. J. Caesar, what he said was, *Veni, vidi, vici.* I came, I saw, I conquered.

And, insofar as the antimatter worlds were concerned, I came, I saw—and I didn't conquer. All I had to show for my trouble was this damned great hunk of anti-iron, and I just couldn't figure out a use for it. It irked me more than somewhat. So, after worrying about it all rather too much, I retired from the field and left it all to my subconscious.

Well, John—that's my son—littered up the house with all sorts of books when he was studying for his latest degree. There was, as I have said, quite a pile of historical material. Not only Julius Caesar and Shakespeare and the learned Herr Doktor Freud, but books on, of all things, the history of transport. Those I read, and they were fascinating. Galleys with sweating slaves manning the sweeps. Galleons with wind power replacing muscle power. The clipper ships, with acres of canvas spread to the gales. The first steamships. The motor ships. The nuclear-powered ships. And, in the air, the airships—dirigible balloons. The airplanes. The jets. The rockets—and the first spaceships.

And with the spaceships sail came back, but briefly. There was the Erikson drive. There were the ships that spread their great plastic sails and drifted out from the orbit of Earth to that of Mars, but slowly, slowly. It was a good idea—but as long as those ships had mass it was impracticable. But if there had then been any means of nullifying gravity they would have superseded the rockets.

Then it all clicked. The oldtimers didn't have antigravity. I *do* have antigravity. I can build a real sailing ship—a vessel to run before the photon gale, a ship that can be handled just as the old windjammers on Earth's seas were handled. A ship, come to that, Captain Listowel, that can be handled just as the topsail schooners on Atlantia's seas are handled . . .

[*He waved a hand towards the model on his desk.*]

There she is. There's *Flying Cloud*. The first of the real lightjammers. And she's yours.

Chapter 5

"Even so . . ." murmured Ralph, breaking the silence.

"Even so, Captain Listowel," echoed Grimes, a sardonic edge to his voice.

"Even so, sir," went on Ralph, undeterred, "I don't think that I'm qualified. I doubt if any of us is qualified."

"You *are* qualified," stated Grimes flatly. "You've experience in sail, which is more than any other master or officer in this employ can boast. Oh, there was Calver. He was in sail, too, before he joined us, but he's no longer with us. So you're the only possible choice."

"But . . . I've no real qualifications."

Grimes laughed. "Who has? There *was* a certificate of competency, Erikson drive, issued on Earth a few centuries ago. But don't let that bother you. The Rim Confederacy will issue certificates of competency for the improved Erikson drive."

"And the examiner?" asked Ralph.

"For a start, you," stated Grimes.

"But, damn it all, sir, there aren't any textbooks, manuals . . ."

"You will write them when you get around to it."

"Even so, sir," protested Ralph, "this is rather much. Don't think that I'm not appreciative of the promotion, but . . ."

Grimes grinned happily. He said, "In my own bumbling way—after all, I'm a spaceman, neither a seaman nor an airman—I've worked out some rough and ready methods for handling this brute." His hand went out to the beautiful model on his desk with a possessive, caressing gesture. "If it were not for the fact that I have a wife and family I'd be sailing as her first master. As things are, I've had to waive that privilege, although not without reluctance. But I can give you a rough idea of what's required."

He took from the top drawer of his desk a little control panel and set it down before himself. He pressed a stud and we watched, fascinated, as the spars rotated on their long axes and then, when the sails were furled, folded back into slots in the shell plating.

"As you see," he told us, "there are now only the atmospheric control surfaces left exposed—including, of course, the airscrews. In appearance the ship is not unlike one of the dirigible airships of the early days of aviation. A lighter-than-air ship, in fact. But she's not lighter than air. Not yet.

"This model, as you've all probably guessed by this time, is a working model—insofar as her handling inside atmospheric limits is concerned. She has within her a tiny fragment of the anti-iron, a miniscule sphere of antimatter complete with induced antigravity." He looked at Ralph. "Now, I'd like you to get the feel of her, Captain Listowel. Go on, she won't bite you. Take hold of her. Lift her off the desk."

Ralph got slowly to his feet, extended two cautious hands, got his fingers around the cylindrical hull. He said, accusingly, "But she's heavy."

"Of course she's heavy. When the real ship is berthed on a planetary surface to discharge and load cargo we don't want her at the mercy of every puff of wind. All right, put her down again. And now stand back."

Ralph stood back, without reluctance. Grimes pressed another stud on his control panel. None of us was expecting what happened next—the stream of water that poured from vents on the underside of the model, flooding the desk top, dripping on to the carpet. Miss Hallows clucked annoyance, but we just watched fascinated. The commodore smiled happily, his hands busy at the miniature controls. There was the whine of a motor inside the model ship and the two air-screws at the after end started to turn. Before they had picked up speed, while the separate blades were still clearly visible, *Flying Cloud* began to move, sliding slowly over the smooth surface of the desk. (I noticed that she barely disturbed the film of moisture.) She reached the edge and she dropped—but slowly, slowly— and then the control surfaces, elevators and rudder, twitched nervously, and her screws were a translucent blur, and her fall was checked and she was rising, obedient to her helm, making a circuit of the desk and gaining altitude with every lap. There was still a dribble of water from her outlets that fell, shockingly cold, on our upturned faces.

"You see," said Grimes. "In an atmosphere you have no worrries at all. Drive her down on negative dynamic lift, start the compressors if you have to to give her a little extra mass with compressed air." (A faint throb was audible above the whine of the motors.) "Open your valves if you think that she's getting too heavy." (We heard the thin, high whistle.) "I'm sorry that I can't give a real demonstration of how she'll handle in deep space, but I can give you some sort of an idea." (He jockeyed the model almost to ceiling level and manipulated the controls so that she was hanging stern on to the big overhead light globe.) "There's the sun," he said. "The sun, or any other source of photons. You spread your sails . . ." (The spars extended from the hull, the complexity of plastic vanes unfurled.) "And off you go. Mind you, I'm cheating. I'm using the air screws. And now, watch carefully. One surface of each sail is silvered, the other surface is black. By use of the reflecting and absorbing surfaces I can steer the ship, I can even exercise control over her speed . . . any questions, Captain Listowel?"

"Not yet," said Ralph cautiously.

"I've told you all I know," Grimes told him cheerfully, "and now you know just about everything there is to know. But I admit that this handling of her in deep space, under sail, is all theory and guesswork. You'll have to make up the rules as you go along. But the atmospheric handling is pretty well worked out. Landing, for example." He looked at his secretary. "Miss Hallows, is the spaceport open for traffic?"

She sighed, then said, "Yes, commodore."

"But it's not," he said.

She sighed again, got to her feet and went to a door, her manner displaying a certain embarrassment. Behind the door was Commodore Grimes' private lavatory. I was rather surprised to see that he had been able to commandeer a full-length tub for himself as well as the usual, standard fittings. Oh, well, rank has its privileges.

"And that," said Grimes, "is a working model of the spaceport of the near future. A lake, natural or artificial. Or a wide river. Or a sheltered bay. Maintenance costs cut to a bare minimum."

I got to my feet and saw that the tub was full.

The model *Flying Cloud* droned slowly over our heads, her suit of sails once again withdrawn and steered through the open door of the bathroom, her airscrews and elevators driving her down in a long slant towards the surface of the water in the tub. While she was still all of three feet above it a tendril snaked from her underbelly, a long tube that extended itself until its end was submerged. Once again there was the throbbing of a tiny pump and the model settled, gradually at first, then faster, then dropping with a startlingly loud splash.

"A clumsy landing," admitted Grimes, "but I'm sure that you'll do better, Captain."

"I hope so," said Ralph gloomily.

II
THE SHIP

Chapter 6

But I think Ralph thoroughly enjoyed himself in the few weeks that followed. I doubt if any of the rest of us did. I know that I didn't. Sailing as a sport is all very well on a planet like Caribbea, but it has little to recommend it on a bleak slag heap such as Lorn. Oh, there's always a wind—but that wind is always bitter and, as often as not, opaque with gritty dust.

I don't think that anybody had ever sailed on Lorn until we, the future personnel of *Flying Cloud*, cast off our sleek, smart (and that didn't last for long) catamaran from the rickety jetty on the shore of Lake Misere, under the derisive stares of the local fishermen in their shabby, power-driven craft, to put in hour after hour, day after day of tacking and wearing, running free, sailing close-hauled and all the rest of it.

But Ralph was good. I have to admit that. I was amazed to learn that so much control of the flimsy, complicated, wind-driven contraption was possible. In my innocence I had always assumed that a sailing vessel could proceed only in a direction exactly opposite to that from which the wind was blowing. I learned better. We all learned better. But I still think that there are easier ways of proceeding from point A to point B, either in deep space or on the water, than under sail.

Yes, all of us had to get a grounding in sail seamanship, Sandra, Doc Jenkins and Smethwick as well as myself. We gathered that Commodore Grimes wasn't finding it easy to find officers for his fine, new ship—after all, even Rim Worlders weren't keen on voyages that would extend over years, even though those years would be objective rather than subjective time. There just weren't that many completely unattached people around. So he'd been dickering with the Astronauts' Guild and got them to agree that anybody, but anybody, could be issued a certificate of competency with respect to the improved Erikson drive.

So we all—and how we hated it!—had to become more or less competent sailors. As I've said, on a sunny world with balmy breezes, blue seas, golden beaches and palm trees it would have been fun. On Lake Misere it wasn't. On Lake Misere it was hard work in miserable conditions—and I still think that it's utterly incredible that in this day and age no heavy weather clothing has yet been devised that will stop the ingress of freezing water between neck and collar, between boot-top and leg.

And when we had all become more or less competent sailors—Ralph called it Part A of our certificates—we thought that the worst was over. How wrong we were! The next stage of our training was to bumble around in yet another archaic contraption, a clumsy, lighter-than-air monstrosity called a blimp. (Like the catamaran, it had been built merely for instructional purposes.) I don't profess to know the origin of the name, but it looked like a blimp. One just couldn't imagine its being called anything else. There was a flaccid bag of gas—helium—shaped like a fat cigar, and from this depended a stream-lined cabin that was control room, living quarters and engine room. There was a propeller driven by a small diesel motor, that moved us through the air at a maximum speed of fifty knots. (Our speed over the ground was, of course, governed by wind direction and velocity.) There was a lot of complicated juggling with gas and ballast. There was the occasion when we were blown off course and drifted helplessly over Port Forlorn just as *Rim Hound* was coming in. Ralph told us afterwards that had the blimp been hydrogen-filled that would have been our finish; as it was, with our gasbag all but burst by the searing heat of *Rim Hound*'s exhaust, leaking from every seam, we made an ignominious crash landing in Lake Misere, from which dismal puddle we were rescued by the fishermen—who were, of course, highly amused to see us again, and in even more ludicrous circumstances than before.

But the blimp was patched up and again made airworthy—as airworthy as she ever would be, ever could be—and we carried on with our training. And we got the feel of the brute. We neither respected nor loved her, but we came to understand what she could and could not do and, when Ralph had decided that we all (including himself) had passed for Part B of our certificates we proceeded, in the little airship, to Port Erikson on the southern shore of Coldharbor Bay.

There's one thing you can say in favor of the Survey Service boys who first made landings on the Rim Worlds, and you can say the same thing in favor of the first colonists. When it came to dishing out names they were realistic. Lorn . . . Port Forlorn . . . Lake Misere . . . the Great Barrens . . . Mount Desolation . . . Coldharbor Bay . . .

The trip was not a happy one. In spite of the heat from the single diesel the cabin was bitterly cold as we threaded our way over and through the Great Barrens, skirting the jagged, snow-covered peaks, fighting for altitude in the higher passes, jettisoning ballast when dynamic lift proved insufficient and then perforce being obliged to valve gas for the long slant down over the dreary tundra that somebody in the First Expedition had named the Nullarbor Plain.

And there was Coldharbor Bay ahead, a sliver of dull lead inset in the dun rim of the horizon. There was Coldharbor Bay, leaden water under a leaden sky, and a huddle of rawly new buildings along its southern shore, and something else, something big and silvery, somehow graceful, that looked out of place in these drab surroundings.

"The ship," I said unnecessarily. *"Flying Cloud."*

"Flying Crud!" sneered Doc Jenkins. He was not in a good mood. His normally ruddy face was blue with cold, and a violent pitch and yaw of the ship a few minutes since had upset a cup of scalding coffee (prepared, somehow, by Sandra in her cramped apology for a galley) in his lap. "And what ruddy genius was it," he demanded, "who decided to establish a spaceport in these godforsaken latitudes? Damn it all, it isn't as though we had the Ehrenhaft drive to contend with and lines of magnetic force to worry about. And both old Grimes and you, Ralph, have been harping on the fact—or is it only a theory?—that these fancy lightjammers will be far easier to handle in an atmosphere than a conventional spaceship."

"True," admitted Ralph. "True. But, even so . . . just remember that on Lorn every major center of population is on or near the equator. And there's a certain amount of risk in having conventional spaceports near cities—and the conventional spaceship isn't one per cent as potentially dangerous as a lightjammer."

"I don't see it," insisted Doc. "To begin with, there's a much smaller pile. A lightjammer is far less dangerous."

"Don't forget what's in the heart of her," said Ralph quietly. "That core of anti-iron. Should the casing be breached, should the antimatter come into contact with normal matter . . ."

He lifted his gloved hands from the wheel in an expressive, explosive gesture. The ship swung off course, dipped and rolled. It was my turn to get a lapful of hot coffee. I decided that there was a lot to be said in favor of the despised drinking bulbs used in deep space.

"Any more questions," asked Ralph, "before we make it landing stations?"

"If you insist on answering with your hands," I said, "no."

He grinned ever so slightly. "All right, then. Now remember, all of you, that this won't be the real thing—but it'll be as near to real as we can make it. To begin with—an upwind approach . . ."

"I can see the windsock," said Sandra, who was using binoculars.

"Where away?"

"A degree or so to starboard of the stern of the ship. On that tower."

"And wind direction?"

"As near south as makes no difference. A following wind."

"Good. Now, Peter, you're in charge of the gas valves, and you, Doc, can handle the ballast . . ."

"The tank's dry," grumbled Jenkins.

"Anything with mass is ballast. *Anything.* Open a port and have a pile of odds and ends ready to dump. And you, Mr. Smethwick, stand by the hose and pump . . ."

We were over the spaceport now. We could see the administration buildings and the warehouses, the long wharf alongside which lay *Flying Cloud.* We could see the little, waving figures of people. And we could hear, from our telephone, the voice of Commodore Grimes speaking from spaceport control: "What are your intentions, Captain Listowel? The ground crew is standing by for your lines."

"I intend to land on the Bay, sir, to make this a rehearsal of landing the big ship."

"A good idea, captain. Berth ahead of *Flying Cloud.* Berth ahead of *Flying Cloud.*"

Ralph brought the blimp round in a long curve and lined her up for the beacon at the end of the wharf. He said sharply, "Don't valve any gas unless I tell you, Peter. That's one thing we shan't be able to do in the real ship." I saw that he was using the control surfaces to drive us down, and I heard the complaining of structural members. But the surface of the water was close now, closer with every second.

"Mr. Smethwick, the hose!"

I couldn't see what was happening, but I could visualize that long tube of plastic snaking down towards the sea. I felt the blimp jump and lift as contact was made and, at Ralph's barked order, valved a cubic centimeter or so of helium. I heard the throbbing whine as the ballast pump started.

We were down then, the boat bottom of the cabin slapping (or being slapped by) the crests of the little waves, and then, a little heavier, we were properly waterborne and taxiing in towards the raw concrete of the new wharf.

It was a good landing—and if good landings could be made in a misshapen little brute like the blimp, then equally good ones should be made in the proud, shining ship that we were approaching.

I thought, with a strong feeling of relief, *There's nothing to worry about after all.*

I don't know if that sentence is included in any collection of famous last words. If it's not, it should be.

Chapter 7

We made fast to a couple of bollards at the foot of the steps at the end of the wharf. The blimp lay there quietly enough, her wrinkled hide twitching in the light, eddying breeze; the high warehouse inshore from the quay gave us a good lee. The linesmen ran out a light gangway and we maneuvered the end of it through the cabin door. Smethwick, who had suffered from airsickness during our northward flight, started to hurry ashore. Ralph halted him with a sharp order. Then he said, in a gentler voice, "We all of us have still a lot to learn about the handling of lighter-than-air ships. One thing always to bear in mind is that any weight discharged has to be compensated for." He turned to me, saying, "Peter, stand by the ballast valve. We shouldn't require the pump."

I opened the valve, allowing the water to run into the tank below the cabin deck. I shut it when the water outside was lapping the sill of the open door. Smethwick scrambled out and the ship lurched and lifted. I opened the valve again, and it was Sandra's turn to disembark. Doc Jenkins followed her. Ralph took my place at the valve and I followed the doctor. Finally Ralph, having satisfied himself with the blimp wasn't liable to take off unmanned, joined us on the wharf.

Commodore Grimes was there, muffled in a heavy synthefur coat. With him were two women similarly clad. The super greeted us and then said to Ralph, "A nice landing, Captain Listowel. I hope you do as well with *Flying Cloud*."

"So do I, sir."

Grimes laughed. "You'd better." He gestured towards the slender, gleaming length of the big ship. "She cost a little more than your little gasbag."

We all stared at her. Yes, she did look expensive. I suppose that it was because she was new. The ships to which we had become used out on the Rim were all second- and even third-hand tonnage, obsolescent Epsilon Class tramps auctioned off by the Interstellar Transport Commission.

Yes, she looked expensive, and she looked new, and she looked *odd*. She didn't look like a spaceship—or, if she did look like a spaceship she looked like one that, toppling on its vaned landing gear, had crashed on to its side. An yet we felt that this was the way that she should be lying. She reminded me, I decided, of the big commercial submarines used by the Llarsii on their stormy, watery world.

Grimes was still talking. "Captain, I'd like you to meet your new shipmates for the maiden voyage. This is Miss Wayne, of the *Port Forlorn Chronicle*. And Miss Simmons, your donkey-man . . ."

I looked at the girls curiously and, I must confess, hopefully. Perhaps the voyage would be even more interesting than anticipated. Oh, I know that most planetlubbers have wildly romantic ideas about the function of a catering officer in a starship—but let me assure you that there's precious little romance. Bear in mind that the catering officer is the ship's dietician—and as such she can determine what the behavior of her male shipmates will be. And in most of the ships that I've sailed in the men have conducted themselves like well-behaved geldings. The exceptions have been vessels in which the catering officers, all too conscious of the passage of years and the fading of charms, have taken steps to insure that they, as women, will not be unappreciated. You may not recall the *Duchess of Atholl* scandal, but I do. Several innocent people took the blame for that unsavory affair and I was one of them. And that was the reason I left the employ of the Waverly Royal Mail and came out to the Rim.

Anyhow, I looked at the two women, thinking (and hoping) that with a little competition in the ship Sandra might ginger up our diet a bit. Martha Wayne was a tall, slim, sleek brunette—and how she managed to look sleek and slim in her shaggy and bulky furs was something of a mystery. But sleek and slim she was. I had read some of her articles in the *Chronicle*, usually towards the end of a voyage, during that period when any and every scrap of hitherto unread printed matter is seized upon avidly. They'd been just the usual woman's page slush—Home Beautiful, Kitchen Functional, Menu Exotic and all the rest of it. Anyhow, she extended her hand to Ralph as though she expected him to make a low bow and kiss it. He shook it, however, although without much warmth.

Then there was Miss Simmons. ("Call me Peggy," she said at once.) She was short, dumpy in her cold weather clothing. She had thrown back the hood of her parka, revealing a head of tousled, sandy hair. Her face was pretty enough, in an obvious sort of way, and the smudge of dark grease on her right cheek somehow enhanced the prettiness.

"Commodore," said Ralph slowly, "did I understand you to say that Miss Simmons is to be our donkeyman?"

"Yes, captain." Grimes looked slightly embarrassed. "A little trouble with the Institute," he added vaguely.

I could guess right then what the trouble was, and I found later that my guess was right. The Institute of Spatial Engineers would be taking a dim view of the improved Erikson drive, the system of propulsion that would rob its members of their hard-won status. They would refuse to allow even a junior member to sign as donkey-man—and, no doubt, they had been able to bring pressure to bear on other engineering guilds and unions, making sure that no qualified engineer would be available.

But a woman . . .

"It's quite all right, captain," the girl assured him brightly. "I'm it. I had an oil can for a feeding bottle, and when other kids were playing with dolls I was amusing myself with nuts and bolts and wrenches."

"Miss Simmons," explained Grimes, "is the daughter of an old friend of mine. Simmons, of Simmons's Air Car Repair Shop in Port Forlorn. Her father assures me that Peggy is the best mechanic he has working for him."

"Even so . . ." said Ralph. Then—"How is it that Mr. Simmons can bear to part with such a treasure? Objectively speaking, this will be a long voyage."

"The usual trouble, captain," Grimes told him. "A new stepmother . . ."

"I hate the bitch," declared Peggy Simmons. She added quietly, "She's young. No older than me. But when this ship comes back to Lorn *I'll* still be young, and she—"

"Peggy!" snapped Grimes.

"But it's true, Uncle Andy."

"That will do. I don't think that Captain Listowel is interested in your personal problems. All that he wants is a competent mechanic."

Her face lost its ugly hardness. "And I'm just that, skipper," she grinned.

"All right," said the super briskly. "That's that. Now, if you feel up to it after your flight in that makeshift contraption, I suggest that we make an inspection of the ship."

"Even so . . ." began Ralph.

"Even so," flared Grimes, "I've got you a donkeyman, and a damn good one. And Miss Wayne has been commissioned to write the journal of the maiden voyage, but she's willing to make herself useful. She'll be signing as assistant purser."

"All right, commodore," said Ralph coldly. "You can hand over the ship."

Chapter 8

Normally, handing over a spaceship is a lengthy business.

But these, we learned, were not normal circumstances. Lloyd's of London had issued a provisional certificate of spaceworthiness—but this, Grimes told us, was liable to be canceled at the drop of a hat. The great majority of Lloyd's surveyors are engineers, and *Flying Cloud* was an affront to those arrogant mechanics. She, as far as they were concerned, was an impudent putting back of the clock, an insolent attempt to return to those good old days when the master, in Lloyd's own words, was "master under God" and, in effect, did as he damn well pleased. The speed of a windjammer was in direct ratio to the skill of her master. The speed of a lightjammer would be in direct ratio to the skill of her master. The donkeyman of a windjammer held petty officer's rank only, messing with the boatswain, carpenter and sailmaker. The donkeyman of a lightjammer would be a junior officer only because the merchant navy doesn't run to petty officers. So the Institute of Spatial Engineers didn't like lightjammers. So they had run, squealing piteously, to Lloyd's. So the heirs and successors to that prosperous little coffee house proprietor, acting on the advice of their prejudiced surveyors, would sooner or later—and, quite probably, sooner—get around to revoking that provisional spaceworthiness certificate.

Flying Cloud was Grimes's baby. He had brought back the antimatter from the antimatter systems. He had worked out a way in which it might be used. He had succeeded in convincing his employers that a lightjammer would be the most economical form of interstellar transport. Now it was up to us to prove him right. Once the maiden voyage was completed successfully, Lloyd's would have no excuse for not granting a full certificate.

So we joined a ship already spaceworthy in all respects. While we had been playing around in the catamaran and the blimp, Grimes had achieved wonders. *Flying Cloud* was fully stored and provisioned. Algae, yeast and tissue cultures were flourishing. The hydroponic tanks would have been a credit to an Empress Class liner. The last of the cargo—an unromantic consignment of zinc ingots for Grollor—was streaming into the ship by way of the main conveyor belt.

We had to take Grimes's word for it that everything was working as it should. Grimes's word, and the word of the Simmons girl, who assured us that she, personally, had checked every piece of machinery. We hoped that they were right, especially since there was some equipment, notably the spars and sails, that could not be actually tested inside an atmosphere in a heavy gravitational field.

Anyhow, that was the way of it. Ralph affixed his autograph to the handing-over form and I, as mate (acting, probably temporary, but not unpaid) witnessed it. And Martha Wayne, as representative of the *Port Forlorn Chronicle*, made a sound and vision recording of the historic moment. And Doc Jenkins suggested that the occasion called for a drink. Ralph frowned at this and said stiffly that we, who would shortly be taking an untested ship into space, would be well advised to stay sober. Grimes told him not to be so bloody silly, adding that takeoff wasn't due for all of twelve hours. So Sandra went to the little bar at one side of the wardroom and opened the refrigerator and brought out two bottles of champagne. Grimes opened them himself, laughing wryly as the violently expanding carbon dioxide shot the corks up to the deckhead. "And this," he chuckled, "will be the only reaction drive as far as the ship's concerned!" And then, when the glasses were filled, he raised his in a toast. "To *Flying Cloud*," he said solemnly, "and to all who sail in her." He emphasized the word *sail*. "To *Flying Cloud*," we repeated.

The commodore drained his glass and set it down on the table. There was a sudden sadness in his manner. He said quietly, "Captain Listowel, I'm an outsider here. This is your ship. I'll leave you with your officers to get the hang of her. If you want to know anything, I shall be in my office ashore . . ."

He got slowly to his feet.

"Even so, sir . . ." began Ralph.

"Even so be damned. This is *your* ship, Listowel. Your donkeyman knows as much about the auxiliary machinery as I do, probably more. And as far as the handling of the sails is concerned, you'll have to make up the rules as you go along." He paused, then said, "But I shall be aboard in the morning to see you off."

He left us then.

"He should have sailed as her first master," said Ralph.

"And returning, still a relatively young man, to find his wife an old woman and his son his senior," said Jenkins. "I can see why we were the mugs. We have no ties."

"Even so . . ." said Ralph doubtfully.

"Come off it, skipper. There's nobody to miss us if this scow comes a gutser. We're expendable, even more so than the average Rim Runner officer. And that's saying plenty."

Ralph grinned reluctantly and gestured to Sandra to refill the glasses. He admitted, "I do believe you're right, Doc. I really do . . ." But the moment of relaxation didn't last long. His manner stiffened again. "All right, all of you. Finish your drinks, and then we'll get busy. I'd like you and Doc, Sandra, to make sure that all's well as far as the farm's concerned. I could be wrong, but I didn't think that the yeasts looked too healthy. And you're the mate, Peter; ballast and cargo are your worry. Just make sure that everything's going as it should."

"Aye, aye, sir," I replied in what I hoped was a seaman-like manner.

He scowled at me, then turned to the donkeyman. "And you, Miss Simmons, can give me another run-through on the various auxiliaries."

"And what can I do, captain?" asked the journalist.

"Just keep out of the way, Miss Wayne," he told her, not unkindly.

She attached herself to me. Not that I minded—I don't suppose that any ship's officer, in any class of ship in any period, has really objected to having an attractive woman getting in his hair. She followed me as I made my way to the supercargo's office. It was already occupied; Trantor, one of the company's wharf superintendents, was there, sitting well back in the swivel chair, his feet on the desk, watching a blonde disrobing on the tiny screen of the portable TV set that he had hung on the bulkhead.

He started to take his feet off the desk slowly when he saw me—and with more haste when he saw Martha Wayne. He reached out to switch off his TV.

"Don't bother," said Martha Wayne. "I've often wondered just who does watch that program. Nobody will admit it."

Nevertheless, he switched off. He saved face by sneering at the new braid on my epaulettes. "Ah," he said, "the chief officer. In person. From office boy to mate in one easy lesson."

"There was more than one lesson, Trantor," I told him. "And they weren't all that easy."

They hadn't been easy at all, I remembered. There had been all the messing around in that cranky catamaran, and the messing around in that crankier blimp, and the long nights of study, and the training that we had undergone in mock-ups of the various control compartments of the ship. The model of the supercargo's office, I realized, had been extremely accurate. Ignoring Trantor, I inspected the gauges. Numbers 1 and 7 ballast tanks were out; 2, 3, 4, 5 and 6 were still in. There was no way of ascertaining the deadweight tonage of cargo loaded save by tally and draft—and the columns of mercury in the draft indicator told me that if steps were not taken, and soon, *Flying Cloud* would shortly look even more like a submarine than she already did.

I went to the control panel, opened the exhaust valves to Numbers 2 and 6 tanks, and pressed the button that started the pump. I heard the throbbing whine of it as it went into action, saw the mercury columns begin to fall in their graduated tubes.

"What the hell do you think you're doing?" demanded Trantor.

"I'm the mate," I told him. "You said so. Remember?"

"If you're taking over," he said huffily, "I might as well get ashore."

"You might as well," I agreed. "But, first of all, I want you to come with me to make sure that the cargo is properly stowed and secured."

"Fussy, aren't you?" he growled.

"That's what I'm paid for," I said.

"But what is all this about stowage?" asked Martha Wayne.

"We have to watch it here," I told her. "Even more so than in a conventional ship. In the normal spaceship, *down* is always towards the stern, always—no matter if you're sitting on your backside on a planetary surface or accelerating in deep space. But here, when you're on the surface or navigating in a planetary atmosphere, *down* is vertically at right angles to the long axis. Once we're up and out, however, accelerating, *down* will be towards the stern."

"I see," she said, in that tone of voice that conveys the impression that the speaker doesn't.

"I suppose you know that your pump is still running," said Trantor.

"Yes. I know. It should be. It'll run till the tanks are out, and then it'll shut itself off."

"All right. It's your worry," he said.

"It's my worry," I agreed. "And now we'll look at the stowage."

With Trantor in the lead, we made our way along the alleyway to the hold. We went through the airtight door, and along the tunnel through the cargo bins. There was nothing to worry about—but that was due more to Grimes's foresight than to Trantor's efficiency. As each bin had been filled, the locking bars—stout metal rods padded with resilient plastic— had slid into place.

As we walked between the bins, the words of that ancient poem chased through my mind. *Argosies with magic sails, pilots of the purple twilight dropping down with costly bales* . . . But there weren't any costly bales here. There were drab, prosaic ingots of lead and zinc and cadmium, cargo for which there was a steady demand but no mad rush. Oh, well, we still had the magic sails.

The stevedore foreman, who had been juggling another set of locking bars into position, looked up from his work. He said cheerfully, "She'll be all right, mister."

"I hope so," I said.

"Just another twenty tons of zinc," he said, "an' that's it. You can have her then. An' welcome to her. I've loaded some odd ships in my time, but this'n's the oddest . . ."

"She'll be all right." I repeated his words.

"That's your worry, mister," he said. "Can't say that I'd like to be away on a voyage for all of twenty years." He gave Martha Wayne an appraising stare. "Although I allow that it might have its compensations."

"Or complications," I said.

Martha Wayne had her portable recorder out. She said to the foreman, "I take it that you've loaded this ship, Mr. . . . ?"

"Kilmer's the name, miss."

"Mr. Kilmer. I wonder if I might ask you for your impressions of the vessel?"

"After the loading is finished, Miss Wayne," I told her.

"From spacefaring office boy to mate in one easy lesson," said Trantor, grinning nastily.

Chapter 9

We finally got to our bunks that night, staggering to our cabins after a scratch meal of coffee and sandwiches in the wardroom. Ralph had driven us hard, and he had driven himself hard. He had insisted on testing everything that could be tested, had made his personal inspection of everything capable of being inspected. Ballast tanks had been flooded and then pumped out. The ingenious machinery that swiveled furniture and fittings through an arc of ninety degrees when transition was made from atmospheric to spatial flight was operated. The motors driving the airscrews were given a thorough trial.

At the finish of it all, Doc and Smethwick were on the verge of mutiny, Sandra was finding it imperative to do things in her galley by herself, and Martha Wayne was looking as though she were already regretting having accepted this assignment. Only Peggy Simmons seemed to be enjoying herself. As well as being obviously in love with her machinery, she appeared to have gotten a crush on Ralph. I overheard Doc mutter to Smethwick, "Following him round like a bitch in heat . . ." Oh, well, I thought to myself, Sandra will soon fix all that once she starts turning out the balanced diet.

Anyhow, with Ralph at last more or less happy about everything, we bolted our sandwiches, gulped our coffee and then retired. I was just about to switch off the light at the head of my bunk when there was a gentle tapping at my door. My first thought was that it was Ralph, that the master had thought of something else that might go wrong and had come to worry his mate about it. But Ralph would have knocked in a firm, authorative manner.

Sandra? I wondered hopefully.

"Come in," I called softly.

It was Peggy Simmons. She was dressed in a bulky, unglamorous robe. She looked like a little girl—and not one of the nymphette variety either. She looked like a fat little girl, although I was prepared to admit that it could have been the shapeless thing that she was wearing that conveyed this impression.

She said, "I hope you weren't asleep, Peter."

"I wasn't," I admitted grudgingly. "Not quite."

She said, "I just had to talk to somebody." She sat on the chair by my bunk, and helped herself to a cigarette from the box on the table. She went on, "This is all so strange. And tomorrow, after we get away, it will be even stranger."

"What isn't strange?" I countered. "Come to think of it, it's the normal that's really strange."

"You're too deep for me," she laughed ruefully. "But I came to talk to you because you're not clever . . ."

"Thank you," I said coldly.

"No. That wasn't quite what I meant, Peter. You *are* clever—you must be, to be chief officer of a ship like this. And I'm clever too—but with machinery. But the others—Sandra and Martha Wayne and Doc— are so . . . so . . ."

"Sophisticated," I supplied.

"Yes. That's the word. Sophisticated. And poor Claude Smethwick is the reverse. So unworldly. So weird, even . . ."

"And Ralph?" I prodded.

Her face seemed to light up and to cloud simultaneously, although there must have been a slight lag. "Oh, he's . . . exceptional? Yes. Exceptional. But I could hardly expect a man like him to want to talk to a girl like me. Could I?"

And why the hell not? I thought. *Put on some makeup, and throw something seductively translucent over the body beautiful instead of that padded tent, and you might get somewhere. But not with me, and not tonight, Josephine..*

"I haven't known many spacemen," she went on. "Only the commodore, really, and he's so much one of the family that he hardly counts. But there's always been something about you all, those few of you whom I have met. I think I know what it is. You all have pasts . . ."

And how! I thought.

"Like Ralph. Like the captain, I mean. You and he have been shipmates for a long time, Peter, haven't you? But I can't help wondering why such a capable man should come out to the Rim . . ."

And him old enough to be your father, I thought. And then I remembered what we had learned of Peggy Simmons' own story. It all added up.

Ralph, by virtue of personality as well as rank, was the ideal Father Image. *Sticky*, I thought. *Definitely sticky.*

"Women," I said.

"Women?"

"Yeah. That's the usual reason why we all come out to the Rim."

"Men," she said, "even the most brilliant men, are such fools where women of a certain class are concerned."

Like your father, I thought.

"With the *right* woman," she went on, "they could go a long way . . ."

Too right, I thought. *Too damn right. All the way to the next galaxy but three, under full sail, and with the right woman manning the pumps or whatever it is that the donkeyman does . . .*

She said wistfully, "I wish . . ."

"You wish what, Peggy?"

"Oh, I . . . I don't know, Peter . . ."

I wish that you'd get the hell out of here, I thought. *I wish that I could get some sleep.*

"Have you a drink?" she asked. "A nightcap, to make me sleep . . ."

"In that locker," I told her, "there's a bottle of brandy. Medicinal. Get out two glasses and I'll have a drink with you. I could use some sleep myself."

She splashed brandy generously into the glasses and handed one to me.

"Down the hatch," I said.

"Down the hatch," she repeated. Then she demanded suddenly, "What haven't I got, Peter?"

I knew what she meant. "As far as I can see," I told her, "you have all the standard equipment. As far as I can see."

She said abruptly, "*She's* with him. In his cabin."

I felt a stab of jealousy. "Who?" I asked.

"Sandra."

So they managed to keep it a secret in Rim Dragon, I thought. *Not that there was any need to. There's nothing in the regulations that says that officers shall not sleep with each other, provided that it doesn't get in the way of their duties . . .*

I said, "But they've known each other for years."

"And I'm just the small girl around the ship. The newcomer. The outsider."

"Miss Simmons," I said severely, "people who affix their autographs to the articles of agreement are engaged for one reason only: to take the ship from point A to point B as required by the lawful commands of the master. Who sleeps with whom—or who doesn't sleep with whom—is entirely outside the scope of the Merchant Shipping Act."

Her robe had somehow become unfastened, and I could see that she did, in fact, possess the usual equipment and that it was in no way substandard. She knew that I was looking at her, but she made no attempt to cover herself. Instead she got to her feet and stood there for a moment or so, posing rather self-consciously and awkwardly, before going to the locker for the brandy bottle. She refilled our glasses, the rosy nipple of her right breast almost brushing my face as she stooped. I restrained myself from pulling her down to me.

"One for the road," I said firmly.

"For the road?" she echoed.

"For the road, Peggy. We're both of us tired, and we have another heavy day ahead of us tomorrow."

"But . . ." She might just as well not have been wearing the robe.

"Damn it all, girl," I exploded, "I may be only the mate, and an ex-purser at that, but I have my pride. You've been making it bloody obvious all day that you were just dying to serve yourself up to Ralph on a silver tray and trimmed with parsley. Sandra beat you to Ralph's bed, so I'm second choice. Or do you think that you're hurting him in some obscure way by giving me what he didn't take? Either way, I'm not playing. So finish your drink like a good girl and go and turn in. By yourself."

"If that's the way you want it," she said coldly.

"That's the way that I want it," I said coldly.

"Goodnight," she said.

"Goodnight," I said.

She set her empty glass down gently on the table. Her face was pale and a tiny muscle was twitching in her left cheek. With her robe again belted securely around her she looked once more like a small girl—like a small girl who is convinced she has been unjustly spanked.

She said, "I'm sorry to have troubled you."

I said, "And I'm sorry that . . . oh, never mind."

"Goodnight," she said again.

"Goodnight," I replied again.

She left then, closing the door quietly behind her. I finished my drink and switched out the light. But I didn't get to sleep for a long time. And I should have slept well, I knew, had I taken the opportunity for the loosening of nervous tension in the most effective way there is. My absurdly puritanical attitude (a hangover from that sordid affair on *Duchess of Atholl?*) had done no good to anybody at all, including myself.

And it was—although this was unforeseeable—to have far-reaching consequences.

Chapter 10

The next morning Sandra was in one of her house-wifely moods; these had been the occasion for jocular comment now and again in *Rim Dragon*. She called each of us individually, with tea and toast. Now that I knew the reasons for these spasms of domesticity I wasn't any happier. "Good morning, Peter," she said brightly (too brightly) as she switched on my light. "Rise and shine for the Cluster Line." (She had served in that outfit before joining Rim Runners.) "I hope you slept well."

"I didn't," I growled. I glowered at her from eyes that probably looked as bleary as they felt. "I hope that *you* slept well."

"But of course," she said sweetly, and left me to my tea.

By the time the breakfast gong sounded, I had showered and shaved and dressed in the rig of the day and was feeling a little better. This was our first real meal aboard the ship and something of a ceremonious occasion. Ralph was at the head of the table and rather conscious, I could see, of the gleaming new braid on his epaulettes. I sat down at his right, with Sandra, when she wasn't bustling to and from the pantry, opposite me. The others took their places, with Peggy Simmons, as the most junior member of the ship's company, sitting at the foot of the table. She blushed when I said good morning to her. I hoped that none of the others noticed, although Doc Jenkins, who never missed much of what was going on, leered in my direction.

"This," said Ralph rather stuffily before we could make a start on the eggs and bacon, "is a momentous occasion."

"We still have to get this bitch off the ground," Jenkins told him.

"Off the water, you mean," I amended.

"Even so . . ." began Ralph severely.

"Good morning to you all," said a familiar voice. We turned to see that Grimes had just entered the wardroom.

We got to our feet.

"Carry on," he said. "Don't mind me."

"Some breakfast, sir?" asked Ralph.

"No thank you. But some coffee, if I may, captain."

He pulled up a chair and Sandra attended to his needs.

He said, "You'll forgive me for talking shop, but I take it that you're secured for space?"

"We are, sir," Ralph told him.

"Good. Well, I have no wish to interfere with your arrangements, but there must be no delay."

"We can take off now, sir, if you wish," said Ralph, pushing away his plate with the half-eaten food.

"For the love of all the odd gods of the Galaxy," pleaded Grimes, "finish your breakfast. I intend to enjoy at least one more cup of this excellent coffee. But, while you're eating, I'll put you in the picture." He patted his lips with the napkin Sandra had given him. "Throughout my career I've never been overly fussy about treading on corns, but I seem to have been trampling on some very tender ones of late. This is the way of it. My spies inform me that this very morning, Metropolitan Standard Time, the *Flying Cloud* issue is going to be raised in the Senate. The Honorable Member for Spelterville will demand an inquiry into the squandering of public money on the construction of an utterly impracticable spaceship. And his crony, the Honorable Member for Iron-hill East, will back him up and demand that the ship be held pending the inquiry . . ."

"Amalgamated Rockets," said Martha Wayne. "And Interstellar Drives, Incorporated."

"Precisely," agreed Grimes. "Well, I don't think that they'll be able to get things moving prior to your takeoff, captain—but if you should have to return to surface for any reason, or even if you hang in orbit, there's a grave risk that you'll be held. I want there to be no hitches."

"There will be none," said Ralph stiffly.

"Good. And when do you intend getting upstairs?"

"At the advertised time, sir, 0900 hrs."

"And you're quite happy about everything?"

"Yes, sir. Even so . . ."

"Every spaceman always feels that 'even so'—otherwise he wouldn't be worth a damn as a spaceman. (Some more coffee, please, if you'll be so good. Excellent.) I suppose that I'll still be around when you return. I hope so. But I shall be getting your voyage reports by way of the psionic radio . . ."

"I'm surprised, commodore," said Martha Wayne, "that the ship hasn't been fitted with the Carlotti equipment."

"It wouldn't work," Grimes told her. "It will run only in conjunction with the Mannschenn drive." He turned to the telepath. "So you're the key man, Mr. Smethwick."

Claude grinned feebly and said, "As long as you don't expect me to bash a key, sir."

We all laughed. His ineptitude with anything mechanical was notorious.

Grimes got to his feet reluctantly. "I'll not get in your hair any longer. You all have jobs to do." He said, as he shook hands with Ralph, "You've a good ship, Listowel. And a good crew. Look after them both."

"I'll do that," promised Ralph.

"I won't say goodbye," said Grimes. "Au revoir is better."

He swung away abruptly and walked quickly out of the wardroom. I hurried after him to escort him to the gangway.

At the airlock he shook hands with me again. He said quietly, "I envy you, Mr. Malcolm. I envy you. If things had been different I'd have been sailing in her. But . . ."

"There are times," I said, "when I envy those who have family ties."

He allowed himself to grin. "You have something there, young man. After all, one can't have everything. I've a wife and a son, and you have the first of the interstellar lightjammers. I guess that we shall each of us have to make the best of what we've got. Anyhow, look after yourself."

I assured him that I would, and, as soon as he was ashore, I went back inside the ship.

The takeoff was a remarkably painless procedure.

When the ship was buttoned up and we were at our stations, the linesmen let go our moorings fore and aft. The little winches, obedient to the pressing of buttons in the control room, functioned perfectly. On the screen of the closed-circuit TV I watched the lines snaking in through the fair-leads, saw the cover plates slide into place as the eyes vanished inside our hull. There was no need for any fancy maneuvers; the wind pushed us gently away from the wharf.

"Ballast," ordered Ralph. "Pump 3 and 5."

"Pump 3 and 5," I repeated, opening valves and pressing the starter buttons.

I heard the throbbing of the pumps, watched the mercury fall in the graduated columns of the draft indicator, a twin to the one in the supercargo's office. But we still had negative lift, although we were now floating on the surface like a huge bubble. There was a new feel to the ship, an uneasiness, an expectancy as she stirred and rolled to the low swell. And still the mercury dropped in the transparent tubes until, abruptly, the pulsation of the pumps cut out.

"Number 4, sir?" I asked.

"No, Peter. Not yet. Extrude atmospheric control surfaces."

"Extrude atmospheric control surfaces, sir."

On the screen I saw the stubby wings extend telescopically from the shining hull.

"I thought that you just pumped all ballast and went straight up," said Martha Wayne, who was seated at the radio telephone.

"We could," said Ralph, "we could; but, as I see it, the secret of handling these ships is always to keep some weight up your sleeve. After all, we shall have to make a landing on Grollor. I intend to see if I can get her upstairs on aerodynamic lift." He turned to me. "I don't think that it's really necessary to keep Sandra and Doc on stations in the storeroom and the farm. After all, this isn't a rocket blast-off, and they're supposed to be learning how to handle this scow. Get them up here, will you?"

"And Claude and Peggy?" I asked.

"No. Claude is hopeless at anything but his job, and Miss Simmons had better keep her eye on her mechanical toys."

I gave the necessary orders on the intercom, and while I was doing so the speaker of the RT crackled into life. "Spaceport control to *Flying Cloud*," we heard. "Spaceport control to *Flying Cloud*. What is the delay? I repeat: what is the delay?"

The voice was familiar; it belonged to Commodore Grimes. And it was anxious.

"Pass me the mike," said Ralph. He reported quietly, "*Flying Cloud* to spaceport control. There is no delay. Request permission to take off."

"Take off then, before the barnacles start growing on your bottom!" blustered Grimes.

Ralph grinned and handed the microphone back to Martha. He waited until Sandra and Doc, who had just come into the control room, had belted themselves into their chairs; then he put both hands on the large wheel. "Full ahead port," he ordered. I pressed the starting button, moved the handle hard over, and Ralph turned his wheel to starboard. "Full ahead starboard," he ordered.

The ship came round easily, heading out for the open sea. From the transparent bubble that was the control room we could now see nothing but gray water and gray sky, and the dark line of the horizon towards which we were steering; but on the screen of the closed circuit TV we could watch the huddle of spaceport buildings and the wharf, to which the little blimp was still moored, receding.

With his left hand Ralph held *Flying Cloud* steady on course; his right moved over the controls on the steering column. And the motion was different now. The ship was no longer rolling or pitching, but, from under us, came the rhythmic *slap, slap* of the small waves striking our bottom as we lifted clear of the surface. And then that was gone and there was only the clicking of our compass and the muffled, almost inaudible throbbing of our screws.

From the RT came Grimes' voice, "Good sailing, *Flying Cloud*. Good sailing!"

"Tell him thank you," said Ralph to Martha. Then, characteristically, "Even so, we haven't started to *sail* yet."

Chapter 11

We should have spent more time in the atmosphere than we did, getting the feel of the ship. But there was the broadcast that Martha picked up on the RT, the daily transmission of proceedings in the Senate. The Honorable Member for Spelterville was in good form. We heard *Flying Cloud* described in one sentence as a futuristic fictioneer's nightmare, and in the next as an anachronistic reversion to the dark ages of ocean transport. And then, just to make his listeners' blood run cold, he described in great detail what would happen should she chance to crash in a densely populated area. The casing around the sphere of anti-iron would be ruptured and, the antimatter coming into contact with normal matter, there would be one hell of a big bang. Furthermore, he went on, there was the strong possibility of a chain reaction that would destroy the entire planet.

It would all have been very amusing, but there were far too many cries of approval and support from both Government and Opposition benches—especially when the Honorable Member, after having divulged the information that *Flying Cloud* was already airborne, demanded that the Government act *now*.

Ralph, as he listened, looked worried. He said, "Miss Wayne, I think that our receiver has broken down, hasn't it?"

She grinned back at him. "It has. Shall I pull a fuse?"

"Don't bother," he said. "If we get a direct order from the commodore to return to port we shall do so, I suppose. Otherwise . . ."

He had handed over the controls to Doc Jenkins and myself; I was steering and Doc was functioning, not too inefficiently, as altitude coxswain. We were rising in a tight spiral, and below us was a snowy, almost featureless field of alto-cumulus. Above us was the sky, clear and dark, with the great lens of the Galaxy already visible although the sun had yet to set. So far all had gone well and smoothly, although it was obvious that in order to break free of the atmosphere we should have to valve more ballast.

Suddenly Sandra cried out, pointing downwards.

We all looked through the transparent deck of the control room and saw that something small and black had broken through the overcast. A tiny triangle it was, a dart, rather, and at its base was a streak of blue fire bright even against the gleaming whiteness of the cloud. Ralph managed to bring the big, mounted binoculars to bear.

"Air force markings," he muttered. "One of the rocket fighters."

Somebody muttered something about "bloody flyboys."

"Better have the transceiver working," ordered Ralph.

Hard on his words came a voice from the RT. "Officer commanding Defense Wing 7 to master of *Flying Cloud*. Return at once to your berth. Return at once to your berth."

"Master of *Flying Cloud* to unidentified aircraft," replied Ralph coldly. "Your message received."

The plane was closer now, gaining on us rapidly. I watched it until a sharp reprimand from Ralph caused me to return my attention to the steering. But I could still listen, and I heard the airman say, "Return at once to your berth. That is an order."

"And if I refuse?"

"Then I shall be obliged to shoot you down." This was followed by a rather unpleasant chuckle. "After all, captain, you're a big target and a slow one."

"And if you do shoot us down," said Ralph reasonably, "what then? We are liable to fall anywhere. And you know that the anti-iron that we carry makes us an atomic bomb far more powerful than any fission or fusion device ever exploded by man to date." He covered the microphone with his hand, remarking, "That's given him something to think about. But he can't shoot us down, anyhow. If he punctures the ballast tanks or knocks a few pieces off the hull we lose our negative lift . . . and if he should rupture the casing around the anti-iron . . ."

"What then?" asked Martha Wayne.

"It'll be the last thing he'll ever do—and the last thing that we shall ever experience."

"He's getting bloody close," grumbled Doc. "I can see the rockets mounted on his wings, and what look like a couple of cannon—"

"Comply with my orders!" barked the voice from the RT.

"Sandra," said Ralph quietly, "stand by the ballast controls."

"I give you ten seconds," we heard. "I have all the latest reports and forecasts. If I shoot you down here you will fall somewhere inside the ice cap. There's no risk of your dropping where you'll do any damage. Ten . . . nine . . . eight . . ."

"Jettison," ordered Ralph quietly.

"Valves open," reported Sandra.

Looking down, I could see the water gushing from our exhausts—a steady stream that thinned to a fine spray as it fell. I could see, too, the deadly black shape, the spearhead on its shaft of fire that was driving straight for our belly. And I saw the twinkle of flame at the gun muzzles as the automatic cannon opened up, the tracer that arched towards us with deceptive laziness. So he wasn't using his air-to-air missiles, that was something to be thankful for. He wasn't using his air-to-air missiles—yet.

The ship shuddered—and I realized, dimly, that we had been hit. There was an alarm bell shrilling somewhere, there was the thin, high scream of escaping atmosphere. There was the thudding of airtight doors slamming shut and, before the fans stopped, there was the acrid reek of high explosive drifting through the ducts. Then, with incredible swiftness, the aircraft was falling away from us, diminishing to the merest speck against the gleaming expanse of cloud. She belatedly fired her rockets, but they couldn't reach us now. We were up and clear, hurled into the interstellar emptiness by our antigravity. We were up and clear, and already Lorn was no more than a great ball beneath us, a pearly sphere glowing against the blackness of space. We were up and clear and outward bound—but until we could do something about getting the ship under control we were no more than a derelict.

Things could have been worse.

Nobody was injured, although Peggy had been obliged to scramble fast into a spacesuit. There were several bad punctures in the pressure hull, but these could be patched. There was a consignment of steel plates in our cargo, and our use of them in this emergency would be covered. The loss of atmosphere could be made good from our reserve bottles. It was unfortunate that we were now in a condition of positive buoyancy rather than the neutral buoyancy that Ralph had planned for the voyage—but, he assured us, he had already worked out a landing technique for use in such circumstances. (Whether or not it would prove practicable we still had to find out.)

So, clad in space armor and armed with welding torches, Peggy and I turned to render the ship airtight once more. As mate I was in official charge of repairs, but I soon realized that my actual status was that of welder's helper. It was Peggy Simmons who did most of the work. A tool in her hands was an extension of her body—or, even, an extension of her personality. She stitched metal to metal with the delicate precision that an ancestor of hers might have displayed with needle, thread and fine fabric.

I watched her with something akin to envy—and it was more than her manual dexterity that I envied. She had something that occupied all her attention. I had not. Although it was foolish, every now and again I had to throw back the welder's mask and look about me. I was far from happy. This was not the first time that I had been outside in deep space, but it was the first time that I had been outside on the Rim. It was the *emptiness* that was so frightening. There was our sun, and there was Lorn (and it seemed to me that they were diminishing visibly as I watched) and there was the distant, dim-glowing Galactic lens—and there was *nothing*. We were drifting towards the edge of the dark in a crippled ship, and we should never (I thought) make it back to warmth and comfort and security.

I heard Peggy's satisfied grunt in my helmet phones and wrenched my eyes away from the horrid fascination of the ultimate emptiness. She had finished the last piece of welding, I saw, and she straightened up with a loud sigh. She stood there, anchored by the magnetic soles of her boots to the hull, a most unfeminine figure in her bulky suit. She reached out to me, and the metallic fingers of her glove grated on my shoulder plate. She pulled me to her, touched her helmet to mine. I heard her whisper, "Switch off."

I didn't understand what she wanted at first—and then, after the third repetition, nudged the switch of my suit radio with my chin. She said, her voice faint and barely audible, "Do you think that this will make any difference?"

"Of course," I assured her. "We can bring pressure up to normal throughout the ship now."

"I didn't mean *that!*" she exclaimed indignantly.

"Then what the hell did you mean?" I demanded.

"Do you think that this will make any difference to Ralph's—the captain's—attitude towards me? After all, the other two women weren't much use, were they?"

"Neither was I," I admitted sourly.

"But you're a man." She paused. "Seriously, Peter, do you think that this repair job will help? With Ralph, I mean . . ."

"Seriously, Peggy," I told her, "it's time that we were getting back inside. The others are probably watching us and wondering what the hell we're playing at." I added, "There's never been a case of seduction in hard vacuum yet—but there's always a first time for everything."

"Don't be funny!" she flared. Then, her voice softening, "There's an old saying: The way to a man's heart is through his stomach. It could be that the way to a space captain's heart is through his ship."

"Could be," I admitted. "Could be. But Ralph won't love either of us for dawdling out here when he's itching to clap on sail. Come on, let's report that the job's finished and get back in." I switched on my suit radio again.

Before I could speak I heard Ralph's voice. Even the tinny quality of the helmet phones couldn't disguise his bad temper. "What the hell do you two think you're doing? Standing there hand in hand, admiring the scenery . . . Mr. Malcom, are the repairs finished? If so, report at once and then return inboard."

"Repairs completed, sir," I said.

"Then let's not waste any more time," suggested Ralph coldly.

We didn't waste any more time. Carefully, sliding our feet over the metal skin, we inched towards the open airlock valve. Peggy went in first and I handed the tools and the unused materials to her. I followed her into the little compartment, and I was pleased when the door slid shut, cutting out the sight of the black emptiness.

The needle on the illuminated dial quivered and then jerked abruptly to the ship's working pressure.

We were all of us in the control room—all save Peggy, who had been ordered, somewhat brusquely, to look after her motors. From our sharp prow the long, telescopic must have already been protruded, the metal spar on the end of which was mounted the TV camera. On the big screen we could see the image of *Flying Cloud* as she appeared from ahead. I thought that it was a pity that we did not have other cameras that would allow us to see her in profile, to appreciate the gleaming slenderness of her.

"The first problem," said Ralph, in his best lecture-room manner, "is to swing the ship. As you are all, no doubt, aware, we possess no gyroscopes. Even so, such devices are not essential. The master of a windjammer had no gyroscopes to aid him in setting and steering a course . . ."

"He had a rudder," I said, "acting upon and acted upon by the fluid medium through which his hull progressed."

Ralph glared at me. "A resourceful windjammer master," he stated flatly, "was not utterly dependent upon his rudder. Bear in mind the fact that his ship was not, repeat not, a submarine and, therefore, moved through no less than two fluid mediums, air and water. His rudder, as you have been so good to tell us, acted upon and was acted upon by the water in which it was immersed. But his sails acted upon and were acted upon by the air." He paused for breath. "We, in this vessel, may consider light a fluid medium. Now, if you will observe carefully . . ."

We observed. We watched Ralph's capable hands playing over the control panel. We watched the TV screen. We saw the spars extend from the hull so that the ship, briefly, had the appearance of some spherical, spiny monster. And then the roller reefing gear came into play and the sails were unfurled—on one side a dazzling white, on the other jet black. We could feel the gentle centrifugal force as the ship turned about her short axis, bringing the Lorn sun dead astern.

Then spars rotated and, as far as that camera mounted at the end of its telescopic mast was concerned, the sails were invisible. Their white surfaces were all presented to the Lorn sun, to the steady photon gale. We were running free, racing before the interstellar wind.

I realized that Ralph was singing softly:

> "Way, hey, and up she rises,
> Way, hey, and up she rises,
> Way, hey, and up she rises . . .
> Early in the morning!"

Chapter 12

So there we were, bowling along under full sail, running the easting down. In some ways the Erikson drive was a vast improvement over the Mannschenn drive. There was not that continuous high whine of the ever-precessing gyroscopes, there was not that uneasy feeling of *déjà vu* that is a side effect of the Mannschenn drive's temporal precession field. Too, we could look out of the control room and see a reasonable picture of the Universe as it is and not, in the case of the Galactic lens, something like a Klein bottle fabricated by a drunken glass blower.

Flying Cloud was an easy ship, once the course had been set, once she was running free before the photon gale. She was an easy ship—as a ship, as an assemblage of steel and plastic and fissioning uranium. But a ship is more than the metals and chemicals that have gone into her construction. In the final analysis it is the crew that make the ship—and *Flying Cloud* was not happy.

It was the strong element of sexual jealousy that was the trouble. I did my best to keep my own yardarm clear, but I could observe—and feel jealous myself. It was obvious that Sandra was captain's lady. It was obvious, too, that both Martha Wayne and Peggy Simmons had aspired to that position and that both were jealous. And Doc Jenkins couldn't hide the fact, for all his cynicism, that he would have welcomed a roll in the hay with Martha. The only one who was really amused by it all was Smethwick. He drifted into the Control Room during my watch and said, "Ours is a happy ship, ours is."

"Are you snooping?" I demanded sharply. "If you are, Claude, I'll see to it, personally, that you're booted out of the service."

He looked hurt. "No, I'm not snooping. Apart from the regulations, it's a thing I wouldn't dream of doing. But even you must be sensitive to the atmosphere, and you're not a telepath."

"Yes," I agreed. "I am sensitive." I offered him a cigarette, took and lit one myself. "But what's new? Anything?"

"The flap seems to have died down on Lorn," he told me. "We're a fait accompli. Old Grimes got Livitski—he's the new Port Forlorn Psionic Radio Officer—to push a message through to wish us well and to tell us that he has everything under control at his end."

"Have you informed the master?" I asked.

"He's in his quarters," he said. "I don't think that he wants to be disturbed."

"Like that," I said.

"Like that," he said.

"Oh," I said.

We sat in silence—there was still enough acceleration to enable us to do so without using seat belts—smoking. I looked out of the transparency at the blackness, towards the faint, far spark that was the Grollor sun. Claude looked at nothing. I heard the sound of feet on the control room deck, turned and saw that the faint noise had been made by Peggy Simmons. She said, "I'm sorry. I . . . I thought that you were alone, Peter . . ."

"Don't let me interfere with love's young dream," grinned Smethwick, getting to his feet.

"You've a dirty mind!" flared the girl.

"If it is dirty," he told her nastily, "it's from the overflow from other people's minds. But I'll go away and leave you to it."

"I'm on watch," I said virtuously. "And, in any case, Peggy has probably come here to report some mechanical malfunction. Or something."

"Yes," she said.

She dropped into the chair that had been vacated by the telepath, accepted a cigarette from my pack. I waited until Claude was gone and then asked, "What's the trouble, Peggy?"

"Nothing," she said. "Nothing mechanical, that is. Although I should check some of the wiring where the shell splinters pierced the inner sheathing."

"Then why don't you?" I asked.

"Because," she told me," "for the first few days in space one has more important things to worry about. There's the file, and the auxiliary machinery, and . . ."

"Surely the wiring is part of the auxiliary machinery," I pointed out.

"Not this wiring. It's the power supply to the trimming and reefing gear—and we won't be using that for a while, not until we make landfall."

"Planetfall," I corrected.

"Ralph says landfall," she told me.

"He would," I said. "He must have brought at least a couple of trunks full of books about windjammers—fact, fiction and poetry—away with him. Mind you, some of it is good." I quoted:

"I must go down to the sea again,
To the lonely sea and the sky,
And all I ask is a tall ship
And a star to steer her by . . ."

I gestured widely towards the Grollor sun, the distant spark that, thanks to the Doppler effect, was shining with a steely glitter instead of its normal ruddiness. I said, "There's his star to steer by." I thumped the arm of my chair. "And here's his tall ship."

"And so he has everything he wants," she said.

"Everything." I decided to be blunt. "He's got his tall ship, and he's got his star to steer by, and he's got his woman."

"But," she said, "I could give him so much more."

"Peggy," I admonished, "don't kid yourself. You're attractive, and you're capable—but Sandra is rather more than attractive. *And* she's a good cook. Take my advice: just forget any school-girlish ideas you may have of becoming the captain's lady. Make this voyage—after all, you've no option now—and then get the hell out . . ."

"And marry and raise a family," she concluded. "But I don't want to, Peter. I don't want to. I don't want to be the wife of some grubby little clerk or mechanic and spend all my remaining days on Lorn."

"All right," I said, "if that's the way you feel about it. But this is an order, Peggy. Lay off Ralph. We're probably in enough trouble already without having triangles added to our worries."

She took a cigarette from my pack, lit it and put it to her mouth. She stared at the eddying wisps of smoke. She said, "That poetry you quoted. Tall ships and stars. That's what Ralph really wants, isn't it?"

"Tall ships and stars and the trimmings," I said.

"Never mind the trimmings," she told me. "And when it comes to trimmings, I can out-trim Sandra."

"Peggy," I said, "you can't. You're not . . . experienced."

Her face lit up briefly with a flash of humor. "And whose fault is that?" she asked. Then, soberly, "But I can give him *real* trimmings. Any woman can sprawl in bed, arms and legs wide open—but I'm the woman who can make Ralph, and his ship, go down in history."

"Judging by the flap when we shoved off," I said, "they already have."

She said, "Correct me if I'm wrong—but the Erikson drive, as it stands, will never be a commercial success. It takes far too long for a cargo, even a non-perishable cargo for which there's no mad rush, to be carted from point A to point B. And there's the problem of manning, too. As far as this ship was concerned, Uncle Andy was able to assemble a bunch of misfits with no close ties for the job, people who wouldn't give a damn if the round voyage lasted a couple of objective centuries. But it mightn't be so easy to find another crew for another lightjammer. Agreed?"

"Agreed," I said, after a pause.

She went on, "I'm new to space, but I've read plenty. I'm no physicist, but I have a rough idea of the modus operandi of the various interstellar drives. And, so far, there's been no faster-than-light drive."

"What!" I exclaimed.

"No, there hasn't. I'm right, Peter. The basic idea of the Ehrenhaft drive was that of a magnetic particle trying to be in two places at the same time in a magnetic field or current, the ship being the particle. But, as far as I can gather, space was warped so that she could do just that. I couldn't follow the math, but I got the general drift of it. And then, of course, there's the Mannschenn drive—but, there, the apparent FTL speeds are achieved by tinkering with time."

"Hmm," I grunted. "Hmm."

"Getting away from machinery," she said, "and back to personalities, Ralph loves his ship. I'm sure that if he had to make a choice between Sandra and *Flying Cloud* it wouldn't be *Flying Cloud* left in the lurch. But . . . but what do you think he'd feel about a woman who made him the captain of the first *real* FTL starwagon?"

I said, "You'd better see Doc on your way aft. He stocks quite a good line in sedative mixtures."

She said, "You're laughing at me."

"I'm not," I assured her. "But, Peggy, even I, and I'm no physicist, can tell you that's it quite impossible to exceed the speed of light. As you have already pointed out, we can cheat, but that's all. And in this ship we can't even cheat. We can no more outrun light than a windjammer could outrun the wind that was her motive power." I pointed to a dial on the panel before me. "That's our log. It works by Doppler effect. At the moment our speed is Lume 0.345 and a few odd decimals. It's building up all the time, and fast. By the end of the watch it should be about Lume 0.6 . . ."

She said, "A fantastic acceleration."

"Isn't it? By rights we should be spread over the deck plates like strawberry jam. But, thanks to the antigravity, this is almost an inertialess drive. Anyhow, thanks to our utterly weightless condition, we may achieve Lume 0.9 recurring. But that's as high as we can possibly get."

"I see," she said doubtfully. Then she added, "But . . ." She shrugged and said, "Oh, never mind."

She got up to leave.

"Thanks for dropping in." I said.

"And thanks for the fatherly advice," she said.

"Think nothing of it," I told her generously.

"I shan't," she said, with what I belatedly realized was deliberate ambiguity.

And then she was gone.

Chapter 13

It was a couple of mornings later as measured by our chronometer, and, after a not very good breakfast, I was making rounds. It's odd how that unappetizing meal sticks in my memory. Sandra was acting third mate now, and Ralph had decreed that Martha Wayne take over as catering officer. And Martha, as the old saying goes, couldn't boil water without burning it. Sandra's scrambled eggs had always been a delight—fluffy but not watery, with the merest hint of garlic, prettied up with chopped parsley and paprika, piled high on crisp, lavishly buttered toast. The less said about Martha's scrambled eggs the better.

Anyhow, I was not in a good mood as I made my way aft from the wardroom. *Flying Cloud* was still accelerating slightly, so "down" was aft. Rather to my disappointment I discovered nothing with which to find fault in the farm, the compartment housing the hydroponic tanks and the yeast and tissue-culture vats. I hurried through the antimatter room—frankly, that huge, spherical casing surrounded by great horseshoe magnets always gave me the shivers. I knew what was inside it, and knew that should it ever make contact with normal matter we should all go up in a flare of uncontrolled and uncontrollable energy. In the auxiliary machinery space I did start finding fault. It was obvious that Peggy had done nothing as yet about removing the splinter-pierced panels of the internal sheathing to inspect the wiring.

But there was no sign of Peggy.

I continued aft, through the reactor room and then into the tunnel that led to the extreme stern. As I clambered down the ladder I heard the clinking of tools and the sound of a voice upraised in song. It was Doc Jenkins' not unpleasant tenor.

"Sally Brown, she's a bright mulatter—
Way, hey, roll and go!
She drinks rum and chews terbaccer—
Spend my money on Sally Brown!
"Sally Brown, she's a proper lady—
Way, hey, roll and go!
Got a house right full o' yaller babies—
Spend my money on Sally Brown!"

I dropped the last few feet into the transom space, landing with a faint thud. Doc Jenkins and Peggy looked up from what they were doing. Doc was wearing only a pair of shorts and his pudgy torso was streaked with grime and perspiration. Peggy was clad in disreputable overalls. She was holding a welding torch.

She said, rather guiltily, "Good morning, Peter."

"Good morning," I replied automatically. Then, "I know that I'm only the mate, but might I inquire what you two are up to?"

"We're going to make this bitch roll and go," replied Peggy happily.

"What do you mean?" I asked coldly.

I looked around the cramped compartment, saw two discarded space-suits that had been flung carelessly on to the deck. And I saw what looked like the breech of a gun protruding from the plating. Around its circumference the welding was still bright. I looked from it back to the spacesuits.

"Have you been outside?" I demanded.

"No," said Peggy.

"Don't worry, Peter," said Jenkins. "We didn't lose any atmosphere. We sealed the transom space off before we went to work, and put the pump on it . . ."

"Remote control," said Peggy, "from inside."

"And you pierced the hull?" I asked with mounting anger.

"Only a small hole," admitted the doctor.

"Damn it!" I flared. "This is too much. Only four days out and you're already space-happy. Burning holes in the shell plating and risking all our lives. And I still don't know what it's all about. When Ralph hears of this . . ."

"He'll be pleased," said Peggy simply.

"He'll be pleased, all right. He'll roll on the deck in uncontrollable ecstasy. He'll have your guts for a necktie, both of you, and then boot you out of the airlock without a spacesuit. He'll . . ."

"Be reasonable, Peter," admonished Jenkins.

"Be reasonable? I am being reasonable. Peggy here has work that she should be doing, instead of which I find her engaged in some fantastic act of sabotage with you, one of the ship's executive officers, aiding and abetting."

"Come off it, Peter," said the Doc. "I'm second mate of this wagon, and I signed the articles as such, and one of the clauses says that deck and engine room departments should cooperate . . ."

"Never mind this second mate business," I told him. "As ship's surgeon, you're still a member of the deck department, ranking with, but below, the mate. And as far as I'm concerned, the prime function of the engine room department is to do as it's bloody well told."

"Then why don't you *tell* me something?" asked Peggy, sweetly reasonable.

"I will," I promised. "I will. But, to begin with, you will tell *me* something. You will tell me just what the hell you two are playing at down here."

"Is that a lawful command?" asked Peggy.

"I suppose so," admitted Jenkins grudgingly.

"All right," she said slowly. "I'll tell you. What you see . . ." she kicked the breech of the cannon with a heavy shoe . . . "is the means whereby we shall exceed the speed of light."

"But it's impossible," I said.

"How do you know?" she countered.

"It's common knowledge," I sneered.

"Way back in the Middle Ages," she said, "it was common knowledge that the sun went around Earth . . ."

But I was giving her only half my attention. Out of the corner of my eyes I was watching Doc Jenkins. He was edging gradually towards the switch of the power point into which the welding tool was plugged. I shrugged. I didn't see why he had to be so surreptitious about it. If Peggy wanted to finish whatever welding she had been doing when I had disturbed them, what did it matter?

Or perhaps it did matter.

I said, "I suppose this welded seam is tight?"

"Of course," she said.

"Then we'll get back amidships. You've plenty of work to do in the auxiliary motor room."

"I have," she admitted.

Then my curiosity got the better of me. "But just how," I demanded, "did you ever hope to attain FTL?"

"This," she said, gesturing with the torch towards the breech of the gun, "is an auxiliary rocket. There is already a charge of solid propellant—Doc mixed it for me—in the firing chamber. We were going to connect up the wiring to the detonator when you interrupted us."

"It's just as well that I did interrupt you," I said. "But how was it supposed to work?"

"I thought that it would be obvious. The ship is already proceeding at almost the speed of light. The rocket is just to give her the extra nudge . . ."

I couldn't help laughing. "Peggy, Peggy, how naive can you be? And with homemade solid propellant yet!"

"Solid propellants have their advantages," she said.

"Such as?" I asked scornfully.

"This!" she snapped.

The welding torch flared blindingly. I realized her intention, but too late. As I tried to wrest the tool from her hands the metal casing of the firing chamber was already cherry red.

I felt rather than heard the *whoomph* of the exploding powder . . .

III
THE WINDS OF IF

Chapter 14

Everything was different, and yet the same.

"Even so," Ralph was saying, "the chow in this wagon leaves much to be desired."

I looked up irritably from the simmering pot of lamb curry on the stove top—and then, obeying an odd impulse, I looked down again, stared at the savory stew of meat and vegetables and hot spices, stared at my hand, still going through the stirring motions with the spoon.

I asked myself: *What am I doing here?*

"You have about three pet dishes," went on Ralph. "I admit that you do them well. But they're all that you *do* do well . . ."

This time I did look up at him. *What was he doing in civilian shirt and shorts?* Then, pursuing the thought, *But why should the Federation Government's observer, even though he is a full commander in the Survey Service, be wearing uniform?*

"Sandra's getting browned off with the lack of variety," said Ralph.

"Mrs. Malcolm, you mean," I corrected him coldly.

"*Captain* Malcolm, if you insist," he corrected me, grinning.

I shrugged. "All right. I'm only the catering officer, and she's the captain. At the same time, I *am* the catering officer, and she's my wife."

"Such a set-up," said Ralph, "would never be tolerated in a Federation ship. To be frank, I came out to the Rim as much to see how the Feminists managed as to investigate the potentialities of this fancy new drive of yours. And this ship, cut off from the Universe for objective years, is the ideal microcosm."

"We get by, out here on the Rim," I said shortly.

"Even so," he said, "you're not a Rim Worlder yourself. You're none of you Rim Worlders, born and bred, except the engineer and that tame telepath of yours. I can understand the women coming out here, but not the men. It must rankle when you're allowed to come into space only in a menial capacity."

"Our boss, Commodore Grimes, is a man," I said. "And most of the Rim Runners fleet is manned by the male sex. Anyhow, there's nothing menial in being a cook. I'm far happier than I was as purser in the Waverly Royal Mail. Furthermore," I said, warming up to the subject, "all the best chefs are men."

Ralph wiped a splatter of curry from his shirt. (I had gestured dramatically with my spoon.) "But it doesn't follow," he said, "that all men are the best chefs."

"Everybody likes my curry," I told him.

"But not all the time. Not for every meal," he said. "Well, Malcolm, I'll leave you to it. And since we have to eat your curry, you might see that the rice isn't so soggy this time."

Interfering bastard, I thought. I brought the spoon to my lips and tasted. It wasn't a bad curry, I decided. It wasn't a bad curry at all. Served with the sliced cucumber and the shredded coconut and the chopped banana, together with the imported mango chutney from Caribbea, it would be edible. Of course, there should be Bombay Duck. I wondered, as I had often wondered before, if it would be possible to convert the fish that flourished in our algae vats into that somewhat odorous delicacy.

Again I was interrupted.

"More curry?" complained Claude Smethwick.

"It's good," I told him. I scooped up a spoonful. "Taste."

"Not bad," he admitted. "If you like curry, that is. I don't have to be telepath to know that you do." He handed the spoon back to me. "But I didn't come here to get a preview of dinner."

"Then what did you come for?" I asked shortly.

"Peter, there's something wrong about this ship. You're the only one that I can talk to about it. Commander Listowel's an outsider, and Doc has gone on one of his verse and vodka jags, and the others are . . . women."

"They can't help it," I said.

"I know they can't—but they look at things differently from the way that we do. Apart from anything else, every one of them is chasing after that Survey Service commander . . ."

"Every one?" I asked coldly.

"Not Sandra, of course," he assured me hastily. (Too hastily?) "But Sandra's got all the worries of the ship—after all, she is captain of the first interstellar lightjammer—on her shoulders, and Martha and Peggy are trying hard to get into Listowel's good books—and bed?—and so there's only you."

"I'm flattered," I said, stirring the curry.

"There's something wrong," he said.

"You said that before," I told him.

"And I'll say it again," he said.

"Well, what *is* wrong?" I demanded.

"You know the *déjà vu* feeling that you get when the Mannschenn drive starts up? Well, it's something like that. But it's not that . . . it's more, somehow."

"I think I know what you mean . . ." I said slowly.

He went on, "You'll think that I'm crazy, I know. But that doesn't matter—all you so-called normals think that psi people like me are at least halfway round the bend. But I've a theory: couldn't it be that out here, on the Rim, on the very edge of this expanding Galaxy, there's a tendency for alternative time tracks to merge? For example, just suppose that the feminist ships had never got out here . . ."

"But they did," I said.

"But they could very easily not have done. After all, it was back in the days of the Ehrenhaft drive, the gaussjammers. And you've read your history, and you know how many of those cranky brutes got slung away to hell and gone off course by magnetic storms."

"So in this alternative Universe of yours," I said tolerantly, "the Rim Worlds never got colonized."

"I didn't say that. You've only to look at the personnel of this ship— all outsiders but Peggy and myself, and neither Peggy nor I can claim descent from the first families. My ancestors came out long after the Feminist movement had fizzled on Earth, and so did Peggy's . . ."

I stirred the curry thoughtfully. "So on another time track there's another *Aeriel*, the first of her kind in space, and another Peter Malcolm in the throes of cooking up a really first-class curry for his unappreciative shipmates."

"Could be," he said. "Or the ship could have a different name, or we could be serving in her in different capacities—all but myself, of course."

I burst into song.

> "Oh, I am the Cook, and the Captain bold,
> And the mate of the *Nancy* brig,
> And the Bo's'n tight, and the Midshipmite,
> And the crew of the Captain's gig!"

"But not," I was interrupted, "the engineer."

I turned away from the stove. "Oh, it's you, Peggy."

"Who else?" She took the spoon from my hand, raised it to her lips, blew on it. She sipped appreciatively. "Not bad, not bad . . ." A few drops of the sauce dribbled on to the breast of her once-white boiler suit, but she ignored them. They made quite a contrast, I decided, to the smears of black grease. She said, "You'll do me for a rough working mate, Peter."

"Thank you."

She absentmindedly put the spoon into a side pocket that already held a wrench and a hammer. I snatched it back, carefully wiped it and returned it to the pot.

She asked, her voice deliberately casual, "Have you seen Ralph?"

"I think he's gone up to the control room," I told her.

She said sulkily, "He's been promising to let me show him the auxiliary motor room for the last three days."

"After all," I consoled her, "he's not an engineer commander."

"But . . ."

"Curry again?" complained a fresh voice.

I resumed my stirring with an unnecessary clatter. I muttered mutinously, "If my galley is going to be turned into the ship's social club there won't be anything. But aren't you supposed to be on watch, Miss Wayne?"

"The old woman relieved me," she said. "She's showing Ralph just how a lightjammer should be handled." She leaned back against a bench, slimly elegant in her tailored shirt and shorts, nibbling a piece of celery she had picked up from the chopping board. "If the Federation Survey Service doesn't build a fleet of improved Erikson drive wagons it won't be Sandra's fault."

"Love me, love my ship," muttered Peggy.

"What was that?" I asked sharply.

"Nothing," she said.

Both women looked at me in silence, and I was suddenly afraid that what I could read in their eyes was pity.

Chapter 15

Everything was different again.

I was relaxing in the easy chair in the captain's day room, smoking a cigarette and listening to a recording of the old-time sea chanteys of distant Earth. I wondered what those ancient sailormen would have made of this fabrication of metal and plastic, with atomic fire in her belly, spreading her wings in the empty gulf between the stars, running free before the photon gale. Then I heard the door between bathroom and bedroom open, and I turned my head. Sandra, naked from her shower, walked slowly to the chair at her dressing table and sat down before the mirror. I had seen her naked many times before. (But had I?) But this was the first time. (But how could it be?) I felt the stirrings of desire.

I got up and walked through to the bedroom. I put my hands gently on her smooth shoulders, kissed her gently behind the ear.

"No," she said. *"No."*

"But . . ."

"I've done my hair," she said, "and I don't want it messed up."

"Damn it all," I told her, "we *are* married."

But are we? I asked myself.

"Take your hands off me," she ordered coldly.

I did so, and looked at her and at her reflection in the mirror. She was beautiful. But I tried to find fault. There was that mole just above her navel. And the feeble gravitational field was kind to her; her breasts were proud and outthrusting without artificial support, her stomach flat. *In a heavy gravitational field*, I told myself, *she would not be as lovely.*

But I knew that she would be.

"Don't maul me," she said.

"Sorry," I muttered.

I went to sit on the bed.

"Haven't you anything better to do?" she asked.

"No," I said.

She made a sound that can only be described as a snarl and then, ignoring me, went on with her toilet. There was a session with the whirring hair dryer, after which she affixed glittering clips to the lobes of her ears. She got up then and walked to the wardrobe, ignoring me. She took out a uniform shirt of thin black silk, a pair of black shorts and a pair of stiletto-heeled black sandals. Her back to me, she shrugged into the shirt and then pulled the shorts up over her long, slim legs. She sat on the bed (and I might as well not have been there) and buckled the sandals over her slender feet. She returned to the mirror and with a tiny brush applied lip rouge.

"Going ashore?" I asked sarcastically.

"If you must know," she told me, "Commander Listowel has a fine collection of films made by the Survey Service on worlds with non-human cultures."

"Good," I said. "I'll brush my hair and wash behind the ears."

"You," she said, "were not invited."

"But . . ."

Her manner softened—but briefly, very briefly. "I'm sorry, Peter, but when senior officers of different space services want to talk shop they don't want juniors in their hair."

"I see," I said.

She got up from the chair. In the form-molding shirt, the abbreviated shorts, she looked more naked than she had when she had come through from the shower. I was acutely conscious that under the skimpy garments there was a woman. *My* woman. (Or was she? Had she ever been?)

"You needn't wait up for me," she said.

"Thank you," I said.

"You're rather sweet," she said, "in your own way."

"Thank you," I said.

I watched her go, then lit another cigarette and stuck it in my mouth. I knew now what was happening. I'd seen it happen before, to other people, but that didn't make it any better. Ashore it would have been bad enough—but here, in deep space, with Sandra the absolute monarch of this little, artificial world, there was nothing at all I could do. Ashore, even in a Feminist culture, a man can take strong action against an erring wife and her paramour. But if I took action here I should be classed as a mutineer.

But there must be something that I could do about it.

There must be *something*.

How much did Martha know? How much did Peggy know?

Women know women as no man can ever know them. There is that freemasonry, the lodge into which no male may ever intrude. There is the freemasonry—but, too, there are the rivalries within the lodge. There is the bitchiness. And all is fair in love and war, and if I could turn the jealousy being felt by both Martha and Peggy to my own account, so much the better. (It would have been better still to have slugged it out with Listowel and then to have dragged Sandra by the hair, kicking and screaming, to bed—but, knowing Sandra, so far as any man can know any woman, I didn't feel like taking the risk. She was still the captain, and I was the cook, and the extreme penalty for mutiny in space is death.)

Peggy, I thought, would be the best bet. As a woman Martha might hate Sandra's guts, but as mate she would be loyal to the captain. Peggy, brought up in the workshop rather than the wardroom, would be less overawed by gold braid and Queen Mother's Regulations.

I still didn't like it. It seemed more than somewhat gutless to go whining in search of outside help, but I was feeling desperate. I threw my cigarette in the general direction of the disposer, then got up and went into the alleyway. I looked towards the door of the guest room, in which Listowel was berthed, and wondered what was happening behind it. I almost strode towards it, my fists clenched ready to start hammering on the featureless panel. Almost.

But I hadn't the guts.

I went, instead, to the companionway leading down to the next deck, to the compartment in which the subordinate officers were housed. From Martha's cabin drifted the faint strains of music—or of what she called music, a recording of one of Krashenko's atonal symphonies. So she was alone, which meant that Peggy would be alone too. (Peggy made no secret of the fact that she liked something "with a bit of tune to it.") Doc Jenkins, as acting second mate, would be on watch. And Claude Smethwick almost certainly would be sending his thoughts ranging across the light years, gossiping with his fellow telepaths aboard distant ships and on distant worlds.

I tapped at Peggy's door and heard her call out what I thought was an invitation to enter.

I stepped into the cabin—then started to back out. She was prone on her bunk, absorbing the radiation of a sunlamp. She was wearing a pair of dark glasses and a thoughtful expression.

I stammered, "I'm sorry. I thought you said to come in."

She said, "I did say come in. Shut the door. There's a draft."

I shut the door, then sat down heavily in the chair. It was rather too close to the bunk. (Or, perhaps, it wasn't close enough . . .) I thought, *To hell with it. If she's not embarrassed, why should I be?* and looked at her with appreciation. There was something hauntingly familiar about her unclad body as well as something surprising. In her overalls she was dumpy and unglamorous—naked, she was rather beautiful. She was plump, but in the places where it counted, and her waist was narrow. I thought that I should be able to get my two hands around it. I thought that it would be nice to try.

She said, "A penny for them."

I told her, "I was wondering if this lamp of yours could be used to make Bombay Duck."

She asked, "What is Bombay Duck?"

I said, "It's fish, uncooked and dried in the sun. It stinks. You crumble it over curry."

She said, "You're a bloody liar, Peter."

"I'm not. That's all that Bombay Duck is. Stinking dried fish."

"I'm not disputing that. Your thoughts, at this moment, may be below your navel, but they're not centered on your stomach."

"Well . . ." I muttered lamely.

"And furthermore, Mr. Malcolm, you needn't expect that I'm going to catch you on the rebound, or that you're going to catch me the same way."

I said, "It would be a neat solution."

"Now, perhaps. But probably a messy one later, when certain persons who shall be nameless decide that their duties to their respective services come first." She declaimed:

> "I could not love thee, deah, so much,
> Loved I not honour more."

I said, "Do you mind if I smoke?"

She said, "I don't care if you burst into flame."

"Not very original," I told her. "And not very funny." I lit a cigarette. She stretched a shapely arm and took it from me, but still succeeded in displaying no more than her rear elevation. I lit another cigarette and put it to my lips. I said, "Come to think of it, it is rather hot in here."

"Is it?" she asked. Then she said, "No, you may not remove your shirt. And you may not, repeat not, remove your shorts. If you do, I shall holler rape. And as you're in my cabin, and not I in yours, you'll find yourself well in the cactus."

"Oh," I said.

"Precisely," she said.

For a while I smoked in silence, and she smoked in silence. I thought,

You can look, but you can't touch. I asked, "Aren't you done on that side?"

She said, "No."

We smoked in silence; this time, she broke it.

"Why did you come to see me, Peter?"

I said, "I thought you might be able to help."

"And why should I want to help you?"

"Just enlightened self-interest," I said. "You want Listowel, God knows why. I want Sandra back. If you get that stuffed shirt commander it'll leave my everloving wife at loose ends—and I don't think, somehow, that she'll make a pass at either Doc Jenkins or poor old Claude."

"All right," she said. "You help me, and I help you. If the old woman returns to her husband that leaves Ralph all on his ownsome. Then Martha and I can fight it out between us."

"This mutual aid . . ." I said.

"It's all rather complicated," Peggy told me. She threw the end of her cigarette into the disposer. "It all hinges on the fact that Sandra puts the ship first. And I think—mind you, it's not a certainty–that you can get yourself well into her good books. How would it be if you could say, 'Look, darling, I've made you the captain of the first FTL ship in history,'?"

"This ship is not faster than light," I said. "But the Mannschenn drive ships are, and the Ehrenhaft drive wagons what few there are left of them."

"Is that so?" she countered.

"Of course," I said.

"Oh." She paused for a second or so, then said slowly, "Correct me if I'm wrong, but the Erikson drive, as it stands, will never be a commercial success. It takes far too long for a cargo, even a non-perishable cargo for which there's no mad rush, to be carted from point A to point B. And there's the problem of manning, too. As far as this ship was concerned, Auntie Susan was able to assemble a bunch of misfits with no close ties for the job, people who wouldn't give a damn if the round voyage lasted a couple or three centuries—objective centuries, that is. Or even subjective. But it mightn't be so easy to find another crew for another lightjammer. Agreed?"

I said, "You drifted away from the script."

"What do you mean?" she asked. Her face looked frightened.

"Nothing," I said. "Nothing. It's just that I seem to have heard you say almost the same words before."

She said, but doubtfully, "You're space-happy, Peter." Then she went on: "I'm new in space, relatively new compared to the rest of you, but I've read plenty. I'm no physicist, but I have a rough idea of the modus operandi of the various interstellar drives. And, so far, there's been no faster-than-light drive."

"What!" I exclaimed, but somehow I didn't feel as surprised as I should have.

"No, there hasn't. I'm right, Peter. The basic idea of the Ehrenhaft drive was that of a magnetic particle trying to be in two places at the same time in a magnetic field or current, the ship being the particle. But, as far as I can gather, space was warped so that she could do just that. I couldn't follow the math, but I got the general drift of it. And then, of course, there's the Mannschenn drive—but, there, the apparent FTL speeds are achieved by tinkering with time . . ."

"Hmm," I grunted. "Hmm."

"Getting away from machinery," she said, "and back to personalities, Sandra loves her ship. I'm sure that if she had to make a choice between Ralph and *Aeriel* it wouldn't be *Aeriel* left in the lurch. Or if she had to make a choice between you and *Aeriel* . . . but what do you think she'd feel about the man who made her captain of the first real FTL starwagon?"

I said, "You'd better see Doc when he comes off watch. He stocks quite a good line in sedative mixtures."

She said, "You're turning down a good chance, perhaps your only chance, Peter."

"Damn it all," I said, "even I, and I'm no physicist, can tell you that it's quite impossible to exceed the speed of light. As you have already pointed out, we can cheat, but that's all. And in this ship we can't even cheat. We can no more outrun light than a windjammer could outrun the wind that was her motive power." I started to point towards something that wasn't there. "That's our log. It works by Doppler effect. At the moment our speed is . . ."

She looked at me hard, a puzzled expression on her face. "A log? Here? What the hell's wrong with you, Peter?"

I said, "I don't know."

She said, "There's something screwy about this ship. But definitely. Anyhow, let me finish what I was going to say. I maintain that we can give it a go—exceeding the speed of light, I mean."

"But it's impossible," I said.

"How do you know?" she countered.

"It's common knowledge," I sneered.

"Way back in the Middle Ages," she said, "it was common knowledge that the sun went round the Earth."

"Oh, all right," I grunted. "But tell me, please, just how do you expect to attain FTL speeds?"

"With an auxiliary rocket," she said. "Just a stovepipe, sticking out from the stern end of the ship. I can make it—and you, with your access to the chemicals for the hydroponics tanks, can make the solid propellant, the black powder. We're doing about Lume 0.9 recurring at the moment, all we need is a nudge . . ."

I couldn't help laughing. "Peggy, Peggy, how naive can you be? And with homemade solid propellant yet!"

"You can make it," she said. "And it's to your advantage."

I looked at her. During our heated discussion she had turned over. The dark glasses made her look so much more naked. I said, "I'm not sure that I'm really interested in getting Sandra back . . ."

She flopped back again on her belly in a flurry of limbs.

She said coldly, "Let's not forget the purpose of this discussion. Frankly, it was my intention to bribe you with the body beautiful to play along with me on this FTL project, but it wouldn't be right. You want Sandra back, and I want Ralph. Let's keep it that way, shall we?"

"But . . ." I extended a hand to one smooth buttock.

"On your bicycle, spaceman," she told me. "Hit the track. Make another pass, and I holler rape. After all, you're in my cabin, I'm not in yours. Come and see me again when you've got two or three pounds of black powder made up. And if you can't make it, then Martha and I will figure out some other way."

I asked, "She's in on this?"

"Of course," said Peggy scornfully. "I hate the bitch, but she's a good mate. I'd never be able to cut a hole in the stern for my auxiliary rocket unless she approved."

My hand had strayed back again and was stroking the silky skin on her back. I imagined that I heard her purring, like some great, sleek, lazy cat. And then, with shocking suddenness, she was off the bunk and bundling me towards the door.

"Out," she snarled. "Out. And don't come back until you have that powder."

"But . . ."

"Out!" she said with determined finality, and I was standing in the alleyway, staring resentfully at the panel that had slammed shut on her golden loveliness.

I don't know whether or not you have ever tried to make black powder, but I can tell you this: it's easier talking about it than doing it. You want flowers of sulfur, and you want charcoal (or carbon) and you want saltpeter. At first I made the mistake of trying to mix the ingredients dry, and all I got was a grayish dust that burned with a halfhearted fizzle. Then

I substituted potassium chlorate for the sodium nitrate, and my sample went off prematurely and took my eyebrows with it. I came to the conclusion then that the powder would have to be properly mixed with water, and then dried out—using, of course, the recommended ingredients. And it worked out, even though I dried the sludge by exposure to vacuum instead of in the sun, as was done (I suppose) by the first cannoneers.

Anyhow, it was as well that I had something to occupy my mind. It was obvious, far too obvious, what was going on between Listowel and Sandra. Peggy's scheme was a harebrained one, but it might just get results. I had little doubt that it would get results—but what those results would be I could not imagine. Meanwhile, everybody in *Aeriel* continued to do his or her appointed duty, even though the ship was fast becoming a seething caldron of sexual jealousies.

And then, one night (as reckoned by our chronometer) I had the last batch of gunpowder mixed and dried. There was a five-gallon can full of the stuff. I picked it up, let myself out of the galley and made my way to the officers' flat. As I entered the alleyway I saw Doc Jenkins knocking on the door of Martha Wayne's cabin. I wondered who was in control, and then wished that I hadn't wondered. The control room would be well-manned, of course. There would be the captain, and there would be that blasted Survey Service commander, the pair of them looking at the stars and feeling romantic.

"Ah," said Jenkins, noticing me, "the commissioned cook. In person. Singing and dancing."

"Neither singing nor dancing," I said grimly.

"And what have you got in the can, Petey boy? You know that I have the monopoly on jungle juice."

"Nothing to drink," I said.

"Then what is it?"

"Something for Peggy."

"Something for Peggy," he mimicked. "Something for Peggy . . ." He quoted:

"When in danger or in fear,
Always blame the engineer . . ."

I tried to edge past him, but he put out his hand and grabbed my arm. In spite of his flabby appearance he was strong. And I was afraid to struggle; there was the possibility that the can of black powder might get a hard knock if I did. (I know that in theory it was quite safe, but I still didn't trust the stuff.)

"Not so fast," he said. "Not so fast. There's something going on aboard this ship, and as one of the executive officers, as well as the surgeon, it's my duty to find out what it is."

The door of the chief officer's cabin slid open. Martha stood there looking at us. "Come in," she ordered sharply. "Both of you."

We obeyed. Martha shut the door behind us and motioned us to chairs. We sat down. With a certain relief I put the can of powder gently on the carpeted deck—and then, before I could stop him, Doc snatched it up. He shook it.

He demanded, "What's in this?"

"Some powder," I said lamely.

"Powder?" He worried the lid off the container. "Powder? What sort of powder?"

"Abrasive powder," I lied. "Peggy gave me the formula and asked me to cook some up for her."

"Oh." He put the can, lid still off, down beside his chair, away from me. He took a cigarette from the box on Martha's desk, lit it, put it to his lips. He inhaled deeply, inhaled again. The burning end glowed brightly, the ash lengthened as we watched. He made as though to use the open can as an ash tray.

Martha's hand flashed out, smacked the cigarette from his fingers and sent it flying across the cabin in a flurry of sparks.

Jenkins looked hurt. "What was that in aid of?"

She said, "You were going to spoil the . . . mixture."

"How? If it's abrasive powder, a little ash might improve it."

"Not this mixture," she said.

"No," I supported her. "No. It wouldn't."

"I'm not altogether a fool," grumbled Jenkins.

"No?" asked Martha sweetly. "No?" She extended a slender leg, and with her slim foot gently shoved the can out of harm's way. "No?"

"No!" he almost shouted. "I've lived on primitive worlds, Martha, planets where military science is in its infancy. And here's Peter, lugging around a dirty great cannister of villainous saltpeter, and there's Peggy, sweating and slaving over something that looks like a breech-loading cannon." He snorted. "If it were a couple of dueling pieces it would make sense. Pistols for two and coffee for one. And then after the commissioned cook and the bold commander had settled their differences, you and Peggy could do battle, at twenty paces, for the favors of the survivor.

"But a cannon . . . it doesn't make sense."

"No, it doesn't," agreed Martha. She got up and went to a locker. I thought that she was going to offer us drinks. There were racked bottles there, and glasses. And there was a drawer under the liquor compartment, which she pulled open. She took from it a nasty-looking Minetti automatic.

She said, "I'm sorry, Doc, but you know too much. We have to keep you quiet for the next few hours. And you, Peter, see about tying him up and gagging him, will you?" She motioned with the pistol. "Down, boy, down. I shan't shoot to kill—but you wouldn't like your kneecaps shattered, would you?"

Jenkins subsided. He looked scared—and, at the same time, oddly amused. "But I don't know too much," he expostulated. "I don't know enough."

Martha allowed a brief smile to flicker over her full mouth. She glanced at me fleetingly. "Shall we tell him, Peter?"

I said, "It wouldn't do any harm. Now."

Martha sat down again, the hand with the pistol resting on one slender thigh. It remained pointing directly at Jenkins. Her finger never strayed from the trigger.

"All right," she said. "I'll put you in the picture. As you are aware, there's a considerable amount of ill-feeling aboard this vessel."

"How right you are!" exclaimed Jenkins.

"We think that the captain is behaving in a manner prejudicial to good order and discipline."

He chuckled softly. "Mutiny, is it? In all my years in space I've never seen one. But why that absurd, archaic cannon? After all, you've access to the ship's firearms." He added, "As you've just proved, Martha."

"It's not mutiny," she snapped.

"Have I another guess?"

She told him, "You can guess all the way from here to Grollor, but you'll never guess right."

"No?" He made as though to rise from his chair, but her gun hand twitched suggestively. "No? Then why not tell me and get it over with."

"If you must know," she said tiredly, "it's a way—it might work and it might not–to distract Sandra's attention from Ralph. She's more in love with her ship than with anybody in the ship but if Peter were to be able to say, 'Look, darling, thanks to me you are now the captain of the first real FTL starwagon,' she'd be eating out of his hand."

He stared at me in mock admiration. "I didn't know you had it in you, Peter."

"He hasn't," said Sandra. "It was Peggy and I who cooked up the scheme. We don't know if it will succeed or not—but *something* is bound to happen when Peggy's solid fuel rocket gives the ship just that extra nudge."

"And all these years," whispered Jenkins, "I've regarded you as just a stuffed shirt—mind you, a well-stuffed shirt—and Peggy as a barely literate mechanic. But there's a streak of wild poetry in you, in both of you.

Mind you, I don't think that Listowel is worth the trouble.—But throwing your bonnet over the windmill is always worthwhile. This crazy scheme appeals to me. I'm with it, Martha, and I'm with you. I've been dreaming about something on those lines myself, but not so practically as you have done . . ."

His hand went to the side pocket of his shorts—and Martha's hand, holding the pistol, lifted to cover him. But it was a folded sheet of paper that he pulled out.

"Martha," he pleaded, "put the *Outer Reaches Suite* on your playmaster, will you? Or get Peter to put it on, if you don't trust me. And, if you would be so good, something to wet my whistle . . ."

"Fix it, Peter," ordered Martha.

I fixed it, first of all pouring a stiff whiskey on the rocks for each of us, then adjusting the controls of the gleaming instrument. The first notes of the Suite drifted into the cabin. It wasn't music that I have ever cared for. There was too much of loneliness in it, too much of the blackness and the emptiness—the emptiness that, somehow, was not empty, that was peopled with the dim, flimsy ghosts of the might-have-been.

Jenkins drained his glass, then unfolded the piece of paper and blinked at it.

> "Down the years
> And the light years,
> Wings wide spread
> To the silent gale . . .
> Wide wings beating
> The wall between
> Our reality and our reality
> And realities undreamed . . .
> And realities undreamed . . .
> Or dreamed?
> Down the years
> And the darkness—"

He broke off abruptly, and Martha stiffened, her Minetti swinging to cover the open door. Peggy was there, demanding irritably, "Aren't you people going to lend a hand? Do I do all the work in this bloody ship?" She saw Doc, muttered, "Sorry. Didn't know you had company."

"*We* have company, Peggy," corrected Martha.

"You mean he . . ."

"Yes. He knows."

"Yes, indeed," agreed Doc happily. "And I'll help you to beat your wings against the wall."

"What wall?" demanded Peggy disgustedly.

It was odd that we now trusted Doc without any question. Or was it so odd? There were those half-memories, there was the haunting feeling that we had done all this before. Anyhow, we poured Peggy a drink, had another one ourselves, and then made our way aft. In the workshop we picked up the thing that Peggy had been making. It did look like a cannon, and not a small one either. It was fortunate that our acceleration was now extremely gentle, otherwise it would have been impossible for us to handle that heavy steel tube without rigging tackles.

We got it down at last to the transom space and dropped it on the after bulkhead. Martha climbed back, with Peggy and myself, into the air screw motor room; Doc stayed below. While Peggy and I climbed into spacesuits Martha passed the other equipment down to Jenkins—the welding and cutting tools, the can of powder. And then Doc came up, and Peggy and I, armored against cold and vacuum, took his place.

Over our heads the airtight door slid shut. I heard the faint whirr of the pump that Peggy had installed in the motor room, and realized that the atmosphere was being evacuated from our compartment. I saw the needle of the gauge on the wrist of my suit falling, and watched it continue to drop even when I could no longer hear anything.

Peggy's voice in my helmet phones was surprisingly loud.

She said, "Let's get moving."

It was Peggy who did most of the work. A tool in her hands was an extension of her body—or even an extension of her personality. The blue-flaring torch cut a neat round hole in the bulkhead and then, after I had lifted the circle of still glowing steel away and clear, in the shell plating beyond. This section I kicked out, and watched fascinated as it diminished slowly, a tiny, twinkling star against the utter blackness. Peggy irritably pulled me back to the work in hand. Together we maneuvered the rocket tube into place. It was a tight fit, but not too tight. And then Peggy stitched metal to metal with the delicate precision that an ancester might have displayed with needle, thread and fine fabric.

I watched her with something akin to envy—and it was more than her manual dexterity that I envied. She had something that occupied all her attention; I had not. I had time to doubt, and to wonder. At the back of my mind a nagging, insistent voice was saying, *No good will come of this.*

I heard Peggy's satisfied grunt in my helmet phones and saw that the job was finished. She unscrewed the breech of the tube, and flipped it back on its hinge. She picked up a wad of rags, shoved it down the barrel, but not too far down. I managed to get the lid off the powder cannister and handed it to her. She poured the black grains onto the wad. Her guess as to the positioning of it had been a good one; only a spoonful of gunpowder remained in the can. This she transferred to a tubular recess in the middle of the breech block, stoppering it with another scrap of rag. She replaced the block then, gasping slightly as she gave it that extra half-turn to ensure that it was well and tightly home.

"O.K., Martha," she said. "You can let the air back in."

"Valve open," Martha's voice said tinnily from the phones.

I watched the needle of my wrist gauge start to rise, and heard after a while the thin, high screaming of the inrushing atmosphere. And then the airtight door over our heads opened and I saw Martha and Doc framed in the opening, looking not at us but at what we had done. After a second's hesitation they joined us in the transom space. Martha helped Peggy off with her helmet; Doc removed mine for me.

"A neat job," said Martha.

"It will do," said Peggy.

"I hope," added Doc, but he did not seem unduly worried.

"You wire her up," said Peggy to Martha. "I can't do it in these damn gloves."

"Anything to oblige," murmured Martha. She handed the double cable that she had brought down with her to Jenkins and started to loosen the thumbscrews on the breech block.

"I know that I'm only the captain," said a cold, a very cold voice, "but might I inquire what the hell you're doing?"

"We're going to make this bitch roll and go," replied Jenkins happily.

I looked up from the makeshift rocket and saw that Sandra and Listowel were standing in the motor room, looking down at us through the doorway. Sandra was icily furious. Listowel looked mildly interested.

Sandra's finger pointed first at Peggy, then at myself. "Spacesuits . . . have you been outside?" she demanded.

"No," said Peggy.

"Don't worry, skipper," said Jenkins. "We didn't lose any atmosphere. We sealed the transom space off before Peggy and Peter went to work, and put the pump on it . . ."

"But you pierced the hull," she said with mounting anger.

"Only a small hole," admitted Jenkins.

"This," she grated, "is too much. Only a couple of weeks out and you're already space-happy. Burning holes in the pressure plating and risking all our lives. Are you mad?"

"No," stated Doc. "And when you find out what it's about you'll be pleased."

"Pleased? I shall be pleased all right. I shall roll on the deck in uncontrollable ectasy. And I'll have your guts for a necktie, and then I'll boot you out of the airlock without spacesuits. I'll—"

"Be reasonable, Sandra," admonished Listowel rashly.

"Reasonable? I am being reasonable. All these officers have work that they should be doing, instead of which I find them engaged in some fantastic act of sabotage . . ."

"Sandra," I put in, "I can explain."

"*You?* You ineffectual puppy!" I saw with shock that there was a pistol in her hand. "Come up out of there, all of you. That is an order." She turned to her companion. "Commander Listowel, as captain of this vessel I request your aid in dealing with these mutineers."

"But—" I began.

"Drop whatever you're doing," she snapped, "and come up."

"Better do as she says," grumbled Peggy. She picked up her welding torch.

"Just let us tell you what it's all about, skipper," pleaded Jenkins, edging towards the power point into which the torch was plugged.

"No," said Sandra flatly.

"But . . ." murmured Peggy, her voice trailing off.

There was the sharp click of a switch and the torch flared blindingly. I realized Peggy's intention, but too late. As I tried to wrest the tool from her hands (but why? but why?), the metal casing of the firing chamber was already cherry red.

I felt rather than heard the *whoomph* of the exploding powder . . .

Chapter 16

Her body against mine was warm and resilient, yielding—and then, at the finish, almost violently possessive. There was the flaring intensity of sensation, prolonged to the limits of endurance, and the long, long fall down into the soft darkness of the sweetest sleep of all.

And yet . . .

"Sandra . . ." I started to say, before my eyes were properly focused on the face beside mine on the pillow.

She snapped back into full consciousness and stared at me coldly.

"What was that, Peter? I've suspected that . . ."

"I don't know, Peggy," I muttered. "I don't know . . ."

I don't know, I thought. *I don't know. But I remember . . . what do I remember? Some crazy dream about another ship, another lightjammer, with Sandra as the captain and myself as catering officer and Ralph as some sort of outsider. And I was married to Sandra in this dream, and I'd lost her, and I was trying to win her back with Peggy's help. There was something about a solid fuel rocket . . .*

"What is it, Peter?" she asked sharply.

"A dream," I told her. "It must have been a dream . . ."

I unsnapped the elastic webbing that held us to the bunk and floated away from it and from Peggy to the center of the cabin. I looked around me, noting details in the dim light, trying to reassure myself of its reality, of our reality. It was all so familiar, and all so old. The ghosts of those who had lived here, who had loved here and hated here, generation after generation, seemed to whisper to me, *This is* Thermopylae. *This is all the world you have ever known, ever will know . . .*

It was all so unfamiliar.

And Peggy . . .

I turned to look at her as she lay on the bed, still held there by the webbing, the bands startlingly white against her golden skin. She was real enough. Her naked beauty was part of my memories—all my memories.

"Peter," she said. "Peter, come back."

From nowhere a tag of poetry drifted into my mind, and I murmured,

> ". . . and home there's no returning.
> The Spartans on the sea-wet rock sat down
> and combed their hair."

It made an odd sort of sense.

Thermopylae—the last stand of the Spartans, back in the early dawn of Terran history; *Thermopylae*—one of the great windjammers that sailed Earth's seas; *Thermopylae*—the last stand of the Spartacists . . .

"Come back," she called pleadingly.

"I'm here," I told her. "I'm here. It was just that I had a little trouble getting myself oriented."

Stretching my right leg I was just able to touch the bulkhead with the tip of my big toe, and I shoved gently. I drifted back in the general direction of the bed. Peggy extended her arm and caught me, pulled me to her.

"Born in the ship," she scolded, "raised in the ship, and you still haven't the sense to put your sandals on . . ."

"There was that . . . strangeness . . ." I faltered.

"If that's what I do to you, my boy, I'd better see about getting a divorce. There's nothing strange about us. I'm a perfectly prosaic plumber, and you're a prurient purser, and our names start with a P as well as our ratings, so we're obviously made for each other. At least, I thought so until just now . . . but when the bridegroom, on his wedding night, starts calling his blushing bride by another woman's name it's rather much!" She smiled tantalizingly. "Of course, I had quite a crush on Ralph once—not that he'd ever notice me. Plumbers are rather beneath the captain's notice. He reminds me so much of my father . . ." Her face sobered. "I wonder what it would be like to live on a real world, a planet, with ample living room and with no necessity to stash parents away in the deep freeze when they've lived their alloted span? I wonder if our fathers and mothers, and their fathers and mothers, will ever be revived to walk on grass and breathe fresh air . . . I wonder if we shall ever be revived after we're put away to make room for *our* children . . ." She reached out for something from the bedside locker—and suddenly her expression was one of puzzlement and disappointment. She whispered, "I wanted a cigarette. I wanted a cigarette to smoke and to wave in the air as I talked . . ."

"I asked, "What is a cigarette?"

"I . . . I don't know . . . I think it would be one of those tiny, white smoldering tubes that characters are always playing with in the old films . . . those men and women who played out their dramas on worlds like Earth and Austral and Caribbea, or aboard ships that could cross the Galaxy in a matter of months." She said intensely, "At times I hate the Spartacists. It was all very well for them, the disgruntled technicians and scientists who thought that they had become the slaves of capital and organized labor—whatever *they* were—and who staged their futile slave revolt, and built this crazy ship because they hadn't the money or materials to construct a Mannschenn drive job—whatever *that* was. It was all very well for *them*, the romantic Durnhamites, pushing out under full sail for the Rim Stars—but what about us? Born in this tin coffin, living in this tin coffin and, at the end, put to sleep in this tin coffin—unless we die first—in the hope of a glorious resurrection on some fair planet circling a dim, distant sun. And we've never known the feel of grass under our bare feet, never known the kiss of the sun and the breeze on our skins, making do with fans and UV lamps, taking our exercise in the centrifuge instead of on the playing field or in the swimming pool, subsisting on algae and on tissue cultures that have long since lost any flavor they once had. Why, even on Lorn . . ."

"Even on Lorn?" I echoed.

"What am I saying?" she whispered. "What am I saying? Where is Lorn?"

"Lorn, Faraway, Ultimo and Thule . . ." I murmured. "And the worlds of the Eastern Circuit—Tharn and Grollor, Mellise and Stree . . . Tharn, with the dirt streets in the towns, and the traders' stalls under the flaring gas jets as the evening falls, and the taverns with good liquor and good company . . . Mellise, and the long swell rolling in from half way across the world, breaking on the white beaches of the archipelago . . ."

"What's happened to us?" she cried. Then, "What have we lost?"

"How can we have lost," I asked, "what we have never known?"

"Dreams," she whispered. "Dreams . . . or the alternative time tracks that Claude is always talking about. Somewhere, or somewhen, another Peter and Peggy have walked the white beaches of Mellise, have swum together in the warm sea. Somewhen we have strolled together along a street on Tharn, and you have bought for me a bracelet of beaten silver . . ."

"Dreams," I said. "But you are the reality, and you are beautiful . . ."

As I kissed her, as my caressing hands wandered over her compliant body, desire mounted. But there was a part of myself holding back, there was a cold voice at the back of my mind that said, *You are doing this to forget. You are doing this to forget the worlds and the ships and the women that you have known.* And, coldly, I answered myself with the question, *Is there a better way of forgetting? And why should one not forget a foolish dream?*

Her urgent mouth was on mine and her arms were about me, and forgetfulness was sweet and reality was all we need ever ask, and—

A giant hand slammed us from the bunk, snapping the webbing, hurling against the bulkhead. The single light went out. We sprawled against the cold, metal surface, held there by some pseudo-gravity, hurt, frightened, still clinging desperately to each other. Dimly I heard the incessant shrilling of alarm bells and somewhere somebody screaming. We felt rather than heard the thudding shut of airtight doors.

The pressure against us relaxed and, slowly, we drifted into the center of the cabin. I held Peggy to me tightly. I could hear her breathing, could feel her chest rising and falling against my own. She stirred feebly.

"Peggy, are you all right?" I cried. "Darling, are you all right?"

"I . . . I think so . . ." she replied faintly. Then, with a flash of the old humor, "Do you have to be so rough?"

There was a crackling sound, and then from the bulkhead speaker issued the voice of Ralph, calm as always, authorative.

"This is the captain. We have been in collision with a meteor swarm. Will all surviving personnel report to the control room, please? All surviving personnel report to the control room."

"We'd better do as the man says," said Peggy shakily, "even though it means dressing in the dark . . ."

IV

JOURNEY'S END

Chapter 17

We were in the control room—those of us who had survived.

We had made our rounds, armored against cold and vacuum. We had seen the results of our collision with the meteor swarm, the rending and melting of tough metal and plastic, the effects of sudden decompression on human flesh. We had seen too much. Speaking for myself, it was only the uncanny half-knowledge that this was only an evil dream that enabled me to keep a hold on my sanity.

We were in the control room, the seven of us.

There was Ralph Listowel, acting captain, strapped in his seat before the useless controls. Beside him, anchored to the deck by the magnetic soles of her sandals, stood Sandra, acting mate. And there was David Jenkins, ship's surgeon, and very close to him stood Martha Wayne, ship's chronicler. There was Peggy, ship's plumber. There was Claude Smethwick, always the odd man out. There was myself.

We had survived.

We had made our rounds of the stricken *Thermopylae* and had found no other survivors. All the accommodation abaft officers' country had been holed, as had been the dormitory, the deep freeze, in which our parents—and their parents, and *their* parents—had been laid away, in stasis, to await planetfall. But they had never known what had hit them. They were luckier than our generation, for whom there must have been a long second or so of agonised realization, the horror of bursting lungs and viscera, before the end.

"Report," ordered Ralph tiredly.

There was a long silence, which Jenkins was the first to break. He said, "We suited up, and went through the ship. She's like a colander. There are no other survivors."

"None?" asked Ralph.

"No, skipper. Do you wish details?"

"No," said Ralph.

"I made rounds with Doc," said Sandra. "The deep freeze has had it. So has all the accommodation abaft officers' country. So has most of the accommodation forward of the bulkhead. Second mate, third mate, engineers, catering officer—all dead. Very dead . . ."

"And outside?" asked Ralph.

"I saw what I could from the blisters. It's a mess. Spars buckled. Twenty odd square miles of sail in ribbons . . ."

"Report," said Ralph, looking at me.

I told him, "I've been through the farm. We haven't got a farm any more. The tank room and the tissue culture room were both holed. Of course, the deep-frozen, dehydrated tissue cultures will keep us going for some time . . ."

"If we had air and water they would," said Jenkins glumly. "But we haven't."

"There are the cylinders of reserve oxygen," I pointed out.

"And how do we get rid of the carbon dioxide?" asked the doctor.

"Chemicals . . ." suggested Peggy vaguely.

"What chemicals?" he demanded. He went on, "Oh, we can keep alive for a few days, or a few weeks—but we shall merely be postponing the inevitable. Better to end it now, skipper. I've got the drugs for the job. It will be quite painless. Pleasant, even."

Ralph turned to Peggy. "Report."

She said, "The generator room's wrecked. The only power we have at our disposal is from the batteries."

"And their life?"

"If we practice the utmost economy, perhaps two hundred hours. But I may be able to get a jenny repaired—"

"And burn up our oxygen reserve running it," said Ralph. Then, to Smethwick, "Report."

"I've tried," the telepath whispered. "I've tried. But there's no contact anywhere. We are alone, lost and alone. But . . ."

"But?" echoed Ralph.

"I . . . I'm not sure . . ." Then, suddenly, Smethwick seemed to gain stature, to change his personality almost. Always until now the shyest and most retiring of men, he dominated us by his vehemence. "Don't *you* have the memories—the memories of the lives you've lived elsewhere, elsewhen? Haven't you any recollection of yourself as Captain Listowel of the Rim Runners, as Commander Listowel of the Federation Survey

Service? And the rest of you," he went on, "don't *you* remember? This isn't the only life—or the only death . . ."

"Lorn and Faraway . . ." I said softly.

"Ultimo and Thule . . ." whispered Martha.

"And the planets of the Eastern Circuit," said Sandra flatly.

"You remember," cried Smethwick. "Of course you remember. I'm snooping now. I admit it. You can do what you like to me, but I'm snooping. I'm peeping into your minds. And it all adds up, what I can read of your memories, your half-memories. There's the pattern, the unbreakable pattern. All the time, every time, it's been just the seven of us—aboard *Flying Cloud*, aboard *Aeriel*, and now aboard *Thermopylae* . . .

"There's the pattern . . . we've tried to break free from it, but we've never succeeded. But we have changed it—every time we have changed it—and we can change it again. Whether for better or for worse I cannot say—but it can hardly be for worse *now*."

Ralph was looking at Sandra—and once, I knew, the way that she was looking back at him would have aroused my intense jealousy. "Yes," he said slowly. "I remember . . . hazily . . . even so, wasn't there some trouble with Peter?"

I was holding Peggy close to me. "There was," I said. "But not any more."

"And what about you, Martha?" asked Sandra. "Do you remember?"

"I do," she said, "but I'm perfectly happy the way things are now. Both David and I are happy—so happy, in fact, that I don't welcome the idea of euthanasia . . ."

"Go on," urged Smethwick. "Go on. Remember!"

"I made a rocket," muttered Peggy hesitantly. "Didn't I?"

"And I mixed a batch of solid fuel," I supported her.

"No," contradicted Doc. "I did."

"Some bastard did," stated Ralph, looking rather hostile.

"Too right," said Sandra. "And whoever it was put us in the jam that we're in now. I was quite happy as catering-officer-cum-third-mate of *Flying Cloud*, and quite happy as captain of *Aeriel*, and I rather resent finding myself chief officer of a dismasted derelict, with only a few days to live."

"*You* might have been happy," I told her, "but you must admit that the way things were aboard *Aeriel* did not, repeat not, contribute to *my* happiness."

"My marriage to you was a big mistake," she said.

"Wasn't it just!" I agreed. "On *my* part! I should have known better. Give a woman a position of authority and she at once abuses it. 'I'm the captain, and I sleep with whom I bloody well please. See?' "

"I resent that," said Sandra.

"Resent away," I told her, "if it makes you any happier. Resenting seems to be your specialty, darling."

"But you were such a bloody lousy cook," she said.

"Like hell I was!" I flared. "I'm a bloody good cook, and you know it. *Aeriel* ate a damn sight better than *Flying Cloud* ever did."

"I suppose," she said, "that you mixed gunpowder in with your curry."

"You wouldn't know the difference," I sneered.

"Who would?" she sneered back.

"I think his curry is good," said Peggy loyally.

"You would," snapped Sandra.

"The rocket!" Claude was screaming. *"The rocket!"*

I told him what to do with the rocket, tail fins and all. I said to Sandra, "It's high time that we got things sorted out. You behaved very shabbily. Even you must admit that. I've nothing against Ralph—in fact I think that's he's more to be pitied than blamed. But if it hadn't been for the way that you carried on aboard both *Flying Cloud* and *Aeriel* there wouldn't have been any rockets. There wouldn't have been any misguided attempts to break the light barrier."

"So it's all my fault," she said sarcastically.

"Of course," I told her.

"And that refugee from a bicycle shop, to whom you happen to be married at the moment, has nothing at all to do with it. Oh, no. And neither has the incompetent pill peddler who mixed the first batch of powder. And neither have you, who mixed the second. But, as far as I'm concerned, what really rankles is this. I don't mind all this switching from one time track to another—after all, variety is the spice of life. What I do object to is being the victim of the blundering machinations of the same bunch of dimwits every bloody time. It's too much. Really, it's too much."

"My heart bleeds for you," I said. "Let me suggest that on the next time track you get you to a nunnery. Preferably a Trappist one. If there are such institutions."

Her face was white with passion. Her hand flashed out and caught me a stinging blow across the mouth. My feet lost their magnetic contact with the deck and I floated backwards, fetching up hard against the bulkhead.

Peggy, her voice bitter, said, "You deserved that."

"No," said Martha. "No. Everything has been Sandra's fault."

"Pipe down," ordered Ralph. "Pipe down, all of you. And you, Malcolm, please refrain from making any more slanderous attacks on my wife."

"*My* wife," I said.

"Not in this continuum," he corrected me. "But what happened in the alternative Universes has a certain bearing upon our present predicament. Thanks to your otherwise unpardonable outburst, we can remember now—"

"And about bloody well time you did," said Claude.

"We can't all be perfect," stated Ralph, with mild sarcasm. "Even so, we can try. We know the way out now—and, this time, we're all of us involved. *All* of us. We must break the light barrier once more, and the only way that we can do it is by giving this wagon that extra push. Has anybody any suggestions?"

Martha said slowly, "We must have been close to Lume 1 when the meteors hit us. But the impact was at right angles to our trajectory . . ."

"Work it out by the parallelogram of forces," Ralph told her. "If you really want to, that is. But we have the Doppler log—it's still working—and that gives us the answer without any fooling around with slipsticks. Even though we are a dismasted derelict we're still bowling along at a good rate. But it'll take more than a powder-fuelled rocket to give us the boost."

"There's the reserve oxygen," I said.

"And there's plenty of alcohol," added Jenkins.

"And Peggy's a plumber in this incarnation," said Sandra, rather nastily.

"So . . ." said Ralph.

Chapter 18

It was dark outside and, despite the heating units and insulation of our suits, bitterly cold. Astern of us was the dull-glowing Galactic lens, a monstrous ember in the black ash of the ultimate night. Ahead of us, flaring with an unnatural steely brilliance, was one of the distant island nebulae. But we were in no mood for astronomical sight-seeing. Almost at once our attention was caught and held by the horrible tangle of twisted wreckage that extended all the way from the stern, where we were standing, to the stem of the huge ship, standing out sharply and shockingly in the harsh glare of our working lights: the buckled spars, the vast, disorderly expanse of tattered sail and snapped cordage, the rent and battered shell plating. But we did not look long, nor did we want to. There was work to do—burning and welding, man-handling the massive pipe sections into place, heating and beating the twisted plating of the stern so that it conformed, more or less, to our plans.

Peggy took charge—and it was Peggy, too, who did most of the work. A tool in her hands was an extension of her body—or, even, an extension of her personality. She stitched metal to metal with the delicate precision that an ancestress might have displayed with needle, thread and fine fabric. I watched her with envy, and it was not only her manual dexterity that I envied. She was so sure of herself, so certain. And I was not certain. Oh, I had no doubts that this was the only way out of our predicament—but once we had won through to an alternative time track should we be any better off? In *Thermopylae* we had achieved what seemed to be a stable grouping, like paired with like, but would it, could it last?

I looked at Peggy, and I hoped with all my heart that it would.

I heard her satisfied, peculiarly feminine grunt in my helmet phones. She said flatly, "That's that."

"Even so," murmured Ralph doubtfully, "will it hold?"

"Long enough," she told him cheerfully. "Long enough. After all, Ralph, this isn't the first time . . ."

"No," said Sandra, a nasty edge to her voice, "it isn't."

"That will do," ordered her husband coldly.

"And now we'll connect up the tanks and bottles," said Peggy.

We clambered back inside through the rents in the shell plating, back into the wrecked lazaret. Intended for use as a sick bay by the ship's builders, it had become over the generations a storeroom, a repository for things that never had been used, that never would be used, that had been stashed away in the belief that somebody, sooner or later, would find a use for them. We had found the piping there, a fine assortment, large and small bore. Some had been damaged by the meteor swarm, most of it had not been. Finding it saved us both time and labor.

The oxygen cylinders and the tanks of alcohol, however, we had to lug through the ship from the centrally situated storage compartments. The work was heavy and awkward, but that wasn't the worst part of it. The trouble was that we were obliged to see again the torn, frozen bodies of our late shipmates. And there was that sense of responsibility that was so hard to shake off. If it hadn't been for the pattern, as we were thinking of it, if it hadn't been for the odd design which made it somehow imperative that the seven of us, and only the seven of us, should be attempting to break the light barrier by means of rocket power, would *Thermopylae* have come to grief? And had we, of our own volition, established the pattern? Or had the pattern existed always, and were we no more than puppets?

But we worked on. We were still alive, and we had every inducement to stay that way. We convinced ourselves that we were in, but not of, *Thermopylae*. We felt that we were innocent bystanders involved by blind chance in a catastrophe not of our making, not of our concern. All that concerned us was getting the hell out, and that as soon as possible. My parents, I knew, were among those who had perished when the cosmic debris destroyed the deep freeze. But my parents, I knew with even greater certainty, were solid citizens of Dunedin, capital of the Empire of Waverly, who, without fail, sent me a canned turkey every year in the pious hope that it would arrive at or before Christmas. Then there was the carroty cat Susan. I had known her before I met Peggy. I had known her very well indeed. I had seen her—what was left of her—as I helped lug the oxygen cylinders back aft from the stores. And I told myself, *That pitiful, broken body means nothing to me. I have never slept with it. When I was in* Flying Cloud, *when I was in* Aeriel, *I never knew anybody called Susan . . .*

I told myself that.

But we worked, all of us, fetching and carrying at Peggy's command, sweating in our suits, gasping in the stale air. We watched the makeshift contraption growing as we worked—the alcohol tanks with the oxygen bottles attached to them to drive the fluid into the firing chamber, the other oxygen bottles that would feed directly into the rocket motor. It was a dreadfully inefficient setup, but it didn't matter. Mass ratio didn't worry us. We weren't concerned with escape velocity; all that we wanted was that extra nudge, the push that would drive us faster than light, that would expel us from this continuum in which we didn't belong.

We worked, stumbling, fumbling automatons, breathing our own stinks, our skin chafed and sore inside our suits. We worked, tired and hungry and thirsty as we were. There was the urgency, there was the feeling that if we failed to meet the deadline we should be marooned here, doomed to die in a little, ruined world not of our making. We worked, half-blinded by the actinic flaring of Peggy's torch, cursing the tools that slipped from our clumsy, gloved hands, cursing each other for carelessness and failure to cooperate.

But we worked.

And, astern of us, the target at which the cannon of our jury rocket was aimed, we could see the dull-glowing Galactic lens, the smear of smoky crimson against the darkness. Whatever happened, we all knew, there was no return, ever, to the warmth and light of the center. We belonged on the Rim. Aboard *Flying Cloud*, aboard *Aeriel*, aboard *Thermopylae*—we belonged on the Rim . . .

"Now," Peggy was saying. "*Now*. Stand by, all of you . . ."

"Wait!" Ralph's voice was sharp. "There'll be acceleration. Unless we've secured ourselves we shall fall through the holes in the plating—and that will be the end."

"Then secure yourselves," said Peggy.

I shuffled to where she was standing, got one arm around a stanchion, the other around her waist. I saw that the others were similarly disposing themselves. Peggy, with both hands free, opened two valves. From the venturi of the rocket jetted a white vapor. Then her right hand went out to a crude switch—and, abruptly, the white vapor became a torrent of fire.

It won't work, I thought. *It won't work. Not this time . . .*

Desperately I clung to the stanchion, fighting the pseudogravity of our acceleration. I tried not to look down through the rents in the shell plating, tried to ignore the light-years-deep chasm beneath us. I clung with desperation to the stanchion and even more desperately to Peggy, who needed both hands to adjust the valves.

The weight on my arms, as acceleration mounted, became intolerable, but I knew that I must not, could not, would not let go.

Then I felt the ominous vibration as the stanchion started to give.

Chapter 19

Ahead of us had been the spark of luminescence that was a planet, astern of us the disc of fire that was a sun. We had done the things that had to be done—mechanically, not too inefficiently. But I was still seeing, in my mind's eye, the dull-glowing lens of the Galaxy, smoky crimson against the sooty depths of the ultimate night, still feeling, in my left hand and arm, the strain—the strain, and the crackling of the weakening, snapping stanchion. What was real and what was unreal? Was this world towards which we were headed some sort of latter-day Valhalla, a heaven (or hell?) for the souls of departed spacemen.

But we had done the right things—shortening sail, trimming sail, rotating the spars so that the black surfaces of some of the vanes were presented to the major luminary, so that their reflecting surfaces were catching the reflected light from the planet. We had slowed down sufficiently for the making of a safe approach.

"Even so," Ralph was saying, slowly and softly, "what world is it? What world can it be?"

I reached out for the big binoculars on their universally jointed mount. I thought, *I'll play this for real. But it must be real. Or must it?* Slowly, carefully, I adjusted the focus. What had been only short hours ago little more than a point of light was now a great shining sphere. I stared at it stupidly. About a third of the planetary surface was cloud-covered, mainly in the polar regions. I could observe clearly the seas and the continents—blue and brown and green, the snowclad peaks of the mountain ranges a sparkling white—the seas and the continents, the utterly unfamiliar configurations of land and water.

"What world is it?" asked Ralph again, addressing me directly this time.

"I don't know," I admitted, adding wryly, "But navigation in this ship—or these ships?—has been rather a lost art of late . . ."

"But not, unfortunately, rocketry," observed Sandra cattily.

"Pipe down," growled Ralph. "Pipe down. We've all of us come through, somehow, and we're back where we belong, in *Flying Cloud*. All we have to do now is to make a landing."

"But where, lord and master?" asked Sandra, too sweetly. "But where?"

"Does it matter?" he growled. "That looks to be a very pleasant world. Frankly, I shall be happy to set this scow down on any convenient stretch of calm water. After we're rested we'll see about getting our bearings . . ."

"In space?" she asked. "Or in time? Or both?"

"Does it matter?" he almost shouted. Then, "It's time we heard something from our tame telepath."

I said, "His amplifier up and died on him."

"I hope he hasn't dumped it," said Sandra, "although I never did fancy dog's brain in aspic. But Peter could make a curry of it."

"I'm not the cook," I told her coldly. "Not on this time track. And neither, my dear, are you the captain."

Ralph glared at us and then turned to the journalist. "Any luck, Martha?"

"Yes," she said, fiddling with the controls of her transceiver. "There are people there, and they're advanced enough to have radio. Their language is strange—to me, at any rate—but their music is human enough, even though it's a little corny for my taste." She switched over from headphone to speaker. There was a man singing, in a pleasant baritone, accompanied by some stringed instrument. The melody was hauntingly familiar, although the words were in that unknown tongue. Then, in spite of the shifts in key, the odd distortions of rhythm, I had it. In his own language, he was singing:

> "Goodbye, I'll run
> To seek another sun
> Where I
> May find
> There are worlds more kind
> Than the ones left behind . . ."

I said, "The Rim Runners' March . . ."

"You could be right," said Ralph doubtfully. Then, with growing assurance, he repeated, "You could be right. Even so, that piece of music is not the exclusive property of Rim Runners. It's old, old—and nobody knows how many times it's had fresh lyrics tacked on to it. But hearing it, on *their* radio, is evidence that Terran ships have been in contact with this world. The Survey Service, perhaps, or some off-course star tramp. But I think that we can expect a friendly reception, assistance, even . . ." He was beginning to look more cheerful. "All right. We'll get the rest of the way off this wagon now. This is the ideal approach, towards the sunlit hemisphere of the planet. You know the drill, all of you. Trim sails— black surfaces towards the sun, reflecting surfaces towards the source of reflected light. Start the pumps as soon as they have some atmosphere to work on."

His strong, capable hands played over the control panel. I watched the telltale screen. There was the ship as seen from directly ahead, scanned by the camera at the end of its long bowsprit, eclipsing the sun. Surrounding her were the geometric array of vanes and spars, some blindingly white, some sooty black. I watched—but there was no change in the design. I heard Ralph curse softly, I looked back to him. The control panel was alive with red lights.

The intercom speaker crackled and from it issued Peggy's voice. "The wiring's gone. The power supply to the trimming motors. Burned out."

"Manual trimming," ordered Ralph sharply. "Get along to the trimming motor room, all of you. And fast."

I was the first out of the control room, with Sandra, Doc Jenkins and Martha hard on my heels. We shuffled through the alleyways at speed, keeping the magnetized soles of our sandals in contact with the deck, knowing that to fall free would be to waste time rather than to gain it. But it was a nightmarish means of progression. As we passed the psionic radio room we ran into Claude Smethwick, who had just come out into the alleyway. I grabbed his arm and hustled him along with us, refusing to listen to what he was trying to tell me.

The trimming motor room stank of burned insulation, of overheated and melted metal and plastic, of ozone. Peggy was there, frantically stripping panels from the bulkhead sheathing, laying bare the damaged wiring. I heard Sandra say, "If you'd done this before, Miss Cummings, instead of playing around with homemade fireworks . . ."

"Shut up!" I shouted. Then, "Peggy, put the manual controls in gear!"

"Peter," Claude Smethwick was babbling. "Peter, I've made contact. This world . . ."

"Later," I snapped. "Tell me later. We have to get the way off the ship."

"But . . ."

"Get your paws on to that wheel, all of you! Now . . . now . . .

together!" The hand gear was stubborn, and our actions at first were clumsy and uncoordinated. *"Together!"* I shouted again.

The worst of it all was that we were having to work in free fall conditions. All that held us to the deck was the magnetism of the soles of our sandals. We had no purchase. Yet, at last, the big wheel started to turn—slowly, slowly. I wondered how much time remained to us before we should plunge, a blazing meteorite, down through the planet's atmosphere.

I snatched a glance at the indicator and gasped, "Belay, there. Belay." So far, so good. The main drivers were trimmed. The auxiliary vanes still presented a greater reflecting surface to the sun than did the mainsails to the reflected light of the planet, but things were coming under control, the feeling of nightmarish urgency was abating.

Ralph's voice came through the intercom. "Trim 1 and 2 spinnakers. Then stand by."

"Turn back!" bawled Claude Smethwick. "We must turn back!"

"Why, Mr. Smethwick?" asked Ralph's disembodied voice coldly.

"I've been trying to tell you, but nobody will listen. I've been in touch with the telepaths on that planet. It's Llanith, one of the antimatter worlds. And they say, 'Turn back! Turn back!'"

"Mr. Malcolm," snapped Ralph. "Trim all sails!"

Again we strained and sweated, again we were driven by the nightmarish sense of urgency. The first pair of spinnakers was trimmed—and then, with the second pair of auxiliary vanes rotated barely a degree on their spars, the hand gear seized up. Peggy said nothing, just relinquished her hold on the wheel and walked rapidly to the spacesuit locker.

I demanded, "Where are you off to?"

She said, "I have to go outside."

"If there's time," muttered Sandra. "If there's time. Why don't you make another rocket, dearie?"

"What's the delay?" Ralph was demanding. "What's the delay?" Then, his voice suddenly soft, "Goodbye, all of you. It's been good knowing you. Goodbye, Sandra . . ."

She said fiercely, "I might be able to make it to control in time."

Dropping our hands from the useless wheel we watched her go. "Very touching," whispered Jenkins. "Very touching . . ." But, in spite of the slight edge of sarcasm to his voice, he was holding Martha Wayne very closely.

I said to Peggy, "This seems to be it. A pity, since everything's been tidied up so nicely."

She pushed the spacesuit back into its locker and came to stand beside me. She said, putting her hand in mine, "But this mightn't be the end, my dear. Even if there's no after life, we know that we're still living in the alternative Universes . . ."

"Or dying . . ." said Jenkins glumly.

And then—it's odd the way that the human brain works in a crisis—a snatch of archaic verse that I must have learned as a child rose from the depths of my memory, flashed across my mind:

> And fast through the midnight dark and drear,
> Through the whistling sleet and snow,
> Like a sheeted ghost the vessel swept
> On the reef of Norman's Woe . . .

But the crew of the schooner *Hesperus* had died a cold death—ours would be a fiery one. I hoped that it would be sudden.

The ship lurched and shuddered, as though she had in actual fact driven on to a roof. There was a rending, tearing noise, felt as well as heard—the spars and sails, I realized, bearing the brunt of our impact with planet's atmosphere, were braking us, slowing us down. There was the thin, high scream of air rushing over and through projections on our hull, the gaps in our shell plating. The temperature rose sharply. I held Peggy to me tightly, thinking, *This is it*.

The screaming died to a faint whistle and was drowned by a new sound, the throbbing of the air compressors.

Ralph's voice from the bulkhead speaker was faint and shaky, yet reassuring. He said, "All hands report to the control room. All hands report to control—to splice the main brace. And then we'll make it landing stations."

Chapter 20

It's not at all a bad sort of world, this Llanith, and I rather think that Peggy and I shall be staying here, even though Ralph and the local scientists are sure that they'll be able to work out just what did happen, just how *Flying Cloud* made the transition from normal matter to antimatter, or vice versa. The commodore will not have achieved the economical means of interstellar travel of his dreams, but we shall have presented him with something better, much better. There's little doubt that commerce and cultural exchange between the Llanithi Consortium and the Rim Worlds Federation will soon be practicable. And Peggy and I will have an edge on those who, in the not-too-distant future, will come to learn and to teach and to trade.

Meanwhile, Ralph has suggested that each of us tell the story, in his own words, of what happened. The stories, he says, will be of great value to the scientists, both on Llanith and back home on Lorn. It seems that there may have been other forces besides physical ones at play, that psychology may have come into it, and psionics. Be that as it may, it seems obvious—to Peggy and me, at any rate—that the attempt to exceed the speed of light was the governing factor.

Not that we worry much about it.

We're doing nicely, very nicely, the pair of us. My restaurant is better than paying its way; even though the Llanithi had never dreamed of such highly spiced dishes as curry they're fast acquiring the taste for them. And the bicycles—another novelty—that Peggy makes in her little factory are selling like hot cakes.

Doc and Martha are settling down, too. There's quite a demand for the sort of verse and music that they can turn out without really trying. And when they get tired of composing they pick up their brushes and dazzle the natives with neo-abstractionism. And Claude? He gets by. A telepath can find himself at home anywhere—he can always contact others of his kind. If the Llanithi were purple octopi—which they aren't, of course—he'd be equally happy.

It's only Ralph and Sandra who aren't fitting in. Each of them possesses a rather overdeveloped sense of duty—although I am inclined to wonder if Sandra, in her case, isn't really hoping to find her way back to that time track on which the Matriarchate ruled the Rim Worlds and on which she was captain of her own ship.

If she ever does, I shall be neither her husband nor her cook.

This Universe suits me.